TIME OF THE DRAGONS

ALSO BY JAMES A. OWEN

Dawn of the Dragons

JAMES A. OWEN

TIME OF THE DRAGONS

SAGA PRESS

LONDON SYDNEY NEW YORK TORONTO NEW DELHI

TO ALL OF THE GIRLS WHO, LIKE ROSE DYSON, GROW UP TO BECOME BRAVE, AND STRONG, AND TRUE, TO CHANGE THE WORLD AND MAKE IT A BETTER PLACE.

SAGA PRESS
AN IMPRINT OF SIMON & SCHUSTER, INC.
1230 AVENUE OF THE AMERICAS, NEW YORK, NEW YORK 10020

 • The text for this book is set in Adobe Jenson Pro. • Manufactured in the United States of America • First Saga Press paperback edition October 2015 • 10 9 8 7 6 5 4 3 2 1 • Library of Congress Cataloging-in-Publication Data • Owen, James A. • Time of the dragons : The indigo king ; The shadow dragons / James A. Owen.—First Saga Press paperback edition. • pages ; cm. • —(The age of dragons ; 2) • Previously published as two separate stories. • Summary: Caretakers Jack and John race through history to discover the identity of the Cartographer, and Caretakers past and present come together to stop the Winter King's Shadow who has gained control of the doors from the Keep of Time and an army of Dragon Shadows. • ISBN 978-1-4814-2997-9 (pbk) • ISBN 978-1-4814-4144-5 (eBook) • [1. Fantasy. 2. Time travel—Fiction. 3. Mythology—Fiction.] I. Owen, James A. Indigo king. II. Owen, James A. Shadow dragons. III. Title. • PZ7.O97124Tim 2015 • [Fic]—dc23 • 2015018358

CONTENTS

II. THE SHADOW DRAGONS

THE INDIGO KING

PROLOGUE

IN THE CENTURIES *that would pass, the spacious stone room known as Solitude would fill with an accumulation of culture; not by design, but because those who would eventually come to seek the occupant's skills would feel the obligation to bring something, anything, as gifts, or perhaps tribute. But that was in a time yet to come. In the present moment, it was empty save for the items he'd brought with him: a torn robe, an empty scabbard, a quill and half-filled bottle of ink, and as many rolls of parchment as he could carry.*

When he entered, the door had swung shut behind him. He knew without touching it that it had locked, and also, with less assurance, that it would probably not be opened again for many years.

He had once had a name—several names, in fact—all of which were irrelevant now. In his youth he had aspired to be a great man, and had been afforded many opportunities to fulfill that destiny; but far too late, he learned that it was perhaps better to be a good man, who nevertheless aspires to do great things. The distinction had never mattered to him much before.

Solitude had not been created for him, but he took possession of it with the reluctant ease of an heir who receives an unexpected and unwanted inheritance. He laid the robe in one corner, and the scabbard in another, then sat cross-legged in the center of Solitude to examine the rolls of parchment.

Some of them contained drawings and notations; a few, directions that may or may not have been accurate, to places that may or may not have existed. They were maps, more or less, and at one time it had been his driven purpose to create them. But that was before, when his sight was clearer and his motives more pure. Somehow, somewhen, he had lost his way—and in the process, ended up on a path that had brought him here, to Solitude.

Still, he could not help but wonder: Was it the first step on that path, or the last, that had proven to be his undoing? He looked down at the maps. The oldest had been made by his hand more than a millennium before; but the newest of them had been begun, then abandoned, a century ago. He examined it more closely and saw that the delicate lines were obscured by blood—the same that marked the cloak and scabbard as symbols of his shame.

Some things cannot be undone. But someone who is lost might still return to the proper path, if they only have something to show them the way.

Taking the quill in hand, he dipped the point into the bottle. Whether the place he drew existed then didn't matter—it would, eventually. All that mattered now was that he was, at long last, finding his purpose again. Would that he had done so a day earlier. Just one day.

As he began to draw, tears streamed from his eyes, dropping to the parchment, where they mingled freely with the ink and blood in equal measure. The man in Solitude was a mapmaker once more.

PART ONE

THE MYTHOPOEIA

CHAPTER ONE

THE BOOKE OF DAYES

HURRYING ALONG ONE of the tree-lined paths at Magdalen College in Oxford, John glanced up at the cloud-clotted sky and decided that he rather liked the English weather. Constant clouds made for soft light; soft light that cast no shadows. And John liked to avoid shadows as much as possible.

As he passed through the elaborate gate that marked the entrance to Addison's Walk, he looked down at his watch, checking his progress, then looked again. The watch had stopped, and not for the first time. It had been a gift from his youngest child, his only daughter, and while her love in the gift was evident, the selection had been made from a child's point of view and was therefore more aesthetic than practical. The case was burnished gold (although it was most certainly gold-colored tin), the face was painted with spring flowers, and on the back was the embossed image of a frog wearing a bonnet.

John had absentmindedly pulled it out of his pocket during one of the frequent gatherings of his friends at Magdalen, much to their amusement. Barfield in particular loved to approach him now at inopportune moments just to ask the time—and hopefully embarrass John in the process.

John sighed and tucked the watch back in his pocket, then pulled his collar tighter and hurried on. He was probably already late for the dinner he'd been invited to at the college, and although he had always been punctual (mostly), events of recent years had made him much more aware of the consequences tardiness can bring.

Five years earlier, after a sudden and unexpected journey to the Archipelago of Dreams, he'd found himself a half hour late for an evening with visiting friends that had been planned by his wife. Even had he not taken an oath of secrecy regarding the Archipelago, he would scarcely have been able to explain that he was late because he'd been saving Peter Pan's granddaughter and thousands of other children from the Pied Piper, and had only just returned via a magic wardrobe in Sir James Barrie's house, and so had still needed to drive home from London.

His wife, however, still made the occasional remark about his having been late for the party. So John had since resolved to be as punctual as possible in every circumstance. And tonight he was certain that Jack would not want to be on his own for long, even if the third member of their dinner meeting was their good and trusted friend, Hugo Dyson.

Hugo had become part of a loose association of like-minded fellows, centered around Jack and John, who gathered together to read, discuss, and debate literature, Romanticism, and the nature of the universe, among other things. The group had evolved from an informal club at Oxford that John had called the Coalbiters, which was mostly concerned with the history and mythology of the Northern lands. One of the members of the current gathering referred to them jokingly as the "not-so-secret secret society," but where John and Jack were concerned, the name was more ironic than funny. They frequently held other meetings attended only by themselves and their friend Charles, as often as he could justify the trip from London to Oxford, in which they discussed matters that their colleagues would find impossible to believe. For rather than discussing the meaning of metaphor in ancient texts of fable and fairy tale, what was discussed in this *actually* secret secret society were the fables and fairy tales themselves . . . which were *real*. And existed in another world just beyond reach of our own. A world called the Archipelago of Dreams.

John, Jack, and Charles had been recruited to be Caretakers of the *Imaginarium Geographica,* the great atlas of the Archipelago. Accepting the job brought with it many other responsibilities, including the welfare of the Archipelago itself and the peoples within it. The history of the atlas and its Caretakers amounted to a secret history of the world, and sometimes each of them felt the full weight of that burden; for events in the Archipelago are often mirrored in the natural world, and what happens in one can affect the other.

In the fourteen years since they first became Caretakers, all three men had become distinguished as both scholars and writers in and around Oxford, as had been the tradition with other Caretakers across the ages. There were probably many other creative men and women in other parts of the world who might have had the aptitude for it, but the pattern had been set centuries earlier by Roger Bacon, who was himself an Oxford scholar and one of the great compilers of the Histories of the Archipelago.

The very nature of the *Geographica* and the accompanying

Histories meant that discussing them or the Archipelago with anyone in the natural world was verboten. At various points in history, certain Caretakers-in-training had disagreed with this doctrine and had been removed from their positions. Some, like Harry Houdini and Arthur Conan Doyle, were nearly eaten by the dragons that guarded the Frontier, the barrier between the world and the Archipelago, before giving up the job. Others, like the adventurer Sir Richard Burton, were cast aside in a less dramatic fashion but had become more dangerous in the years that followed.

In fact, Burton had nearly cost them their victory in their second conflict with the Winter King—with his shadow, to be more precise—and had ended up escaping with one of the great Dragonships. He had not been seen since. But John suspected he was out there somewhere, watching and waiting.

Burton himself may have been the best argument for Caretaker secrecy. The knowledge of the Archipelago bore with it the potential for great destruction, but Burton was blind to the danger, believing that knowledge was neither good nor evil—only the uses to which it was put could be. It was the trait that made him a great explorer, and an unsuitable Caretaker.

Because of the oath of secrecy, there was no one on Earth with whom the three Caretakers could discuss the Archipelago, save for their mentor Bert, who was in actuality H. G. Wells, and on occasion, James Barrie. But Barrie, called Jamie by the others, was the rare exception to Burton's example: He was a Caretaker who gave up the job willingly. And as such, John had realized early on that the occasional visit to reminisce was fine—but Jamie wanted no part of anything of substance that dealt with the Archipelago.

What made keeping the secret difficult was that John, Jack, and Charles had found a level of comfortable intellectualism within their academic and writing careers. A pleasant camaraderie had developed among their peers at the colleges, and it became more and more tempting to share the secret knowledge that was theirs as Caretakers. John had even suspected that Jack may have already said something to his closest friend, his brother Warnie—but he could hardly fault him for that. Warnie could be trusted, and he had actually seen the girl Laura Glue, when she'd crashed into his and Jack's garden, wings askew, five years earlier, asking about the Caretakers.

But privately, each of them had wondered if one of their friends at Oxford might not be inducted into their circle as an apprentice, or Caretaker-in-training of sorts. After all, that was how Bert and his predecessor, Jules Verne, had recruited their successors. In fact, Bert still maintained files of study on potential Caretakers, young and old, for his three protégés to observe from afar. Within the circle at Oxford, there were at least two among their friends who would qualify in matters of knowledge and creative thinking: Owen Barfield and Hugo Dyson. John expected that sometime in the future, he, Jack, and Charles would likely summon one (or both) colleagues for a long discussion of myth, and history, and languages, and then, after a hearty dinner and good drink, they would unveil the *Imaginarium Geographica* with a flourish, and thus induct their fellow or fellows into the ranks of the Caretakers. Other candidates might be better qualified than the Oxford dons, but familiarity begat comfort, and comfort begat trust. And in a Caretaker, trust was one of the most important qualities of all.

But none of them had anticipated having such a meeting as a matter of necessity, under circumstances that might have mortal consequences for one of their friends. Among them, Jack especially was wary of this. He had lost friends in two worlds and was reluctant to put another at risk if he could help it.

He had requested that all three of them meet for dinner with Hugo Dyson on the upcoming Saturday rather than their usual Thursday gathering time, but as it turned out, Charles was doing research for a novel in the catacombs beneath Paris and could not be reached. He'd been expected back that very day, but as they had heard nothing from him, and he had not yet appeared back in London, John and Jack decided that the meeting was too important to delay, and they confirmed the appointment with Hugo for that evening. It was agreed that the best place for it was in Jack's rooms at Magdalen. They met there often, and so no one observing them would find anything amiss; but the rooms also afforded a degree of privacy they could not get in the open dining halls or local taverns, should the discussion turn to matters best kept secret.

This was almost inevitable, John realized with a shudder of trepidation, given the nature of the matter he and Jack needed to broach with Hugo. Oddly enough, it was actually Charles who was responsible for setting the events in motion, or rather, a small package that had been addressed to him and that he'd subsequently forwarded to Jack at Magdalen. Charles worked at the Oxford University Press, which was based in London, and very few people knew of his connection to Jack at all—much less knew enough to address the parcel, "Mr. Charles Williams, Caretaker." Charles sent it to Jack, with the instruction that he open it together with John—and Hugo Dyson.

Invoking the title of Caretaker meant that the parcel involved the Archipelago. And Charles's request that Hugo be invited meant that whether their colleague was ready for it or not, it might be time to reveal the *Geographica* to him.

When they were not adding notations—or more rarely, new maps—John kept the atlas in his private study, inside an iron box bound with locks of silver and stamped with the seal of the High King of the Archipelago, the Caretakers, and the mark of the extraordinary man who created it, who was called the Cartographer of Lost Places. In that box it was the most secure book in all the world, but now it was wrapped in oilcloth and tucked under John's left arm as he walked through Magdalen College. Still safe, if not secure.

John shivered and hunched his shoulders as he approached the building where Jack's rooms were, then took the steps with a single bound and opened the front door.

The rooms were spare but afforded a degree of elegance by the large quantity of rare and unusual books, which reflected a wealth of selection rather than accumulation. A number of volumes in varying sizes were neatly stacked in all the corners of the rooms and along the tops of the low shelves that were common in Oxford, which all the dons hated. Jack commented frequently that they'd probably been manufactured by dwarves, just to irritate the taller men who'd end up using them.

As John had feared, Hugo was already there, sitting on a big Chesterfield sofa in the center of the sitting room. He was being poured a second cup of Darjeeling tea by their host, who looked wryly at John as he came in.

"The frog in a bonnet set you back again, dear fellow?" said Jack.

"I'm afraid so," John replied. "The dratted thing just won't stay wound."

"Hah!" chortled Hugo. "Time for a new watch, I'd say. Time. For a watch. Hah! Get it?"

Jack rolled his eyes, but John gave a polite chuckle and took a seat in a shabby but comfortable armchair opposite Hugo. The man was a scholar, but he wore the perpetual expression of someone who anticipates winning a carnival prize: anxious but cheerily hopeful. That, combined with his deep academic knowledge of English and his love of truth in all forms, made him a friend both John and Jack valued. Whether he was suited for the calling of Caretaker, however, was yet to be determined.

The three men finished their tea and then ate a sumptuous meal of roast beef, new potatoes, and a dark Irish bread, topped off with sweet biscuits and coffee. John noted that Jack then brought out the rum—much sooner than usual, and with a lesser hesitation than when Warnie was with them—and with the rum, the parcel that had been sent to Charles.

"Ah, yes," said Hugo. "The great mystery that has brought us all together." He leaned forward and examined the writing on the package. "Hmm. This wouldn't be Charles Williams the writer, would it?"

Jack and John looked at each other in surprise. Few of their associates in Oxford knew of Charles, but then again, Charles did have his own reputation in London as an editor, essayist, and poet. His first novel, *War in Heaven,* had come out only the year before, and it was not particularly well known.

"Yes, it is," said John. "Have you read his work?"

"Not much of it, I'm afraid," Hugo replied. "But I've had my own work declined by the press, so I might find I like his writing more if my good character prevails when I do read it.

"I'm familiar with his book," continued Hugo, "because the central object in the story is the Holy Grail."

"The cup of Christ, from the Last Supper," said John.

"Either that, or the vessel used to catch his blood as he hung on the cross," answered Hugo, "depending on which version of the story you believe is more credible as a historian."

"Or as a Christian," said John, "although the Grail lore certainly blurs the line between history and myth."

"It's very interesting that you feel that way," Jack said, unwrapping the parcel and casting a sideways glance at John, "because the line between history and myth is about to be wiped away entirely."

Inside the brown wrapper was a book, about three inches thick and nearly ten inches square. It was bound in ancient leather, and the pages were brown with age. The upper left-hand side of the first few pages had been torn, and the rest bore several deep gashes. Otherwise, the book was intact. The cover itself was filled with ancient writing, and in the center was a detailed impression of the sacred cup itself: the Holy Grail.

Hugo stood to better take in the sight. "Impressive! Is it authentic?"

Jack examined the book in silence for a few minutes, then nodded. "It is. Sixth century, as closely as I can estimate."

Hugo gave him an admiring look. "I didn't realize you were an expert in this sort of historical matter."

"I have some knowledgeable associates," said Jack. He turned to John. "Can you read it?"

John dusted off the cover with a napkin. "Absolutely. The forms are Anglo-Saxon, but the writing itself is Gothic."

"Gothic!" Hugo exclaimed. "No one's used Gothic since . . ."

"Since the sixth century," said John. "But it was one of my favorite languages to play with when I was younger."

"That's what makes him a genius," Hugo said to Jack. "It's all play to him."

The two men refilled their glasses (this time adding a bit of hot water to the rum) and stood back to let John work through the translation. After a few minutes had passed, John turned to Jack and grinned.

"It bears closer study," he said. "If I can refine the actual letterforms, I might even be able to compare it to some of the Histories and narrow down who the author might be. If I didn't know better, I'd say it *is* one of the Histories."

"The author?" Hugo exclaimed. "Surely you're having a joke at my expense, my dear fellow. Narrowing down the century would be impressive enough, but I doubt the author signed his work. Not in those days."

"You'd be surprised," said Jack. "In a way, that's why I asked you to come, Hugo."

"It's quite exceptional, really," John exclaimed. "It purports to be a historical accounting of the lineage of the kings of England. And that history is intertwined with the mythology of the Holy Grail. Except . . ."

"What?" blurted Hugo.

"Except," John finished, "it starts at least five centuries before the birth of Christ."

"So, pure mythology rather than history," said Jack.

"That's debatable," said Hugo, "but you yourself said this would wipe away the line between history and myth."

"Indeed," Jack said, turning to John. "Was Charles's note correct? About the writing?"

John nodded. "The cover text is relevant, but it's the first page that really has me baffled, the same as it did Charles." He lifted the cover. "And for that page, there's no need for me to translate."

Instead of the Gothic writing on the cover, the words on the first page were written in a reddish brown ink in modern English. The page had been torn crosswise from left to right, but the message was largely intact:

The Cartographer
He who seeks the means to
the islands of the Archipelago
will follow the true Grail and
Blood will be saved, by willing choice
that time be restored for the future's sake.
And in God's name, don't close the door!
—*Hugo Dyson*

Hugo clapped them both on the shoulders. "I knew it! Well done, you old scalawags! An excellent joke! Oh, this will be a tale to dine out on! But tell me this: Who is the Cartographer?"

CHAPTER TWO
THE DOOR IN THE WOOD

"IT ISN'T A JOKE, Hugo," said Jack. "You can't tell anyone of this. That isn't ink. And you should take a closer look at the handwriting."

Hugo did so, and his astonished gasp confirmed what Jack had suspected and John had just realized: The writing was in Hugo's own hand.

"Mmm," said John, examining the writing for himself. "You're right, Jack. This *is* quite the mystery. I wonder if that's actually Hugo's blood?"

"Hard to say for certain," said Jack. "It's nearly fourteen centuries old, so there's probably no way to tell."

"My blood?" exclaimed Hugo. "Really now, this is carrying things on a bit past the edge, don't you think?"

"Oh, don't be so squeamish, Hugo," said John. "It's dried, after all."

Jack sat on the sofa and leaned back, his hands behind his neck. "Let's assume this is what it appears to be. Hugo and Charles have never met. So why would this have been sent to Charles?"

"And not only that," John interjected, "but to him in his capacity as a Caretaker."

"A Caretaker of what?" said Hugo. "And who is the Cartographer?"

"I think," John said, reaching for the oilcloth-wrapped book he'd brought with him, "that it's time we explained a few things to you, my baffled friend. Beginning with this."

On top of the table, John unwrapped the *Imaginarium Geographica*.

"We're going to need more rum," said Jack.

As Hugo sat in stunned silence, John and Jack took turns telling him a slightly abridged version of all the adventures they had experienced as Caretakers of the *Imaginarium Geographica*. When they were finished, a completely discombobulated and still slightly skeptical Hugo Dyson squinted one eye and looked them over.

"This is all completely on the level, then?"

"As level as it's possible to get," said John. "And as you can see, the *Geographica* itself is fairly compelling evidence."

"Indeed," said Hugo, rising to look at the atlas. "It is extraordinary, I'll give you that. Extraordinary. And you say this Cartographer of Lost Places created all these maps?"

"Yes," Jack said, nodding.

"So who is he, really?"

"I don't think anyone really knows," said John. "Bert might have his ideas. Samaranth as well. But I've never come across any mention of him in any of the Histories. What we know of him is all there *is* to know."

"Perhaps he's the one who sent it," Hugo suggested. "After all, the note I, uh, wrote seems to be for his benefit."

John shook his head. "It wouldn't have come by post. He'd have sent Bert, or a dragon, or a postal owl or something."

"A postal *owl?*" said Jack.

"I was just giving a 'for instance,'" said John. "I don't think it was really delivered by an owl. Everyone knows swallows are more suited for that sort of thing, anyway."

"That's even worse," said Jack. "At least a good-size owl would have a shot at lifting a heavy book. You'd need *several* swallows to match that."

"He has a point," said Hugo.

"Whatever," said John, irritated. "What I mean is that it was sent by someone in this world, not someone in the Archipelago."

"But who here knows that we're the Caretakers?" asked Jack. "And why not just contact us directly?"

"Maybe they couldn't," offered Hugo. "Perhaps whoever sent the book was prevented from bringing it themselves."

"I think that the reason it was addressed to Charles is obvious," said John. "His novel proves his interest in Grail lore, and as a Caretaker he has resources other scholars wouldn't."

"Fair enough," said Jack. "But what initiated Hugo's involvement in all this?" They both turned to their friend, who gulped and grinned sheepishly.

"I'm just trying to keep up, honestly," said Hugo. "As I said, I was familiar with Charles's work, but my interest was in what I *hoped* the novel was, not what it is.

"I'm doing a lot of reading in Arthurian legends, and so of course I'm taking detours into Grail stories. I thought Charles's book might be a nice diversion, but it was rather disappointing to discover it's wholly contemporary. To him the Grail is an object, a device, if you will, to allow him to tell a story of the supernatural. And that wasn't what I was looking for at all."

"I see," said John. "We'll have to speak further about the Arthur legends. I think we can help you there"—he winked at Jack—"particularly with the material about his descendants."

"You can show me the actual Histories?" Hugo exclaimed.

"Better," said Jack. "We can show you the actual *descendants*."

"We're the last one's godfathers," John explained.

"Good Lord," said Hugo.

"What I want to know is the connection between the Grail and the Cartographer," said Jack. "How are they linked, I wonder?"

"Arthur again," said John. "Remember, the seal of the High King is what keeps the door locked in the Keep. There must be a connection there."

Jack snapped his fingers. "Right. I'd forgotten. So what do we do?"

"Let's do this," said John, rising. "Tomorrow I'll use the Compass Rose to summon one of the Dragonships from the Archipelago, and we'll go ask the Cartographer himself. We can answer all these questions in a matter of days."

"You said the, uh, fortress . . . ," began Hugo.

"The Keep," said Jack.

"Yes, the Keep of, uh, Time, was almost destroyed. Will we be able to get to him?"

John and Jack looked at each other, thinking the same thing: They were glad, in this moment, that Charles was not in the room. Despite the fact that his actions had once saved their lives, he was nevertheless responsible for the Keep being set ablaze and would have been embarrassed to discuss the matter in front of Hugo.

"Yes," said Jack. "It's difficult, but still possible. The fire is long extinguished, but the tower itself continues to crumble. We've had to spend more and more time doing damage control with the various Time Storms that have formed as a result, but just going there to speak to him shouldn't be a problem."

"Hmm," said John. "I wonder if a Time Storm might not be the genesis of this book. After all, there has to be some explanation for how Hugo's writing got on it fourteen centuries ago."

"I've never seen a Time Storm here, in our world," said Jack. "Just in the Archipelago."

"There have been crossovers," John pointed out. "The Bermuda Triangle, for one. And of course, the whole business with the *Red Dragon*."

"*Red Dragon?*" asked Hugo.

"You'd know it better as the *Argo*," said Jack.

"Ah," said Hugo. He got to his feet with a visible wobble. "I think I need some air. Anyone fancy a walk?"

"Excellent idea," agreed John.

After rewrapping the Grail book and the *Geographica* (in the unlikely event that one of Jack's students or the college "scout" responsible for tidying up the rooms should wander in and find them), John, Jack, and Hugo left the New Building and headed down the direction from which John had come earlier. Addison's Walk was a favorite stroll of theirs; it made a circuit around Magdalen from one side of the college, leading to Dover Pier, and then around to the other side along the Cherwell. It was lined with trees and grassy meadows and offered beautiful views of Magdalen Tower and the Magdalen Bridge. It was an eminently peaceful path to walk alone or with companions, and all three of them had followed it often.

The night was pleasant for mid-September, and it was perfect weather for contemplating the universe. The only thing that made the stroll disquieting was the occasional shadows cast by the lamps they passed. Jack tried not to look like he was avoiding them, and he hoped John wouldn't notice.

Hugo walked ahead of the other two, hands clasped behind his back, deep in thought. Occasionally he would stop and begin to utter some half-formed thought, then reconsider and keep walking. Finally he fell back with the others.

"So," Hugo asked, "according to your experiences, all myths are real, and they happened someplace within the Archipelago?"

"That's an awfully general statement," said Jack. "I think it's more reasonable to say that much of what we have believed to be myth and legend in our world here was actually derived from real events in the Archipelago. We've been at this Caretaking business for a number of years now, and we're still just getting our feet wet."

"Indeed," said John, who was rustling around in the brush for a walking stick. "Fact and fiction do not fall into the clear patterns they once did."

"So taken as a whole, mythology, or some of it at least, might actually be real history?"

"We're still trying to figure that out ourselves," replied Jack, "although I must admit it's quite a relief to be able to discuss a lot of this openly with you, Hugo. It's sometimes been very difficult to restrain myself during conversations with Owen Barfield, for example."

"I'd imagine," said John.

Seeing Hugo's puzzled look, Jack explained. "In recent years Barfield has made the argument that mythology, speech, and literature all have a common source, a common origin. In the dawn of prehistory, men did not make distinctions between the literal and the metaphorical. They were one and the same."

"The word and the thing were identical," said Hugo.

"Exactly," said Jack. "That can be described best as the mythological meaning—somewhere between reality and metaphor. When we translate a word, we make distinctions based on context, but early speakers didn't.

"Barfield used the Latin word 'spiritus' as an example," Jack continued. "To early man, it meant something like 'spirit-breath-wind.' When the wind blew, it was not 'like' the breath of a god. It *was* the breath of a god. And when it referred to a speaker's self, his own spirit, he meant it literally as the 'breath of life.'

"What made this compelling was that I had already had several discussions along the same lines with John, Charles, and Ordo Maas in the Archipelago."

"The shipbuilder you told me about?" asked Hugo.

"The same." Jack nodded. "It began with the discussion of the similarities between himself, as Deucalion, and the Biblical Noah, and the fact that stories of the flood and great arks go back well before Gilgamesh."

"But some are real, and others are myths based on the realities?"

"There are different kinds of reality," said Jack. "Barfield said mythological stories are metaphors in narrative form—but that makes them no less real."

Hugo shook his head. "Language gives us the ability to make metaphors, but really, that's all myths are, whether or not they were created around real happenings. Pretty them up all you like, but myths are essentially lies, and therefore worthless."

John and Jack stopped and looked directly at Hugo. "No," John said emphatically. "They are *not* lies."

At that moment there was a rush of wind through the trees that pushed past the three friends and swirled down the shallow hill beyond. It burst upon them so suddenly and forcefully from the still, warm night that it sent a cacophony of leaves raining down from the branches, and it was nearly a full minute before the patter subsided and the walk was quiet once more.

They held their breath, standing still on the path.

"What was that all about?" exclaimed Hugo.

"Quiet," said Jack. "Something's changed."

And he was right. Something *had* changed. There was another presence there with them, somewhere among the trees.

Unmoving, the three men looked about, but nothing seemed amiss. The streams burbled, the trees stood, somber, and the night was as quiet as it had been moments before. And then . . .

Something fell.

"Here," John said, pointing off to the right. "It came from this small clearing."

Cautiously the three scholars stepped away from the path and walked down the gentle slope, threading their way among the beeches and poplars to a small meadow that overlooked one of the streams. In the meadow, standing resolutely in the grass as if it belonged there, was a door. Not a building, just a door. It was plain, made of oak, and set into an arch of crumbling stones. A few feet away lay one of the stones—presumably the one they had heard tumble down from the frame.

All three of them noticed something else that was obviously meant for them to see: Painted across the face of the door in the same reddish brown color as the writing on the book was the image of the Grail.

Hugo turned slightly green. "If that's more blood, I think I might lose my dinner."

Jack let out a low whistle. He recognized the door right away. It was unmistakably one of the doors from the Keep of Time.

"But how can it possibly be here?" John said, answering Jack's unspoken question. "And what's the meaning of the Grail?"

"It's not a coincidence," said Jack. "It's here because we are. I sense a trap."

"That's a bit cloak-and-dagger," said Hugo, who was recovering from his initial surprise. "It's just a door, isn't it?"

"A door into some other time," stated Jack, who was examining the door, albeit from a safe distance, "and from a place far from here."

"Remember what the Cartographer told us," John said. "The doorways were focal points, not actually the pathways themselves."

"You say that like you know what it means," said Jack, "when really, we have no clue how the Keep or the doorways worked."

"I think you're both getting all hot and bothered over a piffle," said Hugo. "Besides, look." He pointed with the toe of his shoe. "It's already open."

Hugo was right. The door was sitting slightly askew within the arch. Not open enough to really see through to the other side, but enough to realize it could be pulled open farther—and so Hugo reached out, and did.

"Hold on!" Jack yelled as he and John both grabbed at Hugo. "You don't know what's on the other side!"

"What can it hurt to open the door?" Hugo reasoned.

"You've obviously never been to Loch Ness," said John.

"What does that mean?"

"Never mind," said Jack. "Hugo may be right. Look."

The door had swung open to reveal . . . nothing.

It was just meadow on the other side.

"See?" said Hugo with a chuckle. "It's just a set dressing, perhaps meant to scare us. Or maybe you're taking a practical joke to unprecedented heights. Either way, I think it's harmless."

And then, as if to prove his point, Hugo walked through the doorway, and half a dozen paces on the other side. Then he turned and spread his hands, smiling. "Gentlemen?"

John and Jack both relaxed visibly.

"I was really quite concerned for a moment," said Jack, as he crouched to sit down in the grass. "I—" He suddenly stopped talking, and his brow furrowed.

"What?" said John.

Jack didn't answer but started moving his head side to side, looking at Hugo. Then his eyes widened and he jumped to his feet.

"Hugo!" he exclaimed. "Come back through the doorway, quickly! Hurry, man!"

Hugo chuckled again. "Jack, you sound like a mother hen. How much rum did you have, anyroad?"

John was looking around, anxious and worried. His Caretaker instincts had gone hyperactive—of them both, Jack wasn't the one to panic easily—and he realized something was wrong.

Jack grabbed him and pulled him two feet to the left of the doorway. As John watched, Hugo vanished.

"Shades!" John hissed. "Hugo! Are you there?" He stepped back. Hugo reappeared.

"Have you both gone round the bend?" asked Hugo. "I'm right here."

He was—but only if they were looking straight through the open doorway. If they moved to either side, and looked around the arch, he disappeared.

"Hugo," said John, "we'll explain in a moment, but for now just walk slowly toward me and through the door."

But Hugo was having nothing of it. "This has gone far enough, I think. It's been a grand joke you two have arranged, but I think it's time to go."

He walked forward and then, whether by happenstance or in defiance of his friends' urgent pleading, he stepped over a fallen stone, and then around the frame rather than through it. And just like that, in a trice . . .

. . . Hugo Dyson was *gone*.

CHAPTER THREE

THE ROYAL ANIMAL RESCUE SQUAD

IT TOOK SEVERAL moments for John and Jack to realize what had happened—and when they did, they realized that there was very little they could actually do.

"Hugo!" John shouted. "Hugo, can you hear me?" But there was no response.

"The scenes we could view through the doorways in the Keep were static, remember?" said Jack.

"Until someone crossed the threshold," said John. "I think Hugo put it into motion."

"But we can see right through it!" protested Jack. "How can he have disappeared so completely?"

"It *is* another time," said John, walking a wide circuit around the door. "He's just moved out of earshot. He's still here. He's just . . . Elsewhen."

"I really wish Charles were here," said Jack. "This is more his forte than ours."

"We'll make do," said John, hefting his walking stick with both hands. "Listen, I'm going to step inside, but I'm going to keep hold of this stick. I want you to remain here and hold on to the other end. That way, whatever happens, you can pull me back through."

"What do you plan to do?"

"I'm going to look around the corner and yell at that idiot to come back through," said John. "With any luck, he's stayed here in the meadow and is wondering where in Hades we got to."

Gingerly Jack took hold of one end of the stick, and with a deep breath, John stepped through the door.

"So far so good," he said, looking over his shoulder. "It really doesn't look any different over here.

"Now," he continued, "I'm going to move around the corner and see if I can spot Hugo."

Keeping the stick firmly grasped in his left hand, John cautiously turned and moved to his right, around the arch, where he found himself looking directly . . .

. . . at *Jack*.

"Jack," said John.

"John," said Jack.

"I don't think it worked. Why isn't it working?"

"Maybe it's because you're holding on to the stick," Jack suggested. "It's keeping you anchored here, to this side."

John made a noise of frustration, and then more on impulse than out of reason, let go of the stick. He leaned sideways and saw Jack leaning on the stick opposite the door.

He walked around to Jack, touching his shoulder to make sure it was not some sort of illusion, then went back through the doorway. Still nothing. Whatever it was that had happened to Hugo was not happening to John.

They tried reversing the process, this time with Jack playing the part of the canary, but with the same result.

Hugo was gone, and they were helpless to do anything about it.

✦ ✦ ✦

The two Caretakers sat under a poplar about twenty feet from the door and stared at it, trying to decide what had just happened.

"This is bad," said John.

"I know," said Jack.

"This is very, very bad," John said again.

"I know!" Jack shot back. "We've just lost a colleague!"

"More like we misplaced him, really," said John. "After all, we do know *where* he is—it's *when* that's the problem."

Jack scrambled to his feet. "Regardless, we haven't the time to sit here moaning about it. We need to get to the Compass Rose and summon some help."

"Who should we call?" asked John, standing and brushing the dry grass from his trousers. "Bert? Or perhaps Artus?"

"Whoever can get here the fastest—probably Stephen, with one of his new airships."

"That's right," said John. "The magic feathers. Perhaps there's even a ship not too far from England. It could ferry us to the Cartographer, and we can get to the bottom of all this."

"You make it sound like getting some help is as easy as snapping your fingers," said Jack, snapping his fingers. "If only—"

As if on cue, a ferocious rattling and roaring sound echoed across the fields, and a curious shape appeared on the other side of the Magdalen Bridge. In seconds it had moved swiftly into view.

It was a metallic conflagration of wheels, gears, levers, and belching smoke. It moved with the lurching fluidity of a caterpillar fleeing a swallow, and with the same urgency. It had a vague resemblance to the vehicle driven by their friend, the badger

Tummeler, but only in the same way that an elephant and a goat were both mammals.

"Dear Lord," declared John. "That contraption looks as if it was built by some fiend with his own three hands in the basement of a third-rate workhouse."

"It probably was," Jack said, "but it's a welcome sight all the same."

As the vehicle came closer, they could better see its makeup. It was essentially a truck, but it seemed to have unfulfilled aspirations of becoming a train. Or a fire engine. Or both. And hanging from every available surface were badgers.

In a cloud of dust and smoke, the motorized monstrosity screeched to a halt on the path above John and Jack, and a dozen badgers in emergency gear leaped to the ground. They moved into a loose formation, then saluted. After a moment (and suppressing grins), John and Jack saluted back.

The tallest of the badgers (and the one who had been driving) stepped forward and offered its paw.

John shook the animal's paw. "I'm guessing you're looking for us."

"We are," said the badger. "The Royal Animal Rescue Squad, at y'r service. Have I th' honor of addressing Scowler Charles?"

"No, I'm John."

"Ah," the badger said, turning to Jack. "Then you must be . . ."

"I'm Jack."

"Oh," said the badger, craning his neck to look around the clearing. "Then Scowler Charles is . . ."

"In France," said John.

As one, all the animals immediately slumped in disappointment and began fidgeting.

"Oh," the apparent leader of the Squad said again. "We're happy to meet you, too, but if Scowler Charles isn't here, then p'rhaps we wasn't needed after all."

"How did you know we were here to begin with?" asked John. "What brought you looking for us?"

"We wuz told that on this particular Saturday, Scowler Charles would be in trouble an' needin' our help. We've been waiting for this day f'r as long as I can remember."

"That's all well and good," said Jack, "but he isn't here. We're awfully glad to see you, though."

The badger waved over one of the others, who pulled out a book that they both began examining with great fervor.

"That binding looks very familiar," said Jack. "What is that book, anyway?"

"Th' Little Whatsit," answered the smaller badger. "It's our guidebook of everything that's anything."

"Sort of like the Great Whatsit back on Paralon?" asked John.

"No," said the first badger, "*exactly* the Great Whatsit. Just portable-like, so we have what we need to know when we needs it. Um, what year is this, anyway?"

"It's 1931," replied John.

"It's the right date," the badger said. "Maybe we're in th' wrong place! Oh dear, oh dear!"

All of the badgers' eyes widened in shock, and the bigger ones started smacking themselves in the heads with their paws.

"But, Father—," said the little one.

"Not now," the first badger said, shushing him.

"Here now," said John. "What's going on?"

"We've failed," said the first badger. "We've failed the great Scowler Charles!"

"I assure you," Jack said soothingly, "Charles is fine. He's nowhere near here. But our friend Hugo is in trouble, and you are, ah, exactly what we needed."

"Really?" the badger said hopefully. He saluted again, and the others followed suit. "The Royal Animal Rescue Squad, at y'r service."

"Thanks," said John. "Say, none of you would happen to be related to our friend Tummeler, would you?"

The first badger nodded enthusiastically. "I is indeed! I am the son of Tummeler, and this," he added, pulling the smaller badger with the book alongside him, "is the son of the son of Tummeler."

"Well met!" said Jack. "And how are you properly addressed?"

"Charles Montgolfier Hargreaves-Heald," said the badger, "but everyone calls me Uncas."

"And you?" John asked, looking at the other, slightly smaller animal. "What's your name?"

"Uh, Fred," said the badger.

"Fred?" said John.

Uncas shrugged. "Badgers named Charles Montgolfier Hargreaves-Heald name their children Fred."

"Why not follow the tale completely and call him Chingachgook?" asked Jack.

The badgers wrinkled their snouts in distaste. "That's a very strange name," said Uncas. "Why would I call him that?"

"Didn't you get *your* name from the Cooper story?"

"The who what?" said Uncas, shaking his head. "I was once in a play called *The Last of th' Phoenicians*," the badger explained proudly. "It was written by my father. He gots th' name from there, an' it stuck t' me."

"My mistake," said Jack.

"What can we do for you, Master Scowlers?" asked Uncas.

John and Jack explained what had happened with the Grail book, and the evening stroll, and the door in the wood, and Hugo's disappearance. All the while they were speaking, the badgers listened with great attentiveness.

"Well," said Uncas when they had finished, "we really had expected to be rescuin' Scowler Charles, but seein' as we're already here, an your friend Hobo—"

"Hugo," John corrected.

"Right, Hugo," said Uncas. "Since he's in trouble, we'll see what we can do."

The badgers swarmed around their vehicle—which Fred explained was called the Howling Improbable—apparently preparing for whatever it was that a Royal Animal Rescue Squad did, while John and Jack watched in patient amusement.

"Do you think Charles is aware of the hero worship being spread around the animal community in the Archipelago?" asked Jack.

"Probably," said John, "but if he isn't, I'm not going to be the one who tells him."

Jack gestured at the badger called Fred, who approached the men with a mixture of shyness and awe. "Yes, Master Scowlers?"

"Tell us about your book," said John, crouching down to meet Fred's eyes. "This 'Little Whatsit.'"

"The prince, Stephen," said Fred. "It was his idea, really. He thought it was impractical to have to go back and forth to Paralon every time he needed to look something up in the Histories. So he set Solomon Kaw and the other crows to work compiling important information and distilling it into a single volume.

"It doesn't have everything about anything," Fred concluded, "but . . ."

"It has something about everything," Jack finished for him. "Brilliant."

"I think so too," Fred agreed. "I never go anywhere without mine. Grandfather Tummeler published it, like he did with the *Geographica*. It's only been printed once, but Grandfather says something like this takes time to find an audience."

"Pardon my asking," said John, "but you don't seem to talk in quite the same way as your father and grandfather. You're a bit more . . ."

"Educated?" guessed Fred.

"I was going to say 'articulate,'" said John, "but yes, educated will do."

Fred looked over his shoulder to where Uncas was coordinating some sort of effort involving coiled wires under the chassis of the Howling Improbable.

"I studied with Stephen under Charys, and Solomon Kaw, and even Samaranth himself," said Fred. "I always thought that maybe, just maybe, if an animal could make himself learn everything it was possible to learn, then I could make my grandfather proud of me. I even hoped . . . I thought maybe . . ."

"Maybe what, Fred?" Jack asked.

The little mammal shifted his feet and would have blushed, if not for his fur. "I thought it might be possible that if I could become a good enough scholar, I might even be able to become a Caretaker myself. Like Charles. Like you."

John and Jack looked at each other, then smiled at Fred. "I think you'd make a very good Caretaker," Jack told the badger. "A very good one indeed."

"We've formulated a plan," Uncas announced finally.

"Excellent," said John. "What is it?"

"We're goin' back t' the Archipelago and getting more help," said the badger.

"What!" exclaimed John and Jack together.

"You've been doing . . . *things* around your vehicle for an hour," said John. "And after all this, the best you can manage is to give up?"

"We're not giving up," huffed Uncas. "But an animal has to know the difference between fight an' flight. And we wasn't prepared to handle something like this."

"What do you usually do?"

"Well, t' be honest," Uncas said sheepishly, "this be th' first time we ever went out on a job."

"The first time?" exclaimed Jack.

"Yes," said Uncas. "In truth, the whole reason the squad was formed was for this one night, and after fourteen years, we're, uh . . . we're really not sure what t' do."

The little animal looked as if it might burst into tears at any second. Jack sighed heavily and sat down next to him.

"Fourteen years," said John. "You've really been waiting fourteen years for this mission, tonight?"

"Yes," said Uncas. "The Prime Caretaker is going to be very disappointed."

"The what?" asked John.

"Th' Prime Caretaker," said Uncas.

"I'm the Caretaker Principia," John said.

"Not the Caretaker Principia," said Uncas, "the Prime Caretaker."

"Do you mean Bert?"

"The Far Traveler? No. He is a friend to us all, but he is not the Prime Caretaker. The Frenchman is."

"Frenchman?" asked John. "Do you mean . . ."

"Never mind who arranged for you to be here," said Jack. "You are still exactly what we'd hoped for. If you appeared here, in Oxford, you must have a means of crossing the Frontier."

"We does indeed," said Uncas. "Every principle in the service of th' New Republic is equipped with a Dragon's Feather." He gestured at the cab of the Howling Improbable, where a bright silver case was fastened above the steering mechanism.

"Well then," said Jack, "let's get back to Paralon, posthaste. We can consult with Aven and Artus, and then go together to see the Cartographer. Between us all, we should be able to sort this all out and rescue Hugo from wherever—whenever—he is."

The badgers all let out a whoop and a cheer. "Rescue Squad!" Uncas shouted joyfully. "Clear the site! We're going home!"

As the animals rejoiced, John and Jack gave a last look at the doorway.

"We should go back to my rooms," said Jack. "We need to pick up the *Geographica*, and I'm sure Artus would like to have a look at the Grail book."

"Agreed."

"Fred," Uncas said, "give me a paw with this, will you?"

It took a moment for the Caretakers to realize what the two badgers were doing, and that was one moment too long.

"No!" yelled Jack. "Don't close the—"

But it was too late. John and Jack both jumped for the door just as Uncas and Fred were closing it, and as the four of them touched it, they heard the gentle but unmistakable click of stone meeting wood. In that instant, the door vanished as if it had never been there.

And that wasn't all.

The Howling Improbable and all the other badgers in the Royal Animal Rescue Squad were also gone.

So was Magdalen Tower. And from what they could see, most of the buildings of the college.

The sky had turned dark, the air chill, and a pall settled over the entire landscape. It was deathly quiet. The trees, what remained of them, were scrawny and barren of leaves. Where there had been soft grass and flowers underfoot, there was now only hard, packed earth.

The stench of decay and rot hung thickly in the air, and for a moment, it seemed to John and Jack as if they'd forgotten to breathe.

"Uh-oh," said Fred.

"Mistakes were made," said Uncas.

And the badger was right, thought John, but the mistakes had all been his.

He was the Caretaker Principia. He was the one who was trained, and experienced, and always, always prepared. And all the signs had been there, all the clues he needed. But he'd grown careless and cocksure. His success in the academic world had given him confidence, and the years of relative peace in both the natural world and the Archipelago had made him sloppy. It was bad enough that Hugo was paying a price for that imprecision, but now, now . . .

With a mounting pressure inside his head, the gravity of their situation was becoming more and more evident.

The doorway *had* been a trap. Jack had even said as much. And up until a moment ago, all John had to do to escape it was to listen to the warning he'd already been given by Hugo himself:

And in God's name, don't close the door!

CHAPTER FOUR

THE UNHISTORY

THE MOON ROSE, and the wan glow it cast over the desolation gave an eerie bas-relief quality to everything the companions saw.

What had been the gently pastoral countryside and beautiful city of Oxford only a minute before was gone. In their place was a cold, bloodless terrain that had been drained of life. No, worse, John thought—it seemed to have been drained of the *will* to live. The trees were scrawny and leafless, and the Cherwell and its many streams were reduced to foul-smelling trickles that were little more than open sewers.

John, Jack, and the badgers cautiously moved onto the walking path above the river and scanned the horizon for any recognizable landmarks. There were none. This was no longer England—or at least, the England they knew.

"It's painful just to look at anything," Fred complained, rubbing at his eyes. "My headbone hurts."

Uncas sniffed the air and wrinkled his snout in disgust. "Death. It smells like death all round, Master Scowlers." The little animal shivered and pulled his son close. "I don't like it a'tall."

John took Jack by the elbow and pointed downriver. "What do you make of that?"

It was a tower, obscured partially by cloud and fog. They'd only just noticed it in the increasing moonlight. It seemed to suck in light, to blend with the night sky. It was, Jack estimated, almost four hundred feet tall. At the top, a reddish glow emanated from a strange crown of stones that looked more like a lidded eye than parapets.

"I couldn't say," Jack replied. "It's not Magdalen Tower, but it's the only thing I can see that seems to have been the work of a civilized mind."

"That's what I was thinking," agreed John. "Until we discern just what's happened to us, we ought to get out of the open—and except for *that*"—he jabbed his thumb at the tower—"it's *all* open."

"Fine," said Jack. "But what do we do with Uncas and Fred? We certainly couldn't take them with us into Magdalen."

"This *isn't* Magdalen," said John. "I don't know what it is. But I think that somehow, Hugo changed the past when he went through that door, and we're seeing the result."

"Hugo vanished an hour before this happened," said Jack. "Why do you think it was he who caused this?"

"Because of how the doors worked in the Keep of Time," said John. "The times we viewed through them only became kinetic when the threshold was crossed. I think Hugo set into motion whatever 'past' that door led to when he stepped through. The doorway, while open, kept it in flux and connected to our 'now.' But when the door closed . . ."

"Awwoooooo . . . ," Fred howled softly, putting his head in his paws. "I'm so sorry, Scowler John, Scowler Jack."

"There now," Uncas said, trying to comfort his son. "I'm in charge of the squad. It be my fault, not yours."

"It be—I mean, it is no one's fault," said John, as forcefully as he thought he could sound without rattling the badgers even further. "We shouldn't place blame. But now we have to work together to find a way out of this mess. Are you with us?"

The badgers girded themselves up, wiping tears away with one paw while saluting with the other. "Th' Royal Animal Rescue . . . uh, Team, is ready to serve, Master Scowlers."

"Fine," John said, turning to Jack. "The badgers stay with us."

They made a quick accounting of what they had with them, and the list was scanty. Uncas had a coil of rope, a small hatchet, and a box of oyster crackers ("For real emergencies," he said), while Fred had a remarkably large key ring, festooned with keys of all shapes and sizes, and his copy of the Little Whatsit. John had his Frog-in-a-Bonnet pocket watch and a small penknife. Jack had only an embroidered handkerchief and a few coins.

"So, other than the crackers, we've no food," said John.

"What did you expect?" Jack exclaimed. "We were taking a walk on the college grounds within shouting distance of my own rooms. Why would I have laden my pockets with anything else, especially food?"

"Don't worry about it," John told him. "You're right. There's no way for us to have known. I just hate feeling so . . . so . . . *unprepared.*"

"At least we have the crackers," said Jack.

"Um," said Uncas, quickly brushing the crumbs out of his whiskers, "we *did.*"

"I thought those were for an emergency," John exclaimed.

Uncas spread his paws and tipped his head back and forth in a matter-of-fact manner. "Seems t' me this *is* an emergency."

"We really should have some sort of Boy Scout kit," said John. "An emergency preparedness sort of thing, for use just in case there's a power outage, or an earthquake, or when one of our friends changes history and makes all the shops vanish."

"I'm thinking I wish I'd brought a pie," said Fred.

"I'm thinking I wish I'd brought more crackers," said Uncas.

"I'm thinking I wish I'd brought the rum," said Jack.

Carefully, and trying to stay alert to their surroundings, they began to make their way toward the dark tower, picking their way along the better maintained, passable parts of the path.

John and Jack each had the same thought: Apart from the eerie resemblance to the Shadowed Lands they had once freed, this tableaux was not entirely unfamiliar in another way. They had both seen—and smelled—places very similar, during their days as soldiers in the Great War. Uncas was right—the smell of death was everywhere.

Several hundred yards on, the path broadened out into an avenue that looked to be even more difficult to traverse, because of a large amount of debris that obstructed the roadway. Broken wheels, discarded carts, and half-burned boxes were scattered in large piles, nearly obscuring the fact that it was an intersection. On closer examination, Jack noted that there were great spider-webs strewn across the piles, clumped in some places, but completely clear of it in others.

"We sh-should go round, Master Jack," said Uncas, the fear in his voice making him stutter.

"Agreed," said Jack.

"No cars," John observed. "Nothing modern whatsoever. No

electricity, as far as I can tell. No automobiles. Not even gas lamps. And those wheels and wagons are archaic. I wonder how far back Hugo went, to have caused this."

"Sixth century," said Jack. "The message on the Grail book had to have been written when he went back. And he knew something bad would happen—that's why he told us not to close the door."

"Don't remind me," said John. "My only consolation is that Charles isn't here to see this too."

"I wish Scowler Charles *was* here," said Uncas. "He'd have set things aright already, I thinks."

"And entirely by accident, knowing Charles," said Jack.

"Which still saved you, more than once," Fred pointed out. "Uh, sir."

"You're probably right," John said, as he scratched the little animal affectionately on the head. "He does have a knack for doing the right thing at the right moment—whether he knows it or not."

The tower stood in what should have been the center of Oxford, and was ringed with walls of sturdier construction than anything else they had passed. They were several dozen yards high, and unlike the tower they encircled, the walls shone brightly in the moonlight.

"That's a hopeful sign," Jack commented. "At least whoever is in charge around here keeps the outer walls clean."

"Hmm," said John. "Now that's odd. For a fortification, anyway."

He was looking at the great iron and wood doors that were set into the wall, just to their left. Massive, they were obviously intended to withstand a hefty assault—but the crossbeams and braces were on the exterior, rather than inside.

"Odd isn't the word," said Jack. "That's just stupid engineering. With all the braces out here, it wouldn't keep anyone out at all. It'd be better for keeping people . . ." His voice trailed off as he realized the conclusion he'd drawn.

"Back up," John said, looking around with a growing unease. "Back up slowly, Jack."

The badgers, for their part, had gone no closer, but stood clutching each other, trembling.

"Uncas?" Jack said, concerned. "Fred? What is it?"

"Headbones," Fred whispered. "Lots of suffering."

"Are you hurt?" asked John.

"Not ours," said Uncas. "Human bean headbones."

The little mammal pointed with a shaking paw at the walls, and they suddenly realized why the walls shone. They weren't clean, so much as *bleached*.

It was interesting to realize, John thought, just how neatly skulls could be stacked, and with such precision.

Suddenly a booming cough came from behind the fortified walls, followed by another, and another, and then something of tremendous mass threw itself against the great doors. The doors shook violently, but held. The creature was tall enough that they could see its hairy bulk rising above the crest of the walls as it—they—paced back and forth, testing the doors with another blow now and again.

"Do you think they know we're here?" John whispered. "Jack—did we wake something up?"

"I'm not going to wait around to ask," Jack began, before he was cut off by another cough, which was followed by an even more chilling sound.

"Jaaack . . ."

Jack froze. So did the others.

"Jaaaack . . . We hear you, Jaaack. . . ."

It was the great creatures inside the walls. Even from that distance, they could hear the companions whispering.

"Who are you?" said John.

"Sssss . . . Weee are the children of Polyphemus . . . ," the creature said. *"Be ye alive, or be ye dead . . . we'll grind your bones to make our bread. . . ."*

"Giants!" Jack hissed. "What are giants doing in Oxford?"

"This isn't Oxford," John said irritably. "But if these are giants . . . Perhaps we could use the Binding? From the *Geographica*? Maybe . . ."

"Is that even possible to do without royal blood?" Jack whispered back. "Who'd be crazy enough to try?"

There was a chuffing noise from behind the walls of bone, and after a moment the companions realized that the giants were laughing at them.

"Foolish mansss . . . ," the giant said. *"Nnooo Bindings on the sons of Polyphemus . . . not like before . . ."*

"Before?" said Jack. "Someone *has* tried to Bind them."

"Yess!" rasped the giant. *"You, Jaaack . . . you have tried. . . . Jaaack, Jaaack, the Giant-Killer . . ."*

"Oh Lord," Jack said under his breath, before he remembered they could hear him anyway. "You've got me confused with someone else," he called more loudly. "It wasn't me!"

There was a pause, almost as if denying it was persuasion enough. And then . . .

"Jaack Giant-Killer . . . Caretaker Jaack, Companion of John . . ."

It was a strange moment for Jack, as John looked at him with something akin to astonishment, while the badgers looked at him in unabashed admiration.

"Achaemenides!" the giant bellowed. *"Achaemenides! Loooose usss! Loose us to seize the slayer of our father!"*

With an impact that shook the ground, the giants—four of them, the companions could now see—pressed against the walls, and one began pounding on the gate. The giants were tall enough that the tops of their heads rose above the walls, and the companions could see that below the scraggly tufts of hair and rough foreheads, their eyes had been sewn shut.

"They're blind," said Jack. "At least they can't see us."

"Nnooo . . . ," said the first giant, a triumphant purr settling into his voice, *"but weee can* hearrr *youuuu. . . ."*

"That's it," John exclaimed, grabbing each of the badgers by their collars. "Run, Jack! Run!"

With the calls of the giants echoing in the air behind them, the four companions ran as fast as they could, John carrying Uncas and Jack carrying Fred. There may have been some slight breach of etiquette or decorum in simply carrying the small animals like cabbages—but at the moment, none of them cared. All that mattered, literally, was getting out of earshot of the giants.

John was more than happy to let Jack take the lead again. Of the two of them, Jack was the quicker thinker in situations like this.

Jack led them back to the intersection where the great spiderwebs were, then took the road leading to the right, keeping them at a dead run.

The direction they were running took them to an area that was pockmarked with structures. Most of them were on stilts and stood ten feet or more off the ground. The ones that weren't on stilts were either in a bad state of disrepair, or burned past usability. The road itself was in better condition, and there were fewer obstructions to slow them down. There were still no lights or fires visible, but as they passed, John imagined he could feel someone watching them from the shadows.

When they had finally gone a far enough distance that the badgers could run for themselves, John and Jack lowered them to the ground and slowed to a brisk trot. As they jogged along, Jack realized that he was still the object of intense admiration.

"Did you really kill a giant, Scowler Jack?" Uncas asked. "They sure seemed t' know *you*."

Jack sighed. "I'm sure if I had, I'd remember it, and if I was the Giant-Killing type, I probably wouldn't be as afraid of that lot as I actually am."

"Oh," the badger said, deflating slightly. "But," he added, brightening, "y' did speak t' them very boldly."

"That he did," Fred agreed. "Very boldly indeed."

"Oh, for heaven's sake," Jack said, sitting heavily on a soft-looking patch of dirt. "I think we've run far enough. And I'm knackered at any rate."

John scanned the horizon in the direction from which they'd come. "I think we're okay for the moment. But I think our plan of approaching whoever is in charge of the tower is right out."

Jack pulled off one of his shoes and examined his foot. "Bugger this for a lark. I've gotten a blister. I hope it doesn't get infected."

"A blister?" John snorted. "I've seen you take cudgel blows that nearly took your arm off, you've been stabbed by swords, and even shot with an arrow—and you're complaining about a blister?"

"It's a really *big* blister," said Jack.

"Here," Fred said, hopping forward. "I can help with that."

The little badger started flipping through pages in the Little Whatsit, humming to himself as he did so. Then he seemed to settle on the page he wanted, scanned it twice, then replaced the book in his coat.

"I'm going to need the penknife, please, Scowler John, and Scowler Jack, tell me—are any of your coins silver?"

"One of them," Jack said as John handed over the knife. "What are you going to do?"

"This'll sting a little, and I'm sorry for that," said Fred, "but I can keep it from getting infected."

Jack removed his stocking and let the animal examine his blistered foot. Fred clucked and purred over it a moment, then swiftly lanced the blister with the knife. As it drained into the cloth Jack pressed against it, Fred used the knife to scrape tiny slivers of silver from the coin, which he then ground to a fine dust between two stones. Finally satisfied with the powdered silver, he pressed it to the wound, then bound the foot tightly with a strip of cloth from his coat. Standing back, he handed the coin to Uncas and told Jack he could replace his stocking and shoe.

"It'll sting a bit, there's no helping that," Fred repeated, "but it'll be healed in a few hours, and it won't get infected."

"Amazing," said Jack. "How is it you learned this?"

Fred patted the book in his pocket. "The Little Whatsit," he said proudly. "I told you—it has something about everything in it."

"Handy, that," said John. "I'd like to take a look at it—but later. I think someone's followed us."

There was a bulky shape moving along the road some distance back, coming straight toward them. It was too small to be one of the giants, but large enough to be worth hiding from.

Jack led them under one of the stilt-houses and under the fallen archway of a house that had been burned. With any luck, they'd blend in with the protruding ribs of the frame that were sticking out of the rubble.

"I think something must have died," Jack whispered, wrinkling his nose and checking his shoes. "It smells horrid over here."

"Uh, that would be me," Uncas admitted sheepishly. "I stepped in a puddle. Sorry."

"Wet badger fur," Jack groaned, nodding. "Charles never told me it was this bad."

"Quiet," said John, hunkering down. "It's coming."

The thing that followed them resembled a motorcar, but it had no engine. Instead it was drawn by two skeletal-looking horses with bandaged heads. With horror, the companions realized that these were dehorned unicorns. And the appearance of the carriage's driver gave the impression that he'd happily have done it himself, and then used the horns as toothpicks just for spite. He stepped down from the carriage and looked about, eyes narrowed. From their concealment, the companions could see he wore a great gray trench coat and a matching top hat. His beard was full and black, he was all of eight feet tall, and he wore a blue rose on his lapel. A Cossack, out on the town.

Then he opened his coat.

Where his torso should have been was a great wicker cage,

and through the weave they could just make out the shapes of small creatures moving about inside. At first John thought they might be monkeys, but then the large man stopped and opened his chest to let them out, and the true horror was laid bare in the chalky moonlight.

They were children.

Little boys, perhaps ten but certainly not as old as twelve, and thin as bamboo. They were filthy, and dressed in rags. Each had a thick iron ring fastened around its neck, which was connected to a leash held by the man. The dozen or so boys who emerged from him spread out at his feet, sniffing the ground.

"Ah, my little Sweeps, my precious Sweeps. Finds us the man-flesh. Finds us it, and make Papa happy."

"Yes, Papa," the children answered in unison.

As the companions watched from their hiding place, the Sweeps began a revoltingly fascinating transformation. They bent low, walking on all fours and sniffing the ground. And as they went, they began murmuring phrases that at first seemed like nonsense.

"I love my vegetables," said one.

"I stabbed my sister in the eye," said another.

"My farts smell like flowers," said a third.

And as the boys voiced these obvious lies, their noses began to grow. Some grew longer than others, but all of them soon had noses of extraordinary length, and their search picked up the pace accordingly.

"Good, good, my precious Sweeps," purred their "papa." "Finds us the man-flesh. Finds it now, for your papa and the King."

The man and his Sweeps were looking around the stilt-houses

on the opposite side of the road, far from where the companions were hiding. For a brief instant, John and Jack both harbored the notion that they could sneak away, but then one of the Sweeps stood stock still, like a chipmunk. It sniffed the air several times, and then turned and looked directly at the companions.

The Sweep ran to its master and whispered to him, and the great man and his hideous children all turned around and began to move across the road.

Suddenly a ball of flame erupted in the center of the road, throwing a blazing light over the whole area. For a moment the Sweeps' master locked fury-filled eyes with John, but he retreated from the fire, pulling all the children back inside himself. Mounting the carriage, he wheeled the unicorns about and disappeared over the hill.

"That was lucky as all Hades," John said, rising from where he'd been crouching. "Very lucky."

"It weren't luck, really," came a muffled voice from above. "The Sweeps can withstand a lot, but the Wicker Men hate fire more than anything."

A thin, limber man dressed in tattered clothes dropped down from the stilt-house to the left of them. His face was wrapped in cloth save for his eyes, and his arms were bandaged to the fingertips. From the blackened cloth, they could tell he'd been badly singed in saving them.

"Naw," he said, waving off their concern. "I's been burned worse, see?"

He unwrapped the cloth from his face to reveal old scars along his right cheek and chin. The companions all gasped in shock—but not because of the scars.

It was Charles.

"Scowler Charles!" Uncas said joyfully. "Of course it be you who rescued us! Of course!"

"Who's Charles?" said the man, eyeing the badger suspiciously. "I only helped you out 'cause I hate the Wicker Men. It weren't to save you lot of idiots a'tall."

"These are scowlers . . . uh, scholars, not idiots," Fred said defiantly, "and they are two of the greatest men in all the world."

"It doesn't matter why," Jack said, offering a hand that was studiously ignored. "Ah, I mean, there's no one in England I'd be happier to see right now."

"England?" the man asked. "What's an 'England'?"

"What kind of question is that?" John sputtered, spreading his arms. "*This* is England. This country, where we live. England. Great Britain. Home."

The man looked puzzled. "I don't know where you blokes come from, but this is Albion. Always has been, as long as anyone can remember. There are some what call it otherwise, but not aloud, not unless they be brave, or foolish. The king's minions, like that one what just run off, have seen to that. I shouldn't even be sayin' as much as I have."

"Either way," John said, "we are truly grateful for your help. I'm John." As Jack had done, John stuck out his hand, which the man finally shook.

"Strange, stupid travelers from afar, you can call me Chaz," he said hesitantly. "Welcome to the Winterland."

PART TWO

FRACTURED ALBION

CHAPTER FIVE

TATTERDEMALION

THE FISHERMEN HAD wondered about the cart, and the scrawny horse that pulled it, and the solitary driver who had waited with it by the river's edge for nearly three hours. He was unshaven and unkempt, but wore robes of great quality and worth. His cart was battered and poorly kept but could withstand such treatment because its builders had been masters of their craft. And the steed was thin, but its bearing was noble. This driver was, despite the appearances, a great dignitary, or even possibly a king who sat in his cart next to the river.

The wild-eyed look he wore, coupled with the fact that he seemed to converse only with himself, encouraged them to leave him be. The fishermen moved their nets farther down the river and left him to his own devices.

The king (for that was, in fact, what he was) had been lured to the riverside by a promise. All he need do was wait for the man depicted in an illumination he'd been given, then deliver him to the distant tournament that had already commenced. And for this, the king would be given his heart's desire—or at least, the fulfillment of the family obsession. It never occurred to him to wonder how his benefactor had discovered the location of the

Questing Beast, but the promise itself was enough, and made it worth his effort to try.

When it was nearly dusk, the autumn light had faded to a haze that painted the belly of the clouds gold and crimson. As the sky grew dimmer, the king's patience finally found itself rewarded when a shortish, slightly discombobulated man came staggering up the embankment.

He was more disheveled than in the illumination, but the manner of dress was the same, and he was here, in the appointed spot, at (almost) the appointed time. The king lowered himself from the cart with a grunt and a groan and bowed his head in greeting.

The odd man he'd been sent to retrieve spoke strangely, almost unintelligibly. Perhaps he was an idiot. Either way, the king reasoned, he needed to communicate his intention. With a series of half phrases and pantomimed gestures, it became evident to the man that the king was there to offer transport. He clambered into the cart, sitting next to the king, and stuck out his hand in greeting. The king looked at it oddly for a moment, then gripped the man's wrist, as if looking for a concealed weapon.

The man laughed uproariously at this and said something the king finally realized was his name: "Dyson. Hugo Dyson. Pleased to make your acquaintance."

The king loosed his wrist and nodded. "Pellinor," he said, tapping his chest. "Pellinor." With that he grasped the reins and clucked his tongue at the horse. They were three days late and still had a long way to go.

Following their familiar-yet-still-a-stranger liberator gave John and Jack time to observe and evaluate him. He was, for all that their senses could accrue, Charles. But at the same time he was, as he insisted repeatedly, not.

Some of the scars he bore were fresh, but others were years old. He had not come here in a trice, as they and the badgers had done. It was possible he had gone through one of the doorways, as their hapless colleague had earlier, and found himself thrust backward in time—but that wouldn't explain why he didn't recognize them, or worse, why it seemed as if he had no memory of the Charles they knew at all.

Chaz was obviously uneducated, and he spoke with worse grammar than Uncas. He bore some of Charles's mannerisms, and certain speech patterns were familiar, the cadences, the tone. . . . But both the scholarly rationalism and playful inquisitiveness were gone. What remained was the shape of Charles, his outline, but it was filled with fear, and distrust, and overwhelmingly, the basest of instincts: to survive at all costs. This was made clear right away.

"Get rid of the animals," Chaz had said, to the badgers' great dismay.

"We're not getting rid of anyone," John stated firmly, backed by incredulous nodding from Jack. "They're with us, period."

Chaz shrugged. "Have it your way. But they smell, and that means death here."

"You aren't a garden of roses yourself," Fred pointed out.

"Fred!" Uncas exclaimed. "Mind your tongue! This be Scowler Charles you be addressin'!"

"There you go with that 'Charles' business again," Chaz said, irritated. "My name is Chaz, not that it matters to you. And you owe me a life-debt."

"For what?" asked Jack.

"Saving you from the Sweeps," said Chaz, "but I'll consider it paid if you give me the fat badger to roast."

Uncas couldn't decide whether to be offended at being called fat, or horrified at the idea of being eaten. Fred just bared his teeth and stepped in front of his father.

"You must be joking," said Jack. "These aren't merely animals—they're our friends!"

"Thank you," said Uncas. "I think."

"Where we're from, Chaz, we don't eat our friends," John explained.

"I thinks you're *here* now, not where you're from," Chaz replied. "But I'm not really that hungry anyway." With a last look at the badgers, he turned and trotted off. About twenty yards away, he turned around, a silhouette against the hillside. "Well? Are you idiots coming or not?"

There had been little choice. And as obscured as it was by strangeness, the voice that beckoned to them was their friend's voice. So they—all four of them—followed.

Chaz set a pace that was swift, but not impossible to keep, even for the badgers. They were slowed only by bewilderment, remorse, and no small amount of fear. It wasn't a scholar who had looked at them, but a predator. And it ran contrary to animal sense to follow a predator into its own lair.

A short distance farther on, John unconsciously checked the time on his watch, noted the fixed hands, then smiled ruefully and put it back in his pocket.

"Why don't you carry one that works," suggested Jack, "and

keep that one in another pocket to show Priscilla when she asks about it?"

"I can't quite manage the deception," John admitted. "It seems like a small thing, to be sure—but when I tried it, I found myself fussing about with them and worrying about which one was draped on the waistcoat and which was hidden . . . and then I forgot, and Pris saw the other one, and the hurt in her eyes was excruciating. So it's the Frog-in-a-Bonnet time or none at all, I'm afraid."

"Perhaps you could ask Father Christmas to give her a good watch this Christmas, to be passed on to you," Jack said, grinning.

"That's not a half-bad idea," John said. "I'll have to ask him about it the next time we're in the Archipelago."

Jack turned his head, but not swiftly enough for John to catch the look of doubt that crossed his features. Bantering about home and family was one thing. But mentioning the Archipelago brought them both back to the present dilemma, and the creeping despair that was becoming impossible to push away.

It took longer for the companions to get to the small village where Chaz lived than it might have if John or Jack had been in the lead. The entire area seemed deserted, and the only other structures they saw were more of the odd stilt-houses that pockmarked the roads. But Chaz had insisted on taking a circuitous route that roamed back and forth across the entire countryside.

"It's because of the Wicker Man," he finally explained when the others pressed for his reasons. "He was out looking for you lot in partic'lar, and there's no telling how many more are doing the same. Their Sweeps follow your scent, an' so it's best to leave a trail that'll confuse 'em before they finds you."

"How many more *what* might be out looking?" asked Jack.

"Wicker Men," Chaz replied without turning around, "and their Sweeps. That wasn't the only one, you know. And there are other creatures too. Some better. Most worse."

"We saw the giants," John said. "Should we be talking aloud, with them lurking somewhere back there?"

"Oh, the giants is no worry," Chaz said breezily. "They can't be loosed until they been summoned, an' . . ."

He stopped as if he'd said too much, then scowled at John. "Be that as it may, mayhap we shouldn't ought t' be talking aloud, anyroad."

After another hour of Möbius loops, Chaz finally brought them to his strange abode. Unlike the dozen or so stilt-houses that clustered nearby, it was set into the side of a hill. It had a round door that was lightly camouflaged and heavily fortified. Through the doorway, they could see that the ceilings were low, but it seemed a good enough place, if not really one suited to guests.

The area itself was more intriguing to Jack. It was disconcertingly familiar. The trees, what remained of them, were bare, but the soil itself, the reddish hues, the texture . . . It was all the same, along with the spot nearby where the quarry should be. . . .

And then he knew.

It was the Kilns, Jack suddenly realized. Home. *His* home, at any rate. His and Warnie's, and Jamie's. Chaz had brought them to the one place Jack most wanted to be, except it wasn't that place at all—it was a place that looked like home but was really in some hellish otherworld in which they were trapped, perhaps permanently.

"So how have you managed to survive on your own?" Jack asked.

"I makes do," Chaz said after a moment. "I scavenge, mostly, and trade a little of this, a little of that. But I gets what I needs."

"I think I need some sustenance," said John, "if you have anything you can spare, Chaz."

"My stores is scanty, save for roots and a bone or two," said Chaz, eyeing the badgers while trying to look as if he wasn't, "but it may be enough for a thin soup, since we have nothing else t' put in the pot."

"Soup—thin or not—sounds fine to me," Jack said, folding his arms and standing protectively in front of the badgers. "I just wish we had Bert's magic stone to help it along."

"Ah yes," said John. "His Stone Soup. Meal fit for, well, a king. Or a group of lost scholars."

"Who's Bert?" Chaz said without looking up from his dinner preparations. "Not that I really care, but talking passes the time."

"Are you sure he's not Charles?" Jack whispered to John.

"Heh," said John. "Bert's our mentor, Chaz. A great man. And I really wish he were here."

"Maybe he is," offered Fred. "If Scowler Char—uh, I mean, if Mister Chaz is here, and he's almost like Scowler Charles, than perhaps others we know are here too."

"Everything here is upside down and sideways anyway," Jack said, indicating their reluctant host. "Perhaps Bert goes by Herb or Herbert or George or some such."

Uncas nodded sagely. "Th' Far Traveler can be knowed by many names."

For the first time it seemed as if the conversation had engaged

Chaz's full attention. He stood abruptly, ladle in hand. "Far Traveler? This Bert fellow is also called the Far Traveler?"

"Does that make a difference?" asked John.

"It does if I knows a 'Far Traveler' and not a 'Bert,'" Chaz replied, suddenly animated. "Is he really a friend of yours?"

"Friend and teacher," said John. "I think what we need is to get some food and rest, then get our bearings in the morning and see if Bert really is somewhere hereabouts."

Chaz dropped the bowl of roots he'd been pulling out of a cupboard and turned to them, incredulous. "Are you mad?" he exclaimed. "Why would you possibly go about during the day?"

"Why would that be a worse plan than traipsing about at night?" asked Jack. "What with giants and Sweeps and Wicker Men roaming around."

"There are worse things than them what serves the king," Chaz said slowly, "an' they go about when the sun is high."

The fear in his voice was enough to convince them. The companions ate the meal he prepared, then stretched out on the dirt floor as the sun began to rise, to sleep until dusk. And so none of them saw the raven Chaz kept in the cage in the rear of the house, or the name he wrote on the note he tied to its leg before he turned it loose into the harsh Albion daylight, closing the door behind it.

When the sun had finally dropped to just a sliver of blood-tinted light on the horizon, Chaz finally opened the door again, and they began the journey to find the Far Traveler.

Chaz led them south and west, to the channel that was the nearest access to open waters in that part of Albion. As they journeyed they could see more towers in the distance. None were close enough for the companions to worry about being sighted, but they kept watchful eyes all around, just to be safe.

It was still fully night when they reached their destination, a small hamlet Chaz called Trevena. It consisted of fewer structures than the village that had been the Kilns, but all here were on the strange stilts. The largest of them, made of stone, was at the edge of the beach, surrounded by a courtyard. A wooden bridge ran up at a slope to the front door, which was open.

The courtyard was bare rather than clean; and the shack simple rather than orderly. Spareness might resemble cleanliness, but it cannot disguise the bleak dreariness underneath.

Chaz passed over the bridge and through the shack with a proprietor's ease and opened the door at the rear of the building. "He'll be out this way, on the pier," he said, gesturing. "Follow me close-like."

The pier, which was itself a generous description, was high off the ground, but short. The beach dropped away sharply, since there was no longer any water flowing underneath, and the sand stretched out into the darkness.

"Must be low tide," John observed, "but the beach seems awfully parched."

Chaz chuckled. "'Tis, 'tis," he said in agreement. "Been low tide for almost two hundred years, as I heard it said. The ocean's still out there, somewheres, but no souls alive has seen it."

"Strange pier," Jack said. "If there's no water, where do you moor the boats?"

"Hsst!" Chaz hissed, looking behind them. "You can't just go round sayin' words like that. Words kill, you know."

"Sorry," said Jack.

"Is that him?" John asked, pointing.

At the end of the pier, a shadow stood against a piling. A shadow with a very familiar shape.

John began to move closer, but Chaz motioned for him to hold back. Instead Chaz stepped to the far right side of the pier, where he could be seen in the dim light—but without getting too close to the figure at the end of the pier.

The shadow raised its head in alarm, then lowered it in resignation.

"Whatever it is you've come about, Chaz, I want no part of it. Go back to your game-playing with the Wicker Men, or better yet, go play some pipes outside the bone towers, and let the giants have some fun with you. I don't care either way—just leave me be."

"Weren't my call to come seeking you either, you old goat," Chaz retorted, "but I run into some fellows who says they knows you. Calls you 'Bert' or summat."

At this the shadow stood upright, startled. "Bert? There's no one else still alive who would use that name, not in *this* world, not unless . . ."

He pushed away from the piling where he'd been braced, and hobbled out into the hazy light. For everyone but Chaz, there was a shock of recognition, and for John and Jack, a further shock of seeing nightmares made real.

It was indeed Bert. But he had been *changed*.

The cheerily ruffled tatterdemalion of their first meeting was barely in evidence here. The clothes and hat were the same, but threadbare and shabby. He was thin, nearly emaciated, and his face haggard and drawn. There was no spark in his eyes, no twinkle. Neither of them had ever seen him without the twinkle, even in the grimmest of circumstances. But then again, neither of them had seem him without all his limbs, either.

Bert supported himself by gripping a small ash walking stick with his left hand—his only hand. His other sleeve was folded and pinned just below his elbow. And in place of his right leg, fastened just under the knee was a piece of wood wrapped in leather, which ended with a crude wooden foot inside his shoe.

Before John or Jack could say anything, Bert threw aside his stick and hobbled forward, grabbing John by the lapels. Weakly, but driven by surprise and rage, his hand shook as the younger man tried to steady him. Bert pressed close, eyes wild, and all but screamed at John.

"Where have you been? Where . . . have . . . you . . . *been?!*"

CHAPTER SIX

THE SERENDIPITY BOX

"BERT!" JOHN SAID in choked astonishment. "You know us? You really know us?"

"Of course I know you, John," the ragged old man said, finally letting go of John's coat and brushing him away. "I gave you the *Geographica*. I helped the three of you learn your roles in the great clockwork mechanism of things that are. I stood by you against a great evil, and we saved the world, once. And then you let it degrade to . . . to . . . this," he spat, gesturing with his good arm. "Here, you. Badger. Give me my stick."

Fred jumped forward and retrieved the short ash staff, handing it to the old man. Neither he nor Uncas understood what was taking place, and so they remained quiet while the humans played out the drama.

Bert stood a few feet from John and Jack, forming a rough triangle, but he refused to look at either of them—not directly. Chaz stood farther back, observing.

"Fourteen years," Bert wheezed. "We came here fourteen years ago, to . . . heh . . . *SAVE* you . . . to *HELP* you . . ."

"You said 'we,' Bert," Jack said, interrupting. "Who else came with you? Surely not Aven?"

"No, not Aven," Bert replied. "Your pretty ladylove stayed in the Archipelago, where she needed to be. She doesn't love you, you know," he added, almost conspiratorially. "Never did. Didn't love the potboy, either. No, Nemo was her companion, but you fixed that, didn't you, Jack?"

In earlier years Jack would have reddened at this and become flustered. But he'd matured a great deal in the intervening time, and could face his own shortcomings and mistakes foursquare, as a man is supposed to do.

"I stopped feeling responsible for that a long time ago, Bert," he said calmly. "James Barrie told me things about Nemo, and you, and . . ." He stopped. "Verne. You came here with Jules Verne."

Bert sighed heavily and turned his back to them before answering. "Yes," he said finally. "Jules and I came here together. We came . . . *here*. . . ."

Without warning, the old man suddenly burst into tears. "Why did you have to bring her up, Jack? Why did you have to mention Aven, now that I'd finally nearly forgotten about her?"

Jack started to reply, but John silenced him with a gesture. Bert was speaking from a long, deep pain, and perhaps they might learn something of what was happening.

"If she'd been killed in battle, I might have been able to live with it," Bert sobbed. "But here, after what's happened, it's as if she never existed! She is worse than dead!"

"The Lady Aven is not dead," came a soft voice. "I saw her myself just yesterday."

Fred was standing nearby, head bowed and paws folded respectfully, but when he spoke his voice was firm with conviction. "She is alive. Maybe not here, where we are, but somewheres. She is. And when Scowler John and Scowler Jack, and, uh, Mister Chaz help us t' get back there, maybe you can come with us and see for yourself."

At first Bert reacted in rage, raising the ash stick to strike at the little creature. But Fred didn't move. He barely flinched, and closed his eyes to receive the blow.

Seeing this, Bert lowered the stick, then fell to his knees and grasped the badger, pulling Fred to his chest. "I'm sorry, I'm sorry, little child of the Earth," Bert said through muffled sobs. "I will not strike you. I won't. It's just . . . It's been so long. . . ."

Fred hugged the old traveler, and after a moment, Uncas moved in to do so as well. "It be all right," said Uncas gently.

"Animal logic," Jack said to John. "Loyalty is all, and all things may be forgiven."

"We should go inside," said Chaz. "The sun will be coming up soon."

"Yes," Bert agreed, rising and wiping his eyes. "We have a great deal to discuss."

With the badgers supporting him on either side, Bert moved down the pier to the bridge that connected it to the house. John followed behind, but Jack pulled Chaz aside.

"If this is indeed 'our' Bert," Jack whispered, "how has he survived? *You* knew just where to find him. Wouldn't the king have killed him long before now?"

"He has, in years past, proved himself to be a friend to the king," Chaz replied, "or at least, wise enough to seem as such."

"And this," Jack said, indicating the damaged man walking ahead of them, "is how the king treats his friends?"

Chaz shrugged. "Someone asked him that once. And th' king laughed an' said, 'A friend this valuable you can't eat all at once.'"

* * *

Bert took them all inside the little shack, where he lit two candles, which he placed at opposite ends of the cramped quarters. For a single person, the accommodations were tight; for four men and two badgers, it was practically claustrophobic. There was a table and only one chair, which Bert took. The others sat on the floor, except for Chaz, who remained standing nervously in the doorway.

"You'll have to forgive my lack of hospitality," Bert told the others. "I'd offer you tea, but I haven't any tea. I'd offer you brandy, but I haven't any brandy. In fact, I don't even have any crackers to give you."

"We did," said Uncas, "but there was an emergency."

"There still is," said Jack.

"That's a shame," said Bert, "to run out of crackers before you've run out of emergency. And in Albion, it's always an emergency."

"The king, whoever he is, sounds like an utter despot," John observed.

"Well said, John," said Bert, "for he is just that. A despot. A petty, cruel dictator who hates himself and takes it out on everyone else. He suffers, and so makes the world suffer too."

"That sounds awfully familiar," said Jack.

"More than you know," said Bert. "You've met him. Killed him, actually, more or less."

"That's impossible," said John.

"Improbable, but clearly not impossible," Bert corrected. "In the world you came from, the Winter King fell to his death in the year 1917. But here it is the one thousand four hundred and fourth year of the reign of our Lord and King, Imperius Rex, Mordred the First."

* * *

It took some time for the reunited friends to explain what had been happening to them, and Bert listened to their accounting of the situation with Hugo Dyson without comment. When they at last had finished explaining, he nodded sadly.

"I begin to understand, at long last," he said, still unwilling to look at any of them directly. "If Hugo went back to the sixth century, then he changed history. And everything proceeded apace from there to what we see now, today. Something that happened in the past gave Mordred the means to conquer and rule and emerge victorious against all opposition—if there ever was any."

"Why do you still know us, Bert?" asked Jack. "Chaz is obviously what Charles became in this timeline where he never knew us—but you're still our Bert."

"Jules and I left Paralon right after the War of the Winter King," said Bert. "He had come across a passage in a future history that mentioned the reemergence of Mordred, and so we returned here to England to warn you. When we arrived, we found things as you see them now, and we were trapped."

"We've seen you since then," said Jack. "Many, many times, in fact. How is that possible if you've been here all these years?"

"Where *is* here?" Bert asked. "'Here' wasn't created until Hugo went through the door. And once that happened, everything forward changed."

"I still don't see how that would affect your return to England," said John. "Our past hasn't changed. Why did yours?"

"Jules and I travel via means that take us outside of time and space," said Bert. "If we'd simply come back on one of the Dragonships, we'd never have noticed a difference. Jules has always kept his own counsel, though, and insisted that we needed to travel by his usual method, so we did."

"You've mentioned time travel before, Bert," John said, "but you've never gone into detail about how you really do it. It never came up as a factor in our roles as Caretakers until the problems with the Keep of Time, so I never asked about it."

"And those problems are the very ones that caused this, aren't they?" Bert said, his voice harsh. "If you'd paid closer attention to your responsibilities, then maybe we wouldn't be here now."

"That's hardly fair, Bert," Jack exclaimed. "You were there with us when Charles led us out of the Keep, before Mordred set it aflame."

"Don't bring *me* into this," put in Chaz, "even if it's the other me."

"Jack's right," said John. "There were things you and Verne could have told us—about time travel, for example—that might have prevented this. But you always seemed to be playing your own cards close, Bert."

"You weren't ready yet," the old man replied. "At least, in Jules's estimation you weren't. We had focused on you, John, as the one with the most potential to learn about the intricacies of time as well as space. But then we realized it might be Jack who possessed the greater capacity. We were wrong on both counts, it seems. No offense."

"I can't be offended," Jack said, "when I don't even understand what you're talking about."

"So you get my point," said Bert. "Excellent. No, we realized it was Charles who had a bent for not only time travel, but also for interdimensionality. So we came back to England specifically to warn *him*."

"Same with th' Royal Animal Rescue Squad," Uncas put in. "We were gived our instructions by th' Prime Caretaker fourteen years ago."

"That's what I find intriguing," said John. "Verne obviously knew more than he was telling you, Bert, to set a plan into motion that involved a rescue effort on the very day that these events would be set into motion in your own future."

Bert stood and hobbled his way over to the mantel of the small tumbledown fireplace at the far side of the shack. On it sat a skull, a scroll, and a small box of a unique design.

Bert removed the box and set it in the center of his small table. The box wasn't polished, but it was shiny with age; great, great age. The wood it was constructed of was pale, and there were cuneiform-like markings carved into the top and sides. Across the bottom were signs of scorching, as if it had been held to a flame. Jack reached out to lift the lid, but Bert slapped down his hand with the ash staff.

"Not so quickly, lad," the old man said. "No telling what'll come out of the Serendipity Box. Don't want to let anything out that's best kept in, for now."

"What is a Serendipity Box?" Jack asked as he rubbed his knuckles. "Some sort of Pandora's Kettle?"

"Not so dire as that," said Bert. "It was your mentor, Stellan, who actually named it, John. What it was called before that, I can't say.

"As the legend goes, it was given to Seth, the third son of Adam and Eve, who passed it to his own son, Enos. Where it went after that is mostly lost to the mists of antiquity. But sometime in the past, it came into the possession of Jules Verne, and it was he who explained its workings to myself and Stellan.

"Adam explained to his son that the box could be used but once, and it was his choice alone when to do so. It would give whoever opened it whatever they most needed, and so the old Patriarch advised Seth that he should save it for a crisis, for a time of great peril, and only then open the box."

"What did Seth use it for?" asked John, who still had not decided whether he even wanted to touch the Serendipity Box, much less open it. "I've never heard of it."

"It was too long ago, and there are too many versions of the stories to know for sure," Bert replied. "Some say that he was given a knife with which to avenge his brother, Abel. Others, that it contained three seeds from the Tree of Life, one of which he placed under Adam's tongue when he died, the second of which he planted in a hollow at the center of the Earth, and the last of which he saved. One story even says that his wife, whom some called Idyl, sprang forth fully formed from the box, like Athena from the forehead of Zeus, and that she was not a Daughter of Eve at all.

"There is a fragment of scripture that claimed Enoch and Methuselah both used the box, and another that claimed it had been used by Moses to part the Red Sea. An entirely apocryphal account says that it was the Serendipity Box that held the thirty pieces of silver given to Judas Iscariot. But no historians I know of believed it."

"Why is that?" asked John.

"Because," said Bert, "according to the story, it was Jesus Christ himself who gave Judas the box."

"Who had it between then and now?"

Bert shrugged, then rubbed absentmindedly at the stump of

his right arm. "Jules and Stellan had some theories, and we read through the Histories at Paralon for clues, but apparently miracle boxes that are only good for a single use aren't worth writing about."

"Jules never said where he got it?"

"Here," Bert said, rising and taking the skull from the mantel. He tossed the skull to John, who jumped up and caught it against his chest. "Ask him yourself. And let me know if he answers—I've been talking to him for years now, and he hasn't said a word."

The companions were speechless, except for Chaz, who watched with mild interest. "Kept it, did you, old-timer?" he said blithely as he walked to the window to pull back the curtain and peer outside. "I suppose the king wouldn't notice one more or less in his tower walls."

"This is Jules Verne?" John asked, flabbergasted. "He's dead?"

"The world we knew thought he died in 1905 anyway," said Bert, "and he may well have. But he had a lot of traveling around to do, in time as well as in space, and he had the bad fortune to end up here, with me, in this dismal place."

"What happened?"

"Mordred was waiting for us," said Bert. "He knew we were coming, somehow, some way. And before we could gird ourselves up to work out what had happened to us—hell's bells, to the whole bloody *world*—Jules was killed."

"There was no way to contact the Archipelago for help?" Jack asked, taking the skull from John and hefting it in one hand. "Samaranth, or Ordo Maas? Anyone?"

Bert shook his head and looked at Jack intensely. "You still don't get it, do you, boy? In this place, there is no Archipelago! Mordred destroyed it all centuries ago, and then set about destroying this world as well! The only creatures or lands who survived were those who joined him, like the giants and the trolls! Everything and everyone else—dragons, elves, dwarves, humans . . . all gone! There was no way to contact anyone, and no one to hear the call if there had been a way!"

"Could you have used the Serendipity Box?" asked Jack.

"I did use it," Bert said, sitting again. "And as Jules had said it would, it gave me what I needed. At least," he added, "I hope it did. Only time shall tell."

"I don't know what all the fuss is about," said Uncas. "There's nothing but crackers in here, anyway."

The others turned back to the table to see the box, top flung wide, spilling over with oyster crackers. Uncas was happily shoving them into his mouth with both paws, while Fred stood a few feet away with a horrified expression on his face.

John took a bowl from a cupboard and emptied the box into it, then closed the box and replaced it on the mantel, higher than a badger's reach.

"Oh, great," Jack groaned. "We have one chance each to get something miraculous from that box, and Uncas wastes it on crackers."

"It doesn't work like that," Bert said with a chuckle. "It isn't a magic genie's bottle that you rub to get three wishes. It gives you, and you alone, one time, what it is that you need the most. So," he finished, rubbing Uncas on the head, "it's likely that it doesn't matter when or where or how Uncas opened the box. It would probably have been full of oyster crackers just the same."

"Forry," said Uncas through a mouthful of crackers. "I juff willy wike 'em."

"I think you might be correct," Bert mused, turning to John. "I think perhaps Jules had planned ahead for something only he was privy to. Something that's happening right now."

"Hold on, you old goat," Chaz said, still glancing out the window and fidgeting nervously. "Don't go gettin' any ideas. . . ."

"But don't you see?" Bert exclaimed. "If all of this was foretold—was anticipated—by Jules, then that changes everything!"

"What are you talking about?" asked John.

"The Serendipity Box was left for you, John. Jules left it for you, and Jack, and Charles. He said you'd come for it. I just never imagined it would take fourteen years."

"I'm surprised Mordred didn't take it for himself," said Jack.

"He did," Chaz answered, gesturing to his face. "He opened it, then flew into a rage at whatever it was he saw inside. Then he tried to burn it, but I managed to steal it back. That was the day I got these scars."

"Mordred didn't know the box can't be destroyed," said Bert. "I've kept it here since, waiting."

"He does have a habit of trying to burn things that can't be burned," said Jack, clapping Chaz on the back. "Well done, old boy."

"We met," Bert said, indicating Chaz, "using the same logic you used to come here. I went looking for you, as you came looking for me. For better or worse, I found *him*."

Chaz made an obscene gesture and looked out the window again. "Sky's brightening. Sun'll be up, soonish."

"We're together again, is what matters," said Jack. "Any reunion of friends is a good happening."

But John was not nearly so pleased. He was putting together

parts of the puzzle that made more sense to him than he liked, and he was slowly realizing that as safe as they felt at that moment, they might in fact be in greater danger than ever. There was a connection of some kind between Chaz and Mordred that had not been revealed. But there was one question on his mind that was even more terrible.

"Bert," John intoned dully, "why were *you* spared? Why was Verne killed, and not you?"

Bert closed his eyes and sat silently for a long moment before answering.

"Because," he finally said, "it was what had to happen."

"Practicality," said Chaz. "You did what you had to do."

John stood up and backed toward the door. "What did you do, Bert?"

"What I was destined to do," Bert replied, his face gone cold. "I just never got thirty pieces of silver."

"You sold him," Jack whispered. "You sold Verne to Mordred, to save yourself."

"I won't argue that on the face of it," Bert said plaintively, "but I take exception to your implication. I did what I had to do to survive to this point in time—but it was not of my own volition, and I compromised myself greatly to do so. I've made many more compromises since, all to make certain that we would be here, tonight, to have this very conversation. So were my actions virtuous, or shameful?"

"That," an icy voice said from just outside the door, "depends entirely on one's point of view."

CHAPTER SEVEN

NOBLE'S ISLE

ALL OF THEM save for Uncas and Fred recognized the voice immediately.

"May I come in?" it said, in a tone that made it sound more like a statement than a query.

Bert sighed heavily. "Enter freely and of your own will, Mordred."

The door opened, and silhouetted against the rising sun they saw the imposing figure of the man they had known as the Winter King. The man they had caused to be killed. The man who, more than once, had tried to kill *them*. And their most trusted ally had just invited him into his house.

Mordred was not significantly different from when they had seen him in their own world. He seemed perhaps more aged, more weathered here. He was stouter, and slightly round-shouldered, but his arms were corded with muscle, and his hair cascaded down his back in a mane. He was dressed in royal colors and had the bearing and manner of a king.

He was in appearance, John realized with a shock, everything one would expect a king to look like, to emanate. And he suddenly understood how a man could be a tyrant and still rule: It was a question of the ability to command, to draw respect, even in the wake of evil acts.

Immediately John and Jack took defensive stances in front of Bert and the badgers, but Mordred ignored them, leaning casually against the door frame and addressing Bert.

"My old friend, the Far Traveler," the king said. "We meet again."

Bert glared at him. "Nothing going on here concerns you, Mordred," he said, gripping the staff so tightly his knuckles turned white. "You needn't have come."

"Oh, but everything in my kingdom concerns me, *Bert,*" Mordred replied. John and Jack, still facing their enemy, didn't notice the blood drain from Bert's face at the mention of his name. "The citizens who walk my streets, as well as the Children of the Earth who live beneath them."

This last he said to Uncas and Fred, who both hissed at him in reply. They did not need to have seen him before in the flesh to realize they were facing the greatest adversary of legend, whom Tummeler had told them about.

For his part, Bert simply slumped in the chair, his chin resting on his chest. He seemed already defeated in a game where the stakes had not even been named. "Why are you here, Mordred?"

"Why?" Mordred replied in mock surprise. "I have simply come to meet the two new friends I have waited to meet for so very, very long."

Waited to meet? John thought. Had Bert given them up as well? John looked at his mentor, but the old man simply continued staring at the king.

"That's very bold, to come here alone," Jack said to Mordred, taking the lead in the game being played out in the shack. "Maybe you don't have any memory of it, but we have all clashed before and seen you bested in battle."

"Is that so?" Mordred purred condescendingly. "What battles were these?"

"I beat you on the ocean, with a ship called the *Yellow Dragon* in the Archipelago of Dreams, and he," Jack said, gesturing at John, "beat you in a swordfight."

Technically, everything Jack said was true—although there had been luck and allies aiding him in the sea battle, and John had not precisely won the swordfight. Either way, the bravado didn't faze the king.

"I think not," Mordred said, smiling. "At any rate, the loss of a battle is not the loss of a war—or its victory, either."

"You've certainly learned a few things," John said. "There's no disputing that. It's a shame it didn't make you a better ruler."

"Whether I am a better ruler than others might have been is not for you to judge. There is only one man who ever lived who was fit to judge me, and he—"

Mordred stopped, almost violently, as if he had spoken too openly. "All that is important to a ruler," he continued, "is strength, and mine has been more than sufficient for a very, very long time."

"Bold words, given the odds," said Jack. "I count four to one."

"Five, if you stack the badgers," said John.

"I count far fewer than that," said Mordred. "The Far Traveler—Bert, is it?—really only counts for half, don't you think? And the animals are even less to me. So that makes it even, doesn't it, Chaz?"

Uncas and Fred let out small howls of dismay, and Bert's head dropped farther to his chest.

John looked at Chaz, astonished. "Don't tell me you're taking his side."

Chaz refused to respond—which was response enough.

"Of course," Jack spat, clenching his fists. "He's like the Wicker Men—a lackey and a traitor. He was going to sell us out to the Winter King all along."

It was Bert's turn to be surprised. "Chaz!" he exclaimed in shock. "Why? Why would you do that?"

"You've always known how I gets by," Chaz shot back. "It never bothered y' before."

"It always bothered me, Chaz," said Bert. "I know you're better than this. I always have."

"That wasn't me you knowed," said Chaz. "That was some other bloke called Charles. Not me."

"But . . . but . . . ," Bert sputtered, "you knew I was looking for them. Why would you sell them out to Mordred, only to bring them . . ." His voice trailed off, and he let out a despairing breath. "You gave him my name too, didn't you, Chaz?"

"Actually," put in Mordred, "a little bird told me. Hugin. Or Munin. I forget which. Ravens all look alike to me."

"What's in a name?" Jack said, breaking through the pall that had settled over the room. "Calling Chaz 'Charles' wouldn't make him less of a traitor, so why does it matter whether or not Mordred knows *your* name?"

"True names are imbued with power—and knowing someone's true name gives you some of that power yourself," Mordred said in response. "Enough, at least, to do what must be done. Am I correct, Far Traveler Bert?"

"That's what you did," John said to his old mentor. "You told him Verne's name, and somehow Mordred used it against him."

Bert seemed caught somewhere between lashing out in anger and bursting into tears. He sat, trembling, and glared at Mordred and Chaz.

Mordred chuckled and turned around, his hands clasped behind his back. "That was it, and that was all, and it was enough . . . ah, what did you say your name was again, child?"

"That be Scowler John y' be addressin'!" Uncas exclaimed.

"Uncas, no!" Jack shouted before realizing he'd just made the same unwitting mistake by blurting out the badger's name. "Oh, damnation," he muttered. "Sorry, John, Uncas."

Mordred chuckled again and raised his left hand to his mouth. He bit into his thumb, hard. Blood welled into the torn flesh and he turned around, eyes glittering.

"Don't apologize t' me," said Uncas, who clearly was the only one in the room who did not realize what was transpiring. "A king might talk t' Fred an' I like that, but he should respect men like you, Scowler Jack."

John slapped his forehead in resignation. The Winter King now had all their names. And the hapless Caretaker already anticipated what was coming next.

Before any of them could react, Mordred moved, almost faster than they could follow, first to Jack, then, surprisingly, to Chaz, then John, then the others. He marked them each on the forehead with the blood from his thumb, and as he did so, he called them by name: "Jack and Chaz, John and Bert, Uncas and Fred—I am Mordred the First, thy king."

Then, he began to recite words John did not realize Mordred knew:

By right and rule
For need of might
I thus bind thee
I thus bind thee

By blood bound
By honor given
I thus bind thee
I thus bind thee

For strength and speed and heaven's power
By ancient claim in this dark hour
I thus bind thee
I thus bind thee.

The instant Mordred began speaking, all the companions found themselves unable to move; their arms felt bolted to their sides, their jaws fixed and unmoving. All, that is, save for one.

Mordred finished the Binding and once more looked at each of them in turn. He was triumphant, but there was a trace—the merest trace, John thought—of melancholy in his expression.

Of regret.

"Long ago there was a prophecy," Mordred began, "that mentioned someone called the Winter King. It was said that he would bring darkness to two worlds, and that . . ." He paused, considering, then continued. "It said that three scholars, three men of imagination and learning from this world, would bring about his downfall.

"It was more than a thousand years before some among my

people began to call me by that name—and only then did I remember the old prophecy.

"The prophet never mentioned the Far Traveler, but when he and his companion first came here fourteen years ago, it rekindled the possibility that the prophecy was true. And so since then I have waited patiently for the three scholars it spoke of to arrive: John, Jack, and *Charles*."

This last he said with a wink at Chaz. "Not precisely what had been prophesied, but when the Far Traveler sought you out, I saw a possible connection and decided not to take chances. And when you sent word that you'd found these two, your own fate was sealed.

"My Shadow-Born will attend to you all shortly. We shall not meet again."

Mordred spun about as if to leave, then thought better of it and stepped slowly back to where Jack was standing.

"I was not always as you see me, child," he whispered. "I *was* different, once. . . ."

Frozen in place, Jack could not respond, and after a moment Mordred took a step backward, turned, and opened the door. They heard him striding across the bridge, then nothing. He was gone.

The Binding was absolute. There was no way to move or speak. But it was not so complete that it did not allow tears to flow, and Bert wept. So did Jack, but more from frustration than sorrow. Chaz was still too stunned to weep; and John's mind was racing too fast to stop and worry over the desperate situation they were in. Even without the Binding, Fred would have been petrified by fear. A blood marking was a potent thing, and even more so among animals than men. Combined with the Binding spell, it was impossible to overcome. And so none of them were able to turn around to see what was making the crunching noises under the table.

"Oh, bother," Uncas said. "That's all the crackers, gone. If I'd known we were going to become prisoners, I'd have saved some of the soup, so as not t' die on an empty stummick."

Uncas was unfrozen. The Binding had not affected him at all. He continued complaining, all the while rubbing worriedly at the small silver coin he'd had in his pocket.

Of course, John thought. *Bindings may be broken by silver! Uncas must have been touching the coin, and so he wasn't frozen. There might still be a way out of this after all!*

John's initial rise of hope quickly dropped as he realized that Uncas being free might not be such a big advantage. The badger still had not realized that the rest of them could not move.

"Y'think he's gone?" Uncas asked, peering over the bottom of the windowsill. "What d'you think that blood-marking business was about, anyhow?"

When no one replied, Uncas scurried over to his son, finally realizing that something was amiss. "Fred? What is it? What is it, son?" he asked. "Fred? Can't you answer?"

Fred couldn't, and didn't, and the reality of what had occurred finally dawned on Uncas. And then he did the only thing he could think of, and consulted the Little Whatsit.

"Hmmm hm hm hm hmm," Uncas hummed as he flipped through the pages. John had just enough range in his field of vision to see the pages below. The badger seemed to be following some arcane indexing system based on keywords.

"Spells, curses," Uncas murmured, chewing absently on the coin, "also see: Bindings, counterspells, blood-oaths, and . . . ah, yes, here we go. It's under the section on blood. You know, it be a fascinatin' thing . . . I never would have made th' connection to lycanthropy, but . . ."

Uncas blinked, then looked at the coin. "Well, pluck my feathers," he said. "Silver's good for lots o' stuff."

He repeated the process Fred had performed earlier, grinding the coin to a fine powder. Then, apologizing for the presumption, he sliced five shards of wood from the ash staff, moistened them with his tongue, then rolled them in the silver dust.

"Let's try this with you first, Fred," he said to his son. "If it works, y' can help with th' others."

Uncas closed his eyes and murmured a badger's prayer under his breath, then plunged the ash and silver dart into Fred's forearm.

It worked.

"Ow!" Fred yelped, rubbing at his arm. "Good show! The Royal Animal Rescue Squad, trained an' true!"

The remedy worked equally well on the men. "Sort of a reverse Balder, eh, Jack?" John asked, examining the dart. But Jack wasn't listening. The second he was freed, he had Chaz pinned to the wall.

"Why did you do it, Chaz?" Jack shouted, livid. "Was it really worth selling out your friends for a few lights?"

"You in't my friends!" Chaz howled in reply. "Besides, he froze me the same as you!"

"No time! There's no time for this!" Bert exclaimed. "Mordred's minions are everywhere, and the news we've escaped may reach him any moment—and then we'll all be lost!"

"Where can we go that he won't find us?" John said. "We have nothing to fight him with—not even his true name."

"Yes, you do have something," said Bert. "You have the prophecy. And you have this." He took the rolled parchment from the mantel. "This is what Jules was given when he opened the Serendipity Box. It was then that he said I must give him to Mordred, and then wait for you. He died so that you could have this chance."

"Well, let's have a look at it," Jack began.

"No time, no time," Bert said. "Just know this: It's a map, to the last island in the Archipelago. The only map left, which has been hidden from Mordred all these years. The only one that was made by the Cartographer, but by covenant, never bound into the *Geographica*."

Hearing this, Uncas and Fred exchanged questioning glances, but said nothing.

"Here," Bert said, stuffing the parchment, the box, and Jules Verne's skull into a bag. "Take these, and let's get you on your way."

"How does y' plan t' do that?" said Chaz.

For the first time, John and Jack saw the old familiar glitter in Bert's eyes. "Easy," he said as he opened the back door. "I'm going to use what the Serendipity Box gave to *me*."

The old man hobbled his way out to the far end of the dock. Looking westward, the companions could see nothing but dust. It was, in all ways, a desert.

"Are we going to walk to this island?" Jack asked. "I've already got a blister going."

"Shush," said John. "I think Bert's got better than that in mind."

"Oh yes." Bert nodded. "I do have something good up my, er, sleeve, as it were."

He reached into his pocket and pulled out a brooch. It was an Egyptian scarab beetle, set in a bronze fitting, and the shell of the beetle was translucent blue. It also seemed to be in motion. Bert turned it over. "Recognize the writings, John?"

"Egyptian, obviously, and . . ." He peered closer. "Is that Hebrew and . . ." John's eyes grew wide. "Is this what I think it is?"

Bert nodded. "From Aaron's hand to mine. His brother didn't part anything. The Red Sea was taken up, whole, and put away for safekeeping. And since the Good Lord saw fit to give it to me, I'm sure he won't mind that I've moved it a few thousand miles west."

Bert drew back his arm, and with surprising strength hurled the brooch high into the sky.

It arced high, higher, then plunged downward, hitting the ground some hundred yards away.

"Now what?" asked Chaz.

Suddenly the earth underneath the brooch fissured and split, and it fell into the ground, out of view. A low rumbling sound shook the air, and the pier began to tremble. Then, where the brooch had fallen, a fountain burst into the sky from the center of the fissure, then another, and another.

In seconds it was as if a reverse thunderstorm had exploded out of the dry earth, filling the sky with water, which fell back to ground and began pooling in greater and greater volume.

As the flood gushed up, rain clouds began to form, and almost immediately a downpour started. The water met in the middle with such force that the winds nearly swept the small group off the dock. And then, as quickly as it had started, the storm subsided, and the clouds began to settle, and the companions found themselves looking out upon an ocean restored.

That was not the end of the surprises: In the distance, perhaps a few miles out, they saw a ship.

A *Dragonship*.

"I thought Mordred would have destroyed them all," said John, "all the Dragonships, along with all the lands in the Archipelago."

"Not this ship, and not this island," said Bert. "There *were* no other Dragonships when this timeline changed. And there were reasons this island was never included in the original *Geographica*. This is one of them."

And so it was with mingled wonder and awe, and no small surprise, that the companions watched as the *Red Dragon* glided smoothly through the water and alongside the dock.

"But why, Bert?" John asked as the companions climbed aboard the ship. "If you had the brooch and could do this at any time, why did you wait so long?"

"For you," Bert said simply. "We had faith in you. Jules trusted in your destiny, and so did I. It was hard, terribly so at times. And I regret to say I am not the same, in many ways. I'm worn thin, John. But I'm heartened by your arrival. And overall, considering what Jules sacrificed, I really shouldn't complain."

"Well, you waited long enough," said Jack, offering a hand. "Step aboard, and let's get the hell away from here."

But Bert didn't move. Instead he simply looked at them all with sorrowful eyes, then patted the *Red Dragon*'s hull. "I'm sorry, lads. I won't be going."

"Why not?"

"Because," Chaz called from the far side of the deck, "someone's got t' stay behind, t' make sure we in't followed."

"I nominate you, traitor," said Jack. "Better you than Bert."

"No," Bert said. "My time is past. This is your destiny to fulfill, the three of you—not mine."

"But he's not Charles!" exclaimed Jack. "Don't do this, Bert!"

The old man was not swayed. "Whatever's going on, Jack, is for you to work through. All things happen for a reason. You have to find out what the reason is, and fix what's been broken."

He tapped the hull again, and, as if a signal had been given, the *Red Dragon* came about and headed for open waters.

Sadly, the companions gathered at the aft railing to wave good-bye to their friend and mentor, but he had already left the dock and returned to the shack, closing the door behind him.

For the first few hours, John and Jack had kept watch, fearing pursuit.

Chaz sat at the fore of the ship, sulking. The badgers busied themselves with examining the ship itself and basically trying not to get in the way.

"That's really some book you have, that Little Whatsit," John said to Fred. "It's been pretty handy so far, anyway."

"Sure," said Jack, "except we had only the one silver coin. What happens when we need more?"

"Not everything in th' Whatsit involves silver," Uncas explained. "Some got t' do with gold, f'r instance."

"Hey," Jack said brightly. "We might have a use for your watch, John."

"Funny scowler," said John. "Here now, let's have a look at this map, shall we?"

The map had been drawn on the same parchment and was of the same dimensions as most of the maps they were accustomed to seeing in the *Imaginarium Geographica*, and it had been created by the familiar hand of the Cartographer of Lost Places.

"'Noble's Isle,' it says it's called," said John. "It's a volcanic island, and looks to be in the south. The markings are clear, though, and in classical Latin, so we shouldn't have any problem navigating there."

"The animals have another name for it," said Fred, peering underneath John's arm. "We call it Sanctuary."

"Sanctuary?" asked Jack. "From what?"

"From the world," said Fred. "Both literal and otherwise.

"When Ordo Maas took us into the Archipelago, he gave us many gifts—but they were things unearned. We wanted to grow up, to have a place that was ours, and no others. A place to do our own work, and to learn to be better than we are. And so the animals went sailing through the Archipelago with Nemo's great-great-great-umpteen-grandfather, Sinbad, and he found this uncharted island. He named it Noble's Isle, but we called it Sanctuary. And when the map was made, we asked that it be kept secret, private-like. Only the High King ever had a copy of it."

"And it was the one thing Jules Verne most needed when he opened the Serendipity Box," John mused. "Interesting. Let's hope that when we get there, more of these mysteries become clear."

Bert had spoken true—all the other islands, everywhere, were gone. There was no frontier to cross, no boundary. And the *Red Dragon* never wavered in its course. The only island left in the natural world, or in the Archipelago itself, was Noble's Isle.

"Impossible," said John. "He can't have destroyed them all. He's not that powerful, is he?"

"The king may not be," Chaz said from the rear, "but she is." He was pointing to the deepening sky, where the moon was beginning to rise. "Before the seas went dry, there was a great flood. . . ."

"Of Biblical proportions?" Jack said wryly, leaning over the rail and dipping his hand into the waves. "What the good Lord giveth, he also taketh away. Then he puts it back again."

It took only a few hours for the ship to reach Noble's Isle. "Land ho!" Uncas called out from his perch high atop the mast. "Sanctuary, straight ahead!"

The island was covered with palm trees that thinned out closer to the center as more cultivated gardens took over. The beaches were shallow, of dull gray sand, and offered no easy access for the *Red Dragon*.

Here Uncas took charge and steered the ship (in a more expert fashion than even Fred was expecting) to a narrow inlet on the southernmost tip. The waterway led to a deepwater dock that was both well lit in the approaching twilight, and well cared for.

The companions tied down the ship and stepped onto the sturdy dock, where they were greeted very smartly by a large fox, who bowed deeply at their approach.

He was walking on his hind legs, as the badgers did, and was dressed similarly in a waistcoat, blazer with tails, and trousers.

"I am Reynard," he said in greeting. "Welcome to Noble's Isle, Children of the Earth and Sons of Adam."

The companions returned the bow and, at Reynard's prompting, followed him off the dock to an awaiting principle. It was large and elegant and hummed like a cat. They clambered aboard, and

Reynard pulled onto a paved lane that led directly to the center of the island.

The inlet had lain between two ridges, which flattened out as they passed upward along the road. To one side was a foul-smelling swamp, and to the other, they saw various cultivated gardens, which were punctuated here and there with greenhouses and outbuildings.

As they drove, Reynard kept up an amiable chatter with Uncas, who talked with the fox as if they were long-lost war veterans who'd been separated for a lifetime and had only an hour to catch up. In less than ten minutes, however, the road widened into a circular drive, which was surrounded by a cluster of buildings. These, Reynard explained, were the main dwellings of Sanctuary, and he'd been instructed to bring the visitors there.

"Instructed by whom?" John asked as they climbed out of the principle.

"By the Prime Caretaker, of course," said Reynard, gesturing toward the main house, "and at the request of Ordo Maas himself. Otherwise you would not have been allowed to set foot on this island."

Reynard bowed again as he spoke, but the companions realized that as respectful as he was, he was not altogether pleased that they were there.

"Please, come inside," said Reynard. "The show is about to begin."

CHAPTER EIGHT
THE INFERNAL DEVICE

THE MAIN HOUSES of Sanctuary were familiar in an unfamiliar way. It was as if Oxford had been built for use by scholars three to four feet tall, who may or may not have had prehensile tails. The construction, decor, and layout were practically Edwardian, but allowances were made for those who were actually in residence.

The hallways were lined with doorways far too small for the companions to use. Possums, groundhogs, hedgehogs, and squirrels, all dressed nattily, were scurrying back and forth, seemingly absorbed in the business of the evening. Few if any gave more than a single startled glance to the strange visitors before going on about their business.

There were other doorways, much larger, that would have easily admitted John, Jack, or Chaz, but Reynard discreetly closed these as they passed.

Uncas and Fred were right at home, quite literally, and strode along behind Reynard with an assurance Jack and John had seldom seen in the badgers. It occurred to them that this might be how they had appeared to their students at the colleges. They were all permitted to be there; but some were more permitted than others.

Jack was abuzz with a thousand questions, all of which Reynard answered patiently. Despite the flashes of reluctance he showed at having them on Sanctuary, he was an exceptional and gracious host.

John asked fewer questions, if only because he was still trying to process everything that was happening.

Only Chaz had remained completely silent since their arrival on the island, which everyone else attributed to sulking. Only after they'd passed a number of animals in the corridors did John realize the truth: The man was terrified.

Another creature, a ferret wearing a pince-nez, paused and squinted at the companions before snorting huffily and scampering off in the other direction.

"It's odd that we aren't attracting more attention," noted Jack, "seeing as there are seldom any humans admitted on the island."

"It's not a matter of inattention," Reynard said blithely. "More an excess of it. We've been preparing for you a long while."

"That's our understanding," said John, who was carrying the bag Bert had given them and could feel the slight pressure of Verne's skull against his hip. "What can you tell us about Jules Verne, Reynard?"

"The Prime Caretaker?" said Reynard. "What would you like to know?"

"For one thing," Jack answered, "why he's called the Prime Caretaker."

The fox stopped and looked at Jack as if he'd asked why water was wet. "Because that is what he is," Reynard said. "He is the Caretaker of us all. Is he not, even now, guiding your path to do what must be done?"

"Guiding or manipulating," said John. "I can't decide which."

Reynard nodded. "We had similar concerns, when he first came to us. Had it not been for the blessing of Ordo Maas, his coming here would not have been allowed."

"Fourteen years ago?" asked Jack.

Reynard gave him another look. "Fourteen centuries ago, give or take. As I said, we've been preparing for you a long time."

"It is a remarkable place you have here," John said. "Very civilized. More so than the rest of Albion, that's for sure."

Reynard shuddered. "The Winterland, yes. When he who calls himself the king began to sweep across the world, we closed ourselves off, even from the Archipelago. And when we again ventured outside, we realized we were all that was left."

"The animals?" John asked.

"The Children of the Earth, yes, but we here on Sanctuary were also all who were left to oppose him," said Reynard. "The king had either slaughtered or enslaved the Sons of Adam and the Daughters of Eve, and when they ran in short supply, he turned his attention to us.

"There was a great rebellion, and there were many terrible battles. All the larger creatures were slain. Many more of us smaller animals were lost as well. Some, to our great sorrow, chose to side with him—and in doing so, became truly beasts. These he shaped through his dark arts into terrible, terrible creatures."

Reynard shuddered with the thought, then went on. "Those who could escape him, even temporarily, fled to the edges of the Earth. But even there, in those havens, they will eventually be found, and used—although it took him centuries to realize our fiercest warriors were those closest to the earth."

"The houses," Jack said, snapping his fingers. "That's why most of the houses were on stilts, to raise them up off the ground."

"Human arrogance," Reynard said, nodding, "to think that we are limited to crawling on our bellies in the dirt. To do otherwise was among the first things taught to us by Ordo Maas."

In unison, the fox and two badgers stood at attention and began to recite:

> "Not to go on all fours, not to suck up drink; not to eat flesh or fish; not to claw the bark of trees; not to chase other creatures, to willingly cause them harm. For all those of the earth are bright and beautiful; all creatures, great and small; all beasts are wise and wonderful; for the Lord God made them all."

"Coleridge?" Jack asked.

"Cecil Alexander," said John. "Mostly, anyway. Coleridge may have been a Caretaker, but he was never that sentimental, or poetic."

"Pardon," said Reynard. "A Caretaker of what?"

"The *Imaginarium Geographica,* of course," said Uncas. "The great book, with all the maps of . . ."

He stopped, and his eyes widened in realization as the fox looked at them all with a blank expression. The rest of them realized it too.

In this place, in this timeline, there *was* no *Geographica.* There had been no Caretakers, no Coleridge. All that existed was a single map, one that had never been a part of the atlas to begin with—and the sole Caretaker who had been known by that name was only a skull in John's bag.

"Never mind," said John, patting Uncas comfortingly. "We'll fix that soon enough."

Reynard led them to an ornate hallway, which ended in a great carved door. It was elaborately decorated with sculpted cherubs and angels and, reassuringly, dragons. Inset at the center of the door, on a shield held within a dragon's claws, was the symbol π—the mark of the Caretaker Principia. John's mark.

Jack caressed the surface of the door and exhaled heavily. "As happy as I was to see the Dragonship," he said with a broad grin, "I'm almost happier to see this. It tells me we're on the right path. I don't recognize the dragon, though."

This was the first remark any of them had made that seemed to rattle Reynard. "You actually know a dragon?" the fox said, mouth agape. "Really and truly?"

"We know many dragons," said Jack. "I'm surprised you don't know them yourself."

The fox shook his head. "Not in many, many centuries. They were the guardians of the Archipelago, but something happened to them when the Winter King ascended. After that, there was no one left who could appoint them."

"Appoint them?" John said in surprise. "Isn't a dragon simply a dragon?"

Reynard looked puzzled for a moment, then brightened. "Oh, I see. You misunderstand. No, a dragon isn't the name of the creature—although most of them were the great sky-serpents you're thinking of. 'Dragon' is the name of the office they hold, and it is a title given only by appointment.

"Now," he said, turning back to the door before the companions could ask more questions, "which among you has the Golden Ticket?"

"The what?" said John.

"Golden Ticket," Reynard replied. "This room has been locked for almost fifteen hundred years. Only my distant ancestors, who helped to build it, and the Prime Caretaker himself have ever been inside. And the door can only be opened here," he said, indicating a slit beneath the mark on the shield, "by inserting a Golden Ticket."

John sighed. "I'm sorry, Reynard, we don't—"

"But we might," Jack interrupted. "You've forgotten the box."

They opened the bag John had been carrying and removed the Serendipity Box, careful to keep it out of Uncas's reach.

"Could it be that simple?" John said, turning the box over and over in his hands.

"It can't hurt to find out," said Jack. "At worst, we'll end up with more crackers."

"I only get to open it once," said John. "Do we really want to risk it to gain a ticket? What if we need something more pressing in the future? What if someone's life may depend on when we choose to use it?"

"I think someone's does," Chaz blurted out. He glanced meaningfully down at Verne's skull and gulped hard.

"Good enough," John said. He closed his eyes and lifted the lid.

"Darn," said Uncas. "I was really hopin' f'r crackers."

• • •

The ticket slid smoothly into the slot and engaged a mechanism inside the door that whirred and clicked and hummed like one of the principles the animals drove. Finally a series of bolts slid back inside the door frame, and the door slowly swung open.

Inside was a postcard-perfect Victorian theater in miniature. There were two dozen lushly appointed chairs upholstered in red velvet, and elegant gas lamps placed artfully along walls embroidered with elaborate patterns. The ceiling was pressed tin and reflected the light evenly throughout the room. At the front, a curtained stage extended from one side to the other, and in the rear was a small booth, also curtained, and a table.

The table was the only anomaly in the room. It was metallic and round and slightly concave. On it was a golden ring four inches or so in diameter, and a note written on the cream-colored paper that seemed to be favored by all the Caretakers. It read, simply, *Spin me.*

"You're the Caretaker Principia," Jack said, gently shoving John toward the table. "*You* spin it."

John picked up the ring and examined it, then chuckled and gave it a twirl on top of the table.

The ring spun about in a blur—but instead of slowing down and losing momentum, it began to spin faster, circling the rim of the table in increasingly smaller circuits. When it reached the center, a voice projected from the ring, loud enough for all of them to hear it clearly.

"This is Jules Verne speaking.

"If you three—John, Jack, and Charles—are hearing this recording, then I am in all likelihood dead, or worse."

"Worse than dead?" Chaz snorted. "He's loopy, he is."

"Shush," said John. "We need to hear this."

"What has been closed, may be opened again," the voice continued. "What has been written, may be rewritten. You have already been given warning of your adversary—now I give you the means to defeat him.

"I have become learned in many means of travel through time and space. And I have found that certain boundaries must not be crossed—not if we are to emerge victorious against our enemies."

"Enemies, plural?" Jack groaned. "Great. Just great."

"I have left you the means to the end you must reach," Verne's voice went on, "through the use of what our friend Bert called the 'Infernal Device.' It is the most specific of the devices I use, and also the most fragile.

"You must discover our adversary's name. His *true* name.

"I have left you five slides for use in the Lanterna Magica. Each corresponds to a key moment in his history, and each will afford the three of you the chance to find him. Each slide may be used only once, and the portals they create will remain open for only twenty-four hours, and no more. If you do not return to Noble's Isle within that time, you will be trapped there, and all our efforts will be for naught.

"Only thus, by seeking him out, naming him, and Binding him, may he be defeated. But remember: Our adversary may not be whom you expect. Be wary. Be watchful. And remember your training. All things come about, in time.

"Answer the question unanswered for more than two millennia, and perhaps you may yet restore the world."

The golden ring began to slow, and with a soft clattering, it fell still and silent on the table.

• • •

The companions tried to spin the ring again, to see if there was any further information to be gleaned, but it simply repeated what they had heard the first time.

"Let's have a look at this lantern, then," Jack said. "In for a penny, in for fifty pounds."

"It's here," said Reynard, gesturing to the small booth near the table. There on a small platform sat an unusual if not extraordinary device.

"To leave a message, he can use a magic ring," said Jack, "but for time travel, we need an antique projector. Splendid."

John ignored his friend's sarcasm and set about examining the machine. The slides were already set into a rotating frame in the center, and where the original gas lamp had been in the back there was an incandescent bulb. Below it an electric cord snaked down and across the floor to an outlet.

"Not entirely antique," John said appraisingly. "Shall we give it a go?"

"Not yet," Jack replied, turning to face Chaz. "You're going to stay here, where you won't cause any trouble."

"Fine by me," Chaz said, plopping himself heavily into one of the chairs. "Nothing to do with me, anyroad."

"Wrong," said John. "Verne said all three of us were meant to do this. And even Mordred himself said in the prophecy that we three—"

"Not we three," Chaz shot back. "You, him, and some bloke called Charles, who I in't. I won't be going anywheres with you lot. I'm fine right where I be."

"Oh, for heaven's sake," John said. "Uncas! Stop that!"

While the humans were arguing, the badgers had switched on the Lanterna Magica and were using the light projected through one of the empty frames to make shadow puppets on the wall.

"Look!" said Uncas. "It's a rooster."

"Quit playing with the time machine," John said sternly. "Remember what happened with the door."

"Sorry," said Uncas.

"Since it's already on," John said as Jack continued glaring at Chaz, "we might as well see what we're in for."

At his signal, Fred scurried over to the Lanterna Magica and rotated the disk that held the five slides. The first frame had been empty and simply projected a pool of light against the curtains. But the next contained a slide—a landscape of some kind. And as they looked, it seemed that the images projected through the stationary slide . . .

. . . were *moving*.

"Here," Reynard said, pulling on the draw for the curtains. "Perhaps this will help."

Instead of a screen or sheet, behind the curtains were layers of a gossamer substance, very much like theatrical backdrops. The image from the projector passed through some layers, but not others. It was like watching a film painted on smoke.

The landscape in the projection was unmistakably Greek. There were temples and great statues of ancient gods visible, all entwined with grapevines and at the bases, olive trees. Farther back, they could see a large group of people gathered in a small amphitheater, listening to a man who stood in the center. The details were sharp and clear, and to the companions it seemed as if they could reach in and touch one of the stately columns.

Then there was a gust of wind in the projection, and one of the grape leaves twisted off its vine and twirled through the air to land in the room at Reynard's feet.

"Dear God," John breathed. "It does work. It will work. Just like the doors."

"But with a time limit, remember," said Jack.

Just then a rumble of thunder shook the room, and the projection wobbled. Reynard looked visibly alarmed, and with no comment, hurried from the room.

"A storm must have come up," said Jack. "Funny. It was clear out before."

"That's not thunder," said John. "That's an impact tremor. Something massive just stepped onto the island."

They looked at one another in alarm. It could only be the giants. Mordred had discovered their escape from Bert's shack and had sent his largest servants to reclaim them.

"Oh, that's capital," groaned Jack. He turned to Chaz, teeth clenched and his temper rising. "You had something to do with this, didn't you?"

Chaz stood up defensively. "I been with you the whole time! And I got no loyalty to him! Not now!"

"You mean after he betrayed you the way you betrayed us?" snapped Jack.

"I'm sorry!" Chaz said. "I . . . I didn't know."

Reynard ran back into the room as another footfall rattled the island. "The giants have come, friends of the Caretaker. And it is time for you to leave."

"What about you?" Jack said. "We can't abandon you!"

The fox shook his head. "We have an understanding with the

giants. They only want you. If you are not here, they will leave us be. It doesn't matter where else you go, or," he said, gesturing suggestively at the projection, "when."

Uncas and Fred both agreed with Reynard—they would be safe. So John grabbed the bag with their scanty supplies and stepped quickly between the chairs to the screen, gesturing to the others as he did so. "Jack! Charles! No time to debate! Let's go!"

"I am *not* Charles!" Chaz exclaimed over the din. "I shouldn't be allowed!"

Jack merely shook his head in disgust and stepped into the projection. John turned around and faced Chaz.

"Perhaps not in this place," he said through the crashing sounds that were now all around them, "but in another place, another dimension, you *are* our friend Charles, and I would not think of leaving you behind."

He reached out his hand, imploring the confused man to take it.

"Chaz!" John beckoned. "Come with us! Now!"

With both hands, Chaz took John's outstretched arm and stepped into the picture.

PART THREE

AFTER THE AGE OF FABLE

CHAPTER NINE
THE STORYTELLER

THIS PELLINOR, HUGO decided, was the most loquacious fellow he'd ever met, even if he seemed mostly to be conversing with himself. The fact that Hugo had more than a passing fluency with Anglo-Saxon made little difference: King Pellinor was in his own realm, and Hugo was merely an interested observer and infrequent participant.

That was fine with Hugo, who had at first determined that he was at the center of the greatest, most elaborate practical joke ever devised by an Oxford don. Jack was probably the instigator, but John had certainly played his part, and played it well. That they had both disappeared along with the door he'd passed through could be attributed to some sort of stage illusion; but the fact that they'd made Magdalen, and in fact, all of Oxford itself disappear could only be explained by the idea that he'd been hypnotized, or transmogrified, or whatever it was that the illusionists did to people that made them think they were the Queen or a chicken or some such. But as the hours passed, Hugo began to realize that it was no illusion, and certainly no joke.

The strange old king produced the crumpled photograph of Hugo that had been taken at the University of Reading, where he taught English, but he remained closemouthed as to who had given it to him and why.

They traveled southward throughout the night, their path lit only by the small lamp Pellinor had attached to the side of the cart. The king kept up a rambling monologue (or more precisely, a solo dialogue) for most of the way, only occasionally interrupting the flow of words to incorporate an answer to one of Hugo's queries. Most of the tales the king told seemed to involve his personal genealogy, and an ancestor who had been shamed at Alexandria, but Hugo couldn't really be sure.

With the coming of daylight, Hugo was better able to take in Pellinor's unusual appearance. The clothing was as authentic as any Hugo had ever seen in museums—but so were the scars that laced the old man's arms and neck. There was even a deep gash along his cheek, which had long since healed.

The old king dismissed queries about the wounds with a laugh and a story about the mythical Questing Beast. And after noticing the weapons and armor still reddened with blood in the back of the cart, Hugo stopped asking questions and just listened to Pellinor ramble.

As the light came up, Hugo could make out other carts and horsemen off in the distance all around them, all headed in the same direction.

He asked Pellinor about them, and the old king answered with an uncommon gravity. "They are going to the same place that we journey to," he said, eyes fixed on Hugo. "To the tournament. To the great Debate."

"Debate?" asked Hugo. "What kind of debate requires horsemen and swordplay?"

"The kind that determines the future of the land," said Pellinor. "The kind that may only be held in a sacred place. A place of death and rebirth."

"And where is that?" asked Hugo.

Pellinor answered, but the accent made it difficult to understand.

"Camazotz?" Hugo said.

Pellinor laughed. "Close enough, my odd friend.

"Camelot," the king said. "We are going to Camelot."

Once John, Jack, and Chaz were through the portal, all the din and clamor of the giants' assault upon Sanctuary ceased. It had opened along the wall of a tall building and was framed by pillars and grapevines. Looking back, they could see the faint impressions of the room they had left behind, lit by the glare of the projector. Reynard was near the door of the room, barking instructions to someone in the hallway, and both badgers were giving a relieved thumbs-up to the companions, who would be visible now inside the projection. There was no doubt—Verne's Infernal Device had worked.

The building formations within the plaza where they had emerged were familiar to John and Jack, who had seen similar structures in the islands of the Underneath in the Archipelago. The main difference was that these were clean and undamaged. This architecture was that of a vital, living city.

Chaz couldn't understand the words being spoken by the storyteller in the amphitheater, but John and Jack were both adept at speaking the language and identified it immediately.

"Extraordinary," marveled Jack. "We've actually gone back in time."

"And, ah, across in space," added John. "We're in Greece . . . or perhaps Turkey."

Jack nodded. "The structures are Ionian, definitely. But it must be prior to the Persian conquest," he said, glancing about, "given the manner of dress we're seeing. So what time do you think it is, anyway?"

On impulse, John reached into his pocket and pulled out his pocket watch. He had it open for a few seconds before chuckling mirthlessly and hastily putting it back.

"Force of habit," he said, shrugging and hoping no one had noticed the strange device he'd just held.

Jack voiced a similar concern. "We're not going to accomplish much dressed like this." He gestured at their modern English outfits. "We're going to need to, um, borrow something more suitable."

A robed figure appeared at their side and proffered two robes to them. "Here, take these."

It was Chaz.

"How did you get these?" exclaimed Jack. "We've only just walked through the portal!"

"I'm a thief, remember?" Chaz said drolly. "Just doin' what comes natural."

"Oh, I'm not . . . ," Jack started to protest, as John took both robes and pressed one on him.

"Don't argue, Jack," he said. "We were about to do the same thing—you just resent that it was Chaz who acquired them for us."

Jack grumbled under his breath but put on the robe. With their sleeves and trousers sticking out, they looked more akin to travelers from the east or south than native Greeks, but the disguises would work well enough.

No one was looking at them, anyway. The attention of everyone in the plaza and amphitheater was focused on the young man in the center, who was telling stories. And for good reason—he was positively magnetic.

The man exuded a natural charisma that came with the confidence of knowing that the audience was completely caught up in the tale being told.

Chaz looked bewildered; he clearly could not understand anything being said. John leaned close to him to translate.

"He's telling a story about a great warrior," he whispered, "who came to this land at the behest of a king called Minos, to defeat a giant called Asterius. The giant had horns and six arms and could not be beaten by a display of strength or prowess, but only by a game of logic."

"Six arms," Chaz replied. "Who ever heard of a giant with six arms?"

"He's got the number of arms right," Jack put in, "but if Asterius is a giant, I'm Sir Walter Scott."

Chaz, scowling, continued watching the storyteller. He'd survived in the Winterland by being aware of everything in his environment. And here he was watching with the eyes of a predator; not looking for prey, but trying to spot the competition. And in a trice, he realized that was exactly what he was seeing: another predator.

"The teller," Chaz said, moving closer to the others and speaking in a hushed whisper. "Look closely at the teller."

There *was* something familiar about the young man. The tilt of his head, perhaps; maybe the tone of his voice, even disguised as it was by the rhythms of ancient Greek speech. Even his gestures seemed . . .

"That's it," breathed Jack. "My God, Chaz, you're right. It's how he moves, his body language. It's definitely familiar. Could this boy actually be a young Mordred? Is he the one we've come to find?"

"Possibly," John replied. "This is the place that Verne's machine sent us. It can't be coincidence that the fellow who's the center of attention seems so familiar to us."

The young man was just finishing his tale of Asterius, much to the delight of his audience, who responded with laughter and applause.

"Tomorrow," the storyteller said, "I will tell you a tale of the giant Polyphemus, who was blinded by the great Odysseus, the sacker-of-cities, and then killed by the slayer-of-giants called Jack."

John looked accusingly at Jack, who sighed heavily and rolled his eyes.

"What?" said Chaz, who had caught Jack's name among the gibberish. "What did you do?"

"Don't look at *me*!" Jack whispered. "I don't have the slightest idea what all this 'Giant-Killer' business is all about. It's got to be coincidence, that's all."

"Except the giants back in Albion recognized your voice, didn't they?" asked Chaz. "How do you explain *that*?"

"I can't," Jack said hotly. "But until I actually kill a giant, I'm not taking the blame, whatever rumors have gone around."

"Look at it this way," offered John. "At least you know that whenever it does take place, the outcome is assured."

"Easy for you to say," said Jack. "You're not the one who's going to feel the pressure of centuries of expectations."

"Far easier to do summat about this boy teller," Chaz reasoned, moving around Jack with his eyes fixed on the man at the front of the amphitheater. "We ought t' just kill him here and be done wi' it."

"We can't!" John hissed, grabbing his arm. "We are only supposed to learn his true name and Bind him, remember?"

"And who's t' do th' Binding?" asked Chaz. "You?"

He was right. John and Jack might know the words, but they didn't have the authority to speak the Binding. Only one of the royal bloodline could—and there wasn't anyone left who qualified back in Albion.

"Drat," said Jack. "Maybe we *should* just kill him."

"And risk really wrecking history?" said John. "I don't think so. Look at how much trouble Hugo caused—and he only went back six centuries. We've gone considerably further than that. If we change something now, the repercussions could be disastrous."

"On t' other hand," said Chaz, "there'd be no King Mordred t' trample an' piss all over everything. Might be worth the trade."

John looked down at the possible Mordred, who was conversing with the crowd as they left the amphitheater. "No," he said, shaking his head. "We were given instructions by Verne to discover Mordred's true name, then return to Noble's Isle. And that's what I intend to do."

Jack and Chaz looked at each other, debating. "You're the Caretaker Principia," Jack said. "I'll defer to you."

"Fine," said John. "Chaz?"

Chaz shrugged. "Whatever you say. I'm not even supposed t' be here, remember?"

As they spoke, a short, solidly built man who had been

watching them from across the plaza approached, and before any of them could move, he had pointed a small dagger at John's stomach.

"My name is Anaximander," the man said, smiling politely, "and you do not belong here. Please state your business, or I will slay you where you stand."

Chaz and Jack both tensed for a fight, but John answered first, holding out his hands placatingly. "We are travelers, strangers to your land," he said in fluent Greek. "We've come here seeking knowledge of that man, there."

Anaximander's eyes darted along the line John's arm made to the young storyteller, who was still accepting farewells from his listeners. "Is that so?" he said. "That's very interesting, as I happen to be his teacher. How is it that you know of him at all, that you come seeking to know more?"

"We've got a history with him," Jack said, "so to speak."

"I don't believe you," Anaximander said, pressing closer with the blade. "Tell me something truthful, or your friend will pay the price, and you after."

"Oh, for heaven's sake," Jack said to John. "Mordred's almost as much trouble here and now as he was in the Archipelago."

Jack had switched to English, but Anaximander recognized the word "Archipelago," and it startled him. He lowered the dagger and looked at the three companions appraisingly.

"Perhaps you speak truth after all," he said finally. "You mean him no harm?"

Jack started to reply, but John cut him off. "We just want to speak with him," he said testily. "That's all. And then we plan to, ah, return to our homeland."

"Fair enough," Anaximander said. "We'll be meeting later, at my home. Please, come with me." With that, he turned and strode away. The companions had little choice but to follow.

The home of Anaximander was only a short distance away, but Chaz kept an eye on the streets they traversed so as not to forget where the portal was located. Of the three of them, he was the one most aware that they had a time limit.

Anaximander's home consisted of three low bungalows connected by a courtyard where he could teach small groups of students. A few minutes before, he'd threatened the companions with violence, but now he was acting the perfect host. He offered them wine and a platter of cold figs, which they consumed with great vigor.

"You seem quite hungry," Anaximander commented. "Did you not bring provisions for your journey? You seem ill-equipped for a long voyage."

"We're staying nearby," Jack said, not exactly lying. "Everything we need is there."

"You said you were a teacher," said John. "What do you teach, if I might ask?"

Anaximander bowed his head at the question. "I am a philosopher of the school of my master, Thales, and I teach what I am still seeking the answers to myself: the origin of all things. I call it Aperion."

"Wait now," said Jack. "I've heard of that. It means 'Infinite Beginning,' does it not?"

"Not precisely," said Anaximander. "More 'Infinite Perpetuity.' There is no beginning or ending, but merely an endlessly repeating process of beginnings *and* endings. Thus, an infinity of all things in space . . . and time."

Jack nearly spit out his wine.

"Amazing," said John, and translated for Chaz. "That's a rather all-encompassing subject."

"Indeed," the teacher said. "Presently I am working on a new theory, which I call 'multiple worlds.' Essentially, I believe that our own world is but one of an infinite number that may appear and disappear at any given moment. Some find solidity and remain, while others flounder and disappear."

Jack raised an intrigued eyebrow and looked at John. What Anaximander was describing was the very time paradox that Hugo Dyson had caused: The world they knew had vanished and been replaced by the Albion of the Winter King.

They both had the same thought: Was this Greek scholar in some way involved in what had taken place, or was his theory merely another coincidence?

A few more hours of discussion with Anaximander confirmed the answers to many of the questions that John and Jack had wondered about. The city was Miletus, on the Ionian coast of what they knew as Turkey. And as close as they could estimate from their fellow scholar's calculations, the date was sometime around 580 BC.

The companions held off discussing the specifics of how and when they'd come to be in Miletus until their host had excused himself to fetch some more refreshments.

"Twenty-five hundred years!" Jack exclaimed, slumping back in his chair, "and then some. What was Verne thinking? What can we possibly solve by going back this far?"

"Remember what Bert said," John reminded him. "Whatever it was that Hugo caused to happen in the past—uh, future—well, whenever he went—was anticipated by Verne. And we know who our adversary is. I think before we can do anything about Hugo, we've got to defeat Mordred, just like the prophecy said."

"We already did that," Jack huffed. "What if it was *that* defeat the prophecy referred to?"

John shook his head. "But we didn't. Not in this timeline, remember? That would have happened after Hugo went through the door."

"Drat," Jack said. "I keep forgetting."

Anaximander came back into the courtyard accompanied by a young man who appeared to be a student of his, given the way he responded to the older man's instructions—not with abject obedience like a servant, but more deferentially than a son or nephew would have done.

"Come, Pythagoras," Anaximander said, indicating the low table adjacent to John. "Just set the tray here. That will be fine."

The boy deftly set the tray, laden as it was with bread, cheese, and grapes, on the table and then left.

"I see I've allowed the teacher in me to supplant the good host," Anaximander commented, moving to the center of the courtyard. "You didn't come here to ask about my philosophies; you wanted to know about my student. I assumed it was because of the legend that has sprung up around the stories that have been told."

"What stories?" asked Jack.

"You are familiar with our great storyteller Homer?" Anaximander asked. "He of the *Iliad*, and the *Odyssey*?"

"Of course."

"Not long ago," the philosopher went on, "a rumor began to spread throughout the land that the gods had allowed Homer to be reborn as a youth, to reawaken the Greek people's belief in wonder and mystery. From town to town and city to city, stories were being told in exchange for room and board. Stories the like of which have not been heard for centuries.

"Great, adventurous tales of fantastic creatures—centaurs and Cyclopes; talking pigs, beautiful sirens, and many, many more. And among these tales were scattered references to the place where they all were supposed to have happened—the Archipelago."

John and Jack couldn't resist the impulse to sit up straighter at this. "Your reborn Homer," John said, "has he actually been to the Archipelago?"

"Better than that, if the stories are to be believed as truth, and not fabrication," Anaximander replied. "They were *born* there."

"I beg your pardon," said Jack. "Did you say 'they'?"

Anaximander merely smiled and rose to his feet. He crossed the courtyard and disappeared through one of the doors. The companions heard a muffled exchange of voices, and a moment later the philosopher reappeared, this time accompanied by two young men.

The first was not so much handsome as striking, which came across mostly through the intensity of his eyes. He was swarthy, muscular, and very, very confident.

The second young man was practically identical to the first. He was only negligibly shorter, and a bit more stocky. His complexion was slightly more pale, as if he spent more time indoors than his brother. But it was evident, John realized, that these were not only brothers, but twins.

"Gentle scholars," said Anaximander, "may I introduce my two prize students—Myrddyn and Madoc."

Chaz squinted and peered at the twins as if he'd been conked on the head and couldn't quite register what he was seeing. "*Two* of 'em?" he said to John. "*Two* Mordreds? I think we just went from th' kettle directly inta th' flames."

John and Jack both stood to receive the visitors, but they were nearly as stunned as Chaz. Myrddyn and Madoc took each of their arms in greeting, and the companions realized that if pressed, they would not be able to say which of them had been the storyteller.

"It depends on the day," Anaximander said in response to their unasked question. "That's what has made the rumors of Homer's return both credible and compelling. The 'single' storyteller has at times been reported in two cities on the same night, and has on occasion held an amphitheater full of citizens in thrall for several days with no apparent pause for sleep. These miracles are only possible, of course, because the single storyteller is, in fact, two."

The twins took some fruit and goblets of wine from the table and settled into the chairs opposite the companions. As Myrddyn and Madoc recounted the events of the day with their teacher, John took the opportunity to examine them more closely. Myrddyn was the more outgoing of the two, and John was nearly certain that it was he whom they had seen in the amphitheater earlier. But then again, Madoc, while less forthcoming than his brother, nevertheless was compellingly familiar. Every gesture, every expression, bore some trace of the man they'd come seeking.

"This is impossible," Jack whispered, leaning in close to John. "I can't tell them apart. If they traded chairs, I might not even lose the thread of the conversation."

"I know what you mean," John whispered back. "Verne never mentioned this particular problem."

"You do realize," Myrddyn said, addressing the companions, "that our teacher is very protective of us and rarely speaks of our secret with anyone."

"You mean your names?" asked Jack.

A flash of something indescribable crossed the young man's eyes. "I meant the secret that we were born not here, in this world, but in the Archipelago."

"Almost no one in the Greek empire knows of its existence," said Madoc. "There are legends and stories, of course, but few who know the reality of it, as you seem to."

"We've been there often," Jack said before John could stop him, "and have many friends among its peoples."

"Really?" Myrddyn said, leaning forward. "Such as who?"

John groaned inwardly, as did Jack, albeit a moment too late. He'd forgotten—they were centuries removed from the time that they knew, and their own journeys in the Archipelago of Dreams. Nemo was not yet born, or Tummeler, or Charys the centaur, or . . .

"Ordo Maas," John said suddenly. "We are friends of Ordo Maas."

The only reaction from the young men was a polite stare. The name meant nothing to them.

"Deucalion," put in Jack. "He is also known as Deucalion."

This brought about an entirely different reaction: Surprise

and delight—and was that an expression of triumph John saw?—registered on Myrddyn and Madoc's faces, and even Anaximander's eyes widened in astonishment.

"The Master of Ships?" he said, his voice cracking. "Surely you jest with us."

"Not at all," John replied. "Do you know him?"

"Indirectly," said Myrddyn. "He is our—mine and Madoc's—direct ancestor."

John and Jack looked at each other, bewildered. This was an unexpected complication. If one of these young men was indeed destined to become Mordred, that meant their greatest enemy was actually a blood relative of one of their strongest allies. But surely Deucalion would have known of this connection, wouldn't he?

"How direct?" Jack asked slowly. "What *is* your exact lineage, if I may ask?"

Myrddyn nodded genially. "Of course. That is, in fact, what we have come here to discuss. Our ancestry is tied to both this world and the Archipelago.

"Deucalion, the son of Prometheus, was our ancestor six generations removed from our father, who went on a great voyage through the Archipelago in a ship given to him by his father. Near the end of his voyage, when all his companions had perished, his ship ran aground on an island where he spent seven years, before finally leaving in a small craft he built in secret.

"He left behind the ship of his father, Laertes; our mother, Calypso; and myself and Madoc, his sons."

John was speechless, as was Jack. Only Chaz, who was barely

following the conversation, remained unaffected. "What is it?" he asked John. "What did he just say?"

"Calypso, Laertes . . . ," John said to Jack. "Is it possible . . . ?"

Myrddyn smiled. "We were born in the Archipelago, but we have always known our destiny would lie here, in the land of our father—Odysseus."

CHAPTER TEN
THE SHIPWRECK

"NEARLY A YEAR ago I was sailing with a small crew on a diplomatic mission to establish a colony at Apollonia," Anaximander began, "when we lost our way and fell far off course. We were caught up in a terrible wind and found ourselves run aground on an island that seemed divided in half by a great line of storms."

"Like Avalon," Jack murmured. "Interesting."

"While we repaired our own vessel," the philosopher continued, "we saw another ship being tossed about by the waves, nearly to its destruction.

"The ship ran aground on the coast, crashing violently against the rocks, and I was the first to come to the wreckage. It was still being battered by the surf, but the two passengers aboard had been thrown clear. Before they could drown, I pulled the two of them from the water and brought them here."

"Is it still there?" John asked. "The ship? Can you take us to the wreck?"

Anaximander shook his head. "The island is too far to travel to safely and quickly, and even were we to go, the ship isn't there any longer anyway.

"As they recovered from their injuries, they both cried out for the ship in their fever dreams," he explained, "concerned for the safety of their father's vessel. But when I went back with several men to help me pull it aground, it was gone. An old fisherman who appeared near the rocks at the shore claimed to have seen it pulled back out to sea by seven scarlet and silver cranes."

John looked at Jack. He recognized the description of the scarlet and silver cranes—the sons of Ordo Maas.

"After my duties at Apollonia were discharged," Anaximander went on, "I offered to bring them here to become my students. But it turned out that I became their student as well—for they have told me many extraordinary things. Things unexpected from men of such youth."

"And many tales of the Archipelago, I'd imagine," said John.

"Yes." The philosopher nodded. "Especially those."

"Why are you sharing all of this with us?" asked Jack. "If you are from the Archipelago, the sons of Odysseus himself even, what can we possibly tell you about it that you don't already know?"

Madoc leaned forward, eyes glittering. "You can tell us the most important thing," he said, his face flushed and earnest. "You can tell us how to go *back*."

At once, John and Jack remembered just *when* they were in history. There *were* no Dragonships yet. Ordo Maas had not yet built them. His own vessel, the great ark, had only gotten through the Frontier because it carried the Flame of Prometheus, the mark of divinity. And so the only other passages between worlds, like the journey of Odysseus, and Myrddyn and Madoc's voyage back, were achieved through pure chance.

"We waited a long time to be able to come here, to the land of our father," Myrddyn said, giving his brother an oddly disapproving look, "but we would like to be able to return home, to the island of our birth. And we would be willing to pay a great price to any man who might assist us in doing so."

During the course of the discussion, Chaz had begun to pick up enough of the language to at least follow the thread of what was being discussed, and he brightened visibly when he realized there was an exchange of value being proposed.

John translated the words Chaz had missed as the others waited patiently.

"That's an easy answer," Chaz said when John was done. "We should just figure out a way t' get that Dragonship of yours through the portal, and let *it* take them where they want t' go."

Jack slapped his head in dismay. Chaz had just blurted out several things they'd planned to keep to themselves—the ship, the portal . . . They were lucky that he'd spoken in English, so the philosopher and his students wouldn't know what had been said.

John and Jack were so focused on Chaz at that moment that they did not see the shadow of fear that passed over the twins' faces at the mention of the word "dragon." But the philosopher did see.

Before John and Jack had time to respond further to Chaz, Anaximander pointedly cleared his throat, and Myrddyn and Madoc rose to their feet. "You must forgive us," Myrddyn said, bowing. "We have enjoyed this meeting a great deal, but we have some responsibilities to attend to. May we continue this discourse in a short while? Perhaps in the morning?"

"Of course," John said, also rising. "We have much more to discuss, I think. But please be aware," he added with a glance at Jack and Chaz, "that we are merely passing through and cannot stay past tomorrow afternoon."

While Anaximander saw the two young men out, John and Jack had an opportunity to quickly relate to Chaz everything else that had been said.

"It's all beyond me," he said, shrugging. "I don't know what any of that whose-father-sailed-what-ship stuff has t' do with our job."

"It helps us understand what's at stake," John told him, "and gives us clues to figure out what to do."

Chaz took on a disdainful expression. "Easy-peasy," he said. "We go back to Sanctuary and try both names—Myrddyn and Madoc—on th' Winter King. Whichever one works, well, that'll Bind him, right?"

"I don't think it'll be as easy as all that," John replied. "Not when there may be a blood rite, and the speaking of the Binding itself—if we can find someone who's able. It's too much time to risk on fifty-fifty odds."

"So we have to find out for certain which of them will become a tyrannical despot in the future," Jack was saying as Anaximander returned to the courtyard. "Great."

"Hey," said Chaz, "how do I ask where the, uh, facilities are?"

"Facilities for what?" asked John.

"I have t' pee."

"Oh," John said. He repeated the query in Greek to Anaximander, who seemed not to understand.

"He wants to go to the room where we make water?" the philosopher asked. "We don't have a 'room' for that, but we do have pots in some of the larger buildings. I have one myself, if your friend would like to make use of it."

John translated, and Chaz screwed up his face in disgust. "I'd just as soon not be sharing a chamber pot, t'anks," he said. "Isn't there a nice, clean hollow log somewheres?"

Again John translated, and Anaximander answered.

"He says most everyone just uses the street," John said apologetically. "Welcome to ancient Greece."

Grumbling, Chaz exited the same way the twins had left, and Anaximander moved over to take his chair.

"What do you think of my students?" the philosopher said, sitting between John and Jack. "Impressive, are they not?"

"Do you believe them?" Jack asked. "Do you really think they are the sons of Odysseus?"

"It's impossible to know for certain," Anaximander admitted, "but their tale rings true. We know from our own histories that Odysseus had children with both the witch Circe and the nymph Calypso, but little was known of what became of them, until last year, when I found Myrddyn and Madoc and learned of their parentage. They know more about the details of Odysseus's journeys than any scholar, more than has been recorded in any history. And so I must give credence to their claims, however outrageous they might seem."

"I don't know what we can do to help," John said plaintively. "We've told you all we can."

"Ah, but I think this is not the case," Anaximander replied. "No—don't be alarmed. I'm not irritated that you have chosen to keep things to yourselves—especially in front of an unknown audience. Am I correct?"

Their uncomfortable silence told him he was.

"Well then," the philosopher said, "it seems I must make the first gesture of trust." He stood and walked to the far side of the courtyard, motioning for them to follow. "I have been developing a new science, based on the idea that there are places in the world that cannot be traveled to except by following a very specific and detailed route," he said as he opened a large, stout door.

"The place where Myrddyn and Madoc were born, the Archipelago, is of our world, and not, all at once. And so I reasoned that the only way to discover the location of an unknown place would be to create a means to represent all the places that *are* known." Anaximander lit one of the lamps in the darkened room, and it suddenly blazed with light. "I call it a *map*."

The two Caretakers stepped into the room and looked around in mute astonishment. Maps. The entire chamber was filled with maps. There were also globes, whole and in pieces, and crude sextants, and even a construction that resembled the solar system, hanging from a thin wire in a corner of the room.

"Cartography," John said, his voice trembling with the realization, as he gripped Jack by the shoulder. "Anaximander is teaching them to make maps."

"Better than that," Jack replied. He was also shaking. "He's making maps to unknown lands. To lost places."

"Are . . . are you the Cartographer?" John asked.

Anaximander bowed deeply. "I am what I am," he said simply. "Now, let us speak of the Archipelago, shall we?"

The problem with trying to relieve oneself in ancient Greece, Chaz decided, was that everywhere he went, there was some kind of statue or carving or bas-relief with a face on it—which meant that every time he stopped to pee, something was watching him. And it was flat-out impossible to loosen one's bladder when one was being watched.

Finally he managed to find a decent spot in between a tall, stout olive tree and a great cistern. The shadow underneath afforded just enough privacy to do what needed doing, as long as not too many people passed by.

Chaz had unbuckled his trousers and was just preparing to relax and let loose the torrent, when he heard familiar voices. He pulled up his pants and leaned back to peer around the cistern.

It was Myrddyn and Madoc. They were at the other end of the alley, having a heated if hushed exchange.

Chaz moved closer to listen. He still could not understand most of what they were saying—but he could *remember*. And he was catching just enough—words like "ship" and "dragon"—that he knew it might be important to remember it all.

"And what happens if we're found out?" Madoc was saying. "They claim to know Deucalion—that means they could discover the truth: that we were exiled from the Archipelago."

"No one needs to know that!" Myrddyn hissed, grabbing his twin by the collar. "Least of all Anaximander! Only Deucalion, the Pandora, and the Dragons themselves know what really took place before we came here. And that's the way it will stay until we can return!

"No," he said, finally releasing his grip on Madoc's tunic, "we'll use them for whatever information we can glean, and then we'll dispose of them, as we have the others. He's already prepared the wine, as he has before."

"You know I'm uncomfortable with that, Myrddyn," Madoc said, his voice low. "We could have trusted some of them, I think."

Myrddyn shook his head. "It's too great a risk," he said blithely. "The knowledge of the Archipelago is rare, and it must remain so.

The fewer who know anything of it, or of us and our real reasons for returning, the better. Do you want to get father's ship back or not?"

After a moment, Madoc nodded, still reluctant. Then together the brothers turned and walked back toward the amphitheater.

When he was certain they had gone, Chaz emerged from the shadow of the cistern where he had been watching them and stood in the alleyway, breathing heavily and trying to reason out what he believed he had heard.

For a long moment, Chaz considered his options, looking hard in the direction of the philosopher's house. Then, abruptly, he spun about and began walking toward the amphitheater and the plaza . . . and the portal back to Sanctuary.

Of any scholars of the ancient world who made maps, only Anaximander had conceived of one depicting the entire world.

The maps he showed to John and Jack were crude by their standards, but revolutionary for the philosopher's time. And they were good enough for a beginning. Some, John suspected, might even be *in* the *Imaginarium Geographica*.

Anaximander had already sussed out the fact that John and Jack were versed in the reading and function of maps, and so he proposed that they help him in indexing the ones he and the twins had already made, to see if they could add details to their growing store of knowledge about the Archipelago.

With unspoken reservations, and keeping their objective in mind, the two Caretakers agreed—but while they worked, the same concern played out in both of their heads.

To return home, Myrddyn and Madoc needed two things: first, something to guide them—the maps, which would eventually form the basis for the *Imaginarium Geographica*; and second, a vessel touched by divinity, as Odysseus's ship had been once, able to make the journey and traverse the Frontier.

They could not help with those things, but they could provide a lot of information about the Archipelago itself. Too much, in fact. In their own time, when they'd first met each other, it had been Mordred's objective to seize the *Geographica* in order to conquer the Archipelago. And that was after he'd only been back in the Archipelago for twenty years.

Giving him, whichever of the twins he was, the means to return twenty-five centuries earlier could devastate the world more than Hugo's mishap had. So they would organize, but not contribute to, the philosopher's work.

A not-too-casual mention by Anaximander that he was fascinated by the concept of time was enough of a prompt for John to pull out his gold pocket watch and proudly show it off. He explained the mechanism and workings of the watch, but much to Jack's amusement and Anaximander's confusion, the watch, as usual, didn't work.

"So it's like my gnomon," the philosopher concluded. "A stationary vertical rod set on a horizontal plane. But," he added, still puzzled, "what is the transparent dome for? It seems it would work better if the rods were more vertically inclined."

"Oh never mind," John said, setting the watch on the table and glaring at it. "It's really best as a paperweight."

"It's an excellent paperweight," said Anaximander.

Twice as they worked, the philosopher's younger student,

Pythagoras, brought food and drink. The second time, Anaximander left the companions for a moment to give more instructions to the boy.

"John," whispered Jack, moving around the table so Anaximander would not overhear them, "Chaz went out a *long* time ago. I don't think he's coming ba—"

"I know," John whispered back, his voice bitter. "I know, Jack. We still have time. Let's just do what we can here, and hope . . ."

John let the sentence trail off without finishing and resumed work on the maps.

Chaz made it to within twenty feet of the portal, where he paced through the entire night. He couldn't decide whether to go through or pee, so he merely paced, and argued with himself.

He had paced through the night and into morning before the pressure became too bad, and he finally was forced to relieve himself on the broad wall next to the plaza entrance.

"Aw, geez, Mister Chaz," came a small voice from behind him. "D'you hafta do that out here, where everyone can see? What, were you raised in a barn?"

Startled, Chaz turned around to see who had spoken. It was Fred, tapping his foot and trying not to watch as the human splashed urine all across the wall.

"Fred!" Chaz exclaimed, with a chagrined, half-embarrassed look. "Have you been watching me pee?"

"No," replied Fred, "we've been watching you pace. We thought you must have been sent back t' stand guard. You only just *started* t' pee."

Chaz looked around worriedly. It might be a strange land,

but he suspected a talking badger wouldn't go unnoticed for very long. "What are you doing here? Why did y' come through th' portal?"

The small mammal held up an hourglass. "Th' time limit!" he exclaimed. "It's almost up. You and Scowler John and Scowler Jack must return, right now!"

The badger was right. There was only a thin layer of sand left inside the upper globe of the hourglass. Could it really have been twenty-four hours already? Chaz wondered. Regardless, he wasn't about to be trapped in a place where he couldn't speak or understand the language without getting a headache.

"Okay," he said, heading for the portal.

"Wait!" Fred cried, pulling on the man's shirt. "What about Scowler Jack and Scowler John?"

Chaz sighed and rolled his eyes, then looked from the portal to Fred, and back again.

"This way," he said finally, fastening up the buckle on his trousers. "We'll have to hurry."

By midday Anaximander's entire map room was sorted and indexed, John and Jack were completely exhausted, and they were not one inch closer to discovering which of the twins was destined to become Mordred.

"This would have been easier if he already had the hook," Jack grumbled, yawning.

"At the Ring of Power, when Artus and I were fighting Mordred, he said he was nearly as old as Ordo Maas," John said, rubbing his chin. "I thought it was just bluff and bluster at the time, but the flood that took Ordo Maas to the Archipelago happened at the beginning of the Bronze Age, and the timing is right for the genealogy to work."

"That's still almost a thousand years earlier than we've come," Jack countered. "But I suppose it isn't inconceivable that they both lived a long time, maybe centuries, in the Archipelago before coming here."

Before they could continue the discussion, the door burst open and Chaz and Fred rushed inside.

"Where the *hell* have you been?" Jack exclaimed. "We thought you—"

"Wasn't coming back?" Chaz shot back. "Hah. Fat chance of that, eh, Fred?"

The little badger looked up, surprised, then gave Chaz a thumbs-up and a grin.

"Where have you—," John started to say.

"No time," Chaz cut in. "You have to hear what I overheard last night, an' then"—he pointed to Fred's hourglass—"we got t' go."

Chaz quickly recounted the whole argument he'd witnessed between Myrddyn and Madoc, repeating the strange Greek words as best he could. When he was finished, Jack snorted.

"You don't *speak* ancient Greek, Chaz," he said mockingly. "I think you're making things up out of your head."

"I'm picking up more than you know," Chaz retorted. "An' I didn't need t' understand it all t' *remember* it."

"I don't know, Chaz." John said doubtfully. "It all fits, but Jack does have a point. We don't know you heard what you think you heard."

"If it wasn't me," Chaz asked, glancing down at Fred, "if it was *him*, th' other me, would you trust me?"

"You mean Charles?" said Jack. "Of course."

"Then trust him," Chaz said to John. "Somewhere I'm him, you say. Well, last night he was me. Trust him. I mean, me. Trust me, John."

John looked questioningly at each of the others in turn. Fred nodded immediately, and finally, more reluctantly, so did Jack.

"They want to get Odysseus's ship back, do they?" John began. "He got it from his father, Laertes, who was one of the original Argonauts," he said, rubbing his chin. "Do you suppose the ship Anaximander saw was . . . ?"

"The *Red Dragon*!" Jack said excitedly. "They came here from the Archipelago in the *Red Dragon*!"

"Mmm, no," said Chaz. "They called it something else . . . the 'Aragorn' or some such."

"The *Argo*," said John. "Jason's ship. That means that Ordo Maas, or at least his sons, had gone to the island to take the wreck of the *Argo* back into the Archipelago, in order to transform it into the first of the Dragonships—the *Red Dragon*."

"Exiled, eh?" said Jack. "I bet that's the reason they were shipwrecked, and why the ship was taken back once they were here."

"One or t' other has t' be Mordred," said Chaz, "but if the other is anything like th' first, then wouldn't he still be somewhere in the future, too?"

Jack's jaw dropped. "That's brilliant, Chaz."

"We already *have* met both of them!" John said. "One of them is the Winter King—and his twin is the Cartographer of Lost Places! It's the only answer that makes any sense!"

"But which is which?" said Jack.

Fred tugged on Chaz's shirt and tapped the nearly empty hourglass.

"The twenty-four hours!" Chaz said. "It's almost up! We have to go, else we'll be trapped here!"

"You've labored long and hard," a voice said from the doorway. "I've brought you more refreshments."

Anaximander entered carrying a tray with a flagon of wine and two goblets. He started when he saw Chaz, and he studiously ignored Fred. "I'm sorry," the philosopher said, awkwardly balancing the tray. "I'll fetch another goblet."

"Where's Pythagoras?" Jack asked. "Doesn't he usually fetch the wine?"

"I, er, sent him home," Anaximander said. "I thought as a show of gratitude I would serve you the morning wine myself."

"No!" yelled Fred, leaping up to the table and knocking the tray from the philosopher's hands.

"Fred!" Jack began, but he stopped short as they all looked down at the spilled wine, which sizzled and bubbled on the stone floor.

"Animal instincts," said Fred, "and a good nose."

"Right," Chaz said. His left fist snapped up, and he struck Anaximander brutally in the jaw. The philosopher went down hard, falling in a sprawl at the man's feet. "Y' unnerstand *that*?"

The truth of what was happening slowly sank into John and Jack as Chaz and Fred headed out the door. "You didn't make any of these maps, did you, Anaximander? One of your students did."

"The desire is there, but I have not the skill," the philosopher admitted, teeth clenched. "It was that boy, that *child*. . . . He had such a hand, and such a clear mind for detail. . . . I had saved his life, after all. Wasn't I entitled to benefit from that? Wasn't I?"

Jack cursed in English, then switched back to Greek. "We don't care about that!" he said harshly. "We just want to know which of them it was!"

"Jack! John!" Chaz shouted from the courtyard. "Now!"

"Anaximander! Please!" John called as he backed out of the map room. "We have to know! We need to know! Tell us, please!

"*Who is the Cartographer?*"

But no answer was forthcoming. John and Jack raced out of the philosopher's home as he collapsed in a wreck of tears and regret.

Chaz, with Fred trailing behind, already had a good lead, and the streets of Miletus were broad and uncrowded. There would be no real gathering in this part of the town for another hour or two, John thought wryly. Not until the storyteller, whichever twin it was today, made his appearance in the amphitheater.

To his credit, Chaz had slackened his pace just slightly enough to allow the badger to keep up, so John and Jack had nearly caught up to them by the time the thief and the badger had entered the portal.

Jack raced through next, hardly pausing in the apparent act of running into a marble wall. John was close on his heels and cut the timing tightly enough to see the edges of the projection beginning to close in and lose their shape.

He passed through the gossamer layers and turned around for one final look at Miletus—and saw Myrddyn and Madoc dash from an alleyway and into the plaza.

In seconds the twin sons of Odysseus had spotted the unusual nature of the wall where the companions had vanished, and they moved quickly to follow, swords drawn.

But it was too late. The projection began to fade as the slide was burned dry by the incandescent bulb in the Lanterna Magica, and in a moment, the portal had closed in front of them. Ancient Greece was history.

"Curse it all," said John. "I've forgotten my watch."

CHAPTER ELEVEN
THE GRAIL

THE HARSH WHITE light of the Lanterna Magica cast deep shadows behind John, Jack, and Chaz as they stood, reeling from the chase, and realized they were once again safe in the projection room on Noble's Isle.

"The giants!" Jack exclaimed, looking around in trepidation. "Are the giants still outside?"

Reynard moved to him, making soothing gestures with his paws. "No need to fear. They retreated when they realized you were no longer here. But," he added, almost apologetic, "they may yet return. Were you successful in your mission?"

At that both Jack and Chaz looked at John, who took a deep breath. "Well, yes and no," he admitted. "I think we found the answer we were looking for—Mordred's true name—or at least, we've narrowed it down. But we still don't know how to use it against him."

Sitting to rest, the three men took turns recounting the events of the last day to Fred and Uncas, as Reynard ordered in food and drink.

Chaz hungrily tucked into the pile of cheese and bread that had been brought in by three ferrets. "Truth t' tell, I'm more sleepy than anything," he said through a mouthful of food, "but this may be the best sandwich I've ever had."

Reynard bowed in gratitude and began to pour a cup of wine. Chaz stopped him, covering the cup with his hand. "If it's all th' same t' you," he said, looking at the others, "I'd just as soon stick t' water or ale after this trip."

"Agreed," said Jack, shuddering at the thought of how close he'd come to drinking the poisoned wine. "Thanks for the save, Fred."

The little mammal would have blushed if he could. As it was, he beamed happily and chewed a crust of bread Chaz had handed him.

"One thing's certain," John said. "We went into that completely unprepared. We can't do so a second time."

"To be fair," said Uncas, "there *were* giants at the door yesterday."

Chaz nodded grimly. "An' they could be lurkin' about even now—so we'd best get prepared and decide what t' do right."

"Is it me," Reynard whispered to John, "or didst his countenance change during your journey into the projection?"

"His appearance?"

The fox shook his head. "Countenance. His . . . appearance beneath what we see with our eyes."

"Mmm, perhaps," John mused, looking at his reluctant companion. "Maybe it has, at that."

"So," Uncas began, "how do we prepare you better for the next trip, other than giving you the hourglass this time around?"

"Yes," said John. "You saved us there, too, it seems. As to being better prepared, I don't think there is anything further that we *can* do. We simply don't have enough information to work with."

"Maybe we do," Jack said, a look of excitement on his face. "Remember? The warning! The warning in the book that was sent to Charles!"

John swore under his breath. "I'd completely forgotten about it," he admitted, "not that it would have done us any good where Verne sent us."

"What do you mean?" asked Jack. "Why not?"

"At its earliest, the representation of the Grail wouldn't have had any meaning at all until a few decades after the crucifixion of Christ. And we already know that Hugo was sent back several centuries later than that. So I don't see how his warning is relevant to Verne's mission."

"But it *is* relevant, don't you see, John?" Jack exclaimed. "Hugo gave us the answer in his message! It's the Cartographer! Mordred's twin! His own brother *would* be capable of the Binding!"

John's brow furrowed in concentration as he considered Jack's idea. It might in fact be possible—he was unclear as to the rules that regulated the power behind the Summonings and the Bindings, except that they had to be spoken by someone of royal birth. Artus was able to do it, as had Arthur, generations before him. Aven's son, Stephen, could have done it as well. And they already knew Mordred was capable of doing a Binding—so the same *might* be true of his brother.

"We know the Cartographer's existence predates Arthur's rule," John reasoned, "and we'd already suspected that Mordred did too. And remember—back on Terminus, Mordred did say that he and Artus shared the same blood. So somehow the authority to speak Bindings and Summonings comes from somewhere beyond even Mordred."

"Fair enough," said Jack. "That means his twin—the Cartographer—would possess the same ability. Hugo's note mentioned the Cartographer, and Verne told us we needed to discover Mordred's true name in order to defeat him. We can't do that here," he said, waving his arms to indicate Albion as a whole. "There are no other kings able to do to *him* what he can do to *us*. And I don't think the authority of the Caretakers can overpower the authority of the king."

"Mebbe that's what this 'Verne' meant f'r us t' do," said Chaz, who was sitting against the wall, dozing, but still listening. "Mebbe it's up t' us t' turn one of the brothers against the other."

"That's what it comes down to, doesn't it?" Jack asked. "We have to convince whichever one is the Cartographer that his brother will eventually turn rotten, and that the only way to prevent it is to Bind him."

"But for how long?" wondered John. "Binding can't really be permanent, unless . . ."

Only Chaz and Reynard didn't understand John's unspoken thought, which the others knew as part of their own history: The only way to defeat the Winter King was to kill him. And even that had proven to be problematic.

"Y'r still forgetting one thing," said Chaz. "He in't the Cartographer yet. And *both* of 'em were thrown out of the Archipelago, remember? I heard 'em say it. And they were both in on th' plan t' kill *us*, if you recall. When they was chasin' us out of Miletus, they *both* had drawn swords. That says poison t' me. Both of 'em. They be poison."

"Isn't the Cartographer your friend?" asked Uncas. "Back where we came from?"

John shook his head slowly. "I don't think the Cartographer is anyone's friend, to be honest," he said. "We went to him when we had to, and no more. And he gave us what he needed to, and no more. It wasn't so much a friendship as it was cooperation between interested parties."

"Isn't that what you're seeking now?" asked Reynard, who had been listening from the back of the room all the while. "Not his friendship, but his cooperation?"

"Yes," Jack replied, "but we have less to argue with here. Back in our world, he was a virtual prisoner, locked in the Keep of Time, behind the door that bore the mark of the king."

"Mordred's mark?" asked Chaz.

"Arthur's mark," said Jack. "Different king, but the Cartographer was just as trapped."

"What for?" asked Chaz. "What did *he* do t' piss someone off?"

John shrugged. "No one's ever said. I'm not sure if anyone really knows. None of the Histories ever mentioned it, that's for certain."

"Mayhap we should consult th' Little Whatsit," offered Uncas. "There be lots of unique knowledge there that even some scowlers may not know."

"Thank you, Uncas," John said gently, "but this is bigger than just healing blisters or making magic darts." He sat in the chair next to the badger and looked at the projector. "I wonder if we shouldn't turn it on and have a look at the next slide? That way we can equip ourselves ahead of time for wherever and whenever it lands us."

"Do we really want to do that?" asked Jack. "We can't afford to use up the hours. Once we turn it on, we have twenty-four hours maximum before the slide burns out. And we're going to need every second to convince the Cartographer to join us against his brother."

"You're probably right," said John. "We became acclimated pretty quickly in Miletus, and Chaz was useful in helping us blend in. Perhaps this really will just be a leap of faith."

John's sentiment was punctuated by a loud boom from outside and a faint tremor which shook the room.

"Oh, no," Jack groaned, slapping his forehead. "Here we go again."

"Wait," Reynard said, rushing from the room. "Let me see for certain."

Any doubt they felt as to what had made the noise was dispelled a moment later when the voice of the giant filtered through the walls of the building. *"Jaaackk,"* it said, menacing and persuasive all at once, *"Jaack . . . wee have a preeesent for youuu. . . ."*

There was a crashing somewhere outside the house, and a cacophony of animal noises, then silence.

"They're being a bit more restrained than the last time," John observed. "That can't be good."

Chaz agreed. "They's up t' summat, for sure."

A moment later the fox reentered the room.

"I have good news, and bad news, and worse news," Reynard announced. He was trembling. Whatever had just transpired outside had rattled the fox to his core.

"What's the good news?" Jack said.

"The giants will honor the king's covenant with the Children of the Earth," Reynard answered. "They will not cross our boundary and step onto Sanctuary."

"Excellent!" Jack exclaimed. "We'll be safe here, then."

"Trapped, y' mean," Chaz said glumly. He looked at the fox. "They in't going anywhere, is they?"

Reynard shook his head. "They are at the four points of the compass—one each at north, south, east, and west. They will not permit you and your fellows, or indeed, anyone else to leave Sanctuary while you are here."

"I'm guessing that's the bad news, then," said John. "Should we dare ask what the worse news is?"

Reynard leaned back and motioned for the large jackrabbit that waited in the hall to come into the projection room. The animal was carrying a small burlap sack, tied with a ribbon and bearing a card. The rabbit set the bag on one of the chairs, then hopped quickly away.

John stepped forward and looked at the card. It read simply, *To complete the set.*

He frowned and undid the tie on the bag, which dropped open.

The badgers gasped and turned away, and Jack covered his eyes with his hands. Chaz reacted even more strongly, cursing and clenching his fists in anger. As for John, he simply closed his eyes and murmured a hasty prayer before retying the bag that held his old mentor's head and setting it reverently in one corner of the room.

John turned to Reynard, wiping his eyes with the back of his hand. "There's no more time to waste," he said as boldly as he could manage. "Let's see the second slide."

The companions prepared for the second jaunt through the Lanterna Magica's projections while trying to ignore the frequent taunts of the giants, and even more so the grisly present in the burlap bag.

John decided against including the hourglass in their supplies, making the argument that it could too easily be lost, broken, or upended. "No," he said, "I think what happened before is really our ideal. Uncas and Fred will be our timekeepers. You're both safe here on Sanctuary anyway, and you can come fetch us as the time grows short."

"They were able to do that last time because I, ah, were passin' by the portal," said Chaz. "How will they find us this time around?"

"We'll have to be aware of the time ourselves as best we can," said John, "and try to keep a bearing on the position of the portal so we'll be nearby."

"Don't worry, Scowler John," Uncas stated with a salute. "Th' Royal Animal Rescue Squad will not fail you."

"I know you won't, Uncas," John said, resisting the urge to pat the badger on the head while he was being stately. "The son of Tummeler would never let us down."

Uncas looked so proud at the compliment that John thought he might burst into tears. "Ready?" he said to Jack and Chaz.

Chaz yawned and nodded. "Enough, I guess."

"Ready," agreed Jack.

"All right," John said, signaling Reynard. "Light it up."

The fox pressed the switch that rotated the disc of slides, and the next image slid smoothly into view. John, Jack, and Chaz stepped aside to better get a view of the slide, and Uncas and Fred dutifully turned over the hourglass.

As before, the multiple layers that were projected on the wall gave everyone a slightly disoriented feeling. It took a few moments for their vision to adjust to the shifting perspectives, and then they could see what was on the slide.

In front of them, perhaps thirty feet distant, was the elaborately decorated entrance to a mosque, or perhaps a temple. The architecture was more advanced than what they had seen in the previous projection, but harder to place.

"Persian?" Jack murmured.

"No," said John. "More Egyptian, I'd say."

The wall they faced was dominated by a great arched doorway, in front of which was a broad pedestal. On it was an immense horned owl, which was clutching a piece of chalk in one clawed foot and seemed to be using it to scribble on a piece of slate.

"What do you make of that?" John asked.

"The bird?" said Jack. "I think it's an owl."

John groaned. "I know it's an owl!" he whispered back. "I mean *that*!" He pointed behind the bird.

Jack gasped, as did Chaz. Behind the pedestal, engraved into the door and embellished with golden ornaments and designs crusted with jewels, was the image of the Holy Grail, the same one that was on the cover of the book back at Magdalen College.

"So we're definitely into Anno Domini," Jack said. "Past the time of Christ."

"Or within it," said John, as a man, absorbed in whatever work he was attending to, passed by the scene in front of them. He wore sandals and a simple robe with a sash. "I can't tell from the attire. First century? Second, maybe? We'll have to suss it out for certain once we've crossed over."

"Good enough," said Jack. "Who wants to go first?"

"Don't look at me," said Chaz. "You two are the 'Scowlers.'"

"It doesn't need to be a debate," John said. "We've done it before."

"You couldn't tell from all the bickering," said a trilling voice that was airy and condescending at the same time. "If you asked me, I'd say you're all scared to death."

John and Jack stared at each other in surprise. The voice had spoken in Greek—but it had come from the *owl*.

"What?" the owl asked. "Cat got your tongues?"

The three companions all stepped through the portal and into the hallway they'd been watching. If they were going to converse with a giant bird, John figured it would be less conspicuous to do so in person than to risk anyone seeing the owl verbally upbraiding a blank wall.

"Not scared," Jack said in response to the owl's comment. "Just cautious."

"Caution, fft," the owl scoffed. "That's not really the attitude to have if you want to take over the world, now, is it?"

"Why would I want to take over the world?" asked Jack.

"Why else would you come to Alexandria?" the owl replied. "All the fashionable would-be world conquerors do."

Alexandria. So, John realized, they were in Egypt, but at the edge of the influence of the Greek world. And certainly later than the common era they'd been to in the other projection.

"It's simpler than that," Chaz said in surprisingly passable Greek. "We just need to find someone."

"Mmm," said the owl, obviously losing interest. "And what is this someone's name?"

"We're not really sure," Jack admitted.

"That would make it harder, wouldn't it?" the owl replied with no trace of sympathy.

"What's *your* name?" Chaz asked.

The owl preened. Apparently he wasn't asked his name very often. "Archimedes," he replied. "A pleasure, I'm sure."

"Archimedes? Like the mathematician?" asked John.

The owl hopped up and down in irritation. "Why does everyone ask me that? Why does no one ever think that a bird can't also be a mathematician?"

"Sorry," said John. "I didn't mean to offend."

The owl scowled. "Pythagoras should have built me as an eagle instead of an owl. No one ever questions an eagle."

"A clockwork owl?" Jack whispered. "Intriguing."

"What are you working on, Archie?" asked Chaz, looking at the slate. "Looks complicated."

Any irritation the owl might have felt at being called "Archie" was set aside by the chance to discuss the notations on the tablet.

"It's a math problem," he said, giving John a poisonous look, "for the trials. You know about the trials, do you not?"

"We're strangers here," John began, before Archimedes cut him off with a disgusted noise.

"I *know* you're strangers here," the bird said. "I just watched you walk through a *wall*. Locals don't really do that much. And you aren't here as conquerors, or if you are, you're the most ill-prepared conquerors I've ever seen."

"We're not conquerors," Jack confirmed.

"You're the funny one in the group, aren't you?" asked the bird.

"It depends on the day," said Jack.

"People come here for only two reasons," Archimedes continued, "to start an insurrection to try to unite the world, or to prepare for the trials."

"Trials for what?" asked John.

"To become Caretakers, of course."

"Caretakers? Of the *Imaginarium Geographica*?"

"The what? No," the bird replied, exasperated. "Of the Sangreal."

"The Holy Grail?"

The bird glared at him. "Why do you repeat everything I say? You must be the stupid one of the group. Which isn't saying much, is it?

"Yes," Archimedes said as he went back to his equations. "The trials are to test those who would become Caretakers—of the Holy Grail."

CHAPTER TWELVE

IMAGINARY GEOGRAPHIES

THE THREE COMPANIONS retreated a few feet away to confer privately, while the owl went back to its figures and calculations.

"That seals it," whispered Jack. "It's no coincidence we came here now. The Grail has to figure into our mission to find Myrddyn and Madoc."

"I can't see how," said John, "unless they've become somehow entwined with the Grail lore this far back. Remember, we're still centuries from where Hugo ended up."

"Perhaps he discovered that somehow," suggested Jack, "and that's why he included it in the message to us."

John rubbed his forehead and chewed on his lip. "No," he said finally, "I can think of another reason they'd be here now. They've come for the trials. Remember what they claimed they wanted to do, back in Miletus?"

Chaz nodded. "They wanted t' find a way t' get back to th' Archipelago."

"Right," said John, "and to do that, they needed a route, and directions, and something else—an object touched by divinity that would allow them passage through the Frontier. And at this point in history, can you think of any other object that fits the description better than the cup of Christ?"

The companions turned and went back to the owl, who sighed dramatically. "Now what? I have work to do, you know. The trials won't write themselves, and I only have until tomorrow."

"The Grail trials are math problems?" asked John.

"Yes, oh master of the obvious," retorted the owl. "Or a part of them, anyway. The trials judge one's worth, through tests spiritual, physical, and intellectual. I'm in charge of the intellectual part."

"We'll leave you alone to work, we promise," John said. "We'd just like to ask some directions."

"Oh?" said Archimedes. "To find your nameless friend?"

"We're looking for someone who likes t' make maps," said Chaz. "Y' know anyone like that?"

"I do, actually," Archimedes replied, still distracted by his equations. "Go north three hundred paces, then open the second door. That should be the man you seek."

"Thanks, Archie," said Chaz, turning to the others. "Time's a-wastin'. Shall we go?"

"Wait," John said, still flabbergasted at having somehow become the third wheel of the trio. "He's here? In this very building?"

"Well, where else would someone who's anyone be?" Archimedes asked without looking up. "If you aren't working at the library, you aren't worth paying attention to, anyway."

John and Jack exchanged knowing glances. Of course. The seat of learning, the crossroads of culture for the entire civilized world, wouldn't just be the city. It would be the Library of Alexandria itself.

Heartened by the progress they seemed to be making, the three companions followed the owl's directions down the passageway and opened the door.

They were looking into a broad, high-ceilinged room that was essentially one great, global map. The walls and ceilings were festooned with drawings, and all across them were lines that even connected across the floor, which was also covered with illustrations. The effect was not unlike stepping inside an immense transparent globe.

"Impressive, I know," a voice said from somewhere across the expanse of parchment that lined the tables and shelves scattered about the room. "I call the lines drawn across the maps 'latitude' and 'longitude.' Forgive me if I've forgotten a meeting. I'm not expected to present my discoveries in the rotunda until next week, but they're taking all my attention at present."

A short, pleasantly anxious man stepped around a tall papier-mâché globe he was constructing and offered them a hand in greeting.

He was olive-skinned, and he spoke with an accent that demonstrated both travel abroad and great education, but his mannerisms were those of a tailor who can't decide between creating a more finely cut suit, or a more satisfied customer. He wore a round cap and breeches that seemed to be Persian, or perhaps Egyptian. And shoes, rather than the sandals they'd seen the others wearing through the projection. They'd expected to go straight from Archimedes to one or both of the twins, and so they had not procured any appropriate clothing. However, their unusual dress seemed not to matter at all to the man, who was dressed even more oddly than they were.

John took the man's hand, which was sticky with paste, and shook it firmly.

"Oh! I'm very sorry," the man said, just realizing what he'd done. "Can you forgive?"

"Don't worry about it," said John, wiping his hand on the back of his trousers and smiling. "I'm John."

"Claudius Ptolemaeus. Call me Ptolemy," the man replied. "Did we have a meeting today?"

"We're just here for the trials," Jack answered. "To become Caretakers of the, uh, Grail."

Ptolemy squinted, as if he was having trouble with Jack's accent. "Oh!" he said finally. "Of course! The trials. Yes, a sorry business it is."

"The trials?"

"No," said Ptolemy. "The need for a new Caretaker. One of them—one of the best we've had, in fact—tried to . . ."

He paused and cupped his hands around his mouth, as if he didn't want to be heard speaking the words. "He tried to take the Grail. For himself. And he was caught and shall be executed soon. That's the reason I'm behind schedule," Ptolemy explained, gesturing at the room full of maps. "The betrayer was my own understudy, and perhaps the most talented mapmaker I've ever known."

John, Jack, and Chaz all stiffened at this, but it was a testament to the swift self-control of all three men that Ptolemy never noticed their reactions.

"I was mocked in other places, other libraries," Ptolemy continued, using a small stepladder and a pointer to tap out some locations high on the southern wall. "Here, and here, and, uh"—he turned, pointing east—"and over there. I always believed that imagination plays as crucial a part in the making of maps as education. After all, how else is one to test the spatial boundaries of the world, if one cannot first imagine them?"

John pursed his lips. "That's a great argument, Ptolemy. Is it a viewpoint your understudy shares?"

The mapmaker nodded and climbed down the ladder. "Yes," he said morosely, folding his hands behind his back. "It is. That man has such a mind, such a mind, it's a wonder. And such talent! Just look at these works!"

"These are his?" Jack asked, leafing through some sheets of parchment. "Not yours?"

"Some are mine, some his," Ptolemy admitted. "Our studies we work on together. But our principal works we have done separately—the better to test their merits against each other's work."

Ptolemy pushed his way through two shelves laden with tools and buckets and retrieved a large folio. It was bound in leather and contained sheets of parchment.

"Normally," he said, placing the book in front of them, "I'd just be drawing the maps on scrolls, as scholars always have done. But keeping the latitudes straight in particular necessitated that they be cut into squares and bound thusly."

"These are maps of the entire world?" John asked as Ptolemy began to display his work to them.

"Much of it, yes," he answered. "From the Blessed Isles, here, to Thule, here, and Meroë and Serica, here." He tapped the map proudly. "Pretty good, yes?"

"It's remarkable," John agreed.

"Breathtaking," said Jack.

"The parchments are very clean," observed Chaz.

"I'd worked out most of 'latitude' myself," said Ptolemy, indicating the horizontal lines drawn across the maps. "But 'longitude,'" he added, noting the vertical lines, "didn't really come together until my understudy arrived. He showed me ways to use some underlying cartological principles that haven't been used since the philosopher Anaximander's time to clarify my own measurements. You'd be surprised at how clearly he could articulate them."

"I'll bet," John said dryly.

"I just wish he'd been cleverer," said Ptolemy. "If not too clever to steal, at least too clever to be caught."

"Why is that?" asked Jack.

Ptolemy closed the book and dusted off the cover. "We finished my *Geographica*," he said sadly, "but we'll never have the chance to finish his." He put his book on a wide shelf and removed a second one, which was similar in size and shape but vastly more familiar to John and Jack—even in its much earlier state.

"He calls it his *Imaginary Geography*," Ptolemy said. "It contains maps to places that no one has seen, and now," he added with a sigh, "perhaps no one ever will."

The *Imaginarium Geographica*, the earliest version of it at least, was right there in front of them. It was all John could do not to grab the book and start hugging it.

"I'm happy to see it too," Jack whispered, having noted the flare of joy in his friend's eyes, "but remember—this is not our *Geographica*. Not yet."

Jack was right. As Ptolemy paged through the scant few completed maps, some were familiar, others not so much. Some of the islands of the Underneath were there: Aiaia, and Lixus, and the Island of Wandering Rocks. A few were unmarked, but several others bore annotations.

"An addition of my own," Ptolemy said proudly. "I felt it was essential to know something more about the lands in a *Geographica* than just how to get there."

"We appreciate that a lot," said John. "More than you can know."

Chaz scratched his head. "How d'you annotate a map t' an imaginary place?"

"Just the idea was mine, not the writing itself," Ptolemy said. "But even so, how could you go wrong writing a description of an imaginary land? All that would matter is whether or not you believed in it yourself."

"Ptolemy," John said, "we need to see your understudy. Can you take us to see him?"

"Oh, I'm sorry," the mapmaker said. "He's already condemned and in his cell, awaiting execution. I couldn't—"

"Please," John implored. "It's important."

"Well, if I were to help . . . ," Ptolemy began, tapping at his chin. "How might I benefit by it?"

Jack answered, turning to Ptolemy with a determined look on his face. "If we give you something of great value, will you help us?"

Ptolemy folded his arms. "What are you offering?"

"What if I can show you a land, a new land that really exists, but that no one knows about yet?"

Ptolemy's arms dropped to his sides. "A new land? A real one?"

In reply, Jack took a stylus from a table, then grabbed a fresh sheet of parchment from a nearby stack and began to sketch. A couple of times he stood back, appraising, then kept working. Once

John realized what Jack was doing, he picked up another stylus and began to add topographical details, and even a fish or three swimming in the water. When they had finished, Jack handed the sheet to Ptolemy. "There. What do you think of that?"

"Amazing!" Ptolemy exclaimed. "Where is it?"

Jack pointed to John's notations. "Here—it lies far south of Chi—uh, Sinae.

"We call it 'Australia.'"

"You'll have to wait until dark," Ptolemy explained as he traced out the route the companions needed to follow. "There will be guards attending to him through the evening, but you should be able to sneak past if you use the corridors I've marked. You don't plan to kill anyone, do you?"

John was aghast. "Of course not!"

Ptolemy took this with aplomb. "Oh, I wouldn't take issue if you really needed to. I just want to know if I have to plan ahead for anyone's replacement."

"Why would that be your worry?" asked Chaz. "Are you some sort of supervisor here at the library?"

"Actually," Ptolemy whispered, again with the hand cupped to his mouth, "I'm the king. Of Alexandria."

Chaz started to ask the obvious question: Why did they have to resort to sneaking and subterfuge to see the prisoner, if Ptolemy was in a position to simply order it?

John quickly looked at the others with a slight head shake. If Ptolemy was speaking the truth, he could be helpful; but if he was just a crazy geographer, engaging him more fully in their quest could just complicate things.

Jack rolled his eyes. "Okay," he said to Ptolemy. "We appreciate your help."

The three companions shook hands with the geographer king and started tracing the labyrinthine path he'd marked for them, which wound through the warren of rooms. They moved from corridor to corridor, each one taking them to progressively larger rooms, most of which were filled with racks and shelves laden with scrolls. It was more than tempting for John and Jack to reach out every so often to touch one of the scrolls.

"Why so delicate?" Chaz asked. "Paper don't break."

"You wouldn't understand," John replied, still eyeing a set of scrolls that bore Egyptian seals as they passed to the next room. "This library, and everything in it, represents a collection of knowledge more complete than the world will ever see again. It's tempting to just stay and read. To men like us, this is holy ground."

"Right," said Chaz, who was clearly unimpressed. "If it was so great, what happened to it?"

"The usual," said Jack. "Catastrophe, followed by a couple thousand years of regret."

In the adjacent structure they found the cluster of rooms where Ptolemy said his understudy was being held.

The hall was lined with identical doors set into stone. "Which one?" Jack asked. "They're all the same. It'll take all night."

"That one," Chaz said, pointing. "It's the only one with a guard." Without further discussion, he slipped around to the next corridor and disappeared. A moment later a second guard stopped in front of the cell door and spoke briefly to the first, who got up and began to walk directly to John and Jack's place of concealment. The other went back the way he had come.

The first guard didn't even have time to call out before John clocked him hard on the chin. The guard fell and slumped against the wall, and Jack grabbed him under the arms and dragged him to a less conspicuous spot. Just then, Chaz appeared at the other end of the corridor and trotted to them.

"What happened to the other guard?" John whispered. "I thought there were two."

"There were," Chaz whispered back, "but he couldn't handle his wine."

"You got him drunk? That fast?"

"Nah," said Chaz, pointing to his forehead. "Hit him with th' bottle."

Jack came back just in time to overhear them. "You know, Chaz," he said, only half joking, "for a thief and a traitor, you've turned out to be really useful."

"I resemble that remark," said Chaz.

"Fair enough," Jack declared. "I got the keys from the guard. Let's go see who we find."

Jack fumbled a bit with the keys, so Chaz offered to try. The third key he put into the lock worked, and the door swung open with a gentle push.

The cell beyond was rectangular and made entirely of stone. There was a small window on the far wall, but it was blocked by wooden beams just outside. John saw at once that this room had never been intended for use as a cell at all; it had to have been a storeroom of some kind, only recently converted to hold a prisoner. Even so, it was a cell in name only, and distinguishable from other rooms at the library solely because of the lock on the door and the guards in front of it.

There was a solitary desk and a chair, but the only light came from a small oil lamp that hung near the door, and a second positioned over the desk. In many ways, the room bore a strong resemblance to Ptolemy's workshop. Every surface was covered with maps, and there were globes and statuary scattered throughout. As they stepped over the threshold, the lamp at the door seemed to brighten, and it cast their shadows deep into the room.

"Hello?" John said cautiously. "Is someone there?"

At the desk, a man raised his tousled head up from the work he was concentrating on, and eyes that were more distracted than curious peered at them.

"Is it time already? I still have work to do, and I was hoping for a little more sleep before morning so my eyes wouldn't be puffy when you lop off my head."

"We're not here to execute you," said Jack. "We're here to, uh . . ." He looked at John, who shrugged. What were they here to do? Rescue him?

"We've got a couple of questions," said Chaz. "If you please."

The man at the desk perked up. "Three visitors, and three voices I haven't heard in oh so long," he said, standing and straightening his clothes. "You've picked a good time to visit. Another day and I'd have been unable to answer."

"So we heard," said Jack. "My sympathy would be greater if you hadn't tried to poison us, then chase us with a sword the last time we met."

"Last time, or first?" came the reply. "Not that I really care, mind you. For what it's worth, I do regret trying to poison you. It was a different time then, and I was a different man. What are your questions?"

As he said this, he stepped farther into the lamplight. He hadn't aged much but was perhaps shorter, as if gravity had noticed him more than before. Still, they couldn't quite tell if he was Myrddyn or Madoc.

John suddenly realized that the answer to one question was literally right in front of them. This was Ptolemy's understudy. Whichever of the twins this was would be the Cartographer.

"What's your name?" asked Chaz.

The man's smile was warm, but slightly weary also. "I've had many names, but at present I am called Meridian."

John's mouth twitched imperceptibly, as he tried not to sigh in relief. Meridian was the name of a line of longitude. This was the Cartographer.

"What brought you here?" asked Jack.

"I first traveled here when it was still called Rhakotis, before Alexander transfigured everything in his own image," Meridian said, pacing back and forth in front of them, so that he constantly passed between light and shadow. "That Alexander should later come here to establish a great center of learning in the same place can be called an accident of family, I suppose."

"You're related to Alexander?" John said in surprise.

"A cousin," replied Meridian. "We descendants of the Argonauts are an ambitious lot, it seems. World conquest is in our blood. At least," he added quickly, "for some of us."

"You're not interested in conquering the world, Myrddyn?" John asked, remembering more about the twin they were facing as they conversed.

The mapmaker raised a hand. "Please. I have not gone by that name in almost two hundred years. Meridian suits me better, I think."

"And your brother?" John asked, noting that Meridian hadn't actually answered his question. "Has he changed as well?"

"Madoc is still Madoc, in name and temperament," said Meridian. "He has chosen his path, and it differs from mine. Why do you ask?"

John looked first at Jack, who nodded his assent, then at Chaz, who chewed his lip for a few seconds, looking hard at Meridian, before he also agreed.

"We have some things we need to tell you," he began slowly, "things that may seem impossible to believe. But believe them you must. And when we have finished, we're hoping that you can help us find a way to solve our problem . . .

". . . without killing your brother."

PART FOUR

THE IRON CROWN

CHAPTER THIRTEEN
BETRAYAL

BY EARLY AFTERNOON, Hugo Dyson and King Pellinor had arrived at the place Pellinor called "Camelot." Whatever Hugo had initially envisioned on hearing the name vanished as the cart crested the hill overlooking the shallow valley that was their destination.

Camelot was not a city, or even the castle Hugo had been half hoping to see. Instead they looked out over a broad valley ringed about with low hills and a scattering of scrubby trees. In the center stood a number of upraised stones and a granite stairway that wound its way up a grassy mound, ending at a great stone table.

Throughout the valley were camped the various travelers Hugo had observed from a distance as they rode south. There were mud-and-wattle huts and silken tents, along with a more common scattering of simpler tents and enclosures. But in front of each encampment was a banner representing the champion who had come to compete in the tournament.

To the right, Hugo saw a flag emblazoned with a scarlet roc; and beside that, one bearing a golden griffin. To their left, he saw an immense banner crested with ships and an embroidered fish.

In the distance, he could even make out one that seemed simpler, as if it had been sewn for a blanket rather than a war banner; it bore the image of a white pig.

"So," Hugo said jovially, "uh, have we got a banner to fly?"

Pellinor raised an eyebrow at him, then lifted his foot and booted Hugo out of the cart.

The scholar rolled clumsily for a moment before righting himself, spitting and brushing dirt off his clothes. "I say," Hugo said indignantly. "What's that all about?"

Pellinor shrugged and tossed the crumpled photograph at him. "I was asked to pick you up and then deliver you here. I've done that, done. And now I've my own business to attend to."

Without another word, Pellinor clicked his tongue at the old horse and wheeled it around. In minutes he'd disappeared amongst the other carts and horses and tents filling the small valley.

Hugo blinked a few times, then began to assess his situation through clear eyes for the first time. This was no joke, no illusion. And he was far out of his depth in whatever it was that was happening around him.

As if to compound his concern, a knight dressed in armor and a green-gold tunic noticed him sitting on the hillside and began walking directly toward him.

The knight stopped, towering over the scholar, who was growing more anxiety-ridden by the second. "You look as out of place as I feel," he whispered to Hugo in perfect, unaccented American English. "And that's saying a lot."

"Wh-wh-what?" Hugo stammered. This was unexpected, even after the ride with Pellinor.

"Hank Morgan," the knight said, removing his helmet. "Pleased to meet you."

"Are—are you here to fight in the tournament?" asked Hugo, eyeing the dress and armor. "Whatever this tournament is supposed to be?"

"I'm here as a watcher only," Hank replied. "I'm to observe and record, but never interfere."

"And who are you watching for?" Hugo asked.

Hank blinked in surprise. "Weren't you sent here to watch too?" he asked. "By the Caretakers?"

Hugo brightened, slightly relieved. This might be a friend. "No, I wasn't," he said, proffering his hand. "Hugo Dyson, newly itinerant friend of the Caretakers. I'm here by accident, I'm afraid."

Hank's eyes narrowed at this. "By accident?" he said, repeating Hugo's words as they shook hands. "By *accident*? How is that possible? I thought I was the only one that had happened to. Usually these jaunts into zero points are too well-planned for someone to come 'by accident.'"

Hank turned away from Hugo, muttering and grumbling under his breath. He removed the heavy gauntlets he'd been wearing and pulled a small, leather-bound notebook out of his tunic. He flipped through the pages, occasionally making a notation with a stub of a pencil, and less occasionally, glancing back at Hugo with a halfhearted smile.

Finally Hank finished checking whatever he'd needed to find in the notebook and pulled a silver pocket watch out of a pocket sewn into his sleeve.

"If you'll excuse me," he said to Hugo, "I need to let someone know about you, posthaste. You see, I don't think you're supposed to be here at all."

Hugo swallowed hard. "I keep getting the same feeling, Mr. Morgan, the same feeling exactly. The problem is, I can't decide if I'm in someplace strange, or if this is a joke of some sort, or if I'm only in a dream."

Hank laughed and clapped him on the back. "I know just how you feel. The first time I 'went out,' I'd been conked in the noggin by a fellow called Hercules in a factory back in Hartford. When I woke up, I was here. Well," he added, scratching his head and examining the watch, "not 'here' here, exactly. More like thirty years from now, give or take. But one thing I came to realize was that it wasn't a dream. And you'd best realize that too, if you want to keep your head on your shoulders."

Hugo gulped hard again and fingered his collar.

Hank smiled drolly. "I'm only half-joking," he said, "but I'll do my best to see you're taken care of until we're done here, and then we'll see about getting you back when you belong."

"*Where* I belong, you mean?" said Hugo.

Hank frowned. "You really don't know what's going on, do you?" he asked rhetorically. "When do you think you are?"

"It's the twentieth of September, 1931," Hugo replied.

Hank didn't reply to this but squinted at the silver watch and turned two of the dials set in its side. The watch began to chime, then buzzed harshly. He tapped it on his armor, then shook it. "Dratted machine," he complained. "Something's off. I don't think I can get a message to anyone much earlier than about a decade and a half before your prime time, but that ought to give them sufficient notice to set things aright before you leave."

He said all this as if it would mean something to Hugo, then realized that the scholar hadn't comprehended a word of it. "Never mind," Hank said with a wave. "Just wait here and try to stay out of everyone's way. I'll send the message for you and see if the Frenchman can't help somehow, and then I have to finish my report for Sam. And I can't do either out in the open."

With that, he began to stride off, leaving the hapless Hugo sitting in the grass, holding his helmet and gauntlets. "But wait!" Hugo called. "Who's Sam?"

"The man who sent me here to begin with," Hank answered over his shoulder without turning around. "Samuel Clemens, the Caretaker Principia of the *Imaginarium Geographica*."

John and Jack took turns telling Meridian why they had come to Alexandria, with occasional contributions from Chaz. He seemed to have thoroughly mastered Greek far more quickly than they had thought possible, but however he'd done it, they were grateful. He had a keener sense than they did of which topics should be avoided and when, cutting in if he suspected they were saying too much.

The two Caretakers might have set aside the poisoning attempt in Miletus, but Chaz had not. And they didn't have Fred around to sniff out a second try.

When they had finished, Meridian sat at the table, thinking. A minute passed. Then another. Then five more.

"If all you have said is true," Meridian finally said, measuring out his words carefully, "then I have been working in error for my entire life."

"What error?" asked John. "Trying to steal the Grail?"

"That would only be the least, and most recent, of my mistakes," Meridian replied, "if it had in fact been I who deigned to take it."

"You didn't try to steal the Grail?" Jack asked.

"Of course it wasn't me!" Meridian exclaimed angrily, stopping so his face was half in shadow. "I have my work laid out to do. I'm not interested in some relic that may or may not have belonged to a false god over a century ago! Why would I risk so much, especially with my position here at the library, to gain so little?"

"Historically speaking, it's worth a great deal to many, many people," John said in answer. "Even now, you can see how it's regarded. This entire institution has been retooled to its service. And we in fact do believe it has value to you—because we know you still want to return to the Archipelago."

"What does that have to do with the Grail?"

Jack gave John a look of caution; this was a crucial piece of information to be sharing with a still uncertain ally. John shared the concern, but he was running out of options—and arguments.

"To cross the Frontier," he said, "you need to carry with you an object that has been touched by divinity. For this reason alone, I think you would desire the Grail."

Meridian narrowed his eyes, then snorted disdainfully. "Divinity? Hardly. I was a thousand years old before he was even born, and his mother was never touched by any of the gods I know. The fact that his story has become a myth believed by many people doesn't make anything he touched divine."

"It might if it's a true myth," John countered. "Ordo Maas crossed the Frontier because he carried the Flame of Prometheus—but most scholars would agree that Prometheus was only a myth."

Meridian's eyes flared at the mention of Prometheus, or so

it seemed. He smiled patiently, as if he were explaining a lesson to a slow student. "Most scholars aren't descended from him," he retorted, "and if you want to believe in a new, modern god, that's your business, not mine."

"I don't, really," said Jack. "I believe in a God, but not necessarily in the Christ myth any more than I believe in Prometheus."

"And yet," Meridian continued, "you have crossed the Frontier yourselves, have you not? So you must believe in *something*."

That was an issue Jack wasn't prepared to tackle. And neither was John. Chaz broke the moment with another question.

"Mebbe *you* don't believe," he said pointedly, "but what if your brother does?"

"Yes," Meridian replied. "That would seem like a reason for his actions, to ones such as yourselves. But it would not have been mine, even if it was Madoc's. But he could not have meant to use the Grail in the way that you suggest, to cross back to the Archipelago."

"Why not?"

"Simple," Meridian replied. "We never knew that's how it was done."

John and Jack both groaned inwardly. This might be the Cartographer, but it was a gamble telling him as much as they had. The problem was, the stakes were still unknown.

Meridian smiled. "Don't worry. I reconciled myself to being here in Odysseus's world a long time ago. If—no, when—I do return to the Archipelago, it shall be in the proper time, after the proper order of things."

"One more question," said Chaz, who had clearly taken the lead in the discussion. "Why were you and Madoc exiled from the Archipelago?"

Meridian started, and actually put out a hand to steady himself against the desk. This was not a question he had anticipated, and it seemed to rattle him deeply.

"We made a mistake," he finally said, clearing his throat. "We tried to become more than we were, to become great, but we wanted to take a shortcut. We tried to open a door that was not meant to be opened, and we were caught, and punished. And that's all I can say. I shall not speak of it again."

Chaz looked at the others. All three were making their choice—whether to trust this man before them, or not. There was no way to be sure that they could. The only thing they could be certain of was that they needed to stop his twin. That was their first priority, above all.

"We wanted to know for sure it was you we were dealing with before we liberated you," John said. "No offense intended. But we had to know you were the man we could trust."

"And how do you know I am?" argued Meridian. "We've met twice now, skipping over centuries, and for less than a day each time. And, as you pointed out, I tried to have Anaximander poison you in Miletus. So why trust me now?"

His face was an open book. This was no subversion, John realized. Meridian really wanted to know.

"We trust you," John said, "because we know the man that you will one day become. Not as friends, really, but not as adversaries. And one of the reasons we're here now, the main reason, really, is that we were told by someone we do believe in that the future's sake depends on the Cartographer. So we will trust in that. And in you."

Meridian stepped between John and Jack, past Chaz, and into

the empty corridor. "The Cartographer, you say? I've been called worse, but few have called me better."

"So you'll help us?" Chaz said plaintively. "You'll help us stop your brother?"

"You all have my gratitude," Meridian replied, smiling broadly and nodding. "That should mean something."

Jack quietly closed the door behind them, and it locked with a soft click. Meridian shuddered.

"I think if I'd had to spend one more day confined inside that wretched stone room," he said, with a somewhat restrained tone, "I'd have gone mad. I was grateful that Ptolemy permitted me the materials to continue my work, but I was actually starting to look forward to my own execution, just to escape.

"Now," he finished, rubbing his hands together, "let's deal with Madoc."

With Meridian leading the way, they wound back through the rooms and corridors with greater speed than before. John paced alongside him, asking questions about the rooms they passed, while Jack kept a watchful eye out for other guards, but they moved through undisturbed.

Jack noticed Chaz hanging back, moving more slowly. He seemed to be worrying over something.

"Chaz, what's up?" Jack asked him quietly. "Did you see something that's amiss?"

Chaz glanced ahead at John and Meridian, then gestured for Jack to slow down with him. "It's a couple o' things, really," he said. "F'r one thing, that seemed too easy. Too quick-like."

"I get where you're coming from," Jack retorted, "but I'm not going to complain about something going our way for a change."

"I'm not tryin' t' quiet y'r kettle, Jack, but did that look like a cell to you? Or he, like a man about t' be killed?"

"It was an unusual setting, sure," said Jack, "but Ptolemy wasn't operating on all cylinders either."

"There's summat else, though," Chaz continued. "If he—Meridian—if he does this now, won't it change history even worse?"

"How do you mean worse?"

"If we Bind Madoc now," Chaz said bluntly, "then he might not become the Winter King at all. Ever."

"And that would be a bad thing?"

"Maybe, maybe not," Chaz admitted, "but a lot of good things that happened because of him might never happen either."

Jack realized what Chaz meant. If it hadn't been for the Winter King, John, Jack, and Charles—*their* Charles—might never have met. And if it hadn't been for the events that created Albion, Chaz himself might never have come to be.

"I don't know," Jack said slowly. "It's a risk, certainly. But Jules Verne and Bert both gave their lives so that we could try to do . . . something to stop him. And we're running out of options."

Chaz stared at him for a moment, then nodded grimly and quickened his step to catch up to the others.

Meridian altered the course they took so as not to pass by Ptolemy's workshop. A confrontation with the geographer would only delay them, and might warn Madoc.

"He's here?" John said, startled. "At the library?"

Meridian nodded, his features inscrutable. "He's the other Caretaker of the Sangreal. The only one these past weeks since I was arrested for trying to steal it. It's a fine irony. The one entrusted to the care of the Grail is the very one who tried to take it."

"Madoc tried to steal the Grail?" said Jack. "Then why were you arrested?"

"The three of you are well-educated and seem to know much about my brother and me," Meridian said wryly, "and even you have trouble telling us apart. How much harder is it for that fool Ptolemy?"

"Fool?" John said, furrowing his brow. "I thought he was helping you with your work."

"He's a genius geographer," Meridian replied quickly, "and as an astronomer, he's had some astonishingly astute insights. But as a king, he's a half-full pitcher of stale water."

"So Madoc blamed you for the crime?"

Meridian nodded.

Chaz shook his head in disbelief. "And you were going to just let yourself be executed? For what he did?"

"Hardly," Meridian said with a droll chuckle. "It served my purposes not to disrupt the library more than necessary, and losing him would have done that. And as for myself, I was never in danger."

Jack and John traded skeptical glances, and Meridian laughed and looked at them with a trace of smugness.

"I'm a millennium old," he said. "Don't you suppose that room would only have held me for as long as I wished to be held?"

"Right," Chaz muttered under his breath. He knew bravado when he saw it. And he knew when a truth was whole, and when it was in pieces.

"We're here," Meridian declared. "Hello, Archimedes."

The owl squawked and looked up from his calculations. "Aren't you dead yet, Meridian?"

"I'm not Meridian, I'm Madoc."

"Then who's in there with the Sangreal?" Archimedes asked. "You're not supposed to leave your post."

"That's why my friends and I need to get in," Meridian said. "To do my job."

The bird peered at him with one eye. "How do I know you're not lying?" he asked.

"I always lie," answered Meridian, "except when I tell the truth."

The great bird considered this for a moment, then nodded and walked over to a small opening set in the side wall. He inserted one clawed foot, and the companions heard a lever inside release with a clicking sound. To the bird's right, the door that bore the image of the Grail swung open on mechanized hinges and the companions stepped inside.

"Have a nice day, Madoc," Archimedes said as he returned to his figures.

"See what I mean?" Meridian said. "We used to do that to Anaximander all the time."

"That's an impressive door," John said as it swung closed. "Those mechanisms are remarkable."

"It's a design built by the owl's creator," Meridian said as he pushed open an inner door and ushered them through. "Both were based on a curious device that I sold to him a few centuries ago. That's why it may look familiar to you. I think you called it a 'watch.'"

Grinning, Meridian and John stepped into the inner chamber

and stopped. Jack and Chaz were already inside, and at a loss as to what they should do next.

It was a large dome, with a massive fireplace opposite the doors, which provided both heat and light. Pillars placed through the room supported high arches, and there were two sets of stairs that presumably led to other rooms. All along the walls were pictographs showing points of recent history, a story in pictures of the Christian myth, and below them, various objects that were likely other talismans related to the Grail.

As to the Grail itself, there were several cups and saucers on the low wall that ringed the room. It wasn't readily apparent which, if any, was the true Grail. But none of the companions were focused on any of that. Instead they were transfixed by the sight of the couple sleeping on the blankets and mats that lay in the middle of the floor, as if the Grail room was nothing more than an elaborate bedchamber.

"Brother," Meridian said softly. "What . . . have . . . you . . . *done?*"

At once Madoc was awake. He was startled to see his brother—and the entourage he'd brought with him.

"Meridian!" he exclaimed. "What are you—"

His sentence remained unfinished as the girl, perhaps twenty years old, if that, suddenly awoke and pulled the cloak they'd used as a blanket over herself in fear. She had dark hair, skin that glistened, and eyes that were clear and focused.

"I can explain," Madoc began, rising.

"No need," Meridian said, taking a spear from the wall closest to him. "I now know all that I need to."

"Jack!" John exclaimed, realizing the Cartographer's intentions. "We can't let him kill Madoc!"

Before any of them could move, Meridian lunged at his brother with the spear. He missed, but only just.

The girl leaped to her feet, crying out in fear, and Madoc placed himself between her and Meridian. "Don't do this!" he implored. "You don't realize what you're doing!"

"Wrong," Meridian answered. "I know exactly what I must do."

Jack and John grabbed him, and they were surprised to realize that they could barely hold him. His strength was astonishing. "Meridian!" John shouted. "We can't risk killing him! Bind him! Then we can decide what to do!"

The Cartographer nodded and cast aside the spear.

Madoc turned to the girl, who was pulling away from him, screaming in terror now. He clutched at her robe, which tore in his hands as she ran from him, tears streaming.

"Please!" Madoc cried to her, imploring. "I'm sorry! Forgive me! Please!"

But no answer was forthcoming, and she disappeared through a second doorway at the other end of the chamber. Voices and footsteps could be heard coming from the other rooms. Her screams had alerted the library that something was amiss.

"We're about to have company," Chaz said grimly. "We got t' hurry."

Meridian leaped forward and knocked his twin to the floor, then spun him about. He held Madoc down, pinning his brother's shoulders with his knees. Meridian bit down hard on his thumb, then marked Madoc's forehead with his blood. And then he began to speak the words:

Madoc, son of Odysseus
By right and rule
For need of might
I thus bind thee
I thus bind thee

By blood bound
By honor given
I thus bind thee
I thus bind thee

For strength and speed and heaven's power
By ancient claim in this dark hour
I thus bind thee
I thus bind thee.

As Meridian finished speaking, both brothers screamed and convulsed, spines arching, as if they'd received a tremendous shock. Panting, Meridian rolled away from his brother and staggered to his feet.

"You are thus Bound, Madoc," he rasped. "By blood, and by the Old Magic, I have Bound you. And I command you . . ." He stopped and looked hesitatingly at John. It was the question none of them had any answer to. How, even Bound, could Madoc be stopped without simply killing him?

Suddenly Meridian's eyes glittered, and he turned back to his brother, who was still struggling to rise to his feet.

"Madoc, duly Bound," said Meridian, "I command you to go to the very ends of the known world, there to stay until you are summoned again, by blood."

Madoc looked stricken. For a brief instant, John actually felt compassion for him. This man still had no realization of what was happening to him, of what had been done to him—and of what fate his own twin brother had just sentenced him to.

Madoc stood shakily and reached a hand out to his brother. "I'm to be exiled?" he said pleadingly. "Again? But I don't . . . I don't . . . When?" he asked. "When will you summon me back?"

But Meridian didn't answer. He turned his back on Madoc and gave a grim smile and a brief nod to the companions. Then, without another word, he ran from the room and disappeared.

CHAPTER FOURTEEN

THE SWORD OF AENEAS

MADOC SIMPLY STOOD there, looking at John, Jack, and Chaz with a stricken expression.

"I know you," he said in wonderment. "We have met before."

"Yes," John said, feeling a strong twinge of compassion that he had to fight to keep down. "And for what it's worth . . . we're . . . I—I'm sorry, Madoc."

Jack's mouth dropped open, and Chaz just looked at the others as if they were all insane. But Madoc stared back at John with that same plaintive expression. He really didn't understand what had happened.

"Why?" he asked.

"Because of who you will become," Jack said bluntly. "You needed to be Bound."

"That's not what I was asking," Madoc replied, looking over his shoulder. "Why did Meridian do that? Why did he use Old Magic on me?"

"To protect the Grail," Jack said, "and the rest of the world."

Madoc's demeanor was so confusing to them that Jack, and even Chaz, were beginning to soften.

"Protect the Grail?" Madoc said, clearly perplexed. "That doesn't make any sense."

Before they could press the matter further, a group of librarians, armed with swords and daggers, swarmed down one of the stairways. There were obviously other entrances than the one the companions had come through.

The foremost of them scanned the room, barely noticing the companions, then fixed his glare on Madoc. "The Grail is taken!" he shouted. "Hold them! Hold them all!"

With no warning, a flame exploded in the center of the room, dividing it neatly between the companions and Madoc on one side, and the librarians on the other.

Madoc took one step, then spun about as if he were on a tether. The Binding was good, and he'd be compelled to do as he was commanded. He bent and scooped up the spear, then ran from the room. As he went, his eyes locked with John's, and the Caretaker was stunned to see there was no anger in his expression—only hurt and sorrow.

The fire had caught several floor coverings alight and was threatening the pillars as well.

"This way!" Jack shouted to the others. He led them up another stairway and out of the Grail chamber. The passageway curved around and brought them back to the entrance, where Archimedes was already sounding an alarm.

Jack didn't even pause as he exited, but rounded the corner at full speed and headed back to the main chambers of the library.

"That was lucky for us," John panted as they ran. "Talk about an opportune moment for spontaneous combustion!"

"It weren't luck," Chaz said, opening his jacket to reveal a small cache of cylinders. "I brought my flash-bangs with me in case they were needed, and it seems they were!"

John stopped, aghast, as did Jack still ahead of them.

"You did that on *purpose*?" Jack said, sputtering in anger and confusion. "Why, Chaz?"

"A distraction," Chaz said, completely baffled as to why they weren't delighted that he'd sidetracked their pursuers. "I thought you'd be happy!"

"Happy!" exclaimed Jack. "You fool—you've just set fire to the Library of Alexandria!"

Chaz scowled, still uncertain why escaping with their lives was a bad thing. John swore silently, and they all started to run again.

"Never mind," John said to Chaz. "We did what we needed to. That's what matters most."

"You know," Jack remarked, considering, "Charles is going to be mortified."

Chaz reared back. "Charles? Why would he be mortified? This is my fault."

"I know," Jack replied. "But all he's going to care about is that he seems to keep setting fire to places, whichever timeline he's in."

As they turned a corner in the main corridor, the companions passed Ptolemy, who was dashing in the other direction. He paused slightly, looking at them through narrowed eyes, as if he suspected that they'd been the instigators of the inferno, but then he turned away and kept running. John, to his great relief, had noted that the geographer had been carrying both *Geographicas*—his own as well as Meridian's.

Another one of the librarians, who had been first in the Grail chamber, stopped the king.

"It's too late!" he exclaimed, mouth agape with fear and astonishment. "The Sangreal is lost!"

"What are you talking about, Pelles?" Ptolemy answered. "Lost how?"

"A great winged beast!" Pelles cried. "It took the Sangreal into the air and away from the library!"

"No time for stories," Ptolemy said, "just because you've failed in your duties! Send word to the son of Arimathea, and take what you can to Glastonbury.

"The library," the geographer went on, "is finished."

Reaching one of the main repositories, the two Caretakers and the hapless former thief grabbed some large wicker baskets in both hands and began to shovel scrolls of parchment into them.

"Hurry!" Jack implored the others. "We have to save as many as we can!"

"It's going up too quickly," John said, scanning the rafters of the room, which were already pouring with smoke. "We can't do enough. The Histories said that the most essential works were saved. We'll just have to trust that they will be."

Reluctantly the others agreed. They dropped the baskets and headed for the portal.

All the librarians and various scholars were running in every direction, mostly away from the flames. As the companions passed the doorway to the Grail chamber, they noticed that Archimedes was no longer at his post.

"Smart old owl," Chaz remarked drolly as they turned the corner and headed for the projection.

Chaz passed through first, with Jack close on his heels. John paused at the wall and turned to look at the Grail on the door, now cracked.

Meridian was gone, to who knew where. Madoc was Bound, and banished. It had not even occurred to John that banishment could be done. If he was truly exiled to the ends of the Earth, then perhaps that was enough. Perhaps.

He tried not to think about the fact that at the moment Meridian had spoken the Binding, he had considered just killing Madoc. And he tried not to think about how relieved he'd felt when, with the banishment, he realized he might not have to.

And all it had taken was convincing the brother they trusted that he had to betray the one they didn't.

He hoped they had done enough.

John closed his eyes to the flames as they enveloped the image of the Grail, and he turned and stepped through the portal.

After receiving much more attention than he was comfortable getting, Hugo decided to camouflage himself as best as he could by donning Hank Morgan's helmet and gauntlets. After five minutes of wearing the incredibly heavy, stiflingly hot, and impossibly ill-fitting pieces of armor, he took them off and was immediately accosted by a small band of lithe, well-armed men. Or at least, he assumed they were men—they cursed like men and were dressed like others he'd seen on the field. But when he looked closely, he noticed that their ears were pointed, and they had only four fingers. And while they knocked him about, more for sport than anything else, he thought he heard them refer to each other as "elves."

He quickly replaced the helmet and gauntlets, and the elves, laughing, moved on. Hugo sighed heavily and looked around for Hank, who had at least seemed to be genial, if not a friend. Even Pellinor would be a welcome sight.

Still, Hugo had time to think. Hank had mentioned having been sent here by a Caretaker of the *Imaginarium Geographica* . . . Samuel Clemens. It took a moment for Hugo to remember why that name was familiar, and then he recalled it. The American writer. The one who wrote of riverboats, and slavery, and Adam and Eve . . . That fellow had been a Caretaker, as John and Jack claimed to be?

But wasn't Clemens also dead?

"Sam says hello," Hank said as he dropped down to sit next to Hugo. "Aren't those hot?" he asked, indicating the helmet and gauntlets.

"Terribly so, yes," Hugo replied, removing the armor. "But it seems unless I look a bit more the part of the knight-at-arms, I'm a target for mischief and harassment."

"The elves, I'll bet," Hank guessed, looking over the helmet. "There's a compact not to engage in any fighting until the actual start of the tournament, but that only applies to the champions here to compete—mostly knights and would-be kings. The elves are notorious for skirting the rules. They think they're better than everyone else, mostly because they live impossibly long lives. I think they're a bunch of pansies, myself."

"But you said you weren't here to compete," said Hugo. "So why did you come dressed as a knight?"

"Simple," Hank answered as he put on the helmet. "So I wouldn't be kicked around by a bunch of pansy elves."

* * *

Hank led Hugo around the outskirts of the field to a small campsite, where they could talk undisturbed. Like all the other arrivals to the tournament, Hank had erected a banner in front. It was a long, tapering pennant with a blue and red circular design in the center and the words GO CUBS! on both sides.

"Interesting," said Hugo. "What does it mean?"

"It was a gift from Sam," Hank explained as they entered the tent. "He said it used to represent Triumph over Adversity, but now better represents Impossible Quests and Lost Causes."

"I think I preferred not knowing that," said Hugo.

Hank grinned. "You're a Sox fan too, hey?"

In the relative privacy of Hank's camp, they were able to talk more freely, so Hugo related everything that had happened since the walk at Magdalen, and also about the dinner, and the mysterious Grail book. And he asked a torrent of questions along the way.

"I don't know that much about it myself," Hank said in response to Hugo's inquiry about the *Imaginarium Geographica*. "I know a little, thanks to Sam. But there's a fellow here who might be helpful. All the maps in here are his, as a matter of fact." He swept his arm across the interior of the tent.

Hugo had at first assumed that the stacks were fabric of some kind, or bundles of supplies for the tournament. But looking at them more closely, he could see that they were dozens of carefully drawn maps.

"I daresay he might be able to help, at that," said Hugo. "Did he make these all himself?"

"I haven't asked," Hank replied. "Didn't feel it was my business. But they are the first thing unpacked at every stop, and he handles them as if they're gold. After what you've explained to me, I half wonder if they aren't part of the reason I was sent here to watch him."

"Is he a knight or a king?" asked Hugo.

"Both and neither," Hank said, "but you know of him by reputation alone, if nothing else."

"That is either a charitable description of me, Sir Henry," a stolid, commanding voice said, "or a condemnation. And today I cannot say which I deserve more." A gloved hand parted the opening of the tent, flooding it with light, and a man, shorter than Hank but stouter than Hugo, stepped inside.

"Hugo Dyson," Hank said, rising and bowing deferentially to the new arrival, "I'd like you to meet Merlin, Lord of Albion."

Merlin was dressed formally but practically. His breeches and tunic were elegantly made, but of leather, studded throughout with iron. Not clothes for court, but for combat. He wore a headband, and his hair draped to his shoulders, flowing over the top of a cape that was fastened at his shoulders.

It occurred to Hugo that Merlin's eyes showed a flash of recognition when he entered, but on reflection, that was probably more of a reaction to Hugo's strange clothes.

"So," Merlin said. "You know who I am?"

"I know what I've read of you, ah, sir," Hugo stammered. "You're a very great man."

Merlin didn't react to the compliment, except to frown and raise an eyebrow.

"What I mean is that you are a legend," Hugo said quickly. "Everyone knows you."

"Really," Merlin replied, still unsure what Hugo was complimenting him for. "Would you say I'm a myth, then?"

It was Hugo's turn to look confused. "I might have yesterday," he said, "but I hadn't met you then."

Merlin burst into laughter. "Well met, then, Hugo Dyson," he said, handing a parcel to Hank. "You should find the rest of the day's events very enlightening."

With that, he turned and left the tent.

"Drat," said Hugo. "I should have asked for his autograph." He looked at the tent opening, then back at Hank. "Does he know about . . . ?" He pointed delicately.

"About me?" Hank exclaimed. "Where and when I'm really from? I doubt it. I made up a story when I first got here, which I'm pretty certain he saw right through. But I've been helpful to him, and loyal. So he doesn't press the matter."

"And you're here at the behest of Sam Clemens?"

"His and that of his former apprentice, a Frenchman called Verne. Do you know him?"

Hugo shook his head. "Not personally."

"Well," Hank continued, "he's the one who worked out a lot of the underlying principles behind time travel and zero points."

"Uh, zero points?" asked Hugo.

"The points in history that allow travel, or at least communication, in the case of the lesser points. There was a good one about fourteen years before your prime time that I was able to use to send a message to Verne. I don't know what it was that happened then, but it must have seemed like the end of the world."

"One or the other," Hugo said, "from what I've been told. So," he continued earnestly, "this message you sent. Will it allow Verne to fix whatever it is that happened to me at Addison's Walk?"

Hank shrugged. "I don't know. When you showed up, I thought

I'd better let someone know. Mistakes like that usually aren't mistakes at all."

"You think someone deliberately arranged for me to come here?" asked Hugo.

"I do, and what's more," Hank said, checking the silver watch, "so does Sam. You're to stay here, at least for now."

Hugo was aghast. "But why? Isn't there some sort of . . . I don't know, time machine they can use to whisk me back to Magdalen?"

Hank gave a wry chuckle and scratched his neck. "It doesn't quite work that way. I'm still a novice, a foot soldier, if you will. But even I know you aren't supposed to mess around with time by traipsing to and fro."

"But you're here," Hugo protested. "Isn't that meddling?"

"No," said Hank. "I'm here in part because one of the Caretakers' Histories said I was. So I was meant to be here. You weren't."

"But don't you see," Hugo declared, having suddenly realized something. "I was. I was meant to be here. Or else how do we explain the Grail book that I supposedly wrote in?"

Hank stared back at him, puzzled. "That *is* a good question," he said, removing the silver watch again. "I'd better—"

Before he could finish speaking, the watch emitted a high-pitched squeal and began to spark, then smoke. Hank shook it, then held it to his ear. It had stopped ticking.

"That looks bad," said Hugo.

Hank bit his lip, thinking, then replaced the watch in the secret pocket. "Come on," he said, standing. "Let's see where this goes. It's high noon—the tournament is about to begin, and Merlin will be looking for me."

* * *

Hank loaned Hugo a cloak and spare helmet, which they hoped would lend just enough camouflage to the professor's appearance that he could move about more freely. It worked for the most part—although the elves kept pointing at him to get his attention, then making rude gestures.

"I'm starting to warm to the opportunity I've been given to have this adventure," Hugo said dryly, "but if I never see another cursed elf, it'll be too soon."

The tournament was centered not at the great stone table, as Hugo assumed it would be, but around a field to the west of it. There a great tent had been erected facing a low hill, on which they could see a few crumbling walls that marked rough boundaries around a shallow depression.

The participants had assembled around the front of the tent, waiting for the announcement and a proclamation of the rules.

"Taliesin's tent," Hank murmured as they approached. "Hang back a bit, so we can watch. We don't want to get too wrapped up in events. No telling what could happen if we get involved in something by accident."

Hugo was more than willing to keep a comfortable distance. He'd realized with an alarming clarity that these knights assembled here were not the same as those he'd read about in the great medieval romances. These were warriors; battle-hardened and less likely to be chivalrous than they were to be actors in a play. What's more, he wasn't certain that all of those at the gathering were even human.

There was movement at the rear of Taliesin's tent, and Hugo saw Merlin exit from a flap in the tent, and then walk around to the back of the hill. A few moments later he reappeared at the crest of the hill and strode down into the assemblage.

"What a show-off," Hank whispered, scribbling in his notebook. "He was up there just so he could arrive last and appear to have come down to everyone else's level."

Merlin passed easily through the crowd, which parted to let him through. Apparently his reputation had preceded him. He took a position not far from the front of the tent and crossed his arms, waiting.

He didn't have to wait long. The front of the tent opened and Taliesin appeared. He was tall, bearded, and graying at the temples. He wore a simple tunic, leather breeches, and tall leather boots. There were feathers in his hair, which was swept back and grew long, almost to his waist in back.

Taliesin carried a black staff carved with runes, which seemed to glow faintly, even in the daylight. He walked to the base of the hill, then turned to address the gathering.

"I am Taliesin, called the Lawgiver," he began, his voice low but commanding in tone. "Hear my words, all ye who have been summoned.

"We have come here, to the place where once, long ago, the man called Camaalis earned for himself the mantle of king of Albion and ruled this land as his stewardship. Here he built his first castle, called after his name, and here he died and was forgotten.

"What was lost to history, and forgotten by men, is that he was to be the ruler of two worlds—both this land we know, and another, in the Unknown Region."

"The Archipelago?" Hugo whispered.

"I think so," Hank replied, writing. "This is very intriguing."

Taliesin went on. "Others have ruled parts of these lands since, but never the whole, and never the lands beyond. Those who had appointed Camaalis withdrew the knowledge and the means, until another, one worthy to rule, could be chosen.

"If there is no authority to rule, no chosen leader acknowledged by all, only a group of 'nobles' willing to destroy the land in order to wrest control of it, then the lands beyond will also remain forever apart.

"This is why the tournament has been called. To reestablish the lineage of the authority to rule. The lineage that began with the gods of myth and passed through their heirs—the heroes of the Trojan War.

"Aeneas, one of the great heroes of antiquity, possessed a great sword. When the walls of Troy finally fell, his grandson, Brutus, smuggled it away from those who would use it to further their own ends.

"He sailed far away, taking with him the sword and those who had managed to escape from the marauding Greek armies. He came here, to the island called Myrddyn's Precinct, where he founded a settlement called Troia Nova."

"Troia Nova," Hugo whispered. "New Troy, then . . . It eventually became Trinovantum, then Londinium, didn't it?"

Hank didn't hear the question. "Did he say Myrddyn's Precinct?" he asked instead. "That's rather ominous, don't you think?"

"There was another hero of the Trojan war," continued Taliesin, "called Odysseus, who had a bow that could not be drawn except by the true king. That promise and curse protected his homeland of Ithaka for generations. And the same promise and curse, passed down through the lineage of Aeneas, will protect those who would unite and rule the world—beginning here, in Myrddyn's Precinct, at the place where Camaalis was buried."

Taliesin moved aside, and for the first time Hugo and Hank could see what was in the depression on the hill.

It was a stone block, which bore the mark of the Greek letter *alpha*. It was, Hugo realized, the topmost stone of a crypt.

At Taliesin's signal, several burly men moved forward, grasped the sides of the great stone block, and slowly moved it aside. Underneath, set into the hillside, was a stone box. One of the knights removed the topmost stone and set it aside.

There, lying in state, was a black sword in a scabbard, covered in the dust of the first great king of the land.

"Caliburn," the Lawgiver proclaimed, pointing down at the crypt. "The sword of Aeneas.

"Whosoever is able to draw the sword from its sheath shall henceforth be the High King of all the lands that are. So say we all?"

The question was answered with a thundering shout, which only grew louder and louder as the seconds passed, until Hugo thought he would go deaf from the noise of it. Finally the whoops and hollers died down, and the Lawgiver Taliesin spoke once more.

"The Tournament of Champions is begun."

CHAPTER FIFTEEN

THE STRIPLING WARRIOR

UNCAS, FRED, AND REYNARD clustered around John, Jack, and Chaz as they stepped back through the projection.

"Is everything all right, Scowler John?" Uncas asked worriedly. "You've only been gone about ten hours."

"Fine, Uncas," John reassured him. "Reynard? Shut down the projection, quickly!"

The fox swiftly moved over to the Lanterna Magica and flipped the switch. Immediately the lamp went dark and the slide vanished from the wall, and with it the conflagration in the library.

"Thanks," said Jack, sitting in a chair and slumping over the back. "I don't think I could bear to watch."

"I was more worried about Sanctuary," John said, taking one of the other chairs. "If we could pass through, other things might be able to also. And it won't be too long before the wall we came through is on fire itself."

Only Chaz was still standing at the wall. He was touching his chest and arms, as if confirming his own solidity.

"Mister Chaz?" said Fred. "Are you all right?"

"Did we do it?" Chaz asked hesitantly. "Did we change the world?"

Fred looked at Uncas, who looked at Reynard, who shook his head. "There is no difference outside, if that's what you're asking," the fox said. "The king, Mordred, still rules over Albion, and the giants still come by every hour or so to throw stones in the harbor."

"I really hate those creatures," muttered Jack.

"I think the feeling is reciprocated," said Reynard. "At one point they were offering to tell the king the rest of your companions were dead if they'd just give *you* up."

Jack swallowed hard and managed a weak smile.

"Don't worry, Scowler Jack," Uncas said, patting him on the knee. "We told 'em we'd just as soon do you in ourselves."

"Thanks, Uncas."

Chaz exploded. "So what good did we do?" he exclaimed, waving his arms in frustration. "We found his true name! And we convinced the other one t' Bind him! And it didn't change anything at all!"

"We've only done half the task," John reminded him. "Our friend Hugo is still trapped somewhere in the sixth century, and that's what caused England to become Albion. When we confronted Madoc, and Meridian Bound him, it was only the second century. So obviously something still happens four hundred years later that we have to prevent."

"And how are we supposed to do that?" asked Jack.

"There are three more slides," Reynard reminded them. "I do not think the Prime Caretaker would have left them as mere redundancies. I think each one may have a purpose in and of itself."

Fred nodded enthusiastically. "I agree. Each time you've gone through a portal, you've come back with something you needed to know."

"That's true," Jack agreed. "The trip to Miletus revealed that Mordred and the Cartographer were brothers, and the second, to Alexandria, allowed us to tell Meridian how to Bind his brother."

"Curious, though," John pondered. "He already knew the words to do it. I think he just never would have done it if we hadn't provided the motivation."

"He needed t' know," said Chaz. "He needed t' know what his brother would one day become. And there was no one else t' tell him but us."

"So what now, John?" asked Jack. "I don't think we can handle another jaunt right away. I'm exhausted."

Chaz, already dozing, snored in agreement.

John looked to Reynard. "If we take a short nap and regain a bit of vigor, do you think the giants will cause trouble?"

The fox shook his head. "They can disturb and harass, and they may be able to damage your ship in the harbor by throwing stones. But I think it will be safe enough for you to remain, for a short while."

"Good," John replied, already stretching out on the floor. "I feel like I haven't slept in centuries."

After a few hours, Uncas and Fred regretfully roused the companions. "Sorry t' wake you, Scowlers," said Uncas, "but the giants have rallied."

John groaned and stretched, and Jack rose, looking around the room. His face fell when he saw the burlap bag in the corner, untouched as they had left it.

"Damn and double-damn," he breathed. "I'd really hoped that I dreamed that part."

Chaz jumped to his feet. The brief sleep seemed to have recharged him fully. "So what is the plan?"

John was examining the packs that the badgers had prepared for them. There were rations of food, and containers of fresh water, along with two other items: the Serendipity Box and the Little Whatsit.

"The latter is for any emergencies what may arise," explained Uncas, "an' the former, for when you're well an' truly up t' your necks in it. Just in case."

"I already used the Box," John said.

"I know," said Uncas, "but they haven't."

The badger was right. According to Bert, they could each use it once, and Jack and Chaz hadn't touched it yet.

Before John could ask anything else, they were interrupted by a tremendous crash from outside. There was a cacophony of howls, and what sounded like pounding surf, and worse, the laughter of giants.

Fred indicated to the others that they should remain in the projection room, and he rushed out the door.

A few seconds later he reappeared, helping Reynard, who was limping and bleeding badly from a gash in his skull that had nearly cost him an ear.

The companions hurried over to the wounded fox. "What's happened, Reynard?" John asked, concern etched on his face. "Are you all right?"

"I shall live," Reynard replied, "but you have suffered a loss, I am sorry to say."

"What loss?" asked Jack.

"Your ship," Reynard said, still in shock. "The *Red Dragon*.

The giants have succeeded in destroying her. She's gone, shattered, sunk."

So that was it, John realized. The *Red Dragon* had been their only means of escape from Noble's Isle. Whatever success they were to have in defeating Mordred would now only be found inside the slides left for them by Jules Verne.

"Uncas," John instructed, "fire up the Lanterna Magica. We're running out of time."

The third slide showed a grassy hilltop, on what seemed to be a summer day. There was a single tall oak tree at the crest of the hill, and underneath, a young man, barely more than a boy, sleeping peacefully.

"Do you know who it is?" Chaz asked the others. "He's too young to be Meridian or Madoc."

John shook his head, as did Jack. "Not a clue, I'm afraid," Jack said, "but I mean to find out."

The three companions said their good-byes to the badgers, and thanked the injured fox for his attempts to protect their ship. Then, Chaz leading this time, they stepped into the projection.

Unlike the previous slides, which had opened into cities on the sides of walls, this one opened a portal into open air. The three men moved quickly through the gossamer layers and turned around to look at the odd phenomenon.

"Strange, isn't it?" said Jack. "It's a bit like the door in the wood, John. There's no back side to it when you come around the other side."

"At least this one isn't going to close on us," John replied. "We'll have to remember it's to the east of the tree when we return."

There was nothing else in sight, save for miles of rolling hills and clusters of trees. No buildings, no structures of any kind, as far as they could see. Just the tall oak and the sleeping boy.

He was dressed heavily, with a cloak over his tunic and shirt, and his boots were fur. He'd come from some land that was colder than this, wherever they were.

"It's England, of course," said Jack. "Can't you tell by the light?"

"If you say so," John said, unconvinced. "Shall we wake him up? He's obviously the reason Verne had us come here."

The others agreed, and John reached down and shook the boy's shoulder once, then again. Finally the boy opened his eyes and gave them a half-awake smile. "It's about time," he said, sitting up. "I'd begun to think you would never get here."

His speech was a mix of Gaelic and Old English, but it was not difficult for John and Jack to understand. Chaz couldn't quite make it out, but he seemed to get the gist of it. The boy had been waiting for them.

"You were expecting us?" John said in surprise, offering the boy a hand up.

The boy rose to his feet and dusted himself off. "I was expecting . . . someone," he replied. "I blew the horn almost an hour ago."

He showed them a curved, golden horn that had Greek letters etched into the sides. "My mother gave it to me," he explained, "and said to use it only in a time of great peril."

Jack looked around at the countryside, which seemed empty of life, save for a few mice on the hill and a distant bird, circling in the sky. "Peril?" he asked. "Did we miss it?"

The boy reddened. "I know. I must seem a fool for using it so lightly. But I lost my way, and I'm out of food and have little water, and I didn't think I could hold out much longer just wandering around."

"How long have you been traveling?"

"A month," the boy answered. "I came from high in the mountains, where it is still winter, riding hard. I had to abandon my horse when I crossed the water, and I've been walking for several days now. Then today I decided to use the horn. I'm already late, and if I arrive too weak from hunger and thirst, then I'll have no chance at all in the tournament."

"What tournament?" asked Jack. "Where are you going?"

"The tournament at Camelot," the boy said, "to choose the High King of this world and of the Unknown Region."

The companions looked at each other in astonishment.

"What's your name, lad?" asked John.

"I'm called Thorn," the boy said. "Have you got anything to eat?"

They opened up the packs prepared for them by the badgers and held off asking anything further while Thorn tucked into the food and drink. John stood a few feet away, watching, while Chaz busied himself reading the Little Whatsit to see if there were any language translation aids to be found there.

Jack walked around the other side of the tree, watching Chaz with an odd expression. "Do you get the impression," he said to John, "that the Chaz we've ended up with isn't the one we started with?"

"I know what you mean," John replied, looking over his shoulder at the former thief and self-confessed traitor, who had become completely absorbed in reading the badgers' handbook. "At first

I thought it was just that he had a knack for languages. He is a chosen Caretaker, after all. He had the aptitude, even if he's from a timeline where he never became the educated man we know. But it's more than just remembering Greek, or being able to translate it, then speak it, after only *days* among the native speakers. He isn't struggling—he's *fluent*. He's . . . he's . . . *changing*, isn't he? Almost like . . ."

"Almost like he's becoming a lot like another scowler we know and respect?" said Jack.

"Something like that."

"How can that be?" asked Jack. "Isn't it a different world altogether? He can't be our Charles."

"It wasn't a different world for Bert," John replied. "He was, in many ways, 'our' Bert—at least he claimed to be. Maybe, in some small way, this is still 'our' Charles."

"Hey," Chaz called out, marking a page in the Little Whatsit. "I think I finally found a place that sounds worse than Albion. According to th' book, it's called 'Cambridge.'"

It was a full minute before John and Jack could stop laughing.

"I don't get it," said Chaz.

"Uncas will explain it to you later," John told him.

"Well," Jack said, looking at their empty satchels and drained flagon, "so much for our provisions."

"We haven't even been here an hour," John replied, "and we aren't even sure what we're supposed to do. Why don't you just go back into Sanctuary and restock? That way we'll be prepared for anything and won't go hungry later."

"Good idea," Jack answered, gathering up the bags and heading around the hill. "I'll be right back."

"Is Sanctuary where I summoned you from?" asked Thorn. "When I blew Bran Galed's horn?"

"We weren't summoned," John said. "It was just a coincidence that we came when we did."

"Really?" said Thorn. "What did you come here for?"

Before John could explain, Jack came running up to the tree, a panicked expression on his face.

John took his arm. "What is it? Are the badgers all right?"

"I don't know!" Jack exclaimed. "I didn't have the chance to look!"

"Why not?"

"The portal!" Jack said with rising terror in his voice. "It's gone! We can't get back!"

The tournament had gone forward in a spectacular fashion, overseen by the Lawgiver. There had been contests of not only physical prowess, but of intellect.

"Merlin nicknamed it 'Heart, Hand, and Head,'" Hank told Hugo. "Apparently, the contests are based on a series of trials once used in competitions at Alexandria."

"Like the Gordian knot?" asked Hugo.

"Something like that," Hank answered.

The contests went on throughout the day, and more than half of the hundred or so who had come to compete were eliminated. There were very few life-threatening injuries, and no deaths whatsoever.

"It was the one condition Taliesin insisted on," said Hank. "First blood only. No deaths."

"That's rather civilized," said Hugo.

"You can say that because you're not being stabbed," Hank chortled. "As Sam used to say, 'It's all fun and games until someone loses an eye.'"

By late afternoon there were only seven left standing who had not been defeated in any of the trials. Taliesin motioned for them to take up positions around the crypt that bore the sword.

"Of all those who have come," the Lawgiver announced, "you seven, kings all, have proven your worth to compete for the honor of serving the peoples of two worlds."

"Eight!" a voice bellowed. Pellinor pushed his way to the front of the gathering, eyes watery and face flushed.

"Cheated! Cheated, I was! I was told the Questing Beast would be here, *here*, when I finished the job I was given! And I was cheated! So I demand my right to draw the black sword and become the High King! It is only fair. There are *eight* great kings here!"

The Lawgiver raised an eyebrow and appraised Pellinor for a long moment, then gestured at the sword. "Fine," he said. "*Eight* great kings. If you believe yourself worthy, try to draw the sword from its scabbard."

Pellinor harrumphed and adjusted his belt as he stepped down into the shallow hole. He looked down at the sword, which was shorter and more stout than he'd imagined it to be. It also wasn't very decorative. The hilt was plain, mostly tarnished silver and steel wrapped in blackened leather, and the scabbard was a match in style and plainness. It was not in appearance the weapon of a king—but that, he figured, could be fixed with some jewels and gold flecking, and probably a new scabbard altogether.

"This should be good," Hank whispered to Hugo.

"Why?" Hugo wondered.

"Because he's doing what everyone told him not to," Hank whispered back. "I've seen this sort of thing in power plants, where some hoity-toity fellow with a degree from a fancy school starts directing the engineers on how to change everything. It usually ends when he insists on touching a cable no one else will go near."

"What happens then?" asked Hugo.

Pellinor bent down and lifted up the sword and scabbard in one swift motion. He held it, smiling triumphantly, then grasped the hilt and attempted to remove the sword—which stayed exactly where it was.

Pellinor's smile faltered, and he redoubled his effort, putting the sword between his legs for leverage and using both hands. Finally, incredibly, the sword shifted one-quarter of an inch within the scabbard.

"Aha!" Pellinor exclaimed. "That's—"

A tremendous bolt of lightning erupted from the sword itself, shooting skyward and filling the valley with thunder. It threw Pellinor out of the hole and about twenty feet into the dust, scorched and smoking.

"*That's* what happens," said Hank, shaking his head.

"Is he alive?" the Lawgiver asked.

One of the knights, who had ducked as Pellinor flew overhead, went over to where he lay and put a blade of grass in front of the old king's nose.

"He's breathing," reported the knight. "For now."

"Well and good," said the Lawgiver. "As I was saying, you seven great kings have proven your worth to compete—"

"To be the High King?" one of the seven bellowed. "To be Pendragon?"

Taliesin nodded and raised his staff.

A cheer went up from the assemblage, and the seven kings all looked at one another, each taking the measure of the others, trying to judge who among them might prevail.

"Tomorrow morning," Taliesin said, "we shall have the final contests. The seven shall draw lots, and then may choose whom to fight in single combat. The last to stand shall then be offered the chance to draw the blade from the scabbard. And if that one succeeds—"

"He shall have one more battle to fight," a harsh voice called out, "unless you are willing to admit me now as one who has the right to vie for the office."

From the eastern side of the hill a black horse sauntered in, and its rider, dressed in equally ebony clothes, dismounted. There were murmurs and growls throughout the crowd, but from two, Taliesin and Merlin, gasps of recognition.

He removed a tall, bull-horned helmet and placed it on the ground, possessively near the crypt. His skin was dark, more from weathering than pigmentation, and his features were lean. He moved with grace and the coiled energy of a serpent, which, Hugo realized, was exactly what he was. A serpent had come into Taliesin's well-ordered garden.

His clothes were unusual but seemed tailored for combat, wrapped tightly around his limbs and loosely around his torso. And as for weapons, he carried only a spear, which in contrast to his dress and manner appeared to be of Roman make.

"I declare my intention to compete. Are there any who would oppose me?" the man asked, looking directly at Merlin.

Taliesin's eyes narrowed, and he looked from the new arrival to Merlin and back again. There seemed to be an unseen struggle taking place in the very air. Finally Merlin nodded to the Lawgiver, almost imperceptibly, and Taliesin turned to the stranger. "What is your name, and by what right have you come here to disrupt this tournament?"

The man smiled coldly, as if he had been waiting for, and hating, that very question.

"I come by right of blood," he said quietly but firmly, in a tone that said he would brook no opposition, "honor-bound, after long exile. And I come because it is I, and I alone, who is worthy to draw Caliburn and become the Arthur—the High King."

"What is your name?" the Lawgiver asked again.

"I've been called many names during a long life," the man replied, "and none have served me well enough to keep. But the people who took me in, whom I have called my own for so many years, called me Mordraut. And that should suffice for this gathering."

"What?" Hank said to Hugo, straining to hear. "What did he say?"

"Mordred," Hugo said, shuddering. "He said his name is Mordred."

For almost an hour, John, Jack, Chaz, and a slightly confused Thorn circled the hill around the oak tree looking for a window in the air that was no longer anywhere to be found. Jack was distraught, and John was concerned. Of the three of them, only Chaz seemed unworried.

"Don't take this the wrong way," he said, tucking the Little Whatsit under one arm, "but I'm not exac'ly all broken up at the thought of being stuck here. It in't perfect, but it's better than where I was at."

"Nothing's perfect," said Thorn. "I don't think anything is expected to be."

"Then what is expected?" asked Chaz.

"To become better than you are, one day at a time," replied Thorn. "Progression, not perfection, should be the goal."

"That's a very enlightened attitude," John said, clearly impressed. "How did you come by it?"

"From my teacher," said Thorn. "He ought to be coming back anytime now."

"I thought you were here alone," asked John

"I didn't think to mention him," Thorn explained, using his hand to shade his eyes from the sun. "He went off exploring after I used the horn."

"Why am you looking up?" asked Chaz, his Gaelic still rough. "Are. Why *are* you looking up?"

As if in answer to the question, a bird—the one Jack had seen at a distance, he now realized—began to spiral downward towards the oak. Moments later the great bird, an owl, had lit on Thorn's shoulder.

"You three," the owl said scornfully in flawless Old English. "You can listen to the smart one, there," he told Thorn, pointing a claw at Chaz, "but these other two are a bit slow."

"Archimedes," John greeted the owl he'd last seen in Alexandria.

"Of course," the bird replied. "How many other talking owls have you met?"

"Just you, actually," John admitted.

"See what I mean?" the owl said. "Slow."

• • •

The bird reacquainted itself with the companions as they told it of recent events, then agreed to assist them in looking for the lost window. But the addition of an extra pair of eyes, even those as sharp as Archimedes', did not help them locate the portal to Sanctuary. Jack was right—it was gone.

"Could it have been the giants?" John asked. "Do you suppose they actually went onto the island?"

"I doubt it," Jack replied. "If they were going to do that, they'd have done it much earlier."

"You came through a door with only one side?" asked Archimedes. "That's very interesting."

"I'd love to show it to you, Archimedes," said John, "but I think we've run our luck dry."

"Not luck," said Thorn. "The will of God."

"What do you mean?" Jack asked. "Which God?"

Thorn looked at him, surprised. "There's only one God, Sir Jack," he said plainly. "I don't know much about him, but I know that he sees all, knows all, and has a reason for everything he does."

"Stranding us in . . . what year is it, anyway?" said Jack.

"It's been approximately four centuries since we first met, at the library," said Archimedes. "If I had a chalk and slate, I could work it out more precisely."

"Great," said Jack. "We're in the sixth century. Do you want me to believe that it's God's will that we're trapped here?"

"You came when I summoned you with the horn," Thorn replied. "How can I think otherwise?"

"We didn't come because of the horn," Jack retorted. "We came to . . . to . . ." He stopped and turned to his fellow scholar. "I don't even know, John. What *are* we here to do?"

"I think," John said, carefully considering his words, "that we were meant to be here, now, to help Thorn get to where he's going."

"It seems we have little choice," said Jack in resignation, casting a look around the hill. "We can't go back. We might as well go forward."

"That's very astute," said Archimedes. "One might think you were an educated man."

"I've got an entire section here on Camelot," Chaz said, pointing to the Little Whatsit. "There are a few passages on tournaments and the like, but along with those are some general directions. We should be able to get Thorn where he needs t' be without much trouble."

"It doesn't help us to know where we're going, if we don't know where we're starting from," John said in a slightly officious voice. "It's one of the first things I learned watching over the *Geographica*."

Chaz blinked. "And . . . ?"

"And Thorn was already lost, and we have no way of telling where we are."

"Sure we do," Chaz insisted, pointing at the book. "We're at Grandfather Oak. See? There's a picture."

Sure enough, there was an engraving of the tree that stood next to them.

"That's insane," Jack stated. "Why would that book have a picture of this tree, of all things?"

"It seems to be an important place," said Chaz. "According to the Whatsit, it's where someone called Arthur first met the knights of the Crusade, on the day before he became the High King."

It took a few moments for the full meaning of the words Chaz read to sink in. When they finally did, John and Jack turned to look at Thorn. "Is that true?" John asked slowly. "Are you Arthur?"

"Not yet," Thorn answered, "but I hope to be, soon."

CHAPTER SIXTEEN
THE CRUCIBLE

CHAZ LED THE WAY, with a conversational Archimedes circling low above his head. John, Jack, and Thorn followed closely behind, talking.

Thorn explained that Arthur was not a name in and of itself but a title of rule, and that it essentially meant "High King."

"High King of Britain?" asked Jack.

"You mean this land here?" Thorn replied. "I've not heard it called that before. It is called Albion by some, but most call it Myrddyn's Precinct. But," he added in a conspiratorial whisper, "I'm not allowed to know that."

"Why?" asked John.

"My mother would behead Archimedes if she knew he'd told me," Thorn replied, seemingly unwilling to elaborate.

John already knew the land had once been called Myrddyn's Precinct. But that was before he'd discovered who Myrddyn was. Apparently, in the four centuries since Alexandria, the Cartographer had been busy.

"Archimedes found out about the tournament," Thorn was saying, "and he convinced me that I needed to come and participate. I was against it at first."

"Against the chance to be king?" asked Jack.

"Against the need to fight for it," said Thorn. "As I understand it, the office of Arthur is to go to someone who is worthy to serve the people of the lands. I didn't understand why there needed to be a competition to find such a person."

"You don't worry that someone less worthy might take the title?" John wondered.

"Why would they?" Thorn replied. "What's the point of being in charge of the world if you don't want to help people? Hey!" he exclaimed, running ahead. "Chaz! Race you to the stone!"

"He's a good man," John said as they watched him race with their companion to a large stone up ahead. "Isn't he?"

"Yes," Jack agreed. "He's going to get slaughtered tomorrow."

As night began to fall, the companions built a small fire in the lee of the stone and set up a makeshift campsite around it. Archimedes turned out to be an excellent night watchman, and an even better cook. Using recipes Chaz found in the Little Whatsit, they gathered roots and herbs from the shrubbery and used the last flagon of water and one of Reynard's bottles to make a soup. It was thin, but tasty and warming.

With Archimedes standing guard, Thorn and Chaz soon fell asleep, but John and Jack stayed awake, talking.

"When the owl told us we were in the sixth century," John began, "I thought maybe . . ."

"Hugo would be somewhere nearby?" Jack finished. "So did I. But even if he is here, how are we going to get him back? The portal is gone."

"I know," said John, "but I'm hoping there will be another way back. We never did find out what happened to the door from the Keep."

"True, that," Jack agreed. "This Thorn is an interesting boy."

John nodded, a shadow against the stone. "He might really be Arthur—and I rather like the idea that we're to be remembered as knights of the Crusades."

"We will be," said Jack, "as long as we've gotten here soon enough to prevent whatever it is that Hugo did to create Albion."

"Don't worry about that now," John told him, settling down to try to sleep. "Plenty of time for that tomorrow."

It was a clear statement of intent that Mordred set up his camp not around the basin of the valley, as everyone else had, but on top of the hill, adjacent to the stone table and facing the crypt of Caliburn.

There had been some fighting among the knights and nobles, particularly those who had been eliminated earliest, but it never amounted to a formal protest, much less an outright rebellion.

The assent of the Lawgiver was enough to persuade most of them that there was in fact something substantial to the claims of the mysterious new arrival.

The look on Mordred's face was enough to convince the rest.

The fires were lit, and venison was roasted as the dinner celebrations began. It was more civilized than Hugo expected, but still more raw and primal than he was prepared for, so he and Hank retreated to their own camp to sup and discuss the day's events.

"Mordred," Hugo repeated for perhaps the hundredth time. "That's amazing to me. Did you see how he silenced the crowd with little more than bravado?"

"More charisma than bravado, I'd say," Hank replied as he

crouched over the small fire, stirring the stew he'd prepared for dinner. "He certainly has some kind of history with Merlin."

"I saw the look," said Hugo. "That's the other thing: the idea that 'Arthur' is a title. I wonder if it's possible that one or the other is actually meant to become King Arthur? That maybe he wasn't a separate man after all?"

Hank chuckled. "No, the Arthur is someone else," he said mysteriously. "More than that, I'm not allowed to say. But it's going to be very interesting to see how this all plays out."

Hugo handed Hank their bowls. "Is your watch device working any better yet?"

"Not at all, I'm afraid," he said, filling a bowl and handing it back. "I think . . ." He paused. "I think somehow time itself has been broken."

Hugo stopped, his hand halfway to his mouth with a ladle of stew. "Do—do you think that's my fault?"

"You're an anomaly, that's for sure," Hank said, blowing on his stew. "Careful, it's hot. No, I think something else has happened. But fixing it is out of our hands. It's on someone else now to try to sort out what's gone on. Not only for our sakes . . .

". . . but for the sake of the future itself."

After they ate dinner and cleared away the bowls and kettle, Hank went to sleep immediately, citing the heavy armor he'd worn all day as the reason he was so weary. For his part, Hugo could not close his eyes for a second. He was too intrigued by the turn of events at the tournament and the new arrival.

Leaving the engineer sleeping soundly in the tent, Hugo crept out and began to make his way back to the center of the happenings.

He thought he'd take a closer look at Mordred if he could, his curiosity overcoming his fear, but he was sidetracked by a light he saw emanating from the tent of the Lawgiver.

He made his way around to the rear, where he'd seen Merlin exiting earlier, and peered through the flap.

Inside, Taliesin was standing to one side, while Merlin paced in front of him, obviously agitated.

"I did not know he would come at your summoning, Taliesin," Merlin said brusquely. "I was unprepared."

"You were forgetful," the Lawgiver shot back. "Your Binding exiled him, until he was summoned again—by *blood*."

"That *was* a slip of the tongue, wasn't it?" Merlin admitted. "It never occurred to me, cousin, that another of our family might ever call out into the world for a Gathering."

"We're not family, Myrddyn," Taliesin said with undisguised rancor. "We shared a father in Odysseus, but our mothers were different, and we've never been family."

"If we were not, my dear cousin," Merlin said with deliberate emphasis as he touched the older man on the forehead, "then my Binding on you would never have worked, and we would not be here today."

"Do you believe this will be the way you will get back, Merlin? Back to the Archipelago? By deceiving your way to possession of Caliburn?"

"I believe it's the way I will conquer the Archipelago. And everything else."

"It won't work. You saw the lineage in the book yourself. Only a follower of the Grail—"

"I was a Caretaker of the Grail!" Merlin said, clenching his fists.

"Only a follower of the true Grail," Taliesin continued, "will be able to use the sword. Madoc and his own bloodline—"

"When he betrayed the trust of the Grail, Madoc lost the Mandate of Heaven," Merlin interrupted. "It doesn't matter what his bloodline spawned."

"To betray the Grail is to betray Holy Blood," said Taliesin. "How have you done differently?"

"I've betrayed nothing," said Merlin. "Madoc chose his own path, as did you."

"And my sister?" Taliesin said softly. "Did Nimue deserve *her* fate?"

"She could have ruled with me. She chose otherwise."

"Do you think her blood on your hands will let you touch the sword?"

"Our blood is different!" Merlin shouted. "We *know* our lineage, Taliesin. We know we're descended of gods. The children of the Grail are not."

"Not of our gods, no," Taliesin replied calmly, "but this is a time of new gods, Merlin. I've accepted that, and so should you. You know how his divinity was proven—and you know how this tournament will be won."

Merlin whirled away from Taliesin and was quiet for a long while. "By willing choice and sacrifice," he said at length. "That's Old Magic. It has nothing to do with new gods, Taliesin."

"We will see, Merlin."

"Yes, we shall."

Hugo would have listened longer, but a group of knights were sauntering by, and he worried about being caught and accused of spying. He worried even more that he might have to reveal what he'd heard.

He was about to leave, but his eyes widened in surprise as he noticed something just below him in Taliesin's tent. He snaked a hand inside the flap and snatched it. Then, running as quickly as he could, Hugo hurried back to the campsite to wake Hank Morgan.

"That old snake," Hank said, pounding a fist into his other hand. "That explains an awful lot."

"Can you use your device?" asked Hugo. "The silver dragon watch? Can you use it to send a message, as you did before?"

Hank shook his head. "I've tried. It still isn't working. That's never happened before—not for this long."

"What does that mean?"

"It means," Hank said with a desperate edge to his voice, "that we are completely on our own."

"Perhaps not." Hugo sat upright with a strange expression on his face. "I might be going balmy, but I think I have an idea worthy of a Caretaker."

"What's that?"

"We've been too caught up in instantaneous communication," Hugo explained, "worrying too much about how soon we can contact someone via your watch device, when we really, literally, have all the time in the world."

"You've figured out another way to contact help?"

"Better than that," Hugo said, beaming. "We already *have*." He held up the squarish book he'd taken from Taliesin's tent. The first page was blank, but the rest of the book was filled with writing—and on the cover, embossed deeply in the leather, was the image of the Grail.

"Do you have any ink and a quill?" asked Hugo.

"I have a quill," Hank replied, "but Merlin makes his own ink. I could probably put something together for you, but it would have to be done in daylight."

"No time for that." Hugo rolled up his sleeve and held out his hand for Hank's dagger. "John's going to be pleased that he called this one on the nose."

After more bloodlettings than Hugo expected, he finally had enough to work with to inscribe his message in the book. It was approaching morning before he finally began writing in earnest.

"Not to be critical," said Hank, "but wouldn't 'Help us! Help us! We're trapped in the sixth century!' suffice?"

"Now, now," Hugo admonished. "This has to be done properly. This is a work for the ages—I can't just slop it together."

"It's a plea for help, not a sonnet," Hank argued, holding open the tent flap to look outside. "Just write it out so we can be done before Merlin returns."

"I'm a professor of English!" Hugo retorted. "I don't want to be embarrassed in front of my peers when they come to rescue us, just because I slacked off in my composition efforts."

"Technically, you already read what you're writing," said Hank. "Can't you just write it out from memory?"

"I can't recall it all," Hugo said, leaning over the book. "There was a lot going on that evening, and my head was all a-muddle. I even thought it was all a joke of some kind until I actually got here with Pellinor."

"You're lucky you did," Hank said with no trace of sarcasm. "He's batty. The story goes that his ancestor, Pelles, was a guardian of the Holy Grail, who lost it when it was stolen by a dragon he called the Questing Beast. They've all been on the crazy side ever since."

"I've never seen a dragon, either," Hugo said as he began to write, "but after the past few days, I'd be willing to extend him the benefit of the doubt."

In short order, Hugo finished writing the warning to his satisfaction, and together he and Hank hid it where Merlin would not stumble across it.

"That's that," Hugo said, dusting his vest off with one hand and flexing the other, which was sore from the dagger pokes. "According to the rules of time travel, now that I've actually created the message for us to get later, they should be coming to pick us up any time now."

"The 'rules of time travel'?" Hank said with a smirk. "Do you think they're just going to be able to do some mumbo-jumbo and suddenly appear?"

"Am I really being criticized by a man who travels through time with a silver pocket watch?"

"Sorry," said Hank. "I'm not trying to be discouraging. I just didn't want you to think that even for the Caretakers, it would be as easy as just flipping a switch."

"Ah, but if I know John and Jack," Hugo said with more pride than confidence, "it is."

The final contests began at sunrise, and everyone who was camped in the valley was there to watch. No one wanted to miss the drama being played out on the hill.

Merlin came to Hank's tent to retrieve another pair of gauntlets, a helmet, and a short Roman sword. He strapped it around a Grecian leather skirt that was studded with iron, and he also took a small round shield.

He never so much as glanced at Hugo, except for a curt glance and tight smile as he left.

"Do you think he knows I overheard him last night?" Hugo asked Hank.

"If he had, he wouldn't have left you alive," the engineer replied. "Let's go see this."

The Lawgiver stood at his usual place and extended his hand to show that he held eight small stones. Seven black, one white. Whichever among the champions chose the white stone from a bronze bowl would be allowed to choose the first opponent.

One by one, they turned their heads and drew a stone, Mordred last. He turned back and opened his hand. "Of course," he murmured, looking at the round white stone. "That's just as it should be."

Merlin suppressed a grin and tipped his chin at Taliesin. The Lawgiver raised both hands. "Mordred shall be first to choose. Against which man will you raise your hand?"

Mordred looked over his opponents, considering, then extended his arm and pointed at the burly warrior to Merlin's left. "You. I raise my hand against you."

Taliesin withered slightly, as if he'd hoped for a different response. "Gwydion, son of Don, will you raise your hand against Mordred?"

The king called Gwydion nodded.

Taliesin dropped his hands. "Then it is begun."

✦ ✦ ✦

The first contest was epic, nearly ending in a draw, so evenly matched were its contestants. But then Mordred got a swing under Gwydion's defenses and slashed his right shoulder to the bone.

"First blood," Taliesin called out as the knights helped Gwydion away, and Mordred pointed at another warrior, this time to Merlin's right.

It became obvious to all that Mordred intended for Merlin to be the last, should he defeat the other kings. And with each new contest, that's what Mordred did.

One by one, some more easily than others, six opponents fell before Mordred until finally, only Merlin was left.

"My God," Hank whispered. "This has really gone the distance. I don't believe Mordred defeated them all." He kept glancing around, as if he expected something else to take place. "This is bad."

"Why?" said Hugo.

"Merlin's good, but not this good," Hank said worriedly. "He can't beat Mordred."

"We can't let that happen!" exclaimed Hugo. "We have to stop it!"

Hank shook his head. "It's not our fight, Hugo."

"Mordred," the Lawgiver said again, "against which man shall you raise your hand?"

Mordred pointed at Merlin. "Against him, I shall raise my hand."

"Merlin," Taliesin said, the sorrow in his voice almost palpable, "will you raise your hand against this man?"

Before he could answer, there was a hissing sound, and a gasp of surprise from the crowd—and from Mordred.

A dagger, clumsily thrown, was sticking out of Mordred's side at an odd angle.

Mordred couldn't decide whether to be furious that he'd been stabbed or incredulous that anyone had dared. "Who does this?" he growled, pulling the dagger from his ribs. "What treachery is this, Merlin?"

Merlin's eyes narrowed. "Don't accuse an innocent . . . Mordred," he said harshly.

"He does not," declared Taliesin, pointing. "Your own squire has thrown the dagger."

The Lawgiver was pointing at Hugo, who, in his state of shock and awe at what he'd done, still had his arm extended from the throw.

Immediately two of the knights seized him, holding him fast. Hank, pushed to the side, was too stunned to speak.

"First blood, Mordred," Taliesin said, still uncertain himself what had happened. "You've lost."

"No!" Mordred screamed. "Unfair! A cheat!"

Taliesin shook his head, and a confused smile began to spread over Merlin's face. "Those are the rules, Mordred. He wears Merlin's colors. He drew first blood. You have lost. Withdraw, gracefully."

Mordred stood, glaring mutely at Taliesin, the anger rising off him like waves of heat. Then he turned slowly toward the knights holding Hugo and extended his arm, pointing a finger directly at the terrified professor.

The meaning was clear. If it ever was in his power to make it happen, Mordred would kill Hugo Dyson.

"Hugo!" Hank cried, his head still whirling from the speed of events. "Why did you do that?"

"I had no choice," Hugo gasped. "I had to, don't you understand? I had to stop him! He would have won! Mordred would have become the Arthur! And then who would have been left to stand against him?"

Before anyone could respond, a great bird swooped over the field, screeching shrilly.

Merlin's eyes darkened, and the smile dropped away.

To the south of the hill, the crowd parted and four men strode forward to the crypt.

"Lawgiver," the youngest of them said, "I am Thorn, son of Nimue, and by right of blood and right of honor, I have come to compete."

There was an immediate reaction to Thorn's announcement, and it was harsh. The gathered throng of warriors had allowed one apparent breach of the rules when Mordred came in so near the end of the tournament, but it would not be so easy for this bold boy to breach them again by taking part so late.

He didn't have the fearsome countenance of Mordred, or the reputation of Merlin or Gwydion or any of the others. And no one cared who his mother was.

No one save for the Lawgiver, whose eyes blazed.

"Silence!" Taliesin commanded, raising his arms high. "I am the Lawgiver, and I will decide what is to be allowed!"

The angry cries settled down to a disgruntled muttering as Taliesin motioned for Thorn to come forward.

The other three men stayed at the fringes of the crowd, but Hugo nearly shouted with joy when he recognized two of them as his friends John and Jack.

Hank motioned for him to be quiet. "You're in enough trouble as it is," he said under his breath. "Let's see if the Lawgiver can sort out your mess."

"I wish to speak!" Mordred declared, stepping in front of Thorn. "I have not been given my chance to fight!"

"I have already said that you lost, Mordred," Taliesin said. "First blood."

Mordred clenched his teeth and looked down at the boy, Thorn, with undisguised loathing. Then his expression changed, and he seemed to be puzzled. The boy returned his gaze bravely and unafraid.

Mordred looked at Merlin, then turned back to the boy again. "I think I see it clearly now, Lawgiver," he said, smiling coldly. "It is an old, old story, and one I know all too well."

Without another word, Mordred went to his tent and mounted his horse, taking only his spear with him. He left his tent and everything else behind and rode away without looking back.

"Well," said Merlin, "I think that ends our tournament."

Taliesin raised a hand. "Not quite, Merlin. You, too, are out of the competition. For cheating."

"What!" Merlin exclaimed, suddenly enraged. "I never cheated anyone!"

Taliesin pointed his black staff at Hugo. "He wears your colors. He is your squire. It is you who bears the loss."

Merlin shot a poisonous look at Hugo, then another at Hank. "We'll talk later," he hissed. "This isn't over."

"Did the tall one with the staff call the other one Merlin?" John whispered.

"Yes," said Jack, who was just as surprised. "Meridian is *Merlin*."

"I don't know who that is," whispered Chaz, "but Meridian looks like he wants t' kill that scrawny fellow the knights are holding."

Merlin turned back to the Lawgiver. "The tournament itself cannot continue. None among the champions is fit to fight—even if their challenger is just a boy."

"I am a man, my Lord," Thorn said, "and I will fight my own battles, thank you." He turned to the Lawgiver himself. "May I compete?"

To Merlin's increased rage, Taliesin nodded. "I know your lineage, and you have the right. The only opponent left has been disqualified, unless you choose otherwise."

Thorn looked at Merlin. "I'm not afraid," he said. "What must I do?"

"Will you raise your hand against this man?" said Taliesin.

Thorn looked confused. "What about the other tests? The trials and contests of physical prowess?"

Taliesin shook his head. "None of those matter now. Will you raise your hand against this man?" he repeated.

Thorn considered Merlin, then smiled wryly. "If you're giving me the choice, then no, I won't."

Merlin looked confused. Taliesin turned to him, grinning like a Cheshire cat. "And you? Will you raise your hand against he who will not raise his against you?"

Merlin's face was a mix of emotions. He locked eyes with the youth, and they looked at each other in some test of wills that none around them were privy to.

After an eternal pause, Merlin broke the stare and looked around him at the assemblage. His eyes looked wild, as if he were considering option after option and finding them all leading down dark pathways and ending at stone walls. He shook his head and rubbed his temples.

"Speak it," Taliesin demanded. "Speak the words."

"I . . . I cannot," Merlin finally said, his voice barely a whisper.

It took a few seconds for Taliesin to understand that Merlin had indeed declined to fight. In relief and with renewed vigor, the Lawgiver gestured to Thorn.

"Then," Taliesin said, placing his hands on Thorn's shoulders, "only one test remains."

He pointed the staff at the black sword, which still lay in the shallow grave. Thorn turned and stepped down into the crypt, picking up the sword as he did.

"If you can draw the sword from the scabbard . . . ," Taliesin began. But Thorn didn't give him time to finish. In one swift motion, he drew the sword from the scabbard and raised it high above his head.

There was a moment of absolute stillness as a hush overtook the crowd. Then, in a fluid motion, they all fell to one knee and began to cheer.

In the noise, no one realized that six men had remained standing: Taliesin, Hank, Hugo, John, Jack, and Charles. Merlin had disappeared into the Lawgiver's tent, and the owl Archimedes was flying in tight circles overhead and singing.

Taliesin stepped forward and tapped Thorn on each shoulder with the black staff, then kissed him on the forehead. "Well done, young Thorn. You are victorious. From this day henceforth, you are Arthur."

PART FIVE

THE ISLE OF GLASS

CHAPTER SEVENTEEN

ANIMAL LOGIC

THE PARISH CHURCH was cold, Geoffrey decided. It had always been chill, but for some reason, he'd never thought of it as actually being *cold*. But that morning he'd realized that it was in fact cold, when he noticed that his own breath was obscuring the writing on the parchment in front of him.

Sighing in resignation, he laid the quill inside his leather writing pouch and replaced the wax plug in the bottle of ink, then set about finding some tinder to put in the hearth. He carefully made his way down the steps and then opened the stout wooden door. The weather at Caerleon was always a bit ratty. He could understand why St. Cadoc had never wanted to fight any battles. It would have been too cold to lift his sword.

Still, it was a good enough place to build a church here and name it after him, Geoffrey decided, and if St. Cadoc could bear the weather, then so could he.

As he bent to pick up some sticks of wood at the tree line, a gust of wind caught his attention, and he looked seaward.

He had seen some mysterious storms out over the water of late, and more south of the parish. He didn't know what they meant, but he understood well enough to keep to his work, rather than look too closely.

But tonight the storm seemed different. The clouds were taking shape. . . .

He dropped the sticks and crossed himself as three giants came striding out of the surf, directly toward the town. They were massive creatures that towered over the tallest trees in Caerleon. Behemoths such as these might have cowed even Arthur, Geoffrey thought. Yes, even he.

Then, as quickly as the apparitions had appeared, the giants paled, then faded, then disappeared completely, leaving behind less than smoke in the air.

Geoffrey lifted his robe and hurried back to the church. If nothing else, he intended to get his transcriptions done and turn in early. He could tell a sign when he was given it. No need to burn any bushes for him.

Although, he thought as he trudged back up the stairs, that *would* have made him warmer.

He reached for his door, and oddly, found it jammed from within. He rattled the latch, and from inside he heard a soft cursing, followed by the sound of tearing paper.

He pressed harder, and suddenly the door flew open.

The room was empty save for his small fireplace, his table, his chair, and the parchments he'd been working on. The window was locked. And there, on the floor, lay the ancient book he'd been transcribing.

Somehow the first few pages had been torn out diagonally, from the upper left to the lower right side. Only the left-hand pieces remained. There was no sign of the torn pages themselves.

Shaking his head, Geoffrey crossed himself again and closed the door. Something beyond his ken was happening here, and he hadn't the presence of mind to deal with it. Not while it was so cold. The history of the kings of England would have to wait until later.

Still mulling over what the vision might have meant, and trying not to consider the possible ways someone could have entered his study invisibly, Geoffrey of Monmouth fell into a fitful slumber. As he did, all around him, time itself shook and trembled like a tree in a thunderstorm. . . .

Being declared the High King of the lands both known and unknown has its benefits, and when John and Jack made it clear that Hugo was their friend, Arthur immediately pardoned him and ordered him released.

The Lawgiver took Arthur aside to discuss matters of his new office, and the rest of the knights immediately began to start a celebration—which, Hugo decided, was practically identical to the tournament, with less of a point.

Of the companions, only Chaz had noted that not all the cheers were heartfelt, and not all the new subjects seemed to be pleased with the King, or the process by which he'd been chosen.

Hugo was mostly just relieved to see his old friends from Oxford. "I knew it!" he exclaimed happily. "I knew you'd be here to fetch me!"

"And just in time, it seems," John noted. "It looked like you were about to be drawn and quartered."

"All under control, I assure you," Hugo said with a wave. "But I'm not going to complain about your timing." He turned to Chaz and took his hand, which he began pumping frenetically. "And you, dear boy! So happy to see you, too! What happened to your face?"

Chaz pulled his arm free and tightened his collar. "Ah, I'm happy to see you well, Hugo."

John gave Chaz a quizzical look, and Chaz took him aside, out of earshot of the others. "I didn't want t' give him anything t' regret," he said flatly. "He doesn't know I'm not Charles, and he doesn't need to know where I came from or," he added with a quick glance back, "what else transpired there."

John nodded. "I understand. You're a good fellow, Chaz."

"Don't rub it in."

They rejoined the others, who were now conversing with Hank Morgan. He showed them his watch and seemed as pleased as Hugo that they'd come.

"It still isn't working," he said, shaking the watch. "When you return, can you get a message to Verne?"

"I'm sure we can," said Jack, "one way or another. What year is it, exactly?"

"It's the year 498 AD," said Hank, "give or take a few weeks."

"Not quite the sixth century," said John.

"Close enough," said Hugo. "So," he added, rubbing his hands in anticipation, "when do we go home?"

"That," John said, putting his arm around his friend's shoulders, "is something we need to discuss."

Back at his tent, Hank prepared another stew for his hungry new guests as John, Jack, and Chaz offered an abridged version of what had happened to them.

Hugo had barely begun his reciprocal tale, starting with his trip with Pellinor, when the High King poked his head inside the tent.

"Sorry to interrupt," Arthur said, "but Archimedes has just captured something for our dinner."

"He's an industrious bird," said Chaz. "Tell him to bring it here, and we'll add it to the stew."

"That's the problem," said Arthur. "It's talking—and insisting it's here to rescue something called scowlers."

John and Jack beamed and simultaneously sighed in relief. John dashed out of the tent, and Jack clapped Hugo on the back. "Hang on, old sport," he said, smiling broadly. "The cavalry's here, and they're short and furry."

John followed Arthur to the crest of the hill, where Archimedes was grappling with an extremely agitated Uncas.

"Stupid bird!" Uncas exclaimed. "What are you, a cannibobble?"

"I'm a mathematician, if you must know," the owl replied, still keeping a grip on the badger with one claw.

"Let him go, Archie," Chaz said as he and the others caught up to John.

The bird immediately loosed the badger, who snorted at it, then patted down his fur. "I come on a rescue mission, and nearly get et by a cannibobble," Uncas muttered. "No respect."

"We respect you, Uncas," Jack said, sweeping up the badger in a tight hug. "I'm thrilled to see you."

"Scowler Jack! Scowler John! Mister Chaz!" Uncas shouted. "I finally found you! I knew I would!"

The little fellow was so happy, and they were so relieved, that none of them noted that it was actually the owl who'd brought him to them. "What happened?" asked John. "We went back to the proper spot, but the portal was gone. It had only been a few minutes."

"That'd be my fault, Scowler John," Uncas said, looking as embarrassed and forlorn as they'd ever seen him. "Mine, an' mine only."

Jack knelt down and took the little fellow by the shoulder. "It's all right, Uncas. Mistakes happen. What did you do?"

"I, uh, I tripped over the cord, and accidentally unplugged the projector."

"Okay," said Jack, suppressing a grin. "Then why didn't you just plug it back in?"

"I tried!" Uncas wailed. "But I got all tangled up in it, and then I pulled over the whole thing, and it breaked! I mean, broked. . . . Um, I cracked it, is what I mean t' say!"

"So how did you get here?" asked John.

"We fixed it up—Reynard is a work an' a wonder with lenses—and plugged it back in. But by then you were gone."

"How long did it take you to repair it, Uncas?" asked Jack.

Uncas closed one eye and estimated. "About an hour."

Jack's shoulders slumped. "Then we're still in trouble," he said, shading his eyes and looking at the afternoon sun. "It's been twenty-four hours already, plus the hour it was down. The slide will have burned out by now."

"We thought of that!" Uncas said, preening. "Fred and I looked all over for you around that old oak, until just an hour ago. Then we stopped it before we ran out of time."

"Is Reynard simply going to turn it back on so we can return?" asked Jack.

Uncas looked crestfallen. "That would have been a good idea," he admitted.

"But he would have no way of knowing Uncas found us," Chaz said, "and the slide would still burn out."

"He's right, Uncas," John said, still confused, "how do we get *back?*"

"Easy," Uncas said, bursting with the ingenuity of his plan. "We brung it with us—the entire Lanterna Magica."

They had Arthur ask Archimedes to return to Grandfather Oak, to look for a second badger and a small machine, and to return, as carefully as possible, with them both.

The bird flew off, and inside of an hour returned with the projector in his claws and Fred riding on his back.

"Please don't drop the time machine," said Jack.

"Or the badger," added John.

"I meant to say that," said Jack.

Archimedes spiraled slowly down and lowered the Lanterna Magica to the grass, and Fred leaped off his back and hugged Uncas.

"Did you see, Father?" Fred exclaimed. "I flew! In the air!"

Uncas hugged his son back and glared at the bird. "I had the same trip, under less pleasant circumstances."

John and Jack stared at the projector. The badgers had indeed managed to bring it through.

"It was Reynard who figured it out," Fred explained. "He used an extra lens to keep the projection large as we pulled the machine closer to the screens. Then, when it was almost inside, we pulled it through, and the portal closed behind it."

"It almost didn't work at all," said Uncas. "The cord in the back was barely long enough to let us pull the projector through before it came out of the socket."

"That's actually my next question," Jack said, already knowing—and dreading—the answer. "We're at the end of the fifth century. Where are we going to plug it in?"

The mournful howling of the two badgers was so pitiful that the companions had to move them down the back side of the hill, away from the celebration and into the woods.

It took several minutes and the combined efforts of John, Jack, and Chaz to settle them down. Then the companions began to discuss any ideas they might have to get back to Sanctuary.

"The Lanterna Magica used to be powered by a candle," John suggested. "Maybe we don't need the electricity."

Jack shook his head. "I was looking it over with Reynard. We'd have to take it apart to do something like that, and we don't understand enough of how it works. What if we broke the mechanism that makes it function?"

"I wish you'd thought to bring a generator, too," John said to Uncas. "Not," he added quickly as the badger started to tear up again, "that I'd have thought of it either."

"The Serendipity Box?" asked Chaz. "Could it give us a generator?"

"Not likely," John said, eyeing the box. "It's too small, and too big a risk to wish for something it can't give us."

"We might just as well wish for a generator," said Jack. "It could fall into our laps this very minute."

"Not quite that fast," someone said, "but give me a few days, and I might be able to arrange it."

It was Hank Morgan who had spoken. "I'm only an amateur time traveler," he said with some degree of modesty, "but in my day job, I'm an electrical engineer. I'm certain we could construct an electrical generator in a few days, give or take. And then we can power that thing up and get you on your way."

"Perhaps we could fix your watch," John suggested. "Could you take us back with you?"

"I wish I could," Hank replied, "but I'm afraid the device doesn't work that way. Not yet, anyway. It's a one-person contraption. I've tried to take a passenger, but it just left them standing and clutching empty air. But perhaps in the future something can be done to change that. It's busted, anyway. But if I ever get another one, I'll give it to you. You really ought to have a watch if you're going to be traveling in time."

"I'd appreciate it," said John. "I'm going to catch hell for the last one I lost."

The group returned to Hank's tent, where he kept a large bag filled with various handmade tools and implements, and a second one filled with raw materials.

"Ever the Boy Scout, eh?" said John.

"The what?" said Hank. "No, I just like to always be prepared."

"Couldn't you have just used that watch of yours to pop back and forth in time, and simply bring back the tools you need?" asked Jack. "That would be a lot easier than fashioning everything by hand."

"Would if I could, brother," Hank replied. "It just doesn't work that way. The only thing I can actually take back and forth is the watch. Everything else has to be created or acquired."

"Does that include . . . ?" Jack asked, indicating Hank's clothes.

"Yep," Hank admitted with a slight blush. "First trip out, I found myself absolutely starkers. Should have seen the first knight who stumbled over me. He thought I was some kind of crazy man."

"It didn't say that you were naked in the book," said John. "Not that I recall, anyway."

"A favor from Sam," Hank explained. "I have to preserve my dignity where I can, you know."

"But I've seen you take notes," said Hugo. "Should I even ask how you get them back?"

"Better for us both if you don't," said Hank.

As Hank worked, the companions remained apart from the celebrations and revelry, so as not to risk disturbing the timestream worse than they had. Now that they had Hugo, all John and Jack wanted to do was get home.

Fred, Archie, and Chaz turned into an unexpected trio of friends, who passed the time playing logic games. Uncas mostly stayed at Hank's side, feeling as he did responsible for the entire mess. If he could help, he would.

As it turned out, the Little Whatsit was a great benefit to Hank's efforts, providing him with instructions and diagrams that he otherwise would have had to work out himself.

"With that book," Hank said, wiping his brow, "we should be done tomorrow."

"That quickly?" asked John. "Excellent. Good show, Hank."

Jack seemed a bit put out that Arthur was not spending more time with them. "We are the ones who brought him here, after all," he complained. "If not for us, he'd still be asleep under the tree."

"Now, Jack," Hugo said consolingly, "he is the High King, after all. He's got a lot to do, I'm sure."

Of Merlin there was no sign. And Mordred never rode back to the camp. In his stead, Arthur had moved in to occupy the tent he left behind.

"There's a metaphor in there somewhere," John remarked, "but I'll be damned if I know what it is."

By late the next morning, the generator was assembled and running.

"Should we say good-bye to Arthur?" asked Jack.

"Best not," John replied. "We'd have to explain too much about where we're going and why. And I'd prefer to let history take its course without any further help from us. And you, Hank?" he said to the engineer. "Will you be all right?"

"My device is still not working," Hank said, holding the silver watch to his ear, "but no matter. If I have to stay awhile, so be it. Sam and Verne will straighten it out. Besides, it's good weather—I'm thinking about organizing a few baseball teams and having a tournament of my own."

"Ah . . . Go Sox!" said Hugo.

"Attaboy!" said Hank. "Good luck to you, gentlemen . . . and badgers."

They plugged in the Lanterna Magica and crossed their fingers. "Ready?" Hank asked. Everyone nodded, and he gave a signal to Uncas, who threw the switch.

Against the wall of Hank's tent, the brilliant projection sprang to life. But instead of the room at Sanctuary they were expecting to see, they saw a tree on a hillside, with a young man sleeping underneath.

Jack realized it first and slapped his forehead. "Of course," he moaned. "This isn't like the doors, where it's two-way. The Lanterna Magica only projects a portal into whatever's on the slide."

"In this case, a couple of days ago, when we got here," said John.

"Can we go through there," asked Chaz, "before we got shut out?"

John shook his head. "We'd still have no way to get to Sanctuary, and," he noted bitterly as the edges of the slide began to thicken and fade, "this slide is nearly finished, anyway."

"Can we go through one of the other slides instead?" asked Fred.

"Too risky," said John. "They would just take us to another spot in our past, and presumably, another encounter with Mordred. And now that Arthur's taken control, I don't want to chance another change."

"I'm sorry," Hank said as the slide burned away and the projection turned clear. "I got her going for you, but after that, I'm fresh out of miracles."

"You might be, but we aren't!" Jack said, snapping his fingers. "The Serendipity Box!"

John pulled it out of his bag and handed it to Jack as Chaz explained the workings of it to Hugo and Hank.

"All I want," said Jack, closing his eyes, "is a ticket home." He opened his eyes and the box at the same time, and everyone leaned in close to see what it had given him.

Inside the box was a miniature ship inside a bottle. Jack took it out and looked closely at it.

"A ship?" said John. "I have no idea what that's supposed to do for us."

"Neither do I," admitted Jack, deflated. He'd hoped for

something more clearly useful, but this ship in a bottle was, according to the box, the thing he needed most.

"There's no time limit, remember," John pointed out. "It doesn't seem to be constrained by the urgency of the moment. Bert's scarab brooch wasn't needed for years."

"Grand," Jack said, pocketing the bottle and closing the box. "Now what do we do?"

"Let me try," Chaz suggested. "It is more my world we left from, after all. Maybe it'll be my need the box responds to."

Jack shrugged and handed it over. "I don't see that we'll lose anything if you try."

Chaz rubbed Uncas's head for luck. "If it's not a magic carpet t' home," he said cheerfully, "let's hope for some oyster crackers, eh?"

Chaz opened the box.

"Oh, drat again," said Uncas. "And after you got my hopes up an' all."

Chaz reached inside and removed a small photographic slide. In it they could see the projection room back at Sanctuary, and even a miniature depiction of Reynard, still watching for them.

Jack removed the disk from the projector. "It has a sixth slot," he said with a trace of surprise, "almost as if it had been left open for a reason."

Hank and Uncas fitted the slide into the slot, then replaced the disk. "Here goes nothing," Hank said, firing up the generator again.

In a moment, the image of the projection room sprang up on the tent wall. The image was coarser than the others they'd gone through, but this one seemed no less viable.

"Only one way to find out," said Jack, and he stepped from the tent into the house on Sanctuary.

"Come on!" he implored, waving them over. "It's a bit more like moving through soup than air, but I'm here just fine."

"I think I can duplicate that trick with the lenses," Hank said to John, "so you can take it back through with you."

"Are you sure you don't want to come with us?"

The engineer shook his head. "Not my place or time," he said. "Thanks for the offer, though. Just get a message to Verne."

"I will," John said, and he stepped through the portal, with Uncas and Fred close behind. Hugo gave Hank a warm, two-handed handshake and, swallowing hard, threw himself through the portal, landing in a sprawl in the room, much to the delight of everyone there.

Only Chaz remained in the tent. He made no move to go through.

"Chaz?" called John. "Are you all right?"

"I don't . . . I don't want t' go back," he said.

"But why not?" exclaimed Jack. "We've got Hugo back and assured that Arthur has the throne he's supposed to have. When we get back to Noble's Isle, everything will have changed back to the way it's supposed to be!"

"You mean," Chaz replied softly, "everything will have changed back t' th' way it's supposed t' be . . . for *you*. If everything else changes," he continued, "will I just become 'your' Charles? Will I even remember who I was before?"

"I honestly don't know," offered John. "I hadn't thought much about it—no offense," he added quickly. "It's just that you've become so much like . . ."

"So much like him that you hadn't noticed I wasn't him?" Chaz said with a trace of bitterness. "Well, I'd noticed," he said, jabbing his thumb at his chest, "and I don't want to go anywhere if it means I'm not going t' be me when I get there."

"I don't think it'll work like that," said Jack. "I think you'll stay 'you' no matter what. You're one of those implementing the changes in the timelines. So I think you'll remain unaffected—stay Chaz-like, as it were."

"I agree," John said. "Bert mentioned that he and Verne traveled outside the timelines somehow, and despite going to times and places they'd already been, they always kept a memory of events. I think it'll be the same with you."

"There is another thing to consider," Hugo put in. "If you stay, you will probably affect the timeline for us. After all, isn't that why you all came back? To bring me home, so I don't mess up whatever I, ah, botched in history? What if you stay there, and the same thing happens?"

Chaz looked at each of them through the projection, considering, then stopped at Hugo. "That's really th' best reason, isn't it?" he said. "Whatever else goes wrong, I don't want t' be th' cause of Mordred taking over th' world. So let's just pull me over and be done, hey? Before I change my mind?"

"Mordred taking over the world?" Hugo said to Jack. "What's happened while I've been gone?"

"We'll explain later," Jack told him, "hopefully back in my rooms at Magdalen."

Chaz put his hands through the projection, and John and Jack pulled him through. Then, with some coaching from Reynard, Hank adjusted the lenses on the Lanterna Magica and moved it closer, until the men in Sanctuary could touch it, grasp it, and pull it through its own projection. Hank waved a last farewell as he pulled the cord and tossed it through. An instant later the wall went blank. They were back in the room on Sanctuary.

Jack started to cheer, but John held up his hands. "Wait," he said. He didn't know if Reynard, or the room, or the entire island would have been affected by the change they made in the past by returning with Hugo.

He looked at Chaz, who patted himself down and then shrugged. Chaz was still Chaz.

"Reynard," John said cautiously, "has anything changed in our absence?"

"Changed?" asked the fox. "In what way?"

As Reynard spoke, John realized he was bandaged—he still bore the fresh wounds he'd gotten trying to protect the *Red Dragon* from being destroyed.

"John," Jack said tonelessly, pointing at the corner of the room. "The burlap bag. It's still where we left it."

John sat down heavily in a chair and began to shake. There was too much that had been overcome, at too great a cost. Even when the impossible had been needed, they had still managed, somehow, to prevail. And none of it had done them any good at all.

"It's still Albion. Still the Winterland," John said bitterly. "We haven't changed anything."

CHAPTER EIGHTEEN
THE SACRIFICE

THERE WAS NO choice then but to explain to Hugo the complete story of exactly what had taken place after he stepped through the door in the wood. When the companions had finished, Hugo was shaken, but reciprocated with his own tale, looking askance at Chaz as he spoke.

After the Caretakers had explained who he really was, Hugo had accepted it with aplomb, but a feather's uncertainty remained. If it were not for the scarring on his face, and the occasional lapse into vulgar language, Hugo might have thought it was another joke being played on him.

"The book was sent to Charles, and Pellinor had been instructed by someone to retrieve the man in the photo—you, Hugo," Jack summarized. "Then, a time traveler who was working with Samuel Clemens, another Caretaker of the *Imaginarium Geographica,* appears at a tournament in fifth-century Britain. This is all being orchestrated by someone, somewhere."

"I still think Mordred has everything to do with this," suggested Chaz. "I know him—at least, the Mordred of the Winterland—better than any of you. And this is exactly his kind of scheme."

"It wasn't Mordred I heard scheming," said Hugo. "It was

Merlin—the Cartographer. He's the one I wrote the message to warn you about."

"I understand what you think you overheard, Hugo," John offered, "but remember, we know what the Cartographer became. We've had several encounters with him through the slides in the Lanterna Magica, and we know his predilections. But we know where he ended up, too. And he's an ally, not a threat."

"Fair enough," Hugo said, a bit nonplussed at the easy dismissal of his story. "After all, I share your concerns about Mordred. As a scholar of Arthurian lore, I knew I couldn't allow him to defeat Merlin and become the Arthur. That's why I did what I did. I'm just lucky you came along with the real Arthur."

"Yes, lucky," Jack said, rubbing his chin in thought. "But I'm not certain it was luck.

"Consider this," he continued. "Verne and Bert did what they did in response to Hugo going through the door and altering time. They had no way of knowing what specifically had happened—just that something had. And so they responded, and then left us the means to resolve what had gone awry."

"What are you getting at, Jack?" asked John. "Everything changed after Hugo went through the door and the badgers closed it. Of course the thing to do was to find him and bring him back."

"That wasn't what Verne directed us to do," Jack insisted. "He gave us the mission of defeating our adversary. He never mentioned bringing Hugo back as a means for doing that."

"So all this death, and destruction, and whatnot that happened," Hugo said carefully, "it might not, in fact, be my fault?"

"Not all of it, anyway," said Jack, "no."

"Oh, I'm so relieved," Hugo said.

"I know *exac'ly* how you feel," said Uncas, patting Hugo's knee. "Exac'ly."

Reynard and the jackrabbit entered the room carrying trays of potato sandwiches and a hot drink that resembled tea and smelled of chile and cinnamon. "To revitalize you," Reynard said as he passed out the cups. "It's an old recipe, given to us long ago by the wife of the shipbuilder."

The companions drank the tea, and ate the sandwiches hungrily. Despite the camaraderie of Hank Morgan and the interest they had in young Arthur, they were relieved to be able to rest, even temporarily, in a place where they felt civilized.

"The other slides," John said suddenly. "We still have two slides."

"Like the one Charles got out of the box?" asked Hugo, rising and walking over to John's pack. "I didn't realize there were others in here."

"Hugo, wait!" Jack shouted, leaping to his feet and scattering cups and saucers as he did so. But he was a fraction of an instant too late. Hugo flipped open the lid of the Serendipity Box and peered inside.

"Huh," Hugo exclaimed, holding aloft a flower. "It's a purple rose. Was this in here before?"

"It's not purple. It's indigo," said Jack, sitting back down in one of the chairs. "And no, it wasn't. It was there just for you, because it's apparently what you needed the most."

"Strange little whatchamacallit," Hugo remarked as he handed the box to John, then inserted the rose in one of his jacket pockets. "It's pretty, but I'm not really in need of a flower."

"You may be," said John. "It doesn't give you instructions. And each person can open it only once. We'd expected to save your turn until we were in trouble."

"You just finished explaining to me how the entire world is under Mordred's thrall, our only transportation was a ship, now destroyed, and there are giants waiting to kill us if we go outside. How is this not the appropriate time to open the box?"

John looked to Jack and Chaz, who both shrugged. "He has a point," said Chaz.

"It seems to me," Hugo said, sniffing the rose, "that we should follow the mandate of Jules Verne. He gave you five slides. Two remain. We should use those to see if what's been broken can, in fact, be mended."

All the others considered this, then nodded in agreement and got to their feet to start preparing for another trip through time.

Fred and Uncas assured the companions that there would be no mishaps with the cord, and they promised that it would stay put where it belonged on Sanctuary. As before, the companions took supplies to sustain them throughout the day, but they briefly debated whether or not to leave the Serendipity Box behind.

"The 'imp' may not appear for any of us again," Jack said as he and Reynard placed the box in a bag, "but I'd rather keep a hand on the 'bottle,' if you follow my meaning."

"Fair enough," John declared. He turned to the badgers. "Okay, Uncas. Let's see when we're going next."

The badger turned on the projector, and for a moment it seemed as if the image was unable to focus. It shifted and blurred, and finally clarified to a clear but dark scene in a very familiar setting.

The projection on the wall was almost identical to the one

they had gone through last: an image of Grandfather Oak, in the center of the hill not far from Camelot.

"Did we use the same slide again?" Jack asked Uncas. "Is this the burned one?"

Uncas shook his head. "The other one's all used up, Scowler Jack," he said. "This is slide four, as y' requested."

"It isn't the same," Chaz said suddenly. "Look—the tree. It's taller, older. And the trunk is split."

Looking more closely, they realized Chaz was correct. The tree was the same shape, but taller and stouter, and there was a wicked gash along one side, as if it had been struck by lightning. It was a bad enough split that ultimately the tree would not survive.

Chaz flipped through the pages of the Little Whatsit to the entry on Grandfather Oak. "It says here that the tree is still standing," he said, indicating a passage in the book. "What does that mean?"

"It means," John reasoned, "that whatever caused the changes to the world that resulted in the Winterland already happened. Maybe when we were there, in the fifth century. Maybe after. But whatever happened to the tree might be happening everywhere."

"Is this what Verne meant for us to do?" asked Jack. "Are we supposed to find the exact cause of the change and fix it? Can we do that, if it's already happened?"

"I don't know," said John, "but I'm going to go with Hugo's assessment. These slides aren't redundant. They've all been left for a reason. We've got Hugo back now, thanks to the last one. Perhaps this one will bring us closer to the finish."

"I hope so," Jack said as he stepped through the projection. "I need something to believe in."

* * *

The tree, Grandfather Oak, was indeed dying, and the rest of the countryside looked no better. It was bleak, stricken, as if it was diseased. A thick odor hung in the air, an odor of death and decay.

"What's happened?" Hugo exclaimed. "How long have we been away?"

"Years, certainly," said John. "Decades, perhaps, judging from the size of the tree," he added, stroking the bark. "A shame we won't see it again after this."

"This must be a different timeline," Chaz said. "Different from yours, I mean. This looks more than familiar t' me."

They started walking the same route they had taken before, but other than the topography of the land, nothing was familiar.

There were scattered houses and a number of crumbling and broken walls. There were fires in some of the structures, and a few carcasses of horses and cattle that looked as if the animals had died of consumption rather than in a conflict.

Far off in the distance, they could just make out through the smoke and haze the crenellated towers of a castle.

"Camelot," John said dully. "Or what's left of it."

"Let's make haste," Hugo urged, beckoning them on. "We need to get to the bottom of things as quickly as we can. It's early in the day, from the position of the sun, so we can be there in a few hours if we hurry."

The companions ran as long as they could, finally slowing to a walk to conserve their strength for any unexpected surprises. The closer they got to the place they had known as Camelot, the more barren the landscape had become. It had been stripped bare of trees, stones, and anything else that could have been useful in a siege. And a siege was exactly what was taking place.

From the hilltop where they were, the companions could see the fields in the shallow valley where the tournament had taken place. Massed along the valley floor were thousands of warriors, many bearing banners they'd seen at the competition. There were battering rams, and trebuchets, and various machines of war that were completely unfamiliar in design, but evident in their use. Destruction was their purpose, and they were being used by warriors willing to smash everything in their path.

The armies were circled around the castle that had been built on the hill where the stone table stood. It was a motte-and-bailey castle of raised earth and wood that had been fortified with stone. The traditional courtyard that enclosed the town below had been obliterated by the invaders, who were now pressing their attack with fire and steel up against the walls of the castle itself.

The castle and its defenders would not last the night.

"This is it, isn't it?" Jack whispered, awestruck by the spectacle in front of them. "This is the beginning of the Winterland."

"No," John replied. "This is just the result. Whatever set things on this path has already happened."

"But how can we fix this?" Hugo asked, sitting on the ground and clutching his knees. "This is war!"

Hugo had lived through the Great War—but unlike John and Jack, he had never witnessed the kind of savagery that permeated every aspect of a battle that turned on blood and steel. Hand-to-hand combat with spears and swords was a different kind of warfare, and it was frightening Hugo into a stupor.

"Hey, Hugo," said Chaz, pointing at the Little Whatsit, "give me a hand here, will you? I can't make sense of some of this."

John started to remark that Chaz hadn't had a problem with reading it before, when he glanced at Chaz and Hugo and realized that Chaz still needed no help. He'd asked Hugo to assist him to break the professor's coma of fear. And it worked. With his attention drawn away from the battlefield before them and focused instead on the unusual academia of the Whatsit, Hugo was getting his color back.

Chaz looked up at John and gave him a half smile and a nod, then went back to examining the book.

It occurred to John that it had only been through necessity that they'd brought Chaz with them. But just that degree of contact had changed him, perhaps permanently. He would never be the same Chaz they had first met. Perhaps never Charles—not their Charles, at any rate. But not the same as he'd been.

Jack interrupted John's reverie with a squeeze of his arm. "Someone's coming," he said. "But I think he's a friend."

"Why do you say that?" asked John, already stiffened in expectation of a row.

"Because," Jack replied, "he's carrying a sword, a shield, and a baseball bat."

The figure of the knight trudging toward them finally realized that the men in front of him were not fleeing, but merely watching. He took a defensive stance, and then looked more closely at their clothing.

"Who goes there?" the knight called out. "Identify yourselves, and state your allegiances."

"Hank?" Hugo exclaimed. "Is that you?"

The knight straightened up and lowered the sword, then after a long moment, removed his helmet, which was streaked with blood. His gauntlets and breastplate were similarly stained, but his face was welcomingly familiar.

It was Hank Morgan.

Hugo strode down the slope, arms outstretched. "Hank! Well met, old sock! Well met!"

Hank held out a cautious hand. "I'm sorry, but I don't know you. How is it you're here now?"

Hugo stopped and lowered his arms, confused. "You may not know us, but we know you, Hank."

"You know me?" Hank exclaimed through gritted teeth. "That's impossible."

"No, it isn't!" said Hugo. "We're time travelers as well! We actually met you here, some years ago!"

The bloodied engineer shook his head. "I don't know what you're talking about," he said brusquely. "I've never traveled in time before. I don't know how it happened. I was having an argument at my factory in Hartford, and a crusher named Hercules cracked me in the skull with a crowbar. I woke up underneath a great oak tree not too many miles from here."

"We know the place," said Hugo. "How long have you been here?"

"About six months, give or take," Hank replied. "Just long enough to see the whole place going straight to hell in a handbasket." He dropped the bat and shield and moved up to shake hands with Hugo. "Sorry about the reaction," he said. "It's been a long time since I saw a friendly face."

"What's happened here, Hank?" asked John, pointing at the castle. "Who's attacking them?"

"Who isn't is a better question," Hank replied. "All the tribes and fiefdoms have united against King Arthur."

"*Against* Arthur?" John deadpanned. "Arthur united the tribes and kingdoms. Who would dare raise a hand against him?"

"From what I've learned, the nobles have always resented him," Hank replied. "There's a deep-seated belief that he came by his crown though deceptive means, that he never truly earned the right to become the High King thirty years past. And it all came to a head a few months ago when his own adviser, that bastard Merlin, united the nobles and besieged Camelot.

"Actually, the place would have fallen weeks ago," Hank continued, "if Arthur's uncle, Mordred, hadn't shown up to help defend the castle."

The companions were horrified.

"His *uncle?*" Jack exclaimed, eyes narrowing. "When did *that* happen?"

"It isn't in the histories," said John. "None of the ones I've read, anyway."

"I don't care if Mordred's his nursemaid," said Chaz. "Why is *Merlin* attacking Arthur? I'nt he s'pposed t' be the *good* one?"

Hugo was overcome with a different emotion: guilt. "This is all my fault," he began.

"It's not over yet," John said, cutting him off. He turned to Hank. "We have to get to Arthur. Is there any way we can get close to the castle? Any way at all?"

"There just might be," Hank answered. "Follow me."

About half a mile to the north of the castle, where an assault was impossible because of the thickness of the rocks and trees that bordered the river just beyond, Hank led them to a massive stone.

On the stone, almost completely faded with age, were markings in ancient Greek.

"Arthur showed this to me when I first got here," Hank explained. "A man called Brutus created the passageway centuries ago, modeled after one he'd used to escape the siege of Troy. There are several more scattered around Albion."

The companions all shuddered involuntarily on hearing the name. "Britain, if you please," Jack said, looking around the stone. "Where is the passageway?"

Hank gave the massive boulder a shove, and they heard a mechanism underneath grind into action. The stone levered over on its side, revealing a long-unused set of stone steps that spiraled down into darkness.

"I think it leads to a spot right in the center of the castle, and there are oil lamps throughout," said Hank. "Anyone got a match?"

Lamps blazing, the companions moved quickly through the narrow underground passage. Hugo led the way, having renewed his courage since seeing a familiar face—even if the engineer didn't recognize him in turn. Hank followed behind him, then Chaz, with John and Jack in the rear, making sure they were not being followed.

Suddenly Hugo stopped. There was something partially blocking the narrow passageway. It was a bird, an immense owl, which lay unmoving on the flat stones.

"Archimedes," Chaz breathed, pushing past the others. He knelt down and pressed his ear to the bird's chest. "He's functioning, but barely. I think there might be something in the Little Whatsit I can use to fix him up."

"We don't have time for a stupid bird," Hank hissed. "What are you doing?"

"I'm not leaving him behind," said Chaz, dumping a few other items out of his pack. "I'm taking him with me."

"Your business, not mine," Hank retorted, turning around. "Come on. We're almost there."

"Do you believe," John whispered to Jack as they watched Chaz gently wrap the damaged owl and put it into his bag, "that this is the same fellow who wanted us to give him Uncas to eat?"

"Miracles never cease," said Jack. "Look—the passageway is sloping upward to more steps."

The passageway leveled out, then pitched steeply upward, ending at a stone ceiling. "Stand aside," Hank instructed the others, taking up the bat. He got a solid grip on it, then swung it up into the stones.

They shivered, and a light rain of dust fell. Hank adjusted his grip and swung again, then again, and with a sharp crack, the stones broke apart and crumbled down onto the steps. Above them, they could see a stone covering that was slightly ajar, so light could come down into the tunnel. And they could hear voices; harsh, almost shouting.

"You think I don't know?" one was saying. "Don't you think I knew all along what I had lost?"

"I can't let you do it," another voice pleaded. "I can't let you kill him."

"You must."

"I can't!"

"That's Mordred," said John urgently. "And Arthur! We have to get up there, now!"

Pushing together, Hank, John, and Jack hefted the large stone off the entrance and shoved it aside. They climbed out to an astonishing realization: The stone had been covering the crypt of the old king, Camaalis. The tunnel led to the very spot where Caliburn had lain for centuries until Arthur claimed it.

A short distance away, in the center of the castle walls, Arthur and Mordred were facing each other across the ancient stone table. They had ignored the clamor of the falling stones in the passageway, but ceased arguing when they realized that they had an audience.

Arthur was bewildered at first—he hadn't seen the companions long enough to immediately recall them after three decades. But Mordred recognized them instantly.

"I don't know why you're here," he said, his voice low and dangerous, "but you have followed my brother and me across the centuries, always appearing at these pivotal points in our histories. It's only right that you are here to witness this now."

Arthur, older and bearded but still bearing the youth and noble countenance of the boy they remembered, spun back to his uncle. "I can't allow it, Mordred."

Mordred raised his spear—the one he had taken from the chamber of the Grail in Alexandria. "You cannot stop me, boy. Not in this."

In answer, Arthur began to raise the black sword, Caliburn, as he stepped forward.

"Arthur, please!" Mordred cried out as he stepped up onto the table to meet the younger man's approach. "Please, don't—"

The corner of the table, worn and pockmarked with age, gave way under Mordred's foot, and he fell, twisting, against Arthur, who caught him against his chest.

There was a terrible cracking sound, and thunder shook the castle walls, raining stones down all around them.

The sword Caliburn fell to the ground. The blade broke off just above the hilt.

Mordred looked down at it, disbelieving, and stepped back from his nephew, letting go of the spear.

Arthur looked down at the shattered sword, then at his chest, where the spear, the Lance of Longinus, had pierced his heart. He pulled it free, then fell to his knees on the stone table. He whispered something to Mordred, then fell.

The companions raced over to the table just in time for John to catch the king. He looked up, stricken. "We've arrived too late," he said mutely. "The one, the Arthur . . .

". . . is *dead.*"

CHAPTER NINETEEN

THE ENCHANTRESSES

THE GIRL WALKED along the island's shoreline, idly dragging one foot through the surf. The old fisherman watched her, knowing, as she only suspected, that this was the last day they would spend together.

"You know," he said jovially, "you're going to scare all the fish."

"Sorry, Grandfather," she told him. "I was just thinking."

"I could tell. But you're not afraid?"

She considered her answer. "No," she said finally. "Not afraid. But I know that my childhood is nearly over. And it makes me sad. Leaving you makes me sad."

He nodded. "I understand. It was the same with your uncle Telemachus. But nothing is forever. We'll meet again someday."

"Will we? Does that mean I'll live to see tomorrow?"

"None of us knows that for sure," he replied, "but I'd say the odds are in your favor."

She didn't answer, but simply stared out across the water, toward the line of storms that never seemed to change, and wondered if she would ever see what lay beyond them. She hoped she would.

• • •

Mordred hadn't moved. He just stood there, confused, looking from the bloodied spear that lay on the ground to Arthur and back again.

"What did he mean?" Mordred whispered to no one in particular.

The companions approached cautiously, uncertain of what was happening. John cradled the lifeless form of Arthur in his arms and looked up as Mordred repeated the words. "What did he mean?"

"What did he say to you, Mordred?" Jack said, stepping closer. Once, years before, in his own timeline, he'd shared a connection with Mordred that had been forged more because of his youth than poor judgment, and nearly lost his shadow—and soul—because of it. But he knew a personal struggle when he saw it.

Mordred looked at him, his face a mixture of emotions. "He said, 'You are strong enough to bear this.' What did he mean by that?"

John's mind raced. The crucial moment had passed, and they'd missed their chance to undo whatever had been done. Whichever brother had been their true adversary no longer mattered. Arthur was dead. Now the only hope they had was to prevent the ascent of Mordred to the throne. To keep him from becoming king and turning the world and the Archipelago into the Winterland.

"Mordred," John said cautiously, "what were you and Arthur arguing about?"

The question seemed to snap Mordred out of his trance. "Arguing?" he repeated. "We were arguing about what I am compelled to do. Arthur disagreed. But now," he added ruefully, as he looked at his nephew's body and the realization of what had happened hit him fully, "the path is clear. And there will be none who can oppose me."

"This is what Arthur meant, Mordred!" Jack exclaimed. "You are strong enough to bear this! We saw what happened. We know you didn't mean to kill him. Don't let his death force you into a path—"

"Force me?" Mordred said with a barking laugh. "As with a Binding? Don't you think I worked out long ago who had suggested to my brother that I be Bound? Who it was that was responsible for my exile?"

John and Jack looked grimly at each other. There was nothing they could say.

"If I had not been summoned to the tournament by Taliesin," Mordred continued, "I would have remained in exile. And your treachery"—he pointed at Hugo—"is what cost me the throne that was rightfully mine."

He stepped over the spear, and all the companions reared back in trepidation. "I have a promise to keep," Mordred said as he moved around the table, "and order to restore to the land that has been decimated. But when that is done, we shall have a reckoning of our own."

With that, Mordred glanced upward at the sky, then turned and ran toward one of the great castle doors, where he disappeared.

As one, the companions looked up too. High above, the sun had reached its zenith—but instead of shining brightly, it was obscured by shadow and soon would be in full eclipse.

"Why didn't he kill us?" Hugo asked. "Not that I'm complaining, but I'm certain he really, really wanted to."

"I don't think he can," John answered. "Not here, in this place. And not after killing Arthur." He looked up at the vanishing sun. "I think that's what's happening now. Mordred's broken some law of the Old Magic."

Outside, in the direction Mordred had gone, the din of battle rose. It meant the escalation of the war. Worse—if that was possible to imagine—it meant that the creation of the Winterland was closer than ever.

"We have to find a way to stop this!" Jack exclaimed.

"We will," John said. "But first we're going to take care of Arthur's body. I'm not just leaving it here, uncovered."

As John and Jack wrapped the body of Arthur and laid it in state on the stone table, Hank moved around to the doors, barricading them. "There," he said, breathing hard from the effort. "No one's going to be coming through. Not for a while, at least," he added with a fearful glance at the ramparts, which were being sparsely defended by the king's followers.

Hugo and Chaz sat in the grass, still numb from the events they'd just witnessed. "You know more about this Arthur fellow than I do," Chaz said. "Can I ask you a question?"

"Certainly," said Hugo.

"Is this the first time or the last time that Arthur was killed?"

Hugo's brow furrowed. "I don't understand what you mean by 'first time' and 'last time.'"

Chaz showed him some pages he'd dog-eared in the Little Whatsit. Hugo scanned the passages Chaz indicated, then frowned. Suddenly he sat upright, and his eyes widened in shock and realization.

"John! Jack!" Hugo shouted. "Come here!"

As the Caretakers approached, Hugo gestured to the book. "Here, Chaz!" he said excitedly. "Read them what you've found!"

"I've been trying t' catch up," Chaz explained. "The rest of you knew so much already about Arthur and Mordred and Merlin, that I've been reading up on them. Do you know if this is the first time, or the last time that Arthur was killed?"

"What's the difference?" asked Jack, his tone skeptical. "He's just dead."

"Well, it says here that he might not have t' be," Chaz replied. "The Little Whatsit says that Arthur ruled on the Silver Throne for a hundred years before he died, but that he'd been killed once before—then restored to life."

That got the Caretakers' attention. "Does it say how he was restored?" John asked, trying not to get his hopes up.

Chaz nodded and quoted from the book. "It says that he was 'saved to bring light back into a world of eternal darkness, by blood, by faith, and by the power of the Sangreal.'"

"The Holy Grail," Hugo said breathlessly. "Arthur can be brought back by the Grail."

"Is it true, John?" Hugo asked. "Does the Grail really exist?"

"I never saw it for myself," John answered. "It disappeared from Alexandria while we were there. Merlin was supposed to have tried to steal it, but he claimed Mordred was the real thief. Then we found Mordred in the chamber, sleeping with one of the priestesses who tended the Grail itself, and that's when Merlin Bound him. And the Grail vanished."

Hugo groaned. "So Mordred may have the only thing that can bring back Arthur? How do we convince him to use it?"

"I don't know that he does," said John. "We don't even know that it's an object, really. It's a translation conundrum that no one, not even the Caretakers, have been able to sort out.

"One way of reading *san greal* means 'Holy Grail,' or the cup of Christ," he explained, "but the other way, *sang real,* means 'royal blood.' What we need might be a person. An actual descendant of Jesus Christ himself."

"The legend of Joseph of Aramathea," said Jack. "He was Christ's uncle, and supposedly took his nephew's *children* away from Jerusalem to Glastonbury, in England."

Hugo started. "That night in the tent," he began, excited that he could add a piece of the puzzle, "Merlin and the Lawgiver were arguing about how betraying the Grail meant betraying Holy Blood. And Merlin said something about the children of the Grail."

"So is it the cup, or is it the bloodline?" Jack asked rhetorically. "Not that it will help to know, since I haven't the faintest idea where it can be found."

"But I do," a voice said behind them, "and if you are worthy, you may yet find out the truth for yourselves."

The companions turned as Taliesin the Lawgiver stepped up out of the stone passageway.

"Taliesin," Hugo said in greeting. "How has this happened?"

The Lawgiver's eyes were filled with tears, and he deliberately avoided looking at Arthur's body. "A journey of a thousand regrets," he said simply, "begins with a single step. Follow the path of your adversary to the beginning, and perhaps you will find the means to alter his course."

"If you are who I think you are, then you had as much right to claim Caliburn as Merlin and Mordred," said John. "Why didn't you stop this three decades ago?"

The Lawgiver briefly raised his hand to his forehead, touching it. "I was Bound, and was kept from doing all I might have had I been released. And now the future is certain unless you find the Grail and restore the true king."

"Where?" Jack wondered. "Where can we find it?"

"At your adversary's beginning," said Taliesin, "and my own."

"In the Archipelago?" asked John, his heart sinking as he anticipated the possibility of a long, arduous journey ahead. "Do we need to find Odysseus? Was that the beginning you mean?"

Taliesin shook his head. "Our father is long gone," he said flatly, "but our mothers remain. The Grail may be found with them."

"Calypso and Circe," said John. "They're still alive?"

"They, or an aspect of them," answered Taliesin. "On an island of glass, that is both here and not here. In this time, they are often called the Pandora, after our ancestor."

"The Morgaine," Jack declared, shaking his fist triumphantly. "The Morgaine! Of course! That means the Grail is on Avalon!"

"And of course," Hugo said, "you just happen to know how to get to Avalon."

"Of course," John told him. "Why wouldn't we?"

"Just asking," said Hugo.

"There's a river near the great stone," Jack said to Hank. "Are there any boats nearby? Anything we might use?"

"They've all been destroyed," Hank said. "Used for raw materials in the siege. I don't think there's even a toy boat to be had for a thousand miles."

Jack scratched his ear. "Huh," he murmured. "What do you know."

"What?" said Hank.

Jack stuck his hand in his pocket. "We do have that much at least, right here," he replied, removing the miniature ship in a bottle he'd been given by the Serendipity Box. "Take us to the river."

Taliesin offered to stay with the body, to protect it, and the companions bade him farewell and reentered the stone tunnel. Jack followed last, pausing only to retrieve Mordred's spear. "I don't intend to use it," Jack told the others, "but I'd rather that Mordred didn't have the chance to use it again either."

At the other end of the passageway, as before, the forest was empty. "Thank God for small favors," said Hank. "They're all massed at the gates."

It was not far to a sloping path that led the companions to the flowing water of the river. It was thickly clotted with debris along the shore's edge, but ran clear in the middle, and not too many miles distant, opened up into the sea.

"What do you think, fellows?" Jack asked, cradling the small bottle in his hands. "How do we get it out?"

"Bert simply threw the scarab brooch," said John. "Maybe you should toss it into the water."

"And what if it just sinks?" Jack retorted. "Then where will we be?"

Hank grabbed the bottle out of Jack's hands, and before the others could stop him, he had dashed it against the stones in the shallows. But they realized at once that Hank had done exactly the right thing. The tiny boat, immersed in the water, was beginning to grow.

It took less than a minute for the toy boat to grow into a full-size, functional vessel. It resembled a small Portuguese caravel, with room enough for the companions and their bags, and at the front was the carved representation of a scarlet dragon.

John and Jack nearly cheered at the sight of it. A Dragonship had considerably more meaning for them than it did the others, who were nevertheless still very impressed by the appearance of the instant boat.

"It gave you just what you needed most," Chaz said to Jack. "We just didn't know it at the time."

"Thank God," Jack replied, casting his eyes skyward. "And I mean that literally."

Chaz got in first, still carrying the bag that held the unconscious Archimedes, followed by Jack, then John. Hugo got in next and extended his hand to Hank.

"I'm sorry, fellows," Hank told the others, "but this is as far as I go."

"It's an adventure!" Hugo said brightly. "We're searching for the Holy Grail, don't you see? This is the first Crusade!"

Hank smiled blackly and folded his arms. "I understand your excitement and enthusiasm, Hugo," he said. "I felt the same way when I first got here. But I've been here for too many months, and seen more than I wanted. And I think I've had my fill of adventuring."

"There's a chance this will all change, you know," Jack pointed out. "That's what we're trying to do, anyway."

Hank glanced over his shoulder at the rising clouds of smoke that were darkening an already blackened sky, then up at the haloed sun that was nearly in full eclipse. "I always remain hopeful, but in this case, I think the game's already been called," he said bleakly. "If this isn't the end of the world, it's a damn good imitation. And at this point, I think all I can do is try to stay at the edges of the chaos, and record what I can, before . . ." He let the words trail off.

"Can't you go back?" Hugo implored. "With the watch?"

"The what?" asked Hank. "I don't even know how I got here, much less how I'm going to get home."

"The watch," Hugo repeated. "The one that Sam Clemens gave you, that allows you to travel in time."

Hank looked at the professor as if he were crazy, then chuckled wryly. "I'd say you were losing your marbles, if we weren't where we are. If, by some miracle, you ever come across one of those watches, let me know, will you?"

Hugo turned and looked pointedly at John, who opened up the bag he was carrying. "Maybe you can find it yourself," John said, removing the Serendipity Box and handing it to Hugo, who handed it to Hank. "Open that and tell us what you see."

Obediently Hank lifted the lid and smiled in confused surprise. "You've been having me on the whole time, haven't you?" he asked as he took out the small silver pocket watch that was inside the box. "What does the dragon represent?"

"Hope," said John. "It represents hope."

"How does it work?"

John shook his head. "I don't know. But we were told—by you, actually—that it will let you travel in time."

"There's a note underneath," Hank said. "It reads, 'Midnight takes you back.'"

"The rest is up to you, it seems," said Hugo, clapping Hank on the shoulder. "Remember us to Sam, won't you?"

"Verne," Jack said suddenly. "That's what we need to ask of you, Hank. Remember us to Jules Verne."

"Okay," Hank agreed, still uncertain of what he was being asked or expected to do. "How do I contact him?"

"I think you'll see him when you leave this place," Jack told him, "in another time. Just remember to tell him when and where you got the watch, and from whom."

"I will," said Hank, tapping the dials. "What happens when I turn it to mid—"

Hank vanished.

"That's that, boys," Hugo said, dusting off his hands. "I think he's going where he needs to go, and now, so must we."

He sat in the bow of the boat, which then pulled away from the cluttered shallows and into the swiftly flowing water at the middle of the river.

"So we're on an actual Crusade, then?" Chaz said. "Your Charles would have loved this, wouldn't he?"

"He would, absolutely," said John.

The small boat, which John had dubbed the *Scarlet Dragon*, operated in exactly the way they had hoped. In only a few minutes, the smoke in the air had turned to fog, and it clouded thickly around the craft and its passengers.

Moments passed, and the fog began to thin, then clear completely, and they were sailing in open waters, far from any shore.

"Extraordinary," Hugo breathed, looking around at the horizon. "It's like we've come into another world entirely."

"Not entirely," Jack said, pointing at the sky. The sun above was still eclipsed and hadn't changed. "Avalon lies on the transition line between our world and the Archipelago, so we won't have to completely cross the frontier. But," he added tensely, "if this doesn't work, that may not matter."

Within a few hours, the familiar outlines of the island of Avalon appeared on the western horizon. The sky was already dark enough that they could barely make out the thunderheads beyond that marked the true line of the Frontier—the boundary that protected the Archipelago of Dreams.

As the *Scarlet Dragon* approached, it became evident that this was not entirely the island John and Jack knew. Their Avalon was almost abandoned. Only the three who were one, the witches known as the Morgaine, lived there, with an occasional guest, and were guarded by a succession of old knights. While this Avalon appeared similarly empty, the buildings were not in ruins, as they were in the Caretakers' time. The temples, all Greek, were whole and untouched by time or man.

The shore was clean and afforded an easy landing on the beach in front of them. They pulled the *Scarlet Dragon* up onto the sand, then turned to decide where to go.

"We should be wary," John cautioned. "The Green Knight of this time would not know us, and he won't be as feeble as Darnay, nor as stupid as Magwich."

They approached the centermost temple, but no one greeted them, no knight, no squire. "Well," Jack declared, "I don't think anyone's home."

In defiance of Jack's statement, the torches along the walls suddenly blazed into life, and a chill wind swept through the courtyard.

The companions instinctively backed toward a group of the white marble columns for cover and scanned the buildings to see if they were still alone.

They were not.

From the north a regal woman appeared, hair bound up in the classical Greek manner, underneath a silver circlet. She was dressed in a flowing gown of gossamer silk, with a golden belt that matched her sandals, and walked with the assurance of someone who wielded great power. She strode to the center of the courtyard and stepped up to a dais, where she sat on an elegantly sculpted bench.

From the south another woman had appeared, just as beautiful as the first, but whose countenance shone with a terrible power. Her long, beautiful hair reached nearly to the floor, and she carried a broad golden bowl. Barefoot, she walked to the dais, where she stood next to the other woman. Both faced the companions.

"I am Circe," the standing woman said, "and we have allowed you here on Avallo because you have come bearing the sign of the Pendragon."

"The boat," Jack whispered. "She means the Dragonship."

"Where's the other one?" John whispered back. "There should be three."

"Speak," Circe commanded. "Tell us why you have come here and what it is that you wish."

The companions turned to John, deferring to his authority as the Caveo Principia. He gulped and stepped forward. The Morgaine were unpredictable and usually played games. There was no reason to expect things to be different now, in the past. But what question to ask?

"We've come seeking the beginning of the men called Myrddyn and Madoc," said John.

Circe smiled, but it seemed to John—incredibly—that the other, who must be Calypso, actually winced, then blushed.

"Their beginning," Circe said, "is known to us. They began as all men did, and with the same potential. But they forgot how to choose."

"Forgot how to choose what?" asked John.

"How to choose," Circe answered sternly, as if John were a bit stupid. "They forgot that choosing is always an option. There is always a choice to be made."

"Why are you here?" John said. "On Avalon? I know that your island is called Aiaia."

Circe bowed her head. "It is. And hers was Ogygia, before she came here," she said, indicating Calypso. "We came here to the temple of Diana, which was erected by Brutus, to await our children's return."

"This is the island," Jack interjected. "This is where they wrecked the *Argo*."

Again Circe bowed her head. "Brutus built the temple with those who escaped from broken Troy, before he went to the isle of giants, called Albion, to build a kingdom of his own. No man, save for one, an old fisherman, ever returned to this island until Myrddyn and Madoc were exiled here."

"The fisherman was the one who helped Anaximander rescue them," said John.

"He was," said Circe. "Odysseus was a vain and fickle man, but unlike Iason, he always returned to watch over his children."

"I wanted to ask about the *Red Dragon* . . . ," Jack began.

"Too many questions!" Circe exclaimed. "Enough!"

"I'm getting a good idea which of them turns into Cul," Jack whispered.

"What is it you wish of the Pandora?" Circe demanded again. "Speak."

"We come seeking the Grail," Hugo said. "The Holy Grail."

John swore silently and threw a helpless glance at Jack. Hugo was not accustomed to dealing with the witches; he didn't understand how they responded to direct statements like that.

"At last," Calypso said. "A plainspoken man."

Circe held up the golden bowl. "Choose," she said. "The Cup of Albion, or the bloodline of Aramathea."

"The cup?" John whispered. "That's not a bowl. It's the cup of the giant Brutus slew."

"The bloodline of Aramathea," Jack mused. "That's what we thought of as well. Both have ties to Britain, and to the heritage of Arthur. But I don't know what to choose."

"Don't look at me," Chaz said, paging furiously through the Little Whatsit. "I can't even take a guess."

"Let me," Hugo offered, stepping forward. "I choose the bloodline," he said with no hesitation.

Circe and Calypso nodded at each other, and a third woman, plainer than the others but still lovely, came up the steps behind them to take her place on the dais.

"Are . . . are you . . . ?" Hugo said hesitantly. "Are you the Grail?"

"Gwynhfar," the woman replied, bowing her head. "I am called Gwynhfar."

CHAPTER TWENTY

THE GOOD KNIGHT

"I HAVE SEEN you before, haven't I?" John said gently.

"Yes," said Gwynhfar, glancing at him. "Once, long ago, in a faraway place."

"Alexandria," Jack said, realizing who she was. "You were the girl with Madoc, in the Grail chamber."

"Are you really a descendant of . . . ," Hugo began. "Are you truly of the Holy Blood?"

"Five generations ago, my ancestor was put to death," Gwynhfar said. "He died at the hands of the Romans, who could not bear to see their own beliefs supplanted by those he left in his wake as he traveled, teaching. And so when he returned home, they killed him. And soon after, many who followed him. So my great-great-great-granduncle Joseph gathered the family together and fled the land of our birth for a new world.

"But," she continued, "the beliefs and practices of the old world still held sway there, and it was not safe for us to remain. All who were descended from the great Teacher were eventually killed, save for myself and Uncle Joseph. So he arranged for me to be taken to the one place where I would be guarded, where all the great scholars of the world had come together. A place where new beliefs might be forged and fought for."

"And even there, in the library itself, you were not protected," Jack murmured.

Gwynhfar nodded. "There were those who would use me, and what I represented, to further their own aims."

"So when Madoc forced himself on you . . . ," Jack began.

Gwynhfar looked at him in confusion. This meant nothing to her. "Forced?"

"What I mean to say," Jack tried again, "is that when you were, uh, attacked in Alexandria by Madoc, and he violated you—"

"You misunderstand," Gwynhfar interrupted. "I was not attacked. I was not . . . violated. Not by Madoc. How can you say that I was?"

Jack looked at the others, now clearly confused himself. "But we thought . . . When Meridian spoke of his brother betraying the Grail . . ."

"You are mistaken," Gwynhfar said coldly.

"But we were there," Jack said cautiously, with a quick glance at John. "We saw you with Madoc and heard you scream as you fled the library." He extended his hands, trying to understand. "Meridian defended your honor!"

Gwynhfar snorted derisively. "You assume, and conjecture, and misread everything," she said. "You would have been completely inadequate as my Caretakers."

"We do have our moments," John said, not sure if his own words were a defense or an admission. "Please, tell us what really happened."

Gwynhfar stepped down from the dais to get closer to them.

She was shorter than all of them save Hugo, and surprisingly delicate.

"Meridian and Madoc were there as two of my Caretakers," she began, "but once Meridian discovered who I was, and why I was valued, he lost interest . . . mostly," she added. "His interest in the library had more to do with the objects gathered there, such as the Cup of Albion and the Horn of Bran Galed."

"Old Magic artifacts," said Jack. "But not the New World treasures, like the Lance of Longinus or . . ."

"The Sangreal," Gwynhfar finished. "Except for uses more common."

Her meaning dawned over the companions. "So when Ptolemy said Meridian had tried to take the Grail . . . ," John began.

"He tried to take from me, against my will," Gwynhfar explained, "that which I freely shared with Madoc, whom I loved, and who loved me in return."

"And we believed he was evil," Jack said dully. "We sided with Meridian and helped to Bind his brother. And Madoc was the good one all along."

"Y' mean he might have been," said Chaz, "if we hadn't come along an' mucked him up."

"Both of my sons have made poor choices," Calypso clarified. "Both were exiled from the Archipelago. But of the two, Madoc was the one with a spirit."

"Soul," John said quietly. "She means soul."

"What is the difference?" Calypso asked, hearing the word John spoke. "It is the breath of the gods in him. It is his life. It is himself."

"Spirit, breath, wind," Jack intoned. "My God, John, what have we done?"

"We need to do our duty now," replied John. "We are the Caretakers of the Archipelago." He turned to Gwynhfar. "We need you to come with us. Something terrible has happened, and only you can help us."

She shook her head. "I am of the Archipelago now. The island of Avallo is as far as I will go toward the world that was."

"We should have brought him with us," said Chaz. "Is there time t' go back?"

John shook his head. "It's been too long already," he said, noting the eclipsed sun. "Every moment takes us farther into the Winterland. And we may never be able to reverse it if we don't do it now."

"I must stay," said Gwynhfar, "but the Holy Blood might be taken back with you, to do what must be done."

"You want us to take your blood?" asked Hugo.

"No," she said with a faint smile, "I want you to take my child."

Gwynhfar turned and walked between Circe and Calypso, gesturing for the companions to follow.

They walked out of the temple and down a long procession of steps that ended up splitting into two separate paths. The one to the left followed the ridge of sharp cliffs that rose above the western side of the island. Jack and John looked at each other and grinned in recognition. That path led to the cave where they were most familiar with seeing the Morgaine, and where they would one day meet the distant heir to Arthur's throne. If Arthur might still have heirs, that was.

The path to the right dropped sharply down to a pebbled beach, where a number of rusted weapons and tools were scattered in the sand.

There ahead of them, watching through an old iron grate half-buried in the sand, was a young girl. She was auburn-haired, with wide green eyes and a face that bespoke innocence. She was playing with an assemblage of gears that resembled the insides of a watch.

Gwynhfar walked to the girl, who stood and kissed her mother on the cheek. "I've brought you some visitors," said Gwynhfar. She introduced the companions one by one, and the girl nodded and smiled at each of them in turn.

"And what is your name, my dear young lady?" asked John. "How are you called?"

Gwynhfar answered instead, shaking her head. "She has never been named. Her father has never seen her or spoken her name. So she has waited to choose her own name."

On impulse more than anything else, Hugo reached inside his jacket and removed the indigo rose he'd been given by the Serendipity Box. He looked to Gwynhfar, who gave him a curious look in return, then nodded, and he turned and gave the flower to the girl.

"It's called a rose," he said mildly. "I . . . I think I brought it for you. Will you come with us? Will you come, and help us?"

The girl nodded. "May I give you a thimble?" she asked, and kissed him on the cheek before he could reply. "Thank you for my name. I've been waiting for you a long time."

"It's a flower, not a name," Hugo stammered, still blushing from the kiss.

"A thimble might be a kiss, a flower might be a name, and a dragon might be a ship," said Gwynhfar. "Sometimes things are simply what we need them to be. And sometimes things are not what we expect."

She turned and walked up the steps, expecting the others to follow. Her daughter and Hugo went behind her, then Jack and Chaz.

John was about to follow, when he caught sight of a movement farther down the beach. He stopped and looked more closely, then realized it was an old fisherman, bent over his nets.

The fisherman saw John and lifted an arm to wave. John waved back, then trotted up the steps to catch up to the others. "He always returned to watch over his children," he murmured. "That's the way to do it, old-timer."

Back in the temple of Diana, the companions stood with the enchantresses, Gwynhfar, and the girl.

"Thank you," John began. "We cannot express what this will mean to the world that you are helping us."

"Your gratitude is not necessary," Circe said. "It is a fair exchange, in the manner of the old ways."

Exchange? John thought wildly. *What exchange?* He'd forgotten that the Morgaine rarely gave anything freely; they usually expected something in return. But they had brought nothing with them except . . .

"You don't mean to take our boat, do you?" John said. "We need it to—"

"Not the Dragonship," said Circe. "It has not the value."

"Then what?" asked Jack. "What is it you want?"

"Blood for blood, a life for a life," Circe said simply. "It is the Old Magic, and it is the Law. If the child is to leave Avalon, then one of you must stay."

"You're going to sacrifice one of us?" Hugo gulped.

"No one will be sacrificed." Calypso sighed. "But he who stays will be expected to serve, as our daughter will serve in the Summer Country."

"The Green Knight," Jack said suddenly. "They mean for one of us to become the Green Knight."

John understood. That was why they hadn't seen one of the familiar guardians of the island. There had been no guardian, not until this point in time. And one of them would have to stay behind and take up the mantle, if they were going to have the chance to save Arthur.

Chaz stepped forward. "I can do this. I want to do this."

Jack shook his head. "No," he said flatly. "You don't realize what you're offering, Chaz."

"I know one of us has t' stay," reasoned Chaz. "What else do I need t' know? You two are real Caretakers. You have t' go back. And rescuing Hugo was part of the reason you've done all this t' begin with. I'm the only one who *can* stay."

"We'll find another way," John began. "There must be another way, Chaz!"

"Blood for blood, a life for a life," Circe repeated. "There is no other way."

"I've been wondering all along," Chaz said slowly, eyes downcast, "if maybe things back in Albion might have been different, if I had only been more like Charles instead of Chaz, then. We're not that different now, he and I, I think."

"Chaz," said Jack, "you can't hold yourself responsible. The Winter King was centuries old before you were even born. He had thousands and thousands of minions at his command. Against all that, what can one—"

"What can one man do?" Chaz asked, looking up at Jack with a grin. "Is that what you were going to say, Jack? I've been wondering that myself. Especially with things I've been reading in the Little Whatsit. And it seems that one man, in the right place, an' at th' right time, can do an awful lot. And I could have, and didn't. Not when it meant the most."

He was talking about Bert, John realized. Since the last passage from Sanctuary, they hadn't mentioned the death of the old traveler, but now he understood that it had weighed as heavily on Chaz as it had on him or Jack, and perhaps more so.

"Besides," Chaz went on, "in't all of what we're doing based on one man, anyway? This 'Christ' everyone's been going on about? He was just one man, wasn't he?"

"That's different," Jack replied. "That was . . . well, a mythology. A real mythology, based on a real person, but you can't use that story as a reason for choosing to sacrifice yourself in this way."

"And why not?" Chaz shot back, annoyed. "Isn't that why we come all this way, to this island? T' find the Holy Blood who are his children?

"You say it's just a mythology, a story," Chaz continued, "but here we are anyway, centuries later, pinning all our hopes for the future of the entire world on whether or not this girl is his kin, and carries his blood. And maybe she is, and maybe she isn't—but what else are stories for, 'cept t' learn from, and improve yourself? T' learn t' do th' right thing?"

"Because the story is *mythical*," Jack retorted. "There probably *was* a man called Jesus Christ, and he probably *was* crucified. But all the value of that sacrifice came from the mythology that sprang up around it, and maybe the whole reason that there is power in his bloodline is because people have chosen to believe in it—not because of the value of the literal event itself."

"What's the difference?"

Jack started to reply—then realized he couldn't. Not that he didn't want to, but because he really had no way to answer the question.

Chaz stepped over to Jack and put his hands on his shoulders. "If I do this," Chaz went on, his voice low, "it will be literal, not mythical. Only you, those here with me, will ever know the literal truth of the choice I'm making. But maybe, in time, my friends will make a story out of it, and it might even become a myth. And others can learn from my example, the way I've learned from the ones I've read about, and seen, and become friends with."

Jack met Chaz's eyes and realized that his unlikely ally had indeed become a friend. "You realize," he said, struggling to voice the words, "what we're trying probably won't work, right, Chaz? We're taking this child to a battlefield to resurrect a dead man who may or may not have been the rightful king. And there's no way of knowing if it will work."

"That's where—what did you call it, John? Faith? That's where faith comes in, doesn't it?" Chaz said. "You have t' admit, it sounds familiar . . . sacrifices, and bringing someone back t' life . . . Even if it doesn't work, it'll be a great story. Just don't forget me, hey?"

"Never, Chaz," Jack said, embracing his friend in a tight hug. "I'll never forget."

John also gave Chaz a hug and a solid clap on the back, and even Hugo gave him a warm two-handed shake.

Chaz turned to the enchantresses and spread his arms. "Okay," he said with as much bravado as he could muster. "Y' got me."

Circe looked at Calypso, who nodded and looked at Gwynhfar, who also nodded. Then the three of them beckoned to Chaz to come forward.

He took a few slightly unsteady steps, then strode forward to the top of the dais. Circe moved behind a pillar and reemerged carrying a silver tray. On it was a small cake and a crystal bottle with a stopper.

"Choose," said Calypso. "Choose your form, Chaz, and thus become the Guardian of Avalon."

"I've avoided drinking things lately," Chaz said decisively. "Nothing personal, but everyone in history seems obsessed with poisoning everyone else. So if it's all the same t' you, I'll have the cake."

"As you wish, Chaz," said Circe.

"Don't mind if I do," he replied, taking the small cake from the tray and popping it, whole, into his mouth. "And please, from here on—call me *Charles*."

The cake took effect almost immediately, and Chaz—Charles—bent over in pain. Jack began to rush forward to the dais, but John held him back. "Wait. Just wait, and watch."

The two enchantresses and Gwynhfar stepped around the agonized man, forming a loose circle. All three were murmuring words—words of comfort, or spells? John couldn't tell. His friend twisted about, seemingly in agony. But even through the tears, they could see he was smiling.

Suddenly leaves shot out from his joints, and around his neck and waist, shredding his clothes. His skin began to darken, as if it had been aged and stained to a fine, rich sheen. As one, the three women moved away and removed pieces of armor from the alcoves around the dais. They returned just as the transfigured man was getting to his feet, and they dressed him, reverently, almost gratefully.

Next, Gwynhfar signaled to her daughter, who dashed off to one of the rooms and returned with a great rectangular shield, which she handed to him.

"And now," Calypso stated, "we must choose a weapon for you."

"I think I have just the one," Jack said, and dashed down the steps to the *Scarlet Dragon*. He returned to the temple carrying the Lance of Longinus.

"This was Mordred—Madoc's," he explained, "and it has a history with your ancestor as well, Gwynhfar. I think it being wielded by the Guardian of Avalon would be an appropriate use for it."

"Well spoken," said Circe.

Jack handed the spear to Gwynhfar, who presented it, reverently, to the Green Knight.

"It is done," said Circe. "The Old Magic is satisfied."

The girl kissed each of the enchantresses farewell, then embraced her mother. The companions said their good-byes to the knight, who then stood at the entrance of the temple, ready to assume his duties.

"Tell Fred and Uncas I will miss them," the Green Knight called out as the small boat moved away from the shore. "Tell them I said thank you, for helping me to find my destiny. And look after Archie, will you?"

"We will," Jack said, waving. "Good-bye . . . *Charles*."

The *Scarlet Dragon* passed back into the Summer Country as easily as it had left, and in a matter of hours, the companions were once again racing through the stone passageway that led to the castle.

When they emerged from the crypt, they found Taliesin still watching over Arthur's body. The Lawgiver seemed astonished to see them back.

"The battle does not go well," he said, "and you have increased Mordred's anger tenfold."

"Us?" said John. "Why?"

"He came back for the lance," said Taliesin, "and flew into a rage when I told him you had taken it."

"Hah." Jack smirked. "It's in a far, far better place, and being used for a better purpose than Mordred had managed." He looked down at Arthur's body. "I only hope we've returned in time."

"I don't even know who's supposed to win anymore," said Hugo. "Do we want Mordred to win? Or Merlin?"

"We want Arthur, the true High King, to do what he's meant to do," said John, moving aside to allow the girl to approach the table. "That's what we brought her to do, if she can."

Taliesin gasped in recognition, then bowed his head as the girl approached.

She touched Arthur's face lightly. "Hello, cousin Thorn," she said as if he could hear her. "My name is Rose. And I've come here to help you."

"The blood that took his life must be the blood that restores it," Taliesin murmured.

"He's not going to hurt her, is he?" Hugo asked, eyeing the Lawgiver.

"I don't think so," Jack said, holding him back. "Watch."

Taliesin touched Rose's hand with the black staff, and the runes flared briefly with eldritch light. She looked at her hand and saw the small cut across her palm.

Rose marked both of Arthur's cheeks with the blood from her hand, tracing the line of the bones to his chin. Then, reverently, she laid both of her hands on his head, closed her eyes, and began to speak.

By light's power driven
For need of right
I restore thee
I restore thee

By blood bound
By honor given
I restore thee
I restore thee

For life and light and protection proffered
From blood and will my life is offered
I restore thee
I restore thee.

Rose removed her hands from his head and crumpled to the ground. Hugo rushed forward and caught her, but the others had no time to react to what happened next.

There was a pause, as if the world had stopped.

No sound, no movement. Even the constant rumble of the battle outside had ceased. The stillness was everywhere, and every-when. And then, overhead, the dark circle eclipsing the sun shifted. The light on the edge of the sun brightened, then rays burst forth, striking directly below in the center of the castle, on the ancient table made of stone, which was carved with the runes of the Old Magic.

Suddenly, impossibly, Arthur raised his hand and reached into the light. Then he sat up, swung his legs off the table, and rose to his feet.

The High King, Arthur Pendragon, was alive.

PART SIX

THE SILVER THRONE

CHAPTER TWENTY-ONE
THE FALLEN

A TALL STACK of bound manuscripts tottered, then fell, setting off a chain reaction in the small writing chamber Geoffrey kept on the topmost level of the church.

In seconds, the pages he'd been working on were swept away in a tidal wave of aged leather and the decaying writings of monks long dead.

Geoffrey sat on the floor and sighed. This was becoming a more and more frequent occurrence. He'd gotten into the habit of acquiring old books and manuscripts in his younger days, at the upswing of the twelfth century. But now, at its midpoint, he was beginning to grow weary at the futility of it all.

He reached for the nearest tome and smiled as he realized what it was. Nestor's *Primary Chronicle*. One of the first and greatest of the world histories. Not complete, by any means, and certainly slanted toward the Slavic, but indispensable nonetheless. After all, few chronicles ever attempted to begin as far back as the pharaohs, or even the Deluge. Even his own works were meager contributions to his own library compared to Nestor's works, dealing as they did with the histories of the lineage of Britain's kings, and of the great enchanter and philosopher Myrddyn.

Geoffrey had only just begun to clean up the disaster when he heard a knocking at the door downstairs. He quickly made his way down the stairs, but when he opened the door, no one was there.

Instead he found a parchment rose, which had strange markings on the petals, and a roll of paper, cream-colored and tied with a cord. It was addressed to him. Cautiously he unrolled it and read what was written inside.

He blinked at the rose and the strangeness of the message, then read it again, then a third time.

Quickly he shut the door and hurried back up to his study, where he tossed the rolled paper into the embers of his fireplace, then stoked the coals until it caught fire. He stood and watched it until it was nothing but ash.

"Is this a dream?" Arthur asked. "It must be, because Merlin's War Leader is here and seems to have been weeping over me."

"He was Bound," John said, "by Merlin."

Taliesin knelt and took Arthur's hand. "You are the true High King, the true Arthur."

"Bound?" asked Arthur. "As in Old Magic?"

"Yes," said Hugo. "He's been Bound all along, ever since the tournament."

"The tournament," Arthur said wonderingly. "That's where I met you two before, isn't it? You met Archimedes and me at Grandfather Oak and helped me find my way to Camelot."

"We did," Jack confirmed.

"I wish you'd stayed around," Arthur remarked. "You three seemed reasonable men. And there has been a shortage of reasonable men these last thirty years."

He suddenly noticed his bloodstained tunic and touched his chest, probing. "I . . . I died, didn't I?"

"You did," said John. "It was an accident. Mordred didn't mean to do it."

"Then how is it I am standing here now?"

"Because of her," Hugo said, cradling the still weak girl. "Mordred's daughter—your cousin, Rose. The heir of the Grail."

"I can't believe you have that kind of power," Jack breathed, as he and Hugo helped her to her feet. "You brought him back, Rose."

She shook her head. "Not I, and not my power."

"It was someone's power," reasoned Jack. "He was dead, and then he was not."

"That is the blessing of the Old Magic," said Taliesin, "and the power of belief."

"Oh no," Arthur cried, kneeling. "What happened to my sword?"

"It shattered when Mordred stabbed you," John said. "When his spear clashed against your sword."

"That should not have happened," said Taliesin, looking over the broken halves of Caliburn with Arthur. "Caliburn should have been stronger."

"I don't think it was Caliburn that was weak," said Arthur. "*I* was. I think I was afraid to use the strength that was needed to end this sooner."

"Now is your chance, boy," a harsh voice called out as one of the heavy inner doors splintered apart. The companions whirled about to see Merlin force his way into the castle's center. "It's only right that I should find you here, where it began," he said angrily. "Where you took what was rightfully mine."

He seemed to notice only then that there were others present and, with no small surprise and a rising anger, realized that he knew them.

"You," he said accusingly to the companions. "You have followed me for much of my life. If you value your own, you won't interfere."

"You didn't mind when it benefited you," John pointed out.

"I did mind, when you changed my own history," Merlin spat, "and disqualified me when I was one breath away from gaining my throne."

"You would have lost, Merlin," Taliesin said. "Mordred would have beaten you."

"I lost, traitor," Merlin replied, "when I didn't learn my lesson the first time, to make my Bindings more specific."

He tightened his grip on the short Roman sword he carried and stepped toward Arthur. The companions circled protectively around the king, and then another player joined the deadly game.

"This has been a long time coming, brother," Mordred said, stepping out of the crypt passageway. He stopped in shock when he saw Arthur, and even took a step backward when he saw Rose.

Then he seemed to steel himself. He took a firm grip on the scimitar he was carrying and walked purposefully toward Merlin.

"Mordred," Arthur began.

"Stay back, Arthur," Mordred commanded, "and this shall be ended in a trice."

Merlin acted first, leaping with a snarl at Arthur. His blow was parried not by the king, but by Mordred's scimitar. Mordred pulled back and struck out at Merlin, but found his blow deflected by a short sword, expertly wielded—by Arthur.

"What are you doing?" Mordred asked, incredulous.

"What I must," said Arthur.

"As am I," said Merlin, swinging the sword again. Arthur dodged it easily, then pressed around the table to block Mordred.

Merlin jumped atop the table, only to have his feet knocked out from under him by a vicious blow from the scimitar. Mordred pushed Arthur aside with a shove, then leaped up to deliver a killing blow to the disoriented Merlin.

"This is the end, brother," Mordred said, holding Merlin at the throat with one hand, while drawing back the scimitar with the other.

Merlin screamed.

Mordred struck.

And suddenly he realized that his scimitar was lying on the ground, still clutched in his hand.

He cried out in pain and horror and held the bleeding stump of his forearm to his chest.

"I couldn't let you do it, Mordred," said Arthur, the bloody sword in his hand dropping loosely to his side. "I couldn't let you kill him."

Mordred staggered, then fell. Kneeling in the dirt, he curled in on himself. After a moment, his shoulders began to shake.

Dear Christ, thought John. *Mordred is* laughing.

Mordred threw back his head, eyes wild, and in a moment his frenzied laughter turned into an agonized, soul-searing scream. He rose to his feet, still bleeding, and pushed past Arthur and Taliesin to the crypt, where he disappeared into the passageway below.

The companions moved back to the table, where Merlin was sitting and holding his head in his hands.

"Are you all right, Merlin?" John ventured, staying back out of reach of the short sword.

"I was going to kill you myself!" Merlin cried, looking at Arthur with a bewildered expression. "Why, Thorn? Why did you prevent Mordred from killing me?"

"Because," Arthur replied, "I didn't believe then, and don't believe now, that anyone needs to die to become the High King."

"That," said Taliesin, "is the reason you were able to draw Caliburn at the tournament."

"Then how was it that Mordred's spear shattered Caliburn?" asked Jack. "Arthur is far more noble than Mordred. In my opinion, anyway."

"It wasn't a matter of nobility, but a matter of belief," Taliesin replied. "In the moment that they met, Mordred's belief in his motivation was greater."

A tremendous crashing arose from within the walls of the castle, and the clashing of steel could be heard. The war was coming to the heart of Camelot.

"Is it Arthur's forces, or Merlin's?" asked John.

"It doesn't matter," said Arthur. "My main support had been Mordred's, and the soldiers were his as well. Everyone else, all the other tribes, had been united under Merlin before he tried to overthrow me."

Taliesin agreed, with sadness and regret radiating from his face. "Under the Binding, I had trained them all to respond to the will of Merlin, on Arthur's behalf," he said, "but none of that will matter now. If you have the means to take him away, Arthur must flee, and rule in exile."

John and Jack knew what it would mean if Arthur left now.

Merlin would try to rule until he was overthrown by Mordred. And then, despite all they had done, the Winterland would still come to pass.

"There is a way."

It was Merlin who spoke.

"When you drew Caliburn," he began, "and won the tournament, you were acknowledged as the High King. As the Arthur, Pendragon. The liaison between the Summer Country and the Archipelago of Dreams. But there was one step you didn't take . . . were not allowed to take. One I never allowed those who knew," he said, looking at Taliesin, "to tell you about.

"There are those more powerful than the armies of man," Merlin went on in a somber voice, "and as High King, you have the right to command them."

"Where?" asked Arthur. "Who are they?"

Merlin turned to John. "You know where, and you know how," he said. "Don't you?"

"Stonehenge," John said breathlessly. "We can use Stonehenge, the Ring of Power, to summon the dragons of the Archipelago."

The small group, including Merlin, left the castle through the crypt passageway, pulling the cover stone over it as they went. It would not take long for it to be discovered, but by then they would be miles away.

Taliesin, with some assistance from Jack, secured horses for all the companions and took the lead, heading toward the standing stones John called the Ring of Power. As they left the passageway and waited for the horses, Arthur was anxiously scanning the countryside, looking, hoping, but to no avail.

Mordred was nowhere to be seen.

✦ ✦ ✦

It took several hours for the companions to reach Stonehenge, and all the while they rode, the skies behind them filled with smoke. Camelot was in flames.

Arthur glanced to his left, at the girl called Rose, who was riding behind Hugo on a black mare. There had been little time for discussion, but he was wise enough to have pieced together who she was, and what she had done to save him. He watched her, saddened, and hoped that their support of each other would extend beyond the present moment. That was, he believed, how it should be. In a family.

He patted the bag at his side, taking comfort in the feel of Caliburn, while also feeling shame. Was it possible to betray, even by weakness, a weapon? Even one as storied as Caliburn?

They dismounted and tied the horses in a nearby grove, then walked over to the ancient standing stones.

"The last legacy of the sons of Albion," said Taliesin, stroking one of the massive stones. "And the last connection they kept to the world of their birth."

"Do you know what to do?" Merlin asked Arthur.

"We can show him what he needs to do and say," Jack said, his voice firm, "and if it's all the same to you, I think you need to stand back."

"Of—of course," said Merlin, bowing his head.

He moved to a shallow field where he could watch without disturbing Arthur. The others remained apart from him, until Rose moved over to him and took his hand. Then Hugo followed, and finally Taliesin.

John and Jack took Arthur to the center of the stones and

explained to him what it was they hoped he would do. They explained the means, and the ritual, then left him alone and joined the others.

Arthur stood a long while, arms folded behind his back, head bowed, as if in prayer. Finally, he lifted his head and began to speak.

By right and rule
For need of might
I call on thee
I call on thee

By blood bound
By honor given
I call on thee
I call on thee

For life and light your protection given
From within this Ring by the power of Heaven
I call on thee
I call on thee.

He finished speaking the Summoning and looked around at the mottled sky. Then he turned and called out to the others, "Now what happens?"

"Now," John said grimly, "we wait. And hold out as long as we can."

They did not have to wait for long.

A dozen dragons, of various shapes, sizes, and colors, dropped out of the sky and landed on the hillside near the stone circle. The first among them was not the largest, but was by far the most familiar to John and Jack.

"Samaranth!" John exclaimed. He was almost giddy at seeing one of their strongest allies. Both he and Jack rushed forward—and stopped in their tracks.

The large, reddish dragon with the white mane of hair looked at them with a gaze that was clear in its meaning: Come no closer.

John looked at Jack in puzzlement. Then they both realized what was wrong. They were still in the sixth century and would not meet Samaranth, the oldest dragon, for nearly fourteen hundred more years. He would not know them, here, now. And he, as well as the other dragons, would be wondering who had known to summon them using the Ring of Power.

"Ah, what do I do now?" asked Arthur. "Offer to shake hands?"

"Not a good idea," said Jack. "John?"

John's mind was racing. He hadn't really thought it through this far. He'd simply taken a wild chance that the king would be able to summon the dragons. But he needn't have worried—someone was already in charge and knew how to proceed.

"Why have you summoned us here?" the great, smoky voice of Samaranth rumbled. He swung his head around to Arthur, who, to his credit, stood his ground and faced the dragon fearlessly. "You," Samaranth said. "You spoke the Summoning. What gives you the authority to do so? Who has given you the words that called us here?"

"I called you of my own authority," Arthur answered, emboldened by the fact that the dragon hadn't simply bitten his head off straightaway. "And the words to speak were given to me by your servants, the Caretakers of the *Imaginarium Geographica*."

Arthur made a gesture with his hands, indicating to John and Jack that they should step forward.

"Sons of Adam," Samaranth asked, "what does this mean?"

"It means that we are also Caretakers of the Archipelago of Dreams, and true and loyal servants of the High King," said John.

"And you support his rule?"

Jack and John both nodded. "We do."

"Are there any others who will stand with you, little king?" asked Samaranth.

Screaming a ferocious battle cry, King Pellinor burst through the shrubbery at the edge of the trees, charging straight at the dragons. He was dressed in rags, which were tied around what little remained of his rusted and abused armor, and was running barefoot. Seeing the dragons, the king suddenly skidded to a stop—apparently, when he saw that his legendary "Questing Beast" had finally come to Albion, he had neglected to notice that several others had come as well.

Pellinor stood there, staring mutely at the dragons while his mind reeled. This was not the end to the quest he'd envisioned, nor had his grandfather, or his grandfather's grandfather. Finally he let out a yell in frustration. "Which of you is it?" he shouted. "Which of you is the Questing Beast, appointed by destiny to be slain by the lineage of Pelles?"

The older dragons at the front almost looked as if they were grinning, John thought, if he really believed a dragon was capable of grinning. Then, in the back, a largish orange dragon with a short, stout body and a long, thick neck raised an arm and waved at Pellinor.

"Aha!" the old king exclaimed as he dropped his visor and drew his sword. "Have at thee, beast!"

Pellinor set off at a full run directly at the dragons, who moved aside to let him through to his target. Pellinor barely came up to the dragon's knees—which did not deter him from stabbing the dragon directly in the shin. In response, the Orange Dragon reached out with a great clawed foot and stomped down on the blustering Pellinor with a crunch.

When the dragon lifted his foot, Pellinor's right leg and left arm were twisted at sickeningly odd angles. Still, the old king persisted in stabbing at the dragon with his sword.

"This?" Pellinor bellowed, glancing at his ruined arm. "It's just a flesh wound! I've had worse!"

"Your leg is also broken, you old fool," the dragon noted.

"Making excuses not to fight me, eh, beast?" challenged Pellinor, and he attempted to chop at the dragon's foot. "Coward! I'll have your guts for garters!"

The Orange Dragon sighed and picked Pellinor up by the neck. He walked over to the tree line and deposited the raging king into a stout, hollow oak.

"Think you've won, eh?" shouted Pellinor with a now bark-muffled voice. "I can still see you, beast! I can still, uh . . ." There was a brief pause, as the ratty old king realized that not only was he half-crippled, but he was also completely immobilized within the trunk.

"I can still curse you!" Pellinor yelled, looking through a knothole. "With my last breath, I shall curse at thee, from the very heart of . . . ah, well, this tree!"

The Orange Dragon shook his head and walked back to join the others.

"Any others, little king?" asked Samaranth.

"I think he was the last one who would have backed me," Arthur said, embarrassed, "and he only did that much because my uncle asked him to."

"Ah yes," Samaranth mused. "Your uncle Mordred. He was a favorite of mine. A very good student. But he has always let his belief that events and creatures are unchangeable manipulate his choices. And that, above all, is a stupid way to live."

"And his brother?" asked John. "Was he also your student, Samaranth?"

"He was mine," said a smallish, lithe dragon, who stepped to the fore of the drive. "I was his teacher, and he, too, was an excellent student."

"The Indigo Dragon speaks true," said Samaranth. "The sons of Odysseus have always had great potential. But it has been warped, and misused, and they lost their way."

There was a great, choking sob from behind the companions. Merlin, his eyes filled with tears, stepped forward, hands outstretched. The Indigo Dragon took him, pulled him close, and embraced him. "Ah, little boy-king." The creature sighed. "I had hopes for you. I did. But now it seems another will have to serve in your stead as the Indigo King."

"Was there no time I chose correctly?" Merlin asked. "No chance I had to redeem myself?"

"Almost," said the Indigo Dragon. "Had you chosen—truly chosen—to step aside for the boy, it would have been you who was worthy to wear the Indigo Crown and sit on the Silver Throne."

Merlin looked anguished, then nodded sadly and walked back to the companions.

"Thousands of years ago," declared the Indigo Dragon, "as the world of men ceased believing in magic and wonder, we, the Guardians of the Archipelago, began to draw a veil over it, to prevent passage except by those who traveled in vessels that bore the mark of divinity.

"But that mark had less to do with power than it did with belief, and intention. This was a lesson we ourselves learned, many thousands of years ago. But we also learned that once fallen, we could also rise again if we so chose. And many of us did.

"There are many who will aid you, both in this world and in the Archipelago. There are objects of both power and influence, born of magics old and new. But above all, you must believe in your cause and have the righteousness of intention to see it through, and you shall always prevail.

"This is your secret, young king. Yours, and those who are the Caretakers of the lands that lie beyond," the Indigo Dragon continued, indicating the companions with his great claw. "Guard it well and call on us in time of need. We will aid you, as long as you are worthy."

"You will come, if called by one of royal worth?" said John.

"A misunderstanding," the dragon said. "The authority does not now and never has lain with those of royal blood. Rather, it lies within those of noble worth. And having one does not necessarily guarantee the other."

"These are the duties of your office, young king," Samaranth said. "Will you accept, knowing all that you face? Knowing that the world is united against you, save for these few, and those such as ourselves?"

Arthur nodded with no hesitation. "I will."

The great old dragon looked skyward, as did all the others. Where there was dark smoke obscuring the sky and light of the sun, a thousand pinpricks of light had appeared, breaking apart the darkness.

"Then as you have Summoned us," Samaranth concluded, "the dragons of the Archipelago shall serve."

In minutes the sky was filled with a multitude of dragons, all flying toward Camelot. The dragons in the great stone circle indicated to the companions that they should climb onto them to travel more quickly, and in moments they too were airborne.

CHAPTER TWENTY-TWO

EXILED

WITH THE AID of the dragons, it was not long before order, or at least a more manageable chaos, was established in Camelot. The fires were quenched and the armies routed. And backed by the might of the great winged beasts, Taliesin was able to reassert his authority as war leader over many of the tribes. Not all of them. But enough. And as the sun began to set, it was evident to all the companions that it would be setting on Arthur's Britain, and not on Mordred's Albion.

At the stone table, the dozen dragons who had appeared at Stonehenge converged again with the companions. The Caretakers, Hugo, and Rose had stayed well away from the battles. This was not their war. And Arthur had gone to the front of the conflict, to show to the soldiers that Taliesin was indeed now taking orders from, and obeying, the true king.

Merlin, for the most part, sat at the back of the hill, neither moving nor speaking.

"Have you any further need of us, Arthur?" asked Samaranth. It was the first time any of them had addressed him by the title, and for the first time in thirty years, it felt earned.

"I believe we have it well in hand," said Arthur, "or at least, well enough for all practical purposes. But there is one question I do have." He cast a glance back at Merlin.

"His betrayal of those he trusted in the Archipelago caused him to be exiled here," said the dragon. "It is you who was betrayed here in the Summer Country, and it is you alone who shall decide his fate."

Arthur bowed his head. "Very well."

"Others have been summoned," the Indigo Dragon said. "Your education in the ways of the Archipelago and its peoples is sorely lacking. This must be remedied as soon as can be managed.

"You will have three teachers. The first of them will be waiting for you at the water's edge at sunset. The others will come in time," said the dragon. "All else is now entirely in your hands. Choose wisely. Choose well."

"I will do my best."

The dragons all extended their wings and stroked the air, rising high into the dusk.

"Rule wisely and fare thee well," the Indigo Dragon said again, "Arthur Pendragon, King of the Silver Throne."

The companions gathered together their few belongings and followed Arthur and Merlin to the water, where the river began opening itself up to the sea.

Taliesin remained behind so that a semblance of order might be maintained at the castle. Hugo and Rose took responsibility for the damaged Archimedes. Arthur agreed that the bird would need repairing, and also that he might be a good and eminently appropriate teacher for Rose.

Jack carried the Little Whatsit and the Serendipity Box, and

John, acting as Arthur's squire, carried the scabbard and broken sword Caliburn.

Arthur rode to the rear in silence, with Merlin close at his side. There was little that could be said between them, or perhaps little they felt that they were capable of saying.

At the water, they left the horses near the tree line and walked down to the sand on foot. There, standing starkly against the rays of the setting sun, was a sight that reassured John and Jack even more so than the dragons themselves had.

It was the ship, the *Red Dragon*. And at the helm stood Ordo Maas.

John started to wave at the old shipbuilder before Jack reminded him that Ordo Maas would not know them any more than Samaranth had. So it was particularly surprising when the old man, still carrying his long staff with the eternal flame, disembarked from the ship and came straight toward them.

"Which of you is John?" he asked pleasantly.

"That would be me," said John.

"Here," said Ordo Maas as he handed something to the Caretaker. "I was told you misplaced something very like this a long time past, and a friend didn't want you to go too much longer without."

It was a silver watch with a matching chain and fob, and on the back was a red engraving of Samaranth.

"Is it a time machine?" Jack asked. "Will it let us travel through time?"

"I believe it will," Ordo Maas replied. "I've found for every minute I watch it, I move a full minute farther into the future."

The shipbuilder turned to Arthur. "I am to be your first

teacher, High King. And tonight we go for the first of your many lessons."

"I understand," Arthur said. "May I attend to some business first?"

Ordo Maas bowed. "As you wish."

Arthur took the broken pieces of Caliburn from John and walked to the water's edge. "I drew this sword," he murmured, "and thought I had become a king. Then it broke, and only by going without it at my side, and in my hand, did I truly prove myself to be a king.

"I should like to give it over to the safekeeping of another, until such time as I shall need it again, or until another more worthy than I chooses to seek it out."

"Who is he talking to?" John whispered.

"I have no idea," Jack whispered back. "This is new ground for me, too."

The water near the banks of the river, just past the rushes, began to roil, and a figure rose, spectral-like, out of the water.

She was beautiful in a stern fashion; her eyes were cold for all but Arthur, and she spoke to him alone.

"Will you take it, Mother?"

Nimue reached out and took the shards of Caliburn from her son, then leaned in to kiss him on the cheek before sliding swiftly and silently back into the depths.

John noticed that during the entire encounter, Merlin had kept his back to the woman and stayed far from the water's edge.

"I have one more matter to attend to," said Arthur. "Merlin. Come to me."

The would-be king approached the younger man and dropped

to one knee, but to everyone's surprise, Arthur pulled him to his feet. "You do not kneel to me," he said blithely. "Never do you kneel to me." And then, even more surprisingly, he pulled Merlin in for a tight hug, which Merlin reluctantly returned.

"You understand what I must do?" Arthur said.

Merlin nodded.

"I know you still love your maps," said the High King. "Do you still carry the tools to make them?"

Merlin nodded again. "I have a quill, and ink, and a bundle of parchments," he said, "but I have not used them in almost a century."

"You'll have time to do it again, I think," said Arthur. He rubbed his cheek where he'd been gashed earlier, then touched a blooded finger to Merlin's forehead and began to speak:

Myrddyn, son of Odysseus
By right and rule
For need of might
I thus bind thee
I thus bind thee

By blood bound
By honor given
I thus bind thee
I thus bind thee

For strength and speed and heaven's power
I call on thee in this dark hour
I thus bind thee
I thus bind thee.

"You are thus Bound, Myrddyn," pronounced Arthur, "by the Old Magic, and by blood. And thusly Bound, I command thee to seek out Solitude and to remain there, until released by blood, or by my command."

Merlin looked at him with less sadness than resignation and nodded. "As you command, Arthur."

Arthur took off his torn and bloody cloak and handed it to Merlin. And then, almost as an afterthought, he handed him the scabbard of Caliburn. "Here," he said. "Perhaps one day you will find a use for this. Or choose to use it in the way it was meant to be used, when you are ready."

Merlin stepped into the water and stopped. "How am I to . . . ?" he began.

"My king," said Ordo Maas. "If you'll permit me?"

Arthur nodded, and Ordo Maas raised his staff. A moment later, sailing smoothly along the river, the *Scarlet Dragon* appeared.

"Our boat?" Jack exclaimed. "My boat?"

"Chin up, Jack," said John. "It's not as if we planned to use her again."

Ordo Maas stepped into the water and stroked the *Scarlet Dragon*'s head as he whispered to it. He reared back as if listening, then smiled and patted the boat on the head.

"She will take him," Ordo Maas said to Arthur, "to Solitude. You will learn of it yourself from a teacher other than myself, but for now, there is a place he can go where he can think and dedicate himself to his work."

"Thank you," said Arthur. He gestured at the boat, and Merlin stepped aboard with his few meager belongings. Merlin stood, facing away from the others, and spoke.

"Why?" he asked. "Why wouldn't you allow him to kill me, Arthur?"

Arthur took a deep breath. "You betrayed your brother," he said evenly, "and my mother. And as a child, you even betrayed me, staying only long enough to give me a name. And when I grew older, all that you had feared in me are those things that came from you.

"You have been afraid your whole life. And I cannot bring myself to kill—or allow to be killed—someone who had made the mistakes you've made, just because you are afraid."

The *Scarlet Dragon* took that as a tacit approval to leave, and she pulled away from the shore.

"Thank you, Thorn," Merlin said without turning around.

"You're welcome," Arthur answered. "Farewell . . . Father."

The companions all watched from the shore until the *Scarlet Dragon* vanished from sight.

It took only a short while to arrive at, and cross, the Frontier. *So simple a thing,* Merlin thought to himself. *So simple, when done the right way. It was all I wanted for so long, and now, to have it given to me so easily . . .*

But no—the thoughts themselves caused the blood on his forehead to burn.

He had been marked.

He had been Bound.

And he had returned to the Archipelago.

The *Scarlet Dragon* sailed for days, perhaps longer, before finally approaching their destination.

In the distance, shrouded by mist, the passenger of the small boat could make out the island, and on it a tower that had no end.

And suddenly, with a mixture of shame and surprise, he realized where he was going.

In a short while he would be there, and he would climb the stairs until he found what he had been commanded to seek. Somewhere, there in the Keep of Time, he would at last find Solitude.

Arthur said his farewells to the companions, then stepped onto the *Red Dragon* with Ordo Maas, and the second Dragonship of the evening pulled away from the shores and set course for the Archipelago. The companions watched as the ship sailed away, and then made their way back to the stone passageway.

"One final matter remains," said Hugo. "What is to become of young Rose?"

"We're taking Rose with us," John and Jack said together. It seemed that all three of them had come to the same conclusion.

"Blood for blood, and a life for a life," Rose said, nodding her head in agreement. "Your companion stayed on Avallo, so it seems right that I return with you."

"And if no one has any objections," Hugo added, "I'd like to take Archimedes back as well. Chaz asked that we care for the bird, and Arthur has enough advisers, now."

"Good enough and done, then," said John, looking at the rising moon. "We're running close. We'll have to ride hard to make it."

With horses and best wishes given to them by Taliesin, the companions arrived at Grandfather Oak just as the projection was starting to waver.

"The badgers will be frantic," said John.

"Badgers?" asked Rose.

"You're going to love them," said Hugo. "Ready?"

Rose nodded, and together the foursome stepped through the projection and into the future.

Once more they were back in the projection room on Sanctuary. There was a brief flurry of greetings and explanations to satisfy the badgers' questions—mostly about why they had brought back a sick bird in a bag, and why Chaz seemed to have been turned into a girl.

"I'm not Chaz, I'm Rose," she said. "Pleased to meet you both."

"First things first," said Jack. "We need to know if it worked this time."

From inside the room, nothing seemed different at all.

"Well," John said. "I guess we'll just have to go outside and take a look again, and see if this time it did the trick."

"John!" Jack cried out. "Look! In the corner! The burlap bag is gone! We have changed things, after all!"

"Did you move the bag?" John asked the badgers. "Set it aside, perhaps? Or did Reynard move it?"

Uncas shook his head.

"No, we never touched it," answered Fred. "I never realized it was gone until you mentioned it just now."

"Where's Reynard?" Jack said, looking around the room. "We need to have him check outside, to see if the giants are still lurking about."

"He went out a while ago," said Fred, heading for the door. "I'll go ask after him."

The little badger opened the door and stepped outside—and disappeared with a yelp.

The companions ran over to the door, which opened not into

the hallway they expected to see but into an endless black void. Fred had fallen when he stepped over the threshold, and he was desperately hanging on to the door frame by a single paw.

Jack reached down and grabbed him up, holding him tightly. "Don't worry, little badger," he soothed. "I've got you."

"Thank you, Jack," Uncas said gratefully. "I couldn't bear t' lose my boy!"

"What in Hades is out there?" John said to no one in particular.

"It's Nothing," Hugo said simply. "The door opens into Nothing."

John closed the door and stepped away from it, thinking. "We've changed something," he said, gnawing on his fist in thought. "I think we *did* change the world, after all. Because the one we came from, Chaz's world, is no longer there. At all."

"But this room still is?" asked Jack. "How is that possible?"

"Perhaps we've changed things again," John said morosely. "We left Chaz, centuries ago, in a world that didn't turn into his. And we took away someone who was already there." He gestured to Rose. "Who's to say we didn't do exactly the wrong things?"

"Do you believe that?" Hugo asked. "Do you believe either one of those choices could have been different?"

"No, I don't," John answered. "That's what confuses me. I don't see any other path to have taken other than the one we have."

"Then we should follow it the rest of the way," said Hugo. "We can't go out of this room by the door—so I think we're meant to go through a projection one more time. Why else would it still be here, waiting?"

"I think you're right, Hugo," said John.

"Should we try to take the projector with us again?" asked Jack. "It might be useful."

"To what end?" John replied. "We're out of slides. And unless another one magically appeared, we couldn't use it anyway. No," he said with finality, "I think the room was still here because the projection tied us to the other timeline. It kept it intact, for as long as there's a projection."

"So what happens when the slide burns out?" Hugo asked with a gulp. "Do we vanish into the Nothing too?"

"I don't plan to be here to find out," John said, grabbing his pack. "Take everything we can fit into our bags," he instructed. "We have two choices. We can go back through to Camelot and take our chances, or we can use the last slide Verne left for us and have faith that we're being looked after, even now."

"Do you have that much faith, John?" asked Jack.

John looked at the silver and red dragon watch given to him by Ordo Maas, then at Rose, who had come with them into an unknown future. "Yes," he answered. "I do."

With no more discussion, the companions gathered their few belongings together and prepared for a final trip in time.

"Of course you'll be coming with us," Jack said to Uncas. "We're all going together, wherever and whenever it is."

Verifying that everyone in their small party was ready to go, John gave the signal, and Uncas switched the slide from the sixth-century picture of Camelot, which was already charring at the edges, to the last slide.

It was not what they'd expected.

In front of them, on the wall, a startled monk dropped the bundle of wood he was carrying and crossed himself. That was not what they'd hoped, that the portal was opening in the presence of someone, but not unexpected. But they were unprepared for the effect the last slide had on the projection room itself.

It trembled and shook and began to come apart at the seams and fall away into Nothing.

John and Hugo pushed Rose through the portal, then began to step through themselves. "Hurry, Uncas!" John shouted over the howling winds that were sucking at the walls of the room. "Hurry!"

The door shuddered, then ripped away from the wall, spinning off into the dark. The wall itself followed seconds later. Uncas and Fred rushed forward and jumped through, rolling in the brush on the other side.

Jack tossed the bags and packs through the portal as the other side wall ripped away, and the chairs began flying around the room, then up through the shattering ceiling.

Hugo crossed over, and then Jack. John took one last look into the room and stepped away just as the floor began to disintegrate.

Standing safely amidst the shrubbery and trees that had been visible through the slide, the companions watched in chilling fascination as the rest of the room fell away into Nothing, finally taking the projector with it, and in another instant the projection blurred, then blinked out.

The room, and the Lanterna Magica, were gone.

They found themselves standing in the company of a slightly frightened and extremely bewildered monk.

"Be ye angels, or be ye demons?" he asked in clear Old English.

"We be . . . I mean, we are men," said John.

"And badgers," added Uncas.

"And you?" the monk asked Rose.

"I'm Rose," she answered simply and, to the companions' surprise, in the monk's own language.

"Of course you are," the monk replied. "Are you seeking sanctuary?"

"We've actually just come from there," said Hugo, "but if you've some handy, we wouldn't decline."

The monk looked at him and shook his head. "I'm not sure what you mean by that, but I am happy to help. You are not quite what I expected, but if you carry the sign . . ."

The companions looked at one another with puzzled expressions. The sign? What was he talking about?

Then, on impulse, John reached into his pocket and withdrew the watch that bore the image of the red dragon, Samaranth.

The monk's expression changed from one of cautious surprise to one of relief. "You do bear the sign. That means you are the . . . how did he call you? The Caretakers?"

It was the companions' turn to be surprised. "We are," John said, nodding.

"I'm Geoffrey of Monmouth," the monk replied. "I've been waiting for you."

CHAPTER TWENTY-THREE

RESTORATION

GEOFFREY LED THE companions up the claustrophobic stairway and into his study. "The message said that I was to wait for three scholars, called Caretakers, who carried the sign of the dragon, and that when you arrived, I was to use the, uh, flower to contact the knight."

"You have a Compass Rose?" Jack said, suddenly excited. "Which knight?"

Geoffrey shrugged. "I couldn't tell you," he said, moving aside several piles of parchments. "I'm just riding along on the skiff. I haven't any idea where the river is flowing."

"Jack," John said, looking over the monk's accumulations. "I think I've read some of these! I think these are some of the actual Histories!"

"I can do you one better," said Hugo. "There's one over here that I actually *wrote* in."

The others clustered around Hugo's discovery and realized they recognized it themselves. It was the Grail book that had been sent to Charles.

"Oh, yes, that," Geoffrey said from behind a mound of books. "A very odd Frenchman gave it to me only recently. I had just begun transcribing it, but then parts of several pages mysteriously disappeared. I can't imagine what happened to them."

"That's too bad," said Jack. "I'm sorry your work was interrupted."

"Oh, it didn't slow me down too much," Geoffrey told him. "I'm quite good at, uh, extrapolating details from limited information."

"Making things up out of whole cloth, you mean," said Jack.

"More or less, yes," Geoffrey admitted. "Sorry about the mess, by the way. I've been collecting these writings for years, and I just ran out of places to keep them all."

"I think we can fill in some of the fabric here," said Hugo, "at least where my own contribution is concerned."

On a clean sheet of parchment, Hugo recreated the entire message he'd actually written, which had been truncated by the torn page:

The Cartographer is Merlin, who cannot be trusted.
He who seeks the means to conquer and rule
the islands of the Archipelago and our own world
will follow the true Grail and the children of Holy
Blood will be saved, by willing choice and sacrifice
that time be restored for the future's sake.
And in God's name, don't close the door!

—Hugo Dyson

John breathed hard and rubbed the back of his neck. "If we'd only had this whole message," he said to Hugo, "we might have made all kinds of different choices, starting with never having trusted Merlin."

"Oh, Merlin?" said Geoffrey. "I've written a biography of him. A fascinating man."

"You don't know the half of it," Jack told him dryly.

"Someone sent the book to us," said John. "So someone, somewhere, somewhen, knows more about this than we do."

"Found it!" Geoffrey exclaimed happily. "Now, if I can just remember the working of it . . ."

"Here," Jack said, taking the Compass Rose. "Allow me."

He swiftly found the appropriate place and made the mark that would bring someone from the Archipelago.

"One thing's certain," John said as Geoffrey, accompanied by Fred and Uncas, went to fetch some bread and cheese for his guests. "We prevented Mordred from establishing the Winterland. Geoffrey of Monmouth is in the twelfth century. If Mordred had regained the upper hand, Geoffrey wouldn't be here now, in our England."

"So you've achieved what you set out to achieve, then," Rose said as she examined Archimedes. "This is good, is it not?"

"It is," John replied, clearly uncomfortable discussing Mordred in front of his own daughter. "Now our objective is to simply return home to our own time."

"You're here now," said Rose. "Doesn't that make this time your time?"

John rubbed his temples. "She's another one of those, isn't she?"

"I'm afraid so," said Jack. "And more are on the way, unless I miss my guess." He pointed at the Compass Rose, which had begun to glow. "Company's coming."

Geoffrey and the badgers had just returned with the food when there was a sharp knock at the door below.

Rather than bring someone else into an overcrowded room, they all went down to meet the new visitor.

It was the Green Knight.

Jack and John both cried out in joy at the thought of a reunion with Chaz, but an instant later their faces fell. This was indeed the Green Knight, but it was a different one.

"I am called Abelard," the knight said in a clipped French accent, bowing deeply. "Have I the honor of addressing the Caretakers?"

John and Jack stepped forward. The knight looked confused. "I was told to bring you all with me. You are not all Caretakers?"

"We all are indeed," John said hastily, "after a fashion, that is." The Green Knights were not traditionally known for their intelligence, and the last one he knew personally, Magwich, would sell his own mother, then forget to collect the money.

Geoffrey was taking both the strange appearance of the knight and the invitation with aplomb. John admired that—even if he was a bit bemused at the monk's rather disorganized personal style. Suddenly, looking up the stairs, all the elements of the happening came together for John in a burst of insight.

"Geoff," John said, tapping him on the shoulder, "how would you like to relocate your collection of books and manuscripts and receive a special education on the history of the kings of Britain, all at the same time?"

"That sounds very intriguing," Geoffrey answered, rubbing his hands together. "What must I do?"

John smiled. "Grab your hat," he said briskly, sizing up the Green Knight. "We're going visiting."

• • •

The Green Knight had come to Caerleon in the beasts' ship, the Green Dragon. It was one of the larger of the Dragonships, and also the most wild and free-spirited. With the knight's help, and under Geoffrey's mostly efficient direction, the companions were able to load the monk's entire collection onto the ship in a matter of hours.

With the work done, they all boarded the ship one last time, and slowly it pulled away from the shore and set sail for the Archipelago.

"It was good of you to wait and help us bring all the books and manuscripts," John told the knight. "We appreciate it very much."

The knight bowed. "It was my pleasure, Caretaker."

"Are you the Abelard I would know of?" asked John. "The philosopher poet?"

The knight seemed startled by this, then regained his composure and bowed again. "I am honored that you would remember me as a poet," he said with a lilt of pride in his voice. "It was, in truth, one of the later accomplishments in my life."

"How is it that you were chosen as a knight of Avalon?" asked Jack.

The knight sighed. "It was Bernard of Clairvaux," he said, the shimmying of the leaves on his shoulders attesting to the emotion he felt in sharing the confession.

"He had succeeded in having me accused of heresy. I became ill at the priory of St. Marcel, and it was there that I was approached by my predecessor, a knight called Gawain. He offered me the chance to serve, and I accepted, most gratefully."

"I know of your work too," Geoffrey said quietly. "In fact, I have the only complete copy of your *Historia Calamitatum*."

"I am pleased by this," said the knight, and it showed. He looked near to bursting.

"Your predecessor was Gawain," Jack mused. "Who was his predecessor?"

"The greatest of us all," the knight replied. "He served for many years as the first Guardian of Avalon and set the example by which those who came later follow."

"Are we going to Avalon, then?" Jack said, almost tearing up at the description of Chaz.

The knight shook his head. "That was not my instruction. Tonight we are going to the Chamenos Liber."

"We're going to the Keep?" asked Jack.

The knight nodded. "Someone has asked to see you."

John and Jack looked at each other and traded knowing smiles. There was only one man in residence at the islands of Chamenos Liber—only one man who could have requested them by the title of Caretaker here, in the twelfth century.

At the Keep of Time, the companions all disembarked and began to climb the stairs of the impossibly tall tower. Finally they reached the top of the steps, and the door that was second to last in the Keep.

The door was locked, and the keyhole under the mark of the High King seemed so new it might have just been installed that hour. John was about to knock when Rose reached out her hand and touched the door. The lock disengaged with a soft click.

"Come in," said a now familiar voice. "Enter freely and of your own will."

John gave the door a gentle push, and it swung open to reveal a room that was only just beginning to be filled with the clutter of maps and globes and the accumulated cultural bric-a-brac of two thousand years that they remembered from the first time they'd seen it. And sitting in the center, working at his desk, was the Cartographer of Lost Places.

The Cartographer gave the companions a careful, lingering look of appraisal before speaking again, and when he did, it was to Rose. "Greetings and salutations, daughter of Madoc."

Unexpectedly, Rose walked to the Cartographer and kissed him on the cheek. "Hello, Uncle Merlin."

He shook his head at this and gently pushed her back.

Was that a tear on his cheek? John wondered. Or just a trick of the light?

"No," the Cartographer was saying, "I haven't needed a name in a very long time, and it's doubtful I'll need one again. It's best for all concerned, especially you, dear Rose, to simply call me the Cartographer."

"As you wish," she said, stepping back and taking Hugo's arm. She was trembling, he realized suddenly. The gesture had been more difficult for her than it had appeared.

"You hesitate," the Cartographer said to the others, noting that they had come inside the room but remained clustered by the door, as if they were comforted by the option of easy escape. "With good reason, probably. I was an excellent example of what not to do when you've been gifted with near immortality and unlimited opportunity."

"It's been a revelation, that's for sure," Jack said brusquely.

"Merlin?" asked Geoffrey, pulling at his collar. "As in, the real Merlin?"

John chuckled. The knight made of wood and leaves hadn't fazed the monk, nor had the talking badgers. A living Dragonship was similarly accepted, as was a tower made of time. But the thought of actually meeting the man whose life he'd been chronicling made Geoffrey twitch and shift about as if his bladder were full.

"Real is a matter of perspective," the Cartographer said, "and it's a matter of what is worth remembering and what is worth passing on to those who inherit the future."

"We almost lost, didn't we?" said John. "We almost brought about Mordred's victory."

The Cartographer looked at him for a breathless moment, the nodded. "We almost did. All of us, together, who were there."

"What happened?" Hugo asked. "What did I do to cause the crisis in time?"

"In the history you remember, the one you first came from," the Cartographer replied, "Mordred defeated me as you feared he would, and then was challenged by the boy. Mordred broke the rules of the tournament and attacked Arthur after he'd chosen not to fight his uncle. The boy, bless his scrappy heart, fought back and actually won.

"He drew Caliburn, became High King, and united two worlds. Because he had beaten Mordred in fair combat, the tribes united under his rule."

"So when I interfered by throwing the knife and disqualifying both Mordred and yourself . . . ," Hugo began.

"Arthur won by default when I refused to fight," the Cartographer finished. "And though he was worthy to draw the sword, he did not unite the people. And I . . ." He paused, composing himself. "I used that against him, until you came and set things right again."

"How can you remember all of that?" asked Jack. "What happened the first time? That was a different timeline than the one we changed."

"I have an acquaintance," the Cartographer explained. "One of the more recent kings of the Silver Throne, Arthur's son Eligure, chose to allow me a visitor. And that visitor has shared certain knowledge with me about pasts that were, and a future that may be."

"Verne," said John. "You mean Jules Verne."

"The same," he confirmed. "He has impressed upon me the need to keep detailed Histories of the events of the Summer Country as well as of the Archipelago. That's why I asked Abelard to fetch the monk—what was your name again?"

"G-Geoffrey," came the reply, his voice shaking with trepidation. "Of Monmouth."

"Ah, yes," the Cartographer said. "I understand you have amassed quite a library as it is, am I correct?"

"You are," said Geoffrey. "It's in the ship below."

"Excellent," said the Cartographer. He started rummaging through a stack of maps in the corner. "Eligure's brother, Artigel, has already created a great library within the city they are building on the island of Paralon," he went on, removing a large, leather-bound book from the pile. "All of your collection can go there, but this"—he handed the book to Geoffrey—"must be in your possession always."

It was the *Imaginarium Geographica*. The first *Imaginarium Geographica*, which the Cartographer had begun in Alexandria centuries earlier.

"In this atlas," he explained, "are maps to every land in the Archipelago. At least, those I have managed to remember. Abelard brings me scraps of stories of new lands, and I make new maps. But these, the finished works, should be looked after by those who also write its Histories. Will you accept?"

Geoffrey looked flustered, then bit his lip and bowed gravely. "I am your servant."

The Cartographer shook his head. "You serve the Silver Throne and the peoples of the Archipelago. I am only a mapmaker."

"I have to ask," Jack said. "Did we fix it? Is the world, the timeline, proceeding the way it was meant to after the battle at Camelot?"

The Cartographer nodded. "It was not the last confrontation between Arthur and Mordred—but it was the last that you were witness to. There were other encounters between them, and much more to Arthur's own history that you have not yet learned. The building of the Dragonships. The forging of the great rings from the Cup of Albion. Your learning of these things may yet be in your future, and events must still follow the paths already taken, if you are to return to the world you know."

"We can go home?" Uncas and Fred exclaimed together. "Really?"

"Yes, little Children of the Earth."

"And you'll remain here, Bound by Arthur," said Jack. "It's just, I think. But having been Bound once myself, by Mordred, I can't say I don't have some sympathy for you."

"It must be a strong magic," said Hugo, "to keep you here so long."

"Magic, and Bindings, and Openings, and Summonings have

far less to do with actual power than they do with belief," the Cartographer said. "Belief in what is possible, and belief in what is necessary."

He gestured to Jack. "You say that my brother, Madoc, once performed a Binding on you? With a ritual? And blood?"

"That's right," said John. "On all of us. It took a remedy from within the badgers' book, the Little Whatsit, to free us."

"Did it now?" came the reply. "So ask yourself this: Why did it work to begin with?"

"Because, ah . . . ," John started. He looked at Jack, who shrugged.

"Mm-hmm," said the Cartographer. "And why did the badgers' remedy work?"

John and Jack had no answer for that, either.

The Cartographer nodded, almost melancholy, and rubbed Fred on the head. "And you, little Child of the Earth. Can you tell me why the Binding worked, and why your remedy did as well?"

"Because we wanted them to," Fred answered.

"Because," the Cartographer said simply, "you had *faith* that they would."

"If it's a matter of faith," Jack retorted, "then why wouldn't the talismans you found, like the Spear of Destiny, allow you passage back to the Archipelago?"

"Oh, I found many other talismans," the Cartographer said. "A dozen. Dozens. Maybe a hundred. It doesn't matter. What matters now, as it did then, was the reason that those 'divine' objects wouldn't allow me to pass through the Frontier into another world."

"Because you didn't believe," said Jack. "Because you had no faith that they were, in fact, divine."

"Exactly, my boy," the Cartographer said. "I was searching, and acquiring, and trying to use objects that had value, worth, to other people. Not one of those things meant more to me than that. As a means to an end."

"But if they had . . . ," Jack began.

"If they had," the Cartographer finished, "I'd have crossed over easily, no bones about it. If I'd had a belief in just one of those things, I'd have passed."

"But the sword, Caliburn, was from your world, your gods," said Jack. "Why couldn't you use it?"

"For exactly the opposite reason," the Cartographer said. "I had the belief in it, but I also didn't think I was worthy. And I refused to test myself to have that fear proven for all to see.

"Well," he went on, rubbing his hands together, "I've enjoyed this, but I really must get back to work. Autunno isn't going to annotate itself."

"What are we to do now?" John asked.

The Cartographer blinked. "Abelard is taking Geoffrey to Paralon," he said, "and I expect you'll be going home."

"How do we do that?" asked John. "We used our last means of time travel to get here—and no offense, but it's far from when we want to be."

"Don't you have a talisman of your own?" the Cartographer inquired. "One that can magic up what you need most?"

"Yes," John replied, "but we've all used our turn with the Serendipity Box. It won't work again."

"I haven't," a voice said, small but firm.

It was Fred.

"I haven't opened the Serendipity Box," he repeated. "I've thought about it several times but never did. I wanted to wait until it looked as if there really were no other options."

"Animal logic again," John said gently, kneeling to look the badger in the eyes. "You may turn out to be the wisest of us all, Fred."

Jack and Uncas removed the box from the satchel they'd been carrying and handed it to Fred. The little animal didn't give a preamble speech or make any dramatic gestures, but simply lifted the lid and looked inside.

The box seemed empty at first, until Fred realized that in the corner was a small silver key. He took it out and closed the box.

"It's the key to your future, I'd imagine," the Cartographer said.

"Is that a metaphor?" asked John.

"The future. Upstairs—the next door," the Cartographer replied, exasperated. "That's the problem with scholars. You always think there are layers and layers to everything, when sometimes, the literal meaning is all you need. It is," he repeated pointedly, tapping two fingers into his other palm for emphasis, "the key, to, your, *future*."

Jack and John both realized it at once. The last door in the Keep. The one always out of reach, because the stairs ended at the Cartographer's door, while the tower continued to grow.

"Have you ever gone through it?" John asked. "Have you ever gone into the future?"

The Cartographer turned away from them and did not answer for a long, long while. Finally, still facing the wall, he began to reply.

"I have not gone through it myself," he said quietly, "but it wasn't for lack of desire or effort. It had opened, just the merest fraction of an inch, just enough for a single look, before it was slammed shut and placed forever out of reach."

John realized what the Cartographer had left unspoken. "You didn't get to look through the door, did you?"

"Not I," the Cartographer said, turning to look at Rose, "but my brother did, and what he saw broke his heart, and he spent the next dozen centuries trying to change what he saw. And he never succeeded, because I spent just as many years trying not to. And I will never be able to erase that shame, or ease the pain I caused him."

"That was why you were exiled from the Archipelago, wasn't it?" asked John. "For trying to go into the future."

"Almost," came the reply. "I—we—were exiled not for attempting to see the future, but because we wanted to use that knowledge to shape the world to suit our own purposes. That was not permitted then, or now."

With that, the Cartographer resumed his work, head bowed low to the paper. It was, the companions realized, the end of the conversation.

"Be well, Uncle Merlin," Rose said, as she and Hugo stepped out the door.

Jack bowed his head. "Farewell, Meridian."

"Good-bye . . . Myrddyn," said John.

"I am the Cartographer now," he replied, not looking up, "and that is enough. In truth, it always was."

At the edge of the stairs, the companions found a small keyhole, almost covered over with spiderwebs.

Fred inserted the key into the opening and turned it. There was a small click, then nothing.

Suddenly, as if they were leaves of a plant breaking through soil to sunlight, nubs of stone began to appear along the wall. They pushed outward, groaning and creaking as they grew, until in moments there were several new steps extending from the stairway that ended at a just-appearing platform beneath the last door.

"Lead on, Fred," said John. "It's your key, after all."

Fred and Uncas stepped cautiously up the stairs to the door, which they realized was still standing slightly ajar.

"They never closed it," Jack murmured.

"We'll make sure we do, then," John stated. He pushed it open, and together they moved into the future.

It was dark until John closed the door behind them. Then, just like the door Hugo had gone through, this one disappeared.

They were in the wood, along Addison's Walk, at precisely the spot where the first door had been. And if there had been any doubts whatsoever that they had been returned to the right place, they vanished when the companions heard the whoops and hollers from the Royal Animal Rescue Squad.

The badgers swarmed off the Howling Improbable, which was exactly where John and Jack had last seen it, at the side of the path, just along the trees.

Jubilantly the badgers embraced Uncas and Fred, and even the humans, including an astonished Hugo and a delighted Rose.

Rising above the trees was the comforting, familiar sight of Magdalen Tower, and beyond that, the buildings of the college itself.

"We're back," John said, hugging Jack's shoulders. "We're home."

Jack didn't answer, but just smiled a small smile and watched the badgers dancing around the clearing.

"Never doubted it for a minute," said Hugo.

• • •

The Royal Animal Rescue Squad departed after promising to give a full report to King Artus. As the principle sped away, John also said that he had to get home right away. He looked exhausted.

"It must be nearly three in the morning," he said. "This was quite the extraordinary adventure, wasn't it? Quite the mythopoeia."

Jack responded to the comment with a half smile. "It's certainly going to make a grand story," he said as the four companions walked back to his rooms at the college, "but I don't think I'll ever view the myths again in quite the same way."

"Why is that?" John asked.

"Because," Jack replied, "I've . . . felt them now. I've tasted them. They've become more than stories to me. And I'm going to be thinking about all this a long, long while."

They crossed the quadrangle, and Jack unlocked the gate next to Magdalen Bridge. As they said their good-byes to John, Hugo remained a bit longer as they went to Jack's rooms at the New Building and discussed what would be best to do with Rose.

"There's a boardinghouse in Reading," Hugo said. "It's near the college, and it wouldn't be any trouble to put her up there as my niece. And Archimedes can stay with me so she can see him every day."

He wrapped an affectionate arm around Rose, who yawned. "We'd best be going," said Hugo. "I'll call you up tomorrow to let you know all's well."

Jack closed the door behind Hugo and sat at his desk. His mind was still racing with the events that must have happened in a single night—and had lasted for a lifetime, it seemed.

Sunrise was still hours away, and there would be plenty of daylight in which he could do what he was considering. But he couldn't wait. He had to know if they'd made the right choices, if they had done enough. If they had believed enough.

Jack took out a key that opened the hidden drawer where he kept items pertaining to his duties as Caretaker. It contained some documents, a few items of an unusual nature, and a flower, made of parchment.

He removed the Compass Rose, and with a stick of graphite scratched onto one of the leaves the small mark that would summon a Caretaker from the Archipelago. With John nearby in Oxford, and Charles still in Paris, there was only one other person who might respond to this specific summons.

A tapping at the door an hour later woke Jack from where he'd fallen asleep at his desk.

Bert—all of him, both arms, both legs, and a fully attached head—was standing outside the door.

Jack fell back, stumbling, as his mentor rushed into the room.

"Jack, lad, what is it?" Bert asked, his face a mask of concern. "You look as if you've seen a ghost."

"It—it's good to see you, Bert," Jack said, before his voice finally cracked and he collapsed, sobbing, into the old man's arms. Bert held his friend, not talking, until the sun rose.

CHAPTER TWENTY-FOUR

THE BIRD AND BABY

"UTTERLY UNBELIEVABLE," Charles said.

He returned to England from Paris on Monday, and John and Jack arranged for a meeting in Jack's rooms the following Thursday, so that Charles could come up from London and hear the entire incredible story of what had happened to them.

"Unbelievable," Charles repeated, pouring himself a second glass of rum. "I can't decide if I'm more envious that I missed out, or grateful that I didn't have to go through it all myself."

"You did experience it, in a manner of speaking," said John, who was draped comfortably over the back of a chair. "At the end, Chaz had become very much like you."

"That's fascinating," Charles said. "I've been theorizing about the possibility that different worlds, different dimensions, do in fact exist. Changing the timeline is exactly the kind of method that could be used to travel to those other dimensions."

"Thanks anyway," said Jack, "but I think I like this dimension just fine."

"But don't you see?" Charles exclaimed. "You aren't in the same dimension you started from."

Jack sat upright. "What are you talking about, Charles?"

"You may have prevented the Winterland," Charles said matter-of-factly, "but you did in fact alter the past, and with that change, you affected everything that followed.

"All we knew of the original Green Knight was that he was a Crusader," Charles explained, "but in taking Chaz back, who was from a present that wasn't your own, you inserted a new element into a past that was. You also ensured Arthur's rule—but it came about thirty years later than you say it happened in our Histories."

"You can check that for yourself," said John.

"I have," replied Charles, "and the events happened as you told me they did, after your trip. But that's not how I remember reading about them before."

"You're remembering incorrectly, then."

"No," Charles said. "I just remember it *differently*."

"This is all making my skull hurt," said John. "All this talk of multiple dimensions and whatnot. Are you saying you're not, in fact, 'our' Charles?"

"I'm saying," he replied patiently, "that there are an infinite number of worlds, with an infinite number of each of us in them. There are worlds where we never met. There are worlds where we never became Caretakers. And there are worlds where we might have been lesser men than we are. It may even be possible for the traits of a man in one world to be passed to his twin in another, and vice versa. That might account for Chaz's ability to learn languages so swiftly. He wasn't *learning* so much as drawing on the abilities I already have."

"Does that mean you might start assimilating Chaz's mannerisms?" asked Jack. "I don't know how I feel about that."

"I like to think," Charles replied, "I have hope, that in all of those worlds, there would remain in each of us the potential to choose to better ourselves. And isn't knowing that, believing in that, the most important thing?"

John nodded and raised his glass. "To Chaz."

Jack and Charles raised their glasses too. "To Chaz."

"I'd still like to find out," Charles said as he drained his glass, "who sent this to me and started everything."

He moved over to Jack's table, where the Grail book lay, and traced the image on the cover with his fingers. "It's a shock discovering what the true Histories are," he said wryly, "but at the same time, it's comforting to know that fictionalizing our adventures didn't just begin with Bert."

"Geoffrey was quite the tall-tale teller," said Jack. "You'd have had a wonderful time exchanging Grail lies, I'm sure."

"Yes, but Bert did it out of necessity, to protect the Archipelago," said Charles. "Geoffrey seems to have done it just for a lark."

"Speaking of Bert," John said as he checked the time on his watch, "we'd best be hurrying along if we're to be on time meeting with him and Hugo and Rose at the tavern."

"That's right." Jack got to his feet and grabbed his coat. "It's at that new place that Bert discovered, isn't it? What was the name again?" he said, scratching his head. "The Eagle and Child?"

"That's the real name," Charles said as he closed the door behind them. "But everyone who's a regular there just calls it the Bird and Baby."

The fog had settled thickly around Oxford, hanging low and dense in the air. Usually that meant there would be weather—but on this particular Thursday, the Caretakers knew it meant someone needed cover to land an airship.

"I have to say," Jack commented, "the *White Dragon* being an airship instead of a sailing vessel makes it a hell of a lot more versatile. I wonder if any of the other Dragonships would be amenable to making the conversion?"

"I think Ordo Maas went along with Bert's suggestion just to give him a countermeasure to the *Indigo Dragon*," John said, wincing at having mentioned their long-missing stolen ship as he checked his watch again.

"You really like that thing, don't you?" said Charles. "What did Pris say when you told her you'd lost the other one?"

"She started to get upset," John answered, "but I managed to distract her by telling her a story from the new book. She loves the parts with the elves."

"Oh no," a familiar voice moaned. "Not elves. Give me anything but elves!"

"Well met, Hugo," John called as the professor and his adopted niece rounded the corner in front of them. "Hello, Rose."

"Hello, Uncle John," Rose said, kissing him on the cheek. "Hello, Uncle Jack."

"Oh my stars and garters," declared Charles, stunned. "You must be Rose."

"Hello, Uncle Chaz," Rose said as she kissed him.

Charles touched his cheek and blushed. "I, ah, I'm not Chaz, you know."

"It's hard to tell," she said, looking at him appraisingly. "I only met him once, but he is the reason I could come here. In many ways, he was you, and I think, in all the best ways, you are him. I think he was the bravest knight I've ever known."

"So are you an apprentice Caretaker now, Hugo?" Charles asked, trying to change the subject before he blushed again. "Now that you know where all the bodies are buried, so to speak."

Hugo frowned, then raised his eyebrows. "I rather expect I am, at that," he said. "Do I get some sort of certificate or something?"

"Maybe we'll get you a dragon watch," John said, "as long as it's exactly like the one Verne left for me."

"What does it do?" asked Hugo.

"It tells me the time," John replied, "and nothing else."

"Oh, drat," said Hugo.

At the tavern, Hugo and Rose went inside to secure a table in a private room, where the group could talk relatively undisturbed, while the Caretakers went to the back to retrieve the last member of the party.

They waited only a few seconds before the rope ladder dropped down from the ship hidden somewhere above in the fog. "Dratted ladders," Bert grumbled as he climbed down from the very patient *White Dragon*. "We can build a ship that flies but can't manage a way to get off it that doesn't involve self-strangulation."

"We're already a bit late," said John, "but we can spare a few minutes to unwind you, I think."

"Remember," Bert noted, half upside down, "in the end, it's not the years in your life that count. It's the life in your years. Chaucer said that, I think."

The companions laughed and helped their mentor untangle himself from the ropes. Jack was rather less animated than the others and acted as if he didn't want to miss a second of conversation with the Far Traveler, wrapping an arm around his shoulders and marching him to the door of the tavern. Bert went in first, and Jack held the door for the others.

"Chaucer?" said John quizzically. "He must be mistaken. I've never read that quote."

"You know," Charles said to John, holding him back at the door, "it used to really intimidate me how frequently Bert could quote even the most obscure lines from great works of literature."

"Yes," John said with a smirk. "Jack does it too, and for the same reason—to show up his students."

"Well, I found something interesting," Charles offered, taking a small paperback book out of his jacket. "I pinched it out of his hat when he was tangled up in the *White Dragon*'s rope ladder."

"You *pinched* it?" said John. "That settles it. I'm calling you 'Chaz' for the rest of the night."

"Har har har," said Charles. "Take a look at this, John."

The book was called *Great Quotes from the American Presidents,* and it had been marked on nearly every page.

"He's quoting the American presidents?" John said, unsure whether to be shocked or impressed.

"Why not?" said Charles. "Short, pithy, and designed to rouse the troops. And it makes him look smart. But that's not the best part."

"What is?"

"This," Charles said, tapping on the copyright page. "This book won't be published until 1976. And do you remember that quote from Milton we could never find? It wasn't Milton at all—he was quoting a president who ends up getting killed on"—he checked the listing—"November 22, 1963. I wonder if we should find some way to warn him?"

"That he'll be killed, or that Bert is misattributing his quotes?" Jack said wryly, motioning for them to come inside. "After the adventure we've just had, I want as little as possible to do with time travel, and fate, and destiny. And besides, I don't think any man should know the day he's supposed to die—in any reality."

Together the three men entered the Eagle & Child and were shown to the room near the back where they would be assured of as much privacy as was possible in a neighborhood tavern.

"The Rabbit Room, hey?" said Charles as they walked in. "We'll have to tell Tummeler—" He stopped, stunned, as did John and Jack.

At the mantel, gesturing to them with a glass of beer in hand, was a man John had once described as a "wild-eyed gentleman." But that was before they'd met, which was long after the man was supposed to have died. Then again, if nothing else, Sir Richard Burton was resourceful. Maybe the most resourceful man they'd ever met.

Five years earlier, the companions had found him in the Archipelago, where he had done his best to kill them, their friends, and Peter Pan—after which they rescued his daughter, an act which he repaid by stealing their Dragonship.

"Gentle Caretakers," Burton said cheerfully, "come, let us sup together."

Bert, wearing an angry and pained expression, sat at the far side of the long table, and a bewildered Hugo sat across from him. Rose, who was calmer than anyone in the room except perhaps Burton himself, was sitting next to Hugo, eating a cracker.

John, who was behind the other Caretakers, looked around warily. Was this a trap?

Burton laughed and took a seat at the table near the fireplace. "It's no trap, John. Just a friendly meeting of peers. Or," he added a bit more precisely, "respectful adversaries."

"Burton?" Jack exclaimed as he stepped into the room. "What are you doing here, you son of a—"

"Now, Jack," Burton admonished. "Language."

"Where is my ship, Burton?" Bert demanded, barely containing the fury in his voice. "Where is the *Indigo Dragon?*"

"Where she's been all along," Burton replied. "Serving those who serve the true heirs of the Archipelago."

"Who, you?" John spat.

"The Imperial Cartological Society," Burton replied. "Have you forgotten already?"

"The door," said John. "You're responsible for putting the door in the wood along Addison's Walk, aren't you?"

Burton merely smiled and took a long swallow from his glass.

"It didn't do you any good," Jack said. "We sorted it out, as we've always done."

"Whatever you say, Jack."

"You couldn't even entrap one of *us,*" John said. "You tangled up Hugo instead."

Burton hesitated. The mix-up, apparently, had been an obvious flaw in his plan. "It wasn't perfectly executed," he admitted, looking into his empty glass and reaching for a second ale on the table. "I'll tell you straight out, we were hoping to catch—and convert—*you,* Charles."

"Convert me?" Charles exclaimed. "To what?"

"From your belief and support of the wrong heir," Burton replied. "We at the society know the Histories as well as you. After all, we were all Caretakers too . . .

". . . *almost.*"

"You wanted Mordred to win!" John said incredulously. "Why, Burton?"

"You've been through the Histories," he shot back. "You know what Myrddyn became, who he really is. He's the one who set the path for all the Caretakers. Can you really tell me that is a man you would risk your lives for?"

"Yes," John said evenly. "I can."

"If you'd wanted to convince us the Cartographer was evil," said Jack, "you shouldn't have tried stealing the Grail book. It was one of your people who tore out the pages, wasn't it?"

Burton actually reddened. "Yes, well, some members of the society are being disciplined for that. When they tried to retrieve it, Monmouth surprised them, and one of them dropped it, tearing the pages. He could only bring back that part he'd torn. The fool."

"Harry," said Bert. "You must mean Harry Houdini. He always was a butterfingers. Good for locks, not for espionage."

"Was he the one who put the door in the wood?" asked John.

"He and Conan Doyle," said Burton. "We hoped you'd go through and see what was taking place at Camelot—that Mordred had become a villain only because Arthur and Merlin made him so. We didn't anticipate that you would be foolish enough to close the door. How *did* you get back, anyway?"

"That's a Caretaker secret," Jack replied, knowing the answer, believed or not, would make Burton seethe.

"If you just wanted to make Mordred's case," said John, "why did you need a door from the Keep?"

"To put you in the position to see for yourselves," explained Burton. "So you could see who Mordred and Merlin really were, and which was more noble."

"You didn't benefit," John stated flatly. "All that effort, and nothing came of it."

Burton tipped back the second ale and drained the glass in a swallow. "Oh, I wouldn't say that." He wiped his mouth on his sleeve. "We learned from our mistakes. And we may have found something that I once thought was lost. And it was in our hands the entire time."

"And you nearly caused the destruction of the world!" Hugo exclaimed. "Why, the Winterland that Mordred created—"

"Hugo, please," Jack said, squeezing his shoulders sharply. Hugo realized too late what he'd revealed—Burton had no idea what had been caused by the changes in time, because the Caretakers had managed to repair most of the damage.

Burton smiled. "I think I understand," he said, rising. "And now it's time I take my leave of you. This has been entertaining, but as usual, you Caretakers ask all the wrong questions."

"How can the questions be wrong?" asked Charles.

"You focus entirely on the past, on filling in the holes in events that have already happened," Burton answered. "You are obsessed with what was and miss entirely what is. And that is why we shall control the future."

"What questions?" Charles insisted. "What haven't we asked?"

"All right," Burton said. "Since it is just the six of us in here, all men of learning, I'll give you a lesson you haven't earned.

"You ask why the door was in the wood—but not how we got it, or if there are others like it. You ask why we might want to convert Charles to our cause, without asking what our intentions are in doing so. And you have traveled in time and made choices based on what you experienced in the past—while ignoring the most important revelation of all . . .

". . . that time moves in *two* directions."

Burton took his hat and coat from the rack and bowed. "Farewell, Caretakers," he said, smiling. "Settle my bill, will you?" And with that, he walked out of the tavern and vanished.

"I wasn't pleased to see him," said John, "but at least we know. We know why this happened."

"Was that really Richard Burton?" asked Hugo. "He's charming, but he smells."

Bert scratched his head. "There was something else," he mused. "Something very, very interesting. I don't think he was able to even see Rose. Not at all."

"What would that mean?" said Jack. "How could he not see her?"

"It could be her unique bloodlines, or perhaps the fact she might be from an alternate dimension," said Bert. "At any rate, it's worth discussing with Jules, and it's about time you met him anyway. This latest escapade proves that. We need to accelerate our plans. Soon. Very soon."

None of the companions broached the topic again to ask what Bert meant by this, and Hugo and Rose seemed to be more interested in ordering dinner than in more debates about Archipelago business.

They ordered some food, and more drinks (noting that Burton had left a sizeable tab), and ruminated on what had happened just a few days earlier. One thing was clear—their adversaries were more aware of them than they had been. And they'd been much more active. And that would have to change, John promised himself. It was no longer good enough to simply react.

"So everything Burton did was predicated on the belief Charles would be walking in the park with us Saturday night?" said Jack. "What a stroke of luck that you were detained in Paris!"

"Not luck, but Jules Verne," said Bert, "and the power of cause and effect." He turned to Charles. "Jules deliberately had you detained so that you wouldn't be at risk, then sent the Grail book to Jack."

"But Hugo's warning was incomplete," Jack stammered. "How did that help anything? Why couldn't Jules simply warn us outright?"

"Cause and effect," Bert repeated. "By the time he stopped Charles, he discovered Hugo *had* to go, and in fact, had already *gone*."

"This is very confusing," said Hugo.

Bert nodded in understanding. "It gets worse. He got the first inklings of what was going on when Hank Morgan showed up at Sam Clemens's house carrying the dragon watch. He told us where and when you were, and Jules began to prepare the room on Sanctuary with the Lanterna Magica. Jules arranged for Pellinor—who was meant to be the first Green Knight, incidentally—to be at the river where Hugo would appear, and persuaded him to take you to Camelot by promising him a chance to battle his 'Questing Beast.' You botched that up, Hugo, when you stabbed Merlin.

Our concerns were realized and verified later, when Hank sent us a message that he'd indeed met Hugo Dyson."

"That was the message you got fourteen years ago, when you came back to London to find us," said Jack. "But you—the you in Albion—told us that you'd been trapped there and had to wait for us. How is it you're here now ali—unharmed and whole?"

"That was the risk we took," said Bert, "that you would change what had happened. And you did."

"I'd like to meet Verne for one reason more than any other," put in Jack.

"What's that?" said Bert.

"I want to show him his own skull," Jack said as he took a drink of ale. "It's on the desk in my study."

"It just occurred to me," John said. "Did anyone ever get Pellinor out of the tree?"

Bert pulled a copy of the Little Whatsit out of his bag and thumbed through to one of the back pages. "Ah, no," he replied with a smirk. "They didn't."

"We're going to need to spend some time at the Great Whatsit on Paralon," said Jack. "We have a lot of history that we'll have to unlearn, beginning with the chronicles of Arthur, as the Cartographer was suggesting. We need to know what's changed as a result of this little adventure, and what hasn't."

"Jules has already begun tracking the changes," said Bert. "There have been some discrepancies found here and there in the Histories. One in particular came to our attention fourteen years ago, as Jules began keeping a Chronologue of the various jaunts through time."

"Discrepancies?" said John. "With what?"

"Oh, nothing attached to you, dear boy," Bert said, turning to Jack with a Cheshire grin. "But you, lad, are another matter entirely."

"Me?" Jack exclaimed. "I'm sure I don't know what you mean."

"Then how do you explain the apparently nonfictional, absolutely true, two-thousand-year-old tale that begat the story of Jack the Giant Killer?"

"Oh, for heaven's sake," said Jack. "Not all stories are true, are they? Not all of them really happened." He paused. "Or did they?"

"Time will tell, my boy," said Bert. "Time will tell."

EPILOGUE

CHANCELLOR MURDOCH *entered the small room where the leaders of the world had gathered together to plan and play their little wars.*

The meeting proceeded as he had expected it to; each proposal was met with open enthusiasm and fully proffered support. It would be, he realized, the easiest conquest he'd ever planned, and the most successful, because it would be his last. When this was done, there would be no players on the board but himself.

The rallying offensives of the past year had made his allies arrogant, especially the American president. He was the weakest of them physically, but he commanded the same sort of loyalty as others he had known in the distant past. And he was heading for the same great fall.

If they had not been so concerned with the plans for the war itself, and so enthralled by any credible promise of an added advantage over their enemies, they might have noticed the gentle whirring sounds that the chancellor emitted as he spoke, or the slightly mechanical nature of his movements. But they had not, and so when they left the room, no one looked back at their strange new ally, for if they had, they might have noticed that his shadow had a will of its own and moved of its own accord.

Of course, none among them would have known that it was the shadow that provided the motive power to the Clockwork Man that had been created by talking animals and a man called Nemo, and in another world had been known as the Red King. And if any of them had suspected, they did not care. All that mattered was that he had brought them the weapon that would see them to victory, when the time was right.

It was ironic, he thought. To have sought the weapon once called the Lance of Longinus for so many years, only to discover that it had been in the possession of the Green Knight. Most if not all of their long line, especially the first, would not have entertained the thought of giving it up to one such as he, even if they had been unaware of his plans for it. But the last, Magwich, had been his own servant, and he gave it up for the asking. It had taken time, but the world was once again in flux, and he would have the chance to prove his worth.

And time, the chancellor thought to himself as he cradled the Spear of Destiny in his hands once more, was what it was all about. Time, and how to use it. Because once that question was answered . . .

. . . he would rule the world.

Author's Note

In many ways, the chance to tell the story I created in *The Indigo King* is the reason the Chronicles of the Imaginarium Geographica exist. The heart of it is a very real event that took place on an evening in September 1931, when J. R. R. Tolkien, C. S. Lewis, and Hugo Dyson took a stroll on the grounds around Magdalen College, and discussed the story behind Christianity in the context of its meaning as a mythology rather than a religion.

Lewis had been if not a complete atheist, then something very close to it for most of his life, and although he had finally decided that there was "a" god, he could not wrap his head around the literal truth of the Christian mythology espoused by his friends.

Until that one night.

They walked, and talked, and as Lewis later wrote to his friend Arthur Greeves, "I have just passed on from believing in God to definitely believing in Christ—in Christianity. I will try to explain this another time. My long night talk with Dyson and Tolkien had a good deal to do with it."

Considering how influential Lewis became as an advocate of Christianity, the chance to imagine possible events for my fictional Jack to experience, that might thematically fold into the real events of his life, was too good to resist.

I had a great starting point for the book with the most-asked question about the other books: Who is the Cartographer? I knew

I wanted to tell his complete story, and I'd been careful about dropping hints in the other books. I also wanted to bring my history of the Archipelago into sharper focus, tying it as I have to Odysseus and the Trojan War.

We'd already established connections to Arthurian lore with the lineage of the Silver Throne—but I wanted to go back as far as I could, and it thrilled me beyond words to establish an origin and a pedigree for Arthur's sword, Caliburn. And once I got into it, I decided that I wanted to mess with the conventions of the tales everyone knows.

There are fathers and sons, and nephews and uncles, but they are not who you expect them to be. And the difference between good and evil is not always clear. Sometimes good people make bad choices, and vice versa. And that makes it harder to praise—or condemn them.

The history of the Cartographer is in many ways the history of cartography itself; and the history of the Caretakers is the history of the world. Geoffrey of Monmouth was the first great Arthurian scribe and the first "real" Caretaker. His Green Knight, Abelard, was a contemporary that suited the role I put him in.

As to Chaz, I wanted a way to address Charles Williams's very influential works, which had a great effect on Lewis in particular but are much less well known than either of his friends' tales. His theories of many dimensions gave me a means to create a "what if" story inside my own book.

And as for Hank Morgan, he was the first real time-traveling character from Mark Twain's *A Connecticut Yankee in King Arthur's Court*, and since I'd already earmarked Twain as Jules Verne's predecessor, Hank fit in nicely in several ways.

As to some of the other characters, Reynard the fox was a minor player in Sir Gawain and the Green Knight; Gwynhfar is, obviously, a nod to Arthur while giving me my Holy Grail connection; and as for Rose . . . Well, as Bert said, only time will tell.

James A. Owen
Silvertown, USA

THE SHADOW DRAGONS

PROLOGUE

IT MIGHT BE *said that a mystery is simply a secret to which no one knows the answer. The answers to some mysteries may have been known, once, and then were lost as the centuries passed. But there are other secrets that are so ancient that the truth of them is impossible to discover, and they must forever remain mysteries.*

No one living or dead knew the identity of the Architect of the Keep of Time.

Before Atlantis, before Ur, before any stone of any city was erected upon the Earth in the Summer Country or in the Archipelago of Dreams, the keep had stood.

The Earth was a wilder place in those early days, before the rise of man. Magic and myth mingled freely with history as all manner of creatures tried to make sense of the world around them. Some were more advanced than others, and they took it upon themselves to shape, and to organize, and to look after the welfare of the races that were developing on this young world.

Theirs was the first city, built when there was no division between the worlds, and no need for one. Their sense of wonder was unlimited, for they had no understanding at all of fear. All they knew was discovery, and challenge, and how to overcome. And so they continued to build and to explore and to expand their knowledge.

These creatures soon took note of the keep and realized that it was an anchor against the tides of time that otherwise might have ripped the world asunder. Why it was built, and who had built it, they did not know. But they chose to guard it, and they knew they could learn from it and use it to create a better world.

One among them, the eldest, discovered how to harness the flow of time by fashioning doors and fitting them into the openings that appeared throughout the ever-growing tower. This discovery came none too soon, for a new element had come into the world that threatened the destruction of all that was.

In the guise of a seeker of knowledge from the future, evil had come to their world—and slowly but surely, it was becoming stronger. In time, it would be too strong to resist.

A great council was held among the guardians of the keep to determine how they might avoid the cataclysm that seemed so inevitable, and again, it was the eldest among them who discovered the solution—but it would not be a solution without sacrifice.

Their beloved city would not survive. It would fall. And they themselves would have to accept a new calling—promotions to a new rank that would be permanent, because they would never again be able to lower their guard if the world itself was to survive.

The eldest was first to take the mantle of this new responsibility, then in turn, each of his companions, until all of them had done so. And then each of them chose a door.

To protect the future, they realized that they must also protect the past—and so one by one, they entered the doors of the Keep of Time, until there was no point in the past that did not have, somewhere behind it, its guardian.

The last of them remained behind, watching, waiting, until one among the new races could produce a king worthy of becoming a guardian himself. Only then could he rest, and lay down the seemingly eternal burden.

The world did change; empires rose and fell. Only the keep remained as it was. The great mystery of the Architect's identity might never see an answer; and the secrets of the keep that were known were closely held.

But even so, only two things were sure: first, that to walk through a door was to cross over from the present to some point in the past; and second, that somewhere on the other side, there would be a Dragon.

PART ONE

INKLINGS AND MYSTERIES

CHAPTER ONE
RANSOM

"WE ARE DEFINITELY LOST," John said with decisive authority. "I haven't the faintest idea where we are."

"How can you be lost?" his friend Jack asked with a barely concealed grin. "You're the Principal Caretaker of the *Imaginarium Geographica*. You're probably the foremost authority on maps in the entire world. How is it you've managed to get us lost not two hours' walk from Oxford?"

"I wasn't paying attention," John said irritably. "I was enjoying the conversation and the company. After all, this is the first time in almost twenty years that the three of us have been able to come together as friends out in the open. I like secret societies as much as the next man, but actually having Charles participate as a formal member of the Inklings is going to be delightful."

"Agreed," said Jack, clapping Charles on the back. "The ability to share things with Hugo has been a blessing, but I've been itching to discuss your work at length with Arthur Greeves and Owen Barfield."

"It was fortuitous that Greeves sent you a copy of my new book," Charles agreed, "at the same time that you sent your own to the Oxford University Press. It was just the sort of coincidental happening that's interesting enough to sound truthful."

"That's because it *is* true," Jack insisted, "and all the more significant for it. Although we're going to have to work on our timing for these private walkabouts—I had to bow out of a walking tour with Barfield and Cecil Harwood to come out today."

"And I suppose *you* never get lost?" John said, raising a skeptical eyebrow.

Jack made a dismissive motion with his hands. "Never," he said primly. "We always bring a map, and I am, after all, the best map reader. Honestly, it's a mystery to me why I wasn't made the Caretaker Principia in your place."

John laughed. "I'll gladly give you the job right now," he said, pretending to remove his pack as Jack whistled and looked the other way, pretending to ignore him, "unless we can find someone better qualified, like a badger or a faun."

"I think you're both looney," said Charles, "and it's starting to rain."

They all looked up at the overcast sky, and as one, had the same thought. It had been raining on the night they first met in London—the night their lives were irrevocably changed.

It had been nearly two decades since the three men were brought together at the scene of a terrible crime. John's mentor, a professor of ancient literature named Stellan Sigurdsson, had been killed by a man called the Winter King, who was searching for the book known as the *Imaginarium Geographica*. John was being trained to become the next Caretaker of the great book, and Jack and Charles, as much through circumstance as by design, became Caretakers as well. With the help of another Caretaker called Bert, who became their trusted mentor, they managed to keep the Winter King from using the book to conquer the

Archipelago of Dreams, the great chain of islands for which the atlas was the only guide—but at great cost. Friends and allies were lost, hard lessons were learned; and even then, their nemesis returned again and again like a persistent nightmare at the edge of the waking world.

At the end of their first conflict, a great Dragon called Samaranth had dropped the Winter King over the edge of an endless waterfall. But nine years after that adventure, the three companions returned to the Archipelago to search for the great Dragonships that had vanished—along with all the children—only to discover that his Shadow had survived and was as deadly as the real Winter King himself.

Five years after that, they found themselves drawn into yet another crisis, when rogue Caretakers who had allied themselves with the Winter King tricked their friend Hugo Dyson into going through a door to the past—where he changed history itself.

Only by traveling through the events of two millennia and discovering the identity of the Cartographer of Lost Places, who created the *Geographica*, were they at last able to set things right. But what they discovered was disturbing: The Cartographer, who was once Merlin, was in large part responsible for the Winter King—his twin, Mordred—becoming the twisted, evil man he was. And the Caretakers would not have succeeded at all without the help of a young girl, Mordred's daughter Rose, also called the Grail Child, who returned with them to the present as Hugo's niece.

That was five years ago, and other than a few flurries that necessitated the counsel of the Caretakers—usually just John—there had been no reason to return to the Archipelago. The rogue Caretakers, led by the adventurer Richard Burton, had remained hidden, and there was no sign of the Winter King's Shadow. There were still difficult problems to deal with: The Keep of Time, where the Cartographer resided, had been crumbling apart since their first trip to the Archipelago; and the king, Artus, had tried to replace the monarchy with a republic, to only limited success. But the years of the Great War were far behind them, and all was right enough with the worlds here and beyond to set aside duty and responsibilities for a few hours to better enjoy a pleasant spring walk in the English countryside.

"It's a shame that Hugo could not join us," Jack said. "We've had too few occasions as of late to catch up with him."

"Uncle Hugo wanted to be here," came a voice from somewhere above them, "but he had some obligations to attend to in Reading that could not be delegated elsewhere. He sent me along anyway, because he knew you needed to discuss the Problem."

Rose Dyson dropped down from the birch tree she'd been climbing and dusted herself off, then moved to stand next to Jack.

The "Problem" she referred to was evident to all three Caretakers. When she returned with them to the present from the sixth century, she was barely an adolescent. Tall, perhaps, but the auburn-haired Rose was still obviously a child—and that was, as Hugo put it, the "Problem."

He had placed her in a boardinghouse near his teaching post in Reading, where she was enrolled in school as his niece. And over the course of five years, she had not visibly aged a day.

"It's a natural law without a demonstrable basis," Bert had told them once. "Denizens of the Archipelago age more slowly than we do in the Summer Country. Days and nights are the same as those here, but they're often out of sync."

This much they had witnessed for themselves on numerous occasions. Night in Oxford turned to day upon crossing the Frontier, and vice versa. And once, even the seasons had been reversed: Jack had traveled from Oxford in late summer, only to find the Archipelago in the grip of a terrible winter. So it wasn't just a matter of slight temporal differences—there were rules of time at work between the worlds that no one had as yet been able to decipher.

"Is the fact that she was born there, and brought here, the reason she hasn't aged?" Jack proposed.

"Not necessarily," offered Charles. "She hadn't aged normally on Avalon, either. But given her peculiar lineage, there may be no precedent for the kind of person she'll become."

"I'm a conundrum," Rose said from a few feet up the path, where she was using a branch to lever up a large stone. "Or an enigma. I forget which."

John nodded in agreement. "That's for certain. I've been thinking of contacting Aven and Artus about continuing her schooling on Paralon. At least there she'll not be questioned, no matter her age."

"Plus, she's family," said Jack. "She and Arthur were cousins, so that would make her an aunt, or second cousin, or some such."

"Twenty generations removed," added Charles.

"All of which doesn't change the fact that you've managed to get yourselves lost," came an irritated voice from above. "Of course, I know exactly where we are."

John rolled his eyes. "Of course," he said drolly, looking sideways at the others. "Having him up there is like having a conscience that won't shut up and won't take suggestions."

Complicating matters further was the other teacher the companions had brought forward from the past as a companion for Rose—the great owl Archimedes. That he was in fact a clockwork construct was the least of the problems he caused Hugo Dyson in Reading. He wasn't a predator; he wasn't dangerous; but he was irredeemably sarcastic and wickedly smart—and more than one local had been surprised by an encounter with a talking owl that could insult them while spouting jokes about Plato's Cave.

Archimedes, called Archie for short, stayed in Hugo's rooms, mostly—but it was inevitable that he and Rose would be seen together, and a talking owl combined with a girl who wasn't getting older was a recipe for disaster.

A month earlier they had transported the bird to the Kilns, the residence near Oxford that Jack shared with his brother Warnie and adopted mother Mrs. Moore. Warnie had already been initiated into some of the mysteries of the Caretakers, but it was a more delicate process with Mrs. Moore. However, once she recovered from the initial shock, and once she had accepted the need for secrecy, she and the owl became affable companions. Archie apparently got on very well with females.

Warnie was another matter entirely. The first hour they met, he had made a sudden move that startled the bird, and Archie bit his arm. It left a nasty welt, and thereafter Warnie persisted in referring to the bird as "Lucifer," which didn't endear him to the owl once Jack had explained the reference. The pairing made for a very lively household.

Moving Rose to the Kilns was a second option—but again, they would be risking the same kind of exposure there as they had in Reading. And keeping all knowledge of the *Geographica*, the

Archipelago, and the denizens within a secret was the prime rule of the Caretakers—the very rule that caused Burton and others to rebel. There would be no easy answers—which was why it was important for all three Caretakers to discuss the move as soon as they were able.

Archimedes lit atop a shrub next to where Rose was digging a hole and cast a disdainful eye at John. "Don't you have the atlas with you, Caretaker Principia?" the bird asked. "Isn't it full of maps?"

"Yes, I have it, and yes, it is," John said irritably. "But I don't have any maps of England in it."

The owl hooted in derision. "Only a scholar would go on a hike with a book of maps that are of absolutely no use."

"It's immensely useful!" John shot back. "Just, ah, just not here and now."

It was not all that unusual for a professor to carry books with him wherever he went—even on a walkabout holiday such as this one—so John simply carried the *Imaginarium Geographica* around with him. Too many times in the past circumstances had called for its use, and through misfortune, or lack of preparation, he had found himself without it.

Even after the badger Tummeler had begun publishing an abridged and annotated edition in the Archipelago, and copies were freely available, John still preferred to keep a light hand on the actual atlas. It was impossibly old, and had been written in by some of the greatest creative minds in human history. There were notations that were to be read only by the Caretakers or their apprentices, and so were not available to Tummeler. And there were maps that were left out of the popular edition because the little mammal saw them as unimportant.

What Tummeler didn't realize was that it was often those out-of-the-way places where the turning points of history occurred, in the same way that the men and women who changed the world were not always the ones who seemed to have the power to do so. No one understood this principle quite so well as two professors from Oxford and their editor friend from London.

The owl launched himself back into the air as a stone tumbled into the hole Rose had been digging.

"There," she said, dusting her hands. "That's much better."

"What's better?" Charles asked.

"The stone," Rose replied. "It was in the wrong place. I put it back."

John and Jack blinked at each other in consternation. They couldn't decide if the girl was too simple or too complex to really understand.

"Are you certain he's not going to, ah, rust?" Charles said, casting a glance upward at the bird circling overhead. "Hugo would be quite put out if something befell the owl."

"He hasn't rusted so far," said Jack, looking around the small clearing, "but we're going to be soaked to the skin if we don't find a place to bed down for the evening. We'd best be going, and quickly. It's getting dark."

"Any suggestions?" said John.

Jack indicated a faint footpath to the northwest, which veered off the main walking trail. "There's a faint glow coming from over there. With any luck, it's an inn—or at least a farmhouse where we can get directions and our bearings."

There was indeed a light emanating from somewhere behind a grove of trees. The roadway must have been on the other side, as the path was sparse enough that it could not have seen many travelers. Nevertheless, the companions followed Jack's lead and pressed their way through the trees.

As they walked, the path opened up into a proper road which crossed another going east-west, and there, at the junction, stood the source of the light—a tall streetlamp, which looked as if it had been plucked out of Oxford and dropped here in the countryside.

Underneath it, dressed in a battered topcoat, a man was standing as if he were waiting for a bus, or unwary passersby. Moving closer, John was startled to realize that he recognized him. Or at least, he thought he did.

Jack had the same flash of memory, and both looked back to note that Charles was right behind them.

At first glance, it looked as if Charles—*another* Charles—was standing at the crossroads, waiting for them. The man was tall and had Charles's bearing—but as they walked closer, it was apparent that he was a stranger to them. The three men and the girl nodded politely and began to move past, taking the path to the right and away from the lamp's comforting glow.

"Pardon me," the man said, raising a hand in greeting, "but do you have the time?"

"What?" said John. "Oh, uh, yes, of course," and he turned, pulling his watch from his vest pocket. It was a distinctive sort of watch: silver, untarnished, with a red Chinese dragon on the cover. "It's half past five," he said, snapping the watch closed, "or half past drenched, depending on your point of view."

"Mmm," the stranger mused. "Well put, John. But actually, I also need to know the year, if you don't mind."

At the mention of John's name, he and the others froze in

place. Had the man merely overheard them talking? Had one of them uttered John's name? Or was something more sinister afoot?

"Why do you need to know the year?" John asked cautiously, as Jack and Charles moved protectively closer to Rose.

"Because," replied the man stiffly, "I've come a long way, and I seem to have lost track."

"Lost track of the years?" Charles exclaimed. "If you don't even know what year it is, should you be out and about in the woods all alone?"

"Actually," the man replied, "I came here to protect you, Charles. The year, if you please?"

"It's 1936," said Jack. "April, if you couldn't tell."

The man surprised them by slumping against the waypost in obvious relief. "Thank God," he said, running a hand across his head. "1936. Then I've not arrived too late after all."

"What year did you think it was?" asked John. "And pardon my asking, but how is it that you know our names? Have we met, perchance?"

"You are the Caretakers of the *Imaginarium Geographica*, are you not?" the man replied. "Let's just say we are in service of the same causes. And I was fully expecting to arrive here in 1943."

"You were expecting to arrive in the future?" said Charles. "That's not really possible, is it? I mean, not unless the circumstances are extraordinary."

"You've been in such a circumstance, I believe," the man said. "And it wasn't the future I was aiming for, but the past. I just seem to have overshot my mark, to our benefit, I hope."

John and Jack exchanged worried glances. The man knew enough to be dangerous to them—but he had so far done nothing more than talk while leaning against the post. And he did say he was there to help them.

"Forgive our hesitation," John said mildly, "but we've heard credible stories of every stripe and color from the best of them. How are we to know you are indeed on, ah, our side, so to speak?"

In answer, the man reached into his pocket and pulled out a silver pocket watch. On the back was the clear image of a red dragon. It was identical to the watch John had just pulled from his own pocket. "It was given to me by Jules Verne," the man said, "as, I suspect, he gave yours to you."

"Good enough," John said as he and the stranger compared timepieces. "I've only ever seen one other like it."

"That would probably be Hank Morgan's," said the man. "His is used a bit more frequently, I'm afraid."

"So are you also a time traveler?" asked John.

"Not so much a traveler in time, as in space," the man said, "although thanks to the watch, I have the ability to do so when the need is dire. My mentor has a different set of goals for me than he had for Hank."

"Verne," said Charles. "So he's the one who sent you?"

"Indeed," the man replied. He pulled at his collar and looked around. "We should find a place more suitable to talk, unless you have an objection."

"That was our plan anyway," Jack said, offering his hand. "Do you have some place in mind?"

"I do," said the stranger, shaking Jack's hand, then John's

and Charles's in turn. To Rose he gave only a long, appraising glance.

"You know all of us," Charles said amicably, "but you've not yet introduced yourself."

"Ransom," the man said as he turned and began leading them down the path to the left. "My name is Alvin Ransom."

CHAPTER TWO
THE INN OF THE FLYING DRAGON

"I'M A GREAT admirer of all your works," Ransom said as they walked briskly along, "especially your latest, John. That book about the little fellows with the hairy feet, and wizards, and whatnot. I particularly liked the part where the giants turned into stone. Very moving."

"Actually, those were trolls," John said. "And . . ." He stopped walking. "Hang on there," he exclaimed. "How could you have read that? I haven't even finished that book yet—and I've barely touched it in years!"

Ransom slapped his forehead. "Apologies, my good fellow. I forgot it's not due to be published until next year. That's what I get for trying to curry favor with you by coming up with compliments."

"Oh," said John. "So, ah, you didn't really like it after all?"

"I haven't finished it," Ransom admitted. "But it is on my nightstand, and I fully intend to, as soon as I have the opportunity."

"What is your profession, Mr. Ransom, if I may ask?" said Charles.

"I'm a philologist," he answered evenly, "at the University of Cambridge."

"A philologist?" said John. "Really? A languages specialist? How odd that we haven't met before."

"Not particularly," said Ransom. "The Cambridge that I come from isn't the Cambridge you're familiar with."

"Different country?" asked Jack.

"Different dimension," replied Ransom.

"That sounds *exactly* like Cambridge," said Charles.

"Bert has alluded to the concept of different dimensions once or twice," John said, "but we never got into specifics. Charles is our resident expert in that particular field."

Charles beamed with pleasure at the compliment. "I've actually devoted quite a bit of attention to the topic," he said brightly, "even wrote a book about it."

"I know," Ransom replied, his voice suddenly somber with respect. "It's one of our most important theses on the subject of multidimensionality."

Charles blinked at him. "It was, ah, a work of fiction, actually."

Now it was Ransom's turn to be surprised. He started to make a comment, then paused, his expression softening. "I keep forgetting what year I've come to," he said mildly. "There are things I take for granted that you won't actually know about for a few years yet, God willing."

Jack and John exchanged a glance of concern. God willing? Just what was that supposed to mean? That they wouldn't discover the knowledge Ransom referred to too soon, or that they might not have the opportunity at all?

"You seem to know a great deal more about us than we know about you," Jack said. "I don't know how comfortable I am with that discrepancy."

"That's one reason my Anabasis Machine—I mean, my pocket watch—was fashioned in the manner it was," said Ransom. "There are too many double agents afoot in the lands, and too many allegiances built on the sand. It's difficult to know whom to trust—and so Verne made certain to give those of us who are loyal to the Caretakers' trust an unmistakable symbol."

"A silver pocket watch," John asserted, "with a depiction of Samaranth on the casing."

Ransom nodded. "Exactly."

"Couldn't that be easily duplicated, though?" Charles opined. "I mean, it's a very nice watch, but there are a hundred watchmakers in London who could make a replica in a day."

Ransom almost stumbled as he spun about to frown at Charles. "Haven't you realized by now just how deep a game Verne, and Bert, and the others are playing?" he said with some astonishment. "When the Dyson incident occurred, didn't you think it significant that Verne had already prepared for the eventuality by arranging the Lanterna Magica for you to find, fifteen centuries before it was needed?

"These are the people who *invented* the idea of a secret society," Ransom continued, "so of course there would be safeguards." He snapped open his watch. "The first is the engraved inscription."

Jack and Charles moved closer to peer at the watch cover, which bore two words: *Apprentice Caretaker,* and the Greek letter *omega.*

"Only the Caretakers themselves, their apprentices, and those like myself who have been recruited to the cause know that Bert chose that letter as the Caretaker's mark," said Ransom. "That's the first safeguard."

"And the second?" asked Jack.

Ransom glanced at him in surprise before grinning broadly and turning to resume walking down the path. "I'm surprised that you don't know, considering you are one of the actual Caretakers," he said with a trace of amused smugness, "but then again, the use of the watches and the safeguards didn't really become critical until nearly 1938."

He looked over his other shoulder at John and tipped his chin. "But *you* know, don't you?"

John glanced around to make certain they were alone, then rolled his eyes heavenward. Of course they were alone. They were lost in the English woods following someone from another dimension. If there were anyone lurking about to hear them, it would have to be a stroke of remarkable luck and accidental timing.

"Yes," he said quietly, arching an eyebrow at Ransom. "Bert told me just a few months ago. 'Believing is seeing.'"

"Believe," the philologist replied.

"That's it?" said Charles. "That's a bit simple for a secret code."

"Simplicity is best in cooking, personal combat, and secret codes," said Ransom. "And that statement and response are both more simple and infinitely more complex than you can possibly imagine."

"I can imagine a great deal," Charles huffed.

"Oh, I meant no offense," Ransom said quickly. "That was just a turn of phrase. Of the three of you—"

"Four of us," said John, nodding his head deferentially toward Rose, who smiled.

"Five," came a voice from somewhere above them in the gloom. "Couldn't count in Alexandria, can't count now. Some scholar you turned out to be."

"Sorry," Ransom said, peering up at the owl that circled overhead. "Uh, sorry," he repeated to Rose, with slightly less enthusiasm.

"As I was saying," he continued, "of all of you here, Charles is the one most likely to be able to comprehend what we're about to do. Because, strictly speaking, the place I'm taking you to isn't *in* our dimension."

Without explaining further, Ransom removed a small leather case from inside his coat. It was thick, and about as tall and broad as two decks of playing cards placed side by side. He untied the binding, and inside the companions could see a sheaf of thick, handmade paper with scrawled notes and sketches.

"These pages are for practice," Ransom said as he removed a dozen loose cards from the back of the case, "but these are the real cat's pajamas."

The cards were yellowed with age, and more akin to parchment than paper. Most of the sheets had intricate, nearly photographic drawings on them; only the last few were blank. All of them bore a remarkable pattern on the reverse side: an interweaving series of lines that formed an elaborate labyrinth, at the center of which was the symbol for eternity. Along the borders were symbols of a more familiar nature.

"Elizabethan?" asked John. "These appear to be some kind of . . . I don't know. Royal stationery?"

Ransom smirked. "That's a closer guess than you realize, John," he said, nodding. "Queen Elizabeth commissioned them, but hers was certainly not the hand that made them."

"John Dee," Charles intoned, drawing in a breath. "It had to have been Dee. We know he was an early Caretaker, but his books are missing from the official Histories, and Bert will not speak of him."

Ransom nodded again. "One of the dark secrets of the Caretakers," he said somberly. "Burton was not the only one of your order to betray his oaths of secrecy."

Before the companions could inquire further into what that meant, Ransom fanned the cards out in his hand. "As the Anabasis Machines—the pocket watches—can be used to travel in time, so can these cards be used to travel in space.

"We don't know enough about time travel to do more than journey to what Verne called 'zero points,'" the philologist continued. "We can make educated guesses, but anything outside the zero points is basically gambling without seeing our own hand of cards, so to speak."

"That's how you miss a target date by seven years," said Jack.

"Yes," said Ransom, "although seven isn't bad. If you have the chance, you should ask Hank Morgan about the time he tried jumping to 1905 and accidentally ended up becoming the sixteenth-century Indian emperor Akbar the Great."

"You mean *meeting* the emperor?" asked John.

"No," said Ransom. "*Becoming* the emperor. Like I said, it's a really good tale to dine out on."

"So I'm inferring from what you've said that these cards allow for a bit more precision?" asked Charles.

"Exactly. We actually call them 'Trumps' in honor of your book, Charles," said Ransom. "Dee made them as some kind of literal otherworldly tarot—at least, that's what Verne believes. Only a hundred of the original sheets were discovered intact, and we realized their usefulness when Verne found two with drawings on them."

"And what are they used for?" said Jack.

"Simply put, they are used to travel between places," Ransom replied. "Whatever place is drawn on a Trump can be traveled to."

"Without limitation?" asked Charles.

"As far as we know," said Ransom. "Distance is no barrier, and neither is the ether that separates dimensions. In fact, the only limitation we know of is the number of blank Trumps that can be drawn on. We don't know the process Dee used to make them, and so Verne parceled out the ones we did have with a stern instruction to use them sparingly. Of the dozen given to me, I made nine that I use most frequently, and have three that can be created in case of grave emergency."

"Nine, ah, portals isn't very many," said John. "It seems like a much bigger limitation than you imply."

"Not so," said Ransom. "Verne recruited several agents like myself, and we all have at least six Trumps that are completely unique. The other three are points of conjunction, where we may meet up and then travel together when necessary. They can also be used to communicate—although that risks detection, so we try to do so sparingly."

"Does Hank Morgan have a set?" asked John. "That would explain how he was able to send messages to Jules Verne when we were stuck in the past with Hugo."

"Well deduced, John," Ransom said with a smile of approval. "He does indeed, although we had not worked out all the mechanics of using them at that point."

"Wait a moment," said Jack, confused. "If Hank had these Trumps with him in Camelot, why didn't he just use them to get us out of there as soon as he realized who we were?"

"Two reasons," said Ransom, with slightly less approval. "First, if he had been able to use them to take you out of Camelot, it would not have helped your situation. Trumps don't traverse time, only space. So you'd still have been in the sixth century—just somewhere less useful."

"I'm betting the second reason has to do with time travel," said Charles. "There was already enough damage done by them just being there, and events had to take the proper course to be repaired. Am I right?"

"Eminently so," Ransom replied. He selected one of the cards, then replaced the others in the book, which he put back in his coat. "Everyone, now, if you please—stand behind me and give your attention to the card."

Archimedes dropped down from one of the beech trees and landed lightly on Charles's shoulder. Rose, Jack, John, and Charles moved behind Ransom and stared at the card he held in front of them.

It depicted a cozy-looking, multigabled tavern set in a wood exactly like the one that surrounded the crossroads just ahead of them. At arm's length, the drawing was nearly photographic in nature, so real and precise that it almost seemed to . . .

"Oh!" Rose exclaimed, startled and delighted at once. "The flames in the lanterns! They're flickering!"

The lamps were indeed moving with the light of active flame. The smoke from the chimneys also moved, as did the leaves stirring in the gentle breeze that blew them across the tableau . . .

. . . and onto Ransom's outstretched arm.

The philologist smiled, then concentrated all his attention on the card, which began to grow bigger.

The patterns around the border began to glow with an

ethereal light, and they pulsed with a rhythm very much like a heartbeat.

In moments it was the size of an atlas, and now hung suspended in the air of its own accord. It continued to expand, and within a matter of minutes it was a life-size looking glass that could be stepped through with ease. The only thing that was different about the wood in front of them was that five minutes earlier, there had been no tavern there—but otherwise, every tree and leaf was exactly the same.

Ransom stepped through the frame of the card and beckoned to the others. "Come along," he said with a wry grin. "I assure you, it's perfectly safe."

Charles and Archie went first, with no hesitation. Rose was next, followed by Jack, and finally John, who inhaled sharply, checked his bag for the bulk of the *Imaginarium Geographica* to make sure it was secure, and stepped through.

Once on the other side, the portal shrank rapidly, until it was once more just a drawing on an old sheet of parchment, which Ransom carefully replaced in the book in his coat.

The philologist then turned about and flung out his arm as if he were the host of a party. "My friends," he said brightly, "welcome to the Inn of the Flying Dragon."

"That's fantastic," said John. "I think I like those even better than the doors in the Keep of Time."

"It takes a certain knack to get the hang of them," said Ransom as he walked toward the inn. "We've got our eye on a young fellow named Roger to become my own apprentice. He shows great promise, I think."

Charles stroked Archimedes and frowned. "I'm sorry, old

fellow," he said placatingly. "I know it's a bit dreary still, but we'll need you to stay out here."

Ransom stopped on the front steps of the inn and turned around. "Why is that? Bring him in. I'm sure they can accommodate him."

The companions exchanged confused looks. "I don't know how it is in your Cambridge," said John, "but where we come from, an oversized talking mechanical owl tends to attract a lot of the wrong kind of attention."

"Really?" Ransom said as he opened the door, a knowing smile spreading across his face. "Perhaps in Oxford that's true, but it isn't the case here. Please—come inside and see for yourselves."

Stepping through the door into the Inn of the Flying Dragon was, on first glance, very similar to stepping inside one of their usual gathering places like the Eagle & Child. There was a burly proprietor tending the bar, and scattered patrons seated at the tables, with a few in the back playing a game of cards. The room was well lit and not terribly smoky. There was a scent in the air of charred spices, possibly from a curry being burned in the kitchen. The kegs of ale were stacked high, and the taps flowed freely.

A mop boy scurried over to the companions and offered to show them to a table, taking special notice of the pretty girl in their company. "May I take your owl, sirs?" he offered, trying not to look as if he had noticed Rose. "There's a good spot in the stable behind, where he'll be well looked after."

Before any of them could reply, Archie opened his mouth. "I have very particular needs, boy. Are you prepared for a guest of my composition?"

John sighed. "He means he's not a typical owl," he explained as Rose and Charles both scowled at Archie. "He doesn't really require the normal sort of food and shelter."

"Well," the boy said, "if it helps, there was a wizard here last week who brought a phoenix with him, and they seemed pretty happy when they left."

"A wizard?" asked Jack. "Really?"

The boy nodded. "I forget his name—Bumble or Humble something-or-another. But I took excellent care of his phoenix."

"This bird is, uh, not exactly natural," said John.

"Ah," the boy said. "A clockwork. We've had unusual birds before, and we'll do our best to make him comfortable."

"If that's the case," said Archie, "I want a copy of Einstein's notes on relativity, and a stuffed gopher to chew on as I read."

The boy squinted an eye and pondered this. "I can get you the Einstein notes, but only in German, unless you'll be staying the night. And the only gophers we have are in the stew—but I can get you some mechanical mice instead."

Archimedes beamed and hopped over to the boy's outstretched arm. "Lead on, MacDuff."

"Actually, my name's Flannery."

"Whatever you say, MacDuff."

"Oh, for heaven's sake," said John.

They took seats around a table near the front corner, where they could watch the door and make use of it in a pinch. A stout, ginger-haired man in a floppy hat brought several mugs of ale over to the table.

"There are several such refuges throughout the world," Ransom explained, gesturing around at the inn. "A good term for them might be 'Soft Places,' meaning places where the boundaries are not as solid as elsewhere, and where one might cross between them, with the right knowledge and training."

"Is it luck or good planning that one of your Soft Places just happens to be a tavern?" asked John. "Not that I'm complaining in any way, mind you."

"Not luck," Ransom replied. "It's essentially the power of the crossroads made manifest. A crossroads is important for what it represents, and what it in fact *is*—a junction between paths. Establishments such as the Inn of the Flying Dragon are much the same—junctions between places."

"I've completely overlooked what may be the most appealing aspect of interdimensional travel," Charles said jovially. "Are there more taverns like this, then?"

"A few," said Ransom. "I've heard of one that's supposed to be at the End of the World, but I can't seem to locate it. All that's on Terminus is a bunch of rocks and a gravestone."

"Well, yes," Jack harrumphed. "Where else?"

"There's a nice place that was once called Harrigan's Green, which is difficult to get to, but worth the trip. You can tell stories to pay for your room and board, so essentially, it's merit-based. The best stories get the best room, and the best ale."

"I'll drink to that," said Charles, rising from his chair. "I'll get the next round, gentlemen. Same for all?"

They all nodded. "And you, Rose?" Charles asked.

"I'd really like a glass of milk, thank you," said Rose.

Ransom frowned for just an instant, then started to speak before John interrupted him.

"Pardon," John said, turning to Rose. "I think Charles might need some help with the drinks. Would you be so kind as to give him a hand, Rose?"

"Of course," the girl said cheerfully as she stood, pushing back her chair. "That will also give you and Uncle Jack the chance to ask Mr. Ransom why I make him so uncomfortable."

"She's a smart girl," said Jack as Rose walked over to join Charles at the bar.

"More than smart," said Ransom.

"So, since she brought it up," said John, "why does she make you jumpy, man? Surely you know who she is."

The philologist bit his lip and thought a moment before answering. "I know who she is," he said finally, "but *what* she is is a conundrum."

"Or an enigma," Jack chimed in. "Or both."

"What I mean," said Ransom, "is that she isn't supposed to be here at *all*. In practical terms, the girl doesn't exist."

"But clearly she does," said John.

"What's clear to you and me is not so clear to others," Ransom pointed out. "Did you notice that when we entered, the barman didn't bring anything for her, or even ask?"

"I just assumed that he wasn't accustomed to dealing with children," said John.

"No," said Ransom. "There are children in here all the time, especially during the day. He didn't see her. *Couldn't* see her."

Jack sat up straighter in his seat. "This isn't the first time that's happened," he said, gripping John's arm. "Remember? After we returned to England with Rose and Hugo? At the Bird and Baby?"

John frowned, then glanced over at the bar. "That's right—Burton couldn't see her either."

"But that boy, Flannery, could," said Jack. He eyed Ransom appraisingly. "But why would you say she isn't supposed to exist?"

"Because," Ransom replied, "in the original History, she actually *did* sacrifice herself to save Arthur. It *was* a life for a life. She was *supposed* to die."

"It wasn't necessary," John said, leaning over the table. "She was willing, but that was enough."

"You know that because you were there," said Ransom, "but it wasn't the way history recorded it. And when you chose to bring her here, you somehow removed her from history altogether."

"Then why would some people see her while others can't?" Jack asked. "It doesn't make any sense."

"I can't tell you that," Ransom replied. "But since you returned, everything has been in flux—that's part of the reason I came to find you."

"What's that?" said Charles as he and Rose returned with their drinks. "Hope we haven't missed anything good."

"Just chatting," John said as he took a mug from his friend. "Seems like a fine sort of pub, doesn't it?"

"Yes," Charles agreed, sitting. "But," he added in a hushed voice, "I think the barman has a tail. And I'm all but certain that he has donkey's ears tucked in around that ginger hair under his hat."

"Oh, Lampwick's a good enough fellow," said Ransom as he took a drink, "but I wouldn't mention the ears if I were you. He's a bit touchy about them."

"To your good health," John said, lifting his glass in a toast to his companions. "May all our travels end in such favorable places."

"Hear, hear," said Jack. "This is almost like the Tuesday night meetings with the fellows back at Oxford."

"Except for the fact that we're at an inn named for a dragon, which we can only get to through a drawing on a card," said Charles, "and we're being served drinks by a barman with a tail and donkey ears."

"Well, yes," said Jack. "Except for that."

CHAPTER THREE

PURSUIT OF THE UN-MEN

ONCE THEY HAD settled in with their drinks, John brought the conversation back to the point. "What's so significant about 1936?" he asked. "Since you were aiming for 1943, why would it matter what year you landed in, as long as it was prior to your target?"

"It's significant," came the reply, "because it's the first time the two of you"—he indicated John and Jack—"formally met *him*," he finished, pointing at Charles.

John bristled, and his eyes narrowed. That didn't sound valid. "If Verne did send you, then you both should have been aware that we've known Charles for many years now."

"Sure," said Ransom, "in *this* dimension. But not in others. In most of them, the two of you never met him until the spring of 1936. So there were things that could not be shared with you until the natural greater course of events had occurred. Even you three have realized this at some level," he continued, gesturing at the trio of men, "else you would not have gone to such pains to keep the relationship a secret for all this time."

"Bert said we must, not for temporal or dimensional reasons," said John, "but rather to protect the knowledge of the *Imaginarium Geographica* and the Archipel—"

The quick, curt shake of Ransom's head told John to stop speaking. It was a secret that needed protecting, and even here, in a small, out-of-the way tavern, sitting with an agent of Jules Verne, it was too great a risk to say some things aloud.

"Timelines must be protected as much as possible," Ransom went on, "and even when changes are made, they must be done with an eye toward the ebb and flow of events that have already occurred—past, present, and future.

"You were brought together by the murder of Professor Sigurdsson, but you were already marked as potential Caretakers." Ransom's voice dropped to a whisper with the last word. "The, ah, problem was that you weren't actually supposed to meet for a number of years. You two"—he indicated John and Jack—"in or around 1926, and you"—he pointed at Charles—"in 1936. The Winter King changed all of that. So the fact that some things have been kept from you is no commentary on your worthiness, but rather an effort by Verne to keep the fidelity of this timeline as pure as possible."

"So the me who met them isn't the me who was originally, ah, me?" said Charles. "Does that mean we changed time, or switched dimensions? I'd hate to think there's another me running around somewhere."

"There already is," Rose said. "He's you, but not the same you. I did like him quite a bit, though."

"She's right," Jack declared, his face ashen with realization. "There *is* another Charles—or was, anyway."

John nodded. "Chaz. We took him back in history, where he became the first of the Green Knights. He was from *another* dimension, but he's still in our recorded Histories in *this* dimension. So there have been, in fact, two of you, Charles."

"But not at the same time," Charles retorted. "That's impossible—isn't it?" he asked, looking at Ransom.

The companions all paused as the barman approached. "Another round of drinks?" he asked.

"Yes please, Mr. Lampwick," said Ransom. "And don't forget the milk."

Lampwick went back to the bar, and the companions again huddled closely around the table.

"Hasn't Bert explained it to you?" Ransom began, leaning in to whisper. "Surely you have had occasion to meet with H. G. Wells at one time or another, and surely you realized they were not the same man."

"I had, years ago," said Charles, "and on occasion since."

"As have I," said Jack, "but Bert told us when we first became Care—uh, when we first met, that he was not the same person as our Wells. He told us that he was the time traveler from his book, and that he'd come from eight hundred thousand years in the future."

"I'd always figured that he was exaggerating, for effect," said John.

"He wasn't," said Ransom. "Didn't you ever think it strange that Wells never mentioned you, or your group, or the book?"

"I did," said Charles, "but I assumed it was for one of two reasons: Either he was being discreet, because we were always in some public place and were not able to address those topics; or he was not yet privy to, ah, our secret society. Our Bert is quite a lot older than Wells, you know."

"So you think that his being recruited by Verne hasn't happened yet?" asked Jack.

Charles shrugged and took a long draw from his ale. "Anything is possible with time travel."

"It doesn't fit," said John. "He told us he wrote the books after having the real experiences, which he then fictionalized. So he had to have been recruited at a much younger age, as were we."

Charles and Jack looked crestfallen. "I hadn't thought of that," Jack admitted.

"So what does that mean about *our* Bert?" asked Charles. "Is he or isn't he H. G. Wells?"

"That's the point I was bringing you to," said Ransom. "He's exactly what he said—he *is* H. G. Wells, he's just not the one you know of."

"My head is spinning," said Jack.

"Think of dimensional travel as a sort of 'Othertime,'" Ransom said as Charles jumped up to bring the new tray of drinks to the table. "Not going into the past, or future, or even the present, really—just a different present."

"Or past or future as well, based on what you said," Charles remarked. "You overshot by seven years, if you thought you were going to end up in 1943."

"I was expecting to end up there, but ending up here is an accidental blessing," said Ransom. "It means I have the opportunity to help you avert a terrible event.

"In the future, it is known as the Second World War," the philologist continued, his face grave. "And unless we change events here and now, it may mean the literal end of the world for us all."

"We've been to war, before," said John, respecting the somber tone of Ransom's voice, "both here and in the Archipelago."

"Not like this," Ransom retorted. "The weapons that will be

brought to bear are effective on a continental scale. Cities will be destroyed with single explosive devices smaller than this room. Nations will crack; civilizations will be routed. And millions will die, or be forever enslaved."

"And we're to help you stop all that?" said Charles. "No pressure on us, eh, old fellow?"

"I told you that part of the reason why 1936 is so significant is because it's the first time the three of you came together, publicly, as friends."

"Yes," John said. "What's the other part?"

Ransom shifted about uncomfortably in his seat and stalled for time by sipping his ale. But he could not completely disguise the quick glances over at Rose.

"*She* is the other part of the reason," he said finally. "Her being here doesn't register as a zero point with Verne, but we think that's only because she wasn't meant to be here in this place and time at all. She is the key to everything that happens over the next seven years, which is why I was trying to reach you in 1943—so that we could try to discover alternatives."

"Alternatives to what?" said Jack.

"Alternatives to whom," replied Ransom. "She . . . is not available to us then, but there is no one else we could consult who could replace her."

"Why isn't she 'available'?"

"Sometime in the next few months," Ransom said grimly, "Rose Dyson, the Grail Child, will be murdered. And we have discovered no alternate timeline, or dimension, or world in which that does not take place."

"You might have done that a bit more diplomatically," said Jack, scowling at the philologist and scooting protectively closer to Rose. "She's just a child, after all."

"I don't mind," Rose said, smiling reassuringly at Ransom. "Mr. Ransom was just getting straight to the point. And besides," she added, "in realistic terms, I'm actually older than all of you."

"Maybe," said John. "But I think Jack's point is that you lack the life experience to deal with many of the things an adult might encounter. That's why it's been important for you to be in school."

"And that's why you're taking me to Oxford as well, isn't it?" Rose countered. "So that I can continue to learn from you, and Uncle John, and Uncle Warnie?"

Ransom groaned. "So you've already moved her to the Kilns, then?"

"We hadn't decided," John replied. "Does that matter?"

"That's where it happens in the Histories," said Ransom, gesturing at Charles with his mug. "The ones you've yet to write."

"Is it risking anything, temporally speaking, for you to be revealing elements of the future to us?" Charles asked. "Not to be the damper of the group, especially since this is a topic of special interest to me, but I really don't want to wake up tomorrow finding everything's gone haywire."

"Verne and Bert are very cautious about what we're allowed to disclose," said Ransom, "but bear in mind, from my point of view, I'm not telling you secrets of the future—I'm relating events that have already happened in the past."

"So you expect nothing else to change?" asked Jack. "We will continue as we are, and still do what we've done, even if we know what you say will happen?"

"Yes. Nothing substantial will change."

"Except for our preventing the death of Rose, which you say would cause this 'Second World War.'"

Ransom nodded. "Except for that—which is being allowed for two reasons. Rose is an anomaly, and so her being here does not materially affect your primary timeline. But she does affect events in the Archipelago, which has a ripple effect here, and while it doesn't start the war, it makes it far worse than it might have been."

"Is there anything you can tell us about our future—um, your 'past'—that isn't dire and terrible?" Charles asked with a gloomy expression.

"You are all on the cusp of realizing great success in your careers," Ransom noted.

"Oh, thank God," said Charles. "After all those books, I was beginning to wonder if the things I've been writing about would *ever* catch on."

Ransom squirmed. "Ah, well, yours not so much, I'm afraid," he admitted. "But your association with your friends will keep your status high just the same."

"I'm sure it shall be quite the reverse," Jack said to Charles reassuringly. "Our friendship with you will be our passport to fame."

"Yes, yes," said Charles glumly. "Do you know how many stories I've published? How many poems? And still, I'm best known for works I conceived in part because of my relationship with you fellows, and the adventures we've had. And I'm a little tentative about some of those, seeing as they're little but fictionalized versions of the Histories I've been keeping."

"As have all your predecessors before you, Charles," Ransom said placatingly. "It was their way of processing the myriad experiences they had, and writing the Histories alone was a gargantuan task, assigned only to those most worthy. That you have the skill to fictionalize some of those chronicles is an achievement without peer."

"I appreciate the compliments," said Charles. He wasn't sure if the philologist was pulling his leg for decorum's sake, or if the flattery was sincere. But he wasn't going to argue. "It's just that being well known and respected for one's work has less, ah, emotional resonance when the only ones who do know and respect the work are essentially bound to keep their opinion a secret."

"It's to your advantage, though, Charles," Jack observed. "You're going to be known, in our world, for an increasingly progressive body of work, rather than for the one great book you feel has eluded you. Isn't that what every writer truly wants?"

"It would be a ghastly thing indeed," John chimed in, "to be known for only one or two significant works. That would drain the soul and temper the vinegar of any worthy writer. Don't you agree, Ransom?"

Ransom swallowed hard and waved for the barman. "I think we should get more ales before I answer that," he said, a pensive look on his face. "Several more ales."

He turned in his chair and scanned the great room of the inn, but there was no sign of Lampwick, or of the boy, Flannery—or, for that matter, anyone else.

The card players had gone, as had the three or four scattered patrons who had occupied other tables. The companions were alone in the inn.

"It's only just past seven," John said, checking his watch. "Shouldn't this place be hopping with patrons?"

Ransom pursed his lips and slowly stood up. "It should. There are always travelers seeking a moment's respite, and there is always someone tending to their drinks. Something is seriously amiss here."

Suddenly Flannery's bright face appeared at the edge of the bar, where he gestured to the companions to remain where they were. A finger to his lips told them that silence was also necessary.

"You're being watched," he whispered as he crept toward their table. "Do not let them know that you know. I was told to destroy your owl, but I hid him in my storeroom instead."

The companions sat motionless, save for Rose, who finished her mug of milk. "How do you know this?" she said quietly as she wiped the foam from her lips. "Who are you to us?"

Smart girl, John thought. *Find out if someone is on your side before you place yourself in their hands.*

"I am a friend," Flannery replied. "I'm to help you, if I can."

Charles lifted his drink to his lips to cover his words. "If you're a friend," he whispered, "then you should have a sign that proves who you're working with."

"Oh!" the boy exclaimed, before dropping back to a whisper. "I forgot! I'm supposed to give you a kiss."

Charles choked on his ale. "Pardon me?"

"A kiss," Flannery repeated as he fumbled around in his pocket. "The Valkyrie said if I gave you a kiss, you'd know I could be trusted." He held out his hand and showed them a small silver thimble.

"The kiss," Flannery repeated quietly. "From one of the novice Valkyries of Paralon—Laura Glue."

Instantly the companions' demeanor changed. "He's with us," John said to Ransom.

"What would you have us do, Flannery?" Jack whispered.

"They're outside," he replied. "They're waiting for their leader to come before they take you."

"Who is waiting, Flannery?" Jack pressed. "They who?"

"Men. Un-Men. I—I can't really say," the boy replied. "But I don't like them. They in't natural."

Ransom sat bolt upright. "Not natural? What do they look like?"

The boy scratched his head. "Big bird heads, but on thin bodies of men. And they're dressed like they're in a Shakespeare play."

Grimacing, Ransom slowly rose from his seat. "Yoricks. This will be difficult, I fear."

"Bar the door," Flannery whispered. "It will hold them back a few moments."

Together John and Ransom rose and made as if to approach the bar—then, in a single fluid motion, both men leaped to the door and threw down the large crossbeam. An instant later something slammed against it with a heavy *whump*. The creature outside the door let out a terrible shriek and threw itself against the door again and again. The crossbrace held—but only just.

"No time to waste!" cried Flannery, jumping to his feet. "Quickly! Follow me!"

Protectively shepherding Rose ahead of them, Charles and Jack dashed to the bar, followed by John and Ransom. Flannery led them around an open door to a short corridor lined with doorways. He bypassed nearly all of them, then opened the last one on the right. It showed a dark, candlelit stairway to the cellar.

"Hang on," Jack said cautiously. "If we go down there, we'll be trapped."

Flannery shook his head. "There's a secret passage hidden under a barrel of ginger beer. It leads to my secret storeroom. Even Lampwick doesn't know how to find it."

If the companions were still hesitant to follow the boy, a crashing and splintering sound from the front of the inn convinced them otherwise. The stomping of boots and an otherworldly shrieking from the creatures Ransom called Yoricks was all the motivation they needed.

They all moved down the steps, and Jack and Charles bolted the door, then moved several large crates in front of it to buy more time from their pursuers.

Flannery grabbed a lamp from one of the walls and indicated a barrel among a dozen as the one that concealed his hiding place.

"Lots of travelers come through and need something hid," he explained as Charles and Ransom moved the barrel aside. "I have a place that's secure, and I make a bit of coin on the side. Lampwick doesn't care, because it keeps the customers happy."

"And they trust you to keep the items safe?" asked Charles.

The boy nodded emphatically. "The kind of people who need things secreted away in one of the Soft Places in't the kind of people you want to betray."

"I understand completely," said Charles. "Lead the way, Flannery."

The last of the companions clambered down into the tunnel just as the Yoricks began banging on the door above.

"Won't they find this place eventually too?" asked John. "The room above isn't that large, and the entrance isn't that well concealed."

"I couldn't give a fig if they find this tunnel," Flannery said as he led them down an earthen passage. "Once they get here, they could spend a year looking and never know where we went."

The passage opened into a massive underground cavern that was literally riddled with passageways. It was a honeycomb reimagined for men, and it was a daunting thought to even consider entering one of the holes.

"Did you build this, Flannery?" asked Charles. "Most impressive."

The boy shrugged. "I had help. It's a lot like the place I used to live, so it don't scare me none, neh?"

Jack looked at him more closely. "I don't think we've ever met, but you sound like some other children I know."

Flannery nodded and flashed a brilliant smile, which was missing a tooth on the bottom. "It's nowhere near as big as Asterius's labyrinth back on Centrum Terrae, but it suits me fine," he said as he moved quickly to an opening near the left side of the cavern. "Follow me, but remember—keep turning left."

The passages were dimly lit by glowing moss embedded in the walls and a smattering of luminescent mushrooms, but Flannery was not moving so quickly that any of them ever lost sight of the flame.

Abruptly the tunnel ended, with a sharp upturn and a ladder. Flannery climbed it and threw back the trapdoor at the top.

"It's about time you came back, MacDuff," Archimedes squawked, hopping up and down on a crude wooden table. "These aren't Einstein's papers at all, just a bunch of Newtonian scribbles. And as to those mechanical mice you promised . . ."

"No time, Archie," Charles said as he and the others climbed out of the tunnel and up into the small storeroom. "There's a chase afoot."

The storeroom, which was lit warmly by several candles, was cramped and low-ceilinged. It was carved out of the space underneath a massive oak tree, as evidenced by the roots framing the walls. There were boxes and other parcels scattered around the space, obviously items left in Flannery's care. Higher up, in the trunk itself, were several windows disguised as knotholes. He scrambled up to one and peered outside.

"No one's about," he called down. "They must all be inside tearing the inn apart."

Flannery looked again. "No, wait. I see something." He motioned for the others to move to knotholes lower down. "Have a look, if you wish to see who your enemies are."

The companions clustered around the small openings and peered out into the dusky night air. The moon had come up, and it cast a wan glow over the woods. If they had not known otherwise, they would have been hard-pressed to believe that this place was not just another wood near Oxford.

A clamor from the direction of the inn drew their attention, and off to the right, they saw the glow of firelight, followed by the shadowed forms of their pursuers.

As Ransom had described, the Yoricks were both bird and man. They were seven feet tall, and their heads were the oversized skulls of birds. They had no eyes, only sockets that glowed red, and no feathers. They were garbed in Elizabethan-era clothing, including capes, and had long, skeletal arms that ended in poorly fitting gloves.

Their legs were those of birds, and ended in four-toed avian feet with wicked-looking talons. When they were not shrieking, they communicated with one another in a series of clucks and whistles.

There were nearly two dozen of them—which meant that they were prepared to overwhelm the companions by sheer numbers alone.

Curiously, they seemed to be under the command of a man, who was shorter than they, but obviously in charge. He spoke to them in a brusque tone that was too low to hear, but he was not pleased. Lampwick was also among them, although he seemed more apologetic than anything else. He said something to the man, who responded by striking him brutally across the face. The innkeeper turned and went back the way he'd come.

At the man's direction, half of the Yoricks returned to the inn, and the rest followed him into the wood, on a path that took them startlingly close to Flannery's tree.

All the companions save for Jack dropped away from the knotholes and covered the candles. Jack watched until their pursuers had passed, then joined the others, his face gone gray with fear and, oddly, shock.

"It's all right," Flannery reassured him. "The outside of my den is well concealed. They won't find us easily, and certainly not quickly."

"I don't think that's what's startled him," John said, guiding Jack to a chair. "He's seen and experienced quite a lot, so this has to be something else."

"I'm all right," said Jack. "I'm just trying to rationalize what I saw."

Charles nodded. "I was a bit surprised myself," he said. "Seven-foot-tall birds are not high on my list of expected enemies."

Jack shook his head. "That's not it. We've seen and fought worse than these fellows. But that man who was with them . . ." His voice trailed off, and he rubbed his forehead.

"You recognized him?" Ransom asked. "I couldn't at all. I've never seen the Yoricks under a human's direction before."

"I did recognize him," answered Jack. "I may be mistaken, but I would swear on my life that it was Rudyard Kipling I saw leading the charge."

CHAPTER FOUR
THE PIECES OF TIME

"KIPLING?" RANSOM EXCLAIMED. "That's a fine how-do-you-do. He was Bert's primary rival for the open Caretaker position after Verne took over. It's bad form for such a talented man if he's gone over to the other side."

"I never saw anything of him in the Histories, or in the *Geographica*," said John. "Bert certainly never mentioned him."

"He wouldn't have," Ransom pointed out. "After the Houdini-Doyle incident, when they nearly exposed the Archipelago to the whole world, Verne has kept any information about non-Caretakers or former Caretakers very close to the vest."

"That's just a bloody shame," said Charles. "I wouldn't ever consider putting Kipling and Magwich in the same class."

"You'll have to," Jack said, still a bit shaken. "I have no doubt that he's working with our enemies—probably Burton."

"What makes you say that?" asked John.

"You already know yourselves," Jack replied. "Didn't you see it in the papers? Rudyard Kipling *died* three months ago!"

"That would explain why we didn't recognize him at first," John reasoned, running his hand over his hair. "That man was perhaps forty at most. Kipling was seventy."

"That locks it," said Charles, banging a fist against the table. "Richard Burton's behind this. No one else would know how to manipulate things so as to recruit dead poets to their cause."

"I'm afraid you're right," Ransom said. "His presence here cannot be accidental."

"But yours was," said John pointedly. "If you hadn't met us on the road, then we wouldn't have ended up here, where our enemies now have us hiding under a tree. How do you explain that?"

"I can't," Ransom answered, turning to Flannery. "How did *you* know someone would be looking for them?"

Flannery shrugged. "I din't know nothing," he said. "Lampwick told me to get rid of the bird, so I hid him here. And on the way back up into the Flying Dragon, I saw those Un-Men gathering outside. That's when I knew there'd be trouble."

Jack tilted his head, appraising the boy. "But how is it you were here, today, when we needed an ally?"

"I've been here for two years," Flannery replied. "There are Lost Boys posted at all the Soft Places—the ones we know of, anyways—just in case. We all report t' the Valkyries."

"Well, God bless Laura Glue," said Jack, rising. "What do we do now, Ransom? Do we go back to Oxford?"

The philologist shook his head. "If they're here, they'll be there, too. Don't worry," he added, seeing Jack's look of concern. "They won't hurt your brother, or Mrs. Moore. They're only after Rose."

He removed the book with the Trumps from his coat and fanned out the cards in his hand. "I think it's time to consult someone with a bigger hammer," he said.

"Bigger hammer?" Charles asked.

"When you're stuck with a problem, sometimes the best solution is to hit it with a bigger hammer. I expect he's going to try to contact Verne," said John.

John was close. Ransom held up a card that seemed to depict an ancient Egyptian village, but instead of Jules Verne, they saw the miniature image of an old friend.

"Hank Morgan!" Jack exclaimed. "What a pleasure it is to see you again!"

Hank's face broke into a wide grin, and he waved. "John, Jack. And young Rose, also, I see! And . . ." He paused. "Ah, Chaz?"

"Charles," the third Caretaker replied. "We've not had the pleasure, but I've heard many good stories about you."

Hank raised a questioning eyebrow, then turned his attention back to Ransom. "I wish we had more time to reminisce, Alvin," he said, "but there are too many events cascading together, and it's all we can do to keep track of them."

"We're at the Inn of the Flying Dragon," Ransom reported, "but we've had a bit of a complication develop. Can we come through?"

"You can't," said Hank, shaking his head for emphasis. "Not here, nor any of the Soft Places. I was here in Midian looking to acquire some manuscripts left by Saint Paul of Tarsus, and almost as soon as I arrived, I had to ask the Midians for protection. I've checked the other Trumps—every key Crossroads location is swarming with Un-Men."

"Yoricks?"

Hank nodded. "Those, and worse. Any place you bring Rose will be equally dangerous. I think they're looking for *you*."

"But how?" Ransom exclaimed. "I wasn't even supposed to end up here! It isn't even a zero point. I was aiming for—"

"For 1943, we know," Hank finished for him. "The best we can determine is that your arrival there, near Oxford in 1936, is what *made* it a zero point. And that changed the sequence of events, as well as their relative importance. Where *we* knew without doubt how crucial Rose was to the Wars of the Worlds, our enemies could only suspect."

"Until now," said Ransom, groaning in realization. "Until I confirmed it for them."

"It isn't your fault," Hank told him. "None of us could know. At least," he added with a conspiratorial look, "none of us who could share the information."

John looked askance at Jack and Charles. Was that comment in reference to Verne and his penchant for secrecy? They were the Caretakers of the *Imaginarium Geographica,* and although Verne knew everything they did, they had never so much as glimpsed the so-called Prime Caretaker.

"Have you told them yet?" Hank was asking. "About the Prophecy?"

Ransom swore under his breath and glanced sideways at the Caretakers. "I have not, but I was getting to it. I thought we had . . . well, more time."

"We don't," Hank stated. "Best get them to the Gatherum as quickly as possible."

"The Gatherum?" Ransom repeated. "But that's only possible in—"

"I know, believe me, I know," said Hank. He stepped out of frame for a moment, and the companions could hear muffled shouts and a large crash.

"I'm sorry," he said, moving back into view. "I need to go—I think the locals are about to set fire to the place."

"Anything I can do?" asked Ransom.

"I'll be fine," Hank replied. "Just whatever you do, don't take Rose to any of the Crossroads. Elsewhere she may be safe—but not here. Once you've seen to her security, get the Caretakers to the Nameless Isles, with no delay. Everything may depend on it. Fare thee well, friends."

And with that, the surface of the card blurred and went dark.

"That doesn't sound very promising," said Charles.

"Where do we take her, Ransom?" Jack said as he peered out one of the knotholes. "If the Crossroads places are off-limits, and Oxford will be watched, can we take her back to Reading? Or London?"

"I'm concerned that anywhere we go, we'll be tracked," Ransom answered. "I don't think there's anywhere in this world where she *will* be safe."

Jack snapped his fingers. "Then how about a place that's out of this world?" he said excitedly. "Do you have any Trumps that lead to the Archipelago?"

"I have just one," Ransom replied. "I've been there a few times in the recent past—*my* recent past—but it might be the only option we have left." He shuffled the cards and removed one, turning it around for the companions to see.

On the card was a drawing, precise down to the details of the stonework, intertwined staircases, and windows, of the interior of a place the companions all knew very well.

"The Keep of Time," said John with visible relief. "That will be as good a place as any, and better than most."

"Maybe, and maybe not," Ransom said with obvious discomfort.

"Coming to the Inn of the Flying Dragon is one thing, because I've been here before, and often. But I haven't been to the Keep of Time—not yet, anyway."

"What do you mean?" John demanded. "You just said you've been there several times."

"Yes, I have," Ransom replied, "but all *after* 1936. I made this card in 1943 the first time I was there, which was when I expected to meet you, anyway. I never expected that I'd end up using any of the other cards to transport you away from England to anywhere other than the Flying Dragon."

"Are you implying that if we use this Trump to escape these . . . these Un-Men," said Jack, "we'll risk going into our own future?"

"Yes," Ransom said, looking anxiously through the uppermost knothole. "That's exactly what I'm worried will happen."

"I think we've already got a solution in hand, as it were," John said, reaching into his pocket. "I have one of the watches too, remember? Once we've escaped these Yorick creatures, we can simply use it to return to our own time—as in, *this* time."

Ransom slumped in despair. "I keep forgetting—your watch isn't activated as an Anabasis Machine until 1937."

"But I'm actually a Caretaker," said John with a trace of indignation, "the Caretaker Principia, in fact, not an apprentice. Why wouldn't mine have the same properties as yours?"

"You are indeed a Caretaker," Ransom replied, "but of the *Imaginarium Geographica*, not of . . . well, it's not for me to say. To you, the watches represent badges of honor and a secret way to identify others of our creed—but long before that, they were being used by those of us chosen by Verne to help protect time itself. It was only later that he realized they could serve a dual purpose."

"Wouldn't it have been easier to make all of them time-traveling devices to begin with?" said Jack.

"Maybe on the surface," said Ransom. "It's only been recently that the scope of the Caretakers' responsibilities seems to have expanded to time as well as space, so the watches you'd been given were inert. That appears to have been a miscalculation—but then again, if they'd *all* been fully functional, that would mean your friend Hugo Dyson would also have one. Do you really want *him* meddling in time?"

"Good point," said John. He suddenly snapped his fingers. "Can we use yours, then? If you can tell me how it works quickly enough, that is."

Ransom shook his head. "If I could, I'd gladly hand it over. But it would be more dangerous for you if I did. I've been trained in its use for years by Jules Verne himself, and I still can't manage it with any degree of accuracy. If you were to miscalculate . . ."

Jack groaned. "Never mind—I think we'll take our chances with the Keep of Time. Otherwise, we might end up in the Winterland again, or worse."

"One of you might," said Ransom. "At present, the Anabasis Machine is still a single-user device."

Jack slapped his forehead. "That's right, that's right. I'd forgotten. There's also the problem of arriving naked wherever we'd go too."

Ransom snorted, then chuckled. "Hank probably told you that, didn't he? We actually worked out the mechanics of that particular problem a few years back—Verne and Mark Twain just made a special adjustment to Hank's device as a joke."

"You let him hopscotch through time naked as a *joke*?" John said, incredulous.

The philologist shrugged and chuckled again. "When you are trying to keep order in the entirety of creation, you have to take the opportunities for a moment's levity when you can."

"It *is* pretty funny," said Charles.

"Gentlemen," Flannery said, a tense pitch in his voice, "you'd best make a decision quickly. I think I may have overestimated the usefulness of our hiding place."

He gestured with his thumb for the others to look outside, and they did. About thirty yards away, Kipling and the Yoricks were standing in a clearing—and they were all looking toward Flannery's tree.

"That's it," said Jack. "Ransom, we need to use that Trump. Now. Whatever you feel the risk will be, we'll just have to sort it out when we get there."

The philologist removed the Trump of the Keep from the other cards, then paused. "Remember what I said about the rules that cannot be broken? The rules regarding time and space?"

"Uh-oh," said John. "That sounds like a very bad preamble."

Ransom scowled at him. "All I'm saying is that we don't know everything. Not yet, anyway. And there *are* rules that can't be broken—but we're discovering new rules all the time."

"What are you telling us, Ransom?" Jack asked.

"Instinct counts. Intuition counts. Not everything can be broken down into formulas. There are no equations that can prove that I am in a place where I cannot possibly be. But if I am in that place, then it must be possible—and I think some things can become possible if you just believe that they are."

"'Believing is seeing,'" said Charles.

"Yes," Ransom agreed, handing him the card. "So believe." He turned to Flannery. "I'm betting you have a secret back door to this place, don't you?"

"Three, in fact," the boy replied, pointing at a low door behind the table. "I'll show you where."

"Aren't you going with us?" John asked Ransom, surprised. "You were trying to get to 1943 anyway!"

"My first directive from Verne was to simplify, simplify, simplify," said Ransom, shaking hands with the three men. "The Trumps aren't meant for time travel. I need to find out what's happening here first. I'll try to join you later—and besides, it may not happen the way we think. Hopefully, you'll just end up safely at the Keep."

"I am so filled with confidence at the moment," said Charles. "What do you plan to do, then?"

"I'll lead them away. Don't worry—I've dealt with their kind before. I'll be fine. Just use the Trump as I showed you, and get the girl to safety. And as soon as you are able, you must go to the Nameless Isles."

A terrible screeching filled the air outside—apparently their pursuers had decided to surround the tree. "No more time to explain!" Ransom urged. "We must go!"

"I don't want to seem ungrateful . . . ," John began.

"But I got you into this mess to begin with?" said Ransom. "It's all right—I understand completely. If all goes to plan, we'll be meeting again soon, and I'll try to make it up to you."

"And just how much of your plan has worked out so far?" asked Charles.

"Forget I said anything," Ransom suggested, wincing. "Good luck to you all."

"Thank you, Ransom," said Jack, gripping the other's hand once more. "If we can ever repay the favor . . ."

The philologist winked. "Oh, you will," he said with a chuckle as he ducked into the small doorway Flannery was holding open. "You and I are destined to become great friends, Jack. In one dimension or another, anyway. And Jack," he called back over his shoulder, "call me Alvin."

And with that, he clambered into the tunnel and vanished.

Trying to ignore the clamor of the Yoricks outside, Charles held up the Trump and focused his considerable attention on it. And, as before, it started to expand—but this time, as it grew, the image of the Keep of Time began to lighten and fade.

"Uh-oh," said Jack. "It looks like one of the burned-out slides from the Lanterna Magica."

John agreed. The frame of the Trump was filling the small storeroom now, and the image was almost completely white. "We may be better off trying to negotiate with Kipling," he said just as something massively strong struck the side of the tree. "Or not."

"I'll go first," Charles offered, and he stepped through. Jack and Rose were next, followed by John.

"Archie?" said John. "Are you coming?"

"Coming where?" the owl retorted. "There's nothing *there*."

Another *whump* hit the tree. Archimedes hopped off the table and through the portal. The bird sighed. "Oh, very well. It's obvious you're afraid to go anywhere without my guidance."

The sounds of the Yoricks faded as the portal began to shrink, and in moments it had closed completely. The Trump still bore the illustration of the Keep, but that was not where the companions were.

It was an endless expanse of whiteness. There was no distance, no perspective. Just infinite space. Except for the old man.

"Hello," he said, his voice flat. "Can I help you with something?"

He was slender rather than thin, but hunched with age. He was dressed in a white tunic and cloak, which were embroidered with infinity symbols. His cold eyes were expressionless, and he looked at the companions with all the interest of an architect examining a grain of sand.

Before any of them could speak, Jack grabbed John's elbow and nodded at what the old man held in his hand.

It was a pocket watch. A silver pocket watch.

"You aren't supposed to be here," the old man said dismissively. "You aren't members of the Quorum. You can't be here."

"Begging your pardon," said Charles, "but we didn't plan to be. We had every intention of being elsewhere."

"Then do so, and go," he answered with a wave of his hand. "I have work to do."

"We would if we could," John put in, "but we don't know where—or when—we are."

The old man didn't reply, but merely regarded them with disdain—until his eyes fell on Rose.

To the companions' great surprise, his mouth dropped open in shock and his eyes, cold a moment before, suddenly filled with tears.

"Rose," he said, his voice barely a whisper. "How can you be . . . ?"

Barely taking his eyes off her, he opened the pocket watch, which bore no dragon on the cover, and was festooned with several more dials and buttons than John's own watch.

The old man's forehead wrinkled in confusion. "Most unusual," he murmured to himself. "A new zero point, and here, in Platonia! This must be brought before the Quorum."

He snapped it shut and looked at Rose. His expression had completely changed—he was watching her with a rapt intensity that bespoke familiarity. Somehow, he knew her.

John looked at the girl. Her face was placid. She was observing, and nothing more. She didn't know—couldn't know—who the man was in this strange, infinite space.

"We're trying to reach a place called the Keep of Time," Rose said. "Can you help us?"

"The keep?" he replied in surprise. "Interesting." He consulted his watch again and adjusted a dial. Then he looked up and actually smiled.

"By what means did you come here?" he asked.

Charles showed him the Trump. "Ah," said the old man. "Primitive, but useful in its own way." He moved closer and regarded the companions more carefully, taking furtive, emotion-laden glances at Rose.

"So you're the three," he said rhetorically. "The Prophecy had something to it, after all, did it?"

"We don't know anything about a prophecy," Charles said. "We just need to get Rose somewhere she'll be safe."

"And so you shall," said the old man, abruptly wheeling away.

He stood some distance off, with his back to them. "Use your card once more," he said at length. "It will take you where and when you are meant to be."

Charles did as instructed and held up the Trump, which was already beginning to expand—but this time there was no fading of the image. In moments the frame displayed a perfect, rich picture of the interior stairwell of the Keep.

"Thank you," John called out to the old man as the companions moved through.

He responded with little more than a shrug, and didn't turn around until the frame began to shrink. Tears streaked his cheeks, and he was clutching the watch with hands that trembled.

"I am . . . glad to have seen you, all of you," he said in a shaky voice. "And Rose," he added, "try to think well of me in the future—and in the past."

And with that, the infinite whiteness vanished as the Trump closed, and the companions found themselves standing within the Keep of Time.

PART TWO

ABANDONED HOUSES

CHAPTER FIVE

THE SPANISH PRISONER

IT WAS NOT in the Magician's nature to wait for anything, so it was boredom, rather than the arduous journey or noxious atmosphere, that finally caused him to lose his temper. Fortunately, his companion, whom he had drolly dubbed "The Detective," was accustomed to such outbursts and took them in stride.

"This was not what I signed up for," the Magician grumbled. "I was the toast of Europe. America was at my feet. I had the run of the finest hotels, and the best restaurants valued my opinion of their fare more than they did the critics'. But mostly, I was enjoying myself. And I gave all that up for what? To sit here, in a leaky boat, ticking off the seconds that pass as the stench eats away at my topcoat. I've had it, I tell you."

His companion nodded in understanding. "I don't want to be here any more than you do, Ehrich. But we can't exactly let our attention flag—not at this juncture. You know as well as I do how crucial it is that we are here doing what we're doing."

"I told you, *Ignatius*, don't call me Ehrich," the Magician shot back before settling down, as his look of indignation was slowly replaced by one of resignation. "I know we agreed to do this, and I still believe in our cause. It just feels as if our talents are being wasted. You and I represent the finest in our fields—and yet we have committed ourselves to the role of errand boys."

"Errand boys in the service of a greater calling," the Detective pointed out. "After all, Columbus discovered the Americas, but someone still had to row him ashore."

"Do you remember his name?" the Magician retorted. "Does anyone? I want my own place in the history books, thank you very much. I don't want to change the world by proxy."

"You do have your own place in the history books," said the Detective. "That accomplishment cannot be erased, merely added to."

"It would have been easier to add to before I died," the Magician grumbled. "At least then I was visible on the world's stage."

"You still are," said his companion. "It's just a different world."

The Magician was about to say something in reply, when both men were suddenly silenced by a deep rumbling sound emanating from the sky.

They shaded their eyes from the sunlight and peered upward to a floating structure so distant it appeared to be a dark smudge against the sky. Suddenly several small objects appeared and grew swiftly larger as they fell.

"Row!" shouted the Magician, grabbing an oar. "They're dropping straight for us!"

The two men hastily moved the boat several feet south just as the first stones and part of an archway struck the water where they'd been sitting. A few moments later another object, larger this time, hit the water with a violent splash.

"That's it!" said the Detective, reaching out with a pole that ended in a hook. "I've got it—grab your end, will you?"

"I have it," said the Magician, pulling the object into the small boat, which sank several inches into the water with the added weight. "When do you think it is? Are we up to Victorian yet?"

"I have no idea," said the Detective. "He doesn't let us go through them anymore, remember?"

"That's not my fault, Arthur," said the Magician, using a less provocative name. "I'm sure we'll be allowed to use them again sooner or later."

"I could care less, Harry," Arthur said as he took up an oar and began to row. "As far as I'm concerned, the only value in opening doors to the past is what they can do for our future—whatever world we end up in."

The Magician did not reply, but merely took up rowing with the other oar, and in moments the two men, the leaky rowboat, and a door into time had vanished into the fog.

"What was *that* all about?" John asked Rose. "Who was that man?"

"I have no idea," Rose answered. "But he certainly seemed to know me. And he did help us."

"I'd've thought to try the card again eventually," Charles huffed. "It was only a matter of time before it occurred to one of us."

"Of course, Uncle Charles," said Rose. "He just helped move the process along."

"Well," Charles said, blushing.

"The Trump couldn't have been better placed," said Jack, pointing down. "Have a look, fellows."

There was, in point of fact, almost no floor at all. They had stepped onto one of the landings where the stairways crisscrossed, but just a few steps below there was only open sky. A few yards below, the jagged bottom edge of the tower's stones hung over clouds higher than a mountain, and the stairways' supports had been twisted into chaotic shapes from the weight of the falling stones.

"Another level lower, and we'd have been treading air," said Jack. "We ought to tell Ransom he needs to redraw his card from a higher vantage point."

"I'm not sure he can," John said, pointing in the opposite direction. As one, the Caretakers gasped. They could see the ceiling. That meant there were perhaps forty or so doors left in the tower before the ongoing entropy reached the room where the Cartographer was. And after that . . .

"I say," Charles mused, looking downward. "Is that a boat down there, below us? It's too far to make out properly."

Jack wrapped his arm around a twisted piece of railing and looked to where Charles was pointing. "I think it is," he said, puzzled. "What would a boat that small be doing in the Chamenos Liber?"

Before any of them could venture an answer, the tower began to rumble and shake. A thunderous noise filled the air, and before their eyes the stones in the walls began to separate.

"It's coming apart!" John yelled, scrambling for the landing. "Up the steps, quickly!"

Together the three men raced up the stairs, pushing Rose ahead of them for safety. If one of them fell, as their friend Aven once had, there was no *Indigo Dragon* to catch them before they hit the surface of the water below.

An entire section of stones and steps fell away just before the frame of the lowest door also peeled off and dropped, as, finally, did the door. Abruptly the tower stopped trembling, and the four companions could once again catch their breath.

"That was close," John breathed.

"Too close," Jack agreed.

"I can't see the door," said Charles, peering over the edge of the steps. "Or the boat. I hope it didn't sink the poor devils."

"They probably just left," Jack offered. "It's a terrible place to be fishing, anyway. It stinks of sulfur, and stones are always unexpectedly dropping out of the sky."

"Yes, but anyone in the vicinity would already know that," said John. "Who would come here to fish?"

"Trolls," said Charles. "Or Cambridge scholars."

"Never mind," said Jack, trying to hide a smile at his friend's joke. "Everyone all right? Rose? Archie?"

"I'm fine," Rose replied, looking at the owl. "This is the most fun I've had in ages."

"They're not very bright," Archimedes commented to her, "but they do have a way of keeping things stirred up. Good for the vim and vigor."

"If we could find a way to stir things up less," said Jack, "we'd be very happy men, eh, John? I say, John—are you listening?"

The Caretaker Principia slowly shook his head.

"What's the matter?" Charles asked.

"That door," John said, pointing across the landing. "It's *open*."

"So it is," said Jack. "The last tremor probably shook it loose."

"I've never seen that happen before," John observed. "Remember, the doors are anchored on the reverse by the time they open to. I don't think they *can* be jarred open."

"Should we close it?" asked Charles.

"I'm wondering if we shouldn't have a look," John replied. "So much of what's happening has to do with the Time Storms caused by the collapse of the keep—and Burton is obviously playing at a game we haven't seen yet. I say we have a look."

"We should discuss this," said Jack.

"I agree," said Charles.

"You scholars are worse than three Scots with a match," said Archimedes, "if you have to have a referendum and debate over something as elementary as whether to open or close a door."

Rose did not voice an opinion, but simply walked across the landing and pulled the door open.

"Oh Lord," said Charles. "It's done, fellows. Let's have a look—if it's some prehistoric beastie, we can close it quick."

"Agreed," John said, turning to Rose. "Just don't step over the—"

Rose stepped over the threshold and through the door.

It took a few moments for the frail-seeming, bearded old man to realize that the light falling across the goosedown quilts of his bed was not from the window.

The oil lamps in the room provided enough light for him to read and write. But mostly, he slept. The perpetual twilight kept him in a constant state of drowsiness, and besides, he was tired. Tired to the bone. He'd had a lifetime of adventuring, and this, such as it was, was his reward.

He might have been happier on some island in the outer reaches of the Archipelago, but he would not have lived nearly as long. Here, in this room, Time itself had stopped—or so he'd been told.

And so he waited.

Waited to discover if the so-called Prophecy might indeed come true. Waited, because if it were true, then he would once again be needed. And as often as he had done great deeds and had remarkable adventures, it was all only for the reason that someone had needed him. This, and the love of a beautiful woman, were all the motivation he needed. And so he waited, because the Frenchman had promised that someday he would be needed again.

In his half-drowsy state, he barely noted the new streamers of light in the room, and only then when a shadowy form approached his bed and leaned in closely to speak to him.

"Is it you?" he asked, eyes blinking with tears. "Is it my Dulcinea?"

"My name is Rose Dyson," the girl said as the old man rubbed the sleep goblins from his eyes and propped himself up onto his elbows, "but Dulcinea is a beautiful name, especially with your accent."

"Ah," the old man demurred, "it is in the nature of old Spaniards to speak the name of their one true love as if she were the only woman on earth."

"And how should I call you?" asked Rose.

The old man sat up straighter in his bed and adjusted his nightshirt, then preened his mustache and beard before answering.

"My name, dear girl," he said with gravity and panache, "is Don Quixote de la Mancha. And I have been waiting for you for a very long time."

The three Caretakers and the owl entered the room, but only John paused to examine the door. Any other door in the keep could be opened with a touch, save for the Cartographer's door, which had been sealed by the mark of the king: the Greek letter *alpha*.

Next to the handle on this door was a small Greek letter *pi*—the mark of the Caretaker Principia. John's mark—which he had never made.

John filed the observation away in the back of his head to be addressed later. For now, he wanted to discover the identity of the strange man who was conversing so easily with young Rose.

The man who had introduced himself to Rose as Don Quixote was now making similar introductions to Jack and Charles. Archimedes was ignoring them altogether and had instead focused on the books to one side of the great bed.

The room was almost identical in size to the one farther up where the Cartographer resided. But rather than a clutter-filled workplace, this room had been appointed for comfort. The elaborate four-poster bed was covered in goosedown quilts and draped with finely embroidered heavy silk curtains. There was a tall window with lead-lined panes of milky glass, and several beautiful oil lamps. The books were scattered about, as were the habiliments of a knight: a lance, a sword and scabbard, and authentic—if tarnished—sixteenth-century Spanish armor.

If this is not the real Don Quixote, John thought, *he has certainly made the effort to play the part.*

The old man rose from the bed and straightened his nightshirt. He was impossibly thin and wore a thick beard that pointed in two directions. His hair was more gray than black, and more white than gray.

"If the lady will shield her eyes," Quixote said diplomatically, "I should like to dress."

Rose obediently stood in the corner, looking over Archimedes' shoulder as Charles and Jack helped the old knight dress. His clothing and armor were humble but fit him well. Once he was dressed, he again sat on the bed, and Rose sat beside him.

"You said you were waiting for us," she asked. "Why?"

"Because of the Prophecy, of course," Quixote replied. "You do know about the Prophecy, do you not?"

"We've heard rumors," said Jack, "but we've been a little too pressed for time to ask anyone about specifics."

"Well then, I shall tell you," Quixote declared. "After all, it is your Prophecy."

"Ours?" said John. "How do you know?"

"Because," replied Quixote, "you are the only ones, other than the Frenchman, who have come through that door in nearly four centuries. He said that I would meet three Caretakers, and it would be my honor to aid them in their quest."

The Frenchman. Obviously Verne, thought John, whose interest was suddenly piqued. "You called us Caretakers," he said. "Do you know about the *Imaginarium Geographica*?"

"Know of it?" said Quixote in surprise and mock chagrin. "Why, in all modesty, if it had not been for me, there would be no *Imaginarium Geographica* to take care of. It is one of the greatest, most important books in history—but even great books may, on occasion, be lost. And when that happens, it falls to heroes such as myself to find them again."

"It's hard to imagine a Caretaker losing the *Geographica*," said Jack, winking at John. "The height of irresponsibility, if you ask me."

"Accidents happen," John said, reddening. "People do misplace things, you know."

"Exactly so," said Quixote. "That's one of the reasons there are three of you, did you know?

"The book known as the *Imaginarium Geographica* has passed through a number of Caretakers," he went on. "Dante, and Chaucer; Giovanni Boccaccio; Petrarch. But sometime in the sixteenth century—my century," he added with a bit of wistful pride, "a Caretaker managed to *lose* the *Geographica*—and at the precise time when a terrible conflict was brewing in the Archipelago."

"What kind of conflict?" asked Jack.

"Let me ask you this," replied Quixote. "Have you ever read about a tyrant who called himself the Winter King?"

"Once or twice," John deadpanned. "So to speak."

"At that time, there were rumors of his arrival in the Archipelago," said Quixote. "The first concern was that the *Geographica* be kept safe, and there seemed no safer place than within the halls of Paralon itself. So it had always been kept in the Archipelago. But somehow the book was stolen, and the worlds were plunged into a shadow of fear. No one knew where it had gone, nor what use the thief would put it to. All that was known was that it had been taken across the Frontier, into the real world.

"The Caretaker, Miguel de Cervantes, was summoned to a meeting of the Parliament in Paralon, where all the races of the Archipelago had come together to debate the matter. His guide and messenger, a tall, thin Spaniard, agreed to venture out into the real world to search for the *Geographica*."

"You," said Charles. "That was you."

"Just so," the knight said, bowing his head in acknowledgment. "In my search, I encountered a scholarly detective named Edmund Spenser, who helped me to discover that the *Geographica* was not lost, but had indeed been stolen. The thief was Tycho Brahe, who was a scholar of Ptolemaic geography and had heard of a marvelous book that contained maps said to be created by Ptolemy himself."

"That's mostly true," Archie piped up from the corner, "although he did have some help—and some of his students actually did all the *real* work."

"While Spenser and I pursued the *Geographica,* Cervantes had an adventure of his own, wherein he met an ethereal creature called the Lady of the Lake. He gave her a kiss, and she gave him a bracelet in return and also the secret of passage between the worlds.

"On Cervantes's return to England, he was reunited with myself, Spenser, and Brahe, whom I'd brought to London. I had found the *Geographica* once more, and it was determined that there must always be three Caretakers, to avoid such a catastrophe ever happening again."

"We know about that," John said, opening the book and turning to the endpapers. Below the names of those who had come before, Cervantes, Brahe, and Spenser had signed their names in the front of the Geographica with the same quill and the same ink.

The old knight nodded and beamed at the sight of the book. "I witnessed the signing myself," he said proudly. "It was one of the great moments in a life full of such moments."

"Why didn't you sign?" Charles asked. "You had every right to become a Caretaker, and more than enough reason to justify it."

Quixote shook his head. "I am a messenger at worst, and a knight with noble ambitions at best. I am inquisitive, but it was not my destiny. Also, I asked, but was not chosen."

"Chosen by whom?" wondered Jack.

"By the Prime Caretaker," Quixote replied. "He said that at that time, those three must needs be the Caretakers—that I had had my role to play, and perhaps would again.

"As to the three who were chosen, the *Geographica*, together with the bracelet given to Cervantes, was passed from one to the other, the better to keep it secret and safe. When one of the three died, another would have been in preparation to take his place. And as Geoffrey of Monmouth did before them, the Caretakers, often writers as much as geographers or scholars, shared a fictitious version of their adventures with the world. I know that Miguel did as much with regards to my stories, if not with his own adventures.

"Spenser went on to write *The Faerie Queen*, and that feckless thief, Brahe, passed on the *Geographica* to Johannes Kepler."

"Few men of science have been chosen to become Caretakers," said John, "but it makes sense that Brahe passed it to Kepler. Scientist to scientist, as it were."

"In those bygone days," said Quixote, "science was about explaining things, and thus was as much an art as anything else. But in later years science became about *proving* things—when all that was ever really required of science *or* art was to simply believe."

"Spenser and a later Caretaker—Wordsworth, I believe—both wrote of Arthur's sons, Artigel and Eligure," said Charles. "It's one of the better volumes in the Histories."

"You mentioned a Prophecy," Jack interjected, "and you said it relates to us. How is that? What is the Prophecy?"

Quixote sighed heavily and began again. "As you know, the *Imaginarium Geographica* was passed on year to year to new Caretakers. It was in the care of one of the most recent of their number, a Frenchman called Jules Verne, in the first years of the twentieth century, when mysteriously, the bracelet of the Lady of the Lake was stolen. For a brief time, the *Geographica* itself was also lost.

"Soon after, stories of a dark, evil presence that lingered on the edges of the Archipelago, not quite living, yet not dead, began to reappear. An evil waiting for its opportunity to seize power. An evil referred to in veiled whispers only as 'the Winter King.' For years the stories had persisted, almost fading away into myth and fable, but now the stories began anew. And this time, the whispers went, the Winter King was not waiting and watching—he was at work. He was building a ship called the *Black Dragon,* which he intended to use to cross the Frontier and conquer all of the Archipelago of Dreams.

"It was only then that the Frenchman, Verne, realized that the Winter King was no new villain, but an old threat, who had before plunged the worlds into war. And he recalled a Prophecy, made centuries earlier, that should such an evil once again appear, he would be defeated only by three scholars from your world. And from that day forward, Verne devoted all his time and resources to finding and preparing the three for the battle that was to come."

"What?" declared Jack. "Do you mean us? We're the three?"

"We *were* the Caretakers when the Winter King was defeated," said John, "so it's possible."

"But we *already* defeated him," Jack exclaimed, "so what does that mean?"

The Caretakers looked to one another in resignation. They all knew it could mean only one of two things: Either the Prophecy Quixote spoke of was wrong, and they hadn't needed him to defeat the Winter King at all; or he was right, and a final conflict with their greatest enemy was still to come. The old man in the white place had also referred to a prophecy—and that was too unlikely to be a simple coincidence.

"We must take him with us," Jack suddenly said. "Don Quixote, come with us, please."

At first John was surprised by the urgent tone in Jack's voice, but a moment later he realized what his friend's motive was.

The Keep was still crumbling. And the next tremor would destroy Quixote's room.

The knight needed no further prompting. He, Rose, and Archimedes gathered a few items in a small knapsack, while the Caretakers conversed near the door, which Jack had propped open.

"His story does make sense," Jack whispered. "Cervantes *was* a Caretaker, after all. And we all know Caretakers have fictionalized real events and peoples from the Archipelago in their stories. We've done it ourselves!"

"I can't recall the generalities of his story, much less the specifics," said John. "Did we overlook it, Charles?"

"That's just it," Charles protested. "It's not that I might have overlooked his story in one of the Histories—it isn't in the Histories *at all*. I've been very thorough, especially after the Dyson incident—and I'm telling you, the story he's related to us is nowhere to be found."

"And what was that about Jules Verne losing the *Geographica*?" said John. "I can't believe that. He's always too many moves ahead of any adversary. I can't believe he'd ever countenance such a blow."

"Then again," said Jack, "we were once young and stupid—or at least, younger and stupider than we are now. We learned to become the men we are in part because of the mistakes we made. Couldn't the same be possible for Verne?"

"We've overlooked something else," said Charles. "Hank Morgan also mentioned a Prophecy. So it isn't just Quixote. Something larger is afoot, I'm sure of it. But do we believe him or not?"

"Either way," said Jack, "I don't think we have a choice—we have to take him with us, or he'll perish with the next tremor."

The three companions silently agreed. On that point, there was not—could not—be a debate. Every other door in the keep, save for the Cartographer's, opened into an entire world at a particular point in the past—and when the doors fell, the passageway was simply severed. But this room was actually part of the keep—and to stay within it would be too great a risk.

"All set," Quixote said, having also loaded himself down with a considerable array of weaponry. "What is our destination?"

"Up," said John, pointing. "We go up."

The company, which now numbered six, stepped from the room and closed the door. John felt the small click of a lock under his fingertips, and the *pi* symbol seemed to glow faintly as the door closed.

"What has happened to the tower?" Quixote asked as he looked worriedly over the railing at the damaged keep and the nausea-inducing drop. "It is eternal, is it not?"

"Everything ends," said Jack. "Eventually."

The old knight shook his head sadly. "I fear you are right. But still, it is a fearsome sight."

"Look up, old fellow," said Charles. "That's my answer. Always look up."

Quixote nodded, then took a position behind Jack as together, the companions and their new acquaintance began to climb.

As the group ascended the stairway, the Caretakers explained to the knight whom it was they were going to see.

"I have heard stories of this man, if a man he truly is," said Quixote, "but I have never seen him with my own eyes. Only in stories, and from the things the Frenchman says, do I know him at all."

"He's a difficult man to understand," John said, "but then again, he's also two millennia old. We've all spent time with him in our calling as Caretakers, but we also had the chance to know him at various points in his youth. I regret to say that if we had been more perceptive, or simply better examples and less fearful, he might have become a better man than he is."

"You knew him in his youth?" said Quixote. "Two millennia ago?"

"It was under unusual circumstances," said John.

"Those were indeed unusual circumstances," said Quixote, "if you could manage such a journey through time."

"It was an accident," Jack put in, "involving a scholar and two badgers."

"That would probably be enough," said Quixote. He looked down at Rose. "And you, young Rose? Do you also know this Cartographer of Lost Places?"

Rose smiled. "I've only met him once," she replied, "but in a way I'm closer to him than the Caretakers are. I'm his niece."

"His niece?" Quixote said in surprise, wondering at her obvious youth. "If that is so, then either you have also slept for many years in a tower, so that the days pass you by, untouched—or you have a remarkable parentage."

"You have no idea," said Charles.

* * *

It took very little time, relative to their previous visits, for the companions to reach the top of the stairway and the second to last door. John and Jack took furtive glances at the last door a bit higher in the keep—the door that opened onto the future.

Rose had already guessed her role in this visit. The door was locked, to be opened only by one of the descendants of Arthur—but as had been proven once before, being Arthur's cousin was authority enough. Rose reached out and opened the door.

It swung into the room on silent hinges, revealing what could only be described as organized clutter. Maps and globes and parchment and books filled the space, making it seem smaller than Quixote's room some forty doors below. In the center of the cartological maelstrom sat a familiar figure, who was busy at work.

"Oh, drat," the Cartographer said without looking up from his desk. "Is it already the end of the world again?"

CHAPTER SIX
THE LAST MAP

ROSE ENTERED THE ROOM first, followed by Archie, the three Caretakers, and Quixote, who was still trying to take stock of what was going on—as well as when and where, for that matter.

"Hello, Uncle," Rose said. "You're looking well."

"What?" the Cartographer said, tilting his head and peering over the top of his glasses. His expression softened when he saw the girl. "Looking well for my age, you mean," he went on, putting down his quill and standing to better appraise his visitors. "It feels like a thousand years since I last saw you, child."

"Nearly that, Uncle," said Rose as she moved forward and embraced the old man. After a moment's hesitation, he returned the hug and even kissed the top of her head.

"What do you mean, the end of the world?" John asked, closing the door. "Which world are you talking about?"

The Cartographer sighed. "Your first question is ripe with stupidity, but your second redeems you," he said with a snort. "To make maps, or assist with annotations, or sign autographs for a badger requires only one or two of you to come see me, but for"—he paused and counted heads—"five of you, plus my niece, to come means some kind of disaster is imminent, and at the rate this tower has been crumbling, my guess is that the world is ending."

"So when the tower is destroyed, the world will end?" asked Charles.

"My world will, at any rate," said the Cartographer, "so I don't really make a distinction."

"I've apologized before," Charles offered, "but repairing the keep really is something that's beyond my abilities—or anyone else's, for that matter."

The old mapmaker waved his hands dismissively. "I wasn't chiding you, boy," he said with a huff. "We've all known what the inevitable end would be. But still, it would have been nice if you'd dropped in more often to chat. Brought me some cookies, a comic book or two. A better television would have been nice. You can imagine what the reception is like here in the Archipelago."

"We've come as frequently as we've been needed," John started to protest, "and more often in recent years."

"More often?" said the Cartographer. "You haven't been back at all in at least seven years, if not more."

John glanced around at his companions with a dark expression. Ransom had been correct: Going through a card created in their future had *transported* them to that future. They were in 1943.

"Don't be so sour about it," the Cartographer said, noting the expressions on the Caretakers' faces. "I'm only having a go at you."

"It's not that," John began. "When Ransom sent us here, he—"

"Ransom sent you?" the Cartographer said in surprise. "Alvin Ransom? I thought he'd gotten himself lost in the Southern Isles along with Arthur Pym."

"Ah, that would be me," Quixote said, raising his hand. "And I was not lost—not precisely, in any regard."

"He sent us here through this," Charles said, holding up the Trump. "It worked a bit differently than we'd expected it to, but it did work."

"That's very interesting," the Cartographer said, in a way that indicated he was not used to being interested. He folded his hands behind him and paced across the braided carpet. "Ransom . . . he's Verne's apprentice now, is he not? A very quick study in many ways. In point of fact, he was here very recently, making that selfsame card. But he does have his drawbacks, you know." He stopped and looked at Jack. "Cambridge man, you see."

Jack started. "Why point that out to me?"

"You'll find out in around a decade or so, if there's still a Cambridge by then," the Cartographer replied with a wink. "Just don't let the badgers know."

"What do you know about him?" asked John. "We've only spent a few hours with him, and we only went along because he had one of the pocket watches."

"Ah, he did, did he?" said the Cartographer. "That was one of my ideas, I'll have you know. Something we used to do in the old days of the Mystery Schools, although I'm not really given to joining secret societies—not ones that would have me as a member, at any rate."

He held out his hands and waggled his eyebrows, but got only puzzled looks in return. "Does no one in Oxford watch the Marx Brothers? Never mind," he said with a wave. "Ransom. Bright lad. Unusually adept with spatial perceptions, as you've no doubt noticed. I had him training with me here for a few months before he was seduced by the Frenchman. Not sure if it's a loss or a gain, overall."

"What were you training him for?" asked John. "To be a Caretaker?"

"To be a Cartographer, actually," came the reply. "You don't think I want this job forever, do you?"

"I wasn't aware that you could resign," Charles said mildly.

The Cartographer grinned wryly. "Resign, no, but retire, probably, and whether I like it or not, thanks to you," he said, wagging a finger at Charles, who blushed. "Or hadn't you noticed? I don't have a retirement plan in place, but it would be nice to have a successor.

"I don't hold out much hope for that happening, though," he continued, with a heavy exhalation of breath. "I understand that something's been stirred up back in the Summer Country, and that's causing chaos here in the Archipelago. No one really bothers to keep me updated on things unless they need something from me—but if it's as bad as the wind seems to indicate, I won't be useful to them for much longer anyway. All I do is make maps, and with that," he finished, pointing to the *Geographica* sticking out of John's pack, "you have all the maps anyone needs in this world."

"I think that's part of why we're here," said John. "We have to get Rose to a place that isn't in the *Geographica*."

The Cartographer made a sputtering noise, and his eyes bugged out. "If it isn't in the *Imaginarium Geographica*, boy, then it wasn't worth noting, or no longer exists. And there are even maps of places in the latter category still in it, so—"

Jack interrupted him. "Ransom told us we needed to make

our way to someplace called the Nameless Isles. Do you know anything about them?"

"The Nameless Isles!" the old man exclaimed, eyes blazing with anger. In an unusual show of physicality, he actually stepped forward and grabbed Jack by the lapels. "Are you certain that's what he called them? The Nameless Isles? Tell me, boy! Tell me now!"

All three Caretakers were taken aback at this sudden flaring of emotion. They had seen the man known as the Cartographer at many periods throughout his life—but during his tenure in the Keep of Time, they'd never seen him express anything more than annoyance.

"That's precisely what he called them," said Jack. "We don't mean to upset you, Myrddyn."

At the mention of his true name, the old man was startled out of his anger. He let go of Jack, and with a few deep breaths, he composed himself once more.

"I apologize," he said haltingly. "It's become somewhat of a joke, this 'end of the world' business, especially with the tower crumbling more each day. But the Nameless Isles were something to be hidden away, not named, not discussed, not shown, until and unless the actual end of the world was imminent.

"Far to the north of the Archipelago of Dreams, past the domains of the Troll King, past the islands of the Christmas Saint, lies a circlet of islands that have never been named. No map has been drawn to locate them—well, none that could be duplicated, that is. And certainly none that could be included in the *Imaginarium Geographica*."

"Why couldn't they?" John asked.

"Because the islands themselves are alive," came the response, "or at least as close to living creatures as large masses of stone are likely to get. They have a form of consciousness, and they have will. They are constantly on the move, so they can never be found in the same way twice. A map on paper or parchment would be useless."

John grimaced. "How can we find them if they're always moving?"

Archimedes let out a snort and sidled over to the Cartographer. "He really doesn't listen well, does he?"

"It's been a constant problem," the Cartographer admitted. "I told you the maps could not be included in the *Imaginarium Geographica,*" he said to John, "not that the islands couldn't be mapped at all.

"Finding the route to a living island that is constantly moving," the Cartographer went on, "requires a living map that may constantly change—and so every map I have ever drawn for the Nameless Isles has been drawn on the seekers themselves."

"You're going to draw the maps on *us?*" Jack exclaimed.

"Not all of you," the Cartographer said in exasperation. "I do have other deadlines to meet, you know, and drawing one on each of you would take all day and then some. No, just one of you will do. So," he finished, rubbing his hands together, "whose strong back shall we transform into a map?"

John's face took on a dour expression, and Jack stammered a moment, trying to decide what to say. In his younger days, he would have been the first to volunteer, but age and seasoning had made him much less rash. Still, one of them was going to have to do it if they were to make any progress at all.

Quixote suddenly stepped forward and removed his helmet as

he dropped to one knee. "If I may serve yet again in this humble way," he said in his high baritone, "then I shall offer myself as the canvas for your quill."

The Cartographer looked startled for a moment, then made a clucking sound with his tongue and helped the knight to his feet.

"Your self-sacrificing gesture is appreciated, and your honor and nobility are without question," the old mapmaker said, "but to be most frank, while your spirit is willing, your flesh is wrinkled. I could do it, no question, but it would be akin to projecting a movie reel onto a shar-pei."

"Uncle Merlin," Rose began as the others comforted the crest-fallen Quixote, "I would be willing—"

"Absolutely not," he replied, holding his hands up defiantly. "For all I know you've already got a tattoo or three, and I'm not going to be accused of adding to your delinquency. Also, you're still quite small, and an island is likely to slide off your back altogether.

"No," he said with finality, "If it's to be any of you, it must be one of the Caretakers three."

"We could draw straws," Jack began, when Charles let out a loud noise of exasperation.

"Oh, for heaven's sake," he said as he began pulling off his shirt. "I'll do it, but when my wife starts asking prickly questions, I'm deferring to you fellows."

The Cartographer instructed Charles to lean himself over the drafting table to allow as even a working surface as possible. It was set low to the floor, so Charles's legs dangled at an awkward angle until his companions propped them up with pillows.

"Uncle Charles," Rose said, hiding a giggle, "you look like a bear rug, stretched out to dry."

"More like a bare rug," said John. "The press doesn't let you out to get much sun, does it, old fellow?"

"Do you want to trade places?" Charles shot back.

"Looking good," John said quickly. "Carry on."

The Cartographer rummaged around in the overladen shelves in the back corner of the room, muttering to himself, until he finally emerged with a long, gleaming black quill and a stoppered bottle of ink.

"The quill is made from the tail feather of one of Odin's ravens," he explained as he took his seat behind Charles. "Hugin . . . or maybe it was Munin. I forget. It doesn't matter, anyway. What makes this process work is the ink."

He set the quill aside and gently removed the stopper from the bottle, which appeared to be half-full. The cloudy liquid inside swirled about lazily in the glass and seemed to emanate a faint glow and a familiar scent.

"Apple cider?" John said, sniffing. "The ink you use is apple cider? Will that even work?"

"An unusual map requires an unusual medium," the old mapmaker replied. "It only smells like cider because of its extreme age."

"Did it come from one of the apples on Haven?" Jack asked. "Those trees were quite old, I believe."

"Oh, it's far, far older than that," said the Cartographer as he dipped the quill point into the bottle. "If it didn't come from one of the oldest trees that ever was, it certainly was in their forest. You who subscribe to these newfangled modern religions have a name for it: the Tree of Knowledge of Good and Evil."

Charles nearly bolted upright. "Do you mean the juice you're using to draw with may have come from an apple off the same tree Adam and Eve took an apple from in the Garden of Eden?"

"Same *tree*?" the Cartographer said indignantly. "Pish-tosh. It's from the same *apple*. They only took two bites from it, after all.

"Now," he said, adjusting his glasses. "Hold still—I want to get this right the first time."

Slowly, with deft and deliberate strokes, the ancient man once called Myrddyn, then Meridian, and then Merlin, before at last becoming known only by his trade, began drawing the map that would guide the companions to the Nameless Isles.

He began at the lower left, just under Charles's rib cage, with a vast island large enough to have continental aspirations. Then, pausing only to dip the quill, he quickly worked his way upward, adding smaller islands in a variety of shapes and putting in navigational notations as he sketched. Another sizeable island was situated between the shoulder blades, followed by two half-moon isles that were obviously volcanic in nature.

As he drew, the lines of the cloudy apple ink left only a shiny, moist indication that quill had touched skin; but as he sketched his way down the right side of Charles's back, a curious transformation began to happen on the left.

The lines wavered, faded, then solidified into a rich, reddish-brown color, much like the lines in the older maps of the *Geographica*.

As the map was being created before the companions, all of them were transfixed by the mapmaker's work—except for Rose. While the others watched the line work magically appearing, she remained focused on the maker.

They had only ever met once before, in this very room, but she had known who he was instantly.

She knew because her mother and grandfather had told her stories about him and about her father, who was called Madoc before he took the name Mordred, and through the stories she came to know them. She knew everything about them, including—or perhaps especially—the flaws that had made them who they became. And she learned something else: that when you know everything about a person, it becomes very difficult to hate them, and very easy to love them.

And so there, in that small stone room near the top of a floating tower made of time, six personages watched the old mapmaker create his work on his living canvas. Two, the clockwork owl and the ancient knight, watched with a sense of duty for what was to come. Three, the Caretakers, watched with awe, reverence, and a small inkling of fear for what the map portended. But only one, the Grail Child Rose, watched with love—because she was the only one there who was more concerned with seeing the mapmaker himself than with obtaining what he might provide to them.

The Cartographer halted to consider his work, then again leaned close and completed the circlet of islands that ringed Charles's back. "Now," he said softly, "for the final three."

He dipped the quill one last time, then stoppered the bottle. "Waste not, et cetera," he breathed to no one in particular. Swiftly he drew one final island in the center and added several notations above and below.

The old man leaned back and closed one eye, examining, appraising. Then, with a nod that indicated he was satisfied, he stood up and replaced the quill and bottle where he'd found them.

"One of my better works, all told," he said, wiping his hands on a cloth. "You're quite a good canvas, young Charles. Patient, not fidgety, very few moles to work around. If I'd had a hundred of you I could have done the entire *Geographica* on the backs of scholars and done away with the parchment altogether. We could have kept you in a village somewhere, growing fat and happy on tea and cakes. Then, whenever a captain needed to go somewhere, we'd just call out your particular island and send you off with him."

"An interesting idea," John said as Charles groaned and straightened up. "But what happens when you lose one of the, uh, maps?"

"Interesting doesn't always equal practical," came the reply, "but being practical is always less interesting."

"How do you feel, Charles?" Jack asked as he helped his friend slip his shirt back on. "Does it itch?"

"It's not really too bad," said Charles as he tucked his shirt into his trousers. "It does tingle a bit, but not unpleasantly so. A little like having some friendly ants roaming around searching for a picnic."

"Better you than me," said John. "When you get back to London, you'll just have to remember to sleep on your back to avoid explaining it to your wife."

"No worries there," said the Cartographer. "The map isn't visible in the Summer Country—only here, in the Archipelago."

"Well, if I'd known *that*," Jack huffed, "I'd have volunteered myself."

"Mmm-hmm," Charles hummed skeptically. "I'm sure you would have, Jack."

"Thank you, for . . . for everything," said John, offering his hand to the Cartographer, who paused, then took it at the wrist, in the old fashion. "We should leave. There's no, ah, time to waste."

"We've overlooked one thing," Jack said mildly. "We're still stuck in the Keep of Time."

"It gets easier after the first thousand years or so," said the Cartographer.

"That is a problem," John agreed, realizing they'd come via a one-way passage. "And we don't have a Compass Rose with which to contact anyone either."

"Isolation clears the mind and sharpens the senses," said the Cartographer.

"Perhaps we could fashion some sort of rope and lower ourselves down," Charles suggested.

"And then what?" said Jack. "We swim to the Nameless Isles?"

"We could use the Opening to access the Underneath, and the islands below," John suggested, rubbing his chin. "Autunno is the closest source of allies we have."

"That just creates a whirlpool," Jack countered. "We'd only drop *farther*."

"Why are they arguing about this?" Quixote asked the Cartographer. "Aren't we just going to take the boat?"

The Cartographer shrugged. "I think it's the process they have to go through. They are somehow required to argue pointlessly about things that are completely irrelevant before deciding to do what was staring them in the face all along."

John looked at the old men. "You have a boat?"

"Of course I have a boat," the Cartographer shot back. "You yourselves sent me here in it. It hasn't gone anywhere else since." He jerked a thumb over his shoulder at the chaotic shelves behind his chair.

Sitting there on the edge of the uppermost shelf was a small glass bottle that contained a miniature Dragonship.

"The *Scarlet Dragon,*" John said in realization. "I've never given it another thought."

"I'm not surprised in the least," Archimedes said, preening.

"So it turns into a boat when we break the glass," Jack said. "We still have no way to escape the tower."

"I'm suddenly beginning to see why you're professors," said the Cartographer as he handed Jack the ship in the bottle. "Arguing about the problem instead of asking if anyone has a solution is the best way to ensure tenure. Cambridge is lucky to have you."

"I teach at Oxford," said Jack.

"That's right," the old mapmaker murmured. "I keep forgetting what year it is."

He rustled around in the far corner of the room, where things seemed to be organized in piles rather than piled on shelves. After a minute he uttered a triumphant "Aha!" and turned back to the companions with a wry gleam in his eyes. He was clasping several sheets of parchment as if they were fragile china dolls.

"Here," the Cartographer said, proffering the pages to John. "See what you can make of these."

The old sheets of parchment looked very much like those in the *Imaginarium Geographica,* and John said as much, wondering aloud if they might have come from the same milling.

"Identical, in point of fact," the old mapmaker said with a hint of derision in his voice. "I'm surprised you even questioned it."

John and Jack examined the pages, which were ragged along one edge. "Torn out?" Jack asked. "Were these removed on purpose?"

The Cartographer nodded. "There are secrets hidden within those pages that were too much to handle for some of the Caretakers-in-training," he said blithely. "De Bergerac in particular made unorthodox use of them, and when that idiot Houdini was recruited, the Far Traveler and I were vindicated in our decision to tear them out."

"I thought the *Geographica* couldn't be destroyed," said Charles. "Wasn't that actually a problem when we started all this?"

The Cartographer sighed like a schoolmarm with a worn-out dunce cap. "For one thing, boy, I am the Cartographer. I made the atlas. So I can take out whatever I wish. And for another thing, I wasn't destroying them, merely hiding them. The ones that have been drawn on are dangerous enough—but four or five centuries ago a rogue Caretaker actually stole a stack of blank sheets."

"Is this the moon?" John asked, looking through the pages. "And . . . Mars?"

"Don't get distracted from your goals," the Cartographer said, grabbing the pages and riffling through them. "This here is what you need right now."

The page bore an unfinished drawing of a familiar place that was as comforting in its own way as Ransom's card of the keep had been.

"That's home!" Rose exclaimed. "I would so love to go there, Uncle John!"

"Avalon," said John, nodding. "That would be the perfect place to start the journey to the Nameless Isles. But," he continued, "the drawing is incomplete. Will it still work in the same way as Ransom's card?"

"What Ransom does by practice and instinct, you'll have to do paint-by-numbers," the Cartographer replied in a tone that was only slightly condescending. "I've seen you draw, Caretaker. You should be able to finish what Roger Bacon started."

"If you have the means to travel out of this place," remarked Charles, "then why didn't you leave ages ago? Why don't you come with us now?"

The Cartographer hesitated, and a hard look crossed his features, then softened. "I am bound, if you'll remember, to stay here in Solitude, until such time as Arthur chooses to release me."

"Arthur is dead," Charles said bluntly.

"Charles," chided Jack. "His heirs are able to open the door," he said, turning to the old mapmaker. "I'm sure it is within their power to free you as well."

"When and if they choose," the Cartographer said. He clapped his hands together. "But that is a discussion for a different day. For now, you need to finish the drawing and be on your way."

He provided a pencil and several crayons to John, who quickly began to draw on the sheet, sketching in details of the ruins that existed there now, blurring out the unblemished portrait that Bacon had begun of the structures that were new and unfallen. John had seen the island in both states—pristine and ruined—and he didn't want to take the risk that a drawing of Avalon as it once was would take them further back in time. Better that it take them to the place as he knew it best, even if it was only a shadow of its former glory.

In less than an hour the drawing was completed.

"Simply use it in the same way Ransom used the Trump," the Cartographer instructed them. "Hold the picture in your mind, then merge what you see there with the picture before you. It will expand, and you should then be able to step through.

"I would prefer not to watch, if you don't mind," he said dismissively. "You've distracted me enough today as it is, and I really must get back to work."

The Caretakers each thanked him and bade him good-bye. Don Quixote gave him a stiff and formal bow, which they were surprised to see returned. Rose gave the old mapmaker a hug, then kissed him on the cheek.

"Thank you, Uncle Merlin," she said. "I'm sure we'll see each other again very soon."

"Yes, yes," he said, pressing her away. "Be about your business. I must return to mine."

He turned away from the companions and took up his quill, then began to sketch on the parchment at his desk as if they weren't even in the room.

"Well enough," said John. "Let's take another trip, shall we?"

As they had done with the Trump of the keep, John held up the parchment so they could all concentrate on it. In seconds the soft susurrations of the breezes of Avalon began to swirl through the picture and into the chamber.

The image began to grow, until it filled the entire wall next to the door. Charles, Jack, and Rose moved through, followed by Archimedes and Quixote. John stepped through last, but only after one final glance at the Cartographer. The old man never looked up or ceased sketching with his quill.

The picture began to shrink rapidly, and in moments, it had vanished altogether.

• • •

For the rest of the day, the Cartographer sketched random lines across the parchment, creating the illusion of working, but in reality he was making motions at his desk for their own sake. He continued to do so until the point of his quill snapped, splattering ink across the sheet.

In frustration the old mapmaker crumpled up the page and threw it across the room. His lip quivered, and his eyes welled with moisture. Only a single tear escaped and trailed down his cheek to his chin, dropping to the floor, before he took out another sheet of parchment and a fresh pen and once more began to draw.

CHAPTER SEVEN
THE GROTTO

THE ISLAND OF Avalon occupies an unusual place within the wonder of creation, as it is the only island that exists equally in both the natural world and in that of the Archipelago of Dreams.

As such, it became the first true crossing place between the worlds. In the past there had been other points of passage—usually accidental—but experiments in recent years using dragon feathers and vehicles other than the Dragonships had proven that connections between the worlds are *everywhere*. With the proper preparation, it was possible to cross from any point along the Frontier, the great barrier of storms that protected the Archipelago, into any corresponding point in the natural world.

The steam-powered vehicles called principles had been used on occasion, but most frequently, Bert and other travelers had crossed over in the Dragonships, which Prince Stephen had refashioned into airships. So there was little need to sail on the waters through the traditional crossing point that was Avalon.

A shame, John thought as he stepped through the parchment, *especially considering the glory that this island once was.*

In their journey through the past to rescue Hugo Dyson, John and Jack had been able to see Avalon in its pristine state:

alabaster columns supporting high stone arches; glistening temples of marble and mother-of-pearl; walkways and walls of stone inlaid with jade. It was the Golden Age of the gods made manifest in a single ethereal vision. Only the vision was real, as were the goddesses who inhabited it.

"Well," Charles said once they had all moved through the parchment, "it's a bit more crumbly around the edges, but otherwise, it actually feels good to see this shabby old island again."

John chuckled to himself and winked at Jack. Of course Charles would see it differently than they did. He hadn't been with them on that adventure—not this Charles, at any rate. The "Charles" they'd had with them was from another timeline and was called Chaz. And he made a sacrifice of his own, becoming the first protector of Avalon—the first Green Knight.

"I wonder," said Charles in what was practically a continuation of John's thinking, "where the devil that scoundrel Magwich is? Shouldn't he have appeared by now, waving around a spear and asking us to state our allegiances, or some such?"

"Hmm," Jack mused, looking around the low embankment. "He's probably off taking a nap."

"Well, let's go," John began, turning to instruct the others on a plan of action, when he saw Rose and stopped.

She had dropped to her knees in the sand, and her eyes were full of tears. Quixote had knelt beside her and was gently trying to console her. Archie too was doing his best to make supportive gestures.

"We're all idiots," muttered Jack under his breath to John. "We were so intent on getting out of the tower that it never occurred to us how she would take coming here."

He's right, John thought as they moved over to the girl, *on both counts.*

Rose had been born on Avalon. She was conceived in the city of Alexandria, but her mother, Gwynhfar, had fled the Summer Country and come here. Gwynhfar joined the other two women on the island, the enchantress Circe and the sea-witch Calypso, in becoming the Morgaine—the three supernatural women who may have been the Fates, or goddesses, or simply beings of incomprehensible power.

Sometimes they changed personalities, if not personages—Gwynhfar was not among them when John, Jack, and Charles first met them—but there were always three, and they always reflected aspects of who they truly were. Sometimes they appeared as beautiful women; sometimes, harried old hags. Often the advice they gave was useful, but in John's experience, they were more manipulative than helpful. But whatever else they were, the original Morgaine had been Rose's mother and surrogate aunts. And whatever else Avalon represented, it had been the only home she had known, until John and Jack arrived there centuries earlier and took her with them to resurrect a dead king.

From that experience, she went to England and into a boarding school—and she had never come back to the place of her birth until now. So she had no memories of Avalon except from when it was full of gleaming, glorious edifices fit to rival the finest Greek temples. To come here now and see the island in such a state of disrepair had to be shattering.

"What happened?" Rose was asking as the other men knelt beside her. "What happened to my home? How did it get this way?"

"It's been almost five centuries," John said softly. "Many things change in that much time."

"But wasn't the knight here?" she asked, clutching Charles's hands. "You were here, Uncle Charles. Why did you let this happen?"

Charles stammered a bit under the directness of the question. "I . . . uh, I wish I could tell you, my dear child," he said, looking to John and Jack for support. "It wasn't I who came here, but I know he did the best he could."

"No one lives forever," Jack said, nodding in agreement. "Chaz did everything he could, I'm sure—but when he died, another took his place."

"And another after that," added John. "There have been twenty-six Green Knights, in fact, and I'm sure they all did the best they could. But nothing lasts forever."

"Well, something should," Rose said, still sniffling but calmer now. Quixote produced a beautiful if faded silk handkerchief for her to wipe her face and blow her nose. "Some things should last forever, especially when they exist on an island like Avalon."

"Tell you what," said John. "We'll find the Green Knight, the one who is the Guardian now, and we'll ask him what happened here."

"That sounds like a plan to me," Charles said, rising to his feet and cracking his knuckles. "I'd like to know where Maggot is myself."

The companions searched the island for the better part of an hour, but to no avail. There was no sign of Magwich.

He'd originally been forced to take the role of protector of Avalon by the Dragons, who offered him the choice of service or slow roasting on a spit. Others had become the Green Knight as a form of penance—but only Magwich, who had been a failed apprentice Caretaker, actually saw the role as a means to do as little as possible. He was lazier than he was stupid, but he was not completely irresponsible. If he was not on the island, then he was either dead, or worse.

"Maggot being dead wouldn't break my heart," said Charles with a touch of rancor.

"Whatever else Magwich was," John reminded him, "he also had Caretaker training. Perhaps not much, but enough to be dangerous. We must find where he's gone to."

"But he couldn't just leave the island, could he?" asked Jack. "Wouldn't he turn into dust, or at least set off alarms with the Dragons?"

"Artus sent the Dragons away, remember?" John said. "When he set up his republic, and dissolved the monarchy. If they weren't looking after the welfare of the king, they probably would have cared less about watching the goings-on of a third-rate knight on Avalon."

As they discussed the Magwich issue, Rose, Archie, and Quixote rejoined them from the short walk they'd taken to the western side of the island. Rose used to spend time there fishing with her paternal grandfather—or at least, that was who John and Jack had assumed the old man was—and she wanted to see if he, at least, was still there.

The expression on her face gave them the answer. Rose was still visibly upset, but she seemed to have mostly regained control of her emotions, and she was back to her usual mode of absorbing the information around her.

Rose was unusual in many ways—this had always been evident. But John realized that today was the first time in a long time that they perceived her as what she really was: a child, trying to learn the lessons she needed to become an adult. And finding that some lessons are harder than others.

"Let's go look around the cottages and the cave," Jack suggested. "He's going to be there, if anywhere."

"He's supposed to be here, among the temples," Charles countered.

"That's what I mean," said Jack. "This *is* Magwich, after all. We've just wasted time looking for him where he's supposed to be."

"Good point," said Charles.

The narrow path along the western edge was a bit difficult to traverse for Quixote, and the crosswinds were strong enough that Archimedes stayed well inland. But the companions made quick enough time that they arrived in the clearing where the Morgaine lived while the sun was still high above the horizon.

It was a scene of greater entropy than the temple had been. Where three cottages had once stood, there was only scattered rubble and straw. Nothing remained of the cooking pit, and even the old well had been all but destroyed.

Worse still, all the rare and dangerous artifacts that had also been left there for safekeeping were also missing.

"Pandora's Kettle," said Charles. "It's gone!"

"And the shield of Perseus," Jack added. "And the wands, and armor, and jewels . . . all of it."

"Damn his eyes," said Charles. "Magwich was supposed to guard everything on this island. When I find him . . ." He didn't need to finish the sentence.

"When was the last time we actually saw him here?" John asked. "I can't really recall."

"Whenever it was," said Charles, "remember we're missing seven years. A lot of things may have happened in that time alone."

John nodded in agreement. "The Cartographer said as much. If so many things are going poorly in both worlds, it stands to reason that Avalon would be involved."

"It's the fact that the kettle is gone that worries me," Jack noted, "as well as the only means of capping it—Perseus's shield. Either Artus and Aven took it to Paralon for safekeeping, or else someone else came to get it—to use it. Only a handful of people ever knew what it could do."

John's eyes flicked over to Rose, who was looking down the well and not listening in on the discussion.

"And one in particular who *did* use it," said John, his voice low, "but he's dead."

"His Shadow is still out there somewhere," Charles reminded them, "and the Trolls and Goblins also knew how the kettle was used. The field of suspects is wide open."

"Shall we check the cave?" Quixote asked, peering into the dark cavern. On entering the clearing, he had ignored the cottages altogether in favor of the cave, which seemed to have completely entranced him.

"He's not going to be there," said Charles dismissively. "He never liked it in there to begin with, and after the Morgaine left, I doubt he had any reason to go in at all."

"Where did they go?" asked Rose, obviously crestfallen. She was hoping that some aspect of her memories had survived on the island, but it was becoming more and more clear that the place was completely abandoned.

"I don't know where they went," Charles said. "After the, ah, accident that caused all the trouble at the keep where your Uncle Merlin resides, the Morgaine told us we had unraveled time itself—and we thought we had put things right, but the next time we came here, they were gone. No one knows where."

"Most intriguing," said Quixote. "And no one in the castle could tell you where they went?"

Charles looked at John, then Jack in confusion. "You mean on Paralon?" he said. "No, no one there had any clue, not even Samaranth."

The old knight shook his head and pointed into the cave. "Not on Paralon," he said plaintively. "The *castle*. The castle in the *cave*."

"We've been in there, more than once," Jack said, grimacing slightly at the hint of condescension he heard in his own voice, "and there's nothing in there but dust and cobwebs. Hasn't been for over a decade."

"Pardon," said Quixote, bowing slightly. If he'd taken offense at Jack's tone, it didn't show. "I would not presume to teach such esteemed scholars as yourselves, but I have a special knowledge of this cave. You see, I have been in it before. There is a wondrous meadow there, and a great castle made of crystal. Inside the castle there are wondrous halls of alabaster marble, where the great heroes of history are interred. It is my hope to one day rest among them.

"And," he said in conclusion, "in that place, sometimes, it is possible to commune with the dead. So if we choose to enter, it may very well be there that we shall find the answers you seek."

John blinked, then blinked again. "I'm sure we don't know what you're talking about, my good knight."

Quixote sighed, then smiled knowingly. "I am well used to those around me not believing the stories I tell," he said, gesturing broadly with his hands. "My tales of the adventures in the Archipelago saw me painted with the brush of a teller of falsehoods, never mind that to tell a lie would be ignoble of a knight. So I understand and I tell you with no rancor that it was prophesied that I would sleep until the call came to serve once more. And I believe that I was destined to be here, now, to aid you on your quest."

John pondered the knight's words silently for a moment. In the keep, he had told them that he possessed special knowledge that would be needed by them on their journey. None of them had really believed him, and they had taken him with them out of compassion more than anything else. To do otherwise would have meant his death. But they had never actually considered that he might have been sincere all along.

"Don Quixote de la Mancha," John said, bowing, "I have spoken in haste, and we have not availed ourselves of the counsel you might offer. If you have a special knowledge of this place, I beg you share it with us."

Quixote bowed gravely and blushed at John's respectful speech. He was not accustomed to being spoken to so well, and it took him a few seconds to compose himself.

"To enter the meadow where the castle stands, we must first fall asleep. . . ."

"Fall asleep?" Charles said. "All of us?"

Quixote nodded. "It is through the realm of dreams that we may cross through to the castle."

Charles and Jack each sighed heavily and slumped against the stones lining the entrance of the cave.

"You mean, you dreamed it all," Charles began.

"I'm so glad you understand," said the old knight in obvious relief. "Most people regard it as insanity."

Jack's brow furrowed. "Uh, begging your pardon, but I'm on the fence regarding that myself."

"To be fair," Charles pointed out, "he has been sleeping in the keep for the better part of four centuries. To him, all of this might seem as if it were a dream."

"You're starting to get the hang of it," said Quixote, clapping Charles on the back. "You'd make a fine knight yourself, you know."

"I really don't think we have time for all of us to take a nap," John said diplomatically.

"Oh," Quixote said, deflating. "I suppose we could try the door, if only we had access to a king or queen of the Archipelago. But that's probably too much to ask."

As one, the Caretakers looked down at Rose. "It's worth a try," she said. "After all, I was able to open the Cartographer's door."

Quixote looked from the girl to the companions and back again, gradually realizing what they were talking about. He wheeled around and strode to the remnants of the cooking pit, where he found a solid piece of charcoal, which he handed to Rose.

On the old knight's instruction, the companions all entered the cave. Archie remained behind to be, as John put it, their "canary in the coal mine."

"Isn't the canary supposed to go first, to make certain the air is clear?" asked Jack.

"I didn't say it was a perfect analogy," John replied, "but it's good enough in a pinch."

"If anything happens here," Archie huffed, "your canary will be sure to sing out loud and long."

"Thank you, Archie," said John.

"Humph," said Archie.

Quixote showed Rose what she must do, and the companions watched as she used the charcoal to sketch a broad, high door on the back of the cave wall.

"Very good," said Quixote. "Now, if you'll just recite the poem that opens the door."

Rose blinked. "I don't know what that is."

John stepped forward and opened his pack. "I think I do," he said. He unwrapped the *Geographica*, flipped to a particular page, and held it out for Rose to read.

The girl took the book in her hands and began to recite the verses John had indicated:

By knowledge paid
For riddles wrought
I open thee
I open thee

By bones bound
By honor taken
I open thee
I open thee
For life eternal and liberty gain'd
To sleep and dream, as kings we reign'd

I open thee
I open thee

As she finished speaking, a cracking sound reverberated throughout the cave, and a seam of pure, radiant light appeared along the inside of the charcoal lines. Quixote leaned forward and pushed against the wall—which swung outward, away from his touch.

The light from the other side was blinding after the gloomy twilight of the cave. It took a few seconds for the companions' eyes to adjust, then, cautiously, they all moved forward and through the doorway.

As Quixote had promised, the door opened to a vast meadow of nearly indescribable beauty. There were fields of wildflowers that ended in gently sloping hills of wild wheat and clover. The scents of the flowers and grasses were almost overwhelming, and a sharp, loamy tang permeated the air, as if a thunderstorm had just passed. But the sky was clear and deeply blue, and it appeared to be morning, although there was no sun in the sky.

In the distance, past the golden fields, rose the towers and crenellations of the crystal castle. The blue light, reflected up from the fields, caused the castle to appear bright green, as if it were constructed of emeralds.

Charles gave a low whistle in admiration, and Jack could only continue to stare, slack-jawed in amazement at the sights, as Rose knelt to gather a bundle of clover to press to her face.

As for John, he looked in wonderment at the beauty that surrounded them, then at Quixote, then back again. The old knight had been not only truthful, but extremely precise in his accounting as well.

"Lead on," John said, gesturing for Quixote to take them to the castle. "Your word is good."

Quixote bowed his head and took off at a brisk pace down a well-worn path through the meadow.

The companions followed after, with occasional digressions by Rose and Charles to examine some new patch of flowers that appeared along the way. At first it had appeared that the castle was very close, but as they continued to walk, it became evident that that was not the case. The castle grew taller and more broad the closer they came, but it took nearly an hour to reach the high red gates.

"I had almost thought we'd discovered Macdonald's Fairy Land," Jack said to the others, "but the markings on these gates are Greek."

"This isn't Fairy Land," John agreed. "I don't know what it is."

Quixote said nothing, but instead reached for a corded rope that hung to one side of the gates. He gave it a pull, and a low chime sounded from within.

In short order a gatekeeper appeared, unlocked the gate, and swung it open.

He was aged without seeming old, and more weary than aged. He looked over at Rose with a flicker of surprised recognition, then composed himself. He next regarded Quixote with a cautious eye, before giving his full attention to Charles, John, and Jack.

"I have not seen you before," he said in a voice thick with a French accent. His tone indicated that he was used to speaking with authority. "Why have you come here?"

"Avalon is deserted," John told him. "We're looking to discover why, and what may have happened to the Guardian."

The gatekeeper snorted. "That fool? He has been gone from the isle for many years. Where he went, I cannot say—but the one who might tell you the rest resides here, in the castle."

"Are you the new Green Knight?" Charles asked.

The gatekeeper rolled his eyes. "Do I appear to be made of wood?" he said. "As a knight, I guarded milady, and I guard her still, as well as the others within. What happens outside these walls is no longer my concern."

"May we pass?" asked Jack.

"On what authority do you ask to enter?" said the gatekeeper.

John unwrapped the *Geographica* on a hunch and showed the cover to the old man. "On the authority of the heirs of Arthur, King of the Silver Throne."

The gatekeeper looked as if he had been struck across the face with a hammer. He staggered back a moment, then pulled himself against the gate to stand steady.

"Enter and be welcomed," he said, his voice shaking with barely controlled emotion.

As the companions passed by, they were able to look at the gatekeeper more closely. He had the bearing of a knight but would not meet their eyes, lifting his head only to glance at Rose. There were scars on his arms and face, which had once been handsome. But the sorrow in his eyes and on his countenance was the deepest any of them had ever seen. More surprisingly, under his cloak they could see his own armor, which also bore the mark of the king.

"Who is this?" Quixote asked Charles behind his hand. "He never bothered to say three words to me when I was here before."

"I can't say for certain," Charles replied as they walked into the castle grounds, "but if I were to hazard a guess, I'd say we just met Lancelot himself."

The gatekeeper pointed the companions down a broad avenue between the gleaming green towers, to a pair of white doors. "I must go no farther," he said, "but I will see you on your return. May the gods grant you the knowledge you seek."

"Lancelot?" said Quixote, when they reached the doors and passed between them. "Really? I always thought he was a monk. I—"

The knight stopped talking as the doors closed behind them, leaving them in an expansive room that aspired to be a world, and that rendered them all speechless.

A thousand architectural styles were represented by the miniature buildings that were ensconced in transparent globes placed on gleaming pedestals throughout the room. On closer examination, the Caretakers realized that each miniature city was a world unto itself and contained tiny people and other creatures.

All along the walls were doorways interspersed with crypts, and at the far end of the hall was a bowl of blue fire, set into the floor in front of a massive wall.

Jack clutched at John's coat and pointed. "Look!" he whispered. "I think we've found them!"

Attending to the various globes were three women who floated above the surface of the floor in gossamer robes. One, the closest, was clothed in blue; the next, a short distance away, who was looking into a globe containing a Norse village, wore green; and the most distant of them wore pink.

It wasn't until the woman in blue moved to a globe closer to the doors that John realized he knew her. "Do you know us?" he called out. "Are you of the Morgaine?"

"When one has been a part of the Morgaine," the apparition said, "a part of the three who are one remains ever after. But I am still myself, especially here, in this place."

"And what should we call you?" asked Charles, before John could whisper to him that they already knew this woman. They had met her long ago.

"Call me Guinevere," the apparition said, opening her arms wide to embrace Rose. "Welcome home, daughter."

CHAPTER EIGHT
THE NAMELESS ISLES

GUINEVERE, WITH HER ethereal presence and turquoise hair, seemed more like a fairy than one of the Morgaine—but enough of who she was remained that Rose knew her and recognized her, and it gladdened the companions' hearts to see the girl so fulfilled and happy.

"What is this place?" said John.

"Call it the Elysian fields, or Valhalla, or Vanaheim," replied Guinevere. "It is all and none. But it is a place where the dead heroes of the past may come to rest, before they go on to their afterlife or are needed again."

"Why is Avalon deserted?" John asked. "The Morgaine are gone, and the Green Knight is as well."

"The Morgaine keep their own counsel and left of their own choice," Guinevere intoned. "The Guardian was enticed and easily gave up his post."

"As I thought," Charles fumed. "Once a Maggot, always a Maggot."

"What are you doing here, Mother?" Rose asked. "I've missed you, very much."

Guinevere looked down at her daughter. "As I have missed

you. But we each have our paths to follow, and mine has ended here."

"Ended?" said Charles bluntly. "Are—are you dead?"

She looked up at him and raised an eyebrow. "That would depend on your point of view, Caretaker," she answered. "I left the Morgaine to marry, and saw the downfall of a kingdom. But from the ashes of that tragedy, my children built a kingdom anew—you are its guardians now, and one of you may yet earn your place among the heroes here."

She turned and glided away, gesturing for the companions to follow. She led them to the great marble wall, next to the blue flame.

The marble wall contained three crypts. Guinevere passed the first of them and then paused at the second, resting her hand lightly, almost reverently, on its surface. "Here rests he who was my husband, who breathed his last in my arms," she said, the sorrow in her voice unconcealed. "The first King of the Silver Throne, the first king of Camelot. Here lies Arthur, who will sleep until he is needed again."

"We know a little of his death from the Histories," said Charles, "but Geoffrey of Monmouth was incomplete as a chronicler and fictionalized some things to make his stories more interesting. I didn't realize you had been with him when he died."

She looked pained at hearing this. "I—I wasn't, but I was near," she said, "and I have remained with him ever since.

"Mordred returned to Camelot and brought war with him," she continued. "I had abandoned my duties on Avalon to become Arthur's queen, to protect and watch over him. And I failed. I failed him, in every way. And so it is my penance to stay with him here, to watch over his body and wait for the time when he might rise again to protect all the lands that are, and the people who reside there."

"That's very, ah, loyal," said Jack.

"And optimistic," said Charles.

"It is prophesied," stated Guinevere, "that in the time of greatest need, he will rise once more to defend and protect his kingdom. But," she added before any of the companions could ask, "now is not that time."

"How do you know?" asked Jack.

"There is a Prophecy," Guinevere began.

"I'm starting to get weary of hearing about prophecies," said Charles.

"Does he need me again, Mother?" Rose asked, moving around Charles to take Guinevere's hands. "Does he need my blood to save him, as it did before?"

Guinevere shook her head. "That is not written for you," she said to her daughter in a voice both gentle and firm. "You gave your sacrifice once. In time, it will be for another to do so."

She held her daughter's hands for a moment more, then let them go and crossed her hands in front of her. "What else would you ask of me?"

"Who are in the other two crypts?" Charles asked. "If you don't mind my inquiring."

"In the crypt on the left is the first of the heroes," said Guinevere. "The original, the archetype, the one who inspired all those who came after."

"Hercules?" Jack guessed, only to be slightly embarrassed when the lady responded with a laugh.

"Little mortal, I forget how short a time you have lived, and how little you know of the history of the world. The first hero, who sleeps here next to Arthur, was the one called Gilgamesh."

"And in the third?" said John, whose curiosity had overwhelmed his need for decorum. He really wanted to know: Who could possibly merit being interred next to Gilgamesh and Arthur Pendragon?

Instead of answering, Guinevere glanced almost imperceptibly at Rose, then shook her head. "It is not for me to say," she replied. "Not at this time."

"Guinevere," Jack said suddenly, "may I ask a boon?"

She looked at him curiously, but could not disguise her amusement at the request. "You may ask."

"We first came into the Archipelago to protect your daughter," said Jack. "There are those roaming about, in both this world and in the Summer Country, who seek to harm her. Perhaps even kill her. We don't know of any place where we might take her that will be as safe as she'll be here. Could she stay?"

John and Charles both started to say something, but held their tongues as they realized the truth of Jack's words. If this place was as difficult to enter as it seemed, it really might be the safest place for the girl.

But Guinevere shook her head. "She cannot. This is not a place where the living can long stay. In time she would become as transparent as I. I have lived a full lifetime—more than one, in fact. And so I can accept this ghostly existence. But it is not for her. There is a—"

"Prophecy," said Charles.

"A destiny," Guinevere said, giving Charles a stern look, "that she must seek out. She has an extraordinary life ahead of her, and should not dismiss it so easily by staying here with phantasms. And this is only the beginning. You will need her if your worlds are to survive."

"Why did the Morgaine abandon the Archipelago?" asked John. "Why did they leave?"

"There is nothing gained but futility in weaving a tapestry whose picture changes at a whim," Guinevere said plainly. "Elements of creation are changing, even now, as we speak. Events in history are being made and unmade with every passing moment."

"Is there anything you can tell us?" John pleaded. "For your daughter's sake, if nothing else?"

"A great weapon is being brought to bear against the forces of the Light," Guinevere said, "which you will not be able to withstand. Only by wielding a weapon of equal power will you have the chance to prevail."

"How do we find such a weapon?" said Jack.

"Summon the Lady," the apparition said as she began to shimmer and fade. "The Lady of the Lake. Only she can return what was given. . . ."

Rose leaped forward, but it was too late. Her mother was gone. As the companions watched, the woman in green also faded and vanished, and then, more slowly, the woman in pink, who raised a tentative hand to wave—at Quixote.

"Do you know her?" Charles asked.

Quixote didn't reply for a long moment, then turned to the Caretaker. "It is not yet my time to be here," he said, his voice heavy with emotion. "I must see through this quest and fulfill the Prophecy.

And then, perhaps . . ." He glanced back once more, then quickly turned away. "Perhaps I will have earned the right to join her here. But now is not that time."

All around them, the crystal castle had begun to fade, as if it had been a mirage. The globes vanished, then the walls, and finally the doors. All that remained was the lone figure of the gatekeeper, standing in the expansive meadow.

"Did you find the answers you seek?" he asked the companions as they approached. "Did you speak to her?"

"The fairy with the turquoise hair?" said Charles. "We spoke, and she told us a few things that might prove useful, yes."

"And how did she look?" he asked, trying to mask the eagerness in his voice. "Was she well?"

"As beautiful as ever," said John.

The gatekeeper slumped his shoulders and sighed heavily with relief. "Thank you for that," he said quietly. "It has been too long since I saw her."

"You *are* Lancelot, aren't you?" Charles asked.

The gatekeeper nodded wistfully. "I was. Now I am simply the gatekeeper. Much like your Green Knight, it is my way of doing penance—and part of the agreement is that I may be close, but can never again see her."

"That's awful," said John.

"No," said Quixote, nodding in understanding. "It is the price that must be paid for an unpayable debt. And it is the only choice a noble knight would make."

The gatekeeper lowered his head. "Not noble enough, I fear."

Quixote reached out and lifted Lancelot's chin. "The most noble acts," he said sternly, "are those performed when there is nothing left to be gained. You are not merely a gatekeeper. You are a brother knight. So speaks Don Quixote de la Mancha."

The doorway to the cave lay open in front of them. "Farewell, Lancelot," John said as the companions walked through it.

"May God go with you," replied the gatekeeper.

Rose looked back, just once, in the direction where the green castle had been, as did Quixote.

"Good-bye, Mother," she said.

"Good-bye," Quixote whispered. "Good-bye, my beloved Dulcinea."

And with that last farewell, the door swung closed and was a cave wall once more.

The sun was just beginning to set as the companions reached the eastern beach. Either a full day—or more—had passed while they were in the castle with Guinevere, or their journey had taken scarcely any time at all.

"It had to have been a few hours," John said as he checked on the *Geographica* in his pack. "I'd swear to it."

"I think that grotto, or whatever—wherever—it was that the meadow and castle sit, functions much like Quixote's room in the keep," said Charles. "I don't think time there passes in the same way as it does for us."

"You're probably right," said Jack. "It's frozen, or at the least, passes much more slowly. How much worse would it be if we were to emerge and find out the reverse were true? That while we chatted with a long-lost queen for a few hours, centuries were passing by outside?"

"Brr," John replied. "That would be a bit much. I've already been rather preoccupied with just the idea that we may have lost seven years of our lives by stepping through a drawing."

"That's one reason we should be underway as quickly as possible," said Jack. "We've literally no time to waste."

Jack reached into his pocket where he'd kept the bottle and pulled out their ship. With curt nods of approval from his companions, he windmilled his arm and dashed the bottle against the rocks in the shallow tidepools.

In moments the ship had grown to its full size, much to the companions' great relief. It was much smaller than every other Dragonship, but it was large enough for the four men, the girl, and the owl to be comfortably seated within.

"There's no sail," Charles pointed out, "nor any oars. How do we move her about?"

"I think this is one of Ordo Maas's special ships," said Jack, stroking the Dragon's head. "I think we just need to tell her where we want to go, and she'll get us there. Right, girl?"

There was no audible response from the masthead, but for a few seconds, the Dragon's eyes seemed to glow more brightly, and her neck grew warm under Jack's hand.

With a crunching sound, the boat pulled itself out of the shallows, then glided swiftly through the water at the edge of the storm clouds of the Frontier. A few hundred yards from the island, she stopped and waited.

"Well," John said, standing. "I'd say that's our signal to start navigating." He turned to Charles with a broad grin on his face. "All right, Sir Charles. Strip. It's time to have a look at the map."

"Well?" Charles asked, once he was naked to the waist. "Which way do we go first?"

"First and last," John said, "we need to go north. Due north. That's where we'll find the Nameless Isles."

Traveling so directly north, the only islands they passed that were familiar to them were Prydain and a small group of islands called the Capa Blanca. Prydain was one of the greater islands, second only to the capital island of Paralon, but the Caretakers had never actually traveled to the Capa Blanca islands before.

"I understood from the Histories Bert wrote that they were originally settled by shipwrecked sailors from Spain," Charles remarked, feeling a chill now that the sun was setting. "The sailors built several very lovely towns and had quite a nice culture developing until some British doctor showed up and taught the animals there how to talk. After that it was all downhill. The animals wanted better working conditions and higher wages. You know how it goes."

"Spanish, eh?" said Quixote. "Perhaps we could stop in on our way home. It's been too long since I heard my native tongue."

"Doesn't Verne speak Spanish?" asked Jack.

"Dreadfully," said Quixote. "I made him promise to never again make the attempt."

The last island they passed, the easternmost and most northerly island in the *Geographica*, was a midsize round island called Gondour.

"They're quite the democracy, according to Mark Twain's notes," said John, "although I never did care for his spelling of the name. Always have to catch myself when I mispronounce it 'dour' instead of 'door.'"

"Aren't they assisting Artus with his new republic?" asked Jack.

"I think so. The one oddity is that they are a republic ruled over by an impeachable caliph. I'd imagine it makes for some very lively debates."

After Gondour, there was going to be very little to see for a long while, so the companions made themselves as comfortable as they could in the *Scarlet Dragon*, and took turns sleeping. Jack and Quixote volunteered for the first watch and took up positions at the fore of the boat.

"Jack, may I ask you something?" said Quixote.

"Certainly."

"Have you ever known failure?"

Jack turned to the knight in surprise. "Of course I have. Everyone does, at one time or another."

The knight chewed on his lip as he pondered Jack's reply. "I thought I had failed, once," he said at length, "but I am wondering if that event was not part of my own destiny, Prophecy or no."

"How do you mean?"

"I think I know why I am here, with you," said Quixote. "I think I understand, at least in part, my role. I am owed a debt—and my claiming it may be a key to all that we are experiencing."

"Who owes you the debt?" asked Jack.

"The Lady," Quixote replied. "The Lady of the Lake."

He turned away and said no more, and Jack was reluctant to press him. The rest of the night passed without incident.

In the morning John again instructed Charles to sprawl himself against the masthead so that they could better read the map.

"This is not very dignified, you know," Charles pouted. "Can't you just sketch out a copy in the *Geographica*, so I can keep my shirt on?"

"Sorry, old boy," said John. "Some of the islands have already changed position."

It was true—the locations of several of the Nameless Isles had moved during the night. John made some corrections and adjusted the tiller on the *Scarlet Dragon* to communicate the changes to the boat.

"If all goes as I hope it shall," John said, "we ought to be there by nightfall."

The course the map took them on led them safely distant from the kingdom of the Trolls, farther to the west—which was for the best, as none of the companions had ever liked Arawn, the former prince who was now king of the Trolls. He had been a rabble-rouser during their first encounter with the Winter King, and later allied with him against them. Arawn had been as ungracious in defeat as Artus had been gracious in his victory, and so the Northlands had been a place to avoid ever since—if they could help it.

The islands of the Christmas Saint, past the Troll Kingdom, were the absolute northernmost chronicled in the *Geographica*. All three companions had read the annotations thoroughly, and very early on in their role as Caretakers had conspired to find reasons to correspond with and eventually visit the principal resident. John had even gone so far as to persuade him to write letters to his children, which was one of the great delights of fatherhood. To know beyond a doubt that Father Christmas existed was spectacular enough; to be considered worthy of corresponding with him was a childhood dream made manifest.

Beyond the isles of Father Christmas, there was nothing.

Nothing in the *Geographica*, and nothing as far as the companions could see. None of the previous Caretakers had ever made the effort to sail so far—they had simply assumed that what had been documented was all there was to see. Of them all, only John's mentor, Professor Sigurdsson, had ever taken an active liking to the actual adventuring, the discovery of new lands. He had ventured deep into the Southlands on a fabled voyage, and more than once into the deep west—although John had no clue what he could have been searching for, or what else could be discovered that way, since Terminus and the endless waterfall marked the true End of the World as he knew it.

Charles, when he was not putting on his shirt and taking it off again so the others could check their position, spent his time talking about multiple dimensions with Archimedes, who had proven to be a worthy adversary in a debate.

Quixote preferred to talk to Rose when he could, asking her about the more mundane aspects of boarding school in Reading, with an occasional digression to tales of Odysseus on Avalon.

Jack, for his part, spent the better part of an hour scanning the horizon with a spyglass provided to him by Quixote, until he finally realized that there was no actual glass in the spyglass.

"I never really needed it." Quixote shrugged. "It doesn't help if you're lost, and if you aren't lost, why do you need to see a place you'll soon arrive at anyway?"

Eventually, as the Cartographer had promised, a smudge of land appeared off in the distance, then grew larger at an alarming speed. The Nameless Isles were far closer than they had appeared to be, and had the appearance of a mirage. It took effort to focus on them—a moment of drifting attention found the islands sliding from one's field of vision.

At close range the illusion dropped, and the islands came into sharp relief. There were thirteen all told: a massive island to the south and east of the others, which served as a shield of stone; a small cluster of islands to the west; two larger, half-moon islands to the east and north; and directly ahead of them, a broad, dune-colored island that sloped up from a short beach to a flat expanse of sand, black crystals, and short, blocky trees.

All of the smaller islands had been built up with columns and arches that were all but prehistoric. From their appearance, their construction, and their apparent great age, John surmised that they may have been built in the earliest years of prehistory—contemporary with the first cities, such as Ur and Untapishim. The structures on these outer isles formed a kind of massive arena enclosing the three inner islands. There was no mistaking the purpose: They were defensive, or at least protective, in nature.

On the center island was the unmistakable shape of a house in the distance—and from all appearances it was immense. Directly ahead was a dock, a small boathouse, and a sight that made the companions cheer in joy and relief.

The *White Dragon*, the airship piloted by their mentor Bert, was moored to the north side of the dock, where it floated calmly in the shallows.

"I suddenly feel much better about the prospects of this trip," Charles admitted. "Nothing against you fellows, but Bert always seems to know the score."

"I'm with you there," said John. He guided the *Scarlet Dragon* alongside the larger ship and leaped to the dock to tie a mooring line.

A large orange cat was sitting just past the dock, idly cleaning itself while keeping a watchful eye on the new arrivals to the island.

"I expect you must be the Caretakers," the cat said at length. "Come ashore. You're expected."

"Are you the welcoming committee?" Charles asked as he jumped to the dock and looped the mooring ties to a pylon. "If so, I'm pleased to meet you."

"I am what I am," the cat said, "and if that pleases you, so be it."

"What does that mean?" asked Jack.

"It means," the cat replied, tipping its head toward Rose, "that I am like her. Here, and not here, all at once."

"A riddle?" said John.

"An enigma," said Rose.

"A conundrum," said the cat, which tilted its head, then began to disappear.

"My word," said Charles. "The cat! It's vanishing!"

"No," said the cat, which by now was nothing more than a head, floating in the air. "I'm simply going to a place you aren't looking."

"That makes perfect sense," said Rose.

"It's very confusing," said Jack.

"Thank you very much," said the broad smile that was once a whole cat. "You may call me Grimalkin. Welcome to Tamerlane House."

PART THREE

THE LEAGUE OF POETS

CHAPTER NINE

THE HOUSE OF TAMERLANE

THE MAGICIAN AND the Detective pulled the door out of the ship's hold and dragged it across the field to where the construction was taking place. There were carpenters and bricklayers and all manner of roustabouts scattered across the worksite who were carrying materials and banging on things and generally trying to look busy. But everything always stopped when they delivered a door.

Just so, the Magician thought. *The rabble should stop and take notice when I'm onstage.* It might not be a formal performance as such, but he and the Detective were performing the job that could only be trusted to the betters of these rabble.

"Are you two idiots going to take all day dragging that door over here?" said a brusque voice.

At the top of the rise, holding the project blueprints, stood a solid man whose eyes glittered with purpose and whose scarred cheeks testified to his will. Richard Burton was not one to suffer fools or layabouts—not for long, anyway.

"Bring it up here," Burton instructed them, pointing to a frame that had been erected on a patch of clover. "Carefully, now. The Chancellor will not be pleased if we lose another one. Nor will I."

A few months earlier they had been bringing another door up the rise when some of the workers dropped a wheelbarrow load of bricks from the scaffolding high above. The bricks had struck the door with enough force to shatter it, and splinters were all that was left. Burton had examined them with an Infinite Loupe—a modified set of eyeglasses that could be used to see through time—and proclaimed it to have been linked to the ninth century.

"And to Persia, unless I miss my guess," Burton had said. "That could have been useful—but it isn't a time or place that is wholly unknown to me, so we'll let it go, for now."

Of course, Burton's idea of "letting it go" meant beheading the workers who had spilled the bricks, but since it was also useful in motivating the rest of the workers to be more careful, he didn't see it as a complete waste of effort and resources.

The Detective and the Magician stood the door in place and fitted it to the frame, then stepped back.

Burton wiped his hands on his leather apron and stepped up to the door. Cautiously he reached for the handle and slowly pulled the door open, careful not to step over the threshold.

A bright light emanated from within, giving Burton's harsh features a demonic cast. Baroque-period music could be heard from somewhere deep in whatever place the door had opened to.

"Excellent," he said as he closed the door. "The Chancellor will be very pleased. A few more, and we'll be able to give the order to move forward. A few more doors . . .

". . . and we'll be able to conquer all of creation."

The central island of the Nameless Isles was practically barren of vegetation, save for a number of massive stumps of petrified wood, and the black obsidian crystals that were scattered among the dunes.

At the end of the dock, a path formed of obsidian pieces wound its way up the slope to the front door of the extraordinary dwelling Grimalkin had called Tamerlane House.

It was a Persian palace, both ancient and exotically new all at once. It was massive in an organic way, wings spreading out across the rise like the branches of an enormous tree. There was very little in their experience that it could be compared to, but John had heard stories of the fabled Winchester House in California, which had been built by an heiress to the Winchester rifle fortune to house the spirits of those who had been killed by the rifles. She built endless rooms, and stairways, and closets, and alcoves, and on and on and on. For decades the hammers never stopped. And for the first time, John was looking at a similar structure born of a similar obsession. He wondered with a mixture of curiosity and fear just what kind of spirits were meant to be housed in Tamerlane House.

In answer to his unspoken question, a familiar figure, looking only slightly more presentable than his usual charmingly bedraggled self, appeared at the top of the steps. It was Bert.

The three Caretakers rushed forward to shake hands and embrace their mentor, who appeared equally glad to see them. Rose hugged him tightly as he kissed the top of her head, and even Archimedes restrained himself to a polite greeting that was hardly sarcastic at all.

"You're a tall drink of water," Bert said, shielding his eyes from the sun as he looked up at Quixote, who bowed in greeting. "How did you get pulled into joining this motley crew?"

"He pretty much had to come," explained Jack. "His room was about to fall into the Chamenos Liber."

"His room . . . ?" Bert said. He blinked a few times, then moved closer to the old knight. "Are you Don Quixote?"

A deeper bow this time. "I *am* Don Quixote de la Mancha," he said with a flourish, "and I am your humble servant."

"Does he have to do that every time he meets someone?" Jack asked John.

"It certainly makes him memorable," John replied. "Maybe you should try it with your next reading class."

"Har har har," said Jack.

"I know all about you," Bert said to Quixote with a gleam in his eye, as his old familiar twinkle began to reappear. "Jules has told me many things—and while your presence is a surprise, it is not wholly unexpected.

"Come," he went on, gesturing for them to follow as he turned to enter the house. "There is much to talk about, now that you've finally arrived."

"We were expected?" exclaimed Jack.

Bert grinned wryly. "Of course. Ransom told us what happened seven years ago, so we've been waiting. Otherwise, you wouldn't have gotten past Grimalkin."

"The Cheshire?" said John. "He seemed pretty harmless to me."

"He may look like a simple Cheshire cat," said Bert, looking around cautiously to see if Grimalkin was listening, "but in reality, he's one of those Elder Gods that fellow Lovecraft has been writing about."

"You're kidding, right?" said Charles. "It's a joke."

"Laugh if you like," Bert called over his shoulder, "but if I were you, I wouldn't take off his collar. For *any* reason."

• • •

"As I was saying, we had an idea what had happened to you when Ransom reported in," Bert said as he served the companions tea and Leprechaun crackers in an elaborate parlor, "so we hoped you'd make your way to the Nameless Isles, as Hank had suggested."

"I must admit, Bert," said John, trying not to sound as if he were chiding the older man, "as the Caretaker Principia, I was a bit put out to find there were islands I was unaware of—indeed, islands I was not *allowed* to know of."

"I am sorry about that, John," Bert replied. "Had it been up to me, I'd have said something to you much sooner. It's been a matter of some debate, my position being that if you had been aware, you could have come here directly from Oxford, and not skipped over seven vital years."

"Debate with whom?"

"The Prime Caretaker. But we will discuss that shortly." Bert stood up. "For now, we should make some accommodations for Rose and the good sir knight."

"You rang?" Grimalkin said, appearing on the back of a couch.

"Ah, Grimalkin," said Bert. "Yes, please. If you would be so kind as to show the lady and her gentleman escort to their rooms?"

"Certainly," said Grimalkin, eyeing Archimedes. "Do I get the bird to play with?"

"Define 'play,'" said Bert.

"Oh, never mind," said the cat as his body faded out to nothingness. "Come this way."

"He'll take care of you," said Bert. "Just follow his head."

"I could use a rest, I think," Quixote said. "Thank you, master Caretaker."

As the two companions and the reluctant owl followed the bobbing cat's head down a corridor, Bert turned back to the Caretakers. "Now we can talk as men do, about things of import and consequence."

"Will she be safe here, Bert?" asked John.

"Safe as houses," Bert replied, "or at least, as safe houses. She has nothing to fear here. Grimalkin will look after her, and no one may come here who wasn't invited. That's one of the reasons these islands have remained nameless, and why no map of them exists in the *Geographica*. This place is our own version of Haven, to withdraw to when we must, or when circumstances are most dire."

"Well, we've certainly got a map now," Charles said, scratching at his side. "Does it keep moving even when we've arrived here?"

"The Cartographer cornered you for the duty, eh, Charles?" said Bert with a grin. "It's easier when you're traveling with friends. My first trip here was solo, and I had to use a mirror."

Suddenly a flock of birds barreled down the hallway, each carrying silverware and china place settings. As in the Great Whatsit on Paralon, the servants of the house were large black birds, who were dressed nattily in vests and waistcoats.

"Crows?" Jack asked as the last of the birds flew out of the hallway.

"Ravens," Bert corrected him. "A full unkindness."

"I'll take an unkindness of ravens over a murder of crows any day," said Charles.

"Your jokes are still both literate and unfunny," said Bert, hugging Charles around the shoulders. "It's so good to see you again, lad!"

• • •

Bert led the three friends through room after room, but other than the ravens, the house appeared empty.

"Is there anyone here?" Jack asked, peering up at a stairwell that ended, inexplicably, at the high ceiling. "The place seems to be abandoned."

"The master of the house is indeed here in residence," said Bert, "but he seldom chooses to appear. You may meet him after the Gatherum."

"The what?" asked John.

"Better I simply show you than try to explain," Bert said with deliberate mystery and a touch of glee. "Here—I want to show you the Pygmalion Gallery," he continued, waving them down another long corridor. "In fact, I've wanted to bring you here for a very long time."

"What prevented you?" asked John.

"Those evil stepsisters, Necessity and Planning," Bert replied as they approached a set of tall polished doors. "One always gets too little attention, and the other too much—and they never seem to balance out."

The doors were covered with cherubs, and angels, and all manner of ornate and byzantine carvings. In the center, where the doors met, were three locks. Bert removed a large iron ring with two heavy skeleton keys from his pocket. He unlocked the first lock, then the next.

"Three locks," Charles said, "but only two keys?"

"The third key is imaginary," explained Bert. "It's a safety feature." He made the motions of choosing a key and inserting it into the third lock, and the companions were all surprised to hear a loud click.

"It's always the most difficult," said Bert. "You have to turn it just so."

The gas lamps came up as they entered an anteroom. Beyond was a spacious gallery, with velvet-lined walls, lush oriental carpets, and high ceilings that irised to a circular skylight. The walls were covered with paintings—portraits, John noted, that were almost life-size and large enough to step through.

"An astute observation, young John," Bert said. "Do you recognize any of the portraits?"

"Any of them?" said Charles excitedly. "I recognize them all!"

In the center of the north wall was a full-figured portrait of Geoffrey Chaucer, and slightly smaller portraits of Sir Thomas Malory and Goethe hung to the right and left of it. On the south wall, directly across from Malory's portrait, was an equally large painting of Miguel de Cervantes, flanked by portraits of Franz Schubert and Jonathan Swift. Next to Swift, the companions each noted with barely concealed surprise, was a portrait of Rudyard Kipling, appearing exactly as he had at the Flying Dragon.

Kepler was there, as were William Shakespeare and Nathaniel Hawthorne. Jack was almost as good as Charles at identifying the portraits, but John was having a harder time of it.

"I recognize Twain, and Dickens," he said to Bert, "but I'm really at a loss for several of the others."

"Surely you know Daniel Defoe"—Bert indicated an exceptional portrait set in a rather ordinary frame—"and of course Alexandre Dumas *père*.

"This is where the most important debates about the Archipelago of Dreams take place," he went on somberly, his voice hushed as the four men walked deeper into the gallery proper.

"Within this room is the greatest collection of knowledge and wisdom to be found in any world."

"I thought that was the Great Whatsit, on Paralon," said Charles.

"That is a great repository of learning, yes," said Bert, "but you cannot have a discussion with a book, or debate with a parchment."

"And we're supposed to fare better talking to paintings?" Jack said as he leaned close to examine a portrait of Washington Irving.

"That may depend more on your own skills," Bert replied mysteriously, "than on the conversational skills of any particular painting.

"Gentlemen," he announced with a flourish, "I'd like you to meet your predecessors, those who have gone before you in the most important job in creation: Behold the Caretakers Emeritis of the *Imaginarium Geographica*."

"All of them?" John said in unvarnished awe.

"Mostly, yes," answered Bert. "The only ones we don't actually have here are Wace, Bacon, and Dante. We do have a picture of Geoffrey of Monmouth, but when we told him what it was for he panicked and fled, and so the portrait remains unfinished and cannot be used to bring him through."

"Bring him through what?" Jack exclaimed.

"Through to here—into Tamerlane House," said Bert with a twinkle in his eye. "Watch and learn."

Bert removed his silver pocket watch and walked to the portrait of Hans Christian Andersen, where he inserted the watch into a small, semicircular indentation at the bottom of the frame. He pressed a button on the side of the watch, and a jet of eldritch light shot around the frame. Then, as the astonished companions looked on . . .

. . . Andersen stepped out of the frame and into the gallery.

"Very nice to be out," he said, stretching his arms. "Not that I mind hanging around in here with the rest of the brethren, but in the picture, it's impossible to scratch if you get an itch."

"I imagine it is," Bert said as he inserted the watch into the next frame, and Cervantes joined them on the floor. "Don't frown so, Nathaniel," he called to the painting of Hawthorne. "I'm getting to you next."

As Bert continued the process of liberating the former Caretakers from their frames, Charles commented on the fact that several portraits were turned to the wall, and one even appeared to have been scorched in a fire.

"You already know why," Bert said in answer. "Those are portraits of Caretakers who either failed their duties badly, or betrayed them, or both."

"So, Houdini and Conan Doyle—," Jack began.

"No," Bert replied quickly, cutting him off. "Their portraits are *not* here. And we don't speak of them, not here in this house."

"If their portraits aren't here," said John, "then how is it possible that they exist past the dates of their death?"

"And the burned one?" asked Charles.

"If you get a moment, you might ask Percy Shelley about that one," said Bert. He turned to Jack. "Better yet, you should do the asking."

"What?" Jack said, confused. "I—" He stopped with a lurch. "Oh, dear Lord above," he whispered. The blood drained from his face as he pointed to one they'd overlooked. "Is that . . . ?"

On the far end of the northern wall was a portrait of James Barrie.

"As I told you, a lot has happened in seven years," said Bert, "but now you'll have a chance to catch up. Hello, Jamie."

"Greetings, Bert!" Barrie answered cheerfully. "Boys, it's good to see you again!"

"If you don't mind," a stately, bearded portrait sniffed, "I believe my seniority should dictate that I be released sooner rather than later."

"Very well, Leo," Bert said with a frown, "although technically speaking, Chaucer has seniority here."

"Leonardo da Vinci?" Jack asked behind his hand. "Didn't he steal a lot of things from Roger Bacon?"

"Practically everything." Bert sighed. "If Geoff Chaucer could have done it over again, he'd have picked Michelangelo. But we were still learning the process then, and Leo became a Caretaker instead, mostly because he was older. We've been going after younger apprentices ever since."

"We're not going to let him out, are we?" Jack whispered.

"If we don't," Bert replied, inserting his watch into the frame, "we're all going to hear about it for years."

"Rude," said da Vinci. "I can hear you, you know."

"The effort would have been wasted if you couldn't," said Bert.

In short order, centuries' worth of Caretakers had filled the gallery and were milling about, chatting, arguing, pouring drinks, and getting reacquainted with old discussions, which they were conducting in a variety of languages. John, Jack, and Charles were doing their best just to hold their own in the dialogues. It was hard enough just to keep their composure.

Bert pulled John aside. "There's one more, lad," he said with a smile and a hint of melancholy. "I thought you'd like to summon him yourself."

They stepped over to the last portrait, and John felt his breath catch in his throat. He realized, as he stood there looking at it, that it was the most obvious thing in the world to expect—but he had never even considered the possibility that his mentor, Professor Stellan Sigurdsson, would be included among the throng of Caretakers who were defying space and time to come together at Tamerlane House.

"May I use my own watch?"

Bert nodded his assent. "You may indeed."

With trembling hands, John placed the watch into the frame and watched the light race around the edges. An instant later he could smell that familiar chocolate-tobacco mixture, as his old mentor and teacher stepped down from the frame.

"Hello, my dear boy," said Professor Sigurdsson. "I am very, very happy to see you again."

They shook hands, then embraced.

"I'm . . . very happy to see you again too, Professor," John said. "Perhaps this reunion will last longer than our previous one."

"I hope so, John. I truly do."

While the professor and his understudy became reacquainted, Jack and Charles steered Bert back into the anteroom. "Bert," Jack said quietly, "I wonder if I might have a word with you about Kipling."

They had noticed only at the end, after Barrie had been liberated, that among the crowd of Caretakers were several famous personages who were not, in point of fact, official Caretakers.

"I'd wondered when that would come up," said Bert. "There are a few here in the gallery who were not official Caretakers, but who were loyal to the cause. The practice of naming three Caretakers at a time was a practice born of necessity, and so there are some from days past who were, ah, 'spares,' you might say."

"We're spares?" Charles said, faintly mortified.

"No, not at all," Bert said, comforting him. "You are a Caretaker—but there are those among us who were able to contribute in other ways, but whose, shall we say, temperaments were not well suited to the task. Oscar Wilde, for example. Or Chesterton."

"G. K. Chesterton's dead?" Jack exclaimed.

"Sorry for the surprise," said Bert mildly, "but if it helps, he's pouring a brandy over there with Kepler."

"It's one of those 'apprentice' Caretakers I want to speak to you about, Bert," said Jack. "How well do you know Kipling?"

Before his mentor could answer, Rudyard Kipling stepped around his chair and stuck his hand out in front of Jack. "The name's Kipling, my boy. A pleasure to make your acquaintance."

"Er—um—ah," Jack stammered as he shook the other fellow's hand. "Likewise."

He waved John over from where he was chatting with the professor and introduced him and Charles in turn, each of whom, with some visible reluctance, shook Kipling's hand.

"Wonderful time for a Gatherum, wouldn't you say, Bert?" Kipling said brightly, as he clapped John on the shoulder. "And it's so nice to see the new blood here too, rather than just the usual roster of fuddy-duddies."

"Pardon me, sir," said Jack politely, "but have we seen each other? Recently? In England?"

"Mmm," Kipling murmured, looking inquisitively at Jack. "I don't believe so, unless you were at my funeral, which was the last time I was in England—in which case, I was definitely preoccupied."

"Sorry, I missed it," said Jack.

"No worries, old fellow," Kipling said, smiling. He clapped Jack on the back, then Charles. "After all, that's what we have Tamerlane House for, isn't it?"

John was about to ask something else when Kipling spied another acquaintance among the group and strode away.

"I'm sorry," said Bert. "What did you mean to ask, Jack?"

"I don't think it's important right now," Jack replied. "Don't worry about it."

Bert moved into the next room, and John swiftly pulled Jack and Charles aside. "What do you think that was all about?"

"I've no idea," said Jack, "but he didn't act like a man who had just been hunting us."

"He wasn't, remember?" Charles said. "That was seven years ago."

"Does it really matter to these people?" John asked as Bert reappeared at his side. "They treat things like time, and space, and life and death as if they were playthings."

"Not playthings," said Bert, interjecting himself back into the discussion, "but certainly more flexible than the men of science would have us believe. Come along now, lads. We're about to take our places for dinner."

CHAPTER TEN
THE CUCKOO

EVERYTHING IN TAMERLANE House was evidence of two philosophies: that of excess, and that of quality. Whatever there was of any given category of object, be it china or clocks, was represented by hundreds of examples of the highest caliber. Room after room was filled to overflowing with rare and exquisite objects and items that might have been the plunder from a hundred very cultured pirates. It was, with no embellishment needed, a veritable treasure trove. But the most valued among its contents were just sitting down to what John, Jack, and Charles were certain was destined to be the most extraordinary dinner in the history of history.

The great banquet hall was lit by brass lamps hung high in the air, and had been decorated with silk tapestries that seemed to be a visual representation of every story from every culture that had ever existed, living or dead. The details were such that an entire tale, start to finish, could be depicted in a few square inches, and the stories themselves frequently overlapped.

The table was oak and ash, and fully sixty feet long and ten feet wide. It was set with flawless silver trays and crystal bowls, which promised a great feast to come.

There were many Caretakers the companions knew by name

and reputation, if not for their work, but several were entirely unfamiliar to them by appearance. Bert gladly acted the part of host and made sure that introductions were given all around while the preparations were being finished for the feast.

On the left, Mark Twain and Daniel Defoe sat in deep discussion with Nathaniel Hawthorne and Washington Irving. Charles Dickens, Mary and Percy Shelley, and Alexandre Dumas *père* sat directly across from them, arguing about some arcane poem and the meaning of life.

Next to Dickens, on his left, sat Jakob Grimm, who was pouring wine for Jonathan Swift and, disconcertingly, a smiling Rudyard Kipling.

At the far end of the table were those Bert referred to as the Elder Caretakers—which basically meant everyone who had performed in the role prior to the seventeenth century.

Da Vinci had taken the first chair on the left, opposite Chaucer. Next to them were Sir Thomas Malory, who was dirtier than the companions would have imagined, and the Frenchman Chrétien de Troyes, whom Bert said had to be kept a distance away from Malory.

Tycho Brahe, Miguel de Cervantes, and Edmund Spenser, the first trio of Caretakers, sat together on one side, and across from them, ravishing the fruit plates, were William Shakespeare, Kepler, and the philosopher Goethe. Next to him, Franz Schubert sat with his head down, talking to no one and just twisting his napkin into knots.

"Schubert doesn't socialize," whispered Bert. "There aren't enough women here to suit his tastes, and confident men make him uncomfortable."

"Are there *any* women here other than Mary Shelley?" John

asked, looking up and down the table as he and his companions took seats adjacent to Mark Twain. "We certainly are a boys' club, aren't we?"

"There have been one or two considered as apprentices," Twain offered as he gestured at John with his cigar, "but Mary alone was chosen, I'm afraid."

The Feast Beasts, which were identical to the ones the Lost Boys had imagined on Haven, entered the room with silver trays laden with roasts, and dumplings, and all manner of exotic delicacies. The companions had seldom seen such a repast, and it was only then that they realized how hungry they were.

"I suppose it's been days," said Charles, "although in more practical terms you might say we haven't eaten in years."

As they ate, Jack kept a wary eye on Kipling, whom he was still certain he'd seen at the Inn of the Flying Dragon. John, for his part, was itching to know why no one had taken the chair at the head of the table. He'd come to the conclusion that it had been reserved for the Prime Caretaker, and he knew without a doubt that Jules Verne was that man.

Bert excused himself to go move Malory to a different chair. He'd been making comments about the French spices, and de Troyes was getting red in the face.

After Bert got up, John realized that there was an uneasy truce being negotiated at this end of the table as well. Professor Sigurdsson had not looked up from his plate except to ask for the gravy boat; and across from him, James Barrie was trying desperately to look in any other direction. John decided that if anyone were to break the ice, it would have to be one of the current Caretakers.

He elbowed Charles. "Say something," John hissed.

"What?" Charles hissed back. "I don't want to be stuck in the middle."

"Anything. Just get one of them talking."

"So, Jamie," said Charles jovially, "what happened to your dog? When you died, that is."

"Oh, for heaven's sake," said John.

"What?" said Charles. "You said anything."

The professor and Jamie looked at each other, then burst out laughing. When they caught their breath again, the two old colleagues regarded each other with baleful looks and held them, unblinking, until finally Jamie broke the trance and lowered his head.

"You didn't have to cross out my name," he said without looking up. "In the *Geographica*. That was quite painful to me, Stellan."

"As your choice was painful to me, Jamie," the professor noted. "Of them all, you had the most open mind. You understood the Archipelago better than any of us before or since—no offense, John," he added quickly.

"That may have been the problem, Stellan," Jamie admitted, looking up again. "I would have given myself over to it too fully. And I knew that I had to make a choice, so I did."

"If it will help, yours wasn't the only one, Jamie," said the professor. "We crossed out Houdini and Conan Doyle's names too, and one or two others as well."

"That doesn't really help, no," said Jamie.

"So what *did* happen to your dog?" asked Charles.

"The boys are taking care of him," Jamie answered. "He's in good hands."

"What?" Charles said again as he noticed Jack and John's expressions of exasperation. "I was really worried about the dog, is all."

From the front of the table, Bert signaled for silence by tapping a spoon against one of the crystal glasses. "We've supped and feasted, and had more than a few drinks," he announced with a conspiratorial wink at Percy Shelley, "among other things. And now it is time to call the Gatherum of Caretakers to order. We have business that urgently needs our attention."

He bowed to Chaucer and returned to his seat as the older man rose. "The floor is yours, Geoff."

"As Senior Caretaker," Chaucer began.

"Humph," snorted da Vinci, who then muttered a curse in Latin.

"*As Senior Caretaker,*" Chaucer repeated more solidly, "it falls to me to present the dilemma presently facing the two worlds. It is only the gravest of circumstances that require us to meet, in the flesh, to determine a course of action.

"Centuries ago, an evil man called the Winter King attempted to conquer the Archipelago by slaying his nephew Thorn, also called the Arthur, and in doing so, he nearly destroyed our world.

"Our world and the Archipelago are inseparably linked. What happens in one influences the other. And the Winter King's war in the Archipelago plunged our world into the Dark Ages."

"They weren't all *that* dark," said Malory.

"Now, Tom," said Spenser.

"After a terrible battle," Chaucer continued, "the Winter King was defeated and went into hiding, somewhere on the edges of the world. A new High King, Artigel, was crowned, and the

Imaginarium Geographica was made available to him to help unify his rule of the Archipelago.

"The strength of Artigel and of all the High Kings who followed came from the Ring of Power, which allowed them to summon the great Dragons, who have always been the guardians of the Archipelago and all who reside within. But there was also a Prophecy that one day the Winter King would return, and bring darkness to both worlds."

"Oh, dear," said Charles.

"Shush," said Jack. "He's just getting to the interesting part."

"That's what I was afraid of," said Charles.

Chaucer went on. "The Prophecy said he could be defeated only by three scholars, men of imagination from our world. But as the years passed, the Prophecy, and the warning, was forgotten.

"Then, after centuries of hiding, the Winter King reemerged just as the Prophecy said, leading an army of terrible creatures from all the dark corners of the world. He once again sought to wreak havoc on the two worlds, and would very nearly have succeeded, had it not been for the three Caretakers of Prophecy: the successors of Bert and Stellan."

He gestured to John, Jack, and Charles, and as one the Caretakers Emeritus began a round of vigorous table thumping, punctuated by cheers, whistles, and "Well done's."

John beamed, as did Charles. Jack, however, had learned to be more cautious, and he suspected that the story was not yet finished.

"If we are the three of Prophecy," Jack said when the applause died down, "then why was it necessary to keep it a secret for so long? Especially from us? Why not tell us, before all those events had become history?"

"There are Histories, and then there are Prophecies," Professor Sigurdsson explained. "Histories tell us of what was, and are dangerous only in that they contain secrets that might be cautiously shared. Prophecies tell us of what may be, and thus are full of mysteries that may be spoiled in the sharing."

Several of the others nodded and thumped on the table in agreement.

"A History shared only expands knowledge," said Chaucer, "which may then be used for good or evil. But to share a Prophecy too soon, or in the wrong company, risks a cascade of complications that may change the Histories themselves."

John, Jack, and Charles reddened with shame, each thinking of different situations but with the same cause: Are we here to be reprimanded? Did we do too poor a job?

"Every one of us has made mistakes," Bert said, correctly reading the expressions on his friends' faces, "but that wasn't why we couldn't tell you."

"We didn't tell you," the professor continued, "because that would have compromised what was most important to your performance as Caretakers—your own point of view and natural judgment. If you knew there was a Prophecy about you, then you might start tailoring your responses to fit what you thought was supposed to happen, rather than doing what you believed in your hearts was the best course of action."

"If it helps," added Bert, "we never knew which three Caretakers would be the ones referred to in the Prophecy—not until it came to pass. We realized you were the right three, because you were the ones on the job when the Winter King reemerged."

"Excuse me," Charles said, raising his hand. "May I ask a question?"

Chaucer smiled. "No need to raise your hand, Caretaker. We are all equals here."

"Some of us are just more equal than others," said Defoe.

"Hear, hear," said da Vinci.

"I was just wondering," Charles continued, "what the point is of revealing the Prophecy to us now, when we battled the Winter King so many years ago?"

"Ah," said Chaucer. "So we get to the meat of it. Do you want to answer that, Samuel?"

"Certainly," Twain said, tapping out his cigar on a plate. "You are, of course, referring to your *first* encounter with the Winter King, are you not?"

Charles gulped. "I suppose so."

"We discovered after the crisis wherein all the children and Dragonships were taken that the King of Crickets was actually the Winter King's Shadow in disguise," said Twain, "and for his Shadow to survive, he must also still be alive."

"That constituted your second conflict with him," said Chaucer. "We believe the third is yet to come; the Prophecy speaks of three battles with the Winter King—who, despite your victories, remains our great adversary."

"But we destroyed the Shadow," said John, "or at least, Peter Pan did. And we've come to believe in recent years that our true enemy is actually Richard Burton."

"Where choosing new apprentices was concerned, I had a very shallow learning curve," Dickens said apologetically. "First Burton, then Magwich. We'd all have been better off if I'd never been chosen at all."

"That isn't so," said Kipling. "You yourself were a stellar

Caretaker, and other than those two nonstarters, you've demonstrated exceptional judgment."

"Well, thank you, old fellow," Dickens replied, "but when Burton is one of our primary adversaries, I can't but regret all the training I *did* impart to him."

"Should we say anything about Kipling?" Jack whispered.

"And look like idiots?" answered John. "He's not said a foul word since we got here and hasn't so much as looked cross-eyed at any of us. If he's playing for the other side, he's hiding it well. But if he isn't, we'll have just made a new enemy in our own camp."

"On the whole," said Chaucer, "our record has been one with more victories than defeats, and we have more allies than enemies. And while our enemies are resourceful, and have much knowledge, they do not have it all. We have the Histories, and the prophecies, and the *Imaginarium Geographica*. And most vital to our cause, we also have the Grail Child. The odds are in our favor, regardless of those who chose to turn traitor."

There was more table thumping—but disturbingly, several pairs of eyes flickered toward Jamie as Chaucer spoke. Rather than ignore the glances, Jamie stood.

"I may be unique among this gathering as the only one among us who was once a full Caretaker, and then resigned," he said amidst an undercurrent of grumbles. "But I think my presence here is proof of where my loyalties lie. I have never, nor will I ever, betray our secrets to Burton or any other enemy of the Archipelago."

"That's the problem, isn't it?" asked John. "Burton feels exactly the same way. He believes he's more loyal to the Archipelago by trying to bring all its secrets to light. He truly doesn't understand what kind of havoc will be wrought."

"The Imperial Cartological Society," Dickens said darkly. "They have been a thorn in our side for too long, and Burton has seduced many of our former allies."

"Have *you* been approached, Barrie?" Kipling asked. "Has Burton tried to recruit you?"

Jamie blushed and fumbled with his buttons. "I must admit that he has tried, but not in years," he replied with a glance at the companions. "He believed I might be eager to join him because of my choice to abdicate my responsibilities, but after I explained that my reasons were not the same as his, and that I intended to keep my oaths, he left me alone. And then I died, and it became a moot point."

"Good man," said Kipling. "Would that others of our order had been as strong."

"We should be looking to Jakob," Hawthorne said brusquely. "After all, his own brother was a washout as a Caretaker, and we know he's already sworn allegiance to Burton."

"That's a lie!" Jakob Grimm shouted, standing and placing his fists on the table. "He would not betray us, and never would he betray me!"

"What about Alexandre Dumas *fils*?" asked Defoe. "He made quite a show of leaving us, and was quite loud about his intentions to betray us all."

"Forgive me," Alexandre Dumas *père* said, "and my son. I hope that he would not have sold us out to Burton and his ilk, but I cannot say with certainty."

"And would you betray us, for his sake, if he had?" Kipling asked.

"Never."

"I'd be willing to give you both the benefit of the doubt, Jakob,

Alexandre," said Dickens. "I've been through similar situations myself, and I know how your loyalties have been tested."

"Ah, yes," said Charles. "Maggot."

"Pardon?" said Dickens.

"He means Magwich," Jack corrected. "We've had more than our share of difficulties with him."

"I'm very sorry about that," Dickens said. "It was an awful judgment call on my part to bring him in the first place. He was a very strange sort of fellow, but he had a good core—or so I believed."

"It's well and truly rotten now," said Charles. "He betrayed us once to the Winter King, and I have no doubt that he would do so again."

"I think he should be flogged," said Shakespeare. "Posthaste. That will teach him the error of his ways, I think." He looked around at the others, beaming, as if he'd just solved the world's problems with a single remark—then deflated a little when he realized that no one was paying attention.

"Magwich has already been made the Green Knight," Bert said mildly. "He's paying his dues."

"That's just it," said Charles. "He isn't. The Green Knight isn't on Avalon."

There was a chorus of disbelieving remarks and more than a little grumbling at that.

"Charles," Chaucer said skeptically, "the Green Knight cannot leave Avalon. It's a binding of the Old Magic. Only the Dragons themselves might break such a binding, and they would hardly be inclined, since it was they who bound him in the first place."

"What if he's just faded into dust?" suggested Jack. "That's what happened to his predecessor, isn't it?"

"Charles Darnay had fulfilled his calling and was therefore released," said Dickens. "Do you really think Magwich has fulfilled *anything?*"

"You make a good point," said Jack. "He did prove helpful once, uh, in his own fashion. I don't know that I'd say he could be trusted, but I'd begun to think better of him."

"Extending trust to those who have already proven themselves untrustworthy," Twain remarked, "is a bit like cutting off the end of a rope and sewing it to the other end to make it longer."

John explained briefly the circumstances that had resulted in their arrival in the Nameless Isles, omitting only their suspicion of Kipling as an ally of their still unknown adversary.

"So Quixote is here?" Spenser said with a joyous expression. "My old partner! I would love to see him!"

"I'll pass, if it's all the same to you," Tycho Brahe muttered. "I'm sure he feels the same."

"It's all right," said Cervantes. "The past is the past—I'm sure he's forgiven you by now."

"I would hope so," said Brahe. "If you can't get some leniency after you've died, when can you get it?"

"Hank told us what had happened," said Twain, "and Ransom filled in the holes after. So we knew that seven years hence, you'd try to make your way here."

"That was the plan," said John. "It was a risk to use Ransom's Trump, but we felt that once we had removed Rose from danger and had moved past Verne's zero points, we'd have a better chance of preventing the war."

"Prevent the war?" a quiet voice said. It was Franz Schubert—and it was the first words he had spoken all evening. "Prevent? I'm sure I misunderstand you, young man. You cannot prevent something that has already begun."

"Already begun!" John exclaimed. "You can't be serious!"

One look at Bert's face confirmed that it was true. "The war in the Summer Country has been raging for four years now," the old traveler said, "exactly the same length of time we've been preparing for it here, although they may have fared the worse for it, since our war in the Archipelago has not yet begun."

"But I thought taking Rose away from danger was supposed to stop the war from happening!"

"Stop? No," said Chaucer. "Protecting the Grail Child was of the highest priority, and we are all grateful for your wisdom and diligence in doing so. But her survival was never meant to stop the wars—our adversary was going to see those begun regardless of the safeguards we put into place.

"Her survival was important, because it was the only way to ensure that the wars would *end*."

Chaucer signaled to one of the ravens, who flew across the room and removed a book from a nearby bookcase. The raven laid it on the table and snuck a grape from one of the platters before it flew off again.

The book was roughly the size and shape of one of the Histories. The covers and binding were steel gray leather, and the pages themselves were so white as to appear cold. For leather and parchment to be so bereft of color, the book had to be ancient. More ancient than anything else the Caretakers had ever seen.

In contrast to the *Geographica*, which bore the Greek letter *alpha* on the cover, this book was embossed with an *omega*—the same letter Bert used as his personal emblem.

"This is the only book more dangerous than the *Imaginarium Geographica,*" he said, his voice heavy with responsibility. "It is filled with notations, and formulas, and stories, and even maps. But it is also as close a record as a book can be to a History of the Dragons. It has notes on the first time any dragon has ever appeared in any land, and it lists every one of their True Names. But even more importantly, it contains the prophecies that may yet save the Archipelago.

"In the past, it has been called the *Telos Biblos,* according to the Greek. We simply refer to it as the Last Book. It is one of a set of books—we don't know how many. It was obtained only through great sacrifice, and it is the reason why we have come together today."

"It was taken from the library of the first Caretaker to go rogue," Chaucer continued. "John Dee. Very little is known about him save for rumors and whisperings, but we know that he recorded the True Names of the dragons—and he also planted the seeds for the Imperial Cartological Society, which blossomed under Burton.

"Because of this book, we know many of our enemies who were once friends. Milton. Kit Marlowe. De Bergerac. William Blake. Coleridge. Lord Byron."

"I almost took him out of the game," Percy Shelley commented, "if Mary hadn't thrown the portrait into the tide pool to put out the flames."

"What separates us from them is our belief in order," Bert said sternly. "George Gordon, Lord Byron, was a Caretaker, and his portrait still hangs here, albeit turned over. He'll never participate in a Gatherum, but he'll not aid the enemy, either."

"I knew Kit Marlowe," put in Shakespeare. "He was quite a fair writer—for a traitor, that is."

"The Last Book has remained here in the care of the Prime Caretaker for many years," said Chaucer, "and through it we have learned many things about time, and space, and our own Histories. We also know that our adversaries have gleaned enough knowledge from this, and other books like it, to develop their own methods of moving in time and space, and that makes them more dangerous than ever.

"Because of this book, we know that there is going to be one last great conflict with the Winter King, but not what guise he will take. It may be his Shadow in disguise again, or Mordred himself risen from the endless deep, or both. We know that the three current Caretakers are the key to defeating him. And we know that he has acquired a terrible weapon with which to defeat us."

"How does Rose figure into this?" asked John. "Why was she so important that she was to be killed? And how does her being here now help our cause?"

"Verne can answer you more fully as to the destiny we suspect is ahead of the girl," Edmund Spenser said, leaning over the table to better be heard. "But what little we do know also comes from the Prophecy."

Chaucer turned to a page near the front of the Last Book and scanned it until he found the passage he wanted. "It said that in the final conflict with the King of Shadows, three scholars from the Summer Country will stand united against him. An ageless knight will deliver to them the means to defeat the Shadow King, which will be wielded by a daughter of the Houses of Troy and Aramathea. Rose Dyson, the Grail Child, is the only person in all of history who has that specific heritage. And we believe that she is the key to his final defeat."

"Dear God," said Charles.

"It's a lot to take in, isn't it?" asked Twain.

"That's why we've taken the steps we have," said Bert. "We needed to make sure you were here, now, under the right circumstances, to see that Prophecy fulfilled."

"I think I need a drink," said Jack. "Or five."

"We should adjourn for brandy and a bit of air," suggested Irving. "We've been at this so long it might be a good time for a break." He looked at his watch and frowned. "Drat. I think my watch is running a bit fast. What time do you have, Rudyard?"

Kipling blanched. "I'm not sure," he said, craning his neck. "Do we have a clock in here, Bert?"

"Just check your watch," said Irving. "You *do* have a watch, don't you?"

Kipling went pale. "I, uh, I seem to have left it elsewhere," he said with a weak laugh. "Sorry—no watch."

The room went still.

"A Caretaker is never without his watch," Spenser said coolly. "Where is yours, Kipling?"

In response, Kipling turned out his pockets like a circus clown and grinned sheepishly—then shoved Irving off his chair and leaped onto the table.

"Hell's bells!" Twain exclaimed. "What the devil are you doing, Rudyard?"

Kipling ignored the question and the shouts of the others and instead threw over the candles on the table. Then, amidst the confusion, he bolted from the room.

"Someone stop him!" Irving shouted. "He's heading for the gallery!"

Jack was closest to the doors, and the most able-bodied of the Caretakers—or so he thought. He had exited the room and was racing after Kipling when Jakob Grimm passed him by.

Kipling wheeled about and pushed open the doors to the gallery anteroom, then threw them shut just as Jakob caught up to him. Jakob was struggling with the doors as Jack and then the rest of the Caretakers ran down the corridor.

"He's locked it!" Jakob exclaimed. "I can't get it open!"

"Stand back," said Hawthorne. He took the measure of the doors, and then smashed into them with a powerful, well-placed kick. They didn't budge.

"You thought one kick would do it?" asked Jack.

"Well, I *am* Nathaniel Hawthorne," he answered, gesturing to the others. "All together now!"

Hawthorne, Jack, Irving, and Jakob threw themselves against the doors, which cracked open in a shower of splintered wood.

"There!" said Jack. "He's going back inside the painting!"

At first glance, that seemed to be precisely what Kipling was doing—until the Caretakers rushed forward to capture their colleague and suddenly realized that the portrait of Kipling . . .

. . . was *shrinking*.

"What kind of enchantment is this?" Irving declared.

Whatever was happening, it was too late to catch the Caretaker-gone-wild. The image was the size of a playing card now, and there was no way to reverse or halt the process. In seconds the image would disappear completely.

"Be seeing you," Kipling said with a wink. And then he was gone.

CHAPTER ELEVEN
THE MASTER

"IT WASN'T A PORTRAIT at all!" John exclaimed. "It was a Trump, just like the ones Hank and Ransom use!"

"You're right, young man," Twain said, examining the painting. "A rather ingenious ploy—creating a Trump that opens on top of a painting of the same image."

"He must have used a similar one to come into the gallery," said Jamie, "and merely pretended he was being summoned from his portrait as the rest of us were."

Bert moved over to the painting and tapped on it lightly with his fingertips. "No," he said. "This was an actual portrait done with Pygmalion resins, as all the rest have been. He only needed a means of escape that we couldn't easily duplicate."

"Can we follow him?" asked John. "Through the painting?"

Bert grimaced and shook his head. "They're meant to be one way, and they don't actually go to a place," he said resignedly. "When the Caretakers go back, they aren't somewhere—they're just in a painting."

"He's going to report to his masters," Jakob cried. "We've got to do something! He must be stopped!"

"I left the doors to the gallery unlocked," said Bert. "How was it that Kipling locked them so quickly, since I have the only three keys, and one of *those* is imaginary?"

"I don't know," Jakob said. "He closed them behind him, and as I caught up, I found I couldn't get them open. But believe me, I was pushing as hard as I could."

Defoe stood behind Jakob and closed his hands into fists. "Perhaps we have another turncoat in our midst," he said with obvious menace in his tone. "Where's *your* watch, Jakob?"

With a few fumbles born of fear and haste, Jakob rummaged around in his pockets and finally, with a great sigh of relief, produced his watch.

"You're good, then," Defoe said. "I'm sorry I doubted you, Brother Grimm."

"Thanks," said Jakob, still visibly shaken. "I'm sorry about the doors. Wilhelm would have been smart enough to do it the right way."

"So Kipling knows all our secrets," said Defoe.

"Not all of them," Bert said in admonishment. "He was only a part of the whole. We have the books, and we have the three Caretakers of Prophecy. They will see this through, regardless of Kipling's betrayal."

"This may be the worst possible time to bring this up," said John, "but we had already suspected Kipling was a traitor. We just didn't tell anyone."

Quickly he related the rest of the details about their flight from the Inn of the Flying Dragon, and the fact that Jack believed Kipling had been leading their pursuers.

"Why didn't you tell us this before?" asked Hawthorne. "We might have found him out all the sooner."

"He didn't tell," Twain said, lighting up a fresh cigar, "because he is not an ass, and neither are his two compatriots. They came here today and have listened to a great many impossible things without blinking. But they also saw us turning on our own like a pack of hungry dogs.

"We questioned Charles Dickens' loyalty because two of those he trained turned out to be traitors themselves—never mind the fact that he also trained our Prime Caretaker. We questioned Alexandre Dumas, not for what he chose to do, but because of the choices of his son. And we were one minute away from lynching poor Jakob because we know his brother to be allied with Burton, and he couldn't produce his watch quickly enough.

"No," Twain said with finality. "Young John did exactly the right thing. He watched, and waited, and when it was time to act, he used his best judgment. And that's all anyone can ask of a Caretaker."

"Thank you, Mr. Clemens," said John.

"You don't have to thank me, boy," said Twain as he stepped out into the corridor, puffing on his cigar. "I'm deceased, remember? At this point, I'm just here for the entertainment."

"I am sorry," Jakob said again. "Not just for myself, but for . . . for my brother."

"He made his own choices," said Bert, "but of the two of you, we got the better man. Come," he called to the others, gesturing broadly. "Let us retire to the conservatory for drinks and more discussion. Our schedule has just taken an unexpected leap forward."

The conservatory was in the very center of Tamerlane House, and the ceiling inside the room rose to an impossible height. It had to be ten stories high and was capped by a glittering, translucent dome.

Windows rose along two sides, above a second-floor landing and stairway, with massive tapestries hanging in between. Below were a walk-in fireplace and several shelves lined with busts and sculptures amid a number of chairs, which surrounded a long table much like the one in the dining room. As before, John noted that none of the Caretakers took the seat at the head of the table.

"There's nothing outside that's this tall," John said wonderingly as he looked up at the dome. "Have we gone down somehow, below ground?"

"Oh, no," said Bert. "The earth here is impossibly hard. Just putting in a basement was a trial and a tribulation. This room was built specifically to house the tapestries"—he pointed at the explosions of color that were draped on the walls—"but Marco Polo had underestimated their size when we acquired them from him, and we had a dilemma. So we installed a tesseract, and that's made all the difference. Isn't the dome lovely?"

"Nice, very nice," said Charles. "Egyptian?"

"Hittite," said Bert. "But you were close."

Once drinks were poured and all of them had again settled down from the commotion Kipling had caused, Bert called for silence, and Chaucer stood to address them.

"It has been many years since one of our number has turned," he began, "but we must press forward. Kipling's betrayal changes nothing."

"Perhaps he should be flogged," put in Shakespeare.

"Changes nothing?" Hawthorne exclaimed. "He knows about the girl!"

"They already knew about Rose," Twain corrected. "What they didn't know was that there were other players in the game. They didn't know that John, Jack, and Charles are to play a key role in the final defeat of the Winter King. And they didn't know that Quixote would deliver the weapon of his downfall. So in my opinion, our mission has not changed—we must protect the girl. She is the endgame."

"They may not have known all those things," said Charles, "but we've given them something else: We've confirmed that we know who our adversary is. The Prophecy itself has confirmed it. In some form, we will be facing the Winter King."

"And now that they know we know," said Jack, "he will be making his move."

"I concur," said John. "The war in the Archipelago begins right now."

"I think, given this turn of events," Chaucer said, "we should bring in the Grail Child and her guardian. We need to have all the players on the board, and we all need to know what everyone else knows."

Bert signaled to the ravens, and they flew out of the conservatory, returning a few minutes later with Rose, Quixote, and Archimedes in tow.

It took most of an hour to make introductions. Rose was unusually timid, but polite. Quixote was typically formal in his greetings, except when he got to Edmund Spenser. The two men gripped each other's forearms and laughed. It was a reunion of true friends and colleagues.

"It has been far too long, you old Riddle Master," said Spenser. "How are you?"

"Riddle Master?" answered Quixote. "Pish-tosh. Without your detective skills, the Sphinx would have defeated me."

"Hello, Quixote," said Cervantes.

"Miguel!" Quixote said, shaking his hand. "How goes the new book?"

"I'm almost finished," Cervantes told him.

"Which new book is that?" John whispered to Bert.

"It doesn't really matter," Bert replied. "He always says he's almost finished."

When Quixote came to Tycho Brahe, the best they could manage were polite, if curt, nods at each other. Room was made for Quixote to sit next to Spenser, and Rose went to sit between Jack and Charles. A raven flew in and placed a glass of milk in front of her.

"Thank you, Warren," she said.

"Welcome, miss," said the bird, bowing its head.

They began by having Quixote relate the tale of the cave on Avalon, and what the Lady Guinevere had said to him regarding their enemies.

"She said a great weapon was being brought to bear against the forces of the light," he said somberly, "and that we would need a weapon of equal power to combat it. I asked where such a weapon could be found, and in reply she said to seek the Lady, that she may return what was given."

"The Lady of the Lake," said Malory. "She cannot be summoned on a whim."

"Ah," said Quixote, "that point of fact is exactly the reason I believe I am to play a role in this matter, and why the Frenchman believed I was the knight of the Prophecy.

"Many years ago I was called upon to perform a service for the Caretakers."

"And a job well done," said Cervantes. "You traveled to the Summer Country and to the edges of the Archipelago itself, and you brought back the *Geographica*."

"Indeed," said Quixote, "but what none of you knew, save for my partner Edmund, was that in the course of events I performed a service for the Lady of the Lake. And to this day, she owes me a boon."

"This wasn't in any of the Histories," Irving said with an irritated glance at Spenser. "Where was it chronicled, Caretaker?"

"It's in one of the appendices," replied Spenser, "under the title 'The Thin Man and the Queen of Stars.'"

"Ah," said Irving. "Your pardon, Edmund."

"If you are able to summon the lady," said Chaucer, "what weapon do you believe she will give you?"

"'Return what was given,'" Jack said suddenly. "That can only mean one weapon. We saw it given to her ourselves, John."

"That's right," said John. "It's in one of the, ah, less accurate chronicles written by Geoffrey of Monmouth. After the first battle with Mordred in Camelot, when we brought Rose to restore Arthur's life, he called on the Lady of the Lake—his mother—and gave the shattered pieces of his sword to her.

"The weapon we need to defeat the Winter King is the weapon he wanted for himself," John finished, now visibly excited. "It's the sword of Aeneas! It's Caliburn!"

"I concur," Chaucer said, after all the murmuring and table thumping that had followed John's statement had died down. "That *must* be the weapon mentioned in the Prophecy. But that still leaves us with many unknown pieces on the board. Even if Quixote should succeed in obtaining Caliburn from the Lady, it must still be repaired—and there is no one living who knows how it was forged."

"The Cartographer," said John. "It may be worth consulting him."

"A possibility," allowed Chaucer. "A better one may be the Ancient of Days—the shipbuilder Ordo Maas. He has knowledge of techniques long lost to the rest of the two worlds. He might be willing to help."

"And then what?" said John. "We wait for our adversary to make his plays and then respond in kind? You said the war had not yet begun in the Archipelago, while it's been raging along in the Summer Country. What if he's there already? What if he's planning on turning it into the Winterland first—and then returning here?"

"He hasn't been in the real world," Bert said. "We'd have known, or seen some aspect of his movements there. But we've seen nothing."

"He has to be operating somewhere," said Jack. "Burton and the others of the Imperial Cartological Society are operating in both worlds—why can't he?"

"You've hit the problem on the head, boy," said Twain. "They must have a base of operations, but we just haven't been able to locate it. And believe me," he added, tapping out his cigar, "we've looked. In *both* worlds."

"It isn't there," a soft, slight voice said from somewhere above them. "The place you're seeking—it isn't there."

As one, the assembly looked up to the figure standing at the railing above and gasped in unison.

It was the master of the house.

He stood to the right side of the landing, which was still steeped in shadows. His smallish frame seemed to implode upon itself as he stood there, moving his hands nervously, trying to decide what to do with them. His eyes glittered from under a deep brow and his hair was strewn about as if he'd just risen from a long nap.

He finally gripped the railing to steady himself, then repeated the words he'd spoken: "The place you're seeking isn't there."

Edgar Allan Poe quietly descended the staircase and moved around the table to take his place at the head—a place John had assumed was reserved for Jules Verne.

"Is Poe the Prime Caretaker?" he whispered.

"You've already guessed that Verne has that title," Bert whispered back, "but we can discuss that another time. Poe is something else altogether. He may have a mild manner and bearing, but believe you me—he functions on an entirely different level from the rest of us."

The regard the Caretakers Emeritis held for Poe was evident in their treatment of him. Not a one among them stirred or spoke. The slight man sat and moved some stray strands of hair out of his eyes; then he leaned back, clasping his hands together.

"One of the reasons I shared my discovery of the Soft Places," he began, "is because they are not just places of sanctuary, but may also be used as beachheads against us in the war. We have sent our agents out among the myriad dimensions not only to act as our messengers, but to serve as our spies. The enemy's refuge must be somewhere."

"But most of the Crossroads end at taverns or inns," said Jamie. "Even accounting for a portion of the lands around them, they just aren't large enough. It would have to be a hidden village, like Brigadoon."

"Brigadoon is simply a story from the Encyclopedia Mythica," Poe said, "but in principle, you are correct. There must be a township, or a village, or an island somewhere among the Soft Places large enough to contain the armies of the Winter King and his allies. If we are to gain an advantage, we must find that place."

"Whom do we have out?" Chaucer asked.

"Hank Morgan, Alvin Ransom, and the Rappaccini girl," said Twain. "And Dr. Raven. You know what happened to Arthur Pym."

"Yes," said Poe. "Most unfortunate."

"They should be reporting in soon," said Twain. "I've sent them messages via the Trumps, and their information may prove very useful, especially now that all the major players are here."

"I agree," said Poe. "We shall adjourn for the evening, to rest and recharge, so that we are prepared for what is to come."

The Caretakers all stood up from the table with Poe and moved to various parts of the house to commiserate in small groups. Quixote sat with Spenser, Cervantes, and Brahe by the great fireplace, and in one of the anterooms, Defoe and Swift were showing Rose how to make treasure maps. "You see," Defoe explained as he drew on a sheet of parchment, "you make any shape that seems right. Then you use the names of anyone around you to name the geographical details, like marshes, and rivers, and mountains. And then you make an *X* where you want the treasure to be. And I promise you, if you find an island that matches the map, you'll also find the treasure."

"Or you'll be shot by tiny people with tiny arrows," said Swift. "And you don't want to know about the talking horses."

"I swear, I thought they were centaurs," protested Defoe.

"Daniel, Jonathan," Twain said in warning. "Watch your tongues when there's a lady present."

"Sorry," Defoe and Swift said together.

Professor Sigurdsson was fascinated by Archimedes and retreated with the owl to the library for a game of chess before John could pull him aside.

He had wanted to speak to the professor at length, but Bert tugged on his arm before he could follow them. "There'll be plenty of time to speak to Stellan later," Bert said. "The master of the house would like a private audience with the three of you upstairs in his quarters."

"Poe wants to talk to us?" Charles exclaimed. "Wonderful!"

"Just be careful," Bert cautioned as they ascended the stairs. "He is most trusted, but he is very eccentric. He doesn't always make sense—not at first, anyway. But he is always worth listening to, and he is responsible for everything we have. Even Jules defers to him."

"Lead on, MacDuff," said Jack.

"That bird is a bad influence," Bert said. "On *all* of you."

Four flights up, Poe's own space in Tamerlane House was a room barely sixty feet square. In one corner was a shabby little camp bed, under which a pair of shoes were neatly placed. In the opposite corner were a writing desk and a simple tallow candle. There was no other furniture, or indeed, decoration of any kind in the room. It was the one place in that entire exceptionally colorful house that seemed to have had the color leached from it. John thought it was the most melancholy room he'd ever seen.

Poe was sitting at the desk, writing.

"What do you think of utopias?" he asked without turning around.

"I'm for them, myself," said Charles.

"It would depend," said Jack. "I worry that we'd grow stagnant as a civilization if we truly lived in a utopia."

"Your mentor, Master Wells, had the same worry," said Poe. He turned around and looked at John, his eyes huge in the dim light of the candle. "Do you know what kind of problem I have with utopias?"

John blinked. "I'm sure I have no idea," he said.

"Pistachio nuts," Poe said. "None of them mention pistachio nuts. I love them myself—but they seem to get left out of all of the perfect societies. Would you like a pistachio nut?"

Without waiting for an answer, he held out his hand and dropped a nut into each of the companions' hands. He popped one into his mouth and crunched on it, so the others did the same.

"Follow me," Poe said, rising from the chair, still chewing. "I'd like to show you something."

He led John, Jack, Charles, and Bert down a long hallway that became taller and narrower as they went. Near the end, they found they had to turn sideways just to squeeze through.

"You all right, Jack?" asked John.

"Yes," Jack grunted. "Just regretting eating so many of Mrs. Moore's meat pies."

At the end of the hall was a wide atelier lit by a massive chandelier, and at the far side of the room, near a window, sat a man, painting.

"Basil Hallward, our resident artist," Poe said in introduction. "Oscar Wilde discovered the young man at Magdalen and found he had a remarkable gift for portraiture. We brought him here and commissioned him to create the portraits of past Caretakers."

Hallward glanced over at the companions and nodded distractedly, then did an abrupt double take. He jumped to his feet and threw a sheet over the canvas in progress.

"I say," Charles remarked, "were you by chance painting a portrait of *me*?"

Hallward choked, then looked to Poe, who calmly returned the artist's gaze before looking up at Charles.

"Ransom," Poe said simply. "He was painting Alvin Ransom."

"You do look quite similar, Charles," said Jack.

"My word," Charles exclaimed. "I hope nothing's happened to the poor fellow."

"Oh, no, not at all," Poe answered. "It's just a precaution. What's useful for us Caretakers is also useful for our apprentices."

Hallward nodded. "Useful, yeah. Useful."

"I agree," a voice said behind them. It was Defoe. "Nothing like having someone handy who can—literally—paint the illusion of life," he said cheerfully.

Poe looked askance at Hallward. "You've painted pictures for some of the others?"

"I've considered availing myself of his services once or twice," Defoe said, smirking.

"Now, Daniel," said Bert, wagging a finger in warning, "we've cautioned you about that before. Caretakers only. It's too dangerous to have others hanging around the gallery who might overhear our secrets without the oath of secrecy to bind them.

"And you," he finished, pointing at Hallward. "No freelancing."

"Yes, sir," the painter said, chagrined.

"Caretakers only?" Jack whispered to Charles. "But didn't he just say that Hallward was completing a painting of Ransom?"

"Poe said apprentices, too," Charles reminded him.

"May I have a word?" Defoe said to Poe. "I'd like to discuss the Kipling situation."

"Don't worry," said Bert. "I'll see the lads to their rooms."

He led the companions back out of the atelier and closed the door. "Defoe and Kipling were close," he explained. "This has got to be quite a blow for him."

"For us all," said Jack. "I just wish we'd said something earlier."

"Not everything can be forecast," said Bert. "Not even the things we already know will happen."

"Isn't it risky that so many future events are known and being acted on?" asked Jack. "Won't that disrupt the future—or worse, corrupt the prophecies?"

"Jules and I decided some time ago to view everything as being the past," said Bert. "That's one advantage of having lived eight hundred thousand years in the future. If I view it all as history, then all we're doing is trying to shape the best history possible. Sometimes that means keeping information, such as the prophecies, a secret. And other times it means sharing as much information as possible about the immediate future so that the right preparations can be made."

"Or so that you can pinch books of American presidential

quotations from thirty years hence, so you can sound erudite and wise," John said, winking.

"Will you let that go?" said Bert irritably. "I tell you, if Milton had heard Kennedy speak, he'd have swiped it himself."

"What do you mean by 'immediate future'?" asked Charles.

"No more than a century or two," said Bert, "but that's one of the reasons we do use the knowledge. My own chronicle warned of that."

"*The Shape of Things to Come,*" said John. "I read it, but it came out in the thirties and was written by *our* Wells, wasn't it?"

"Yes," said Bert. "It was based on my own version, but with two major differences. While both predicted World War II, and both saw it as lasting for two decades and ending with a plague that nearly destroys the world, his ends with an eventual utopian society, and mine does not."

"What's the other difference?"

"His was fiction," said Bert, "and mine is not; it is occurring as we speak."

"So the Winter King is trying to create the Winterland," said Jack.

"That's why we hoped to start our countermeasures in 1943," said Bert. "I fear he already *has*."

CHAPTER TWELVE
THE ADVERSARY

THE NIGHT PASSED quickly, and when the Caretakers all gathered again in the conservatory for breakfast, the sun was still low on the horizon.

"The Caretakers keep Oxford hours, it seems," Jack said, yawning. "Early to bed, early to rise. I can't believe we're the last ones awake."

"I don't think they have to sleep when they're in the paintings," said Charles. "Or if they do, it's not because of exhaustion."

"Maybe we'll be paintings here someday," said John. "Won't that be a nice thing to look forward to in our old age? The chance to do it all again?"

Jack started to respond, but Charles scowled and walked away, waving a hand in greeting at some of the other Caretakers.

"What's gotten under his hat?" said John.

"I think he's just worried," Jack replied. "There's a lot to process, even for someone of Charles's perception."

The Feast Beasts had once again served an extraordinary repast. Fresh fruit, of varieties both identified and not; vegetables of unusual shapes and colors, which nevertheless exuded fantastically saliva-inducing aromas; eggs Benedict; milk from eight kinds of cows, three kinds of goats, and one more animal—the pitcher of which no one would touch. There were green eggs and ham, hashed brown potatoes, and country-style omelets.

"I'm normally as carnivorous as the next man," Jack said to Bert, "but we have lots of friends here in the Archipelago who are talking animals, and there are at least three dishes on the table featuring ham. It's making me a little uncomfortable."

"Worry not," Bert said as he sat at the table and tucked a napkin into his collar. "For one thing, there are certain dishes, such as my beloved eggs Benedict, that just aren't the same without meat. And for another thing, it's no one you know."

"Very comforting," said Jack.

The Caretakers were just finishing up the breakfast feast when Charles, Jack, and John pulled Bert into the corridor for a word in private.

"I hesitate to bring this up too loudly," Charles said, looking around almost guiltily, "but you'll understand, considering the reaction everyone had when Kipling couldn't produce a pocket watch."

Bert grinned. "You're worried because you and Jack don't have watches."

"Precisely."

"Understandable, my boy, totally understandable," said Bert. "But you needn't have worried. For one thing, you are current Caretakers. If we didn't trust you, you would not have kept the job this long, especially given some of the, ah, hiccups of your tenure.

"For another, we believe you three to be the scholars mentioned in the Prophecy. No amount of precaution would prepare us if you chose to cross over to the other side.

"And lastly, it wasn't until after 1936 that we realized we had to discover some way to identify our own agents—and we'd already used the watches to do so in a limited capacity. So in short, the reason you don't have watches yet is because you disappeared for seven years, and we hadn't had the chance to give them to you yet."

"Whew," said Charles. "I'm very relieved."

"So am I," said Jack. "Everyone here seems fairly civilized, but for an instant I flashed on the distressing notion that I might have to go toe to toe with Hawthorne."

Bert led the three companions up a winding flight of stairs to a hallway that was so cramped and tiny that they had to crouch to make their way down to the door at the end, which was even smaller.

"Is this where the watches are made?" asked John. "The Watchmaker must be a very compact fellow."

"This is just our storeroom," Bert replied as he knelt on the floor. "The Watchmaker is a very secretive creature. Verne has met him more often than I, and the only other thing I know about him is that he's an old friend of Samaranth."

"So he's a Dragon?" asked Jack.

"I asked the same question," said Bert, "and all he would say was that he had declined the promotion."

"What are you doing down there?" said Charles. "I don't think we can even get through that door."

"It's a voice-released lock," Bert explained, leaning low to the small wooden door. "Who knows what evil lurks in the hearts of men?" he said in a baritone voice. A pause. Then he added, "The Shadow knows!"

There was a click, and then the wall—not the door, but the entire wall—swung open into a stone-lined room.

"The Shadow knows?" said John.

"I got the idea from some radio dramas I gave to the Cartographer," said Bert. "It's a safety feature."

Inside, the walls were lined with small drawers and shelves laden with silver watches.

"Many of them resemble my own," Bert said, "but it was an earlier model. Most of the rest look very similar to yours, John."

"I'd like one of those, if I may," said Jack.

"And I'd like to have one like yours, Bert," said Charles. "If you don't mind, that is."

Bert selected two of the watches and handed them to the Caretakers. "Remember," he said as he placed the watches in their open hands, "Believing is seeing."

"Believe," John, Jack, and Charles said together.

"Don't go yet," Bert said quickly. "I have something else for you." He handed each of the companions another watch.

"Spares?" asked John. "In case we lose the first one?"

"No," Charles said, understanding. "These are for our own apprentices, aren't they?"

"Exactly," said Bert. "There may be a time when you will want to know, without doubt, that someone will be there to come to your aid—as I have always counted on you. You'll choose your apprentices when you give them the watch.

"But be very careful about whom you choose to give them to," he continued. "They are the only means of telling whether or not someone is a true emissary or apprentice of the Caretakers. They cannot be duplicated and cannot be bought or sold—only earned.

If they are stolen, they will crumble into dust. If they are sold, they will crumble into dust. If they are used for evil purposes, they will crumble into dust. But if they are cared for, and used properly, they have the potential to become much, much more, as the wearer earns the right to learn of their powers.

"But if nothing else, value them for being what they are—a symbol that the wearer belongs to the most honored and honorable gathering of men and women who have ever drawn breath.

"So," he said in conclusion, "choose wisely, and choose well, whom you give them to. Your very life may depend on it."

"So if Kipling is in league with Burton," John said as they returned to the conservatory, "his watch probably crumbled to dust."

Bert nodded. "That was all the evidence we needed that the wrong choices were being made, and we had a cuckoo in our midst."

As they approached the conservatory, they could hear the noises of a heated discussion taking place. Quickening their pace, they rushed into the room and found that a new arrival had come to Tamerlane House.

"Ransom!" Jack exclaimed. "It's very good to see you!"

"You made it!" said Ransom with obvious relief. "When I lost the Yoricks, I tried jumping back to this time, but it took a few tries to nail the date. It's all been a botch of things from start to finish."

"We're just happy to see that you made it away in one piece," said Charles.

"Yes, yes," Ransom said distractedly. "It's good to see you alive and well too, all of you. I'm sorry if I'm a bit brusque, but something terrible has happened. I have to show you, right now."

"Whatever you need," said Chaucer, gesturing broadly. "Please."

Ransom cleared a space on the table and hefted a small case onto it. He popped open the twin latches on top and spread it open to reveal a curious device. It had coils and lenses, and two sets of frames that held slides in front of a turntable.

"It's called a Hobbes stereopticon," Bert explained as Ransom assembled the machine. "You can use a lens built into the side of the case to record events, and then it replays them for you later."

"A camera *and* a projector," said Jack. "Very nice."

"Better than that," said Bert. "It projects images and sound in three dimensions, and you can walk through them to observe a scene from every angle."

"Do you have somewhere I can plug this in?" Ransom said, holding up the cord. "I used up the batteries making the recording."

Jakob Grimm took the cord from Ransom and scrambled under one of the tables, searching for an outlet. "Got it," he called after a moment. "Give it a go, Ransom."

The philologist flipped a switch on the back of the stereopticon, and suddenly an incredible light show blazed to life. As Bert had said, the projection was displayed in all three spatial dimensions, filling the room. It was the coastline of a massive island, reduced to the size of a play set—except the tin soldiers were real, as was the battle they were witnessing.

Because the projector was on the table, the ground level of the film was at the Caretakers' waist level. And so, as they walked around examining the scene, they looked like leviathans wading through the channel.

There was a great deal of destruction evident past the coastline. Fires raged, and in the distance, they could see buildings being toppled. According to Ransom, it got worse.

"The island is called Kor," he said, looking back at John. "Do you know it?"

"It's one of the oldest and largest in the Archipelago," John said. "But what would cause all this destruction?"

"This is a declaration of war," stated Ransom. "And a message to us all. If Kor can fall so easily, then it bodes ill for the rest of us. But there is something else."

He pointed to several small objects on the surface of the water that disappeared as they watched. "Seven ships," he said grimly. "Seven ships—and an army comprised of children—caused all this damage."

"This is not an event in the future history," said Twain, "but a continuation from one *past*."

"Agreed," said Bert. "This *must* be the Winter King."

"Were those ships what they appeared to be?" John asked with a rising feeling of dread. "Surely they couldn't be. Not here. Not *now*!"

"The Dragonships lost in time," said Jack. "From the Underneath, in 1926."

Ransom grimaced. "I can't say for certain, but I believe so. And I think he's put them to use in places other than in the Archipelago."

"Then why wait so long to begin the war here?" asked Jack. "The Summer Country has been at war for years—what was he waiting for?"

"He hasn't just been waiting to make a move in the Archipelago," said John. "He's been planning to conquer them *both* all along."

"This must be discussed with Artus and Aven," Bert said as he paced the floor. "We need to go to Paralon."

"That's a good idea," said John. "We need to see what Artus's plans are. He needs to know, if he doesn't already, that the war has finally come to the Archipelago."

"I'm sorry, John, but you must remain here," Chaucer said, almost apologetically. "As Caretaker Principia, there are responsibilities to attend to with the Gatherum."

"Rose and Quixote should also stay," said Bert. "Until we have a plan of action, it's safer for them here. But I'd like Jack and Charles to come with me, to advise the king and queen."

"Of course," Jack said. Charles also nodded his assent.

"Do you want to go by Trump?" Ransom asked. "It's easily done."

Bert shook his head. "I need to take the *White Dragon* in for repairs and restocking," he said. "From the looks of things, we'll need more armament as well."

"Fine by me," said Jack. "I could use the fresh air."

It took only a few hours to make the preparations to leave in the *White Dragon*. Ransom went on ahead to announce their impending arrival, while Jack and Charles said their good-byes to their friends and the Caretakers.

"We'll be back soon," Jack promised Rose. "Artus and Aven will help us sort things out, you'll see."

Charles pulled Quixote aside. "Just a caution," he said softly. "We were surprised by Kipling. I don't want to be surprised again, so stay with Rose. If there are enemies here, they could be anywhere."

"I understand," said Quixote. "I shall guard her with my life."

Bert, Jack, and Charles boarded the *White Dragon*, and, with a last wave, they lifted off into the air.

The airships were faster by far than the original seafaring-only ships had been, and it was only a matter of hours before they were over familiar waters.

It was a pleasant day, and Jack and Charles spent most of their time enjoying the trip, rather than rehashing the earlier events and the terrible situation in England. There would be time enough to do that soon.

Charles did a double take as he thought he saw something in the sky just ahead. He shaded his eyes and took another look.

"Bert!" he exclaimed. "We're steering right into a flock of enormous birds!"

Bert laughed and rushed past the confused Charles to the railing. "They aren't birds," he said, waving his hand in the air. "They're our royal escort!"

The cluster of birds suddenly split apart and flew into formations that spiraled around the *White Dragon*. It was then that Charles realized they weren't birds at all—they were flying children.

For several minutes the ship was surrounded by shifting patterns of laughing, aerodynamic children—no, young adults—most of whom Charles had last seen on an island called Haven.

Three of the winged dervishes glided close, then landed smoothly on the deck.

The tallest of the three, obviously their leader, was dressed in tight leathers and laced boots, and she wore goggles that pinned down her light brown hair, which was sticking out in every direction. Her wings, long and majestic, were attached with a harness that crisscrossed her chest. She lifted up the goggles and flashed a dazzling smile.

"The first time I saw you," Charles said, beaming, "you had

smudges on your face, and you weren't nearly as accomplished at flying. Also, you were shorter."

"It's wonderful to see you again, Charles," she said, embracing the only slightly taller man.

"It's wonderful to see you, too, Laura," he replied.

"That's Laura Glue," she chided him gently, "as if you'd forgotten!"

"I haven't forgotten, Laura my Glue," said Jack as he came around the cabin to give her a welcoming hug. "That was the most impressive display I've ever seen!"

"Aw, we was just fooling around," said the second flyer, a thinner girl with dark, spiky hair. "You should see us when we're actually *trying*."

"Sadie!" Laura Glue admonished. "Discipline."

The girl snapped back to attention. "Sorry, Captain."

"Captain?" said Jack. "Laura Glue—are you the leader of this group, then?"

"I am." The girl nodded. "Captain of the Valkyries."

"That reminds me," said Jack. "I need to thank you for sending all those Lost Boys to the taverns and inns at the Crossroads to watch out for us. We would never have gotten Rose out alive if not for your boy Flannery." He craned his neck to look at several of the other Valkyries who had landed on the *White Dragon*. "Is he here with you? I'd like to thank him myself."

Laura Glue bit her lip and looked at her shoes. Sadie cleared her throat loudly, and Laura Glue looked up again. There were tears in her eyes.

"Three years ago, there was a skirmish with the Yoricks at one of the Soft Places," she said, her voice steady. "It went up in flames. Flannery didn't make it out."

"I'm sorry," said Charles.

"As am I," said Jack. "We left him only a few days ago, but to everyone else, we've been gone for seven years. A lot can happen in that time."

"A lot *has* happened in the last seven years," said Laura Glue. "Not much of it is good. They'll fill you in at Paralon. Artus is waiting to receive you."

She moved over to speak to Bert about other arrangements that needed to be made at Paralon, and Jack pulled Charles aside.

"One thing's for certain," Jack whispered. "When this is all over, and we've gotten back to the time we're supposed to be in, I'm going to make certain that Flannery is nowhere near that tavern, wherever it is."

"Changing a history?" asked Charles.

"Making a prophecy," said Jack.

As the crew of the *White Dragon* gently guided the airship to its customary spot in the Paralon harbor, a tremendous racket sprang up from the docks. It had the vaguest resemblance to music, but was more on the order of a collision of train cars that happened to be carrying musical instruments.

"The Royal Animal Rescue Squad," Jack explained to Charles. "I'd forgotten you haven't met them yet."

Jack went through the group of mammals and made introductions, giving special attention to their friend Tummeler's son, Uncas.

"I have a speech prepared," announced Uncas. "Would you like to hear it?"

"A speech? In our honor?" said Charles, puffing out his chest. "But of course!"

"I think it's honor enough that you chose to write it," said Jack. "To hear it read aloud would only be anticlimactic."

"Oh, uh, great!" said Uncas brightly while Jack winked at the deflated Charles. "Well then, since it's on the way, would you like to come by the shop? We've now got the biggest operation on Paralon, and my son Fred would love to meet the great Scowler Charles."

"You don't say?" Charles said heartily. "Lead the way, Uncas."

The badgers' publishing enterprise, which had begun with Uncas's father's editions of poorly selling cookbooks, had grown exponentially with the release of the popular edition of the *Imaginarium Geographica,* then again with the abridged edition of the guidebook to everything, the Little Whatsit. But even then, the whole venture consisted of a single storefront and a backroom printing facility. It was nothing like the Herculean complex that Uncas was so proudly ushering them into.

The main building itself was the size of an airplane hangar, and was tall enough to have its own weather patterns—*indoors.* There were badgers of every size scurrying to and fro, very occupied with the business at hand. They were all smartly dressed in white shirts and frocks, and all wore black armbands.

"Grandfather Tummeler will be very sorry to have missed you," Fred said earnestly. "He still speaks of you often."

"Good old Tummeler," said Charles jovially. "How is he?"

"Well enough," Fred replied, "but quite far along in badger years. He's basically in retirement at a house Artus had built for him next to the Great Whatsit. That way, he can use it for research as often as he likes."

"Research?" exclaimed Charles. "Is he working on another book?"

"Several," Uncas said, handing a stack of papers to his son. "He's constantly offering revisions on the Little Whatsit, but he's also working on his memoirs. I think he's titled it *There and Back Again: A Badger's Tale*."

"Really!" said Charles. "That's extraordinary. I can't wait to read it."

"The title's a bit bland, though," said Jack. "We'll have to mention it to John. Maybe he can think of a way to improve it. He's very good with titles, you know."

"Uncas," Charles said, "what is the meaning of the black armbands? Are you in mourning for someone?"

On hearing the question, all the badgers nearby stopped what they were doing and, almost in a single motion, turned to look . . .

. . . at Jack.

"What?" said Jack, looking around at his feet as if he'd inadvertently stepped on someone's tail. "Did I do something wrong?"

Uncas hemmed and hawed and stuttered and stammered until Fred sighed and stepped forward to answer. "It's not so much what you done, Scowler Jack," he began, "as it is what you're *going* t' do."

Charles frowned. For Fred to both address Jack formally and to lapse into the slipped vowels of the less-formal badger-speak meant it was a grave matter indeed.

"This isn't about the giants again, is it?" said Jack. "I told Bert—"

"No, no, nuthin' like that," said Fred. "It's just that . . . that . . . well, y'r an *Oxford* man, Scowler Jack!"

"As I always plan to be," Jack said with a trace of defensiveness.

"Well then," said Uncas morosely, "in th' Summer Country, in the year of our Lord nineteen hundred and fifty-four, y'r in for a *big* surprise."

"All this because I supposedly—in the future, mind you—take a post at Cambridge?" Jack whispered as he gestured around at the armband-wearing badgers. "Is it possible to feel guilt over something I don't plan to do, and won't do anyway for *years?*"

"That's an interesting question," replied Charles. "I wonder how the intention or non-intention plays into the concept of repentance."

"Repentance?" Jack sputtered. "But I haven't done anything! Or at least, not yet! And even then, at worst it's because I go teach at another university?"

"Not just another university," Charles said. "*Cambridge.* Not only have we been joking about it for all these years, but according to Bert, the only Caretakers who have ever really botched the job came from Cambridge, not Oxford. It's basically a cursed place, as far as these little fellows are concerned."

As if to punctuate Charles's point, a smallish badger intern carrying a bundle of ribbon markers stopped and looked at them, whiskers quivering.

Jack gave it a little wave, and in response the tiny mammal burst into tears and went running from the room.

"Oh, for heaven's sake," said Jack.

"I'd better do all the talking while we're here," Charles said, laying a comforting hand on Jack's shoulder. "Apparently I don't do anything controversial at all in the fifties."

• • •

The great palace at Paralon was still recognizable, as it was a massive edifice that would resist change or alteration—but the regal air that had permeated the entire island capital of the Archipelago had been replaced with something . . . *different*.

"Mmm," said Charles, inhaling deeply. "Smells like bureaucracy."

"I'm sure you meant to say 'democracy,'" said Jack.

"What's the difference?" Charles replied. "Either way, I suspect that Artus got in over his head."

"He's probably been reading too many American Histories, I'm afraid," said Jack. "There's a lot to advocate for, and I believe his ambitions are nobly based—but I think he may have been better off with his parliamentary-oriented monarchy."

Instead of the Great Hall, where visitors would normally have been received, the Valkyries led the companions to a large storeroom which had been converted into an office. Artus, the former king of Paralon, rose and greeted them warmly.

"My dear friends," he said happily. "It's wonderful to see you. I'm so glad you're not dead!"

"As are we," said Jack, "but we've apparently missed out on a lot of new developments, including, ah, fashion trends."

"Oh, yes, the armbands," Artus said with a sheepish expression on his face. "I'm sorry about that."

"Apparently the controversy that's fired up the badgers involves my future," Jack said, "or one of them, at any rate. We've accidentally leaped some seven years ahead of where—uh, when we were meant to be, so I realize that there will be articles of common knowledge to you that will be incomprehensible to us. But how is it that the badgers know things that won't happen for another decade?"

"It's the Time Storms," Artus explained. "They ebb and flow, and occasionally deposit something here that shouldn't be. It's all fallout from the destruction of the Keep of Time. So Bert has occasionally had to share something he knows about the future, so we don't completely derail it in the present."

"Is there any way, maybe something Samaranth or the Cartographer might know, that can keep the Time Storms from getting worse?" asked Charles.

"That's the problem," Artus said with a grimace. "They haven't gotten *worse,* they've gotten *better.* In fact, they've almost completely stopped."

"Pardon my ignorance," said Charles, "but wouldn't that be a good thing?"

"No," Jack interjected, realizing what Artus was getting at. "It wouldn't. If the fall of the keep and the loss of the doors are what threw a myriad of portals into time itself to the four winds, then the only way that they can be reined in again is—"

"Is if someone's repaired the tower," finished Charles, "and restored the doors."

"Worse," said Artus. "Someone may be building *another* tower altogether."

As they talked, Artus ordered some food and drink to be brought in. A short time later Bert and Ransom joined them, and the philologist relayed the terrible news about Kor.

"This is awful," Artus said. "Kor was one of the islands fighting against protectorate status."

"I'm sorry," said Jack. "What does that mean?"

"The Senate has been preparing for an eventual attack by the

Winter King," Artus explained, "by promising increased protective measures from the republic in exchange for oaths of fealty. It was a plan presented by a very influential man on the rise named Chancellor Murdoch."

"Chancellor?" said Jack. "Which land does he represent?"

"That's the strange part," said Bert. "No one seems to know. He appeared out of nowhere, with no history, no credentials that I can find, and yet all the primary leaders in the Archipelago—save for Artus and Aven—have embraced him and his counsel."

"It's surprising that I've never heard of him," said Jack. "I consider myself very well up-to-date on events in the Archipelago."

"We've also missed seven years," Charles reminded him.

"I'm hoping you might still know something about him," Artus said. "There's a belief that he might actually be a leader from your world."

"One of our people?" exclaimed Charles. "Here? That smacks of Burton's involvement, if you ask me."

"I hope not," said Artus. "The Chancellor is proving to be very popular—and in a republic, that alone can carry the day. Burton is already a thorn in our sides, but if a world leader from the Summer Country is becoming our best ally against the Winter King, then I don't see how he wouldn't be involved."

"What does the Chancellor look like?" asked Jack.

"Our agents, particularly Ransom, have managed to acquire a few photographs of him," Artus said as he spread several pictures out on the table. "The one thing that's peculiar about him is that in all of the pictures, he's seen holding this spear."

"That looks very familiar," said Charles, "but I can't quite put my finger on it."

"I can," said Jack with a groan. "And I *have*. It's the spear we took from Mordred in Camelot. It was called the Lance of Longinus, but you'd know it better as the Spear of Destiny."

"Great Scott!" Charles exclaimed. "But what did *you* have to do with it?"

"John and I gave it to Chaz, when he became the first Green Knight," said Jack. "And every Green Knight since has carried it, including . . ."

"Magwich," Artus said.

"Well, now we know where that idiot Maggot went," Charles fumed. "He threw in with this Chancellor, and he gave him the spear."

"What's the connection between the Green Knight and the Chancellor, though?" asked Jack. "How would someone from our world even know about Magwich or the spear?"

"Here's your connection," Charles said darkly. "Look at this photo—the close-up in profile. Do you recognize him?"

"Yes," Bert declared. "I *have* seen him before!"

"The Red King," said Jack. "From the Clockwork Parliament! But I thought they'd all been destroyed after our first trip into the Archipelago!"

Artus was crestfallen. "So did we," he said. "Apparently, we were mistaken."

"That's not all we've overlooked," said Ransom. "Look more closely at the photo."

"Hmm," said Charles. "That's a puzzler."

"You see it, don't you?" asked Ransom.

"I think so," said Charles. "The light source is on the right, so all the people are casting shadows to the left. But the Red King,

Chancellor Murdoch, or whoever he is—well, he appears to have *two* shadows."

"Lord preserve us," breathed Jack. "Now we know where the Winter King's Shadow went. It wasn't destroyed after all."

"The Chancellor isn't preparing the Archipelago to *fight* the Winter King," said Ransom. "He *is* the Winter King."

PART FOUR

THE TOWN THAT WASN'T THERE

CHAPTER THIRTEEN
THE LEGENDARIUM

RICHARD BURTON WAS a man used to responsibility. What he was not used to was accountability, especially when the rules of the game he was playing suddenly changed.

"The last door was defective," he said gruffly. "I don't know what the problem was."

"Define 'defective,'" said the Chancellor.

Burton could always tell when the Chancellor was upset. There was a strange whirring sound emanating from his chest, and his neck made an odd clicking noise when he spoke. Not good.

"It didn't open into a time, it opened into a place," said Burton. "A small stone room that was completely empty. No exit, and no dragon. We've already discarded the door."

"Fine," said the Chancellor. "We'll be done soon enough anyway."

"What about the Caretakers?"

"They know where to look now," the Chancellor said, glancing at Kipling. "And they will be coming, make no mistake."

"Should I summon the others to return as well, before they're found out too?" Kipling asked.

"No," the Chancellor said after considering the question. "They may yet be useful where they are."

"You realize I can't go back. They'll be watching now."

"That's what we want," came the reply. "They'll be looking for you, and not watching their backs. That's how I was able to procure this." The Chancellor held up an object.

Kipling went pale. "How did you get that?"

The Chancellor laughed, and it was a harsh, grating sound. "Let's just say your report was useful, and two of your colleagues have finally redeemed themselves."

"The timing of the attack on Kor is no coincidence," said Artus. "The next scheduled referendum at the Senate is regarding whether or not to give increased powers to the Chancellor. And as the islands that have joined the protectorate remain untouched, while a powerful nation such as Kor is in flames, I have no doubt the motion will be overwhelmingly passed."

"When is the referendum scheduled?" asked Bert.

"Tonight."

"Can't you stop it?" asked Jack. "Or postpone it? Or something? You're the king!"

"An honorary title within the republic," said Artus. "I have more influence than power, and with the Chancellor's allies, I have far less influence than he."

"I'm guessing his allies include the Goblins and the Trolls?" asked Charles.

"The Goblins remain apart from the rest of us," said Artus, "but the Trolls were early participants in the protectorate."

"And this didn't set off any alarm bells for you?" asked Jack.

"Why would it?" Artus replied. "While war has run rampant in the Summer Country, we've had relative peace here—and the protectorate initiative has been taking care of the lands rather than invading them. We've been watching for an attack from the Winter King, not a fruit basket."

"He's attacked you now, though," said Charles. "Can't you use that against him?"

"How?" asked Artus. "The Chancellor will decry the attack and want to rally to Kor's aid! Anything I say, with only suspicion and photographs as evidence, will look like a personal attack."

"Not to mention that it will alert the Chancellor—uh, Winter King—whatever he is that we know what he's up to," Bert put in. "I have an alternate suggestion. We should consult Samaranth for advice. Outside of Verne or Poe, he'll have a better idea of what to do than anyone."

Reluctantly, Artus agreed. It felt a bit like cowardice, to slip away from the palace to plan and prepare, but it was the only sensible option if their beliefs proved true. "We'll leave shortly," he said as he threw the photos into a leather satchel. "I'll take some precautions here first, and I'll meet you at the badger's garage."

"I have other matters to attend to for the Caretakers," said Ransom, "but I'll stay close."

"Let's go," said Bert. "The clock is ticking."

Fred was more than happy to see the scholars again, particularly Charles. He took great pride in showing the Caretaker every part of the garage where the principles were maintained, while Jack and Bert outfitted a vehicle for the trip to see Samaranth.

"So, Fred," Charles said, "other than the family traditions of publishing and automotive care, tell me what else you've been studying these years past."

"As much as I can of just about everything, Scowler Charles," replied Fred. "I read what I can when I'm not working with my father at the press—although if it were up to my grandfather, I'd still be in cooking school."

"If it hadn't been for your grandfather, we would never have defeated the Winter King," Charles explained, "and if not for you and your father, Jack and John would never have been able to rescue Hugo Dyson."

"T' be fair, Scowler Charles," Fred said, "it was partially our fault Hugo got trapped in time t' begin with."

"Sure," said Charles. "And your willingness to acknowledge your mistakes, and to learn from them, is one of the main reasons I've decided to give you this."

Fred looked down. In Charles's hand was a silver pocket watch, emblazoned with a red dragon. The symbol of an apprentice Caretaker.

"A Samaranth watch!" Fred exclaimed, still unsure of what was happening. "But—but—Scowler Charles—you don't really mean t' give that t' me?"

Charles nodded. "I do. Jack has told me how much help you were to Hugo, and of how diligently you were studying to become a true scholar. So I know of no one who deserves it more." He placed the watch into the small mammal's trembling paw, then closed his fingers over it.

"You know what this means, and you understand the responsibility that comes with it. So don't disappoint me."

Fred was shaking with excitement. "I won't! I promise!" He stopped and furrowed his brow. "Does this have to be a secret? Or can I tell someone? I mean, someones?"

"It's supposed to be a very secret thing," said Charles, "so just be careful about who you do choose to tell. I'm guessing your father and grandfather?"

The badger nodded. "Yes, Scowler Charles."

"That should be fine. And Fred—you're my apprentice now. You can just call me Charles."

"Thank you Scowl—I mean, thank you, Charles!" Fred said as he walked away in as dignified a manner as he could without appearing to want to run.

"Holy hell, lad," Charles called after him. "Run. Run and tell them!"

Without a backward glance, the badger broke into a dead run, his feet barely touching the ground.

In short order, Bert, Artus, and Jack had joined Charles and his newly appointed apprentice in a spacious six-wheeled principle called the Strange Attractor. Fred took the wheel and soon revealed himself to be an expert driver. The trip was innocuous enough, and the engine loud enough, that the companions could talk without being overheard as they traveled.

The first time John, Jack, and Charles met the great dragon Samaranth, he was the only dragon left in the Archipelago. All the other dragons had abandoned the lands and the service of the king, because he had proven himself to be unworthy to call on them.

Now Jack and Charles were again going to see Samaranth, and again he was the only dragon left—but this time, it was because Artus, as the king, had sent them away in the belief that as long as the dragons were always there to solve any problems, he and his people would never fully mature as a race.

"Of course I went to Samaranth first," Artus explained to Jack and Charles, "and when I told him what I planned to do, he was quiet for a very long time. Then, when he finally answered, he asked a question."

"What did he ask you?" said Jack.

"He asked if I had ever seen a baby bird that pushed past its parents and tried to leave the nest before it was ready. I told him I had. And then he asked if I knew what birds like that were called, and I said no."

"What did he say they were called?" asked Jack.

"Lunch."

"That's terrible," said Charles. "Is that all he said to you?"

"No," said Artus. "He told me that I was the King of the Silver Throne, and the dragons served at my pleasure and could be released from service by blowing a horn that he kept in his cave. He said it was very old, and then he said something I didn't understand—he told me it was from a time and place before he was a dragon."

"That's interesting," said Jack. "So what did you do?"

Artus sighed. "I blew the horn. Then I came back to the castle and formed a republic. Everything has been utter chaos ever since."

"Well," said Jack, "sometimes the magic works."

"And sometimes, you really wish it hadn't," said Artus. "I wonder if it's possible to unblow a horn?"

"It isn't possible to unblow a horn," Samaranth said disapprovingly. "You're intelligent enough to know that, Artus."

It had not taken the companions long to reach Samaranth's cavern, and once they were there, it took even less time for them to realize that he was not pleased to see them.

"The Caretakers have not remained steadfast in their jobs," he said in a raspy voice, "and the King of the Silver Throne has handled his stewardship with even less aplomb."

"We've dealt with every crisis we've been called to," Jack pointed out. "Minor and major. And we've always emerged triumphant."

Samaranth snorted one, twice, and then three times—and they realized he was laughing. "Triumphant? Really? With the Keep of Time nearly destroyed, the Morgaine and the Green Knight gone from Avalon, and a new power rising in the Archipelago who may in fact be the enemy you were brought to defeat to begin with? In what way do you consider that triumphant, little Caretakers?"

"We're learning the value of persistence," said Charles. "That's a start."

Samaranth sighed heavily and regarded the companions with weary eyes.

"That you are," he said, blowing out a thin cloud of smoke. "I'll tell you this much. The Prophecy you are meant to fulfill is true—and you have been in the midst of it since the first time we met.

"So, consider everything that has passed before now to be a test. A test of your worthiness to survive."

"As Caretakers?" asked Jack.

"As a king?" said Artus.

"No," Samaranth replied. "As a *race*."

"We'll meet the test," said Charles. "We just need to know if we'll be seeing it through alone."

"You aren't alone unless you believe you are," said Fred.

"The Child of the Earth speaks wise," Samaranth said to Artus. "Ask what you're here to ask."

Artus swallowed hard and took a deep breath. "Can I still summon the dragons?"

The great red dragon ambled over to one of the metallic compartments that lined the walls of the cave and removed a horn. It was stained ivory and curved in on itself like a lily.

"There's one call in it left," he said as he handed it to Artus. "Do not use it until there is no other option. Once the horn is blown, it will be useless to you. So choose your time wisely and well."

"It will bring back the dragons?" said Artus.

"It will do whatever you wish for it to do," said Samaranth. "The Horn of Bran Galed was one of the great treasures of the world. It was acquired by Merlin before he became the Cartographer, and it originally belonged to a centaur who was slain by Hercules. Most of those whose hands it passed through believed that its particular value lay in the fact that it would contain any drink one wished for. The truth was, it gave one *anything* one wished for, and stupid, stupid man-creatures wasted almost all of its wishes on ale and wine."

"So when you told me that blowing it would free us from our dependency on the dragons . . . ," said Artus.

"That's what it gave you, because that's what you wanted the most," said Samaranth. "The desire for independence. It's one of the qualities that makes you a good leader—but you also lost the ability to use the Rings of Power. Not because you were no longer worthy, but because you wished for it.

"Far too much has been made about royal blood meaning more than noble worth, and there is far too much concern about spells and summonings and process and prophecy. If you want something, ask. If you are willing to pay the price, to earn what you desire, then pay it, and take what is rightfully yours.

"Some of the Caretakers have touched on one of the great truths of creation," Samaranth continued, "and like all great truths, it is elegant in its simplicity."

"Believing is seeing," said Fred.

"So believe," said Samaranth. "Good luck, and farewell."

The drive back to the palace was much quieter, as each of the companions was digesting what the great old dragon had said. Of them all, only Fred was certain that the visit had yielded great results. None of the others were quite so sure. The Caretakers, including Bert, were stinging from the dressing-down Samaranth had given them. And Artus was told in so many words that he had essentially made a bad decision for good reasons. But the one thing they all understood was that there was still a chance to win—for all of them.

In his first years as King of the Silver Throne, Artus had proven to be surprisingly effective at governing the vast, eclectic kingdom that was the Archipelago of Dreams. A large part of his success came from his willingness to delegate to others who were more qualified in certain areas than he was. Another factor was his declaration of equal status for his queen, Aven. But the greatest part of his accomplishments came from the fact that he was unafraid to take risks and then stand behind them. There was little point in being responsible if one could not also be accountable.

As the Strange Attractor pulled up to one of the boulevards that led to the main part of the city, a badger jumped out of the brush next to the road and flagged them down.

"Uncas!" Jack exclaimed.

"Dad!" Fred shouted as he slammed on his brakes. "What are you doing out here?"

"You can't go into the city, and nowhere near the palace," said Uncas. He was obviously very upset—he'd twisted his hat into a knot.

"Why not?" said Artus. "What's happened?"

"The Senate convened early, and the Chancellor was granted sovereignty over the entire Archipelago!" Uncas cried. "He started by putting out a call to have you arrested for instigating the attacks on Kor!"

"And so it begins," Artus said, his face darkening.

"This is a put-up job," exclaimed Jack. "You're being set up for a fall, Artus."

"What should we do?" Charles asked.

"Already in the works," Uncas said as he climbed into the back of the Strange Attractor. "We're to meet everyone at Halsey Cove."

"Who's everyone?" asked Charles.

"Y'know," Uncas said. "*Everyone*."

Halsey Cove was an old, seldom-used port several miles south of Paralon proper. It was more archaic, but architecturally more elegant than the main seaports. It was also occasionally used for covert meetings of any kind. Ransom was standing at the head of the docks when they pulled up.

"I trust you heard there's a party being thrown in your honor back at the palace," said Ransom.

"I heard," Artus said. "I think I'll skip it."

"While you've been having tea with a dragon," Ransom said, grinning wryly, "I've been gathering a few friends."

The companions climbed out of the vehicle and realized that Uncas had been telling the truth: Everyone was indeed waiting.

Five of the seven great Dragonships of legend were assembled at the docks. Their captains, along with many personages and creatures who remained loyal to the Silver Throne, were waiting in formation for the king. And foremost among these were the queen, Aven, and her son, Prince Stephen.

The companions rushed forward and greeted them joyfully. Bert, Aven's father, embraced her with tears in his eyes. She hugged him tightly, then stood up straight to take Jack's measure as he was taking hers.

She had aged, as had he, but she was still the pirate girl he had adored, and she still had the mettle in her eyes that made her the greatest captain in the Archipelago.

"Hello, Jack," she said, embracing him tightly.

"Hi, Aven," he said, smiling. "It's good to see you."

"Well, um, yes," said Artus. "Jack, Charles—you remember our son, Stephen."

Both men took turns shaking Stephen's hand—and reeling. They'd known Artus at an age younger than this, and he was always a hero at heart—but Stephen was a heroic figure in every sense of the word.

Artus had been thrust into the role of king as a young man, after a childhood that had consisted of being raised by three witches who occasionally dropped him down a well; one remarkable journey to become a knight and slay a dragon, which had turned out successfully at the time, but which became less so as years went by; and then a sudden revelation that he was the heir to the throne of the entire Archipelago. It was all very heady and would have been hard to process for anyone. For someone who preferred to be on an equal status with his own subjects, and who preferred his friends to call him "Bug" when in private, it was nearly impossible. But he had managed to survive, and to prosper.

His son, Stephen, on the other hand, was born to authority, and he proved to be a stunningly effective commander. He was the perfect synthesis of leader, explorer, and inventor. It was he who first proposed that all the legendary Dragonships be converted into airships. And under the watchful eye of the shipbuilder Ordo Maas, and with the permission of the Dragonships themselves, he performed every conversion himself.

Thus he had a personal rapport with every Dragonship that was second only to those they had with the captains who piloted them. This was more impressive when one realized that he had spent the last years of his childhood as a brainwashed prisoner of the King of Crickets, who was really the Winter King's Shadow in disguise.

As a young man, he had been impressive enough with his noble features and proud bearing. But as an adult, Stephen cut a majestic figure. He wore a leather vest and trousers that mimicked those of the Valkyries, but he also wore the symbol that marked him as a man of legend: the horns and pelt of the Golden Fleece. Together with the mighty double-edged ax he wielded, there were few men in any world who would not pause at his arrival.

"He's the first mate on the *Green Dragon*, under the new Captain, Rillian," said Artus.

"I don't think I know him," said Jack, looking around at the group.

"He's a unicorn," said Uncas.

"Really?" said Jack. "The only ones I've seen were those poor beasts in the Winterland. And what that Wicker Man had done to them," he added, shuddering. "Awful."

"Unicorns?" Fred asked. "Oh, you mean the Houyhnhnms. The larger ones, probably pulling a cart, or some such."

"There are unicorns *smaller* than horses?"

Fred laughed at this.

"You human scowlers," he said, "have always gotten that wrong. Unicorns aren't another name for a horse with a horn. It's a classification for *any* animal with one. In fact, most unicorns are mice. It's just that no one ever really notices the ones *here*"—he crouched low and waved at the ground—"because they're always looking for the ones up *here*." He stood on tiptoe and pointed upward.

"So this Captain Rillian . . . ," Charles began.

"Pleased t' meetcha," said a voice from below. Charles bent low and shook the unicorn mouse's paw. "And I you, Captain."

"Ho, Caretakers!" said a tall, graying centaur. "Are we up to picking a fight?"

"Charys!" Jack exclaimed, clasping arms with the centaur. "It's a pleasure to see you again!"

"The pleasure is mine, Caretaker," Charys replied. "I very much enjoyed those books you wrote. Traveling to other planets, oh ho?" The centaur laughed and clapped him on the shoulders. "What an imagination you have!"

"What books was he referring to?" asked Charles as the centaur trotted over to shout some orders at another group arriving in the cove. "When did you write about space travel?"

Jack shrugged, bewildered. "I haven't the foggiest. It's something I've been toying with, and Ransom certainly sparked some interesting ideas. But I'm a blank slate."

"That's the annoying thing about time travel," said Charles. "You always feel like you're late to the party, even when you aren't."

There were other familiar faces as well: Eledir the Elf King; Falladay Finn, of the Dwarves; and the Valkyries, led by Laura Glue.

"We have everyone," she said to Aven and Artus. "Everyone still loyal to the Silver Throne. We're almost ready to go."

"Are you abandoning the Archipelago?" Jack asked in astonishment.

"No," said Aven. "We're moving the base of operations for the true government to a safer place."

"We're consolidating our power," said Bert, "and we're going to do it in the Nameless Isles."

"Is this a coup?" asked Laura Glue. "I think we're starting a coup."

"We might be at that," said Aven. "We're only waiting for one more ship to arrive."

"Oh, yes," said Artus. "Of course."

"He came through with one of the Time Storms a year ago," said Artus, pointing out into the cove. "I think you're in for a real surprise, Jack."

Just past where the *White Dragon* was moored, the surface of the water had begun to bubble and roil about. A ship was surfacing. A very familiar ship.

The great, gleaming bulk of the *Yellow Dragon* rose up out of the water, and the port hatch lifted. A man both familiar and not stepped out onto the hull and crossed his arms defiantly.

Charles looked on in wonderment, while Jack reeled with the shock of the sight before them.

The man was scarcely out of his teens, if that, but his manner and bearing—and his arrogance—were instantly familiar.

"Speak, and be recognized," called out Uncas. "Who be ye, and where be y'r allegiance?"

"My allegiance is to my ship and crew," the youth replied, dropping off the ship onto the dock, "and to the Archipelago and those who serve her. And as for me," he finished, jabbing a thumb at his chest, "I am the seventh son of the seventh son of Sinbad himself, and I'm here to pick a fight."

He strode over to Jack and stuck out a hand in greeting. "Nemo is my name."

CHAPTER FOURTEEN
Abaton

GEOFFREY CHAUCER CALLED the Gatherum of Caretakers to silence, then addressed the first order of business. "This is one of the reasons we required you to stay at Tamerlane House," he said to John. "We are the historic Caretakers of the Imaginarium Geographica, but we are also past our times. Outside of these walls, we can influence very little, and for too short a time.

"But you are still young and vital—and you are the current Caveo Principia. The Principal Caretaker. And so while we may debate, and offer opinions and counsel, the ultimate decision must be yours."

"Which decision is that?" asked John.

"Whether or not," Chaucer said evenly, "Richard Burton is right."

The concept stunned John into silence. Right about what? About the Archipelago? Were they actually considering the position of their enemy as being more worthy than their own?

"I understand what you must be thinking," Charles Dickens said. "After all, I was the one who recruited him as my apprentice. But ever since your first clash with him, we have been debating whether or not there might not be some merit to his point of view."

"Secrecy has been the mandate," added Twain. "It always has

been. But there comes a time when we must acknowledge that the horse may have left the stable long before we barred the doors."

"What do you mean?" asked John.

"These," Hawthorne said, tossing a copy of Tummeler's *Geographica* on the table. "They're everywhere."

"Everywhere in the Archipelago," John corrected. "We were very clear about that. Tummeler was more than happy to comply, and I know Artus was keeping an eye on his operation."

"That's part of the problem," said Chaucer. "This move Artus made to turn the kingdom into a republic has only made his affinity for the ways of our world grow stronger. We fear that an embargo may not be sufficient."

"Copies are bound to slip across the Frontier," said Irving, "and we no longer believe that Artus would see that as a threat to the Archipelago."

"Wasn't the Silver Throne established to unite *both* worlds?" John asked. "Under the rule of Arthur?"

"That was the original plan, and one of the reasons to have Rings of Power in both," said Chaucer, "but that was effectively ended when Mordred returned and killed Arthur. His heirs were able rulers, but they constrained themselves to rule in the Archipelago, not in the Summer Country. And as the years passed, the divide simply grew broader."

"And now," continued Twain, "we fear that Artus may seek to reestablish a foothold in the Summer Country. And if that happens, even in the attempt, he will compromise everything that is here."

John leaned back and steepled his fingers in front of his face. "If it's as risky as you say, then isn't the debate about Burton moot?"

"Burton cares less about rule and authority than he does about the welfare of the Archipelago itself," said Dickens. "He was, and is, an explorer at heart—and he simply wishes to share his discoveries with the world."

"That's something I've often wondered about," said John. "If Burton believes so strongly that the truth of the Archipelago should be known, why hasn't he spread copies of the *Geographica* far and wide a long time ago? All he'd have to do to expose all of us is tell the truth—so why bother with the cloak-and-dagger machinations and plotting?"

"For the same reason that Houdini and Conan Doyle chose discreet silence," said Twain. "Without the permission of either the dragons, the king, or the Caretakers, Samaranth would hunt them down and roast them otherwise."

"Which alludes to my point about Artus," said Chaucer. "Our oath of secrecy was to protect the Archipelago as well as the atlas itself."

"It seems to me we've strayed far afield from our point," said Twain, "which is that as the *Geographica* becomes more widely known, it becomes far less rare—and less dangerous."

"There are still many things within the actual atlas that are secret," said John. "We certainly didn't allow Tummeler access to *those*."

"There will always be secrets, just as there will always be mysteries," said Chaucer. "But stories will go on regardless. All we are really given is the opportunity to shape how the stories are told."

"There is one great difference between them," a soft voice said from somewhere above. Poe was watching, listening.

"Mysteries are meant to be solved, to be discovered. But secrets are meant to be kept, to remain hidden," he said, "and sometimes one doesn't discover a secret was actually a mystery until it's too late."

"What is it?" asked Twain. "What's happened?"

"The book," said Poe. "Someone has stolen the Last Book."

The entire room was pin-drop silent for a few seconds before it exploded into an uproar. Caretakers were yelling at one another, and yelling for order, and one or two were simply yelling.

"That's done it," said Irving. "We're done for."

"Someone should be flogged," said Shakespeare.

"It was bound to happen," said Defoe.

"Will everyone please be quiet!" said Chaucer.

Suddenly a shot rang out, and the entire room went silent again.

Mark Twain blew the smoke off the barrel and pocketed his small silver gun.

"A gentleman never fires a pistol unless it's to defend a lady's honor or to quiet a herd of braying jackasses," he said. "Luckily, since Lady Shelley and Miss Dyson are among us, I got to do both at once.

"We like to pretend that we're civilized and organized," Twain continued, "but when we're taken by surprise, we suddenly fall apart like clay soldiers. We have the Caretaker Principia with us, and the Grail Child. The Prophecy will be fulfilled—as long as we don't derail it ourselves."

John stood up to better take advantage of the momentary lull. "Samuel's right. We need to organize, and I think the most important concern isn't that the book is gone, but that it was taken at all."

"I concur," said Chaucer. "We still have an enemy in our midst."

"Well," Grimalkin said as he appeared in the center of the table, "you'll have plenty of help discovering who he is. There's an entire armada pulling into the harbor."

John flew to the window. "Well, this is a fine how-do-you-do," he said to the other Caretakers. "It seems the Dragonships have come to the Nameless Isles."

"Which ones?" asked Twain.

John pursed his lips. "All of them."

It took the rest of the day to receive the new arrivals, which was still extremely expedient, considering Tamerlane House had never had so many guests at once.

The flight from Paralon had happened quickly, and so the only provisions the refugees had were what they had had onboard the ships. Bert, Twain, Defoe, Hawthorne, and John took charge of assigning quarters to the newcomers, and the other Caretakers began converting the conservatory into a war room. A meeting of the king and queen, the ship captains, and the Caretakers would have to be held as soon as possible.

Charles, on the other hand, had a plan of his own—which Jack was only too eager to share in. At present, there were at least three conversations Jack had managed to avoid on the trip to the Nameless Isles, and if he could delay them longer still, all the better.

"You heard about the book?" Charles asked as he, Jack, and Fred walked to the Pygmalion Gallery.

"Yes," said Jack. "We keep ending up one step behind! I wonder if Kipling had something to do with it?"

"I was thinking the same thing."

"What would be helpful is if we knew where Kipling went,"

said Jack. "I can't get past the feeling that if we'd said something when we got here, we might be a lot further along." He opened the doors to the gallery, and the three of them walked in.

"I wonder if they'll keep his picture here now that his portrait is just a landscape?" asked Charles.

"I think we ought to just burn it," Jack said irritably. "He won't be returning to Tamerlane House now that we know what he is, so there's no further use for the painting."

"Maybe there is," said Charles, running his hand across his head. "I have a strange idea, but I believe it will work."

"What do you mean?" asked Jack.

"We're going to try taking this battle to the Chancellor's doorstep," Charles called back as he took the stairs two and three at a bound. "Fred, find Bert and bring him upstairs to the atelier. Jack, find Ransom, and bring him up as well. We need to talk to Basil Hallward."

"It *is* possible," Ransom mused after Charles had explained what he proposed to do. "Difficult, perhaps. But not impossible. What do you think, Basil?"

Hallward shrugged and chewed on the end of a brush. "It was a different painting," he said. "When I created Kipling's portrait, it was different."

"So he had to have already been liberated from the real portrait beforehand," said Charles, "and when Bert thought he was bringing him out, he was really just stepping through the Trump. It's quite ingenious."

"Remind me to be impressed later," said Jack. "My question is, can you duplicate the painting as a Trump for us?"

"I don't see why not," said Hallward. "The only real criteria is that it has to be a real place, somewhere, and I have to know exactly what it looks like. And this place must exist, or else he couldn't have gone through."

"And if he can," said Bert, "what then?"

"If we have a Trump," said Charles, "Fred and I can go through and discover where their base of operations is. At present, they don't know where we are, and we don't know where they are. I'd like to shift the balance in our favor."

Bert considered this a moment, then nodded. "Just one thing," he said sternly, "no adventuring. Reconnaissance only. Learn what you can and come back. But don't take any risks."

"Fair enough," said Charles.

Together the group of men and the badger went into the Pygmalion Gallery, where Hallward set up a makeshift easel in front of Kipling's picture.

Ransom gave Hallward one of the blank Trumps, and slowly, carefully, the artist duplicated the scene depicted on Kipling's portrait. "That should do it," said Hallward. "It's already dry, if you'd like to give it a whirl."

Charles held the Trump up in front of him and concentrated on the picture. Slowly it began to expand, and in moments it was large enough to step through.

"Are you sure you don't want any of the rest of us to go with you?" Bert asked.

"You can't spare the resources," said Charles. "And besides, Fred and I are basically reprising another successful espionage partnership. His grandfather and I made quite the team."

Fred beamed. "That you did," he said proudly. "May our venture be as successful."

"Very well," said Ransom. "I'll keep the card open here on this end. If you have any trouble, come running. But remember, Charles . . ." He let the sentence trail off.

Charles nodded. "I understand. If the portal is discovered, you'll have to close it."

"We've opened it this time," Ransom said, "but I don't know if we can do it again. Time is of the essence, Charles."

The two men shook hands, Ransom shook Fred's paw, and Charles thanked Bert and Hallward for their help. And then he and his apprentice stepped through the portal in search of the Town That Didn't Exist.

In his own explorations, Charles had once come across a place in Germany where a narrow alley between a distillery and a seed merchant actually led to an entire district outside space and time.

The entire community seemed sickly and poorly maintained, with faded whitewash on the houses and holes in the cobblestone streets. The seasons themselves were confused in that place, and the trees were barren even in springtime.

He had always planned on exploring it at greater length, but others in the area had stumbled on it and ransacked the hidden village. Not long after, a series of grisly murders occurred in all the nearby German towns, and people whispered that it was the vengeance of the dark spirits who dwelled within.

It was only then, at the moment he was passing through the Trump, that he recalled that the townsfolk who claimed to have seen the spirits described them as men with oversized bird skulls for heads.

He tried to contain the shiver that rolled up his spine,

and only just managed to disguise it as stretching before Fred noticed.

"Are you worried?" asked Fred.

"Not in the slightest," said Charles.

"Good," said Fred. "So am I."

There was a signpost pointing to Abaton that stood just before a half-crumbled gate. The gatekeeper was a blind man, dressed in a loincloth. Every inch of his body was covered in tattoos—some pictorial, but most were words and random markings.

He perked up as he heard them approach. "What business have ye in Abaton?"

Charles sighed. It was not good espionage to declare your intentions. "Our own, if it's all the same to you."

"It's my job to ask, no need to be twisty about it. Sign your names, and enter."

"Sign?" said Charles.

"With the stylus," said the man. "On my skin. I am the keeper of the gate, and all who enter and leave must sign."

"Certainly," said Fred. He took the steel-pointed tool from the man's hand and quickly scribbled two names, which flared with silver fire. As they watched, the writing turned blue, as if it were changing ink.

"Thank you," said the tattooed man, and promptly went to sleep.

"Just a word of advice," Charles began.

"Oh, the names?" said Fred. "Don't worry—I didn't use ours. That might get us into trouble."

"Very perceptive!" Charles said, surprised. "Whose names did you write?"

"Harry Houdini and Arthur Conan Doyle," said Fred.

"This is already a great partnership," Charles said as they entered the town.

It was a pastiche of a town that seemed to have been assembled from a dozen cultures. There were gabled roofs topped with elaborate weather vanes sitting side by side with Turkish domes. The overarching theme was vaguely eastern European, but that might have been an impression generated by the age of some of the structures. The very air was ancient here. And although it was dressed up in familiar garb, that was just the wool covering the wolf underneath.

"There are stories," Charles whispered, "of a German village called Germelshausen, which fell under an evil spell cast by a witch. I've also heard of a similar tale from Scotland, about the Brig o' Doon, in Bobby Burns country, where Tam O' Shanter raced to safety across a stone bridge to escape from a village full of witches."

Fred swallowed hard. "An awful lot of references t' witches, Scowler Charles," the little badger said. "I hope this village in't like those villages."

"You and I both," said Charles, hitching up his belt. "Nothing to do but follow the path and see where it takes us."

As it was, their path led them right past a bakery, which was filled to overflowing with cakes, and pastries, and puddings, and on and on and on. It was a culinary wonderland in the middle of a virtual medieval village.

"Grandfather would be sorry he missed this," Fred said, reaching for a muffin from a cart near the door.

"Don't," warned Charles, grabbing Fred's paw. "I don't think it's wise to eat anything here. I've read far too many stories about travelers being trapped in places just because they ate a morsel of food—and if it's all the same to you, I'd rather be able to get home!"

"No problem, boss," said Fred.

"This also smacks of a witch's gambit," said Charles. "The minute you set foot in the gingerbread cottage, you suddenly find you're in an oven being roasted for dinner."

"Good call," Fred said, pointing up.

In the sky above them, silhouetted against the apricot sky, was a gaggle of witches—but Charles commented that they were wholly unlike any witches he had ever seen.

"How many have you seen?" asked Fred.

"Practically none," said Charles, "but I've read a lot about them, and these don't fit any of the descriptions."

The witches were not on brooms—they were riding bicycles. Each one was sitting upright with ramrod-straight posture and was wearing a dour gray dress, topped off with a black shawl and a pillbox hat.

The bicycles were as average as any he'd seen, except for the fact that they flew. Each one had reflectors on the front (for safety, he assumed) and a small wicker basket behind the seat. They bobbed and wove exactly like a flock of birds, each following in formation behind the others.

Charles and Fred ducked down an alleyway to stay out of sight, splashing through some puddles and tripping into a laundry line as they ran.

The witches were gradually moving southeast to northwest. They had nearly moved away from Charles and Fred altogether when one of the last witches in the gaggle pulled away from the group and stopped, hovering in the air above them.

She squinted her eyes and turned her head from side to side, then lifted her head up to the air and sniffed, then sniffed again.

A smile spread across her face, and she looked down directly at Charles and Fred's hiding place.

"Oh, no," said Charles. "She can smell us."

"You mean me," Fred groaned. "Wet badger fur is a curse—a curse, I tell you!"

"This way!" Charles yelled. "We'll try to lose her in the alleys and switchbacks."

No sooner were the words out of his mouth than he ran headfirst into a solid brick wall. Fred plowed into him a second later, and they both ended up sprawled in a heap.

Charles had led them into what was a blind alley. There were a few open doors on the adjacent walls, but the wall at the end was too high to scale.

"That's an unexpected turn of events," said Charles. "I don't think we can outrun her now!"

"We'll get you, my lovely boy," the witch cackled, "and make a fine pie of your dog!"

"I'm not a dog!" Fred shouted. "I'm a badger!"

The witch swooped down with terrifying speed and swung something at Charles as she passed.

He threw himself aside just in time, but she caught his sleeve. He rolled over as the witch spun about for another pass, and he realized that the elbow of his jacket was in tatters.

Rather than brandishing a wand, the witch was wielding a long, razor-edged fork.

"Oh, come on," Charles groaned. "A fork? What kind of a witch are you?"

"The kind who eats lovely little children like yourself!" she screeched as Charles again threw himself aside, protectively shielding Fred.

"Children!" Charles huffed, jumping to his feet. "I'm no child! I'm an *editor*! With *tenure*!"

The witch just laughed in response—a sound that was like grinding metal gears. She made another lightning pass that reduced Charles's jacket to a ragged mess.

"Curse it," Charles exclaimed. "There wasn't supposed to be any fighting. We're the espionage division, for heaven's sake!"

The witch continued to laugh as she came around again, but this time she wasn't targeting Charles. She was aiming at Fred.

Charles threw himself in front of her just before she ran down the little mammal, and the bicycle bounced violently off of his back. It knocked the wind out of him and only irritated the witch.

"Fred! Run!" Charles shouted. "I'll buy you some time and keep her attention on me!"

"I'm not leaving my partner!" Fred yelled back. Then he turned and dashed inside one of the houses.

"I didn't really expect him to go," Charles said under his breath. "That was just something you're supposed to say."

The witch stopped laughing as she realized that she'd just lost track of one of her quarry. She rode the bicycle more slowly now, and a dark rage settled over her face.

"I can catch you anytime I want," she said with menace as she brandished the fork, which was tipped with crimson.

My blood, Charles realized. This was not going at all well, and it promised to get worse.

"I enjoy the game," the witch said, "but now it's time to finish it."

She dropped down to a height just level with Charles's head and hovered in front of him.

"You aren't going to escape," she said, grinning wickedly, "and neither will your dog."

"He's a badger, actually," said Charles.

"Did you really think you could defeat me? Was that your plan?"

"Not precisely, no," Fred responded as he appeared in a nearby doorway. "The plan was to get you to come closer and hold still."

Before she could react, Fred threw a handful of a thick, cream-colored substance at her. It struck her in the face and stuck like glue.

The witch shrieked in fury and wheeled the bicycle about. She let go of the handlebars to clutch at her face with her hands, and the bicycle spun crazily around, finally flipping end over end, completely out of control.

The bicycle crashed into a wall and plummeted to the ground. The witch fell off it just before it struck, and she rolled several times before she finally came to a stop against a barrel. She didn't move.

"Betcha no dog can do *that,*" Fred said, wiping his paws and smirking. "Stupid witch."

"What was that?" Charles asked, flabbergasted.

"You said I couldn't eat anything, but you didn't say I couldn't use the food as a weapon," said Fred. "There were no muffins in there anyway. So I used the next best thing. Tapioca pudding."

"Fred," said Charles, "I'm completely impressed!"

"It's not as good as a poke in the eye with a sharp stick," said the little badger, "but it'll do in a pinch."

Charles and Fred had finished binding and gagging the witch, whom they hid behind a bushel of potatoes in the cellar of one of the houses. She only narrowly avoided being put into an oven.

"I still say we should have flipped the coin for three out of five," Fred grumbled. "She wouldn't have given us that much of a chance."

"That's what separates her from us," Charles said in admonishment. "We try not to eat anyone else."

"Oh, I wasn't going to eat her," said Fred. "But she would have made a nifty chunk of charcoal."

"At least she provided us with transportation and a disguise," Charles said as he pulled the shawl over his shoulders. "What do you think?"

"You make a pretty good witch," said Fred.

"Thanks a lot," said Charles. "If anyone asks, you're a dog."

"That's very insulting," said Fred.

"Hey," said Charles. "If I have to go in disguise, then so do you."

"Fair enough."

"How do you think this thing works?" Charles asked, examining the bicycle.

"It's not mechanical like the principles," Fred said, crouching to examine the gears. "I think it's purely magical."

"Oh, excellent," said Charles. "No risk there," he added with obvious sarcasm.

"Unless you've got a better idea, this is our best means of

seeing the entire area at once," said Fred. "Time is of the essence, remember?"

"Okay," Charles said as he straddled the bike and lifted the lid on the wicker basket. "Hop in, Rover."

"This is very humiliating," said Fred as he clambered into the basket.

"Better than taking on another one of the witches, or something worse," said Charles. "Hold on—I'm going to attempt a takeoff."

He started pedaling and found he had to hold the handlebars tightly to counter the wobble from one of the bent wheels. He had no idea if a damaged wheel on the ground would have any effect on the contraption's ability to fly.

It didn't. With a few shaky hops, the bicycle bounded into the air. Pedaling furiously, Charles had cleared the rooftops in a matter of seconds, and soon they were high enough to see all of Abaton.

They were still on the eastern edge of the town, which sprawled all across the hilltops and into the valley below. They could see clusters of flying bicycles, but none near enough to cause immediate alarm.

There were several fires burning throughout the town, and the smoke obscured much of the sky. But it was clearer to the west, and Charles and Fred realized in the same instant that the western edge of the valley was where they needed to go.

There, in the distance, was the unmistakable form of a tower, stark and black against the twilight.

CHAPTER FIFTEEN
THE CONSTRUCT

THE COUNCIL OF WAR at Tamerlane House looked as if a library of fairy tales had collided with a library of literary biographies, and someone had turned the result into a full-color, three-dimensional frieze.

The king and queen sat opposite Edgar Allan Poe at one end of the table; Charys, the centaur, sat between Mark Twain and Charles Dickens; Rillian, the unicorn mouse, sat on the table in front of Washington Irving; and Stephen, in full Golden Fleece regalia, sat next to his mother across from Geoffrey Chaucer. The Valkyrie Laura Glue, her wings discreetly folded behind her, was standing behind John and Daniel Defoe, and the improbable young Nemo stood next to her; while the Elf King Eledir, the Dwarf leader, Falladay Finn, and several surly fauns stood behind the rest of the Caretakers. It was, to put it simply, a remarkable group.

"Geoff," John said, still assimilating the recent events, "where should we begin?"

They had already decided to conceal the covert operation Fred and Charles were engaged in. If there was still a traitor among the Caretakers, serving him a play-by-play summary of their own efforts wouldn't be helpful.

The Last Book was already a secret from almost everyone—and so it would be difficult to express the concern the Caretakers were feeling at its loss.

Thus, once Bert, Artus, and Aven had addressed the group and detailed the events that had occurred on Paralon, the next order of business became the Prophecy itself.

"We believe that the Chancellor has spies within these walls," said Chaucer, "and so we must prepare for the inevitable. We will be attacked. And I believe that it will happen sooner rather than later."

"I concur," said Bert. "To move so in Paralon itself, he must be exceptionally confident."

"With good reason," said Artus. "He's been amassing power and influence for a long while. His allies will be our former allies—and so this will not be a war of armies. It will be a last stand."

"What Artus is trying to so cheerfully get across," said Aven, "is what my father was explaining earlier—this is not a new battle, as far as the Prophecy is concerned. This is the endgame."

"Oh, that was much more cheerful," said Defoe. "We have the Caretakers and the knight—when do we acquire the weapon the girl is supposed to use against the Winter King? Or Chancellor? Or whatever we're supposed to call him."

"The Shadow King," said Poe. "The Winter King is no more, and the Chancellor is a fiction. We are dealing with a Shadow King, and we will prevail. I have seen it."

"How do you know this?" asked Eledir.

"Because," said Poe, "in the future, there are still pistachio nuts."

"I'm going to assist Quixote and Rose," said Bert, "in their efforts to acquire the weapon. Artus and Aven have asked Jack to assist the captains in fortifying the Nameless Isles in preparation for the Shadow King's move against us. And John and Stellan are going to continue in the effort to learn more of what our adversary is planning."

"We should have someone trying to suss out other spies," Defoe said with a sideways glance at Jakob Grimm. "Whoever they might be."

"That's a good idea," said Chaucer. "Will you take charge of that, Daniel?"

Defoe nodded. "I will."

"Excellent," Chaucer said. "Then for the moment, we've work to do."

Jack realized that being in charge of the war preparations meant that he was going to have to speak to the young Nemo. The appearance of the youth and the gleaming Dragonship was not as unusual to those in the Archipelago as it was to him. There had been numerous events caused by the Time Storms that had changed many things in the lands. But this was a harder thing to process. After having caused the older Nemo's death during the great battle at the Edge of the World, Jack made sure to visit Nemo's grave every time he'd come to the Archipelago, and he always had plenty to say. But now, with a young Nemo in the very next room, alive, he realized that he couldn't find any words.

Jack's musing was interrupted when a strong hand clapped down on his shoulder.

"When first we met," Charys said, "you were a student who was playacting at being a warrior. Now you are a teacher. And as a descendant of Charon himself, I can truly say there are few callings more noble."

"A teacher, yes," Jack replied. "But still playacting at being the warrior, I'm afraid."

At this the centaur grew serious. "Not playacting, Caretaker. Your deeds are well known throughout the Archipelago, and your bravery and skill are without question. The Far Traveler himself told me that you were a soldier of note in the Summer Country as well. Is that true?"

Jack nodded. "It is. But I'm afraid I didn't fare much better there than I did here. I still failed to protect the ones who depended on me."

"We are all here of our own choosing," Charys countered. "None among us has been coerced, or compelled against his will. Nemo knew what he was doing, and he knew, as do I, the day of his death."

"I know, and I accepted that, long ago," Jack said with a fleeting glance over at the young captain he was avoiding. "But I was hardly prepared for . . . for *this*."

"I have some of my own troops to attend to," Charys said as he wheeled about on his hind legs, "but consider this, Caretaker: What if you are the one who makes Nemo into the warrior he becomes? What if this is the opportunity to teach him what he needs to know to truly be a good man?"

"But for what?" Jack said, protesting. "We know what happened to him in the end."

"If for no other reason," Charys called back over his shoulder, "teach him well, so that when the time comes in his own future, he will be prepared to pass on what it means to be a man . . .

". . . to *you*."

• • •

Charles and Fred landed well short of the tower. They concealed the bicycle in a thicket a few hills to the south of it, then stood up to take stock of their target.

Charles let out a long, slow whistle. It was the Keep of Time, remade as a patchwork lighthouse comprised of doors, rough-hewn stones, and creaky scaffolds. The space between the doors was only broad enough to allow one to open without compromising those adjacent to it, and there were few landings on the stairways—as if the opportunity to pause between doorways were an unthinkable folly.

Unlike the authentic keep, wherein the stairways were on the interior and the doors opened out into whatever time they were anchored to, this construct was exactly the inverse. The structure was built as a hollow tower, and the doors were then inserted into frames, which allowed them to open inward.

"That can't be safe," Charles murmured. "It's practically insane."

"Why?" asked Fred.

"Because all of the doors are linked to some point in the past," Charles whispered. "Just harnessing that kind of energy is almost impossible to conceive. But at least in the real keep, the doors opened out—that let each portal have its own space, so to speak. But if the doors open inward . . ."

"There's no space," said Fred. "They'll all be jammed in together."

"That's my worry," said Charles. "I don't think anything good can come of this."

The tower was all but impossible to approach. It was positioned high enough that any two guards could see everything approaching in any direction, and that would have been hard enough to bypass.

The tower's scaffolding was a beehive of activity, with workers shoring up the base, adding to the top, and building new frames for doors to be set into.

Even worse, two more men approached the tower from the west, dragging another door behind them. Charles had briefly entertained the idea of disguising himself as a laborer, but there was also the possibility of running into Burton, who would easily recognize him. These two new arrivals tripled the odds of that happening.

"Houdini and Conan Doyle," Charles whispered. "The rogue Caretakers."

"I've heard tell of them," said Fred. "That's why I signed their names when we got here—although just mentioning them makes Bert very sad."

"I don't doubt it," said Charles. "They're worthy men—they've just made some very poor choices."

They watched as the Magician and the Detective carried the door to a frame that was built in a nearby field and placed it upright. Another man was called over from the tower to examine it, and Charles shuddered in recognition.

"And there he is," he hissed. "Burton. All the players but one have come to the stage."

Burton opened the door and looked inside. From their position, Charles and Fred couldn't see what he was looking at, but he seemed to declare it satisfactory, as two other workers came over to help carry it up to the top of the winding scaffolding.

"Do you think they're arranged the same way as they were in the real keep?" Charles wondered aloud. "Oldest at the bottom, and getting younger as they rise?"

"That would make sense," said Fred, "if they have been harvesting them as they fell. They would want to fix each door in place as they brought it here."

"I agree, apprentice," said Charles. "We've got to get over to that tower for a closer look. They're building it for some purpose, and we must discover what it is."

"Someone's coming this way," said Fred, pointing.

A very familiar-looking figure came clomping along the cobblestones. He was muttering to himself and walking with a strange, clumsy, high-footed gait.

As he came closer, they could see why. Bags, which were leaking sand in copious amounts, were bound around each of his feet and were tightly bound mid-calf. With every step he took there was a whumping sound and a small cloud of dust.

The figure stepped under one of the lights, and Charles swore softly and rolled his eyes in exasperation.

"Why am I not surprised in the least?" he said under his breath. "If there's something shifty or untrustworthy to be done, it's a level bet that Maggot is somewhere about."

Fred squinted to see better. "The Green Knight, you mean? He's a maggot?" He frowned. "He doesn't look like a maggot."

"You'd be surprised," Charles replied. "There's nothing under that armor but slime."

"Then how did he get to be the Green Knight?"

"It's supposed to be a penance."

Fred looked over the crates again. "Well then, he's doing it wrong."

Charles grinned. "We'll fix that. Follow me."

✦ ✦ ✦

The Caretaker and his apprentice slipped silently along the tree line just on the outer edge of Abaton's southernmost wall, mirroring Magwich's movements along the cobblestone path. When he came to an entrance into the town itself and turned his back to them, they leaped out and seized him, dragging him back into the bushes.

At first Magwich thought he'd been grabbed by a witch and an overly large familiar, but then Charles pulled off the hat and shawl and revealed his identity to the hapless knight.

"Eeep!" Magwich shrieked. "What—what are you doing here? You aren't supposed to be here!"

He stopped and looked at Charles more closely, puzzled. "You're dressed like a witch," he said, fear giving way to curiosity. "What's *that* all about?"

"I'm in disguise," said Charles.

"It works for you," said Magwich.

"Oh, shut up," Charles fumed. "How were you able to leave Avalon?"

In answer, Magwich pointed to the bags strapped to his feet. "In point of fact, I haven't left, not really. These bags are full of beach sand from the island. That means I can go anywhere I want to. I'm finally free of that stupid, empty, lonely island!"

"Your job wasn't done, Maggot," said Charles. "You abandoned your post."

"What post?" Magwich retorted. "After the Morgaine left, there was nothing left there to guard."

"You're wrong," said Fred. "There was a lot left."

"What is he chattering on about?" asked Magwich.

"Where's the spear?" Charles asked. "The spear that has been carried by all the other Green Knights in history?"

Magwich's jaw dropped open, and his eyes grew wide. "I—I couldn't say," he finally answered. "I must have lost it."

"Lost it, or sold it?"

"I wouldn't sell it!" Magwich exclaimed. "Burton would have had my head if I'd—"

Too late he realized his slip.

"He isn't too bright, is he?" asked Fred.

"That's a major understatement," said Charles. He grabbed Magwich by the breastplate and pulled him close. "Listen, Maggot," he said in as threatening a tone as he could manage, "we need to know what's going on here. We need to know what Burton's doing with the tower, and with the spear. And we need to know right now."

"You can't scare me!" Magwich retorted. "I have rights, you know. And when the Chancellor finds out what you've done, there'll be consequences, I promise you!"

"The Chancellor will never know," said Charles, drawing him closer. "Do you know what happened to the last Green Knight who tried to leave Avalon?"

Magwich gulped and swallowed hard, shaking his head.

"He set foot on a boat," said Charles, "and his arms and legs caught fire. And then his chest exploded."

Magwich's eyes were huge.

"Then," Charles went on, "insects began to nest in his chest cavity, where they laid eggs. Eventually the eggs hatched into worms—and the worms burrowed their way up his neck and into his head, and he got to watch the entire time. And the last thing he saw before he perished in terrible agony was the worms eating into his eyeballs. That's what happened to him."

"I—I don't believe you!" Magwich stammered.

"It doesn't matter if you believe me," Charles said with finality, "but if you don't tell us what we want to know, we're going to take those bags off your feet, and you can find out the truth for yourself."

Magwich paused to consider whether he was serious, and on cue, Fred reached out with a sharp claw and snicked open one of the straps that held the bags in place.

"All right, all right!" Magwich yelled. "I'll tell you everything!"

And he did. It took only a few minutes, but when he was through, all the blood had drained out of Charles's face.

"We've got to get back right now," he said to Fred. "This is too important to wait."

Fred tied Magwich's hands and legs and gagged him. They threw him over the handlebars of the bicycle and tied him down; then Fred climbed into the basket as Charles began to pedal.

It was much harder to take off with the added weight, but Charles did not want to risk leaving Magwich behind. It took several tries, but finally they became airborne. Once they were at altitude, it was much easier to navigate the bicycle, and they set course for the Trump portal that lay past the eastern gate of Abaton.

"Uh-oh," Fred said as he peered through the weave of the basket. "There's trouble a' comin'."

Flying straight toward them were three witches, also on bicycles.

"I hope the disguise works," said Charles.

"So do I," said Fred. "I don't have any more tapioca."

The witches stopped in midair and greeted Charles. "Hello,

sister," said the first witch. She pointed at Magwich. "What have you got there?"

"Uh, lunch," Charles said in a terrible falsetto.

"Lunch?" said the second witch. "He's a Green Man. You can't eat a Green Man, even in Abaton."

"We're going to use him to start the fire," said Charles.

"That's just asking for trouble," said the second witch. "The rest will burn *us* out if you do that!"

"Hey," said the third witch, who had flown around to look at the wicker basket. "What have you got here?"

"It's, ah, my dog," said Charles.

"Woof," Fred said helpfully.

"It's the ugliest dog I've ever seen," said the witch. "It looks more like a badger."

"That's very rude," said Fred.

"Oh dear," Charles said before the witches could react. "Hold on tight, Fred!"

Pedaling as if the devil himself were at his heels, Charles put the bicycle into a steep dive and aimed for the eastern gate. He had almost reached the tattooed man when Fred pointed out that the witches were right behind them.

Charles grimaced. Of course they were. The witches were better bicyclists than he was—or at least they were much more experienced—and they weren't carrying a badger with lousy self-control and a Green Knight made of wood.

The bicycle careened past the gate, and they could finally see the portal, hanging in the air just ahead.

"Hang on," he said again. "We're going to come in hot!"

Without slowing, Charles aimed the bicycle straight for the

portal and went screaming through, crashing hard against the opposite wall of the gallery in Tamerlane House.

He staggered to his feet. "Ransom! Somebody! Close the Trump, quickly!"

Ransom ran in from the anteroom and took hold of the Trump just as the witches were coming into view. Rapidly the illustration began to shrink; in moments it was the size of a card again, and Ransom placed it in the pages of a book.

All the Caretakers were summoned, along with Aven and Artus. The still shaken Charles hurriedly explained what he and Fred had been doing, and why the Green Knight was bound and gagged.

Jack and Dickens dragged Magwich off to lock him in a closet, and John brought a kettle of hot tea for Charles and Fred as the other Caretakers arrived in the gallery.

Once they had regained their breath, Fred and Charles took turns relating what they'd seen in Abaton, giving special emphasis to the tower of doors.

"What are they doing with it?" John exclaimed. "What can they be using the doors to do?"

"That's the worst part," said Fred. "The Chancellor's using them to find the dragons one by one."

"Good luck with *that,*" said Jack. "What's he going to do? Poke them with the spear?"

"He's discovered a use for the spear that no one ever anticipated, no one ever dreamed . . . ," Charles said, his voice trailing off. "There's just . . . there's no way to . . ."

"What is it, Charles?" demanded Jack. "What is he doing with the spear?"

"He's using it to sever shadows," said Fred. "*Anyone's* shadow."

"So he's creating another army of Shadow-Born, then?" asked Jack. "We've dealt with that before."

"Not like this, Jack," said Charles. "*Any* shadow. From any creature, whether it walks—or flies."

It took a moment for Jack to realize what he was being told, and when he did, his eyes widened in disbelief. "You can't mean . . . How? How is that even possible?"

"We don't know how he's doing it," Charles said, rising and pacing. "We just know that he is. He's using the Spear of Destiny. Somehow, Chancellor Murdoch is severing the shadows from the *Dragons themselves*. And the army he is building with them will be unstoppable."

CHAPTER SIXTEEN

THE BROKEN SWORD

"THERE IS A Ring of Power here, in the Nameless Isles," said Bert. "It's not made of massive standing stones, as the others are. This one is closer to a fairy ring, in that it can be used only to summon a single entity—the Lady of the Lake.

"You have the authority to use the ring," he told Rose, "and Quixote has the right to request a boon. So only the two of you should go, if she's to appear at all."

"One more thing," said Chaucer. "There is a guardian. He may or may not let you pass. It's our hope that he will. But tell him your request, simply and honestly, and I believe that he will see you through to the Lady."

"It's low tide," Bert said. "You should be able to walk to the upper crescent island. You'll find the guardian and the Ring of Power there."

They watched as the girl and the old knight walked out of Tamerlane House and toward the northern part of the island.

"Will it be dangerous for them?" asked Chaucer.

"No," Bert replied with a sad smile. "As a great poet once said, 'It ain't nothin' but a family thing.'"

* * *

The guardian was tall and bearded, and his hair was white, with two streaks of gray. He was dressed simply in a tunic and leather breeches, and he carried a black staff.

He started when he first heard them approach, then relaxed when he could see them more clearly, and he even smiled as they stepped into the circle of firelight.

"Greetings, niece," the man said, rising from where he was tending the fire. "What brings you to the island at the top of the world?"

"Niece?" Quixote exclaimed, startled by the unexpected greeting. He had fully expected to have to answer a riddle, or perform a feat of skill to be allowed to approach.

"Don Quixote," Rose said in introduction, "this is my uncle, Taliesin the Lawgiver."

Taliesin bowed his head in greeting. "It is simply Taliesin these days. I no longer deal with laws, or those who would see them broken. I am more than content to spend my days here, tending the fire and guarding the circle."

"So it's true," Rose said. "From here, we can summon the Lady of the Lake?"

"Yes," he said. "She may be summoned here. But I fear you may not like the reception she gives you."

"Why is that?" asked Quixote. "I have met her before, and found her to be most gracious."

"I have heard of you, O Riddle Master," Taliesin said with a lopsided grin, "but I was speaking about the Grail Child. I have come to terms with her existence, but my sister has not."

"What did you come to terms with?" asked Rose. "Have I offended you in some way?"

Taliesin shook his head. "Not you, my dear, but your father."

"I know what he is," said Rose. "I hope that I've learned better lessons than he did."

Taliesin gave her a long look, then gestured for them to sit by the fire. "Do you know," he asked when they were seated comfortably, "how Arthur died?"

"I don't," said Rose. "Not really, other than knowing that Mordred was involved."

"Mordred was always on the fringes of the kingdom, waiting for his chance at vengeance," Taliesin said. His beard glowed red from the fire, and his eyes sparkled as he talked. "But it was not Mordred alone who caused Arthur's downfall. He was betrayed by one of his own knights, his most trusted and loyal friend."

"Lancelot," said Quixote, nodding. "I have met this knight."

Taliesin looked surprised at this, but simply continued his story. "There had been decades of peace in both worlds, thanks to Arthur. It was, in every possible way, a Golden Age. And then Lancelot fell in love with the queen, Arthur's wife—your mother, Guinevere. He became consumed with the idea of being with her, of having her to himself. And so he conceived of a plan to see Arthur, his own best friend, killed on the battlefield—and he arranged with Mordred to do the deed."

"D-did my mother participate in this plan?" Rose asked.

"She did not help, but she knew about it—and she did nothing to stop it until it was well in motion," said Taliesin.

He paused, and poked some embers from the fire with the staff. They sparked and danced in the air.

"Mordred was successful in his revenge," Taliesin continued.

"Arthur was slain. Together with her sons, Artigel and Eligure, Guinevere removed his body to Avalon. Lancelot was banished for his part in the murder, and Mordred was cut off completely from entering the Archipelago.

"Artigel assumed the Silver Throne and began to draw a curtain of secrecy over the whole Archipelago, to ensure that Mordred never found his way back. And that was the beginning of the separation of the two worlds.

"Because of the contention between our sibling-cousins, Merlin and Mordred, our family has known little else but suffering and grief," said Taliesin. "Only Thorn, who became the Arthur, has ever brought a glimmer of light into our circle. And even he was born only because Merlin forced himself on Nimue, who became the Lady of the Lake. She raised him to be a good, strong, and noble man—and then he was killed by your father's hand, and your mother's betrayal. So can you understand, young Rose, why she might not be so eager to speak to you?"

"I do understand," Rose answered, "at least as much as I am able to. But I must try, nevertheless. Many people are counting on it."

"Very well," said Taliesin. He looked at Quixote. "Are you prepared for the challenge?"

Quixote nearly fell off his rock. He composed himself and stammered something that sounded like an acceptance. Would it be a trial of skill? Or a battle of wits?

"If you can answer my question, you may pass," said Taliesin. "How long is a rope?"

"Eh . . . What?" said Quixote.

Taliesin chuckled and waved his hands. "I but jest. It's a joke

I heard from a bird once. Of course you may pass." He stood up and gestured to them. "Come this way."

He led them up and over a small, grassy rise, then down to a hidden cove. It was more placid than silent, and was unremarkable: just a sandy beach, a few grasses, and the occasional petrified log. Then they saw it.

It was a small ring of standing stones, which glittered in the light of the rising moon. A miniature Ring of Power.

"I will leave you to your business," Taliesin said. "Do you know what to say?"

Rose nodded. The old man shifted his staff to his other hand, clapped Quixote on the shoulder, and walked back over the rise.

With an encouraging nod from Quixote, Rose stepped inside the ring and began to speak.

By right and rule
For need of might
I call on thee
I call on thee

By blood bound
By honor given
I call on thee
I call on thee

For life and light your protection given
From within this ring by the power of Heaven
I call on thee
I call on thee

At first she was afraid it hadn't worked—that she had done something wrong, or, worse, that she simply hadn't been worthy enough to speak the summoning.

Then a ripple appeared on the placid surface of the water in the cove, then another, and another.

A greenish blue light began to emanate from somewhere below—far deeper than the water actually seemed to be. Then she appeared.

To describe the lady as an apparition would not have done her justice. The folds of her gown floating in the water, twinned with the long strands of her auburn hair, gave her a spectral appearance, but as she rose higher and broke the surface, she was revealed as a creature of flesh and bone. But whatever else she appeared to be, she was not to be toyed with.

Her eyes were stern and cold, and her bearing was haughty. She glided closer to the shoreline, her feet never losing contact with the water.

"Who has summoned me in the old way?" she asked, barely containing her fury. "Who has called the Lady of the Lake?"

Rose knelt in the sand, careful not to touch the water. "I have," she said simply. "I am Rose Dyson, daughter of Guinevere."

The Lady moved closer. "I know who you are," she said coldly. "Tell me why I should not take you now and drag you into the deeps of the sea to drown."

"I gave my lifeblood once to save your son," Rose said softly. "Would you take it again, just to avenge him?"

The Lady retreated, just a little, and the mask of anger slipped, then fell.

"Would that I could," she answered. "Your kin have always been a vexation to me."

"Your kin as well, milady," Rose reminded her, "and I cannot say I disagree with you."

The Lady smiled at that—this girl was an odd mix, she thought. Confidence and boldness, but coupled with an openness that made her hard to dislike.

"Why have you summoned me, child? You may not like the answers I have for you, whatever you ask."

"I summoned you because I could," Rose answered, "and I do have many questions, but there is someone else here who would speak with you."

With that cue, Quixote strode forward next to the ring and removed his helmet.

"Greetings, milady," he said, bowing his head. "It is good to see you again."

"As it is good to see you, brave sir knight," the Lady said. She moved forward almost to the water's edge and pulled gently on his shoulders, permitting him to rise. "I have often thought of the great service you did for me, so long ago. It is among my fondest memories."

"It is one of mine as well, milady," said Quixote, "and that is the reason I have come. I seek a boon."

Her eyes flared up briefly before she softened again. "Of all who seek me out to ask for favors," she said, "only you have the right to do so. What do you seek?"

"Milady," Quixote said, "we seek the return of the sword Caliburn."

The Lady drew back a few feet, then drew back again, holding her hands to her chest. "My son's sword?" she exclaimed. "You wish me to give you the sword of Arthur?"

"We do."

She shook her head. "It is shattered. It is useless to you."

"Surely there must be a way to repair it?" Quixote asked. "It is a matter of the gravest importance."

"You are speaking of the Prophecy, are you not?"

He nodded. "I am."

The Lady seemed to shrink in on herself at this. "The only thing more destructive than limitless ambition," she said, "is a Prophecy, and the fools who follow it."

Turning, she sank into the water and disappeared. For a moment Quixote and Rose were worried that they had offended her, but an instant later she rose back through the water and approached them again, arms outstretched.

In one hand she held the hilt, in the other, the blade. She handed them both to Quixote.

"Thank you," he said gratefully. "Now that we have the sword, we can repair it and—"

"Repair it?" said the Lady. "It cannot be repaired by any smith in the Archipelago or in the Summer Country. It was forged in a time before the age of the Old Gods was over, and none remain who can match the work."

"There must be someone," said Rose. "Taliesin, perhaps?"

"If it were only that, then it might be possible," said the Lady, "but this sword was not shattered by force—it was shattered by a breaking of the Old Magic. And only by Old Magic may it be restored.

"There is only one way to repair Caliburn," she continued, with a tone in her voice that defied argument. "Only he who broke it may restore it. Only Madoc."

"Madoc!" Rose exclaimed. "My father? But he may be the very enemy we are fighting against—or at least, an aspect of him."

"I told you that you would not be so happy to hear the answers I had to give," said Nimue.

"I am not sad," said Quixote. "I asked for a boon, and you granted it. We needed this sword, and you gave it to us. We needed to know how to restore it, and without seeking more for yourself, you shared the secret with us. There is nothing that has happened here today that has saddened me."

"Just remember," Nimue said as she turned and began fading back beneath the water, "do not make the mistakes your forebears made. Do not sacrifice that which you want the *most*, for that which you want the most *at that moment*."

"And do not forget," she said, almost gone.

"Only Madoc may repair Caliburn. Only Madoc."

"But he's dead—isn't he?" asked Shakespeare. "The great Dragon dropped him over the waterfall at the Edge of the World."

"His Shadow survived, and plagues us still," said Bert, "so we believe that somehow, somewhere, he must still be alive."

The war council had been reconvened to decide what to do. They had the sword—but making it whole seemed impossible.

"There's no way to even find him if he lives," said Defoe. "No one's ever gone over the Edge of the World. No one who has returned, that is."

"That's not exactly correct," said Twain, "is it, Professor? It is indeed possible that Mordred—pardon, Madoc—survived, and it's equally possible to find where he is."

"What does he mean?" John said, turning to his mentor.

"It's very simple," said Professor Sigurdsson. "Rose must find Madoc, and I must accompany Rose as her guide. There is no other alternative."

The room went silent, as every Caretaker to a man looked over at the professor.

"That makes sense," John said reasonably, not realizing how much more gravitas was evident in the faces of everyone else. "You certainly have the training, and the experience, and if I were in your place, I wouldn't want to miss a chance for one last adventure."

Defoe let out a bark of a laugh and was elbowed in the ribs by Hawthorne. The professor responded only with a smile that was more melancholy than admonishing.

"That's more true than you realize, John," he said, clapping his protégé on the shoulder.

"Have we missed something?" Jack asked. Charles shrugged and looked at Twain, who merely observed the three companions and puffed on his cigar.

"Rules of time may be broken," said Professor Sigurdsson. "Rules of space may be broken. But not together, and not at the same, ah, time, so to speak. Bent, sometimes, in the rarest of circumstances. But not broken."

"There are limitations," Bert explained. "It's one of the reasons that this place has been kept such a secret. Yes, using Verne's technology it is possible to do as we have done, and summon personages from the past to dine, and discuss, and determine the fate of the world. But the price they pay is that this is all there is—none of them may pass beyond the threshold of Tamerlane House and live."

John sank back in despair. "Then we're handicapped before we start."

"Seven days," came a voice from the upper floor, ghostlike and ethereal. "One may pass outside this door, but unless he crosses back before the end of seven days, he will vanish back into the ether."

"Is that true?" said John, looking at Bert, then the professor.

"I'd trust in Poe," said Bert. "It is his house, after all, and much of what Jules learned was based on his writings. If he says seven days, then you can plan on it."

"You can't do it, Professor," John said, already anticipating his mentor's decision. "We'll find some way to communicate your instructions, to transfer the information they need to navigate to them without sending you in person. There must be some other way."

"It's a bit odd, isn't it?" said Charles. "We have the ability to travel around in time, and into alternate dimensions. We can summon people from the dead. And we're at an impasse to save the world because no one thought to install a telephone system in the Archipelago."

"Actually, we tried," Bert replied. "Nemo was keen to do it, but we could never get all the lands to agree to hook it up. And when you add to that the peculiar weather patterns, the temporal shifts, and mermaids who had a tendency to chew up any cables strung underwater, the result was the lostest of lost causes. The badgers have set up a rudimentary version, but it's not much more advanced than a telegraph, I'm afraid."

"There is no other way, John," the professor said. "Other than Bert, I'm the only one who has ever traveled that far west—at least, the only one willing to act as a guide."

They all knew from the professor's hangdog expression that he was thinking of his old friend Uruk Ko, the Goblin King.

The Goblins were among the most ancient and noble races in the Archipelago, and Uruk Ko and Stellan Sigurdsson had shared a love of adventure and discovery that had culminated in an unprecedented journey. But when the first war with the Winter King took place, Uruk Ko chose to side with Mordred. And after they were defeated, he closed the borders of the Goblin lands to all outsiders.

"We can persuade the Goblin King to do it, somehow," John pleaded. "It's worth trying, and better than you going to a certain death."

The professor laughed heartily at this. "My boy, I have already suffered a certain death, as you put it. Anything from here on out is just gravy."

"But you're *alive* again! It's such an opportunity!" John cried. "We can't just waste it!"

The professor took his young study—who was now nearing the age he had been when he died—firmly by the arms and looked into his eyes.

"John," Professor Sigurdsson said gently, "the reason we were given the chance to come here, now, to this extraordinary place, was to discuss the gravest of crises at the most crucial time in history. Only we Caretakers, gathered here in this way, have the means to decide the future of all that exists. And it seems I am to play a significant role in that. There is nothing wasted in this, John. Not for three days' sake, or three thousand years. It is not wasted. And you should never think it so."

Suddenly a wild idea crossed John's mind. "Hallward!" he exclaimed excitedly. "If the journey takes longer than seven days, can't he just paint another portrait of the professor?"

Bert and Stellan looked at each other, then at their protégé. "No," Bert said after a long pause. "He can't. Didn't you notice, among the Elder Caretakers, that one significant member was missing?"

John chewed on his knuckle and thought, and suddenly realized that there had been one more canvas in the gallery—but one that was only a pastoral background, with no portrait.

"Dante," he said at length. "It can only be Dante Alighieri. His is the missing portrait, isn't it?"

"Yes," said Bert.

"I just assumed he'd been liberated earlier for some reason. What are you telling me, Bert?"

"He was one of the earliest portraits Jules arranged for Basil to paint," Bert explained, "mostly so that we could glean from him more details regarding the Underneath at Chamenos Liber. Dante decided he wanted to actually go there, and he was with the Lost Boys when the time limitation had passed. They reported back to us that he simply faded away into bits of light and dust.

"The others who were here promptly reentered their paintings and only ventured out again after much cajoling. But when they remained as they were, we realized the confines of Tamerlane House were the only limitation to their existing in perpetuity."

"Hang on a minute," said Charles. "If the Caretakers Emeritis can't leave without risking disintegration, then hasn't Kipling just cut his own throat? He certainly won't come back, but if he doesn't, he's doomed."

Bert screwed up his face a moment, considering. "I don't know," he said finally. "We've never tried sending any deceased Caretakers through a Trump. Not because it hadn't occurred to us, but because to have persons who should be dead running around in the open could change too many things. Plus, it scares the horses."

"Can't you go, Bert?" said John. "You wouldn't be at risk the way the professor would be, and you said yourself that you were the only other one who'd ventured that far."

"He might," said the professor, "but he's needed here, more so than I. And I cannot captain the *White Dragon*."

"But—but there has to be some way," John began.

The professor shushed him with a gesture. "Our forces are few, and those of our enemy are many," he said, smiling. "We must use the resources we have to the fullest capacity—and when it comes down to it, I can be the most helpful by doing this."

"But you'd be risking your life!" said John.

"We're all risking our lives, John," the professor reminded him. "And anyway, all I'm risking is my second go-round. I'm willing."

The rest of the Caretakers murmured their agreement and thumped the table for emphasis, and John resigned himself to the fact that this course was indeed the most practical. "All right," he said. "That sounds like a plan."

PART FIVE

BEYOND THE EDGE OF THE WORLD

CHAPTER SEVENTEEN

STRATEGIES OF WAR

"WE HAVE TO destroy it," said Artus. "We have to destroy it now."

The rest of the collective at Tamerlane House were in agreement. The new Tower of Time in Abaton needed to be destroyed.

"He can't reach the dragons without the tower," said Bert, "and until we have the means to fight the spear, this is our best means of attacking him."

"I agree," said John. "There's no way of knowing how many Dragons he's gotten to already—so we should be prepared for anything."

A stealth team was assembled to go back through the Trump into Abaton. No Caretakers were included other than Jack and Charles—it was too great a risk to send them through to an unknown region. If a mishap occurred, it was possible for the still living to find a way to return. The lives of any Caretakers who had come through one of the portraits would be limited to a week if they could not get back.

Charles and Fred were the guides, and Jack was the commander of the small group, which included Stephen, Nemo, three of the Elves, and Laura Glue, along with five of her Valkyries. The latter six were included in the event the witches were still hovering near the entrance to Abaton.

The Elves were coming along specifically to guard Magwich. Charles suspected that his involvement might be necessary at some point, and as reluctant as he was to include the traitorous Green Knight, he couldn't discount the possibility that he'd be needed.

At first John objected to Laura Glue's inclusion—until Aven diplomatically reminded him that she was a veteran warrior and was already older than he had been the first time he went to war.

Artus, Aven, Charys, and the other ship captains set about deploying their small armada along the inner borders of the ring of islands in preparation for the pending attack. There was no way to know how large an army to expect, nor did anyone know what they might do if the Dragon shadows arrived. There was no way to defeat the Dragons themselves—and to combat the shadows was unthinkably terrible.

"That's why we have to repair Caliburn," reiterated Professor Sigurdsson. "It's the only possible way."

"Do you think it will restore the Dragons?" asked John. "Basically reverse the effects of the spear?"

The professor shrugged. "I've no clue. We simply have to trust in the Prophecy and do the best that we can."

"I'll take Rose, the professor, and Quixote to Terminus in the *White Dragon*," said Bert, "where they will be able to continue on using the *Scarlet Dragon*. I'll return as quickly as I can."

John didn't say it, but he knew what they were all thinking: In the coming conflict, one more Dragonship might make little difference, if any.

"Let's go to it, then," said John. "There's no time to waste."

• • •

"How many poets does it take to change a lightbulb?" asked Twain.

"I give up," said Swift. "How many?"

"Three," Twain replied, cackling. "One to curse the darkness, one to light a candle, and one to change the bulb."

"What's a lightbulb?" asked Shakespeare, scratching his head.

"Samuel, Jonny, leave William be," said Bert. "We're trying to save the world here, remember?"

"Sorry," said Twain. "I'm just trying to keep ourselves distracted while everyone else is being productive."

"Pardon," said Hawthorne, "but has anyone seen Jakob? I can't find him anywhere."

"That's not a good sign," said Defoe. "I'm starting to wonder if we haven't discovered who the traitor is who stole the Last Book."

"Jakob is a good man," said Bert, "and I trust him."

"Well enough and fine," Defoe said, rising. "I'm going to go look for him just the same."

The passage into Abaton went as easily as before.

The skies were clear—wherever the witches had gone, they weren't waiting about for a scholar and his dog.

They passed through the gatekeeper by signing with the names of members of the Imperial Cartological Society.

"As a precaution," Charles had advised them, "just in case anyone's checking."

In short order they reached the vantage point where they could observe the tower without being seen—but unlike before, there were no workers milling about.

"This doesn't bode well," said Charles.

There were several dozen Yoricks congregating at points all

along the base of the tower, and among them, dressed as he had been at Tamerlane House, was Kipling.

"So he really is a traitor," Jack said, his temper rising. "He's mine."

"Agreed," said Stephen, "if we can get there at all. We don't have enough warriors with us to take on all of those Un-Men."

"I wonder," said Fred. "Would you call them a flock of Yoricks, like birds? Or something else?"

"They knew," Stephen whispered. "They knew we were coming. It's a trap."

"How could they know?" said Charles. "No one saw us! And Kipling didn't know we'd been here!"

"Maybe they realized I went missing," Magwich sniffed. "I'm very vital to their plans, you know."

"There's how they knew," Laura Glue said, pointing.

The tattooed gatekeeper was standing in front of Kipling. His arms were raised, and he was turning around, giving the rebel Caretaker a full view of the fraudulent signatures.

"Drat," Charles exclaimed. "I thought it was a clever idea."

"So what should we do?" said Stephen. "If we leave to bring reinforcements, they might do the same."

"I say we simply attack," said Nemo, rising. "We're all warriors here, are we not? Then let's have a battle!"

"Sit down!" Jack whispered, pulling the young captain off his feet. "You'll get us all killed!"

"Are you afraid to fight?" Nemo scoffed. "Perhaps you ought to stick to your books."

"I'm not afraid," said Jack calmly, "but I'm not stupid, either. You should learn that a good plan beats a swift attack."

"So what do you propose?" said Stephen.

"We brought the Valkyries along as defense against the witches," Jack said. "I think they'll serve us better as a distraction."

"But the bird-men," Nemo began.

"Are flightless," said Jack. "They can't fight what they cannot reach."

Torches were lit, and Jack's plan was put into motion. The Valkyries were sent aloft, and almost instantly they caught the attention of the Un-Men.

Laura Glue, Sadie Pepperpot, Abby Tornado, and Norah Kiffensdottir each took a compass point above the tower and hurled the torches into the scaffolding. Then, as one, they flew to the north.

As Jack had hoped, Kipling sent half the Yoricks up into the tower to douse the flames, while he led the other half in pursuit of the cackling Valkyries.

"Nonny, nonny, nonny!" Norah called down. "Stupid birds!"

"Discipline, Norah," said Laura Glue. "If you're going to taunt them, remember to stick out your tongue."

"Sorry," said Norah. "I forgot."

"Aren't you worried about the Valkyries?" asked Nemo. "What about the witches?"

"They'll be fine," said Stephen. "Laura Glue can outmaneuver any bicycle ever made, flying or not."

"Now," said Jack, "we finish the job."

Suddenly Magwich let out a howl and threw himself over the bushes, past his surprised guards. "Chancellor!" he cried out. "Wait for me! I'm coming!"

"Nothing to do now but follow that idiot," said Charles as he grabbed a torch. "Let's go."

The small group ran after the Green Knight, who was losing sand with every footfall. They caught up to him just as he reached the tower.

"Magwich, you fool," Charles exclaimed as the knight started to climb the steps. "We're going to burn it down! Come back here!"

"I'm not coming down!" yelled Magwich. "One of these will open for me! I know it!" But every door he tried was locked.

"What do we do?" asked Jack.

"He made his choice," said Charles, "and we have none." He thrust the torch into the lumber at the base of the tower.

Once the flames caught the first planks, the rest of the base burst into flame in a matter of minutes. In no time at all the entire tower was a raging inferno of blue flame.

"Look at that thing burn," said Fred. "You're really good at setting fires, Charles."

"Thanks," said Charles. "It seems I have a special knack for destroying Keeps of Time."

The Valkyries circled back around just as the others reached the Trump portal. By now, the flames from the burning tower could be seen from many miles away.

"We lost them," said Laura Glue. "They'll not catch us before we're long gone."

"Excellent," Charles said as he stepped through the portal. "With the exception of Magwich, this couldn't have gone better."

Jack felt the same way—but as he was preparing to step through the portal himself, he glanced back to where the gatekeeper had been . . .

. . . and he saw Kipling, who waved, then stepped through a Trump of his own.

The war council cheered at the news of the successful raid against the tower, then despaired as Jack told them what he had seen.

"They have been a step ahead of us the entire time," Defoe complained. "They knew about the raid, and after it was carried out, Kipling waves at you?"

"It could simply be an act of chivalry," said Spenser. "Acknowledging the victory of a superior opponent."

"I'm not feeling all that superior," said Jack. "Just a bit weary."

The Caretakers were left to debate the next course of action, while Jack and Charles joined Artus on the large island to the south to help prepare their defenses.

"There are a number of people on the ships I don't recognize," said Charles. "Are these all vetted allies?"

"Each and all," said Artus. "The reason some are a bit unfamiliar is because some of them came through in Time Storms just like young Nemo. The person who conceived of and trained the Valkyries came through to the Underneath, actually, during our battle with the King of Crickets. Amazing woman."

"Would her name be Earhart?"

"Yes," Artus said, surprised. "Do you know her?"

"By reputation only," said Jack, "but she's a good match for Laura Glue."

"That explains why Falladay Finn has been ignoring us, then," said Charles. "He must have come through from a point before we met."

"Mmm, no," Artus said, shaking his head. "That's the same

Falladay Finn—he's just in a particularly bad mood. We found we can't just summon armies and allies willy-nilly, like picking fruit from a bowl. We've had to be much more precise than that."

"Precise how?" asked Jack.

Artus grinned. "If Mordred can pull allies from out of the past, then so can we. Come and take a look."

He opened the hold of the *Blue Dragon* and revealed a giant clockwork man. It was covered in silver and carried a great ax.

"We call him the Tin Man," said Artus, "but really, his name's Roger."

"I thought you were done with clockworks," said Charles, "after the Parliament fiasco."

"Shh," said Artus, closing the doors. "He's sleeping, and I don't want him to hear you.

"This fellow's not exactly a clockwork," Artus continued. "He's more of an old friend who's managed to, ah, enhance his physicality."

"Fair enough," said Charles. "We'll take all the allies we can get."

"I heard how things went on the raid," Aven said to Jack as Charles and Artus continued to check the ships. "Stephen told me. I think you handled Nemo well."

"He's headstrong, and he just won't listen," said Jack, exasperated. "I'm not really sure what to do with him."

"He sounds very much like a young man I once knew," Aven said, raising an eyebrow. "He didn't listen much either."

"That's an angle Charys already tried," said Jack. "I'm certainly not the same person I was, and neither is Nemo."

"That's right," Aven replied. "You aren't. You're an experienced, mature teacher—and he's a spoiled youngest son of royalty, who thinks he's invincible."

"I just don't know how to talk to him, Aven," Jack said. "How can I, when I'm the reason he ends up dying?"

"Maybe because you must, if for no other reason," she said. "It hasn't been any easier for me. Nemo will one day become Stephen's father, and I know he will die. And Stephen knows it too, having never known his father at all. But now, here, we all three have the chance to say things unsaid, and to help this spoiled boy fulfill his own potential.

"My father always talks about how even in time travel, we are always moving forward," she continued, "so consider all this talk of Charles's and Ransom's about causality, and timelines, and different dimensions. What if one of the reasons Nemo took an interest in you then was because you've taken an interest in him now?"

Jack rubbed his chin. "Charys said something similar," he murmured. "You may both be right."

"There's a reason the centaurs have been the great teachers of the ages," Aven said as she walked out of the room, "and there are reasons why both you and Artus come to me when you need advice."

She walked away toward the *Yellow Dragon*, leaving him alone.

The *White Dragon* eased slowly down to the beach on the southern shore of Terminus, which rose over the westernmost edge of the sea. Bert disconnected the harnesses that had bound the *Scarlet Dragon* to the larger vessel and turned to his companions.

"You know how badly John wanted to come, Stellan," Bert said, almost as an apology.

"Yes," replied Stellan. "I know it. But he would have wanted to continue past the Edge, and he has other responsibilities to tend to."

"You must lower the *Scarlet Dragon* into the water," Bert explained, "and go over the edge as if you were a twig caught up in the current. Only then, once you are over and falling, may you deploy the chute, and then unbind the balloon and rotors."

"Isn't that awfully risky?"

"There's nothing about this venture that isn't risky," Bert replied, "but it's the only way past the falls. We've tried to sail airships at altitude, but we always get forced back. The only way over . . . is down."

"It's quite a dilemma, isn't it?" a voice said into John's ear. He sat up straighter in his seat and spun around. A cat's head was grinning at him and floating in midair above his chair. "This business of saving the world."

"Grimalkin," John said, sitting back. "You startled me."

"I seem to be good at that," said the cat. "It's a Cheshire thing."

"Is it also a Cheshire thing to be trusted?" said John. "No one here worries much that you appear and disappear at will."

"I'm trusted, because I'm bound," said the cat. "Do you see my collar? It's a Binding."

"I thought Bindings were spoken spells, involving True Names and blood."

"They are—so consider how terrible a creature I must have been to require a physical binding as well."

John gave Grimalkin a quizzical look. He really wasn't sure whether the cat was just playing with him, or whether the words spoken were serious. "I'm not quite sure what to make of you."

"That's why I trust *you*," the Cheshire cat said, grinning. "You aren't hasty in your judgments."

"I should be quicker to speak, though," said John. "If I had, we'd have caught Kipling. And we might be further along than we are at resolving all of this."

"Things are not always as they appear," said Grimalkin. "An ancient Elder God may appear to be a cat, or vice versa. But which is which depends entirely on when you look."

"What does that mean?"

The cat shrugged. "I can't explain. If I did, I wouldn't be a cat."

John sighed. "You're worse than Samaranth."

"I'll take that as a compliment," said the cat. "If I wasn't, then I'd feel undistinguished. He is still just a young creature, after all."

"Samaranth?" John said in surprise. "He's the oldest creature in the Archipelago. He's even older than Ordo Maas."

"I was ancient when Ordo Maas was still chasing young desert girls in the Empty Quarter," said Grimalkin, "and I was with him on his first voyage into the islands, during the flood. It seems to be my fate to be present whenever someone does something that alters the composition of the world."

"Is that what I'm about to do?" asked John. "Change the world?"

"What do *you* think?" asked the cat. "Would you be doing all these things if not for the Prophecy? Or would you be doing the things you believe to be right, even if they were in spite of it?"

"I don't know what to think," John said miserably. "I don't know who to believe."

"Decide what you want to do," the cat said before vanishing completely. "Then do *that*. There's no other way to move forward—with anything. If you don't believe in yourself first . . . then no one else will either."

With a final wave to his old friend, Bert signaled to the crew of the *White Dragon* to take the ship aloft. He pointed the ship to the east, and it began to pick up speed. In moments it was gone.

"That's it," Rose said. "We're on our own."

"Clears the mind, to have solitude," said Archimedes. "Relative solitude, that is."

"I agree," said Professor Sigurdsson. "We are each appointed to our tasks, and that should be sufficient."

"I concur!" Quixote exclaimed. "I am thy protector, Milady Rose. The good professor is our guide. And Archimedes is, ah . . ."

"I'm the muscle," said Archie.

"Methinks I miss your meaning," said the knight, "but I admire your resolve. Shall we be away?"

"No time like the present," said the professor. "Rose?"

There was nothing more to be said. Rose gave assent with a simple nod of her head. The old knight adjusted the trim and moved the *Scarlet Dragon* forward and over the edge of the falls.

"It is time," said the Shadow King.

"I concur," said one of the others. "We may have lost the tower, but they still have no idea how to discover the spies within their own house."

"Indeed," said the Shadow King, "we know where they are hiding, and we will take the battle to them, and end this, once and for all."

He unrolled a sheet of what appeared to be leather, but was pliable, pale, and . . . *moist*?

"This map will tell us where we need to go," said the Shadow King. "Its previous owner was reluctant to supply it to us, but all things come to pass, given time."

"Have you converted them all, then?" said Houdini. "All of the dragons?"

"Enough," said the Shadow King. "One remains elusive, but only because I cannot find his True Name."

"You can't just sneak up on him?" said Houdini. "*I* could sneak up on him."

The Shadow King didn't answer, but instead shot the Magician a withering look. Houdini lowered his head and stepped back.

The Shadow King looked down at his new map, which was leaving a red puddle on the ground. "It was clever of them not to include this in the atlas," he murmured. "When we find these islands, I will make certain that the world knows just where they are."

Burton blinked. "Hasn't that been the goal of the society all along?" he asked. "To open all the borders and reveal all the secrets? Why else have we been doing all this for you, if not to usurp their power and change the world in the way it's meant to be changed?"

"The goals of the Imperial Cartological Society are of interest to me," said the Shadow King, "so long as they serve my own. Don't forget your place, Burton."

"But Mordred," Burton began.

"*I am not Mordred!*" the Shadow King hissed. For a moment longer, the explorer and the clockwork king stood looking at one another. Then Burton dropped his eyes.

"Good," said the Shadow King. "Anyone else?"

No one spoke.

"Then it is time for the Wars of the Worlds to begin."

The Shadow King and his minions left the Great Hall of Paralon, but Burton lagged behind, pensive.

Kipling turned at the doorway. "Coming, Sir Richard?"

"After a moment."

Kipling paused. "You aren't having second thoughts, are you? About your support of the Chancellor?"

Burton's eyes glittered. "You've had them yourself."

Kipling raised an eyebrow. "Come, Burton," he said, gesturing with his hand. "We should talk."

"You want to talk about what I think?"

"No," replied Kipling. "I want to talk about what you *believe*."

CHAPTER EIGHTEEN

THE DESCENT

"THE ELVES HAVE annexed Abaton as one of their territories," said Artus, "and with my blessing. All in all, I'd say we've achieved a great victory. We destroyed the tower of doors into time that was giving the Chancellor his power, and we've taken over his base of operations. Not too shabby."

"Of course, he still has control of the rest of the Archipelago," said Jack, "and Lord knows how many Dragon shadows at his command."

"It's a start," Artus said defensively.

"I still believe it was the right course of action," said John. "Having access to his secrets was going to do little good if he could still cause damage by using the doors and the spear. Now he's lost one of his tools."

"I just wish we still had eyes and ears in his camp the way he seems to have them in ours," said Artus.

"Pardon the interruption," said Defoe, "but there's some sort of commotion going on outside."

"Is it an attack?" John exclaimed, bolting from his chair. Was it possible for the Shadow King to retaliate so quickly for the raid on Abaton?

"It's another Dragonship," Artus said, pulling aside the curtains for a look. "Have we had another Time Storm?"

Jack groaned inwardly. Dealing with two *Yellow Dragon*s was already more than he could handle even without Nemo. Adding a third was impossible to even contemplate.

"I don't think so," John said. "This one looks like it's come voluntarily."

The others crowded around the windows for a look, and Bert was unable to contain the cheer that left his lips.

It was the *Indigo Dragon*. *His* ship.

"But if the *Indigo Dragon* is here," said Charles, "then that means . . ."

Nemo and several of the Elves marched a prisoner up the steps to the front door of Tamerlane House.

"Greetings, Caretakers," Burton said. "I seek asylum with you here in the Nameless Isles."

The roar at the top of the falls was deafening, but Rose and her companions soon realized that it was only the sound of the endless sea crashing against the rim of the world past Terminus that produced the noise. In a normal waterfall, that sound is reflected, amplified, and added to by the water thundering against the rocks below. But as the little craft dropped farther and farther away from the crest of the falls, they realized that falling water produces no sound, only a gentle susurration, as if it were wind blowing through willows.

It took just moments for the light to recede as well. Above and past Terminus was only darkness, so the only light was that which spilled over the top of the waterfall.

Quixote and Professor Sigurdsson quickly released the parachute, which slowed their fall with a violent jolt, but instantly settled them into a much more comfortable and controlled descent.

A few miles down, there was no light at all save that which they'd brought with them: a silver lantern, fastened to the fore of the boat; and a portable tallow lamp and three candles that the professor had persuaded them would be necessary to complete their task.

Archie's eyes cast a faint greenish glow when he turned away from the light of the lanterns. "We've still picked up a great deal of speed," he said pointedly. "Shouldn't we try to deploy the balloon before we're moving so fast it's simply torn away?"

"We've gone past the Edge of the World," the professor said. "I don't know if physical laws apply. In truth, I don't even know if this is water we're seeing fall, or air we're passing through, or if we only think it is. I just know that we have to keep going down."

"Well, at some point 'down' will end, correct?" said Archimedes. "You know what they say—it isn't the fall that kills you, but the sudden stop at the end."

Quixote and the professor exchanged blinks and rapidly unpacked the balloon. It took no time at all to inflate, and it rose up underneath the parachute, which would serve as a sheath.

Their descent slowed enough that even with no warning, an impact at the bottom would cause minimal damage to the boat. Thus prepared, they settled in to pass the time, and wait.

Professor Sigurdsson pulled a small book out of his pocket and read by the light of the lantern. Quixote, ever vigilant, kept at the prow, watching the darkness. And Rose and Archie stayed busy playing games of logic and inventing word puzzles.

After a while, Rose fell asleep as the professor continued reading—so it was Archimedes and Quixote who were watching out as the light came up below them.

They woke Rose, worried that an impact was imminent, but the diffuse light that surrounded them was part of the very atmosphere some several miles above the bottom of the falls.

"Professor," Rose asked, "what time is it?"

"Oh, we're making good time, my dear Rose. Worry not," he replied. "Just sit back and try to enjoy the ride. I'm sure we're having a better time of it than Mordred did."

The waterfall was ever present, but was more visible now. The *Scarlet Dragon* kept a wide expanse between itself and the falling water, just in case there were any surprises, or other falling objects.

The noise began again, but to nowhere near the degree that they had expected. The water roiled where it struck the earth below, and foam and spray rose up hundreds of feet into the air. It would have—should have—been louder, but there were no rocks or crags for the water to crash against. It simply fell into a smooth basin that rose up to transparent shallows.

The professor guided the *Scarlet Dragon* over the spray and then down to the water, where he instructed Quixote to deflate and store the balloon and parachute.

"Wouldn't it be faster to continue flying?" asked Rose.

"Faster, perhaps," the professor answered, "but we have no idea where Mordred—I mean, Madoc—is, if he survived at all. We need to be closer to the islands if we're to discover what's become of him."

"I thought speed was our first priority."

He shook his head. "Our first priority is success. Speed will be a luxury to indulge in after."

✦ ✦ ✦

They had expected to find all manner of detritus along the bottom of the waterfall, but there was nothing to be seen. It was as if they'd crossed over into a pristine world where no human or creature had set foot.

"Apparently, people have taken the warnings seriously," said Quixote.

"That's why we put it on the maps," said the professor.

After promising not to fly out of sight of the *Scarlet Dragon*, Archimedes lit out to do a little exploring. He was gone only a few minutes when he returned, jabbering excitedly.

"A ship!" he squawked. "I've found another ship! Well, most of one, anyway."

"How do you find 'most of' a ship?" asked Rose.

"Part of it is there, and part of it is not," Archie replied. "You've obviously been spending too much time with those idiots at Oxford."

Archimedes was correct—not a mile away from the falls, on a due west heading, was a ship. It had been badly wrecked and lay in the shallows, with various pieces scattered in the waters nearby.

It was elegantly simple in its design, and several times larger than the *Scarlet Dragon*. On one side, the painted letters peeling from the effects of weather and age, was the name of the vessel: the *Aurora*.

"My old ship!" the professor exclaimed. "I'd always wondered what happened to her!"

"You left her here?" Quixote asked.

"No," replied the professor. "We took her back to Paralon, but that was many years ago. Apparently someone tried to duplicate our voyage to the End of the World. But when we went, it was through the Southern Isles, not here."

"There is an End of the World in the south as well?" Quixote said in surprise. "How can that be?"

"It's a curious cartological principle," the professor replied. "If you are standing on the top of the real world at the North Pole, every step you take in any direction will be south. Similarly, the world ends in the same way no matter which path you take to reach it."

"How did you get it down here, Professor?" asked Rose. "Was it an airship too?"

"The first of them, I believe," the professor said proudly. "It was a creation of my old friend, Uruk Ko, the Goblin King. Of all the races in the Archipelago, theirs was the most technologically advanced. They had been testing airships for decades before Ko and I decided we wanted to undertake this journey."

"The ship," Rose said. "There's no dragon on the prow."

"Oh, it wasn't a Dragonship," the professor said. "Those were not to be used on a foolhardy exploration such as ours. It was built solely for the journey we took—and it came back in one piece. It was the first time Bert and I had the opportunity to really become friends, and it is one of my fondest memories."

"But aren't all the ships similarly equipped with balloons and sails?" Quixote asked. "I understood that to be a recent development."

"After the old *Indigo Dragon* was rebuilt as an airship, Prince Stephen initiated the program to convert them all," said the professor. "He was the only one brave enough to propose doing it to all the Dragonships themselves."

"I wonder why they were here?" said Rose. "That's very sad, to have come all this way down the waterfall only to wreck so short a distance away."

"It weren't a wreck," a faint voice said from somewhere ahead of them. "It were a dread sea-beastie, and the crew never even saw it coming."

The voice had come not from the *Aurora,* but from the wreckage just below the surface.

Resting amid some coral and sea plants was an oval-shaped frame with the portrait of a well-to-do pirate under a piece of heavy, curved glass. It was halfway hidden by some of the undersea flora and seemed to have gone down with the *Aurora,* judging by the amount of silt that had accumulated around it.

"I am Captain Charles Johnson," the portrait said, looking up through the water. "Who is it that you be?"

"I am Don Quixote de la Mancha," the old knight said, bowing deeply, "and these are my companions, the lady Rose, the teacher Archimedes, and the Caretaker Emeritus Professor Sigurdsson. We are on a quest."

Captain Johnson sneered. "Caretaker Emeritus?" he said to the professor. "I didn't realize Caretakers could retire."

"How is it you know of the Caretakers?" Sigurdsson said in surprise.

The portrait blinked. "Are you daft, man? I'm trapped in a painting of myself on the other side of the waterfall at the Edge of the World. I didn't just fall here by accident, you know. Of *course* I know about the Caretakers. I know that you, Professor, are the only one of their number who has ever come over the waterfall—just as I know I was betrayed and left here by one of your predecessors."

"Really?" said Sigurdsson. "Which one?"

"That snake-in-the-grass Daniel Defoe," said Johnson. "He and I were training as apprentices to Cyrano de Bergerac, along with my best friend, a silversmith named Eliot McGee. Cyrano had his eye in particular on Eliot, whom he thought might make a suitable apprentice for the Cartographer himself."

"He was a mapmaker?" the professor said.

"One of the best," Johnson replied. "His father, Elijah, had been approached by a pirate to help him create a map to his own hidden treasures, and he was so successful at it that McGee became the de facto mapmaker to all the pirates in the Caribbean. Elijah trained Eliot in the discipline, and it was then that Daniel and I made his acquaintance."

"What had distinguished you, if you don't mind my asking?" said the professor. "Why did Cyrano seek you out?"

"I was compiling a history of the pirates," Johnson replied. "Basically, as an audition to become the Caretaker after de Bergerac."

"'*A General History of the Robberies and Murders of the Most Notorious Pyrates*,'" said the professor. "I know it well."

"Really?" Johnson said, beaming.

"Yes—but I thought Defoe wrote it. *Everyone* thinks Defoe wrote it."

"Arrrgghhh," the portrait growled. "I hate that! He stole it from me, every jot and tittle!"

"To be fair," Sigurdsson said, "most of the editions carry your name—everyone just thinks it was a pseudonym for Daniel Defoe."

"Daniel Defoe murdered me in 1723," Johnson stated. "He and Eliot were working on a companion book they called the *Pyratlas*. It was to be Eliot's audition to become the Cartographer's apprentice, and with me having my own book, Defoe was going to be shut out altogether. So he had me killed, and published the book himself."

"That's very interesting," Sigurdsson said as he made a shushing gesture to his companions out of Johnson's view. No point in antagonizing the fellow by letting him know they'd just had dinner with his old-friend-turned-adversary. "So how is it you came to be here, in this, ah, state?"

"Apparently, at some point Defoe betrayed Eliot as well, and faked his own death to go into the Archipelago," said Johnson. "In the years that followed, Eliot's son, Ernest, had also become a mapmaker, thus continuing in the family trade. What Defoe only discovered later was that the McGees had been hiding secret clues to the pirate treasures in duplicate maps—maps that young Ernest subsequently burned. A few survived, but not enough that Defoe could use them to find the treasures without consulting a second book I had been writing, which I called *The Maps of Elijah McGee*.

"Somehow Defoe had discovered a process to resurrect the dead by way of painting their portraits—so he commissioned one of me to ask me the whereabouts of the book. The minute I could speak, I spit in his face."

"You can spit?" said Archimedes.

"Well, I could make the gesture," said Johnson. "As long as he knew my intent, it didn't matter if I couldn't really spit. Anyroad," he went on, "after he realized I couldn't be coerced, he sold me to someone who'd just stolen one of the Dragonships—the *Indigo Dragon*, I think he called it—so I ended up in the possession of actual pirates. Ironic, isn't it?"

"That would be a correct assessment," said the professor. "Did any of these pirates have names?"

"Most of them flat-out ignored me," Johnson said, "except when they needed something. So I never got more than the occasional name, like 'Coleridge' or 'Blake.' But I did catch what they called themselves as a whole—they said they were part of the Imperial Cartological Society, and that they'd been commissioned by royalty. That makes them privateers, which is as bad as pirates in my book."

"I agree," the professor said, looking somberly at his companions. They were all thinking the same thing: that Defoe, who was among the Caretakers Emeritis, was in league with Burton—and they had no way of telling anyone at Tamerlane house. "Did any of them survive the, ah, sea-beastie attack?"

"I couldn't tell you," said Johnson. "After the first blow, I ended up where you see me—and my peripheral vision isn't what it used to be."

"I'm impressed that you even made it this far," said the professor.

"We used your own notes, Professor," Johnson replied. "Yours, and those of someone called Bert. They were given to the society by someone called Uruk Ko."

Professor Sigurdsson lowered his head. That was the hat trick. If the Goblin King had aided the Imperial Cartological Society, the Goblins had to be in league with the Winter King's Shadow.

"The notes," he said suddenly. "Did any survive the wreck?"

"I doubt it," said Johnson, "but I can recall most of what was written on them. They had to do with the precautions, I believe."

"Precautions?" asked Quixote.

"There are seven islands that must be crossed," said Johnson.

"You cannot simply bypass them. Each one is akin to a gate, and gates must be entered properly."

"I remember," said the professor. "We've come prepared."

"That's good," said Johnson, "since we weren't. We didn't take the cautions seriously, and as a result, the *Aurora* was lost."

"Professor," Rose whispered, "you have one of the pocket watches—is it possible to release Captain Johnson from the portrait?"

"An interesting thought," said the professor. "Let's find out."

They explained what they wanted to try, and Johnson responded with considerable enthusiasm. Archimedes retrieved several scraps of cloth and timber from the wreck, and Quixote fashioned a sort of sling-on-a-pole to scoop up the portrait.

It took only a few tries for him to succeed, but when they had the picture onboard, their expressions fell.

There was no place on the frame to insert the watch. Johnson was trapped within.

"That's all well and good," he said. "I've gotten used to it, anyway."

"It may be for the best," said the professor. "There's a time limit unless you're at a particular location. And that would literally ruin your week."

"Will you still take me with you, anyroad?" asked Johnson. "I'm really tired of seeing the same fish and coral day after day, and there's only been one other person come over the falls since I got here, and he died straightaway. He's just over there, to the right."

Quixote steered the *Scarlet Dragon* over to where Johnson had indicated, and sure enough there was a skeleton, facedown in the water. It could not have been there very long, as the coral had not yet begun to form around the bones, and scraps of his clothing that had not yet rotted were still floating about.

"I think this is Wilhelm Grimm," the professor said sadly. "He must have displeased his master."

"And he was simply dropped over the waterfall?" Rose exclaimed in horror. "If he died, then what hope do we have of finding Madoc alive?"

"Your father is a man of unusual mettle," said Sigurdsson, "and I suspect, as Samaranth probably knew, that just dropping him over the falls would not be enough to kill him. The same might not be true for mere mortals like myself."

"No, look," said Quixote, pointing. A dagger was lodged firmly between two of the skeleton's ribs, next to its spine. "He was killed, then discarded. Truly, an ignoble act."

"Do you think it was Burton who did it?" Rose asked quietly. "Or someone else?"

"Whoever it was, my dear child," the professor said, turning her away from the sight, "this person is past worry. The troubles of this world are no longer his."

"Pardon," said Quixote, "but that is a strange platitude to hear from someone who is himself dead."

"I am a Caretaker," Sigurdsson replied. "The troubles of this world *are* my business."

No one spoke any further, and Quixote adjusted the sails, pointing the little craft to the west.

CHAPTER NINETEEN
THE RUINED CITY

THE PORTRAIT OF Charles Johnson struck up an immediate friendship with Archimedes, who was fascinated by the tales of pirates and privateers. Their Golden Age, which had been documented by Johnson, Defoe, and the McGees, was an era that the owl had missed completely when Jack and John had brought him into the future with Rose.

"You actually hid clues to the treasures in the maps themselves?" Archimedes asked. "Ingenious!"

"It was Ernest's idea," said Johnson, "because of his connection to the Empress Josephine, and Napoleon's hidden fortune."

"You're more interesting than most portraits I'm acquainted with," said the owl.

"Thank you," said the captain.

With Johnson thusly preoccupied at one end of the boat, the professor, Quixote, and Rose were able to discuss their concerns with a bit more privacy.

"The *Aurora* belonged to the Goblins," said the professor. "If Burton was able to procure it from them, along with my notes, it's all but certain they are in league together."

"What worries me more," Quixote mused, "is what Johnson told us about Defoe. That isn't the behavior of a Caretaker."

"It isn't," said the professor, "but we shall just have to trust in the Caretakers' ability to look after themselves. We have a hard enough task of our own."

"Heads up," Johnson called. "We're approaching the first gate."

The first of the seven gates was a lighthouse.

"That's rather small for an island, and rather odd for a gate," said Quixote.

"It's a most important one," said the professor, "and one I'm guessing the society disregarded."

"I tried to tell them," Johnson said, sighing, "but they wouldn't listen."

"What must we do?" said Quixote.

The professor picked up the tallow lantern. "Simply take this to the room at the top and replace the lantern that's there."

Quixote looked at him in surprise. "That's all?"

The professor nodded. "That's all. But hold fast to the empty lantern. It's our receipt, so to speak."

"On whose account?"

"This is the land of the dragons," said the professor. "Somewhere up there in the darkness, they're watching. And somewhere here below as well. The lantern is marked with the letter *alpha,* and replacing a light in the lighthouse is a show of our good intentions."

"Sort of like leaving the milk out for the faery folk, or the brownies," said Rose. "I think I understand."

Quixote hopped from the boat to the narrow steps of the lighthouse and quickly ascended the steps. While the others waited, they scanned the waters around them for any signs of life, and it was Johnson who found it.

"Oh, dear," he moaned. "Look."

They looked in the direction Johnson was facing and saw a rising swell of water. Something massive was swimming just under the surface, and it was coming toward the *Scarlet Dragon*. It grew closer, and larger, and the professor was just about to suggest deploying the balloons on the boat when a brilliant beam of light cut through the gloom above their heads. The light shone in two directions: one beam back toward the waterfall, and the other forward to the west.

The swell disappeared.

"Whew," said Johnson, as Quixote descended the steps with the empty lantern and rejoined them. "That was excellent timing."

"I'm sorry it took as long as it did," Quixote replied. "I forgot to take a match. Fortunately, someone had left some behind."

He held up a small brown coin purse. "There were a few matches inside, along with some coins and a few pebbles," he said. "We got lucky."

"The luck is accidental," the professor said, taking the small purse. "I must have left it there myself. I've been wondering what happened to it for decades.

"Here, look," he said, examining the contents. "This round black quartz is actually the tear of an Apache princess that I found in Arizona. And this"—he held up a small white stone—"I took from a stream in France that is said to cure all ills and heal all wounds."

"And the coins?" asked Quixote. "Of what significance are they?"

"I kept those in case I needed to buy an ale," said the professor. "This adventuring life is hard work, and it makes one very thirsty."

With the offering to the dragons made, they sailed on toward the next island gate.

"Professor," Rose asked suddenly, "do you know what time it is?"

"I'm not sure if time works the same way here as it does up top," the professor replied. "Worry not, dear Rose. We'll get there, by and by."

"But professor," Rose started to say.

"There," the professor interrupted, pointing. "The second gate!"

The next island was wildly overgrown with foliage and was almost perfectly divided down the middle by a large swamp.

"Anything dangerous here?" asked Quixote.

"The usual," said the professor. "Ligers and tigons, and the occasional gorilla, who will leave you be if you throw the names of books at them."

"Throw books?" asked Rose.

"No," said the professor, "just the names. They're usually content with those. The only creatures to watch out for here are the crocodiles—they fly, you know."

Sure enough, the moment the *Scarlet Dragon* moved into the swamp, the air was suddenly filled with winged crocodiles. They swooped and wove as if they were a great flock of leathery cranes, flying south for the winter.

It took only seconds for them to focus their attention on the tiny boat and its edible occupants, and they changed their formation to envelop the *Scarlet Dragon*.

Before the others could react, the professor reached into a

satchel and flung a handful of small objects into the air. The crocodiles immediately dispensed with the formation to chase the treats. Professor Sigurdsson threw two more handfuls for good measure, and soon all the flying crocodiles had retreated into the jungle.

Rose peered inside the satchel. "Lollipops?"

"Indeed. The crocodiles here are fond of lollipops," the professor explained, "and I made certain to raid the store of them Bert keeps onboard the *White Dragon* so that we'd be prepared."

"I don't think it likely that you carried many lollipops on your first voyage here in the *Aurora*," said Quixote, "so how did you discover the crocodiles' weakness for them?"

"Completely by accident, I assure you," replied the professor. "As we were fighting them off, one of the crew was yanked overboard—and it was in watching the crocs tear the poor devil to pieces that we realized what they were really after."

"The lollipops," said Rose.

"Just so," said the professor. "He had a penchant for them. Claimed it kept him from eating too much, as he hoped to keep his weight down. Ironic, isn't it?"

"This is not a gate where we must pay a toll to get through," the professor said at the third island. "To pass here, one must simply resist the urge to take something."

"How do you mean, professor?" asked Rose.

"I'll show you," he said, "but this is a place we'd best cross in the air."

He and Quixote deployed the balloons, and the little craft rose into the air.

The island was small, and unremarkable in most respects. It

had palm trees, sandy beaches, and a few gently rolling hills. And in the center was a large, glistening lake.

"Look," he said, pointing over the edge of the *Scarlet Dragon* at the water below.

The lake was filled with gold.

Not just raw ore, or coins, but every manner of object one could think of: fruit, and fish, and mugs, and swords, and on and on—all made of the gleaming yellow metal.

"A pirate's repository, perhaps?" asked Quixote.

"No," said the professor. "Death. The waters here bring death. Look farther."

All around the edges of the lake were larger golden masses, which the companions had at first assumed to be simple piles of gold. But they weren't—they were people.

"The water turns everything it touches into gold," said the professor, "including those who seek to take some of it for themselves."

Quixote was holding Johnson so that he could also see the spectacle below. "Look!" the captain said. "There's one of those sorry privateers!"

Professor Sigurdsson looked more closely, then lowered the *Scarlet Dragon* a few yards.

"Hmm," he said. "That's William Blake, unless I miss my guess. Surprising—I would've thought he had a stronger will than that."

In a few more minutes they had passed over the lake, and the professor said it was safe to drop back into the waters past the western beach.

According to Johnson's memory of the professor's notes, the next island gate had a name. "It's called Entelechy," he said.

"Both are," said the professor. "The island, and its queen. They share the same name—although it's more politic to refer to her as 'the Quintessence.' As far as I know, she's Aristotle's goddaughter, and so is at least two thousand years old."

"Finally," said Rose. "I'll get to meet someone my own age."

Entelechy was a prim and proper island, with a well-kept harbor and several soaring towers of blue stone. They stopped at the dock and left Archimedes and Captain Johnson to guard the boat. The professor led the others to a great turquoise-tinged reception hall.

The Quintessence was seated on a throne at the head of a magnificent banquet table. She was perhaps twelve feet tall and had all the presence of a giant. Her gown billowed around her immense chair, and her hair was piled high above a glittering crown.

"Great Quintessence," the professor said, bowing. "We seek passage through your gate, if you please."

"Come closer," she commanded, "that I may better see you."

A curious look of . . . happiness appeared on the queen's face as she watched the professor. She considered them all, briefly, then turned back to Rose.

"You have the look of the Old World to you, girl," she said. "I may allow you to pass. Who are your forebears?"

"My father's father was Odysseus," she replied.

"Ah," said the queen. "I might have guessed. You are familiar to me. And your mother's parentage?"

"No one you'd know."

"Hmm," said the queen. "And you?"

Quixote bowed. "I am the lady's humble protector," he said simply.

"I see," said the queen. "And you?"

"I am a simple traveler," said the professor, "seeking out what beauty there is in the world."

"And what have you found?"

"If seeking beauty was my only goal, I should be happy to stop here," said the professor, "but we have other needs, and thus must go on."

The queen smiled. "That's an excellent answer," she said, smiling. "I believe I will let you pass, for a price."

"There's not much left to barter with," Quixote whispered to the others, "only the candles!"

"Those are for a different gate," said the professor. "Name your price, milady."

"Will you give me a kiss?" the queen asked, bending down so he could reach her.

"I shall," said the professor. And he did.

"Ahh." The queen sighed. "I have missed that—it was as nice as before, so long ago. It does grow lonely out here, you know," she said with a look of sorrow on her face. "There have been few other visitors of late.

"Another descendant—or was it an ancestor?—of Odysseus passed this way not long ago, and I allowed him through, because he knew my godfather."

Rose and Quixote were silently thrilled by this—the first proof they'd had of Madoc's survival, and passing.

"There was another," said the queen, "but he was rude, and a bit delusional. I let him pass, but I kept one of his arms."

"We really ought to be going," said Quixote, his eyes wide. "Begging your pardon."

"You won't stay to dine with me?" said the Queen.

"We really must go," Rose concurred.

"So we must," the professor said. He bowed deeply and kissed the queen's hand.

She bowed her head in assent, and the companions returned to the boat. Shortly after, they were again underway.

"I don't know what to say, Professor," Rose said with a broad smile. "That was an impressive display of personal charm."

"Thank you," replied the professor. "Bert used to refer to it as my 'shield of charisma.'"

"She seemed to remember you," said Quixote, "and very fondly at that."

"And now you know one of the reasons that Bert could not be your guide," said the professor. "The Queen of Entelechy would never have allowed him to pass."

"Why not?" asked Rose.

"Because," explained the professor, "when we came here before, the first words out of his mouth were, 'You're the largest woman I've ever seen in my life!'"

Both Johnson and Quixote groaned. "A terrible mistake," said Quixote.

"Awful," said Johnson.

"I don't get it," said Rose.

"You're still very young," Quixote told her, "but I will tell you what my grandfather wisely told me. Never, ever mention a woman's size, or her age. Women are timelessly young and eternally beautiful."

"Always?"

"Yes, always," Quixote and Johnson said together.

"That's part of the reason it took Bert eight hundred thousand years to find a wife," said the professor. "No tact."

The fifth gate was a trio of tall, spikelike rocks standing only yards apart from one another. The professor lit the tallow candles and instructed Archimedes to place the first one atop the center stone, the second on the stone to the right, and the third on the stone to the left.

"That's it?" said Quixote.

"That's it," said the professor. "We may now pass."

"What would have happened if we hadn't placed the candles there?" asked Quixote.

The professor shivered and drew his coat closer. "I don't even want to think about it," he said. "I've been dead for a quarter century, and the idea *still* gives me nightmares."

After the fifth island gate, they passed into what must have been night. The haze was replaced by complete darkness, and then, eventually, a night sky full of stars.

"Do you recognize any of them, Professor?" asked Rose. "I don't see any of the constellations!"

"I don't believe those are stars, per se," said the professor in a hushed voice. "I believe those are the *dragons* themselves."

It was a sobering, fantastic thought: that they were actually somewhere underneath thousands upon thousands of dragons—and so, the companions slept.

In a few hours, still under the night sky, they came to the sixth island.

Broad, with no hills or cliffs on the beaches, it was not a small island, but it had been completely overbuilt with temple after structure after edifice, until it was practically a city. And the city must have been deserted for countless years, because it was all but ruined.

The crumbling remains were more ancient than those they'd seen on Avalon, and even more ancient than the islands of the Underneath.

Standing among the ruins was a man, dressed in rags and clutching a book. He was staring up at the stars.

"Ah, me," said the professor quietly. "It's the last of the society pirates."

They pulled the *Scarlet Dragon* onto the beach, and the professor took a few steps toward the man, who had not yet acknowledged their presence.

"Hello, Coleridge," said the professor.

The man looked up at the mention of his name. He squinted at the boat on the beach, then at the passengers who were now standing in front of him.

"Sigurdsson?" he asked eventually. "Is that you? What are you doing here at the end of all that is?"

Rose wrinkled her brow at the question, but Quixote's discreet touch on her arm signaled her not to speak. This man should be dealt with by the professor.

"This isn't the end," the professor said, his voice calm and soft. "This is just one more stopping place."

"Dreams come true here, you know," said Coleridge. "I've seen it happen. But no one told me . . ."

His voice trailed off, and he turned away again.

"No one told you what?" the professor asked.

"Nightmares come true here as well," said Coleridge.

"Are you all right?" asked the professor.

"She took my arm," Coleridge said simply, "but she let me go past. I had to come here. I had to see . . ."

"Come with us," said the professor. "There's no reason for you to stay. Do come. Please."

The emaciated figure turned to look at him. "I cannot, for it may yet change. And there is nowhere else to go. There is nothing further. This was the last place in the world. This was the great city I saw in my vision, and it's all a shambles. Destroyed."

"You know it was once great," said the professor. "You know how it began."

"I did not know how it ended," Coleridge said, looking up at the sky. "I did not know."

He did not turn around again. The professor motioned for the others to get on the boat, and they sailed around and past the city.

"What a sad man," said Quixote. "What happened to him?"

"On this island, dreams do eventually come true," said the professor, "but true things are also real, and real things eventually fade. What we saw was the end of his particular dream."

"What was this island called?" asked Rose.

The professor smiled, but it was a melancholy smile. "Xanadu," he said. "It was called Xanadu."

The waters after the Ruined City were placid, with no indication of currents or tides. Above them, disturbingly, the stars began to go out—but soon they realized it was because the light was coming up again. Strangely, it appeared that the sun was rising in the west—until they realized that it was not the sun at all, but the last of the seven island gates.

The island, emerald green with a thick blanket of grasses, was smaller than the last, and had no structures on it—only a ring of standing stones.

A Ring of Power, virtually identical to that on Terminus, save that the stones were larger.

They were pristine, and spread far enough apart that the areas between were paved with smooth stones. In the center was a long stone table draped with a crimson cloth, and seated at the table was a tall, silver-haired man.

As the companions approached, he rose to greet them. His tunic was also silver, shot through with crimson down the left side of his chest, and he was almost as tall as the Quintessence had been.

"Greetings," said the professor. He introduced himself and the others, then asked if the tall man had a name.

"I am a star," he said with an air of haughtiness, "or at least, I once was. I think I may be still, but it is difficult to say. However, when I was still in the sky, those who worshipped me called me Rao."

"Is this a Ring of Power?" Rose asked. "Like the one used to summon the Dragons?"

Rao frowned. "Dragons? I know of none here who may be called to this place, save that I call them. And I would not deign to call Dragons, for they would not come for one such as I."

"A Dragon would not come at the call of a star?"

"One, perhaps," said Rao. "He would not look down upon me as the others might, for not having ascended. He himself chose to descend to the office of Dragon for the sake of a city, so he is, as you might think, different."

"What was his name?" asked Rose.

"Samaranth," said Rao. "But enough of this. Will you settle the dispute?"

"What dispute is that?" asked Quixote.

"There is a dispute between some of my children," said Rao. "Have you come to arbitrate for them? To judge which is in the ascent, and which must descend?"

"We have not come to judge anyone," said the professor. "We have merely come seeking someone who may have passed this way. He is called Madoc."

Rao's eyes narrowed. "None come here save that they fell. Are you saying you have come seeking one of the fallen?"

Before the professor could answer, Rose stepped forward again. "Not everyone must fall, great star," she said, bowing her head respectfully. "We have come here of our own accord, and we did not fall. We flew."

"Hmm," Rao mused. "This I see, Little Thing. But take a caution—others before you have chosen a similar path, and fared the worse for it. Flying is not always ascending."

"Are you one of the fallen?" Rose asked.

Professor Sigurdsson winced. That was not a question he thought would get a good response from a former star.

Strangely enough, Rao looked at her with gentleness, and even touched her head. "I was not," he said. "I had not yet ascended, and thus did not have to choose. But soon, soon."

"If I may," said the professor.

"Little Thing," Rao said bluntly. "Why have you come here?"

"We seek passage beyond your island," said the professor, "in search of the man Madoc. May we pass?"

"You may not," Rao said blithely. "None may pass save that one must stay. That is the Old Magic, and the old rule."

"Then I offer myself," said the professor. "I will stay, so that the others may pass."

"No!" Rose cried. "You can't!"

"That, dear Rose, is the other reason Bert could not come," he replied. "Years ago, we turned back when another star made the same request. And we both knew it would be made again. A life for the passage. That's the rule."

"But we need you!"

"No," he said gently, "you don't. You needed me to get you to your father—and you're nearly there. Quixote is your guardian—I was merely your guide."

"We still have to convince him to repair the sword," said Rose. "We can't do that without you."

"Rose," the professor began.

"I'll stay," said a voice behind them. "I'll do it."

It was the portrait of Captain Johnson. "I'd be willing," he stated, "if the fact that I'm essentially an oil painting doesn't count against me."

"Can you arbitrate?" asked Rao. "Will you arbitrate the disputes of my children?"

"I witnessed more than seventy pirate trials," said Johnson. "I could give it a go, I suppose."

"Little Thing," Rao said, "this is acceptable to me. You shall stay, and the others may pass."

Rose took the portrait from the boat, kissed it quickly, and handed it to Rao.

Quickly, before the star could change his mind, the companions hurried back to the boat and put her to sea.

"Thank you, Captain Johnson," Rose called out.

"Farewell, Captain," Quixote said.

"I'd rather have left the Caretaker," said Archimedes. "There's an entire *houseful* back in the Archipelago."

"Remember," Johnson called out, his voice growing faint as the island vanished behind the mist, "don't trust Daniel Defoe!"

CHAPTER TWENTY
THE BARGAIN

"ABSOLUTELY NOT," said Dickens. "It's the most insane thing I've ever heard of in my life."

"I concur," said John. "He's caused us more grief than almost anyone except for the Winter King himself, and he almost single-handedly brought about the Winterland when he tricked Hugo Dyson through that door. Letting him have asylum here, in Tamerlane House . . ." He paused and took a deep breath. "Well, it's just unthinkable."

"I think it's worth at least a debate," said Defoe. "He knows a great deal about the Shadow King's plans."

"Because he was his chief lieutenant until just a few hours ago!" said John. "We should consider him a prisoner of war, not a refugee seeking asylum."

"I think he should be flogged," said Shakespeare.

"But just yesterday," Chaucer pointed out, "weren't we debating whether or not his beliefs about the Archipelago and the *Imaginarium Geographica* were in fact superior to our own? That alone should change our perception of him."

John rubbed his temples. This discussion was not progressing in a reasonable direction. "All right," he said finally. "Bring him in."

Richard Burton entered the conservatory, flanked by Nathaniel Hawthorne and Daniel Defoe. He grinned and nodded at John as he took a seat at the table.

"You should realize, Burton," John began, "that none of us here trusts you in the least."

"I don't trust you any more than you trust me, John," Burton said, "but desperate times make for strange bedfellows, and you don't have to trust me—just my motives."

"Which are?"

Burton raised his hands and smiled. "The same as they've always been," he said simply. "No more secrets. My goals and those of the Caretakers have seldom been far apart—we just differ in how we approach them. But I've realized that the goals of the Chancellor are not mine—and whatever he is, he is not the man I would willingly serve. I believed he was. I was wrong."

"Would you be willing to give us the information we need to defeat him?" asked Chaucer.

"I will share what I know," said Burton.

"We haven't yet decided whether to give you what you're seeking," said John, "but we're considering it. In the meantime, you're not to be left alone at any time. Either Charles and Fred will be with you, or Defoe and Hawthorne."

"Fine."

"You won't be allowed to go near the docks," John continued. "You must not leave Tamerlane House under any circumstance, and your men must remain within the bounds of their quarters. No exceptions."

"Agreed."

"Very well," said John. "Do you have any questions?"

"Yes," said Burton. "Where's the kitchen? I'm starving."

Charles, Defoe, and Fred took the first shift watching Burton, as the Caretakers continued the debate; and the kitchen was as secure a room as any other in Tamerlane House.

"You're eating quite heartily for a prisoner of war," said Charles.

"Asylum seeker," said Burton, "depending on which way your friend's wind blows."

"Has anyone seen Jakob?" Hawthorne asked, peering around the corner. "I was supposed to help him with some notations an hour ago, and his cat is looking for him."

"There's a hall of mirrors in one of the rooms here," Defoe said. "I think he wanted to go have a look at them, maybe see if there are any trapped princesses or lost treasures in them."

"Very well," said Hawthorne, sighing. "I'll tell Grimalkin."

"What the devil are you eating, Burton?" asked Charles.

"Aardvark," he replied, chewing. "Will you have some? It's delicious."

"It looks a bit greasy to me," said Charles. "Where did you get it? It isn't something the Feast Beasts usually bring out for the banquets."

"Oh, we brought them ourselves," Burton said. "We didn't want to impose on—or expect—your hospitality. The northern lands are crawling with them, and they're easier to hunt than a baby deer."

"How's that?"

"Well," explained Burton, tearing off another piece of flesh with his teeth, "do you know the old joke about how you can hunt deer with an apple and a hammer? Aardvarks are even less trouble than that, mostly due to their sensitive natures, and the fact that they're very slow."

Burton leaned over the table and spoke in a conspiratorial whisper. "To catch an aardvark," he said, grinning, "all you have to do is find one, then start insulting it."

"Really?" said Charles.

"Yes. Instead of running away, it gets offended and sits down, whining about how no one likes it and everyone just wants to be mean to aardvarks."

"And then what?"

"Then, WHAM!" Burton exclaimed, slamming his fist to the table. "We wallop it with a hammer and marinate it in garlic and butter."

"That's positively barbaric," said Charles.

"I *am* a barbarian," said Burton, stroking his scarred cheeks with a bowie knife. "And besides, what else are aardvarks good for?"

"Good point," said Charles.

The loss of their newfound friend was sobering to all four of the companions. In an unfamiliar place, Captain Johnson had been a comforting voice of reason and tact. Granted, being an oil painting, he had less to lose overall, but a life is a life, Sigurdsson told them, and his sacrifice was as meaningful as anyone else's would be.

Past the island of the star, the waters grew still, but they remained cloudy, so it was difficult to estimate their depth. There were no other islands in sight in any direction, and only a smudge of color on the horizon, which hinted at thunderstorms. Other than continuing in the direction they were going, there was no strategy or plan of action they could employ. There was not even an expectation, said the professor, of what they might encounter next.

"Haven't you been here before?" asked Rose.

The professor shook his head. "Remember, we only got as far as the star. When we had to leave someone behind just to go on, Bert and Ko and I decided that we'd gone far enough, and returned to the Archipelago."

"So," said Quixote, "we are truly journeying into an unknown region. This is truly the quest to end them all."

"I know it's just a turn of phrase," said Sigurdsson, "but that really isn't a comforting thought."

"Professor," Rose said gently. "Can you tell me what time it is?"

Professor Sigurdsson opened his mouth to reply, then saw the look on her face and stopped. He turned back to look out over the water and sighed. "Third time's the charm, eh, Rose?" he said quietly.

He reached into his pocket and removed his silver pocket watch. Flipping the lid open, he took a quick glance and snapped it shut again, swallowing hard as he did so.

"How long have we been gone, Professor?"

"It took less than a day for Bert to fly us to Terminus," he said matter-of-factly, "but more than a day to descend the falls. And from the time we discovered the *Aurora*, we have traveled for two full days. All told, we've been gone for just over a hundred hours."

Rose closed her eyes as she realized what that meant. They were past the halfway mark that would allow the professor to return to Tamerlane House and the safety of the Pygmalion Gallery.

The professor reached an arm around her shoulders and gave

her a comforting squeeze. "No time to worry about the trip back when we've yet to reach our destination, hey? Let's see to that first, and we'll worry about the rest when we have to."

"Wall ho," Quixote called out.

"Land ho, you mean," said Archie.

"Land is land and a wall is a wall, and I know the difference between them," Quixote retorted. "Look."

In the near distance, what they had assumed to be storm clouds on the western horizon was now revealed to be more substantial than clouds, and taller besides.

It was, as Quixote said, a wall.

As high as the waterfall at the world's edge had been, the wall was tall, and it stretched away in both directions, north and south, to the vanishing point on each horizon.

"I wonder what's on the other side?" Professor Sigurdsson mused, squinting as he looked up for a glimpse of the wall's summit. "I wonder if there's a way over?"

"This is how people are chosen as Caretakers of an atlas like the *Geographica*," Quixote said to Archimedes. "They can't escape it. It's in their blood."

The wall was so massive that even once they had sighted it, it took another two hours to reach the base. It stood on a narrow beach that was perhaps thirty feet wide and, as far as they could tell, ran the length of the wall. It was as if an infinite barrier had been placed on an equally infinite sandbar.

They pulled the *Scarlet Dragon* into the shallows and clambered out to examine the wall. It was made of stones that were placed so closely and precisely that Quixote could not get his sword point between any two of them.

"Impressive," he said with grave sincerity. "I would not have believed such a wall was possible."

"I can't find a top," called Archie, who was spiraling back down to the others. "I could fly higher, but the air was getting too thin to keep me aloft."

"Is this the end of our journey, Professor?" asked Rose. "If we can't get over it or through it, then how do we go on?"

"It is the end of all that is," a voice said from farther down the beach. The words were spoken calmly, but were tinged with menace, and perhaps . . . fear?

The companions turned around to see a man standing about twenty feet behind them. In one hand he held a hammer. The other was not a hand at all; his arm ended in a hook, which was tarnished and rusty. He was heavily bearded, and his clothing was in tatters. And on his face was a look that was almost indescribable, a mix of fury and what might be relief.

"Hello, Father," said Rose. "It's nice to finally meet you."

There was none among them, other than the professor, who might say how the fall over the water's edge had changed the man called Madoc.

Rose had seen him only once before. At the time he was known as Mordred; he had just tried to kill her uncle Merlin, and had lost his hand to her cousin Arthur. Quixote had also never seen him, but knew of him only through stories about the Winter King, as his enemies had called him. Archimedes had known him when he was still called Madoc, but that had been many centuries earlier. Only Professor Sigurdsson had seen him as the man he was now—and that was moments before Madoc, Mordred, the Winter King, had killed him in his study.

Madoc's hair and beard were long and greasy. His arms were thick and corded with muscle, and he watched the new arrivals with suspicion. Slowly he paced back and forth across the width of the sand, never taking his eyes off them. Finally he decided to speak—to the owl.

"Hello, Archimedes," he said. "You're looking well."

"You're not, Madoc," Archie replied, lighting onto Quixote's shoulder. "You look like you've been hit by a train."

"Actually, I was dropped over a waterfall," said Madoc, "but the net result is probably the same."

"How did you bypass the gates, then?" asked the professor. "And once below, why didn't you try to return to the Archipelago?"

"I was compelled," Madoc said, "and I remain so. I briefly thought of trying to repair that ship, the *Aurora*, but I was unable to even pause to appraise the vessel's damage. I may have been swimming, or walking, or otherwise moving perpendicular to the waterfall, but make no mistake—I was always falling, and am falling still."

"Until you reached this wall," said the professor.

"Yes," said Madoc. "Until I came here. As far as I can determine, it is endless. I spent years doing nothing but walking, first in one direction, then the other. After a while, I began to hallucinate. I dreamed that as I slept, all my progress was undone, and I had been returned to the place I started. Even if that had been true, there was no way to know for certain.

"It's impossible to climb—believe me, I've tried. I wasted a year on *that*. Then I considered trying to dig my way through, but other than this," he said, holding up his hook, "I had nothing that was capable of even scratching it. I built a forge and created several tools, using metals I've scavenged from the beach, but they've all proven too soft for the stone as well. That was almost two years ago. I've spent all of my time since planning my revenge."

The professor started, and Madoc laughed.

"I'm only joking," he said to the old Caretaker. "Really, though—what were you expecting me to say? That I've had time to reconsider my choices, and I've turned over a new leaf?"

"I'm pretty sure that's a lie," said Archimedes.

Madoc rolled his eyes. "Of course it's a joke, you stupid bird," he said, more exasperated than irritated. "I used to be the villain of the story, or hadn't you heard?"

"Actually, you still are, after a fashion," said Sigurdsson. "Or at least, your Shadow is."

"Now you have my attention," Madoc said, sitting cross-legged in the sand. "Tell me."

The companions sat on the sand across from Madoc, and Professor Sigurdsson told him everything that had happened in the quarter century since the conflict on Terminus.

Several times the professor nearly paused in his narrative, concerned that he might be sharing something that would better remain a secret—but each time he reminded himself that without Madoc's help, they would not be able to defeat the Shadow King. And while they were still a long way from being friends, or even friendly enemies, Madoc was at least listening to what they had come to say.

"We need your help, Madoc," the professor said. "Show him, Rose."

She walked back to the *Scarlet Dragon* and retrieved a bundle, which she placed on the sand in front of Madoc. Slowly, carefully, she folded back the oilcloth to reveal the shattered remains of the sword Caliburn.

"We need you to repair the sword, Father," Rose said simply. "Can you do it? Please?"

Madoc stared at the sword for a long moment, as if he couldn't comprehend what he was seeing. His face was inscrutable, and Quixote and Sigurdsson exchanged worried glances. What did this mean, that he didn't react at all?

Suddenly Madoc fell to his knees, dropped his head into his hands, and began to shake violently.

Quixote was about to step forward, and Rose was reaching out a hand to comfort him, when they realized together that Madoc was not sobbing.

He was *laughing*.

He laughed so hard that he could not speak, could not stand. Tears ran down his face as he erupted in a paroxysm of laughter, choking, sobbing, guffawing, all at once.

"If you only realized, child," he choked between spasms. "If you only understood how important this object was to me, once . . ."

"We do understand, Madoc," Sigurdsson began.

"You understand nothing!" shouted Madoc, his anger rapidly sobering him. "Nothing!

"My brother was the one who wished to conquer the world!" he cried. "I only wanted to do what was right! But each time, he forced his way ahead and did as he wanted—only I paid the price!"

"He paid a price too, Father," Rose said. "He was imprisoned in the Keep of Time, never to leave. And it was his own son who banished him there."

Madoc blinked at her, as if he didn't understand. "Arthur?" he said. "Arthur banished him?"

"Yes," said Rose.

"He—he never said," Madoc began. "Even when I returned to Camelot, if he had only told me . . ."

"Would that have changed anything?" asked the professor.

Madoc grew cold again. "No," he said, his voice edged with hatred. "He took my hand, and then he took my wife. He deserved everything I brought down on his house."

"All you've ever brought down is darkness, Madoc," said the professor. "And that darkness has continued to fester and grow, until it now threatens to cover two worlds. And you still have the ability to choose the right thing."

"It's too late for that," Madoc said, shaking his head. "After what was done to me—"

"Spare me," said Archimedes. "You were always the rational one, Madoc. But nothing you've said is rational in the least. So Merlin wanted to conquer the world, and sacrifice his own son in the process. You defended the boy, then lost your hand trying to kill your brother. And after all that, you set out to basically subjugate everyone else who has ever lived. And you failed at that. So why don't you show some of the mettle you used to have, and just do the thing you know to be right?"

Madoc glared at the bird and trembled a little, but then he steadied himself and spoke. "All right."

"All right, what?" said Archimedes.

"It's very simple," Madoc said. "I will do as you ask, and repair the sword. But I want you to do something for me."

"I'll consider it," said Rose. "But I cannot promise anything."

"This is not a negotiation," said Madoc. "This is a barter. I am the only one who can give you what you want, and so I am asking you for something I want. You either say yes, or you say no. Whatever happens now is entirely up to you."

"What is it that you want, son of Odysseus?" said Quixote. "Ask, and we shall consider."

"As I said," Madoc repeated, "it's very simple. I'll repair the sword, and you can go back and defeat whatever evil it is that my Shadow has perpetrated. But when you are victorious, I want you to return to Terminus and drop a door from the Keep of Time over the waterfall."

"You want us to provide you with a means of escaping your prison, you mean," said Professor Sigurdsson. "I don't know if that will be permitted."

"I'm not asking for escape," said Madoc, "or else I'd be demanding to return with you now. I know that there are lines no one will cross for me, and if nothing else, I don't relish the idea of encountering Samaranth again anytime soon. All of which is why I'm asking for the door—any random door will do. It won't be a means of escape so much as a sort of parole."

"Freedom is freedom," said Quixote.

"I say we agree to it," said Archimedes, who had continued listening and observing during the entire discussion. "I've actually known him longer than any of you, and honestly, I always liked him better than the other one."

At the mention of his brother, Madoc winced, as if the words stung. But he said nothing.

"Even if we do agree," said Quixote, "where do we find a door from the keep?"

"If this is successful," the professor said, "then we will have recovered all of the doors that are being hoarded by Burton. We can have our pick of them."

"And if you're not successful?" said Madoc. "What then? I will have done this service for you for no benefit to myself."

"Once you would not have asked a boon for yourself, to do something that cost you so little and helped so many," the professor replied.

Madoc regarded him with a rueful stare. "That was a different time, and long past. Don't try to sway me with what cannot be reclaimed."

"I've read the Histories," the professor said. "I know as much about you as any man, save for my protégés, and I know the caliber of man you once were."

Madoc brandished his right arm, which bore the tarnished hook. "It was your students whom I have to thank for this," he said, waving the hook in the air. "And also for making me the man I am now. And that you cannot change."

"Will you take my word of honor?" Quixote said suddenly. "My word, as a knight, that whatever it may take, we shall deliver you one of the doors?"

Madoc tipped his head back and laughed. "I might, if you were a real knight," he said brusquely. "Go back and play your little games with windmills and shrubberies and fat, useless squires. There's nothing for you to promise here."

"My word then," offered Sigurdsson. "As a Caretaker of the *Imaginarium Geographica*."

"A bit more appealing, but no," said Madoc. "Not that I doubt your sincerity, but from what I can gather you appear to be dead—and dead people have a way of living down to one's expectations."

"Then will you take *my* word?"

Rose stepped between the knight and the professor and laid a comforting hand on Madoc's hook. He started to protest, but after a moment lowered it. Rose took his other hand in hers and looked up at him, her face serene.

"I am your daughter," she said softly. "I am the child you never knew, who was raised by someone you claimed to love. In her name, and on her blood, which also runs in my veins, will you take my word that whatever we must do, we will somehow find a way?"

At first, as she spoke, Madoc would not meet her gaze. Then, slowly, he lifted his eyes to look at her.

"Green," he said quietly, "flecked with violet. Her eyes were not violet."

"But yours are, Father."

He looked at her a moment more, then, almost imperceptibly, he nodded. "Your word I will take."

"Then we agree," Rose said. "If you will repair the sword, we will give you one of the doors from the Keep of Time."

PART SIX

REIGN OF SHADOWS

CHAPTER TWENTY-ONE
THE RETURN

IT WAS NOT by accident that it began in Oxford.

The darkness that began to spread over the cities of Europe covered England first, then moved east.

The Allied forces had been assured that it was all according to some greater plan—but calls to the Chancellor went unanswered, and it was no comfort to them when they received reports that their enemies' strongholds were also being plunged into darkness.

It had been unsettling enough to receive the strange reports of ships manned by children that appeared and disappeared, mounting raids against friend and foe alike before disappearing into the mists. But this strange darkness was worse, because it had been foretold. It was worse because it was darkness with form, and with purpose.

One by one, the cities of the world were made dark by the shadows of the Dragons.

Hank Morgan watched numbly as the shadows covered Oxford, then London, and Paris, and Berlin, and Cairo, and Amsterdam, and Tokyo, and Rome, and on and on.

He returned to the Kilns in Oxford and looked around at the tumbledown wreck the cottage had become in the last seven years.

Reaching behind a cupboard, he retrieved a hidden Trump and quickly began to sketch in the details of a destination he'd been told never to draw.

A few moments later he stepped through the card to Tamerlane House.

With Quixote and Archimedes' help, Madoc soon had the forge glowing hot. He had several rough but still incredibly inventive tools, which could be attached to his hook for a multitude of uses. Once the coals were turning white with the heat, he waved off the knight and the owl and went to work.

Rose watched from the sand not far away, while Professor Sigurdsson was content to sit in the boat and read. "It's John's book, you know," he said in explanation. "I'd like to finish it before the trip is over."

Rose knew what he was avoiding saying, and she resented slightly that he was not more direct—but at the same time, she was a little bit grateful for the lie.

Quixote quickly realized that the work Madoc was doing was far beyond his own experience, and he wisely kept his distance. But Archimedes was a different story. The sword, and its original creation, were not so far removed from his own time, and from the culture that had created him.

He offered a word of advice now and again, and eventually Madoc offered him a modified apron to wear to protect him from the showering of sparks, and Archie took an active role in restoring the sword.

Rose watched this in wonderment. Archie had been Madoc's teacher before he was hers. He had been present when her mother fled Alexandria, during the first betrayal. And now, here he was, centuries later, helping Madoc to create the weapon that would destroy a piece of himself.

Archimedes did not judge him, and was no more or less critical than he was with anyone else. *Is that because he's mechanical, and not truly alive,* she wondered, *or is there something more? Is it perhaps because he knew Madoc before he was Mordred, before the betrayals—and is helping the man he was, not the man he is?*

Is there a difference? And is the difference in the man I see, or in how I choose to see him?

She also looked back at the professor, reading in the *Scarlet Dragon*, and wondered what had motivated *him*. This trip would very likely cost him his existence—an existence that was essentially a second chance at life. But he had risked it to seek out the very man who had killed him, to ask for his help. Why? How could he have believed it was even possible? And yet there Madoc was, doing the very thing they needed the most.

Rose suspected she knew what her uncle John would say if he were here: *This is what it means to grow up, to learn why we do the things we do and make the choices we make. It just comes down to how much you believe in something, and doing it, and not worrying about the outcome.*

Come to think of it, she reconsidered, that was more along the lines of what her uncle Jack would say.

Madoc worked for one hour, then two, then four. The sweat was pouring off him in rivulets, and his arms had gone brown with the heat.

Again and again he flipped the sword with the tongs and

hammered away at it as if possessed. Slowly, ever so carefully, the pieces of the sword began to coalesce into a whole again.

Finally he swung the hammer high over his head and struck the last blow.

Tossing the tongs to Archimedes, he dropped the hammer in the sand and walked over to the water's edge.

He stood there for a long moment, examining the glowing red metal. Then he bowed his head. "Thank you, Nimue. Forgive . . ."

Madoc knelt and plunged the sword into the water.

A cloud of steam issued up and enveloped him, and for a moment he was completely enshrouded in the whiteness. But then it evaporated, and he rose to his feet.

Madoc turned around to face the others. In his hand, he held the gleaming black sword Caliburn.

He clenched his jaw. "This is what I wanted," he said numbly. "This is what I fought for, what I . . .

"Here." He flipped the blade around to offer the hilt to Rose. "Take it. I no longer want it—not when I know what it's already cost me, and everyone else who has touched it. Take it."

But Rose merely stood there with her hands at her side.

"You have the sword Caliburn in your hand," she said. "You have a Dragonship. You could return and take the throne if you wish. You could defeat your own Shadow easily—and then you would be master of the world."

Archimedes let out a squawk, and Quixote stared at the girl in astonishment. Was she suddenly insane?

Madoc met her eyes, trying to read what he saw there. She was inscrutable, and worse, there was no guile in her. She was really offering him the sword and the ship.

"Madre de dios," Quixote muttered.

"Choose," said Rose.

"I shattered this sword the first time," Madoc told her evenly, "because I truly believed that was my destiny. I return it to you now, whole and unbroken, because I know that it is not."

"That," Rose said as she took the sword from his hand, "is why you were able to hold it at all. And that, if nothing else, means there is worth in you still."

Quixote raised his eyes heavenward in a silent prayer, then held his hand out to Madoc. "Thank you."

Madoc looked down at the outstretched hand, then turned his back to the companions and strode over to the forge to start breaking it down.

"What if you need to use it for something else?" said Archimedes. "Shouldn't you leave it be?"

"I won't use it again," Madoc said as he continued his dismantling effort. "Once you've repaired the sword of Aeneas and Arthur, everything else is just metal."

It took only a few minutes for Rose, Quixote, Archie, and the professor to ready the *Scarlet Dragon* for the return voyage home. They wrapped the sword in an oilcloth and secured it under a crossbeam in the prow. Then they went to say good-bye to Madoc.

He had finished dismantling the forge and had strewn the pieces all across the beach. He was standing with his back to them, forty or fifty yards away—far enough that he couldn't feel them behind him as they prepared to leave, but not so far that the echoing properties of the wall wouldn't conduct their farewells.

"Thank you, Madoc," said Archie. "Farewell."

"I am grateful to you," said Quixote, "and we shall not forget our promise."

"I forgive you," said the professor. "This visit has been far more enjoyable than the last time we met."

"Good-bye, Madoc," said Rose. "Good-bye, Father."

Madoc did not turn around, nor acknowledge that he had heard them.

The four companions boarded the *Scarlet Dragon* and inflated the balloon. In seconds it was aloft and pointed east.

The *Scarlet Dragon* flew rather than sailed, because on this trip there was nothing to search for but the horizon. The little ship sped along through the gloom and mist as quickly as they could compel it to go.

It was difficult to estimate time or distance, because there was no real day or night here—it was all varying degrees of light and dark.

Every so often, one of them would glance over at the bundle under the cross-brace, as if to reassure themselves that they had really done it, that the sword was there, and whole. Once Rose offered to unwrap it, but Quixote placed his hands on hers and shook his head.

"It is not a frivolous thing, to be displayed for our amusement or comfort," he said. "You will know when the time is right, and you will hold it as it is meant to be held."

"Also," said Archimedes, "you might drop it over the edge. And that would be a bad, bad thing."

"We don't want to spoil the trip now, do we?" said Professor Sigurdsson.

"Professor," Rose began to ask—but she could not find the words to finish the question. It didn't matter. He knew what she wanted to know, and his answer was that he refused to turn and look at her.

"Faster," Rose whispered to the *Scarlet Dragon*. "We must go faster."

It was difficult to tell, there in the twilight of the place past the Edge of the World, if the ship was flying any faster because of her prompting, but she felt it was, and that gave her hope.

Their altitude was such that they could not see the waters below, and had no way of knowing if they had passed most or all of the islands. Their only hope was an eastward course—and speed.

The professor fell.

He did not faint, but suddenly his legs would not hold him upright in the boat any longer.

Rose and Quixote knelt next to him and sat him upright. "Are you all right, Professor?" Rose asked. But she could read the answer on his face. He was pale—but not from exertion or anemia. He was beginning to become slightly transparent. Ethereal.

He was starting to fade.

"No, no, no, no," Rose said, squeezing his hand. "We're almost there, Professor! You have to hold on!"

He tried to stand, but it was too difficult, and he slumped back down. "Here," Quixote said, folding the professor's coat into a pillow. "Lie down a moment. Gather your strength."

"I fear my strength has all but left me, Don Quixote," said the professor. "I just wish it wasn't so dark out here. I suppose it's all right for the Dragons, but I really prefer the sunshine."

"Really, Professor?" Rose asked, anxious to keep him talking. "Tell us about it."

"It was among my greatest joys of living," Professor Sigurdsson said weakly. "That may sound odd for someone who lived in London, but in my youth, I often traveled to sunnier climes. I had just hoped, when my time finally came, that I would be able to expire in some golden field somewhere."

"There is such a place," Quixote said quietly. "I have seen it, and it is the most wonderful place. There is indeed a golden meadow, the most glorious you can imagine, filled with grasses and flowers that cover every inch of earth. And just beyond is a castle made of crystal, where the great heroes of history may go when they have earned their final rest.

"I am certain," he went on, laying a hand on the professor's forehead, "that there is a place there for you, my noble friend. And there are three beautiful women who watch over the heroes, so that if any have lost their way, they can help them find the road to Paradise."

Tears filled Rose's eyes, and they ran down her cheeks and dripped onto the professor's face. "Don't worry, my dear," he said, consoling her. "Things have happened the way they were meant to. I got to see my dear friends one last time. I was able to make peace with the man who murdered me. And I got to be a hero one final time. There is nothing more I could have asked or expected in this world or any other, and truly, I am content."

"A light!" Archimedes shrieked. "I see a light!"

The companions looked past the prow of the ship to see what had gotten the owl so excited—and then they became excited themselves. There was indeed a light.

The edge of the waterfall was in sight.

Rising swiftly out of the darkness, the light that spilled over from the Archipelago created an artificial horizon—but it was still distressingly far away.

"We're going to make it, Professor," Rose said, gripping his hand. "I know it."

But he shook his head, and touched her cheek. "My dear, we might—just might—make it to the surface again, but it will be too long a journey back to the Nameless Isles for me to survive. You must accept this."

She bit her lip and nodded, then hugged the old man tightly, for she knew it would be her last opportunity to do so.

"Is there anything I might do?" Quixote asked.

"Just one thing," the professor answered. His voice was little more than a whisper now. "I don't want to go while I'm lying here on my back. Will you help me to stand?"

"Of course, my friend."

Together, Quixote and Rose lifted Professor Sigurdsson up until he was on his feet, but he was already too weak.

"It's all right," he said, slumping in their arms. "I can meet my fate sitting."

"You shall not!" said Quixote. "Not while I am with you. By God, you will stand!"

The knight stood next to the professor and pulled his arm around his own shoulders. "I will be your legs," Quixote said. "I shall be your strength."

"The light!" Archimedes called. "We're almost high enough!"

Rose threw aside the parachute to lighten the ship and wring out every ounce of speed. "We're nearly there, professor!" she exclaimed. "You're almost home!"

"So nice," the professor murmured as the first rays of light struck his face. "I can almost see that meadow, Quixote."

"As I knew you would, my friend," the knight said through his own tears. "You will never be in darkness again, only in the light of a glorious, endless day, where every sleep is brief, and at every waking you shall rise up to meet the sun."

The light swept over the little craft as the professor's eyes closed, and his body began to shimmer and fade. In moments he had burst into an explosion of light and joy, and tears, and then he was gone.

There was no time to mourn the loss of the professor. The *Scarlet Dragon* had reached the limits of its endurance, but a respite was within reach, if they could only reach the water past the falls.

The wind-battered Dragonship rose to the crest of the immense waterfall and edged its way over, just barely skimming above the surface. They made it several yards in before the ship started to flounder—but the current was still an immediate danger.

Off to the left, not a mile away, was the island of Terminus.

"There!" Rose exclaimed excitedly. "If we can make it to the island, we may be able to repair the ship!"

Quixote was doubtful that anything could salvage the *Scarlet Dragon,* which had been pushed well past its limits, but after all they had endured with the journey down to find Madoc, and the terrible sacrifice made by Professor Sigurdsson, he was not about to dampen the girl's unflagging spirits.

"We'll make it," he said encouragingly. "Upon my word as a knight, we'll make landfall, my dear, dear girl!"

The knight grabbed the tattered remnants of the balloon and wrapped a rope around the tears. "Ho, Archimedes!" he called out over the roar of the falls. "Take one of the starboard lines and give us a pull!"

Between the port propeller, which was functional but sputtering badly, and the strength of the clockwork owl, the ship skipped slowly across the surface of the water. When it dipped too low, the tremendous current yanked the boat downward, but Archie and Quixote resolved to hold their course. In a matter of minutes, the little craft settled safely onto the sandy beach that lined the southern shore of Terminus, and the balloon finally deflated completely.

Rose and Quixote staggered from the boat and collapsed among the sand and grass. Archie joined them, for once too drained to go circling about.

Rose propped herself up on one elbow. "We can't rest here too long," she told her companions. "We have to find a way to repair the *Scarlet Dragon*. Everything depends on our getting the sword to the king."

"But how, my lady?" Quixote asked without raising his head. "There is nothing on this island but grass, and rocks, and a gravestone."

"Not quite," a voice said from over the low hill behind them. "There's also a friend, who is very, very happy to see you here safe and sound."

Rose and Quixote sat up in astonishment, and Archie let out a squawk of happiness. Just coming over the rise of the hill toward them was a man they had not expected, but were not surprised to see.

"'Believing is seeing,'" said Ransom.

"'Believe,'" answered Rose. "It's wonderful to see you, Mr. Ransom."

"As I told your uncle Jack, dear girl," Ransom admonished, "call me Alvin."

Ransom had with him a small store of food and water, and had even remembered to bring a wind-up mouse for Archie, so the four friends sat down and had an impromptu dinner, while Rose and Quixote took turns telling Ransom about the journey over the waterfall.

His face grew dark when they related what had befallen Professor Sigurdsson.

"He is one I would have liked to know better," Ransom said after offering his condolences. "I have heard great things about him, especially tales of his younger days. He was renowned as an archaeologist and had many adventures even before he was recruited as a Caretaker."

"He did as he told us he would," Quixote said, "and he paid the price he knew must be paid. Now it is for us to make certain it was not a sacrifice made in vain."

"How is it you're here on Terminus, Mr.—Alvin?" asked Rose. "It is, after all, the last place in the entire Archipelago where anyone might go."

"I found my way to the elusive Inn at the World's End," Ransom said as a broad smile spread across his face, "so I was able to sneak in a drink or two before coming here to wait for you. The passage through the Trump requires quite a leap of faith, and when I did get there, I found the place packed. Some sort of metaphysical funeral was going on outside. I asked the innkeeper, and all he would say was that a dream had died. Odd, but a nice tavern nevertheless."

"You came here for us?" Rose exclaimed. "Why? How did you know?"

"There are friends and allies waiting for you all along the edge of the falls," said Ransom, pointing to the water's edge. "Every vessel that wasn't commandeered into battle with the Shadow King. Boats, bottles, bathtubs—whatever would float. I'm not a fan of boats myself, so I elected to wait for you here—where they'd have brought you anyway."

"But why?" Rose repeated.

"In case your quest succeeded," replied Ransom. "We needed a way to get you to the heart of the war as quickly as possible. And since it's partly my fault all this happened, I volunteered to be the one to take you back." He paused. "You were successful, I take it?"

"Oh!" said Rose. "We forgot to show you!" She bounded over to the *Scarlet Dragon* and pulled out the sword, which was still wrapped tightly in the oilcloth.

Reverently she unwrapped it and held it up to the light. The black sword was gleaming and unbroken.

Ransom whistled in appreciation. "Now that's a sword. Let's get you back to Tamerlane House. There's no time to lose."

"Back?" Quixote said, scanning the beach. "Did you bring one of the Dragonships?"

"Better," said Ransom. He opened up his jacket and removed the Trumps. "Remember the ones I reserved in case of an emergency? Well, if the End of the World doesn't qualify, I don't know what does."

At that moment several voices called out to them from the water, and they turned to see a flotilla of small boats and rafts converging on the beach. They were occupied by fauns, and a few badgers, and several old men and young boys from the various islands. All those who were not able to fight in a battle had come here to risk their lives anyway, to be of service to the one who could bring hope to the Archipelago. The hopeful and anxious looks on their faces said everything the companions needed to know.

"Show them," said Ransom. "Show them what it looks like when a hope is fulfilled and a dream comes true."

Rose stood and slowly held the sword high over her head. The response was a wave of cheering and sobbing and chanting of her name. Everyone in the boats was filled with excitement and joy—and, as Ransom had said, hope.

"If you've recovered enough of your strength," said Ransom, "we need to get going. There are a great many people waiting for you back in the Nameless Isles."

"I thought you weren't supposed to create a drawing of the islands there, to keep it a secret?" said Rose.

"All the secrets are out," said Ransom, "and all the cards are on the table except one—and that's you. If this doesn't work, there won't be any place left to keep a secret."

"Is it really that dire?" asked Quixote.

"It is," said Ransom. "But look at all those out there, in the boats. They believed, and here you are. Others believe in you too."

"And believing is seeing," said Rose.

"That's the grand thing about dreams," Ransom said as he held the card up to the light. "Some may eventually pass on, but there's always another one to take its place."

CHAPTER TWENTY-TWO

PAX TERRA

"SO THE ENDGAME has begun," said Twain. "The Shadow King is making his move to conquer the Summer Country."

"I believe so, yes," Hank Morgan said, nodding. "Otherwise, I wouldn't have taken the risk of crossing directly here."

"It was a flaunting of the rules," said Spenser.

"Says the man sitting next to *Richard Burton*," Morgan shot back.

"The boy has a point," said Burton.

"It was the right call," said John, "and Ransom will hopefully soon be putting the Trump to even better use. But the question remains as to what we should do now. We can't possibly fight a war on two fronts, in two worlds."

"Maybe we can," said Artus.

"What do you mean?" asked John.

Artus held up the horn Samaranth had given him. "It still has one call in it, remember? What if I used it to call the Dragons? Do you think they'd come?"

"I don't think it would help," said John. "Remember those whose shadows became Shadow-Born? They were little more than wraiths, drained of life. I think the Dragons might be the same."

"It's worth a try, isn't it?" asked Twain. "If the dragons have any strength at all, it's only a blessing to our side."

"Actually, that wasn't what I was thinking at all," said Artus. "I've already given up the Dragons for lost. But I think they—or at least, their shadows—might still be summoned by the horn."

"Forgive me if I missed something," said Hawthorne, "but aren't they under our adversary's control?"

Burton chuckled. "That's exactly his point, you idiot."

"Burton's right," John said, looking at Artus with admiration. "I think it might work, Artus."

"What might, John?" asked Jack.

"The Horn of Bran Galed will summon the Dragon shadows—and draw them all away from the Summer Country," said John. "It might make our job harder here, but at least for the moment, it would spare the rest of the world."

The Caretakers looked at one another, then nodded their agreement, and the King of the Silver Throne walked outside, put the horn to his lips, and blew.

The note was clear and pure, and took long moments to fade.

"What happens now?" asked Jack.

"We wait," said Artus. "The last time, I—"

Suddenly, without warning, the skies went dark all around the Nameless Isles.

Swirling up like an impenetrable fog, the darkness rose on all sides, leaving only a small circlet of open sky above the ring of islands.

"Is it an eclipse?" Nemo asked.

"I wish it were," said Jack through clenched jaws. "Do you see what I'm seeing, Charys?"

The centaur nodded grimly. "I fear there is no way to strategize, no way to rally for opposition like this," he said, wheeling about. "All we can hope for is a quick, noble death."

"What is it?" Nemo asked as Charys trotted away to organize the captains of the Dragonships. "What are you both so afraid of?"

"That's not just darkness," Jack said. "It's *shadow*. And it's not just any shadow. It's the shadows of the *Dragons*."

"What can we do?"

"We fight as long as we can," Jack said, "and pray for a miracle."

"Why hasn't the darkness covered the sky completely?" John said. "Why haven't the Shadows simply fallen down and overwhelmed us?"

"It's why I built Tamerlane House here," said Poe. "This grouping of islands is among the oldest lands on the Earth, or hadn't you noticed? They form a giant Ring of Power. The original rings were built by the giants—but they modeled them after this place. The shadows cannot come in, but neither can we leave."

"And in the meantime, the armies of the Shadow King will sweep through and devastate us," said Charles. "Wonderful."

"We have our own armies," said John, "and I have faith in them. We just need to hold out until Rose can return with the sword."

Burton laughed. "Do you really believe that that's going to help?"

"You've chosen your side, Richard, whether or not we've accepted you back," said Twain. "Our fate is now yours—so if you have something useful to contribute, now's the time."

"I'll tell you what I can," said Burton, "although it may be too late. He is bringing an army you cannot fight."

"Cannot defeat?" said Charles.

"No," said Burton. "Cannot *fight*."

"Shadow-Born?"

"No. He took the cauldron only so that it could not be used against him," said Burton. "The Spear of Destiny is more compelling, and easier to use. All he need do is speak one's True Name, and bind them, then he can take the shadows with the spear. Using the doors of the keep, we could catch the Dragons unawares, and with the shadows of the Dragons, he has no need of anyone else's."

"But if the Dragon shadows cannot cross into the Nameless Isles," said John, "then it's a stalemate."

"Aren't you listening?" Burton exclaimed, pounding his fist on the table. "Stupid little Caretaker. Years ago I warned you, and still your vision is too small.

"Once you have been defeated, his conquest of the Archipelago will be complete, and the shadows of the Dragons will sweep across the Frontier and back into the Summer Country. But he won't need them to defeat you, because he has an army you cannot fight."

"The only enemy a man cannot defeat by combat is himself," said Shakespeare.

"Finally the idiot savant speaks wise," said Burton.

"What are you talking about?" said John.

"This," Burton said, rising to his feet. He strode to a curtain and threw open the shutters. "Look and see for yourselves. Your enemies have arrived."

The Caretakers crowded around the windows and looked in the direction Burton was pointing.

A Time Storm was forming out over the water. The clouds roiled about, flashing with lighting, as seven shapes emerged and entered the Nameless Isles.

"Oh, no," John whispered. "It isn't possible."

"I've been waiting for them all these years," said Burton. "I'm surprised you haven't been."

Out on the edge of the harbor, in front of the defensive line of Dragonships, seven more ships drew up close and stopped.

They weren't just ships—they were the Dragonships *themselves,* brought out of the past by the Shadow King and led by a fourteen-year-old Stephen and the half-clockwork sons of Jason of myth.

"And thus is the history fulfilled," Bert murmured. "If Stellan and the others don't return soon, this is truly the end for us all."

On the large, outermost of the Nameless Isles, Artus despaired.

"Are those what I think they are?" he said grimly.

"Yes," Jack said, stunned. "Those are the ships we saw in the Underneath, and attacking Kor! But how could he do this? How did he bring them here?"

"It doesn't matter," said Artus, summoning Laura Glue and the Valkyries. "We can't fight them. They are our own children. The best we can do is try to hold them back long enough for—"

"I know," said Jack.

"Spread the word," Artus told Laura Glue. "All ships to the air, where they cannot follow us. And those of us on the ground should be instructed: defense only. No child is to be harmed, if we can help it. They are being compelled, and their wills are not their own."

"Consider this," Jack said as Laura Glue sped off. "When they returned to us during the conflict in the Underneath, after being pulled away in Time, they were battered and bruised, but unharmed. This was when they were pulled *to*. Things may yet turn out in our favor."

"Or it means that they wiped us out here," said Artus. "Whatever happens, we'll hold them, won't we Jack?"

"We will," Jack said, gripping his friend's shoulder.

There was a stirring of a westward breeze in the Pygmalion Gallery, and Rose, Archimedes, Quixote, and Ransom stepped through the portal from Terminus.

"What must we do now?" asked Rose.

Ransom went to the window and looked up at the sky.

"I just pray we haven't come too late," he said. "The Shadow King is here."

"Archie," Rose said. "Get to Bert and the Caretakers, right away! They need to know about Defoe!"

Obediently, Archimedes flew from the room.

"We have to go outside," Rose said to Quixote. "I don't know what's to be done, but we need to get to the king or queen."

"According to the Prophecy," said Ransom, "the sword is for you to use."

"It never occurred to me to ask," said Quixote. "Do you even know how to use a sword?"

"The one good thing about British boarding schools," Rose said as they left the gallery, "is that the better ones all teach fencing. And I wouldn't be my grandfather's heir if I hadn't taken first place in the competition."

"John!" Hawthorne shouted from down the corridor outside the conservatory. "Come quickly! Hurry!"

John and several other Caretakers rushed out to see what the matter was. It was Jakob Grimm. Hawthorne was half carrying, half dragging him down the hall, trailing blood.

"It's how they found us!" Hawthorne said as they pushed open a door to one of the spare rooms. "They took Jakob's map off his back!"

"I'm sorry!" Jakob cried through the tears and mucus running down his face. "I didn't want to bring them! I fought it, as hard as I could! But then they took what they wanted anyway, and it's all for nothing!"

"What is, Jakob?" asked John, getting his arm under the poor man's shoulder to help Hawthorne place him on a settee. "What's for nothing?"

"The Shadow King promised," Jakob sobbed. "He said if I cooperated, he would let my brother live. And I resisted!"

"If he promised something like that," said Chaucer, "then I suspect your brother is already dead."

Jakob collapsed in a heap of shuddering sobs as the Caretakers and several of the ravens began tending to his terrible wound.

"Grimalkin and I found him in one of the upper rooms," Hawthorne said, looking appreciatively at the Cheshire cat that had appeared at their feet. "Somehow, a spy is still among us."

"How are they getting in?" John asked, pounding a wall in frustration. "We've sealed off the gallery and posted guards at both ends. Is it possible there is another Trump hidden inside the house somewhere?"

"Doubtful," said Twain. "There are very few of those sheets unaccounted for, and even fewer people trained in making them. So unless you know someone with a magic box that people can just pop in and out of, I'm at a loss."

"Magic box!" John exclaimed, snapping his fingers. "You're a genius, Samuel!"

"Was there ever a doubt?" Twain called out as John tore from the room. He looked down at Grimalkin, who was missing his torso. "What did I say?"

John burst through the doors of the conservatory. "Jamie!" he said, panting from exertion. "When you died, who handled your estate?"

"My boys, of course," Jamie replied. "Why?"

"For your personal belongings, certainly," said John, "but what about items relating to the Archipelago?"

Jamie shrugged. "I had practically nothing left there in London," he said. "Only a few papers, and the old wardrobe—and I left those to you, Jack, and Charles."

"That's what I was afraid of," said John. "Because we jumped forward in time by going through the Trump, we weren't there to claim anything."

"But the wardrobe is still useless without the second one," said Jamie, "and it's—"

"Safely in Paralon?" John finished. "Under the control of the Senate, and the new Chancellor?"

"Oh, my stars and garters," said Jamie.

At that moment, Archimedes flew into the room.

"Archie!" John exclaimed in shock. "You've come back! Is the professor—"

"No time, no time!" the owl squawked. "I know who the traitor is!"

Quickly Archimedes related to the Caretakers what he had

learned from Captain Johnson, and as he spoke, they became more and more resolved.

"We must talk to Poe," John said. "Right away!"

The new Dragonships commandeered by the children pulled onto the beach, and the spellbound young warriors began to pour from the holds.

"There are thousands of them!" Charys cried. "How can we do this? How do we fight children?"

"We don't," said Jack, looking quickly around the island. "There!" He pointed behind them to one of the cliffs. "They can't hurt us, and we won't have to hurt them if we reduce the size of the target."

The other allies on the ground quickly realized what Jack was referring to, and under the cover of the airships, they swiftly retreated to a narrow isthmus between the cliffs. As Jack had hoped, the masses of children followed.

Once on the other side, the allies would only have to deal with a narrow trickling of the children, rather than all at once.

"How did you learn to do that?" an astonished Nemo asked.

Jack grinned. "*You* taught me how to do that," he said. "About a quarter century ago."

"We'll still have to fight them," said Charys. "It's unavoidable."

"Not completely," said Jack. "Artus! It's time for your secret weapon!"

Artus nodded and grinned, then he signaled to the Elves. They lowered the *Blue Dragon*'s enormous bulk and opened the hold.

The Tin Man jumped out with surprising agility, and without

any instruction, he rushed forward to the narrow pass. Between his bulk, and the gentle sweeps of his ax, he managed to effectively block the advance of the children.

Many stopped, but those who pressed forward received only bruises, and the worst injuries were broken bones.

"That's incredible!" Nemo declared. "You're winning the battle without having to fight!"

"Not winning," said Jack. "Delaying. That may be the best we can do."

"That is the least you can do," said a chilling voice beside them. Jack and the others spun around in time to see Kipling and the Shadow King step out of a Trump portal and onto the hilltop. Kipling held a sword, and the Shadow King carried the Spear of Destiny.

"Get into the airship," Artus said to Nemo and Jack as he stepped forward and drew his sword. "Protect Aven."

"We're not leaving you," Jack began.

"I know that!" said Artus. "But we have to hold on! I believe! Do you?"

"Yes," said Jack, as he eyed Kipling. "I believe." But he didn't climb into the ship, and neither did Nemo or Stephen.

"Stay clear of his reach," Jack warned. "He has the spear, and we don't have anything that can defeat it. Not yet. All we can do is try to hold him off," he finished grimly, with a silent prayer.

"Come, let us reason together," said Artus.

"No reasoning, no discussion," said the Shadow King. He glanced up at the Dragon shadows circling overhead and smirked. "You may have delayed my plans for the Summer Country, but that is all you have done—delay. There is nothing to discuss but your defeat. And you have nothing that can overpower my spear."

"I don't have to defeat you myself," said Artus. "I just have to hold you back long enough for Rose to get here, to do what she's destined to do."

"I've read your Prophecy," the Shadow King hissed, "and it means nothing to me."

"It means something to *him*," said Kipling, "and you shouldn't underestimate that."

"Kill him," the Shadow King said. "Kill him now."

"You know," Kipling remarked, "I really don't think I'm going to be able to do that."

The Shadow King looked at him in confused fury. "What about that order didn't you understand?" he shouted. "Kill him!"

"What about my refusal didn't you understand?" said Kipling. "I'm not a violent man, and I detest war." He dropped the sword to the grass. "I quit."

"You forget what I promised you, Caretaker," the Shadow King said as he touched a contact on his chest and a circlet of mist began to swirl behind him. "You forget what I can do, whom I can return to you."

Kipling paused, and started to look back. In the swirl of mist, a face began to appear—a young man, a soldier.

Kipling steeled himself and bit his lip. "I haven't forgotten. I've just managed to keep the things that are truly right ahead of the things that I want for myself."

"Your son, Kipling—"

"Is dead."

With a snarl, the Shadow King released the contact, and the young soldier vanished.

Kipling walked around the reach of the Shadow King and stood behind Jack. "Greetings, Caretaker."

"I don't understand," Jack hissed, "but I won't argue with your choice."

"I see," said the Shadow King. "There are more traitors than I knew, here in the Nameless Isles."

"Not traitors," Artus said, turning to smile at Kipling, "just friends. And that's how I know we're going to win."

"You won't," the Shadow King replied. With a single motion, he thrust the Spear of Destiny through Artus's heart before anyone could cry out a warning. "I'm not going to take your shadow, boy," he rasped. "I'm just going to end your life."

"Ah, me," Artus said, looking down at the spear sticking out of his chest. "Aven, I—"

The King of the Silver Throne dropped to his knees, then fell over on his side, dead.

When Defoe stepped out of the wardrobe secreted away in the uppermost room at Tamerlane House, a contingent of Caretakers was there to greet him.

"Well, this is a fine how-do-you-do," he said, "to borrow a phrase. How in Hades did you find me out?"

"Traitors are themselves easily betrayed," Poe said softly. "Friends may quarrel, and the bond may remain unbroken. But a traitor can have no friends who will not eventually side against him."

"I can see that," said Defoe. "You welcomed Burton into your midst easily enough."

"Don't take my name in vain, Daniel," Burton said as he strode into the room. "I knew there were more moles about, but I thought you'd at least have been brave enough to be up-front about it."

"Says the original traitor," Defoe spat. "Physician, heal thyself."

"Oh, I'm feeling just fine," said Burton. "I finally realized that there was a price too high to pay to achieve my goals. It serves no one and nothing to seek after truth as an ally of evil."

"You got cold feet, you mean."

"I came to my senses," said Burton, "and you've let the Shadow King's hunger for power color your judgment."

"Chain it," Poe ordered, pointing at the wardrobe. "I'm guessing wherever the other one is, we'll find Houdini and Conan Doyle."

Defoe just glared at him.

"That's answer enough," said Poe. "We'll strand them, and retrieve them when this is finished."

"It'll be finished soon enough," snarled Defoe.

"I agree," said Poe. "It will."

"I'll take responsibility for the Detective and the Magician," said Burton. "They're my apprentices, not the Shadow King's. They'll be penitent enough, I think."

"You didn't bring them with you," said John. "Why?"

Burton grinned. "Self-preservation first. I *am* a barbarian, after all."

Suddenly Defoe ripped a mirror from the wall and smashed it against Archimedes, who'd been perched atop the wardrobe. The owl screetched and flapped his wings, scattering silvered glass all over the Caretakers. John shouted to Bert, and together they calmed down the bird, who was ruffled but unharmed—but the distraction had served its purpose. Defoe had disappeared down one of the endless hallways.

"Never mind," said Poe. "We've cut off his means of escape. We'll find him later."

"If Archimedes is here," said Bert, "does that mean Stellan and the others are too?"

"Not Stellan," said Poe, looking at his watch. "It's been too long."

"We must mourn later," Bert said, grabbing John's shoulders. "We have to find Rose!"

"I agree. I've had enough of debate," said John. "We're going out to join the battle."

The Tin Man, staunch as he was, was being overrun.

The masses of children were finally proving too much, so others of the allies, still under the instruction to delay and not harm, tried to aid his efforts.

The Valkyries were the most effective of the allies' forces, because they were more mobile and flexible than any of the other groups. But they were also the most vulnerable, because they couldn't wear armor and still fly—and any blow that could knock them out meant a fall to the death, unless one of their companions caught them.

The warrior children started hurling stones with slings when they realized their closest enemies were airborne. Sadie Pepperpot had taken a terrible blow to her shoulder, and her left arm was hanging nearly useless at her side. Several others were also injured.

The Tin Man started to pull back, and the others realized that combat with the children might be inevitable.

Stephen cried out when the Shadow King had speared Artus, and he rushed forward, but Jack held him back.

"Look!" Jack cried out. "There! Down the hill!"

The companions, keeping one eye on the Shadow King, edged away from him and risked a glance to where Jack was pointing.

It was Ransom, Quixote, and Rose. And she was holding Caliburn. The sword was whole again.

On the opposite side of the beach, John and Bert had landed and were coming forward at the same time.

Across the bottom of the cliffs, Charles was leading Charys, Falladay Finn, and Eledir to where the fallen king lay in the grass. And Aven leaped down from her airship to stand next to her son.

"Now we're going to finish this," Aven said, drawing her sword. "You can't take all of us, demon."

"I don't need to," said the Shadow King, indicating the children in the pass. "They can."

His words were confident, but the companions noticed that he had not taken his eyes off Rose—and the sword.

"We're going to get him," Stephen called up to Laura Glue, reaching for her. "Can you give us a little more time?"

"We'll keep them off you as long as we can," gasped Laura Glue, swooping down to take his hand.

"Thank you," Stephen said. He gripped her hand tightly for a moment, as words unspoken passed between them in a long, lingering glance. Then she pulled free and rose into the air like a shot.

"Valkyries! To me!" she called out with a loud, trilling battle call. "Norah! Sadie! Abby Tornado!" The Valkyries, aided by the centaurs Charys had summoned, were holding the pass, if barely.

Rose and Quixote reached the top of the hill.

"I don't believe it!" said Charles. "You did it!"

"It's a fraud," the Shadow King hissed. "This is your last chance to surrender."

"No," said John, as he and Bert topped the hill, "it's *yours*."

Rose looked at Artus's fallen body and winced. Then she looked up at Stephen and offered him the sword.

"You brought it back," Stephen replied. "It's yours to wield, just as the Prophecy said."

"There is no Prophecy!" the Shadow King said as he took another step back. "I don't believe!"

Rose drew the blade across the palm of her hand, leaving Caliburn's edge slick with her blood.

The winds of the Time Storm suddenly increased and began to howl around the island, as high above, the shadows of the Dragons circled, waiting.

"What are you doing?" the Shadow King whispered, his voice full of menace. "What do you think you are doing, girl?"

"I'm fulfilling my destiny," she said. Her voice was barely audible over the howling winds. "I'm going to heal my family. I'm going to heal my father."

"I *am* your father!" the Shadow King spat. "Give me the sword! Give me Caliburn! It is mine! It always was!"

"You are *not* my father," Rose said calmly. "You are the darkness in his soul, which he chose to set aside. You are the strength, which takes no responsibility, and the will, which has no desire but to consume. You are his spirit, and when you have joined with him once more, it will be his choice what kind of man he is. Now, and forever."

She leaped forward and pressed the tip of the sword against

the Shadow King's armor—right at the point where it curved into shadow.

The Shadow King froze in place. Caliburn had trapped him in the shell of the Red King.

"What are you doing, girl?" he screamed. "Stop! Stop this! Release me! I command you!"

"That's exactly what I intend to do," said Rose. "I'm going to release you, from everything." With both hands, she drew the sword across his chest, making a lopsided figure eight. The point of the sword never left his armor, and where it passed, it left a mark of blood.

"I Bind you, Shadow," she said softly, not caring if he or anyone else could hear. "With the mark I have chosen for myself, I Bind you."

Then, as the Shadow King continued to scream, she spoke the words:

Shadow of my father
By right and rule
For need of might
I thus bind thee
I thus bind thee
By blood bound
By honor given
I thus bind thee
I thus bind thee
For strength and speed and heaven's power
By ancient claim in this dark hour
I thus bind thee
I thus bind thee

Rose stepped back and lowered the black sword to her side. On the Shadow King's armor, the infinity symbol she had drawn glowed briefly with a blue fire, then faded.

"Let me see who's really in charge," said Rose. "Show yourself, King of the Shadows."

A tearing sound ripped across the hilltop as a thick, dark form pushed its way out of the Red King's body. It had no face, only roiling hatred that crackled in the air.

"That's good enough," she said, gripping the sword with both hands. "I just wanted you to see my face."

Rose swung the sword through the middle of the dark form, and it shattered apart, screaming, at the touch of Caliburn.

"Now," she said to Stephen, "avenge your father, as I've avenged mine."

"Gladly," Stephen said. He stepped forward as the Shadow King's body howled in dismay.

"I'm sorry!" the frozen king cried. "I—I didn't mean for all of this to happen!"

"Good or evil," Stephen said, clenching his jaw, "that's the first thing you've said that I really believe."

He swung the ax and cleanly lopped off the Shadow King's head.

A burst of sparks and flame shot out of the neck as the body dropped to its knees, then fell over onto its right side, unmoving. The head went spinning down the hill and bounced several times, before at last coming to rest against a petrified log.

The body had only its own shadow. The second shadow had been destroyed by the touch of Caliburn.

Charys approached the spot where the head had fallen and looked down. Nothing remained of the countenance of the Shadow

King—all that was left was the original clockwork once called the Red King.

"This is all very unorthodox," the head of the Red King said. "Is the Parliament out of session?"

"It is now," said Charys. He reared up with his forelegs and brought them smashing down onto the head, which exploded into gears and wheels and wires.

At that moment, all the Timelost Dragonships and the thousands of spellbound children crusaders, including young Stephen, vanished.

A cheer rose up from the hovering airships and the allies alike.

"The clockwork!" Bert said in amazement. "It was a giant Anabasis Machine, like the pocket watches! That's how he was able to manipulate the Time Storms to capture the children and the ships!"

"That machine is no more," Charys bellowed, "and I think all debts have been settled!"

"Not entirely," a voice called out from farther down the rise. "There are still other claims to be made, and I'm claiming the Archipelago as my own."

It was Defoe. And in his hands he held the Spear of Destiny.

He looked at John and smirked. "You should act more swiftly against those you discover to be your enemies."

"Don't be a fool, Daniel," said Bert. "You cannot do this!"

"I think I can, and I shall," said Defoe. "We've often searched for the means to make the Society dominant over the Caretakers, and I always believed it would be in the service of Mordred. But I realize now that it was my destiny all along to do it myself."

"Rose has Caliburn, Daniel," said John. "You're outmatched."

"Ah, I think not, young Caretaker," Defoe replied. "I have the shadows of the Dragons. And that makes me the victor, even before the battle is begun. You are trapped here in the Nameless Isles, and I get the rest of creation. That sounds like a fair exchange."

"Overconfidence was Mordred's downfall," said John. "It will be yours, too."

"It's hard to be overconfident when I control all the Dragons," said Defoe.

"Oh, I wouldn't say all of them," Bert noted, looking up. "You missed one, Daniel."

With a terrifying rush of speed and a sickening crunch, Samaranth dropped out of the sky and crushed Defoe beneath his feet.

"I learned my lesson about banishment last time," said Samaranth. "This is now done and done."

The battle was finally over.

"Why didn't the Shadow King go after you?" Jack asked the Dragon. "I'd have thought he would have made certain to get you first."

"He tried," said Samaranth, "but he could never find my True Name to bind me. His mistake was in believing it was in the book. It wasn't."

"Where is it?" asked Jack.

"That would be telling," said Samaranth.

"We saw something similar happen in the battle with Peter Pan," said Jack, referring to the destruction of the Shadow. "How is this time different?"

"Dissipated is different from destroyed," said Bert, "and silver pixie dust is different from the sword of the gods. The Shadow is gone. Forever."

"That begs an interesting question," said Charles. "The Shadow could not survive if the owner was dead—but what about the reverse? With his Shadow destroyed, what will happen to Madoc?"

But Bert didn't answer. He smiled grimly, then strode off to find Aven to move Artus's body. The king had been the only casualty.

Jack wondered if Bert hadn't answered his question because he couldn't . . .

. . . or because he *wouldn't*.

"Answer my question," said John. "Which side are you on?"

Kipling's only response was to reach into his breast pocket and pull out a silver pocket watch. A pocket watch with a red dragon on the cover.

"How did you get that?" John exclaimed. "Haven't you turned traitor?"

Kipling smiled. "I got it in the usual way, and no," he said blithely, "I have not become a traitor."

"The Shadow King had Defoe and poor Jakob in our camp," said Bert with a weary smile, "but we had Kipling in theirs."

"Don't worry, lad," Kipling said. "We'll explain it all to you by and by. Just know that everything's gone as it was supposed to go."

"Everything?" John said, looking at Artus's body, which they had moved to the deck of the *Blue Dragon*.

"Yes, John," Bert said sadly. "Everything."

John gestured skyward at the shadows. "The Shadow King created this terrible army, and he never even used it."

"He tried," said Kipling, "in the Summer Country. But we summoned them away, then defeated their master. We *won*, lad."

John smiled bitterly. "It just seems to have ended too quickly."

Kipling whirled around, eyes flashing. "Were you hoping for a bigger battle, John? A valiant, vain struggle against foes we could not possibly defeat? That would have made a very dramatic story—for anyone who survived to tell it. But can't it be enough that we won? That our enemy was beaten, and only Artus paid the ultimate price? You were a soldier once," he continued. "How many deaths did you have to witness to make you hate war?"

"One was enough."

Kipling nodded. "I lost my son, and my world changed. If a million more had died in grander battles, it would have made no difference to me—it was already more of a burden than I could bear.

"No," he finished, looking at the sky, "what great things we did today were done despite the terrible cost. But they would not have been made greater had the price we paid been more terrible still."

Kipling clapped John on the shoulder and turned away. "We don't always get the ending we hope for, lad," he called back, "but if we work hard enough to earn it, we sometimes get the ending we deserve."

"So my ancestor was your cousin, hundreds of years ago," Stephen said. "Does that make you my aunt?"

"That's probably as close as anything," said Rose, as she looked up at the still dark skies. "What do we do now?"

"How do we go about freeing the Dragons?" Jack asked Samaranth. "The Shadow King didn't create them the same way he did the Shadow-Born, so I'm guessing the cauldron is going to be of no help."

"You guess correctly. The Dragons are not creatures such as yourselves," Samaranth said slowly, his voice a low rumble. "They cannot be restored with a magic jar, as you did with the Shadow-Born. For a Dragon, its shadow is too intrinsically a part of its being to be severed. So when the Shadow King was cutting into them with the spear, he was not merely severing their shadows—he was ending their lives as Dragons upon this Earth. And he was only able to do that much because he knew their True Names.

"Rose can do nothing now but release the spirits that are left."

"They'll die?" said Rose. "I can't do that! I won't!"

"You must," Samaranth said sadly. "They cannot return to what they were. All we can do now is liberate them."

The Caretakers and the others on top of the hill circled around Rose in support, as she slowly realized that it was indeed her responsibility.

The sword suddenly felt a great deal heavier as she realized that in some way, she had known all along what she would be asked to do.

"All right," she said finally. "What must I do?"

"You know the words of Summoning," said Samaranth, "and this entire group of islands is a Ring of Power. Summon them here, and then you'll be able to release them."

It took a very long time.

CHAPTER TWENTY-THREE

JUSTICE AND MERCY

THE FUNERAL FOR Artus was small. Later, there could be a full ceremonial service on Paralon so that the entire Archipelago could mourn. But for now, only the three Caretakers and Bert, Aven and Stephen, Rose and Quixote, and the Dragon Samaranth were present as the king's body was lowered into the earth.

He was buried opposite the grave of Nemo, on Terminus. Both graves were within sight of the ring of stones.

"This is where he wanted to be buried," said Aven. "He said that this was the place where he grew up."

"I thought he'd always lived on Avalon," said Charles.

"Not that kind of 'grew up,'" said Jack. "This is where he stopped being a boy and became a man. It's where he became a king, when he summoned the Dragons."

"He fulfilled his destiny," said Aven. "He was the last king of the Archipelago, the last to sit upon the Silver Throne. And he honored his calling more than anyone could have imagined."

"The first time we met," said Samaranth, "he had a bucket on his head, a wooden sword, and a deep desire to become a great knight. I knew, even then, what his destiny was to be, and so I encouraged him the best that I was able."

"This may be an indelicate time to address this," said John, "but do I understand you correctly that Stephen will not be assuming his father's place on the Silver Throne?"

"The Silver Throne will be kept," said Stephen, "and I'll keep the title of king, if only to continue to manifest the changes my father began."

"It's going to make for a fragile peace," said Jack. "The races of the Archipelago are still as fractured as ever—and the first real unifying personage they've ever had turned out to be a despot. That'll be hard to overcome."

"A fragile peace is what we've always had," said Stephen. "I don't think it was any different with a republic than it was with a monarchy. Mother told me there was a Parliament of Kings guiding the lands before, and it really wasn't any more successful at preventing wars and conflicts than we've been these last decades."

"So what are you going to do?" John asked.

Stephen grinned and shrugged. "We're going to pick up the pieces and start all over again," he said wryly. "Just because we're terrible at making it work in practice doesn't mean the principles aren't still sound in theory. That's what my father believed, and it's the reason he sent away the Dragons in the first place. As long as we always had a fallback position, we were never truly committed to the battle."

"Can the Dragons be reunited with their shadows and made whole again?" asked John. "We're going to be returning to our proper time, before these events all took place. Is there a way to save all the Dragons whose shadows were taken as well?"

Samaranth looked away for a long while without answering, and when he finally did turn to face the companions, they were shocked by his expression. As long as they had known him, Samaranth had always appeared ancient. But this was the first time he had ever appeared . . . *old*.

"They are finally free—free of a choice I compelled them to make aeons ago. I believe they should remain so.

"The Dragonships remain ships, but they are no longer living and cannot cross the Frontier. They lost their lives when their shadows were taken. Those that may have escaped the Shadow King in the past will never return to this place, now or ever. And those lost cannot be restored.

"I am now in fact as well as name the last Dragon," said Samaranth, "and you are, as a race, now well and truly entirely on your own."

"Defoe survived?" John exclaimed when they returned to the Nameless Isles. "But we saw Samaranth crush him to death!"

"Correction," said Bert. "We saw Samaranth crush him. He was *already* dead. Now he's just a bit more disorganized and upset than usual. But no," he finished, sighing, "he didn't die."

"What's to be done with him, then?" asked John. "He's far too dangerous to just be released or banished. And I doubt anyone would consider making him the Green Knight. After Rose's report, and after what happened with Magwich, it'd be foolhardy in the extreme to release someone as willful and resourceful as Daniel Defoe."

"The Caretakers Emeritis have penalties of their own," said Bert. "I don't think there's any way he can escape what's planned for him."

"Fair enough," John said. "And what of Burton?"

"That's going to be a matter of some debate," Bert replied. "Poe for one believes him. We weren't exactly winning when he chose to defect—which lends credence to his claim that he and certain other members of the Imperial Cartological Society did indeed have goals more noble than world domination."

"Pull the other one," said John.

"Don't ascribe to evil what can be attributed to well-intentioned stupidity, John," Bert cautioned. "Burton caused more damage than Defoe, but at the end, he wouldn't betray his ideals. For Defoe, the cause was just a means to an end, which was to gain power over others. That made him a stronger ally for the Shadow King, and a weaker man than Burton. But rest assured—everyone pays a price for the choices they make, no matter what their reasons were."

"Burned alive?" Charles exclaimed. "That's a terrible way to go, even for Maggot—er, Magwich. I can't say I'm sorry that . . ." He paused. "Oh, curse it all." He sighed deeply. "As despicable as he was, there was something I *did* like about Magwich. Maybe it was his constancy."

"His constant whining, his constant lying, his constant cowardice," said Jack. "Is that what you mean?"

"Pretty much, yes," said Charles. "There was less pretense about him than almost anyone I've ever known. I think I might even learn to miss the old bugger."

"I can't believe you just said that," Jack said.

"I'm a bit surprised myself," said Charles.

"Then you may find this cheering," said Eledir, the Elf King. He approached the companions and handed a small bag to

Charles. It was filled with soil and tied around a small, slightly charred plant.

It had only three offshoots, and the leaves had only just begun to bud. In the center, at the top, was a curiously shaped bulb.

"Several of my captains discovered this as we were sweeping the field," Eledir said. "I meant to give it to Samaranth, but I overheard your discussion, and I think it more appropriate that you have it."

"Well, uh, thank you," Charles stammered.

The King of the Elves gave the Caretakers a staunch salute, then spun about and walked away to finish gathering his people and return home.

"Imagine that!" Charles said. "The Elf King gave me a plant. I wonder if it symbolizes something in his culture."

"You'll have to bring it along when you move to Oxford," said Jack. "It'll look good in the window. I wonder what kind of plant it is?"

"Oh, no," John said as he rushed over to his two friends. "I thought Eledir was going to give it to Samaranth." He sighed heavily and rubbed his temples. "It's too late to refuse it now. Eledir would only get offended."

"Refuse it?" asked Charles. "Why would I possibly want to refuse it?"

In answer to his question, a strange, high-pitched whistling noise emitted from the plant. The companions leaned closer to hear better.

"Oh, for heaven's sake," said Jack. "It's talking."

And indeed it was: "Help meee . . . ," the plant said in a tiny, tinny voice. "Help meee. . . ."

Charles's mouth dropped open. "I'm cursed. Cursed, I tell you."

Jack let out a loud guffaw. "Now I have indeed seen everything. Charles, old sock," he said, patting his friend on the back, "you've just become the proud owner of a Magwich plant."

There were a few more good-byes to be said. Aven and Stephen prepared to return to Paralon, and the other captains and kings went off to their respective lands. But some farewells were more difficult than others.

"Ho, Jack," said Nemo.

"Ho, Nemo," Jack replied. "What's to become of you now?"

"I have to go back," he said, casting a furtive glance at Aven, and a more lingering and direct one at Stephen. "I have a future to live, and many things to do. And," he added with a grin, "a young soldier to teach."

"You still have a lot to learn," Jack said, clapping him on the shoulder. "But you are already becoming the man I knew and admired, and I have no doubt you'll get there, in time."

"Literally so," said Nemo. He held out his hand. In it was a silver pocket watch. "Bert instructed me in how to use it, and when I return to my proper time, I'm to turn it back over to him."

"You don't want to keep it?"

Nemo shook his head. "I'm the captain of the *Nautilus* and the heir of Sinbad. I'm meant to be sailing in the Archipelago, not through time."

"Fair enough," said Jack, offering his hand. "Be well, Nemo."

They shook hands, and the young captain strode away. He did not look back.

✦ ✦ ✦

Quixote noted that one other friend in particular struggled with saying farewells.

Uncas was finding it difficult to adjust to the idea that Fred was an apprentice Caretaker—and to the fact that his son was going to probably have the kind of adventures he had only dreamed about.

"I believed myself too old for adventuring," Quixote said to the little badger, "but apparently, I was mistaken. There may be a few more journeys left in these old bones yet."

"I wish you luck, brave sir knight," Uncas said glumly, while trying to appear pleased for him. "I guess I'm going to go back to work at the press. Scowler Charles said I have the temperament to be a fair editor."

He chewed thoughtfully on a paw. "I wonder if he meant 'fair' as in 'just,' or 'fair' as in, I won't be really awful at it?"

"I'm sure he meant the latter," Uncas's son Fred said in consolation. "You've been a mainstay there for years. Editing might be the next natural step."

"With which," Quixote said, "a journey of a thousand miles may be taken. But as always, it is for you to choose the direction."

"And which direction are you going?" asked Fred.

"A knight must needs have a squire," Quixote proclaimed as he knelt before the badgers, "and at the moment, I find myself sorely lacking." He leaned closely to Uncas and pointedly raised an eyebrow.

"Well," Uncas said thoughtfully, "we could help you advertise, put up flyers and whatnot. Maybe we could get Aven t' sponsor a competition or summat, like a contest for a maiden's handkerchief, except you'd be the handkerchief. But not a maidenly one," he added quickly. "More like a manly kind of handkerchief."

Fred rolled his eyes heavenward and elbowed his father in the back. "He's talking about *you,* Pop. He wants you to become his squire, right?"

Quixote nodded, and Uncas's eyes grew wide with the realization of what was being offered to him.

"Y'—y' mean, go with you? On adventures, and heroic quests, and, uh, adventures? Do I get a sword?"

"A dagger, perhaps, would better suit one of your stature," Quixote replied. "But you get a hat with a feather in it."

"And a horse?" said Uncas. "I get to ride a horse?"

"Actually," said Quixote, "I know of an ogre who has a donkey that might be just the right size and temperament for you."

"What's the donkey's name?"

"Donkey," said Quixote.

"That's perfect!" Uncas said, hitting a fist into his other paw. "I can remember that! But . . . ," he continued, his expression suddenly sorrowful, "I have responsibilities here. I mean, the press . . ."

"Will do just fine without you, Father," Fred said hastily. "You've trained me well, and it practically runs on its own, anyway."

"True, true," Uncas said. "But I'm the seniormost member of the RARS. I can't possibly deprive them of my wisdom an' guidance an' . . . uh, smartness."

Fred continued to press the point that this was a great opportunity, but it wasn't until a dozen other badgers who'd heard of Quixote's offer rushed forward to reassure Uncas that somehow the Royal Animal Rescue Squad could struggle along without him, that he finally acquiesced.

"All right," Uncas said to his son. "As long as you'll be able to muddle through on your own." He turned to Quixote. "It would be my privilege," the little mammal said as he bowed deeply, "to become the squire to the great knight, Don Quixote Enchilada."

"De la Mancha," said Quixote.

"Gesundheit," said Uncas.

"We have one last matter to attend to," said Poe. "Caretaker Principia? If you'll come with me."

"Of course," said John.

Poe led John to the atelier, where Basil Hallward was just completing the varnish on a painting. Even from across the wide room, the visage was impossible to mistake.

On the easel was a portrait of Daniel Defoe.

"Are you crazy?" John said to Poe. "We'd just gotten rid of him, and by his own choice, essentially! Why do this now?"

"He was a Caretaker once," said Poe, "and we look after our own. We could not let him die the final death, when we had the means to prevent it."

"By creating a new portrait?" asked John.

Poe shook his head. "By creating the *first* portrait. And the last, for him. The other portrait was a fake, very much like the one we created for Kipling to use. Defoe had prolonged his life through other means. He had never truly been among those Caretakers in the gallery."

"And no one noticed the painting wasn't one of Basil's?"

"It was close enough to fool us all," said Poe, "because it had been painted by Basil's teacher—William Blake. He'd created other portraits, such as the painting of Charles Johnson, but never one of Defoe."

"Good," said John. "Two Defoes would be twice the trouble."

"By a strange quirk of the Pygmalion resins," said Poe, "they can be used for a person only once, and never again. So this picture cannot be duplicated. And he will never again leave Tamerlane House."

"That's good for you lot," said Defoe's image. "If there were more of me, I'd already rule the world."

"Oh, do shut up," said John. "You aren't going to put him in the gallery now, are you?" he asked Poe. "Even being turned to the wall seems too light a sentence, considering you've already saved his life, so to speak."

"No," Poe said, lifting the still wet painting off of the easel. "I have something else in mind for him."

With Defoe cursing all the while, they carried the picture down endless corridors and flights of stairs until they were in the basement, which seemed to be a repository of unused furniture.

Poe walked straight to a tall grandfather clock and moved the hands to midnight. The clock chimed and swung open to reveal a door, and more stairs.

Underneath was an immense cavern, which was chill and dark. Offshoots of the tunnels led in every direction, with the largest carrying the scent of salt water.

"Does that lead outside?" John asked.

"Yes," said Poe, "but the entrance is guarded by a forty-foot-tall flaming red bull. No one comes in or out without my permission—and even then, it's a crapshoot."

The cave had been built out with brick walls that formed dozens of rooms, as if someone had tried to impose a sense of order on the chaos of the cavern.

Poe moved down several levels until he came to a shallow niche, where he placed the painting.

"You think putting me down here is a punishment?" Defoe sneered. "Someone's bound to come exploring and find me."

"They won't after we're through," Poe said, as he picked up two trowels and handed one to John. "The mortar's in that canister. I'll fetch the bricks."

"You are not seriously considering this," Defoe exclaimed as John and Poe laid down the first row of bricks. "This is barbaric."

"Well," said John, "I have been accused of worse."

"But—but you're Caretakers!" Defoe said, eyes grown wide with panic. "You're supposed to help people."

"That," said Poe, "is precisely what we are doing."

The wall was almost complete. John spread the mortar on the last row, and Poe put two more bricks in place.

"Stop!" Defoe shrieked, having dropped all pretense that he was not bothered by his situation. "You *can't*! John, don't do this!"

"Ironic," said John. "That's the last thing I remember someone saying to *you*."

"For the love of God!" Defoe screamed as Poe slid the last brick into place. "For the love of—"

Then, nothing. It was a good wall.

"There's another irony for you, John," Poe said, wiping his hands on his trousers. "Everyone thinks I wrote that story as entertainment. No one ever realized it was actually an instruction manual."

"You promised *what* to *whom*?" John said in astonishment. "Absolutely not."

Rose had finally been able to reveal what she had promised to Madoc in return for restoring the sword—and she chose to tell the three Caretakers in the presence of her uncle, the Cartographer, in his room atop the Keep of Time. It was an appropriate place to do so, she said, because she had made a second decision in concert with Aven and Stephen—to release the Cartographer from the keep.

"It was the only way," said Rose. "He would not have repaired Caliburn otherwise."

"You didn't see what happened when Hugo Dyson went through one of the doors," said Jack, his face flushed with emotion. "The entire world changed into the domain of the Winter King. We had to traipse through two thousand years of history just to fix it—and that was all mostly by accident. Do you know what kind of damage he can cause if we give Mordred himself the means to go into the past?"

"I agree," said Charles. "He went into exile, and that's where he should stay."

"I gave him my promise," Rose said firmly. "And so did Professor Sigurdsson," she added, looking askance at John. "And we didn't give that promise to Mordred, we gave it to Madoc."

"It's the same person," said Jack. "What difference does his name make?"

"Jack," said Bert mildly, "of all of you, I would have thought you would be the most receptive to the idea of giving the door to Madoc."

"Me?" Jack said in surprise. "Why?"

"Because you alone have had the experience of getting a second chance you never expected to have."

"You mean Nemo," said Jack, nodding. "I've considered that. It's a strange loop to be caught in—to know I'm still the one responsible for his death in his future, while having had the chance to teach him, to mentor him, in my present creates conflicting feelings I don't quite know how to process."

"It's very simple," said Bert. "Your actions now redeem your actions then. Nemo knew his part and valued you for what you would one day become—a good man."

"How can we do any less for Madoc," John said, "considering it's in large part *our* fault that he became the man he is today?"

Throughout the entire discussion, the Cartographer had remained silent, observing but not offering any opinion either way. Rose stepped over to his desk and laid a hand on his arm.

"You knew him best, Uncle Merlin," she said plaintively. "What would you choose?"

The Cartographer looked at her for a long moment, then swallowed hard. "I—I have no right to suggest a course of action here," he finally said. "I betrayed him at every turn, and if we're laying our cards out on the table, I have to take as much responsibility as anyone for the evil he's done."

"What would you choose?" Rose repeated, more firmly this time. "You cannot answer badly, Uncle. And whatever you say, it won't change my decision to free you from the keep."

"That's the reason I hesitate," the old man replied. "If we are discussing justice, then he should stay, as punishment for his crimes. But if so, should I not continue to pay for mine, and also his, which he committed because of what we made him into?

"But if we are discussing an act of mercy, which you are offering to me, then would it not also be an act of mercy to offer freedom to him as well?"

"There are no longer any Dragons to compel you to stay," said Rose. "None save for Samaranth, and I think he'd agree with my decision."

"Then . . . yes," said the old mapmaker. "If you are asking, I would choose freedom for myself—and for Madoc."

The keep trembled, and below them they could hear the muffled sounds of stones ripping away from the walls.

"You'd best hurry," said the Cartographer. "There are only a few doors left."

Quickly the Caretakers raced down the stairway to where a door was hanging precariously from a half-fallen archway. They grabbed it just as the stairway below was starting to buckle, and then secured it onboard their own airship.

"Good enough and done," said John.

"Yes," Jack said, grimacing. "Heaven help us all."

"What will you do?" Charles asked as they returned to the Cartographer's room.

"For centuries I have made maps based on the descriptions of others," he replied. "I have long wished to return to the journeys I abandoned so long ago in my youth, and I think that's exactly what I'm going to do."

"Would you like to take anything with you?" asked Rose.

He looked around the small room of Solitude, which had been his only home, and shrugged. "I brought very little with me, and there's little here I wish to keep."

He bent down and retrieved a black scabbard from behind his chair. "Here," he said, handing it to Rose. "Give this to your cousin Stephen. It belongs with his sword, anyway."

The Cartographer gathered together a few rolls of parchment, some bottles of ink, and several pens, and wrapped them all together in a large sheet of oilcloth.

"That should do it," he said as another rumble shook the remains of the tower, "and just in time, from the sound of things."

"Then it's time, Rose," John said, stepping back.

Rose used a small knife to cut into her palm, which she then placed against the old man's forehead as she began to recite the words of power:

Myrddyn, son of Odysseus
By right and rule
For need of might
I thus free thee
I thus free thee

By blood bound
By honor given
I thus free thee
I thus free thee

For strength and speed and heaven's power
By ancient claim in this dark hour
I thus free thee
I thus free thee

As she spoke the last word, the lock on the door popped open with a quiet click. It would lock no longer.

The Cartographer was free.

They stepped out into the tower, onto the last landing that remained, then down to the awaiting airships: the companions onto the *Indigo Dragon*, and the Cartographer onto the *Scarlet Dragon*.

Both airships descended, then pulled away from the tower as another rumble shook a few stones free.

"Farewell," John called out. "May the wind be at your back, Myrddyn."

"Oh, hell's bells, lad," he said over his shoulder as the *Scarlet Dragon* picked up a crosswind, "call me *Merlin*."

Their task completed, the companions laid a course for Terminus one last time. They had one errand to complete, and then they could at long last return home. None of them chose to look back. None of them were even tempted.

And so, no one was watching at the isles called Chamenos Liber when the last stones fell from what was once the Keep of Time. The final door never fell, but simply swung open as the archway around it crumbled. The sky darkened for a moment, as the future became the present, then vanished into the past.

CHAPTER TWENTY-FOUR

THE NOTION CLUB

"YOU REALIZE, you cannot return to the Archipelago," Bert said with obvious remorse. "It may be impossible for you to do so now. At least," he added, "for the next seven years, anyway."

When all the loose ends had been attended to in the Archipelago in 1943, the companions had returned to Tamerlane House, where Poe activated all their pocket watches as functional Anabasis Machines. He then instructed them in the use of the time travel devices, and after Ransom delivered them back to the Inn of the Flying Dragon, John, Jack, and Charles returned to 1936.

"You went back only minutes after you originally left," said Bert, "so Ransom had already led the Yoricks away. And without Rose, they will have no reason to return to Oxford."

That had been the most difficult decision—to leave Rose at Tamerlane House, where she could continue her education under Poe and Jules Verne.

Bert had arranged for them to meet again a week later at the Inn of the Flying Dragon, and he and Ransom brought Rose and Fred with them.

"You can meet her here whenever you like," he said, handing them a card with a drawing of the inn. "And with the Trump, you can contact her if a need arises. But you cannot return to the Archipelago. Not until after the point you left in 1943."

The companions were stunned. "But we're the Caretakers," said John. "How are we to look after the Archipelago if we can't go there at all?"

Before Bert could answer, the mop boy brought a tray of drinks to the table.

"Thank you, Flannery," Jack said, smiling. "It's good to see you again."

"It's good to see you too, sir," the boy said as he put the tray of drinks on the table. He bent closer so that only Jack could hear.

"I just wanted you t' know," Flannery whispered, "Mr. Ransom spoke t' me as you'd asked, an' he warned me about the you-know-what in the you-know-where that you-know-who told you about. And I'll be nowhere near there then. I'm going to finish school on Prydain."

"Really?" said Jack. "On Prydain? That's exceptional, Flannery. What do you plan to study there?"

The boy stood up and took the now empty tray. "Music. I plan to learn to sing, and play an instrument or three, and tell stories in epic songs. The next time you see me," he said proudly, "I won't be mopping up at a tavern—I'll be Flannery Flem the Bard."

Jack winced, as did Charles and John.

"You know," Charles offered, "if you do plan to study on Prydain, you might want to consider changing your name ever so slightly to something more local."

"Change my name?" said Flannery.

"All performers have a stage name," said Jack. "Like Houdini, and . . . well, other performers."

"I'll do it!" Flannery said. "Thanks!"

"You cited *Houdini?*" Charles chided as he lifted his ale. "What kind of example does that set?"

"Says the man raising a Magwich plant," said Jack.

Charles spit out the ale he'd just drunk. "Good point," he said, coughing.

"You knew," John said to Bert. "You and Verne knew how this would go. So why not just take Rose to Tamerlane House to begin with?"

"It was necessary," said Bert, "because it would have been impossible to hide Rose otherwise. To some, she is all but invisible. But to those who know how to look, she shines like a beacon. There was nowhere and nowhen in space and time where she could be safely hidden—so we arranged for her to skip ahead in time to the point where she would be needed most. The point the Shadow King never wanted her to reach. But more important, we needed the three of *you* to skip ahead in time as well."

"Why?" asked John.

"Because," Bert answered, "according to a future History, you already *had*."

"Did you know?" Jack asked, looking at Ransom. "Did you know the Trump would move us in time as well as space?"

Ransom shrugged, then shifted uncomfortably in his chair. "I, ah, suspected it was possible, but I couldn't have said for sure. We were whistling in the dark, really. Making things up as we went along. Hank has more of a knack for time travel than I, and Rappaccini's daughter is better at spatial concepts. But yes, I did think merging the two was possible. We'd just never tested it before, nor assessed the risks."

"I don't think it would have worked," Charles remarked, "if it hadn't been for that old man in the infinite white room."

"We have some associates looking into that," said Ransom. "We don't know who he is, but we do suspect you're right, Charles. Somehow he aided you. We just can't tell how. Or why."

"The old man's technique may work," said Bert. "Using a Trump twice. But we have too few agents to have risked anyone in a test."

"As you did with us," said Rose.

Bert sighed. "Yes. We had to try it. And the theory *was* sound."

"That was a dangerous way to test the theory," John said, casting a watchful eye at the girl, "given Rose's importance."

"But won't that danger still exist now?" said Jack. "If she's there, in the Archipelago where she can be discovered, won't the work we accomplished be undone?"

"The work has already been done," said Bert, "but your concern is also ours—so Jules plans to take her Elsewhen to continue her training."

"Elsewhere?" asked Charles.

"No," said Bert, signaling to Flannery for more drinks, "Else*when*. And Tamerlane House is as safe as . . . well, houses. At least in the Archipelago."

"We still have a lot of questions," said John. "Almost all of them about the Caretakers. I just can't seem to keep the rules straight—but I suspect in part it's because you haven't yet told us what all the rules are."

"Secrets make you sick," Fred commented.

"Didn't Freud say that?" asked Charles.

The badger shook his head. "Beats me if I know. I figured that out watching Magwich."

"All the secrets are out now," said Bert, "and the Prophecy has been fulfilled. There's no need for more secrets, so ask what you will."

"So we have to stay in England, while all of this unfolds, without changing anything," said Jack. "How is that resolving the war that will come?"

"You already *have*," said Bert. "When Ransom sent you into the, ah, 'future,' you changed the events that needed changing. So there's no need to do it again. But if you try, if you alter anything now, and in the coming years, you risk the very victory that you've already won."

"But there will still be a war," said John. "We know it's coming, and we know how and where it's going to start. Shouldn't we try to do something about that? Isn't it the right thing to do?"

Bert sat down across from John and clasped his hands together in thought. After a moment, he looked up and answered. "That's how a man should think, John, yes, and it's to your credit that you would take such a large thing upon yourselves. But there is, as always, a greater canvas to consider, and the matter of free agency among the rest of humanity."

"Haven't we already tampered with that," said Jack, "and more than once? We've gone back in time two millennia when it was necessary. Wasn't that considering the greater canvas and taking away the free agency of two thousand years' worth of the entire world?"

"You didn't initiate that," Bert replied in soft rebuke, "you were responding to the actions of our adversaries. They put the causes into play, and your job was to make sure the effects preserved the free agency of the world. Had you not done so, we would be living in Albion still, under the rule of the Winter King."

"But things will change anyway," said Charles. "Jamie's wardrobe, for example. Burton only got it because we supposedly weren't here to claim it. How do we deal with that?"

"You must remove yourselves from any and all dealings with the Archipelago, and anything associated with it," said Bert. "To take care of the future, you have to become invisible in the present. Throw yourselves into your work. And try not to think about altering events—else we risk changing the result we wanted all along."

"That's a terrible answer," said Jack.

"There's something else, Bert," said Charles. "We've spent a lot of time in the company of seemingly dead men—some who have eluded death via the portraits in Tamerlane House, which I understand. But there are others, like Burton, who never had a portrait painted but are still walking about. Are they traveling in time, like yourself, or have they managed to avoid death by some other means?"

Bert tipped his head back and laughed. "By my bones, Charles, you've quite a mind! And you're more right than you know.

"There are indeed several ways of defying death, but very few that are moral, and fewer still that are honorable."

"How do you mean honorable?" asked Jack.

"Death has little to do with sorrow," said Bert, "although that's what we feel when someone dies. The veil between this life and what comes after is surprisingly thin. Life persists. Consciousness persists. Spirit persists. It's only those of us on this side, who don't see it firsthand, who feel sorrow.

"Life is about the fulfillment of one's duty, and for most, their duty extends past what we know as 'death.' But for some, such as the Caretakers, there is a need to have them here, in this life, after their allotted time has passed. And so Basil paints the portraits in the gallery. But only the one time, and only under the limitations of Tamerlane House.

"There are other ways that allow more freedom—but the reasons to choose one of those methods must be carefully examined, as must one's motives for wanting to do it at all."

"That's why the option of a portrait or one of the other methods hasn't been used to bring back Artus or Nemo, isn't it?" asked Jack. "Neither of them would have chosen to do it."

"That's why. There are certain costs, and other drawbacks to having made such a choice. But it *is* a choice. And in their cases, they had done the work they had been here in this life to do—and it was their time to go forward and continue their work in the next life."

"And what about Professor Sigurdsson?" asked John. "Why couldn't he choose another option, and live on?"

Bert and Ransom exchanged pensive glances, as if they'd expected this question to come, sooner or later.

"As I said, there are several ways for a person to survive past death," Bert began. "The one preferred by the Caretakers Emeritis is the method you have already seen: the creation of the portraits by use of the Pygmalion resins. But there was also another means available to the Caretakers, which was discovered long ago by our first renegade."

"Dr. Dee," said John.

"Yes," Bert said, sighing. "Dee discovered a method for creating a new body, a virtually immortal body, into which one can 'move' upon death. It's basically willing a new self into existence. The

Tibetans call this creation a *tulpa*, and the strength of the creation depends only on the will of the creator. And Caretakers are very strong-willed.

"Roger Bacon scorned the process and disavowed it as a tool of darkness. But some, like William Blake, embraced it and taught the method to others, such as Burton, who has made spirited use of it. He went back in time to recruit his allies in the Imperial Cartological Society before their own deaths occurred, and before portraits could be painted. Most of his recruits were either not yet full Caretakers, or like Doyle and Houdini, not yet dead when he got to them. Only one actual Caretaker has even gone through the process upon his death—and it was at the request of Poe and Verne that he did so."

"Kipling," said Jack. "It was Kipling, wasn't it?"

"It was the only way to ensure that he was accepted into the enemy camp," said Ransom. "It was a heavy price to pay, but he did so willingly."

"How is virtual immortality a heavy price?" asked John. "It sounds like an easy decision to me."

"That's because you're going to live for several more decades," said Ransom. "You and Jack both have plenty of life ahead of you, so it's not a test of your convictions to suggest a way to live forever."

"It is, as with everything in life, a choice," said Bert. "The Caretakers decided long ago that to meddle in the world past our allotted spans was not the ethical choice. As residents of Tamerlane House, through the use of the portraits, we could advise, and counsel, and be a living repository of information for those who came after. But we would not walk about messing around in the affairs of a world we were not meant to be in."

"*You* do," said Jack.

"I haven't died yet," said Bert, "but when I do, I shall join the others in the gallery. Stellan chose to live at Tamerlane, and then to die, finally, on Terminus. And he did so as a hero, John. Do not begrudge him that."

"There was no portrait of Poe in the gallery at Tamerlane House," said Charles. "What does that mean?"

"It means it's his house," said Bert. "He doesn't need a portrait, because he's never actually died."

"There was another one missing," Jack said. "Jules Verne. He died many years ago—but he seems to be pulling all the strings from backstage on everything that's happened. Is he a portrait, or a tulpa?"

"He'll answer that for himself," said Bert. "He should be along shortly. It was he who requested this meeting."

"You said there were other ways to survive death," said John. "Could none of them be used to help the professor?"

"I'm sorry, lad," said Bert, "but none that I know of. Had he been a tulpa first, as Defoe was, we might have created a portrait. But as he was a portrait first, there were no other options. And as Poe told you, the resins can only be used once, so his portrait cannot be recreated. I am truly sorry, John. For all of us.

"What I was referring to by mentioning other methods was other Caretakers, like Bacon, who never needed a portrait at all. He still serves the Archipelago, in his own fashion. You met him in the battle, I believe."

"Bacon?" Jack exclaimed. "I met Roger Bacon? When?"

"He saved your life, and Nemo's beside," said Bert. "Charys calls him the Tin Man."

"I thought that was just another clockwork," said Charles.

"In a way, he was the *first* clockwork," said Bert. "The only difference is, his mind remains inside. All he needs is the occasional spare part, and he can keep wandering the Archipelago until the end of time, if he so wishes."

"That's why the Shadow King was frightened by him," said John. "He saw what he was trying to be, but with, you know, less evil."

"We all learned lots of lessons there," said Bert. "That's one benefit of traveling to your own future, and making the trip part of your past."

"So are all the members of the Imperial Cartological Society immortal?" asked John.

"Only virtually," said Ransom. "They haven't aged, from what we can tell—and while they *can* be killed, it's much harder to manage, as you saw when Samaranth stepped on Defoe. So it's more like they have a second life."

"A very resilient one, and without the restrictions of the portraits," said Charles thoughtfully. "It would be very tempting."

"Everything has changed now," said Ransom. "Hopefully the members of the society truly are more misguided than traitorous."

"Why didn't Jakob Grimm's watch dissolve?" John asked suddenly. "We know he was a traitor, even there, in Tamerlane House."

"The magic that governs the watches is not one of mere cause and effect," Bert replied. "It is attuned to the desires of your heart. Jakob did what he did out of a sincere belief that he was doing what he must to save his brother."

"Even to the point of aligning himself against the Caretakers?" Charles said. "That's a long stretch."

"Jakob has paid his price," said Bert. "And it was more than just the physical damage he suffered. He knows he chose poorly, and he will have to overcome that. And regaining his self-worth will not come easily."

"I'm still unclear what Kipling's role was," said Jack. "Did he switch sides, as Burton tried to do? Or was he your man all along?"

"When we realized that there were traitors among the Caretakers, we seeded Kipling among them so that we would have a means of keeping track of them. The Shadow King found the means to quite seriously tempt him and make it appear he had betrayed us—but we discovered that someone else was already feeding pages from the Last Book to the Shadow King."

"The True Names of the Dragons," said Jack.

"Precisely," Bert replied. "Kipling realized that once Poe revealed the details of the Prophecy and our plan of action to the Caretakers, the traitor would probably try to steal the book itself and get it to his master."

"So Kipling went first, to draw attention to himself?" asked John.

"Again, precisely," said Bert. "If Kipling went, then all the Caretakers' attention would be on him, and any other defection would be much more difficult. It also gave him the opportunity to give Burton the nudge he needed when it was evident that the Shadow King cared more about conquest than anything else. And Burton was still more Caretaker than traitor."

"But Defoe stole the book anyway," said Charles. "That was the one action that devastated the Dragons and nearly lost the entire conflict."

"Yes," said Bert, "and he covered his betrayal well. Kipling never suspected him, nor did any of the rest of us. But Kipling was still in a position where he could continue to report to us, and then, when the time was right, betray the Shadow King. If he'd uncovered Defoe's true allegiance sooner, before he'd taken the book itself, then it would have been too difficult for Kipling to follow after without arousing the suspicions of all the Caretakers."

"So you knew where Abaton was all along," said John.

"We didn't know, but we suspected," said Bert. "Defoe provided Hallward with the image for the painting, and Poe told him to go ahead and paint it. We didn't know *where* it was, just that it went *somewhere*. We weren't sure how to follow up Kipling's actions, until Charles made his suggestion to duplicate Defoe's painting as a Trump. That proved to be the perfect solution in more ways than one."

"All of this started when Kipling tried to capture us here," said Charles. "What would have happened if he had succeeded then?"

Bert grinned. "He wouldn't have. He just needed you to believe he might, so you'd go along with Alvin. His only real problem was making sure the effort looked good so the Shadow King would never suspect he had a cuckoo in his nest."

"Who planned this bit of espionage?" asked Charles. "It seems to have been a very deep game."

"Who else?" said Bert. "Jules is called the Prime Caretaker for a reason. And Poe has perceptive abilities that are far and away the best I've ever witnessed, in any era. Outside of we three, only Chaucer and Hallward knew."

"I knew," said Grimalkin, who was gradually appearing on John's shoulder, "but then again, cats always do."

"I think you've been adopted," Bert said, winking at the cat.

"He's quite unusual," John said, reaching up to scratch the cat's ears. "I wouldn't mind keeping him."

Bert chuckled. "I was talking to *you,* not the cat."

"I'll trade you," said Charles. "I'll give you the Magwich plant for the cat."

"Don't do it, John." Ransom laughed. "You end up with Magwich in 1945 anyway."

"Why is that?" Charles asked. "Do I finally get tired of him?"

Bert scowled at Ransom, as all the blood drained out of the philologist's face.

"Not exactly," Ransom finally managed to stammer. "John gets him because Jack wins the coin toss at your funeral."

"Ah," said Charles. His face betrayed no emotion, but his hands trembled as he set down his beer. "I see."

"When we met," said Ransom, "I said I had come to protect you, Charles. And that was true. Protecting Rose was my primary objective, but you were also in danger. And in some versions of the histories, you did not survive 1943."

"Oh?" exclaimed Charles. "Well, uh, well done, then. I think."

"It's one of the reasons I requested the assignment from Verne," said Ransom. "Of all of you, Charles has a particularly resonant influence on the different dimensions. He seems to be a key figure in all the worlds, and that makes him—in whatever form, or whatever he's called—worth looking after."

"So in some, he's called Chaz," said Jack.

"And in others, something else?" asked John. "Alvin, perhaps?"

Ransom smiled. "Some things aren't just coincidences," he answered. "And some things are just what they appear to be."

"Well, thanks for spilling the beans," Fred said, scowling at Ransom.

"You weren't supposed to know," Bert said to Charles. "No man needs to know the day of his death until it's upon him."

"Nine years is close enough," said Charles. He raised an eyebrow at Ransom. "That portrait Hallward was working on at Tamerlane House," he added with a sudden realization. "It wasn't you after all, was it? It *was* my portrait."

Ransom bit his lip and nodded.

"Sorry, old fellow," Jack said supportively.

"I'm not dead yet!" Charles retorted. "And from what we've been discussing, maybe I won't have to be."

"What are you thinking?" asked Bert.

"Well," said Charles, "what if I was to suggest that I didn't believe my duty would be fulfilled by 1945? What then?"

Bert nodded, as if he was expecting to have this particular discussion. "Come with me," he said, rising. "Let's discuss this privately. I think you'll be relieved and more than a little surprised by what I want to suggest."

"I'll hold down the fort here," said Fred. "Me and Rose, that is."

Rose winked at the little badger. "I'll have Flannery bring over more Leprechaun crackers."

"Y' sure know the way to a badger's heart, Miss Rose."

"Bert never really answered my first question," John said to Ransom. "Communicating with Rose by Trump is one matter, but how are we supposed to fulfill our responsibilities as Caretakers if we aren't allowed to return to the Archipelago?"

"It isn't a certainty that you can't return, not yet," said Ransom. "You resolved a terrible conflict—but you did so in the future. We want to make certain that that future is preserved in this and every other dimension it touches, and so for the time being, we have to move forward as we already have. And that means we must act as if you were not in the Archipelago again for seven years."

"That would apply here as well, then," said John, "because we were completely removed in time. But records still existed of our accomplishments here in Oxford, so somehow, we *were* still present."

"That's his point," said Fred. "The records we had of you *then* are of the deeds you'll perform *now,* and over the coming years. That's what you're meant to do. But here, and not in the Archipelago."

"Time does move in two directions," said Ransom, "but the lives we lead only move forward. That's how a 'Charles' from one world can become the Green Knight in this one."

"And how a 'Charles' from another can arrive here to protect the one we already have, eh, 'Alvin'?"

"Precisely," said Ransom.

"At any rate," John said reflectively as he lit his pipe, "it *is* only for seven years, after all. We went longer than that between our first two visits. And in a way, we've already been there anyway."

"This is making my head spin," said Jack as Charles and Bert returned to the table. "I can't keep track!"

"Jack," Ransom said, "were you able to spend much time with Poe while you were at Tamerlane House?"

Jack shook his head and grabbed a handful of Leprechaun crackers. "Not much, I'm afraid. After the initial Gatherum, I went off to Paralon, and then everything went to hell after that. So it was mostly John who was there, and he was usually locked in a debate with the Caretakers Emeritis."

"So you never got to discuss any of the other *Geographica*s with him?"

Jack choked on a cracker and washed it down with a gulp of

ale. "*Other Geographicas*? What the devil are you talking about, Ransom? The whole point of the last quarter century of my life has been to protect the one, unique atlas—and now you're suggesting that there are *others*?"

"The *Imaginarium Geographica* is unique," Ransom replied. "To *this* world, anyway."

Jack started to sputter a response when Ransom shushed him. "Later, later," the philologist said. "There's someone just about to join us whom I think you're all going to want to speak with."

"Greetings, Caretakers and company," said the stout, bearded man who had just entered the Inn of the Flying Dragon. He was elegantly dressed in a manner more dapper than stylish, and he had a twinkle in his eyes. "I'm Jules Verne, and it is my great pleasure indeed to finally meet you all."

John, Jack, and Charles were stunned into silence. After all that had happened, not just in recent days, but over the last twenty years, they were unprepared to meet the man who seemed to have been the architect of everything they had experienced.

"Let's order a round of drinks, and an assortment of foodstuffs, and get caught up," Verne said as the door opened behind him and three more figures entered the inn. "But first I'd like to introduce you to the last three gentlemen I've invited to our little gathering. I believe you've all made their acquaintance before."

Fred let out a yelp of surprise, and Rose pursed her lips. Bert and Ransom said nothing, for they had expected this—but John, Jack, and Charles were slack-jawed with astonishment. Behind Jules Verne were Harry Houdini, Arthur Conan Doyle, and Sir Richard Burton.

"Greetings, little Caretakers," said Burton.

"What is this about, Bert?" John said, rising. "What are they doing here?"

"I was waiting until Jules arrived to tell you," Bert said placidly. "The Caretakers Emeritis have reached an accord with the leadership of the Imperial Cartological Society."

"'But how was the play otherwise, Mrs. Lincoln?'" Charles commented drolly. "The enemy of my enemy is my friend, eh, Bert?"

"Not enemies," said Verne. "Differing philosophies. We have managed to persuade Sir Richard that complete and unfettered openness would be disastrous."

"But," said Burton, "Poe and the others have conceded that total secrecy has not been the Archipelago's salvation either. So we have agreed to compromise."

"Compromise how?" asked John.

"Sir Richard, Sir Arthur, and, ah, Harry, have agreed to abide by Poe's request that no unauthorized information about the Archipelago will be made public. In exchange, we have agreed to formally sanction the establishment of the Imperial Cartological Society. They will no longer operate in shadow, so to speak. And we need not fear being exposed, because the eventual goal of the society under the Caretakers' purview is to open the knowledge of the Archipelago to all those who prove worthy of it. As it was, once, a long time ago."

"Your apprenticeship program writ large," Burton said, nodding at Fred. "Just imagine—where you are now three, there could be thousands of Caretakers, sharing the secrets and wonders—"

"And responsibilities," said Charles.

"That won't just happen overnight," said John.

"No," said Bert. "It may take a generation or three to implement, but we believe it *is* possible."

Jack slapped his forehead. "And who's to be in charge of this grand endeavor? We probably shouldn't set it up at Oxford—that would be pressing our luck, with John and I teaching there, and Charles having joined the Inklings. Too much risk of exposure."

"It wouldn't be set up at Oxford," said Houdini.

"Then where?"

"Uh-oh," Fred said to Rose. "Here it comes."

Burton grinned wickedly. "Cambridge."

"And the other shoe finally drops," Jack said, leaning on Charles. "I think I'd rather find out when I'll die."

"I'm not convinced," said John, eyeing Burton and the others. "Will this change our future?"

"There will be time enough to explain that as we sup, young John," said Verne, sitting down. "But in this, you may rest assured: There will be time enough for *everything*."

EPILOGUE

Madoc stood looking at the door, considering. His daughter had kept her word—but he had fully expected that. It was not in her nature to be deceptive, although he was certain that the others advising her had argued mightily against it. After all, he was indirectly responsible for all of the trouble that had occurred back in the real world—both in the Summer Country and in the Archipelago. And to be honest, he was surprised to find himself still alive.

It had been proven that a Shadow could not persist if its owner was deceased. And he had long known that he and his Shadow could exist, even function, with great capacity, independently of each other. But he was not sure, not until the recent events had taken place, that he could survive the destruction of his Shadow.

Apparently, he could.

He felt it, the moment it happened, as if an imperceptible weight were taken from him. He had long ago cast it away by choice, so he felt strangely mournful to realize it was now gone for good. Even that had been his own doing, since he gave them the means to defeat the Shadow after naming a price he never believed they'd pay.

And now, standing before him, was the means to end his exile. The Dragons were gone. No one would know where or when he might go if he stepped through the doorway—and they fully knew the kind of consequence that might occur if he changed the past.

The thought gave him pause. They would know. He could *create great chaos, no matter where or when he went. So why would they have allowed Rose to drop the door over the waterfall? What possible argument could she have made, that would have persuaded them . . . ?*

And then he knew.

Redemption.

She had argued that the chance for his freedom would also be a chance for redemption. And for a moment, the thought made him seethe—but that passed as he considered the door, and his choice.

Even after one has fallen into the abyss, it was once said, redemption still might be found in how one chooses to accept the consequences of one's actions. To some, even the smallest act of nobility carries within it the seeds of redemption—but was his choice to repair the sword noble, or selfish? Or did Rose hope that the noble act might come in the future?

Whatever the motivations, Madoc reasoned, the door ensured that there would be a future for him, even if it lay somewhere in the past. He took a deep breath and opened the door. Sunlight steamed through from a distant horizon, which framed a seaport and a bustling marketplace. The styles of dress were unfamiliar to him, but he would adjust and adapt, as he always had.

As Madoc stepped through, pulling the door closed behind him, the lingering notes and cheerful lyrics of a song being sung on the other side echoed past him and into the void: "Yankee Doodle went to town, riding on a pony, stuck a feather in his cap and called it . . ."

Then the door was closed, and the Deep was silent once more.

Author's Note

Since the release of the first book in the Chronicles of the *Imaginarium Geographica,* the aspect of the story that has drawn more reader interest than anything else is the idea of the atlas having had Caretakers before John, Jack, and Charles.

The previous Caretakers (or Caretakers Emeritis, as they prefer to be known) were what justified my conceit of presenting this particular trio of authors as the guardians of this most valuable book. If H. G. Wells and Jules Verne could be Caretakers, then why not Sir James Barrie? And if he could be a Caretaker, then why not Dickens, Poe, Twain? And from there it was easy to make a list of authors, scientists, thinkers, and creatives who might have been so inclined to take the offer to explore and document an imaginary world.

Some were obvious choices (Shakespeare); others, like Schubert, a bit more oblique. A few, such as William Blake, were good choices creatively, but temperamentally more suitable as comrades-in-principle to Richard Burton. This was the basis for the rival organization, the Imperial Cartological Society, and for a corresponding list of almost-Caretakers, failed Caretakers, and could-have-been Caretakers.

The differences between those who were chosen and those who washed out became the core of this book. It was less often a matter of good versus evil as it was a differing of philosophies—and sometimes it was a difference of degree only. This realization is what prompted me to create a subset of the Caretakers: the apprentices. I wanted to be able to examine more formally the characters who were in that position of deciding what they really believed. I wanted to have them face situations that were morally and ethically cloudy, so that when their choices were made, it would be with full knowledge of the decision, and with full responsibility for the results.

All of this was to help refine what I believe is a Thing That Is True: that it is less important to become a Great man than it is to be a Good man who aspires to serve a Great cause.

This book was also much more complex, due in part to the time travel aspects. The real-life counterparts of John and Jack wrote time-travel stories that are more obscure than their greater fantasy works; and Wells and Twain were well known for theirs. So it was inevitable—and a lot of fun, to boot. But, as was underlined by Charles's discovery near the end of the book, time does pass; people do grow older (mostly). And my Caretakers are aging. So the next most ardent questions are these: Who are the Caretakers that follow John, Jack, and Charles? And are there Caretakers today who look after the *Geographica*?

To these, I can only answer that I've already dropped hints about other modern-day Caretakers: men and women with names like Ray, and Madeleine, and Lloyd, and Arthur. The apprentices, and the new status of the ICS, are also markers of where things might go; and the prominence of Rose Dyson in this book should not be underestimated. At some point in every story, real and imagined, the students become the teachers as the torch is passed on to a new generation. In a manner of speaking, everyone who reads these books and shares these stories has become an apprentice Caretaker, in spirit if not yet in fact. And as for the Principal Caretakers themselves, I've already written how they can be identified: They carry the silver watches with the red Chinese dragon on the case. . . .

Just like mine.

James A. Owen
Silvertown, USA

ACKNOWLEDGMENTS

The Indigo King was the book that I most looked forward to writing; the book I dreaded writing; the book that was the hardest to write; and my favorite book so far. Writing *The Shadow Dragons* was also an interesting challenge. It's a "middle book," and so brought with it both the expectations generated by the first three, as well as those anticipated by the stories to come. It was the most complex book to work on, and the easiest to understand—because the characters involved are now old friends. And so are the ones in the book itself. Neither of them would be the books that they are without the hard work and dedication of my editors.

David Gale is exceptionally patient, and knows how to persuade rather than push a writer. He gave me support when I needed it, and room when I needed *that*. Navah Wolfe, whom I got to know as an online friend prior to her employment as an editor at Simon & Schuster, is an invaluable first reader, and is as first-class as they come where this author is concerned. She is smart, and caring, and she kept me on my game. Dorothy Gribbin remains an editorial rock in my world. I've often rethought certain passages just because I knew she'd question them. And it's always been for the better. And Valerie Shea is a rock star. I sometimes feel like she's been more exacting with details than I am, and that fact both impresses and humbles me.

Julie and Ellen at the Gotham Group, and my attorney, Craig

Emanuel, continue to keep the contracts pulled together and make sure that everything I need to keep doing this for a living flows smoothly and well. Without their support I would be hoeing a much tougher row.

It's also gratifying to know that I have the support of all the executives at Simon & Schuster. Justin Chanda, Jon Anderson, and Carolyn Reidy have all made it easy to work with this house, and my art directors, Laurent and Lizzy, have always made the books shine.

My family, in particular my wife Cindy and children Sophie and Nathaniel, are the reasons that I love what I do. Watching Nathaniel and Sophie come into their own as creative individuals gives me the steam I need to keep my wheels turning, and hopefully tell the kind of stories that will inspire them throughout their lives, and I would not be able to keep the schedule I do without my brother Jeremy, who is my protector and advocate in more ways than I can count.

And not least, I want to thank a friend who remains with us in spirit, and (in his brother's words) who often seemed more committed to my goals than I was: James Chapple. He was not a writer or an artist, but was a very good man who saw virtues in me I could not see for myself, and was and is one of my great friends and inspirations.